I0650234

The Second Moon

Bob Marx

Second Edition

Publishing History

Syton Publishing April 2011, June 2011

All Rights Reserved
Copyright 2011 Robert Marx

ISBN 10: 0-615-46791-1
ISBN 13: 978-0-615-46791-7

Printed in the United States of America
10 9 8 7 6 5 4 3 2 1

Dedication

The Second Moon is dedicated to my wonderful family, especially my wife, Vicki. Far too many nights, she retired alone, while I struggled to form coherent sentences.

The Human Prohibitions

Negotiated by the Sytonian Council and Dai Avram Elstrada.
Ratified by the Human Caucus 8 A.H. 16th of the Fifth Septet

1. No harm or interference.
Humans may not cause harm to or interfere with the native population of Syton.

2. No advanced technologies.
Humans may never possess, use, store, manufacture or cause to be utilized any device or process which is determined to embody scientific principles not currently developed or in use by the native population. Nor may such scientific principles be taught or passed on.

3. No property.
Humans may use what is given, found, or provided but ownership of all things on Syton resides with the natives and any and all goods must be returned upon request.

4. No weapons.
Humans may not carry, possess, manufacture, or store any object that could be construed as a possible weapon.

5. No travel in the Kull or Soto Harbor.

6. No unsanctioned or undue fraternization with native populations.

7. No use of boats or other deepwater conveyances beyond Lake Chook, except for Bistoun Ferry.

8. No hunting or destruction of natural resources.

Prologue

His son's mind was slipping away. He had seen the signs in other towan countless times before—the blank stare, the discolored shoulder patches, the loose pleats of the boy's food sacks beneath a slack jaw, his long arms hanging limp in the frigid lake. His son would soon die. Ninety-seven years, it was a long life for an average towan, an honorable life, so perhaps he was wrong, even cruel to have forced the empty husk of his son's body to endure this desperate journey. Perhaps he should let there be an end.

But the Black Rocks were close now. There was hope. They had both been lucky to avoid serious accidents and to steer clear of the sick, but if they didn't hurry a dead brain in an otherwise healthy body would be all that remained. Still, he hesitated.

Fearing failure, he had avoided bringing the boy last year when he first noticed the death signs, but as the septets passed he had convinced himself that with this son it would be different. This one deserved a chance at the life only he knew. They were so alike. And he was so lonely.

He gazed at the familiar landscape, the impenetrable darkness of the water, the jumble of boulders they now rested upon, the gravel shore that gave way to green stubble and the path that led into the canyon. In the beginning he and his dying children had made this trip many times. He had always returned home alone. But that was many wives and mistakes ago. He was sure he understood the mystery now and this boy was special. He was, after all, his son of the towa, Mo Sy, his daughter. How much more of himself could he impart? Yes, this time it would be different. This boy would not die in his arms as tiny Mo Sy had.

Iridescent air plankton, fleeing the frigid surface of the lake, had begun to swarm. The microscopic organisms rose like a mist and drifted up the canyon. It was time. If he couldn't get his son to rise from the gray, lake boulder on which he rested, they would miss their opportunity.

Wrapping an arm around his son's waist, he lifted the two-meter towan from the boulder. He doubted that he would be able to carry his son very far. Thankfully, the lethargic body responded and they were able to travel beneath the living cloud and enter the narrow canyon. Had others ever followed the plankton swarm, drawn by the warmth and well being it radiated? He swiveled his head, taking measure of the glowing mass, the largest he had ever seen. They would make it.

The dark alcove wasn't far from the lake. It wasn't hidden and wouldn't have been of particular note had he not sought refuge here from a swarm so many lives ago. He positioned his son slightly off-center, nearer the jagged edge of the black rocks where he knew the effects would be the strongest. Looking deeply into the boy's expressionless eyes, he told him, without expecting any response, not to worry. Surprisingly, the boy's eyes momentarily focused and he awkwardly lifted an arm to run his double thumbs across his father's heavily crosshatched initiation scar, a clear demonstration of his son's love and respect.

A moment later, billions of electrically charged organisms enveloped them, leaving them blind and deaf, erasing their real world. Only garishly painted images flickered on the canvas of their minds. Unnatural sounds and distorted pictures burst forth and fought each other for dominance. Memories exploded, vivid dreams blossomed, all converging in a whirlwind of emotions and ideas. Feeling the familiar rush of euphoria, the father opened his mouth and allowed the tiny energized plankton to flood into his food sacks until the folds in his neck billowed. He knew eating them wasn't necessary, but they tasted good and he enjoyed immersing himself completely, their flavor enhancing the tingle that danced through his body.

Currents flowed through the airborne plankton initiating their reproductive cycle. Normally the lake water would ground them, but the iron-rich black rock was a much better conductor. It made no difference to the microscopic life that two beings stood in their field, hoping to recharge the small gland in their brains that stored and supplied energy to the rest of their nervous systems.

Afterward, father and son lay crumbled on the floor of the black magnetite alcove. Sight and reality slowly returned. Swallowing the last remnants from his food sacks, he raised his head stiffly from the boy's dull gray shoulder and searched for signs in his son's lifeless eyes. For a brief moment his deceased wife Mo Sy stared back…and then his son too was dead.

It took a while, but he was able to drag the body back to the shore of the lake. The sky was clear now. The plankton swirled and thickened on the surface of the water. This would be where his son's journey would end. He searched along the water's edge, among the smoothly tumbled stones, until he found a piece of laskic shell and sharpened an edge before returning to the body. With a single slice, he opened a hole into the torso then reached inside, tore out a dark organ, and ate it. The aspic was most flavorful. While he savored it a discordant hiss suddenly filled the sky. He peered upward. A thin gray streak split the air as if someone from above had taken the laskic shell from him and cut the heavens. He tried to follow the head of the streak as it disappeared behind a distant mountain range. Streaks in the night sky were familiar, but he had never seen one during the day. Even for one that had lived so long and had seen so much, it was novel. Leaning back on his middle leg, he finished eating the aspic. A froth of memories and thoughts still bubbled inside his mind. Why, when the experience in the alcove left him exhilarated, did it destroy others? Why, when it fueled him, giving him so many years of extra life, did it also bring death? He had no answers, but until he did, he wouldn't risk bringing anyone else to the Black Rocks.

Before leaving, he glanced at his son's body with pride and knelt down beside it. He slowly ran his two right thumbs along the raised initiation scar, feeling each of the nearly dozen crosshatches, one for each towan that the boy had mentored during his long and honorable life. Now, if his son were lucky, the cyliths would come.

Foul Wind

Elizabeth straightened and looked down from the top of the pyre at the human body wrapped in coarse linen. The corpse had begun to smell days earlier, but Hyland's last request—to be cremated on the lake—had been odd and it had taken her a long time to gather sufficient cottonbark to build a raft and still have enough to incinerate the body.

Several steps below, Jorge peered up at her. She gathered the rough cloth of her skirt, pretending not to notice his indiscreet stares, and continued stacking and binding the precious branches. At twenty-six she wasn't particularly modest, but still found the lecherous attention of a man twice her age unsettling. After two years of being his father's nurse, Elizabeth had learned to avoid Jorge, but today even the assistance of a lazy, middle-aged man helped. Without him, the pyre would not be finished in time. Neither of them had ever done anything like this. No one, native or human, had ever been cremated on Syton before.

They had begun building the wooden raft before the brightening, planning to be finished with their makeshift crematorium by the time people arrived, but now it was already past noon, the dimness fog had long disappeared from the lake, and mourners, along with the curious, were trickling in.

Suddenly, a section of the pyre beneath Jorge collapsed, sending him crashing to his knees. Jagged branches tore through a trouser leg. He winced.

"Shit. Damn crazy idea," he sputtered, picking himself up out of the brambles.

Elisabeth paused, taking a few breaths through her scarf to soothe the burn in her throat. "Are you all right?"

"No, I'm not all right. Do I look all right? Does any of this seem the least bit all right to you? Let's get the old man on top of this heap before one of us ends up joining him. One funeral is enough."

With as much dignity as the chore permitted, they lifted Hyland, and then using short lengths of rope, fastened the body to a frame meant to keep the guest of honor from rolling off when the raft containing the pyre was towed out onto the lake.

They gathered a tinder pile of small twigs and kindling at the base of the cottonbark tower, and then quickly cleaned the area where the ceremony would take place. Grabbing what remained of their bundling twine, they made their way up the dirt path that led from the shoreline.

After a few meters, the smell of death was replaced by fresh dung. The offending blaython, burdened with packs and supplies, stood guard over her master, napping just off the path. Elizabeth kicked the muddy boot protruding into their path. A deeply wrinkled red face appeared from beneath a worn leather cap.

"There's plenty of space in back of the cabin where you can hitch your smelly friend there," said Elizabeth. "A lot of people are going to use this path."

The man glared up at Elizabeth. With difficulty he got to his feet, massaged his knees, and took a menacing step towards her, but stopped. She towered above him by almost a half meter. The man stared up at her face, strong and determined, streaked with dirt and sweat, a memorial tattoo beneath her ear. Her brown eyes held his without blinking. He looked down noticing her strong arms and legs, then laughed and turned to Jorge.

"Are you Hyland's kid?

Jorge opened his mouth to answer.

"Yeah, yeah, I can see it now." The stranger turned back and surveyed Elizabeth once again—wide set eyes, a strong chin accented a pleasing oval face, dark auburn hair cascading past her athletic shoulders. He reached under his grimy hat for a quick scratch and then shook his head. "Nope, I give up. Never met you."

Elizabeth ignored him and turned her head down the path. "You should clean up after your animal."

"I have no control over the beast. Does what he wants." He laughed, holding up both his hands, then extended one. "Membomba, Engineer Second Class, Henri Membomba, I worked with his father."

Elizabeth looked down at his filthy hand, but decided to shake it anyway. It was strange that a man who looked like he couldn't afford a bar of soap could afford a blaython. "Elizabeth Tournell." She tipped her head and looked under the animal. "If I'm not mistaken, he's a she."

"Was and is the horniest he you'll ever lay eyes on. Plumbing's a bit messed up." Membomba shrugged. "I was a better engineer than surgeon."

"Well, just get…whatever it is…off the path. If you'd like to freshen up; we're done at the lake."

"I'm fine," Membomba said, not picking up on the hint. He turned back to Jorge, "Listen kid, I'm sorry about your dad. We had good times together. Smartest man I ever knew. Taught me more than—"

Jorge gave a small nod. "I don't remember you."

"And why should you? That was a long time ago." The rare donkey-like creature began to fidget. "Yeah, well maybe he would like a drink. I don't think Hyland will mind, do you?" He chuckled, the only one that thought it the least bit funny. "Don't let me keep you." He started down the trail, casually kicking the dung aside. "Sure ya have work to do."

Laughter and screams greeted Elizabeth and Jorge as they approached the straw bale home. A wet naked boy burst through the cloth flap that served as a front door and ran into Elizabeth's arms. She lifted him easily. A grinning middle-aged woman with a towel over her shoulder followed him out.

"Elizabeth can't protect you!" yelled the woman, her fingers outstretched and wiggling. She began tickling the squirming child.

Smiling, Elizabeth let him down. The boy hugged her legs and looked up at his father. The older woman took the towel from around her shoulders and reached out for the boy. "Jorge, tell Wilem to let Elizabeth go. It's time to settle down and get dressed."

Jorge looked at his ex-wife with disdain. "Nanc, how will he ever respect you if you won't bother to learn how to talk to him?" He crouched down and used his hands to make signs while he spoke directly to the deaf boy. "Wilem, it's time to get dressed. Obey your mother."

Elizabeth pried Wilem's tight grip from her legs. He looked up at her, his big almond-shaped eyes begging. Wilem's features were distinctly oriental, yet neither of his parents appeared to carry any similar genes. Elisabeth had often pondered whether that fact could have aided the collapse of their marriage, She brought her hand to her lips and kissed her fingers. Gently she placed them on the boy's forehead. Reluctantly, he returned to his mother and they all went inside.

Elizabeth had come to Lake Chook two years ago to help care for the ailing Hyland Wynosk. At the time, Jorge and Nanc's marriage was already in trouble and the household barely functioned. Elizabeth couldn't count the nights she endured the screaming, usually followed by Nanc escaping into Elizabeth's small corner of the cabin, into her bed, crying. When Nanc, after tiring of Jorge's abusive behavior and accusations finally ran away to join the women in the mountains, Elizabeth suddenly became Wilem's nanny and the family's housekeeper as well. Without Nanc, organized meals, regular bedtimes, clean clothes and discipline disappeared altogether. Elizabeth provided what little structure the Wynosk family had left, but her principle duty had been to Hyland. Today, even under these strained circumstances, it was a relief to have Nanc back.

With Wilem being taken care of by his mother, Elizabeth could relax. She removed her depleted breathing scarf, crushed a meita and dropped them both into the red liquid of the communal treatment pot. Humans could breathe Syton's atmosphere without great trouble; it was a close match, but not perfect. The sore throat was really a small inconvenience and eliminated entirely by the chemicals in the red tablets. Jorge handed Elizabeth his scarf and she soaked it before retreating to her small corner of the large one-room shelter. She drew the privacy drapes making sure they were pulled tightly against the irregular walls. Jorge's leering had only become worse since Nanc left and she didn't think his ex-wife's presence would restrain his wandering gaze. If Wilem and Hyland hadn't needed her, she'd have left months ago. But now...well, now it was different. She was free.

A cool breeze entered through her window opening. Elizabeth closed her eyes and inhaled deeply. Exhaling, she relaxed, feeling an inner peace soothing her. She turned, knelt down in front of the chest next to her straw mattress, and withdrew the only dress she owned—the funeral dress, as she had begun to think of it. It had been her mother's before she died. Laying it out carefully on the bed, she recalled how beautiful her mother had looked in it, dancing with her brother Michael at her graduation. Her family had been so close then. It was just a few years ago, but she felt like it was a different lifetime. She absently touched Michael's memorial tattoo beneath her ear. Two, now three funerals in as many years, and with each loss her life had become darker. At first, her fragile emotions hid just below the surface, but her brother's recent death had forced them even deeper and now she was numb, her passions were in full retreat, her emotional core as frozen as the surface of Syton.

She unwrapped the filthy skirt she wore and let it drop. A jug of water, her washbasin, and a few personal items stood on a small table in the corner. From a crude clay dish she took a piece of gray soap and cleaned her hands and face. The faint sweet flowery smell of keets calmed the harsh detergent smell of the lye and lingered briefly. She dipped an old rag into the soapy water and used it to wash the dirt from her feet.

As she wrung the washcloth, the sound of approaching boots drifted through the open window, and then a knock against the doorframe. Instinctively, Elizabeth began to grab for her dirty wrap but remembered there were others to take care of the visitor and relaxed. Jorge or Nanc could find out who it was.

Two more raps...

"Hold on! I'll be right there." Jorge yelled out. He moved to the doorway and pushed the heavy woven cloth aside. Standing alone was an extremely tall, regal man with an immense broad hat. His shirt not only covered his arms but extra fabric had been sewn on the cuffs, which extended partly over his hands. The collar rose up high on his neck. He looked to be at least 80 years old, but his skin, what you could see of it, was pale, almost white, and unwrinkled.

"Jorge, I'm not sure you will remember me," began the man.

Jorge held up his hand. "Stop. I know you've come a long way, Avram, but... this, you being here, isn't right."

"Please...just give me a moment." Avram Elstrada spoke softly, "I'm truly sorry about your dad and whether you believe me or not, he was a dear friend." He hesitated. "If you would...I'd like it if... I mean, maybe I could help."

"Hyland never had much good to say about what you did, Avram. And I'm sure he wouldn't want you here. I think it best if you just go." When the tall stranger made no signs of moving, Jorge said boldly, "I'm asking you to leave, Avram."

"I loved your dad. I worked with him side by side for over thirty years. Without him...he must have saved us a hundred times. When I heard, I had to come. Please, we've been traveling for three straight days. May I come in out of the sun? Just for a moment."

Jorge stared at Avram as if he could detect the truth of the man's statements from his appearance, and then past him, across the field, where two figures stood. Only one was human.

Relenting, Jorge stood aside for Avram to enter. "Just for a moment and only you."

Elizabeth who had remained almost motionless throughout the exchange quietly rose and stepped into her funeral dress. She could hear heavy boots enter the house.

"Those boots had better be clean," Elizabeth said as she threw open her drapes and confronted the visitor. They locked eyes for a moment and even though she was slightly taller, Elizabeth felt small in the man's presence. She glanced down, pretending to look at his boots, then up at his smooth unwrinkled face. Avram was smiling. Squaring her shoulders, Elizabeth insisted, "Don't be tracking dirt in here." She turned, and walked out through the doorway.

"Who is she?" asked Avram watching her leave.

Jorge waved her off as if she was a household pest. "Don't mind her. Why are you here? What did you think you could possibly do to help?"

Avram turned back to face Jorge. "I would like to speak at the funeral—just a few words at the graveside."

"That won't be possible."

"I'll keep it short."

"Absolutely not! Besides, there's no grave."

"I don't understand."

"No grave, he wanted to be cremated on the lake."

Avram smiled. "Even in death your dad has a sense of humor. I guess it's fitting."

Jorge returned a rare smile. "I thought so. I'm glad you appreciate the irony."

"Of course. Then it's even more important for me to say a few nice words, to explain."

"We don't need you to explain anything. No one will understand why we'd let you speak."

"I'll make them understand. Listen; what's done is done. The disagreement was between Hyland and me. It was a long time ago and I did what I thought was necessary. Your father understood. What's important now, today, is that he's properly remembered. Who else can speak personally of those years and pay your father the proper respect?"

There was silence. The question hung in the air.

Avram continued. "There're not many shipborn still alive. You know I've been giving speeches for the last thirty years, but this one's special. It's important to me that Hyland has an appropriate eulogy."

"I am more than capable of eulogizing my father."

"Avram nodded. "Of course you are. But this is his final farewell. Let all that knew him and loved him speak. I'll make you proud to be his son."

"I am proud to be his son."

"I'm sorry, I know that. But others should know why you're so proud. Let me tell them."

Confused, Jorge walked to the doorway. Elizabeth had kept the front cloth open in order to better hear the conversation she pretended to ignore. She sat, her long legs stretched out, relaxing on a rough hewn chair gazing at Avram's companions. They were the true puzzle here. Whether Jorge knew yet what his answer would be, she knew from the beginning that Jorge would be unable to dissuade this man. The question of the moment was who those two were. The human was a young man, possibly thirty, dark hair, almost black she thought, and although shorter than his native companion, a strong athletic build. He looked familiar, but at this distance she couldn't be sure. He held onto the reins of two additional blaython. Before today, she hadn't seen more than three or four of the beasts. Standing next to the young man was a towan, nearly two meters tall. Surprisingly, they were conversing.

Delaying a decision, Jorge asked the question that Elizabeth pondered as well, "Who'd you bring?"

"Jasin came with me, and Sy Toberry."

Jorge considered this. "We don't see many natives this far into the cold country."

"No. Sy Toberry's a hardy one," said Avram.

"And where's Julian?"

"She…she wanted to come, but said it would be too hard. She said you'd understand and sends her love."

"Anyone else coming from Nova Gaia?"

"Do you remember Beloit McMaster?"

Jorge nodded.

"He went down to investigate some trouble in Bistoun. He should be here tonight." Avram walked up behind Jorge and gently put a reassuring hand on his shoulder. "Everything will be all right." Avram said softly.

Jorge took a deep breath and let out a groan reflecting his battle of indecision and doubt. He looked up at Avram. "Make it nice, okay?"

"You have my word." Then, as if it were an afterthought instead of the planned reward it truly was, Avram added, "By the way, have you thought about joining the Caucus? We'll need someone from Lake Chook now that Hyland's gone." Without waiting for an answer, Avram put on his broad-rimmed hat and began to leave. "When are you going to have the ceremony?"

When Jorge didn't answer, Elizabeth spoke up. "We figure at beginning of dimness, before planet rising."

Avram turned to her and nodded. "I'm sorry we weren't introduced. I'm Dai Avram Elstrada," he said using the full honorific.

Elstrada...no wonder the young man was familiar. "I'm Elizabeth Tournell. Actually, my brother Michael and Jasin were friends at school. I met your son once when I was visiting."

"Tournell...from Panvera? Jasin and your brother were roommates. I knew your mother, Sidrah, and your father quite well."

Elizabeth straightened and lifted her head, "Dai Warren and Di Sidrah."

"Of course, I'm sorry. You are correct and they both deserved the honor." He grinned. "Is your father coming?"

"No, I don't think he had much contact with Hyland."

Avram considered that for a moment. "Well, I'm pleased to meet you, Elizabeth. I'm sure Jasin will be happy to see a familiar face. I had to force him to come along. He hates going to funerals. These days that seems to be all I'm doing. Tell me, how is your family? Your dad, is he well?"

It was apparent he hadn't heard about Michael. That wasn't unusual as news from Panvera was a rare commodity in the lower settlements. Elizabeth nodded. "As well as can be expected."

"Good." He appeared genuinely pleased. "But you must have much to do. We can talk tonight."

Elizabeth watched Avram rejoin his son. Jasin tied up their animals, and then the three of them took the path down to the lake. Elizabeth marveled at Avram's charisma and power of persuasion. Of course, Jorge was weak and easily manipulated – even she had taken advantage of that over the last couple years – but nonetheless she was quite impressed. Over the years, she had heard of Avram Elstrada. Who in the settlements hadn't? It was he, who after nearly seven years of study, finally broke down the communication barrier between Humans and the Sytonians, and almost single-handedly negotiated the settlement agreement. There were a few, Hyland being the most outspoken, who thought Avram had given up too much to the natives, had too easily agreed to the Prohibitions, in order to be allowed to live in the Syton gorge. It was an old debate, which became academic over thirty years ago and of little interest now to anyone... well, almost anyone. Family grudges died hard. She was surprised that Jorge could still be so upset and was anxious to hear what Avram would say.

Elizabeth and Jorge rejoined the others inside to complete preparations for the ceremony. Nanc had baked tiela gourd and flaxmeal biscuits earlier, and many who had come brought various sweet treats and spiced finger foods that needed to be organized. With Wilem's eager help, Elizabeth prepared several pitchers of sweet melon drink and put together special trays for the keetah ritual. The time went quickly and soon it was time. As they made their way down to the lake, Jorge lit a dozen torches along the trail. The dimness would soon be upon them.

When they arrived at the clearing next to the pyre, they were shocked to see nearly thirty of their Lake Chook neighbors. Fifteen families had come from other villages. Elizabeth recognized several from her hometown of Panvera and enjoyed small talk until the conversation would inevitably turn to Michael's death and how she was coping.

Excusing herself, she would slip away until cornered by the next. Three human families along with several male Sytonians had come from the fishing village of Bistoun at the other end of the lake. Of course there was Avram's group from Nova Gaia, and Membomba, who appeared to have no permanent home. People mingled and exchanged news from the human villages. Almost all of the settlements were represented. Growth and expansion were the main interests. Nearly seven hundred humans now lived in six small towns or villages. Elizabeth guessed that many of the elderly, now frail and bent, had served with Hyland.

Sy Toberry and the few other towan gathered with their cyliths and Elizabeth gave them wide berth. Jorge was right; she had rarely seen the pentapods and their animals this high in the gorge, except of course during Initiation season. As a child growing up in frigid Panvera, she had never seen a native. Even leaning back upon their third legs, the towan towered above most of the humans, she and Avram being the obvious exceptions. She paid special attention to the cyliths. More than mere pets, the towan treated their fierce dog-like companions with more deference than their towa, their wives. After all, throughout their lives, a towan never captured and trained more than a single cylith to provide company and protection. Towa, collected and exchanged as desired, were another, less important matter.

Occasionally a towan would reach out and trace another's fresh ritual scar. Their speech sounded like stuttering. Jasin Elstrada sat on a rock outcropping near the group and engaged in their spirited exchange. Natives, she knew, easily grasped Human, but few beside Avram, and obviously Jasin, could comprehend, much less speak the native's language. Jasin looked up and smiled at her. She looked away, unsure of how to react to his glance. Hyland's creamation had certainly attracted a mix of intriguing company.

The sun was disappearing over the high, far ridge, and the pale yellow-green crescent of Conboet, the mother planet was making a final appearance. The dimness would soon be upon them. Elizabeth searched out the owners of the fishing boats and asked if any would be willing to tow the raft out a couple of hundred meters and ignite the wood pile when signaled.

"We'll pull the raft out, but we're not starting any fires," one of the fishing men apologized. The others nodded their agreement. "The towan are barely tolerating this whole circus."

"More than the wood, they don't understand the wasting of the meat," another spoke up.

Elizabeth explained the problem to Jorge and Nanc. "Screw the lot of them!" Jorge cursed. "I'll set the damn fire." Jorge stormed off, away from the crowd, to calm down.

Nanc followed her estranged husband to the shore of the lake where she took his arm. Elizabeth watched as he lowered his head onto her shoulder. He shuddered and Nanc hugged him. Several blundering visitors took the inopportune moment to approach Jorge and Nanc with their own heartfelt condolences. They talked of Hyland and often about Wilem. Genuine pride shone in the parents' eyes when anyone referred to their son. If they had done anything right with their lives, it was having this spirited boy.

Soon the dimness was upon them. Jorge reluctantly made his way over to a tumble of large rocks jutting out from the shoreline that could act as a convenient speaking platform. Before he could begin to climb them, he felt a strong hand on his arm. Turning, he found Avram standing beside him. "There is no need for you to burden yourself," Avram began. "If you would like, I could—"

Jorge shook off the hand. "You'll have your time. This is mine." And he climbed up on top of the rocks to address the crowd. The chatter quieted and all eyes turned to Jorge.

"My family and I would like to thank you for coming and for bringing your memories and sincere words of love and concern." Jorge took a moment to survey the upturned faces. "We, appreciate the effort many of you have taken to be with us today. I know that Father would appreciate you all being here. He cared for you all. The past thirty years since leaving the ship have been difficult for our family of engineers. They were especially difficult for Hyland. Except for the birth of our son Wilem, the time here on Syton meant little to him. For Father, Tanis was everything. He used to spend hours talking about life aboard her and the challenges we all faced. He remembered how we once fought to keep our home alive. For us... for us engineers, it was the most exciting time of our lives—using every trick, every tool, and every scrap of knowledge to keep Tanis running. For my father, those were the times that mattered."

Jorge hesitated, uncomfortable with the direction his tribute was taking. Many of those listening had only known Hyland as the old man of Lake Chook. He was talking as if only Hyland's time aboard the ship had meant anything. He took a deep breath and continued.

"Be assured that even in his last days of pain, Hyland never lost hope for this human settlement. It has been difficult for many of us to get used to this way of life, it has been difficult to accept this moon as our home, and it has been difficult to obey the Prohibitions. Father would say to me, 'Don't forget who you are. Don't forget how far we've come and what we humans have accomplished.' So I will never forget, because it was important to him. Hyland was important to me, not just as a father, but as a mentor, as a teacher, and a confidant."

Jorge paused, and tried to collect his thoughts, unsure of what he would say next. "I don't know if it is wrong for a son to tell others how great a man his father was." His voice strained. "I'm not sure I can even put it into words...." At that point Jorge gave up trying to control his emotions. He raised his head, sniffled, and with a voice racked with pain and with great effort he finished. "All I really know for sure is I loved him."

Unbalanced, he stepped down from the rocks. Avram reached out to help him, but Jorge refused the hand. Little Wilem watched his Daddy. Sensing that something wasn't right, the boy ran into his father's arms. Jorge hid his tears in a great hug.

Watching the two of them comfort each other, Elizabeth felt her own tears surface. It was the first time she had cried since coming to Lake Chook. Father, son, grandfather, they had a special love, the kind she didn't think she could ever share with anyone ever again. She turned away from the crowd embarrassed, realizing she wasn't crying for Hyland. Self-pity did not suit her. She saw herself as strong and confident, riding above the waves of despair, but she was drowning and had been sinking deeper for months and like all life shielded from the sun's rays below the water's surface, hers had lost its color.

Jorge and Wilem took a flaming torch and approached the pyre. A peculiar chorus of discordant Sytonian refrains rose out of the alien group. Elizabeth turned towards them expecting trouble, but they lowered their voices. Jorge looked out over the faces, then turned, took a last look at the body, and then plunged the torch into the dry kindling. The thin cottonbark twigs caught immediately, sending off a loud crackling and an oily smoke, which surrounded the body before staining the air black above the corpse. The fishing boats slowly towed the flaming pyre out into the bay.

Avram waited patiently until the boats returned and their crews rejoined the crowd. Then he slowly climbed the rock outcropping. He had removed his oversized hat, revealing a short black ponytail that was heavily streaked with white. His soft gray eyes spoke of kindness and sincerity. With a natural grace, he waited until everyone turned their attention towards him. For a brief moment, he lowered his head, as if in prayer. Raising his head, he spoke in a strong voice. "Hyland's family has graciously allowed me to add a few words in memory of our friend."

Those in the crowd that knew Avram realized that it would probably not be just a few words and found comfortable spots in the clearing to sit. Others took the hint and joined them on the ground. Elizabeth moved to stand within a bright circle of one of the torches. Again, Avram waited until he had everyone's attention.

"For the few I haven't had the privilege of meeting, I am Avram Elstrada, founder of the Human Caucus for our settlement here on Syton, the second moon of Conboet. Hyland Wynosk was my closest friend for nearly forty years. We grew up together; our families had quarters next to each other. He served as Chief Engineer for nearly twenty-five years and during my tenure as second-in-command of Tanis he was without a doubt the single most valuable member of the crew."

Jorge spoke of Hyland's devotion and dedication to preserving our home aboard Tanis, but few can truly understand just what a remarkable man he was without knowing the daunting challenge he continually faced maintaining our fragile old ship. When Hyland and I were born, Tanis was already over 650 years old. She had housed at least 25 generations and during our time she carried nearly 400 of us. The records aboard Tanis told us that she, and others like her, were built to carry our ancestors into space, to settle colonies such as this one, that would insure that the Human race would continue to grow and survive. No one knew how long it would take for those ships to find suitable new homes, but I'm sure the original designers and builders never anticipated that Tanis would have to last almost seven centuries."

Before we discovered Syton, many of the ship's systems were failing. The ship was literally falling apart. Hyland and the other engineers worked around the clock performing one miracle after another. There were countless days that my friend never slept. We all would have perished if it were not for him. We stand here today, able to hold our loved ones, able to raise our families, able to complete the dream our ancestors began, all because of Hyland."

Avram glanced over his shoulder to look at the lake and the cremation taking place in the bay. He dipped his head into his medicated scarf and took a few deep breaths before continuing. "Once before, nearly thirty years ago, we gathered at this spot for another ceremony where Hyland was the central figure. I am sure many of you remember, but let me tell the others."

After we all transferred from Tanis to our new home here in the Syton gorge, Hyland sent the dying ship crashing into the sun. He then piloted the last existing shuttle to this very spot where it remained for years. At the Sytonians request, and as a sign of our commitment to the adopted rules of conduct, specifically the second Prohibition restricting the use of advanced technology, we agreed to destroy the shuttle and all that it represented. For sentimental reasons, the idea was difficult for Hyland to accept at first. Finally he agreed, asking that he, as the Chief Engineer, be allowed to demonstrate his acceptance of this most difficult Prohibition. In one of his finest—and I'm sure most difficult acts—Hyland sent the shuttle out into the center of this deep bay, not far from where his body burns tonight, and there he set the shuttle on fire by exploding the fuel supply. It was a spectacular display that none of us will ever forget. She burned for quite a while, and then sank, disappearing into this lake forever."

I believe Hyland is sending us a message today by his unusual request to follow the shuttle into the depths of Lake Chook. He wants us to remember his brave and symbolic act of acceptance and sacrifice. He wants us to remember how important it is to be committed to the ideas of peace and to remember that our toys of technology are not as important as our humanity. So I beg of you to remember this great man, remember his selfless deeds, both aboard Tanis and here, in this very bay on Syton. My friend was a true hero and will be an inspiration to me and our people forever."

By the time Avram finished, the pale algae green crescent of the planet Conboet was just setting. The flaming raft painted a colorful mural of orange, red, and yellow flames against a darkening greenish-blue sky. The effect was temporary. The background colors faded and soon the flames fought against the growing light of Syton's sister moon Eian, as it made its way into the evening sky. The crowd knew the formal speeches were over. If anyone else had anything to say, no one had the courage to follow Avram's eloquence. There was an awkward moment when no one moved, waiting until they were told what to do next. Elizabeth broke the silence.

"We'd like to thank you all for coming," announced Elizabeth. "Please join us for refreshment and in a few minutes we'd like to offer those who are interested a ceremonial cup of keetah."

Nanc gratefully accepted a few last cakes and platters of cookies from neighbors and placed them among the other food on a flat board that served as a table. Glasses of sweet melon juice were passed around. Elizabeth started a small cooking fire and heated a kettle of water. She portioned out the powdered keetah into as many cups as she had, and when the water boiled she poured it into the cups.

Most of the humans were helping themselves to the other refreshments, but Avram, Jasin, and the Sytonians clearly had their eyes on Elizabeth and her preparations. Jorge came over to help pass out the dozen or so cups of steaming keetah. Sy Toberry carefully took a cup from Elizabeth, managed a strange sounding "Thank you" in Human, and then held it between his thumbs, supporting the bottom with his other hand. The other Sytonians held their cups in identical fashion. The few humans in this group pretended to support the cup with their other hand, as the aliens were doing, but the cups were much too hot to be placed on a human palm. Still, they knew it was proper etiquette to try.

Jorge began the keetah ceremony, but was immediately interrupted by Membomba. "Excuse me, son...but this isn't right. Don't get me wrong," he hesitated, looking for an inoffensive way to phrase it, "I mean your father was a fine man and all that, but you shouldn't have to do this. You're family."

Everyone else just stared at Membomba. Avram looked at Jasin and raised an eyebrow. Jasin returned the look and shook his head. Even Elizabeth knew it was bad manners to interrupt once the keetah had been handed out. The natives let out a low grumbling sound. Sy Toberry stepped forward and confronted Membomba. "You must not stop him. The keetah is hot. The ceremony has begun. Now you must continue." Toberry towered above Membomba and thrust a finger at the engineer's chest. Henri Membomba looked up at the scarring on the alien's chest. This male had initiated so many young that his scars overlapped and blended together. He was a Sytonian adult male, a towan, of significant stature. He and the other towans took these ceremonies seriously.

Membomba looked around at the other humans searching for support but found none. He looked back at Sy Toberry and nodded his acquiescence. He stepped to the center of the group with his cup before him and proclaimed in a loud voice, "We raise our cup in honor and respect, in remembrance and brotherhood, to my mentor and our friend Hyland Wynosk. May his spirit live on in all of us. Tyhinga!" and then he drank deeply from the steaming cup searing his mouth and throat.

In unison, the group immediately echoed the traditional salute and swallowed the burning liquid. The narcotic effect of the keetah quickly deadened the pain, but not before several of the humans in the group let out small groans of agony. The natives burst forth with a triumphant howl. Everyone then spilled the remaining keetah from their cups and returned them to Elizabeth. All except Avram, who held on to his cup and sipped at it while the others disbanded.

Noticing this behavior, Sy Toberry walked over to Avram. "Dai Avram, you must not continue. This is bad for you. I have told you before not to drink cold keetah. It is bad here." He pointed at Avram's chest.

"Sy Toberry, I thank you. I am fine. You are most wise, but I have drunk keetah for nearly thirty years and prefer it cooler." Avram replied.

"Keetah is only for important times. It is only drunk hot."

Avram smiled at his friend Toberry and turned the cup over, spilling the keetah at their feet. This satisfied the towan, who then turned and rejoined the other natives. Avram shook his head and walked over to where Elizabeth was standing with the other cups and handed his to her. "It's silly to waste keetah of that quality. Where was it from?" Avram asked.

"A trader sold it to us earlier this week. I believe he said it came from T'Matte." Elizabeth answered. "He claimed it came from the same stock as the keetah of the Council of Seventeen. I didn't believe him."

"It's possible," mused Avram. "I have tasted this quality before during other their ceremonies. Do you have anymore?"

"We just used every bit we purchased. It is not the sort of thing we keep in the house."

"I suppose not." Disappointed, Avram turned his attention towards the dispersing crowd and together they watched the arrival of a short stocky man. Sy Toberry also paid close attention to this bald newcomer who approached Jorge and began talking to him. Elizabeth and Avram stood in silence. Finally Avram spoke, "You've done a fine job here considering the family..." He paused searching for a diplomatic word. "dynamics. Impressive. It must have been especially difficult after Nanc left."

"It wasn't so bad," Elizabeth lied.

"No?" Avram turned to face her, looking for deceit in her face. Elizabeth stared back. "Well, you've done well. Do you plan on staying?"

Again she lied, "I haven't thought about it."

"Well, if you do think about it, we're looking for help in Nova Gaia. Sy Toberry there," he indicated the towan, "decided he needed a new fourth wife, so we lost our housekeeper. You would have room and board as you have here...maybe a bit nicer."

"It depends on what they decide to do about Wilem" She looked over and saw Jasin playing with the Wilem. Normally, adults avoided the boy, uncomfortable with his handicap. They seemed to be getting along fine.

"Did you teach him to sign?" asked Avram.

"No, it was Hyland."

"I wonder if he made up the language. Can't say we ever had a case of deafness aboard Tanis."

Elizabeth shrugged. "Hyland knew many things."

"You have no idea," Avram turned and watched as the new arrival and Sy Toberry walked purposefully towards him. "Please excuse me Elizabeth, it was a pleasure." He stepped away to greet them.

Elizabeth nodded but took her time gathering the last remnants of the keetah ceremony. She hoped to overhear what had delayed the Enforcer.

"Avram, I'm sorry to have missed your eulogy. To tell you the truth I was surprised that Jorge even allowed it," began Beloit McMaster. He was a powerfully built man, who carried a strange intensity of purpose. Over two decades ago, Avram had convinced the Human Caucus to give McMaster the responsibility of enforcing human compliance to the Prohibitions, the eight rules of conduct that Avram had negotiated on behalf of the settlers and accepted, with considerable heated debate, as a condition for their colonization.

"I left Bistoun as soon as I was able. The place hasn't changed. What a crazy collection of characters!" continued Beloit. "Avram, just be glad you didn't come with me."

"Bistoun is a wonderful place," Avram argued. Then looking straight at Toberry with a twinkle in his eye, "You can get or do anything you want there, and no one would ever stop a man from having a simple cup of keetah."

"You might even get something there you'd regret," Beloit said playfully.

Avram smiled. "So I gather you're not moving back there."

"This might be a bad time." Looking around, he caught Elizabeth eavesdropping. "We need to talk…in private."

They moved away from Elizabeth. Then Avram turned to Toberry, and although the native spoke Human well, Avram addressed him with respect in his native tongue. "Sy Toberry, respectfully sir, Beloit and I need to be alone. Would you tell Jasin to prepare a sleeping place for all of us?" Together they watched the departing towan to make sure he was out of range.

"It's an odd town, Avram. Native and human working and living together, young towan initiates from the warmer region passing through on their way to the wilderness areas, others returning starved and bloodied, many with their new cylith pups. A lot of keetah is being traded and drunk. And there's always a few young women looking for...accommodations. It's a busy place." McMaster hesitated.

"Bistoun has always attracted a special assortment. You of all people shouldn't be surprised. I doubt it's changed much since you left. What's the problem?"

"A woman's been raped—one of the tavern whores. It was difficult finding anyone that would talk, but once the ice broke...they said it was savage and brutal."

"It's a stupid, dangerous game those girls play, Beloit, a different partner each night. But what's the problem? How do you know it wasn't just, you know, just a little rougher than normal?"

"You don't understand. I think we have a real incident here, a diplomatic incident."

"Beloit, the Sytonians don't care about some aberrant human behavior. Considering a son just set fire to his father while we all drank and ate...they already think we're crazy. Humans raping each other on this fractured rock, where the males treat their females like breeding stock, is hardly a diplomatic emergency."

Beloit shook his head and moved closer. "This attack was apparently horrendous. From what I gathered, rape might be too tame a word for what happened to this woman. No one I talked to had a better word for it, Avram, but she was apparently ravaged, ripped and torn. Avram...no one believes a human could have done it."

"That's impossible and you know it! What you're implying is ridiculous. Did you see her? Know who she is?"

"No...I wasn't there long enough. I don't know what happened to her."

"Is she dead?"

Beloit shrugged.

Avram shook his head. "Human history is full of the most awful physical deprivations you can imagine. We just haven't dealt this kind of depravity here before, but now that our numbers have grown we're bound to see some aberrant behavior. To think it might be a towan, however, is more perverted than the attack itself. The Sytonians are the most peaceful race I can imagine. To my knowledge, since we arrived, there hasn't even been a single incident of violence amongst the natives, much less against a human. How can you assume a totally different species would be sexually interested, able, or violent enough?" Avram didn't wait for a reply. "No. There is no viable record, outside of mythology, of any interspecies rape. The rape of a human is a human act of violence. Without question, Beloit, we are the most violent race on this moon. Don't even let yourself consider anything else for an instant."

The prohibition enforcement officer stood momentarily silenced by the strength of Avram's conviction, but eventually he shook his head. "Avram, if there was fraternization; it could be a violation of the sixth Prohibition."

"That Prohibition is meant to avoid undue influence. Don't misunderstand me," Avram put a hand on his Enforcer's shoulder, "this is bad. You're probably right; this could be a diplomatic problem. If the humans in Bistoun start to worry about the Sytonians there, it could spread to other villages. The peace and our settlement could be at risk from this misunderstanding. The end result could be real violence, not just imagined, and that would be a definite breach of the Prohibitions. We can't afford friction. There aren't even seven hundred of us here. I want you to go back, I know it isn't strictly within your responsibilities, but we must uncover the truth and you're the best we have. Find the man who did this and bring him before the Caucus. We need to do it quickly before this gets out of hand."

"That will be nearly impossible, Avram. The trail's cold. It took me most of a day before I could find a person who'd talk to me. No one believes it could be a human. No one's ever heard of a human capable of that kind of violence."

"No one's heard of a towan who's capable of it either. Trust me Beloit. This is the kind of lie that will spread fast. Go back tomorrow and take Jasin. He's been working with you for a year now and he's hardly been out of Nova Gaia.

He needs the field experience and you could use the help. His ability to speak their language will be an asset."

McMaster took a deep breath through his breathing scarf and looked out at the flaming raft. It was still burning strongly, creating strange shadows among those few who had not departed. The mixed scents of the burning drifted through them like spirits happy to be liberated.

"Avram...ever think about your own death? About how we might die? Whether anyone will be left to speak at our memorial service?"

Avram threw an arm around Beloit's shoulders. "You look exhausted. Grab some food and relax."

Beloit shrugged off Avram's embrace. "I've thought about my own...and I don't think many people will care. Most will probably be happy to be rid of me. You may have been the one to approve of the Prohibitions, but I'm the one who enforces them. People are unhappy to see me arrive and glad to see me leave. You can't believe the hatred I felt in Bistoun."

Avram began to respond but Beloit cut him off. "You haven't the slightest idea what I feel, the reaction I get from people once they know who I am, why I'm there. To you they bestow honor. Dai Avram Elstrada." He spat out the name like it was poison. "You must realize that a lot of humans secretly hate you for forcing us to live like this, for giving up thousands of years of human progress, but they would never treat you poorly. When you die, they will sing your praises. They will talk of your breaking the language barrier, of your patient negotiations and guidance of the Human Caucus. You helped create the restrictions and rules we must live by, but you'll be remembered fondly." He shook his head trying to find understanding in irony. "I just make sure we follow those rules and they hate me for it. They take out their anger on me so they don't have to hate their hero. You want me to find a deranged human so it doesn't become a huge incident, so the peace you helped create doesn't disappear. But it means I will be questioning my own kind, generating resentment wherever I go. I'm not sure I want to go back to Bistoun. I'm tired of being the hated one. Are you sure you want your son to share in that?"

"Forgive me, Beloit. I was insensitive. You've traveled a long way without rest and the first thing I request is for you to make the trip again. I'm sorry. It was thoughtless of me."

Beloit slowly shook his head again. "Avram, don't play with me. Give me at least that much respect."

Avram grinned. "We've worked together too many years...but honestly, you do look tired."

"I'll be fine. Tell Jasin we'll leave at first light."

"I'll tell him, and do be careful." This time Avram sounded sincere.

Beloit pressed his lips together and nodded.

"While you're there—" Avram began.

"I'll see what I can find."

"Elizabeth said there was a trader from T'matte. His stuff was exceptional."

"You really shouldn't be using so much."

Avram smiled. "I use it only for ceremonial purposes."

"I think perhaps you celebrate too much."

Avram grasped Beloit by the shoulders and faced him squarely. "My friend, we need to celebrate. We're safe and secure, due in no small part to you and Hyland. We couldn't have been luckier than finding this moon when time ran out."

Beloit shrugged off Avram's embrace. "I'm going to get some rest. Tell Jasin to be ready." He turned and headed up the path, leaving Avram standing alone.

"Beloit!" Avram shouted after him. Elizabeth looked over towards them.

McMaster stopped and turned.

Avram took a few steps toward him. "I'll speak at your funeral, my friend...if I'm still alive."

"And what will you say about me? Do you really know what I've been through, what my life's been like?" Beloit turned away and continued up the path, alone.

After everyone had departed, Elizabeth sat alone on the shoreline surrounded by four bright torches. She gazed out into the dark bay, watching the dying embers of what had been the raft. In the last year she had begun to hate the dimness, afraid of what lay just beyond the light, but the bickering in the cabin had started up again and she knew Nanc would be seeking refuge in her bed tonight. Experience had shown that it was better to share the mattress after Nanc had fallen asleep.

It was time to leave Lake Chook. She knew father and son would be just fine. Jorge loved his son and could be an attentive father, especially if there were no distractions. Avram's offer intrigued her. While it wasn't health care, it allowed her to move on, without retreating back to Daddy and the icy village of Panvera. She had never been to Nova Gaia. It was larger than Lake Chook and more developed. Lost in thought, she was startled by a deep, calm voice. She flinched.

"You shouldn't sneak up on someone like that," Elizabeth complained. She recognized Jasin Elstrada as he entered the ring of light. His black hair was quite long and tousled; she had remembered him as neatly trimmed.

"Sneak up? I made so much noise coming down the path I was sure you heard me. I'm sorry that I scared you," he said, brushing a loose strand from his eye.

"You didn't."

"Do you remember me?" asked Jasin.

She decided not to make it easy on him. "I'm sorry. There have been a lot of people here today."

"I'm Jasin Elstrada. We've met before. I was your brother Michael's roommate."

"I think I remember you."

"I didn't have a chance to talk to you earlier. You were so busy. Do you mind if I sit?"

"I was just about to go in," Elizabeth said, hoping he would realize she wasn't in the mood to talk, not in the mood for anything.

"Just for a second? I know you must be exhausted but…"

"But?"

"I was wondering about Michael. How's he doing? Last time I talked to him, he was going back to Panvera after school. I lost track of him."

Elizabeth turned away to stare out into the water. She said softly, "They say you are going to be an Enforcer like Beloit McMaster."

"I am an Enforcer."

"Then you should be more aware of what happens around here." Elizabeth turned slowly to face him. "My brother is dead."

"No…" Jasin's pain was evident. He sat down near her. "I'm sorry. I hadn't heard. What happened?"

"I'd rather not talk about it."

They sat in silence for several long minutes until finally Elizabeth relented. She took a deep, soothing breath through her breathing scarf. "We were camping along the fringe of the wilderness area where the young towan go for Initiation. It was already hours into the dimness when some Initiate flushed a small pack of cyliths into our site. They surprised us. Michael tried to fight them off, but there had to be a dozen of them."

"Were you hurt?"

Elizabeth shook her head and pretended to be looking out over the water. For the second time today tears formed and rolled down her cheek. Not wanting to embarrass her, Jasin looked away. The bright circle of torches now made sense to him.

"How long ago?" It was obvious her grief was fresh.

"Not quite a year ago, it was nearly the dark time, a week before the last Rhan-da-lith," she said in almost a whisper.

"I'm so sorry."

Elizabeth just nodded. There was an awkward pause.

Jasin stood up. "I'll let you be. I just wanted…it was nice seeing you again Elizabeth. I'm sorry…about not knowing…about your brother."

"It's okay."

"I was wondering…" Jasin hesitated until Elizabeth turned toward him. Her moist eyes sparkled in the light of the torches. "If I return this way when we're through in Bistoun, would you mind if I stopped back?"

"You're going to Bistoun?"

"In the morning."

"Both you and your father?"

"No, my father is returning to Nova Gaia. I'm going with Beloit. Did you have a chance to meet him?"

Elizabeth shook her head and then hesitated before asking, "Jasin, your Dad mentioned that you had lost your housekeeper, and that there might be a job available?"

Jasin shrugged. "I don't really know. I've heard that Sy Toberry is taking Seanne Sy to replace his Fourth."

Once again silence enveloped them. Not a single ember glowed in the bay. A few stray insects flickered about the torches sending eerie shadows darting back and forth on the ground. After a moment of thought, Elizabeth stood and grabbed a torch, and while one was sufficient, Jasin took a second. Together they walked up the path.

Bistoun

Maelstroms of ice and snow scour the frozen surface of Syton with enough force to tear off human flesh and then sand the bones smooth. Looking for a possible home, it was no wonder the crew of *Tanis* initially rejected this moon in favor of Eian, the inner, warmer moon of the mother planet, Conboet. If Eian's atmosphere had been breathable, they would never have taken another look at the second moon, Syton, and would never have discovered the mammoth fissure and plume of steam rising from its depths. At the bottom, thirteen kilometers below the ice fields, molten rock and gas escaped the inferno hidden deep within the moon's core. There, blood would boil. But between this hell and the frozen surface, on a vast plateau three hundred kilometers wide that formed where the canyon walls rested momentarily from their relentless descent, the planetary geologists discovered a temperate zone, and a fragile ecosystem that could provide salvation for the desperate crew of Tanis. They also discovered the natives that already lived there.

The snow and ice that swept into the gorge, melted and trickled down its steep sides, the frigid water ran through peaks and mountains, and cascaded in gushing waterfalls to eventually fill Lake Chook. The Andoree River then sucked out the water and delivered it to an even greater lake beyond. The tidal forces of Syton's mother planet and its sister moon yanked and pushed the water back and forth before it spilled over the lip of the great basin and onto the superheated rocks below. There it turned into steam, and rose out of the gorge to freeze and fuel the ferocious storms that ravaged the surface.

Jasin waded out into the icy water of Lake Chook until he was waist deep and washed off the grime of the trail, finishing by a quick dunk under the frigid water. Shock and an immediate headache served to dissolve the last cobwebs of sleep from his mind. Ashore, he retrieved his filthy pants and shirt from the same rocky outcropping that his father had spoken from the night before. He dressed, and waited for Beloit McMaster. The sun had barely risen, but the dimness was waning.

His unsettled thoughts bounced between Michael's horrible fate, beautiful yet impenetrable Elizabeth, and the investigation that awaited them in Bistoun. Jasin forced himself to concentrate on the days ahead. Once before he had experienced the fishing village of Bistoun and the guilty pleasures it afforded, but it was with Michael. Vivid memories of an indulgent break from school should have left little room for thoughts of anything else, but soon the image of Elizabeth surrounded by a ring of torches, her captivating eyes, and the gruesome thought of her brother's death by the pack of wild cyliths returned like a flood. Again he tried to put it out of his mind, but again Elizabeth and Michael returned—a torturous loop.

Chilling wind blew through Jasin's wet hair. He squeezed the water out. There should be time to get it cut in Bistoun, he thought. Being from high Nova Gaia, he easily tolerated the cold; he was quite accustomed to it. With the exception of Panvera, his hometown was probably the coldest human settlement on Syton, but this morning, the cold moist breeze off the lake penetrated his clothes and chilled him. Perhaps he shouldn't have taken that dip. A few days ago, he had looked forward to visiting Lake Chook, but now he couldn't wait to leave. If only last night had been different, if she hadn't been so unapproachable. He shivered; evidently everything was cold in Lake Chook.

Things would heat up in Bistoun. Jasin smiled. While it was still on the water's edge, at least it had redeeming qualities. He remembered the bathhouse Michael and he had gone to, and the accommodating girls in the barbershop next door...but Michael was dead. Jasin's thoughts again began to repeat themselves. Thankfully, McMaster broke the cycle.

"You didn't bring a razor either I see," said Beloit, eyeing Jasin's stubble. "I thought I'd be heading home. Well, there are plenty of talented blades ahead."

Jasin rubbed his cheek, "Maybe I'll grow a beard."

"Girls don't like a rough face."

Jasin shrugged. "You cleaning up?" he asked.

Beloit looked out across the bay. Fog obscured its cold surface. He shook his head. "Let's get going. We'll take a break in a few hours. I'll freshen up then."

Without much conversation, the two made their way to the clearing where they had spent the night. Avram squatted next to a crackling fire chewing a hard biscuit. A pot of water nestled in a bed of glowing embers.

"Want something to warm your insides before you go?" he asked. "Got some tea left and a few stale biscuits from home."

Jasin looked to Beloit who answered, "We'll take what you can spare."

Avram stood up slowly and went over to his blaython. From his pack, he drew out a full package of unopened food and handed it to Beloit. "Leftovers from Nanc. A gift from one of their neighbors they didn't use or need." He shrugged his shoulders.

"Thank her for us," Beloit said. He stuffed the package inside one of his travel sacks, then carried them over to his blaython and slung them over the animal's bony haunches.

"Do you have time for a warm drink?" Avram asked.

"Sure," answered Jasin.

"We need to get going," Beloit said abruptly. "I'd like to make the Fork before dimness."

"Well then, you two have a safe trip. I'm anxious to hear what you find out."

Jasin cocked his head. This was cold behavior between friends. Fork Camp wasn't that far. Beloit knew it. His father was well aware of the distance. He walked over to his own animal and closed his bags. His father came up beside him.

"Be careful in Bistoun," Avram said. "Someone won't be happy you're there."

Jasin nodded and glanced over to Beloit, then back to his father. "Is everything ok?"

"Everything's fine. Don't worry about it. Just be safe."

Jasin searched his father's face looking for more, but his father just smiled. "As usual, you're concerned about the wrong things." Avram placed a hand on his son's shoulder. "I'm very serious; take care of yourself," Avram insisted.

Jasin grabbed the reins, placed his foot on the blaython's extended center leg and climbed up.

Beloit mounted then spoke over a shoulder to Avram. "We'll probably see you in about a week,"

"Whatever it takes," replied Avram.

Jasin lifted his hand in farewell. In response, his father tossed him the biscuit he had been holding.

Leaving Lake Chook, they rode past small fields of purple flax fighting for life in the alien soil, and then they turned towards the lower canyon pass. A damp wind blew in from behind, forcing them to raise the collars of their oiled overcoats. There was no satisfactory way to ride a blaython comfortably. The towan's double knees allowed them to wrap their longer legs around the animal's bony midsection, but human's, especially shorter ones like Jasin and Beloit, usually ended up with bruises and cramps in exchange for the quicker ride.

The fastest route to Bistoun was by boat, but then they would have had to give up the valuable pack animals, making for a long walk back to Nova Gaia once they had completed their investigation. They could have tried to forge a trail along the lake and then the river, but Beloit decided to travel the established path, temporarily away from Bistoun, even if it wasn't the most direct. Once they got to Fork Camp they would angle back towards the Andoree River instead of continuing up into the canyon.

After two hours, sunlight broke through the steam clouds and the brisk wind subsided. Beloit pulled them off the main trail. "There are dozens of creeks and streams flowing out of the canyon and down to the Andoree," explained Beloit. "Look for the stiff grasses and umbrella weed. They seem to prefer wet soil." A minute later they arrived at a slow moving stream. "The shallow water will be much warmer than the lake if you want to freshen up," Beloit said removing his clothes.

Jasin washed the trail dirt from his face and relaxed while Beloit finished bathing and rinsing his hair. Beloit must have been amused at his dip in the freezing water this morning, Jasin reflected. "What's going on between you and my father?"

"Why do you ask that?"

"Just felt it."

Beloit left the water and gathered up his things. "Nothing much, a small difference in opinion."

"Small?"

"Minor really. You ready to get going?"

"It didn't seem minor."

"Did the animals get water?" asked Beloit.

Jasin looked over to the blaython resting not far from the stream's edge. "I suppose so."

"Make sure, then let's go."

Jasin walked over to the pack animals and brought them right to the stream's edge. They weren't interested.

"They're fine," reported Jasin.

Beloit finished tying his boot and, without another word, led them out of the grasses.

It was still early afternoon when they arrived at Fork Camp. From here, you could either continue up into the canyon and eventually farther into the cold country towards the Great Falls and Nova Gaia, or you could head around the lower side of Mount Schtolin and then ascend to Panvera. They planned to follow yet another trail and descend toward the Andoree and to the ferry landing across from Bistoun. Being at this crossroads, the camp was heavily used. At least three distinct groups were busy making camp before the dimness returned. Jasin recognized several people who had attended Hyland's funeral. Getting to the next higher camp was a full day's travel from here. No one traveling higher would be starting this late in the day.

"What do you think?" Jasin asked.

"There's plenty of room for two more if you're tired," Beloit said.

Jasin heard the challenge in Beloit's voice. "There's plenty of light. Let's head towards the river."

"We won't make it before we lose most of the light."

"So?"

"We'll have to make camp. Not scared of the cyliths?" asked Beloit.

"I doubt any packs are this close to Bistoun. The Initiates have probably cleaned out the area." Jasin looked over to Beloit to see if his answer satisfied his boss. He couldn't tell. "Ever see any between the falls and the river?"

Beloit laughed. "Never even heard of anyone who has."

They refilled their water bags and took the trail angling back down towards the river. It was less used than the trails to Lake Chook or up into the canyon, but they made good time, stopping only to stretch their legs.

The day had passed without them having eaten anything substantial, so an hour or so before dimness, they made camp, fixed a quick dinner, and then scouted the area. While they walked, they gathered several small bundles of sticks. Beloit asked Jasin to make the fire while he retrieved the sleeping blankets and ground cloths. He laid them in the small clearing, propped himself up, crossed his arms, and watched Jasin work on the fire. Almost immediately, Jasin heard snoring.

Digging in his backpack, Jasin found his remaining flint needle. On their way to the funeral, Avram had requested boiling water almost every night. Keetah didn't dissolve well unless the water was extremely hot.

From the wood they had collected Jasin made a small mound of kindling, and then searched along the edge of the clearing for a few fresh popper thorns that hadn't yet split.

He found several and snapped them off, careful not to break them too close to the stem and risk releasing their methane gas. Bending over the kindling, he held the flint needle and poppers together, and then with a practiced flick of the wrist, snapped them in two and plunged the resulting tiny blue flame into the dry kindling. A blaze soon bathed their campsite in a flickering glow.

The crackling woke McMaster and he distributed the greasy pemmican Avram had provided. Jasin nibbled at the mixture of jerky, nuts, and dried fruit, but gave up, preferring to be hungry rather than sick. He leaned back and watched the sparkling ashes rise into the evening sky where they mixed with the half dozen stars visible overhead.

"I can't believe how many stars you can see on a clear night," Jasin said.

Beloit laughed. "And I will never get used to how few you see from down here."

"Do you really miss being trapped inside that small ship?"

"Wasn't small."

"I mean compared to this world. It must have been like living your life inside a single home, never able to leave, seeing the same walls year after year."

"We never knew any different. Most of us never wanted to leave. The thought of leaving the ship petrified us. It was our world. It took a long time to understand that we had to leave, that the ship was dying, and that we couldn't take the chance that we'd find another world before the ship failed. If it weren't for that, I don't think anyone would have left. Even after most of us understood that staying on the ship meant eventual death, there were a few that refused to leave. The doctor and a couple of the older ones had to be drugged. Hyland carried them from the ship himself."

"How about you?" asked Jasin.

"I left standing."

"Hyland?"

"People misunderstood Hyland's reluctance. When it was time for Hyland to leave, he went willingly. He wasn't the rebel your Dad was. Everyone trusted Hyland and his staff. It was Avram who was always a little radical."

Jasin sensed the reemergence of the morning's coolness. "I take it this trip to Bistoun wasn't your idea."

"Hardly, but we need to go. We need to find out what happened to that whore and try to keep the peace."

"How do you know she was—?"

"A whore? All the misfits run away to Bistoun to find something better, but sooner or later the girls find the only thing they have of value is between their legs."

"What about the local authorities?" asked Jasin. "Why are we involved?"

"The relationship with the natives is our responsibility. The Prohibitions are intended to avoid conflict," answered Beloit.

"But no Prohibition has been broken here. A woman has been molested. There's no technology involved, no weapons, no restricted travel, no sale of human artifacts or land issues."

"You're right, if it were up to me I'd skip it, let this one alone, but this is the first instance of this level of violence since we arrived and it has everyone, especially your dad, on edge. From what little I've heard, some believe a native was involved. That would be a violation of the sixth. Anyway, Avram's right about one thing, the quicker this incident is resolved, the better."

Jasin leaned over and picked up a dried branch of poppers and threw it into the fire. It caught instantly and burned brighter than the other twigs. They sat quietly watching. Jasin finally broke the silence. "Do you spend many nights on the trail?"

"You get used to it…comes with the job. Just don't get involved…" Beloit's voice trailed off thoughtfully.

"Involved?"

"Relationships. You involved with anyone? I saw you last night with Hyland's nurse."

"She's the sister of someone I once knew."

"Pretty."

"Kinda tall, not really my type."

"Don't get involved," Beloit muttered under his breath. "Don't get involved with any of them. They're all whores." Beloit yawned and laid his head back looking up at the thin sliver of Conboet. Finally he asked, "So how'd you learn to speak Sytonian?"

"Avram pushed me hard when I was young. He thought it was important. That's why he always had one of the natives around, like Sy Toberry. When I went to advanced studies in Panvera, the language courses were the easiest."

"You obviously have an ear for it. I can hardly make out a single word of their stupid tongue." Beloit rose and took a few steps before peeing into the darkness.

"Being able to speak their language is going to come in handy tomorrow," Beloit said, returning and making himself comfortable. Within minutes he was asleep.

Jasin built up the fire and leaned back against one of the supply bags. He stared at Beloit's sleeping form. How was it possible to snore so loud and not wake yourself? At least the noise should scare off any wild animals that might have gotten a whiff of their meal.

While he wasn't sure of their exact role in the rape investigation, he understood how important it was to keep the peace with the natives. The Human colony's survival depended upon it. When he had finished school, he was thrilled when his father suggested he help Beloit enforce the Prohibitions. He had grown up with a deep conviction that the Prohibitions were as important to their existence as air or water.

Humans, especially those ship-born, resented the rules Avram had bound them to, but the ship-born were also the most likely to lapse and introduce some technology from the past. When the few hundred humans landed on Syton, they had technology and weapons a thousand years more advanced than the natives.

Avram understood that knowledge and its offspring technology were powerful tools that could easily divide a society, or even be used as a weapon to control those that didn't possess them. The natives and the shipborn both recognized that the inhabitable land in the gorge was too limited to attempt segregation so, in return for permission to settle, the Sytonian Council had insisted that humans abandon their technology and live as they did. Avram had been convinced that the natives were ready to die to enforce their demand and realized the slaughter would have been horrific. Humans would have had to kill tens of thousands of towan and severely maim the developing Sytonian civilization all so they could keep their lifestyle. It was ultimately a moral question. Where did Human rights end and the Sytonians' begin? Even if war could have been avoided, were the technical conveniences of a few hundred humans worth creating a race of second-class individuals and altering the course of an entire planet's culture?

Jasin knew Avram was right to agree to the Sytonian Prohibitions. And he knew how important enforcing them was. It wasn't a difficult choice for a morally advanced race to make. As sleep overcame him, Jasin was first filled with pride, and then admiration, not only for his father and Beloit, but also for the Sytonian Council of Seventeen, who had the foresight and moral compass to insist on the Prohibitions in the first place.

When brightness returned they broke camp, and within an hour stood at the empty ferry landing on the bank of the Andoree River. To their left, the river eventually widened to become Lake Chook. If they followed the river to the right, they would travel beneath high cliffs for a stretch before coming to a group of small islands and the intersection with the Canyon River. Beyond that was the Great Lake. Today their thoughts were on Bistoun just across the narrows where the ferry, a crude raft of bundled reeds and grasses, bobbed in the river's swell. It was tied to the shore with a thick rope of fiber robe. No one was aboard.

Beloit tied the blaythons to a bush so they could easily be seen from the other shore, and made himself comfortable against some boulders. Jasin paced.

"Relax, sit down," Beloit suggested. "It'll be a while. He won't bother moving the ferry until it's calmer. It's too much work to fight the current."

"How long?"

"Check the high water mark." Beloit indicated with a lift of his head. "The water is still flowing in. Looks like maybe an hour."

"Can't we wade across?" asked Jasin. "It looks like it might be shallow enough,"

Beloit just looked up at him, shading the sun from his eyes with his open hand. Jasin realized how dumb the question was. Why build a ferry where you could simply walk across?

"I'm just anxious," He felt extremely stupid. "I think I'll stretch my legs."

Beloit barely acknowledged his leaving.

Jasin headed back up the trail they had just come down. As he rounded a slight bend, he raised his breathing scarf and began to jog, a slow comfortable pace. It felt good. He hadn't run in nearly a week, since before leaving for Hyland's funeral. At home he ran almost daily. It relieved stress and he loved the feeling of freedom and self-confidence it gave him. As a young boy he began running to relieve tension and discovered the adrenaline high that running in the dimness would bring, especially when there was barely enough light to see where he was going, when his feet would hardly touch the ground and the fear of falling, just barely in control, combined with exhilarating speed would leave him breathless.

Now when he ran, there wasn't that same intensity, but he still enjoyed it. He circled a small hill and sprinted along a winding path up the backside until he was at the top. The hill dropped off steeply towards the river creating a lookout over the ferry landing and to Bistoun beyond. Jasin sat on the edge to catch his breath and survey the town.

Along the river were several empty boat slips, defined by short finger piers jutting into the muddy water. A long flat barge, heavily laden with salted paddlefish, fantale, and dried gilia root lay secured against the shore down stream. Straight across the river, Jasin could see the raft still tied up at the opposite ferry landing. Just beyond the landing, across the frontage road and next to a ten meter tall tree was a three-story inn that he remembered from his previous visit. He assumed they would sleep there tonight. Jasin could see smoke rising from the cooking area behind. He wondered whether they still made deepfish stew. The memory of its unique sharp taste and the mellowness one felt afterward was hard to forget. It had been several days since he had a good meal and was famished. Right next door, between the inn and the boat construction yard was one of the two taverns in town. The larger one had rooms on the second floor rumored to rent by the hour.

Jasin surveyed the roads leading to the riverbank. Where was the owner of the ferry? Surely the current wasn't strong enough to delay much longer. He wasn't sure who controlled the ferry these days; probably still a towan. Last time across, he remembered, it was a young towan, but you never could tell in Bistoun where fortunes and property changed hands frequently.

The door of the small tavern next to a fish smoker opened and a young blond woman appeared carrying a bucket. She started across the frontage road. At first, Jasin hoped she might have operated the ferry, but it became obvious that she was much too petite to pole the raft across. She walked out on to one of the finger piers and emptied the garbage bucket into the river. He watched the bits of refuse gather around the piers. It was slack tide.

With a shock, he realized that the raft was moving. He had been distracted and missed the arrival of the ferry operator. Jasin jumped to his feet and ran down the hill.

It took less than five minutes for the raft to arrive. Operating it was an ancient towan who probably couldn't remember his youth. He moved slowly and carefully. His legs were deformed from a severe case of muscle bulge, a common ailment among older towans that caused the muscles to contract into tight knots making it difficult to bend their upper knee joints or even move. With great effort, he threw a rope to Beloit, who immediately handed it to Jasin. He tied it to a post that had been wedged between rocks next to the landing. The towan made no effort to help as Beloit and Jasin moved their belongings and the blaythons aboard. Getting the animals to be still took great effort. Finally, they were calm enough for Jasin to handle them alone and Beloit went to pay for their passage.

He handed the towan several small, clear, cut crystals from a leather pouch he dug from his traveling pack. The towan pointed at the animals with his main large finger that was also deformed with muscle bulge. Beloit nodded his head in agreement and counted out each of the four passengers, "One, two, three, four," and then he turned and repeated the count for the crystals in the towan's palm. The towan let out a low tone and again pointed at the animals. One of the scared blaythons was urinating. Its pungent scent filled the air as it splattered on Jasin's feet. Jasin swore, and jumped out of the way, but he couldn't go far.

Beloit chuckled at Jasin's dismay. The old towan's expression didn't change. He voiced another series of words, again in low tones and once more held out his hand. "Listen," Beloit said with a note of aggravation, "Four of us, four clear crystals, that's normal passage."

"He wants more because of the mess," explained Jasin.

"He wanted more even before the animal peed on his raft," complained Beloit.

"Maybe he knew it was coming." Jasin shrugged. "Looks like he's been at this a long time. Probably not the first time some scared animal made a mess of his raft."

Beloit took out his pouch and found a tiny, round, blue crystal, and added it to the four clear ones. This satisfied the towan, who stood with difficulty. Jasin retrieved the binding rope and pushed the raft away from the shore. With considerable effort, the towan poled the raft slowly towards the opposite shore. Jasin turned and looked back at the hill he'd run up. He felt as if he was leaving his familiar world behind, crossing an imaginary line that separated Human from Sytonian.

The river *was* a natural boundary. Most humans lived on the cold side of the river, in the higher towns and villages where the alien air was thinner, cooler, and easier to breathe. The Sytonians, however, found the warmer, lower altitudes more comfortable. Of course, there were a few scattered exceptions. Bistoun was an anomaly. It was the coldest town that the Sytonians regularly inhabited, but the warmest where humans could feel comfortable year round. This made it unique — humans and natives living and working together. Jasin knew he could help Beloit here.

On the opposite shore, Beloit and Jasin left the crippled towan and walked across the frontage road to the large inn. Jasin took the two blaythons around back to the stables while Beloit went to see about rooms. Rounding the corner of the inn, Jasin was assaulted by the stench of the large inn's open sewage system. Breathing through his mouth, he hastened to the stable, tugging the blaythons behind him. He located two empty stalls and left the animals with a good portion of sungrass. The inn had a back entrance and Jasin, wanting to vacate the stinking yard, rushed to take advantage of it. He entered the kitchen breathing heavily. Large boiling pots of deepfish filled the air with their unique tang, not spicy, not really a true scent at all, but a sharp sensation in the back of the nose like a smell.

Suddenly he stopped. At first he thought the kitchen had been deserted, but there, huddled together against a greasy, soot covered wall, were five diminutive towas—Sytonian females—standing absolutely motionless. The dark, naked, identical forms stared at him, unblinking. He had obviously scared them. They made such a dramatic counterpoint to the large towan or Sytonian male. He returned their gaze. Suddenly he felt warm. Blood ran to his cheeks, and he became dizzy. Turning to leave, he crashed to the floor, conscious, but unable to move a muscle.

Sy Fask

With caution, the towas moved to inspect the body sprawled on their kitchen floor. One of them leaned over, close to Jasin's face, and sniffed his breath, evidently familiar with other humans flat on their backs. Another began roughly prodding Jasin in the ribs with her foot. Completely paralyzed, all Jasin could do was stare up at their naked bodies. An interesting view, he thought, if he weren't so confused and helpless.

Although he was sure he was still being kicked, there was no sensation of pain. Panic began to creep in. After a moment or two, several towa took hold of each of his arms and dragged him into the main entry area of the inn and then disappeared like a whiff of smoke back into the kitchen. Jasin could hear Beloit talking to someone. Muffled unintelligible conversation, then silence, footsteps, until Beloit and a frail, spindly young boy towered above him.

"Damn, you all right?" asked the boy. The raw exclamation felt out of place coming from this frail boy who couldn't have been more than ten years old.

Jasin couldn't answer. Numbness had spread throughout his body. He was having trouble breathing.

"He'll come 'round soon," declared the boy. "Musta wandered into the kitchen. They boiling deepfish for tonight. Smell it?"

Beloit raised his head and sniffed. "Let's move him farther away."

The boy nodded. With a grunt, Beloit lifted Jasin, carried him out the front door, and deposited him on the ground.

"It's great eatin'...deepfish I mean, once they done adding everythin'," the boy continued to explain, "but you got to boil them out. You know, boil out the toxes...the poison stuff. Anyway, one, two fish dancing in a pot ain't nothin', but a big kettle like that...not a good place for us no way."

After a few minutes, Jasin began to feel better; he could move his arms and legs. He tried to speak but only a garbled mumble escaped. "No talkin' fer awhile. If you do, you'd soundin' stupid," said the boy.

Beloit cracked a grin and quickly looked away. Jasin smiled to himself. If Avram heard this boy's speech he'd be upset. One of his father's regrets since settling on Syton had been the falling level of general education among the human population. The rapid decline in the ability to read, and write, and just speak well was striking.

"So, young man," said Beloit digging into his leather bag and extracting a small pink *meita*, "We want to thank you for your help. Please see that our blaythons have plenty of water and feed during their stay at your stables." Beloit gave him the tiny pill Humans traded containing the chemicals that saturated their breathing scarves.

"Ya sir! Certain I would sir but..." he held his palm open. Even in his little hand the meita looked miniscule.

"Don't be greedy boy," Beloit scolded. "There'll be more *if* the animals are well cared for."

The young boy quickly closed his hand. "Don't blame a business man fer askin'. Wouldn't be right didn't try, heh? Anything you need here, I'm your man. Anything." He turned to go and started for the stables.

"Well, there is one more thing..." Beloit said. The frail boy swirled around anxiously. "What's your name?"

"My name? Call me Samson. Sami is my real name. No one calls me that anymore."

"Well Samson, I have a friend who's more than a little fond of good keetah. I wouldn't imagine that a young boy like you would know where I could pick some up. I'm only interested in the best."

"Best's not cheap," said Samson.

Beloit reached into his little pouch and pulled out a large red meita and held it up so the boy could see. "Think this might cover it?"

"Would rather have crystal. Keetah is towan trade. Only humans care 'bout meitas."

Beloit dug out a large blue crystal. Samson reached out to take it, but Beloit pulled it back. "Of course, I would have to see it. We'll be back tonight. Think you can find what I'm looking for? We only want the highest quality."

"Told you, I'm your man."

Beloit turned to Jasin as the young boy headed off to the stables. "Do you feel well enough to try walking?"

"Think so." Jasin mumbled, attempting to stand. Beloit put a hand around his waist to keep him upright. Jasin's hair was full of grease and dirt from lying on the kitchen floor and again on the ground. His side was aching from being kicked and he could feel a bump over his right ear where he had hit the floor. He smelled from two days on the trail and was a mess. It seemed like a long time since his cold dip in Lake Chook.

"Beloit…can you get my pack and help me get over to the bathhouse?" His speech was becoming clearer.

"And how would you know about the bathhouse?" Beloit asked with a smile.

Jasin managed a weak grin. "Bathhouse, then maybe a shave and haircut next door with one of the ladies. We all deserve a little pampering now and again."

"Is that what they're calling it these days?"

Beloit retrieved Jasin's pack, and together they slowly walked across the main street leading from the river to the bathhouse. Before separating, they arranged to meet for dinner at the tavern next to the inn. Neither of them felt like deepfish stew tonight.

Jasin opened the door to the bathhouse and entered a small antechamber with a rectangular table jutting out from one side. The air was heavy with warm moisture from tubs hidden behind a drape hung across a doorway in the back wall. He swung his pack onto the table and steadied himself.

"Anyone here?" he asked loudly. His voice broke up slightly, but he was beginning to feel normal again. He heard muffled voices from behind the drape. It was drawn aside and an older woman entered. Jasin thought she looked at least sixty.

"Would you mind?" she lifted Jasin's filthy pack from the table and handed it back to him. It left a ring of dirt on the table. She ignored the dirt and looked Jasin over.

"Sorry," Jasin apologized. "Do you have any hot water left?"

The old lady continued staring.

"Listen, I said I was sorry." Jasin began to wipe the table down. "But I was hoping to wash up."

"Are you Julian's kid?" she asked.

Jasin stared back, locking his eyes on hers. He nodded.

"You need a shave. Want one with the bath?"

"Have we met before?" he asked.

She shook her head and waved off the question. "It's the thick black hair and eyes; same as your mom's. Listen...I'll throw in the shave for nothing. I owe her."

"Just the bath for now, but thanks. I'll see one of the ladies next door for the shave." Jasin hoped she'd understand and wouldn't pursue it. He didn't have a very respectful reason to refuse her generous offer except...

The old woman, trying to hide a tiny smirk, was amused. "I would be happy to help you out myself..." she paused for the effect. Jasin felt the blood rush to his face. Finally, her smile escaped. "I know the girls next door very well, but only one is as good with a blade in her hand, as without one. My treat, I'll have her come over." Then abruptly, "Well, let's say we get you cleaned up."

Within minutes, Jasin was soaking in a tub of hot, soapy water. He washed his hair and then closing his eyes, let the dirt, and aches from the towa's kicking dissolve away. The warm water revived his numb muscles, removing the last effects of the fish toxins. He drifted, semi-conscious and totally relaxed, listening to vague snippets of sound and unintelligible voices until he was asleep.

With a start, Jasin realized he wasn't alone. He sat up, instantly awake. At the foot of the tub stood a young woman who looked up from the bath water to meet Jasin's gaze. Her oval face was framed by long black hair falling over her shoulders; a simple thin white sheath covered her nubile form.

"You were sleeping, I'm sorry." Her beautiful round eyes caught a glint of light and sparkled. He leaned slightly to get a better look around the tub. She held up a bar of soap in one hand, and a blade in the other. She walked gracefully towards him. Light shone through the gauzy fabric of her dress revealing her sensual curves. "I'm from next door. I was told you wanted a shave." She lifted the blade as if to remind him why she was there.

It was difficult for Jasin not to stare at the girl; she was simply stunning, but her razor competed for his attention. It was a most unusual shade of dark greenish-blue—unlike any knife blade he'd ever seen…for that matter, unlike any metal he'd ever seen. "Do you know what you're doing with that?" he asked, indicating the razor.

"I've never had any complaints."

Jasin's gaze traveled the length of her body. "I'll wager that's true." But his eyes were drawn back to the blade. He held out his hand, "It's most unusual. Do you mind?"

"Be very careful," she replied laying it in his palm, "It's awfully sharp."

The blade lay like a feather in his hand. It was practically weightless. He thought it must be paper-thin, but when he held it between his fingertips he realized it was actually as thick as a regular knife blade, just incredibly light. He brought it closer for a better look. There were no manufacturing marks, no sign that it had ever been hammered or filed, and yet, the edge appeared perfectly smooth. Very carefully he checked for sharpness with his thumb.

"Oh!" he flinched and dropped the blade, which struck the side of the metal tub before hitting the floor. A drop of blood oozed out of Jasin's thumb. "I'm sorry... I didn't realize..."

"You dumb animal!" exclaimed the girl, kneeling to pick up her razor. "I told you to be careful. I just got this blade and it cost me plenty." She lifted the blade. They could both see that the razor's sharp edge had a nick in it where it had hit the tub. She shook it at Jasin. "You owe me."

"It's not that bad," Jasin tried to calm her. In fact, it actually didn't look as bad as he thought at first glance. Both Jasin and the girl stared at the blade. The nick was slowly disappearing.

Astonished, the girl handed it to Jasin. He too had trouble believing what he had witnessed. The blade was perfect now. The strange material had repaired itself, reforming a perfect edge.

"He just said it wouldn't need to be sharpened," the girl whispered.

"Who?" Jasin's professional curiosity was aroused. This was advanced technology and prohibited by the Second Prohibition. It might also be considered a weapon, a violation of the Fourth.

The young lady shook her head. A few strands of black silky hair fell over an eye. She brushed it away, but it immediately returned, falling seductively across her face. "A gift from a private client," she said evasively. "He enjoyed my services. Said he got it from a trader and thought I could use it."

"A gift? I thought you said it cost you plenty. Who was it?" Jasin asked again.

"Why do you care?"

"He could be in trouble. You could be in trouble for having it."

"It's just a razor. I have many."

Jasin raised the blade. "Like this?"

"No," she said softly, then reached out and took it back. "Listen, do you want the shave? I'm not paid to answer stupid questions."

The water had turned cold. They had been distracted and Jasin's mood had changed. "Perhaps another time," Jasin said. "Are you working tomorrow?"

"I work everyday. Just ask for Tabiya." She moved closer and smiled. "I could come to your room tonight...I'm not expensive." Again her hair fell sensually across her cheek.

Jasin reached out and gently moved the errant strands of hair behind her ear, then let his hand run lightly along her smooth skin. Her offer was very tempting, but she was awfully young, maybe seventeen at most. He began to feel guilty even touching her face. She tilted her head, pressing her soft cheek into his hand.

"Tabiya, you're too young, and too beautiful, to be selling yourself to anyone with a crystal. Don't waste your life in a bathhouse. You should still be in school, having fun with decent young men your own age. Get out of here before you get yourself in trouble. And don't show that blade to anyone."

Jasin's admonishment confused her. "What's your name?" she asked softly.

"Jasin Elstrada."

"Well Jasin, shave or not, I'm still charging the house my fee." As she turned away, her long silky hair brushed his face, leaving a faint floral scent behind. He climbed out of the cold water, dressed in the least dirty of his clothes and left the bathhouse for the tavern.

Beloit was pacing outside waiting for him. As soon as he saw Jasin, he hurried across the street. "You're looking better," he said. "No shave?"

"Nah, just hungry. Don't you want to eat?" asked Jasin.

Beloit glanced over his shoulder and across the street. "Of course, but that's the wrong tavern. The woman who was raped usually worked the other one. Let's go."

At the intersection of the main street and the frontage road, they passed under the huge tree and continued past the potter's shop. A dim glow from the river drew them to its edge. Beneath the surface, shining like a thousand stars, tiny one-celled plankton twinkled.

Continuing along the river, they wove between broken, salt-encrusted barrels standing like dock sentinels for the preservation house that shared a wall with the tavern. Crossing the frontage road, they approached the bar. A fish smoker abutted the establishment's other flank. Short stuttering phrases escaped open windows—a spirited conversation between natives.

Jasin and Beloit entered. A lingering smoky aroma confirmed their suspicion that this had once been part of the smoker. They carefully surveyed the room. Several small groups of towans stood eating or talking. A few tables, looking extremely short, had been provided for human guests, of which there were quite a number. Jasin was ravenous and didn't waste a second in procuring two huge portions of the day's fare — a raw minced tuber the natives called *fantale* and salted fish. They ate native style, without utensils, but sat instead of standing. The fish made them extremely thirsty and they quickly drank several mugs of the local beverage before realizing how really dreadful it tasted. They sat back, fully sated, and watched a young towan and his mentor. From the lack of cross-hatching on the elder's maturity mark, this would have to be one of his first Initiates. They were just starting their journey up the gorge into the colder climates.

When a young Sytonian male came of age, he chose an older, respected towan, who would accompany him and pass on the necessary skills needed to live alone, entirely off the land, for at least a week. The Initiate is required to steal a young male cylith pup from its protective pack and bring it home to train as a guardian pet. If the Initiate is successful, a long horizontal mark is burned across his chest and his mentor receives a short vertical one.

Jasin and Beloit were among the last to eat and it appeared the proprietor didn't expect any further guests. He was now relaxing, finishing his own meal.

"I was told his name is Sy Fask," said Beloit, indicating their host. A few days ago, when I tried to question him, he wouldn't speak. I don't think he understands us, or wants to understand us, but it's important to find out what he knows."

Jasin waited a few more minutes until the towan had finished eating before approaching. Beloit followed. A few of the others watched expecting an unusual confrontation.

"Respectfully, sir," began Jasin in his best Sytonian, "you are Sy Fask?" As in his human language, it was important that the melody of the voice intoned a question and not a statement. The order of the words had less meaning than the lilt, and the stuttering came from the expression of past, future, or present tense.

The towan looked down at Jasin. There was at least a half-meter difference in their height. Looking a towan directly in the eyes was a sign of equals on Syton. Those of lesser stature, their young and their females looked up. It was a problem for the average human, especially Jasin who hadn't inherited his father's height; just one of the reasons Avram had made such a good negotiator and diplomat. The towan slowly looked around the room, making note of who was there. "I am Sy Fask," he acknowledged. "Who are you and why do you come here?"

Jasin turned to Beloit and nodded. Then he answered, "I am Jasin, son of Avram Elstrada, and this is Beloit McMaster." He had decided to trade on any recognition of his father's name, but there was no sign that Sy Fask had ever heard of Avram. "The food here is good. We were very hungry. Thank you."

"Many humans eat here," said Sy Fask, indicating the occupants of the other tables. Two flirtatious young ladies, looking to earn a few meitas or crystals before the night was over, had joined the other men.

Jasin would have liked to invite the large towan to sit at a less conspicuous table to ask the next questions, but he knew that the request to lower one's height might be taken wrong. Instead, he turned and indicated a quieter corner of the room far away from the others. "Respectfully, sir," he said, lowering his head further. The towan straightened, extended his exceptionally long arm, and repeated the gesture to move to the corner. He made it appear as if he were requesting it and Jasin quickly honored him by nodding his head and saying, "Thank you, thank you," loudly enough for others to hear and followed him to the corner. Beloit wasn't far behind.

"Sir, a human female was hurt," began Jasin. "You know her?" Again, he was careful of the tone. But then he added, "She was here often." This time he made it obvious that he wasn't asking a question.

"This is sad," The towan replied. Jasin waited for him to admit knowing the woman, but the towan said nothing more.

"Yes, this is sad," Jasin repeated and waited again. Finally, "She was your friend?"

"No, not my friend."

Jasin felt a small sense of victory. At least Sy Fask had admitted the woman existed. "She had friends here?"

"Many human friends. Many women find friends here." He glanced over to the table of men who were laughing and talking to the two ladies. One of the women was in her mid-thirties, pleasant looking, but tired and disheveled. It looked like she had already entertained too many this evening; the other was a scrawny blond, twenty, and extremely fidgety, continually glancing over towards Jasin. He was sure she was the young girl he saw from across the river.

"The last time you saw her, do you remember who her friend was?" asked Jasin.

"No," Fask answered.

"No?"

When Sy Fask didn't answer, Jasin turned to Beloit, "He says she had lots of human friends but won't tell me who she was with that night."

"Ask him if she had any native friends," said Beloit.

Jasin was surprised at this change of direction. Weren't they looking for a human? Jasin feared that the question would be insulting, but asked anyway, "Respectfully sir, did she have any towan friends?"

"No," Fask repeated.

Perhaps the concept of friend is standing in our way, thought Jasin. "Very respectfully sir, did any towan talk to her that night?"

He was right. After a brief hesitation Fask answered, "Yes, Sy Loeton talked to her. He liked to talk and look at her. He talked a long time that night. Sy Loeton talks to many women."

Beloit heard the name and bolted upright in his chair. "Is he saying Sy Loeton? Ask him again, Sy Loeton?"

Jasin didn't have to ask again. The towan stood tall at the mention of the name. "Sy Loeton comes here. Sy Loeton eats my food."

"Who is this Sy Loeton?" Jasin asked Beloit.

"Ask him if they left together."

"Sy Fask sir, Sy Loeton knows good food. Did Sy Loeton leave with the girl the night she was hurt?"

"Sy Loeton was not a friend. The girl had many friends. Not Sy Loeton; he has many towas." Fask replied.

Jasin knew there were several words the natives used for friend. The form he had been using evidently had a sexual connotation. "Did she want to be a friend for Loeton?" Jasin could hardly believe he was asking this absurd question. The idea that a woman would want to have a sexual relationship with a native was unthinkable.

But the towan considered this idea thoughtfully. "Sy Loeton liked this girl. Sy Loeton likes many human women. He likes to look and talk. He likes to touch. This woman was tall and liked Sy Loeton. This female had many friends...I do not know." Sy Fask decided the conversation had ended. He turned and walked away, but after he had taken a few long strides he turned and proclaimed quite loudly, "It is sad." Several towans looked up. The table of humans also glanced over. The blond girl stared at them.

"Well? Did she leave with Loeton?" asked Beloit.

"Who in the world is this Loeton?" Jasin exclaimed.

"Did she leave with him?"

"He didn't say. Now who is he?"

Beloit looked around. They were still being watched by a few. "Not here. Let's go back to the inn. We'll talk on the way." They paid and left quickly, but before they had a chance to exchange a single word, the younger woman burst from the tavern and ran up to them.

"Who are you?" she shouted angrily. "What do you want with Fask?"

"Why is that of interest to a tavern whore?" Beloit asked.

"Just is. What did Fask tell you?" she asked.

Jasin thought Beloit's reaction a bit strange. Here was obviously someone they needed to talk to. "We're investigating the death of another woman who worked there. Know anything about it?"

"She's not dead!" the young woman lashed back. "Not dead," she repeated under her breath as if to convince herself.

"You know her?" asked Jasin.

"You're some idiots. Don't even know if she's alive or dead. Don't even know who or what to ask. You're lucky Fask even talked to you. I can't believe you just walked in and started asking questions about that alien pervert. Loeton was born here, you morons, spends a lot of time here. He's a local big shot. They don't care what he did to her."

"Are you sure she's alive?" Beloit asked.

"Of course I'm sure. I been staying with her since."

"She's still alive?" asked Beloit. "Did she say anything? Why do you say it was Loeton?"

"Who else could it be? I seen them, everyone in the tavern seen them together that night. He was attentive, if you know what I mean. She liked that; she liked all kinds. I mean if you're in the business you have to pretend to like it all...even girls, but doing girls ain't really bad, I don't think so anyway...not like them." She hesitated, searching their eyes for a reaction that never came. "Anyway, I didn't believe it when I first heard she might be fooling with those monsters. None of us are that stupid."

"Then it could have been another native," suggested Jasin.

The girl shrugged. "Didn't see no one else. She left. He left."

"Has she spoken?" Beloit asked again.

The girl looked at Beloit with disgust. "She can't say a blasted thing, you fool. Her face is all busted. I sewed her up best I could, but she's still bleeding. She can't...I don't...I don't think she's going to make it." With this last outburst, she lost all her bravado and strength. Tears started to flow.

"What's your name?" Jasin asked, taking a softer approach.

"Cherri," the girl replied.

"I'm sorry, Cherri, but I have to ask," Jasin began, "if no one actually saw Loeton do it, and she's never been able to accuse him...isn't it possible, just consider it for a moment, couldn't it have been a human?"

The girl looked over to Beloit for any support he might give. Finding none, she turned to Jasin and whispered, "You'd have to see her."

It didn't take long to gather their belongings and the blaythons from the inn, but when Samson learned of their plans to leave with Cherri to see the injured woman, he wouldn't let them go until he had completed his keetah sale. Within seconds of finishing with Samson, they left the inn and were heading out through the center of town. They passed along the outlying livestock yards where the natives raised their styke and traveled into the surrounding countryside. Unlike the uneven terrain on the cold side of the river, this land was fairly flat with an occasional dry riverbed to add interest.

"Beloit, I wanted to ask you something. I saw something in town...Do you know of any material or technology that could mend itself?" asked Jasin.

"Mend itself? What did you see?"

"A blade, a greenish-blue razor."

"What do you mean mend itself?" Beloit cocked his head, truly confused.

"Well, it just sort of repaired itself."

"You know it's against the Prohibitions for a human to own a weapon."

"Of course. But did we ever have such technology?"

"Never saw anything like that...probably from Cernai." Beloit said, referring to the small human village. Jasin recalled the many times they had traced the origin of some new toy back there, but he wasn't sure Beloit was right this time.

Slightly more than an hour had passed when they arrived at a cluster of dwellings huddled around a stone well. These homes, Jasin counted six, were near the border of the Kull, Syton's cold desert, which the fifth Prohibition declared off limits to humans. Through the windows, Jasin could see candles burning and movement within all but one of the homes. They tied up the animals outside the deserted one. An unlit lantern hung from a cornice of the broken down porch. Stepping carefully to avoid a rotten board, Beloit lit the lantern. They moved inside.

Foul air, and dread, overwhelmed them. From the dim, flickering light, they could make out a crude table and two straw mattresses next to each other on the dirt floor. Neither bed looked occupied, but as they walked forward, the lantern began to illuminate a crumpled form covered in a pile of rough blankets and clothes. Bloody sewing needles and bits of thread lay on the floor near by.

"Kait...it's Cherri," said the young girl softy as she knelt down. Beloit brought the light closer. Cherri reached out and pulled the blankets back, then gently cleared a lock of hair from her friend's face, caressing her cheek. With a gasp, she drew her hand away and fell back onto her own mattress. The body was cold and gray. Cherri curled up, hugged her thin blanket, and rolled over, turning her back to them. She began to shake. Jasin, worried that she might be going into shock, looked around vainly to find something else to keep her warm.

"It looks like Cherri used most of what they had to cover her," observed Beloit, nodding towards the dead girl. There were several different blankets and jackets draped over the body. Beloit took a ratty blanket and recoiled as tiny bugs dropped from its folds. He shook out the vermin before laying the blanket over the trembling young girl. Jasin took the lantern and turned his attention to the lifeless form, now almost completely uncovered.

She had been a tall woman, thirties, he thought, certainly not older than forty. He lifted the light and held it close to the bruised face. Clearly her jaw had been broken, and the blond hair on one side of her head was matted and crusted with dried blood, indicating a massive blow that may have cracked her skull. The blood from her head had flowed down her neck and stained the collar of her blouse before seeping into the straw mattress under her shoulders. With some hesitation, Jasin tenderly lifted the last of her bed sheets; her naked lower torso lay revealed in a pool of congealed blood that spread beyond her wide hips. A thin shallow cut ran straight down from her neck, between her breasts, and over her stomach where it crossed another deeper horizontal slash that had been crudely sutured in her lower abdomen. Jasin gasped. The woman's vulva seemed ripped apart, exposing a gash of raw meat. Stunned, he momentarily averted his eyes. Beloit, standing a few steps away was completely transfixed. Such mutilation was impossible to imagine, but Jasin forced himself to complete the gruesome examination. What appeared to be pieces of her shredded, prolapsed vagina hung inside out between her scraped and deeply gouged thighs. He had seen more than enough and quickly replaced the few bed coverings before retreating outside to compose himself. Beloit joined him.

"I'm amazed the girl survived long enough to make it back here," Jasin whispered.

Beloit nodded. "I'm going to find a neighbor to take care of Cherri. Are you going to be all right?"

Jasin looked vacantly at Beloit, his eyes wide and moist. Beloit placed a hand on his shoulder. Jasin turned away, suddenly becoming aware of his own labored breathing. He took deep breaths through his scarf as if to cleanse himself of the hideous image, an image that would haunt him over the next four days while they travelled home.

Nova Gaia

"Damn," Avram swore under his breath. With care, he swept finely ground keetah off the stone table into his cup. Wasting even the smallest amount of such quality felt like a crime. It promised a strong brew, he mused, but why bother at all if it wasn't potent. He poured the last of the boiling water over the rusty powder. With a spoon, he coaxed it into solution. This would be his third cup of the morning. He smiled at the indulgence. Seanne Sy had finally learned how he enjoyed his keetah, but the towa always disappeared with the precious powder after his first cup. No matter, now that Sy Toberry had claimed her, he could refill as many times as he liked. Avram leaned back in his chair and closed his eyes while his cup of keetah cooled. The tradition of intentionally burning oneself, even if the pain was fleeting, escaped him.

He yawned. It was early into the brightness and he should have been well rested, but sleep had once again escaped him. Churning over minor issues that in years past would not have warranted a second thought, he wasted the darkness tossing about without relief. Useless, that's what he'd become. Old age was punishment for an exciting youth. Better to burn out young than live to deliver eulogies for dear friends, and he had been doing more of that than he cared to think about. Over the last few years of his declining influence, he had given advice on the lower school curriculum; asked to settle a dispute between some ship-born, animal phobic parents and their teenagers who wanted to raise a cylith pup; and then there was the request to speak at the opening of Rahfi's new restaurant. What other challenging and weighty subjects would he face before someone stood over his dead body, scratching their head wondering what this bag of bones had ever done to deserve their passing respect? He sipped the keetah, relishing the heightened awareness and adrenaline it brought to his aged body. The drug provided a poor substitute for purpose.

Warming his arthritic hands around the steaming cup, he walked over to the window of the study and peeked between the drapes. Jasin and his friend, Mas Baurchart, were stretching. Mas was a tall handsome young man, ship-born, just a few years older than Jasin, and blessed with a strong body and other natural gifts. With his long blond hair and easy-going nature, he effortlessly attracted the attention of eligible young ladies, causing Jasin constant aggravation. And even though Jasin ran often, Avram knew that Mas could easily keep pace and, without much effort, surpass his son in any footrace, or any other athletic endeavor for that matter. Yet Avram knew Jasin continually felt the need to challenge his friend, to push himself regardless of the inevitable outcome.

Avram watched as the young men raised their breathing scarves and jogged off, Jasin's shorter, measured strides keeping pace with Mas's long, easy ones. They disappeared from sight just as the sun breached the canyon rim. Instinctively, he pulled the heavy drapes together, sealing himself off, his ship-born mind unable to accept that Syton's atmosphere could protect him from the dangerous rays.

He was fortunate to have been given this beautiful two-story home, huge by any measure and one of the few private residences to have a second story and mineral windows. Gardens, now overgrown and hidden beneath years of neglect, surrounded the house in stark contrast to the broad open courtyard. Beyond the gardens were several cabins; each larger than the average straw bale and stucco homes the humans had been given. All the cabins sat empty, except one that Jasin had moved into upon returning from Advanced Studies in Panvera.

Avram often wondered who had owned this magnificent compound before they arrived, or for that matter any of residences that the humans were given to occupy. Where were those that lived here before? He had never gotten a clear answer about that from any Sytonian. Perhaps he'd ask Sy Lang when he arrived. The towan was the closest thing he had to a native friend. Sy Lang would tell him…if they were still speaking after their morning meeting.

Friend or not, this would be a difficult discussion. The Council of Seventeen needed to know about the possible trouble brewing in Bistoun. But since it could involve Sy Loeton, also a Council member, diplomacy would be the order of the day. He still wasn't convinced that a towan could be responsible for the gruesome acts Jasin and Beloit had described, but the tension from the incident was real enough to cause concern.

This, at least, was a problem worthy of his experience and talents.

Avram took a cautious sip. The keetah was strong and cool enough not to burn and he quickly emptied the cup. The drug produced a soothing wave, relaxing him, yet helping to focus his mind. He refilled the small water pot and set it over the fire.

"Hello, Avram," said Sy Lang, entering the study. Without looking, no one else would have suspected a native. The towan's grasp of their language was flawless. Lang was at least a hand taller than Avram's two meters. He carried a large rolled parchment.

"Honorable sir," Avram replied. "Which shall it be, my humble Human language or the beautiful tongue of your planet? Perhaps today we should speak Native," suggested Avram. He switched tongues, "Thank you for making the trip." Avram's linguistic skills were the reason he had been chosen to negotiate the original settlement agreement.

"I've brought a small gift to add to your collection." Sy Lang gave Avram the parchment. "It's the Kaysop mountain range." Avram moved the bag of keetah and his cup from the table and unrolled the topographic map detailing in elegant and precise hand the natural barrier between the human towns and the lower, warmer Sytonian cities of Fistulee and T'Matte.

"It's wonderful. Please thank the artist when you return to T'Matte."

"This mapmaker lives in Bistoun. I told him I needed a special map for a special friend."

Avram hesitated. He had assumed Sy Lang had traveled by ship from the port of Fistulee to Soto, and then directly to Nova Gaia through the farmland. "Then you passed through Bistoun?"

Lang leaned over and indicated the pass though the Kaysop mountain range and the road to Bistoun that he'd taken. "It's quite easy, Avram. Good safe roads the entire way."

"Then you're aware of the incident in Bistoun."

Lang didn't answer. He looked away from the table and walked over towards Avram's collection of maps. "Yes, it is why I traveled that way." He picked up an ancient book that lay on a shelf above the other maps and opened it with his large center finger. The brown dry edges of the pages flaked off. "Curious."

"Please be careful. It's one of the only items of its kind that survived the voyage aboard Tanis. It was once a very popular book of ancient religious myths printed on our home planet nearly a thousand years ago." Avram paused, thinking of Hyland. "A good friend gave it to me when we settled here...but now, on this other matter...we have to find a way to keep the peace. Many humans believe the woman was killed by a towan. I have my doubts, but others believe it was Sy Loeton. He has never liked the thought of humans settling on Syton. We must find out the truth. If it was Sy Loeton...I think it would be an important matter for the Council of Seventeen to consider. Humans must see that justice is done, that a native can't kill or hurt one of us and not be punished."

"And why is that?" Sy Lang continued to move around the room. When he spied the pot of steaming water, he turned angrily. "Avram, I've told you before. You mustn't continue using keetah everyday. It is for special ceremonies. It isn't good for your heart."

"Sy Lang, my friend, let's not be distracted. The peace you and I have nurtured between our races is threatened. That is why violence should not be tolerated…What did you learn in Bistoun?"

"It is not a secret. Sy Loeton never wanted humans to settle here. Nor is it a secret that your human females fascinate him. He is quite odd."

"My friend, Beloit McMaster, has been asking other towans about Sy Loeton. They say he is quite…physical, that he has many wives, some of them from killing his enemies and seizing their towas. He is always looking for more. Many are afraid of Sy Loeton. McMaster believes that he is capable of violence."

"All that is true," agreed Sy Lang, "but the act of taking a wife widowed by violence or by accident is honorable. It is an important tradition and you shouldn't disparage him for that. There is no denying, however, that Sy Loeton is different. He acts quickly with surprising energy when angered. You humans have a word for it."

"Temper, he has a bad temper."

"Yes, a bad temper. But it is unlikely that he has committed this attack." Sy Lang leaned back on his middle leg. A long finger relieved an itch along his puffed out food sacks.

"But, if he is guilty, will the Council act to punish him?" Avram asked.

"Punish? No. We can only dismiss him from the Council of Seventeen. Only those highly respected can serve on the Council, but there are no other laws covering the interaction of our two races, other than the Prohibitions that you must follow."

"Perhaps that was an oversight."

"My friend, you weren't in a position to demand anything then…nor are you now. Besides, there isn't any proof of his guilt."

Avram lowered his head in thought. "If there was?"

"Loeton might be removed from the Council; his respect would be certainly diminished. He would be disgraced."

"If Sy Loeton hurt a Sytonian and they died, what would be the punishment?"

"Towa or towan?"

"It matters?"

"Of course! If it is his towa, nothing. If someone else's towa, he would have to replace her. If he killed another towan, death."

"You understand, our human females have the same rights as our males."

"I have always thought that odd, but the rights you speak of refer to your laws—not ours."

"Unfortunate."

Sy Lang turned abruptly and confronted his friend. "Why must you be so provocative? You have no idea how destructive your ideas could be to our society. Be careful where you speak of such things."

"But if I can prove to you that Sy Loeton was guilty, would you help convince your Council to create a new Sytonian law protecting all humans from dishonorable acts by Sytonians? It would calm a lot of people and help keep the peace. I'm just talking about improving the relationship between our races."

"I would try, but I'm only one towan. It is unlikely that humans, especially your females, would be granted these rights. And just how do you intend to prove such a thing?"

They could hear voices in the courtyard and Sy Lang walked over to the window, drawing back the heavy drapes to observe Sy Toberry in the process of greeting the returning runners. Sunlight streamed into the room. Avram backed away from the light. "I'm sorry, Avram." Sy Lang pulled the drapes together.

"I know it's irrational, but I've never gotten used to it. Honestly, Sy Lang, I wasn't convinced a towan was capable of it, but no one else was seen with her that night. And the wounds...well, a human female simply cannot withstand intimate contact with a towan without suffering just those types of wounds. Our women don't develop the hardness as towas do."

Sy Lang shook his head and prepared to leave. "This entire episode is senseless. Please be careful how you pursue this, Avram. It is sad that the woman is dead, but you must remember, it is clearly forbidden by the Prohibitions for you to harm any Sytonian." Sy Lang headed for the doorway.

"Thank you for coming, and for the gift. I promise to be careful, but I fear the anger in Bistoun—"

"It will subside if you allow it to. She was not an important human; only a woman who had no male in her life. Soon she will be forgotten."

Only a woman…soon forgotten…the words sickened Avram. Despondently, he watched Lang leave. The native may have spoken the truth, but it was immoral not to pursue her attackers—Sytonian or Human.

Sy Lang continued into the courtyard and slowed to watch Sy Toberry conduct traditional towan physical training for Jasin and Mas, and Toberry's own son, Sy Jelick. Concentration and focus were crucial or your opponent, who whirled, kicked, and swung in a tightly choreographed high-speed attack, would strike you. Mas seemed calm as he easily avoided the towan's long arms and multi-jointed legs. Jasin, on the other hand, appeared unsure and hesitant. Several times he received a rough kick or barely escaped a swift punch from Sy Jelick, who completed the moves as if no thought were required. At a break, Sy Lang approached them.

"You men are lucky to have Sy Toberry as a teacher. Many of us are proud to have been his Initiate." He reached out and traced one of the hash marks on Toberry's highly decorated chest.

"Respectfully sir, may I speak to you in private?" Sy Lang asked in Sytonian. The two towans walked off to a far corner of the courtyard leaving Jasin and Mas to catch their breath. Even in the coolness of the Sytonian air, the boys' shirts were drenched. Sy Jelick stood apart, neither included with his father and Sy Lang, nor able to understand the Human language Mas and Jasin spoke.

"Even Council members come to learn from Toberry," said Mas quietly.

Jasin nodded. "Avram believes that Sy Toberry is one of the most respected natives on either side of the Andoree."

"He's a spy for the council," declared Mas.

"Of course he is, but we're not hiding anything. We prefer to think of him as a conduit— the communication is, in fact, two-way. Avram believes that it's actually an advantage to have someone so well connected so close."

"He makes me uncomfortable. When he's around, I have to think about everything I say."

"It's a good habit. We have to be careful."

"Why? You think we should be scared of them? I can't worry every time I open my mouth or continually be concerned that someone is breaking some silly rule. Really, Jasin, you've got to loosen up, relax, and enjoy life a little more. We can't live in a continuous state of fear." Mas looked up towards the window of Avram's study. "It's like your father and sunlight. I couldn't imagine hiding from it, but when I see you, it's like you're afraid to have fun, to expose yourself to risk, scared to lose control. You're so cautious about everything."

Jasin didn't know what to say. There was a lot of truth there, but Mas just didn't understand what was at stake. Mas's lack of fear, his dismissal of consequence was both his source of strength and his blind spot. Jasin searched for his father's reassuring form in the window. His phobia was understandable. On board ship, Avram had avoided direct exposure to radiation his entire life. Jasin thought he saw the drapes move. Yes, Father was there, but it appeared he wasn't watching them. He was looking out beyond the courtyard gate. Jasin turned to see what Avram was looking at. A solitary figure with a backpack trudged along the road towards them. Whoever it was looked tired.

Following Jasin's gaze, Mas said, "You've got company." A few moments later he smiled and added, "I think you should leave this to me."

Jasin bristled at his cockiness. "It's Elizabeth Tournell," he said, identifying the approaching figure. "Remember her brother, Michael, from Advanced Studies?"

"Sure, but I don't remember him having a sister...and I don't think I'd forget her." Mas stared appreciably at Elizabeth's tall, athletic body. The towans hardly glanced at her as she entered the courtyard. Mas stepped forward to help with her backpack. Jasin, rooted to the ground, awkwardly gave her a nod. Elizabeth's long auburn hair was tied up, exposing her long neck streaked with dirt and sweat from the road. For the first time, Jasin noticed the memorial mark below her left ear.

"Thanks," she rewarded Mas with a smile. Then she turned to Jasin. "I decided to see if Avram was serious about the job."

"He's up in the study." Jasin turned and indicated the section of the house. "But it's really my mother you should meet. It looks like you've been on the road awhile."

"Couple of days." Elizabeth surveyed the huge house. She'd never seen a home of this size.

"Any problems?" Jasin asked.

"No." Then she looked over at Jasin's lanky, blond friend and acknowledged him with a small nod of her head. "Hi, I'm Elizabeth." Jasin completed the introductions including the towans.

Elizabeth asked, "How many families live here?"

"Actually, just Avram and my mother. I grew up here, but I'm in one of the back cabins now."

"What about them?" She indicated the towans.

"No, just my folks. Sy Lang is visiting and Toberry has another home nearby. Let's go inside and find my parents."

Jasin was happy to have an excuse to separate Elizabeth and Mas, and led her though the courtyard and entered the house. It was quiet and their footsteps echoed in the vast emptiness. "She sleeps later these days, but she should be up by now. I think Avram saw you, but I'll make sure."

"Do you think I might have a chance to freshen up a bit before I meet your mother? It's been a long dusty walk."

Jasin showed her an empty room and brought some water and a towel, then left to inform Avram.

Elizabeth quickly washed, changed her dusty clothes, untied her hair and ran a brush through it. As she repacked, she heard faint music—possibly a flute, she thought—coming from another room nearby. She considered waiting for Jasin's return, but the melody was enchanting. Hesitantly, she followed the music until she stood in the doorway of a huge, two-story room. Bright sunlight blasted through large multi-paned windows illuminating a petite musician she assumed was Jasin's mother. Dwarfed by the imposing space, she played with practiced confidence. Abruptly, she stopped and turned to Elizabeth.

"I'm sorry. I didn't mean to interrupt."

"Then why intrude uninvited?" Julian Elstrada stood up and took a few steps towards her. She appeared to be about seventy years old. Her thinning hair was completely gray.

Embarrassed, Elizabeth hesitated, frozen with doubt and insecurity. With effort she approached awkwardly. Julian needed to tilt her head back to look into Elizabeth's eyes. Julian's frailness did not extend to her penetrating eyes and through them Elizabeth could feel the lady's strength and poise.

"Please excuse me. Jasin kindly allowed me to freshen up and your music caught my attention. I'm Elizabeth Tournell. Avram told me you might be looking for a housekeeper or assistant?" Before Julian could answer, Jasin and Avram joined them.

"Elizabeth, how wonderful! I'm so glad you took me seriously," said Avram. "Juls, I thought without Seanne you might appreciate some help. Elizabeth worked for Hyland. You'll remember her parents, Sidrah and Warren Tournell."

"Di Sidrah and Dai Warren, of course. It's nice to meet you, Elizabeth. I used to enjoy your mother's lectures on ancient earth history."

Elizabeth beamed at the respect and dignity Julian paid her parents. Her heart calmed. "I'm sorry to have intruded, but I heard you playing. It was wonderful."

"Have you heard many other musicians?" asked Julian, "Or perhaps, you play yourself?"

Again, Elizabeth felt awkward and strangely challenged by Julian. It was just a simple question she told herself, but it felt like she was being tested. "I'm afraid not," she answered softly.

Julian finally smiled. "Well, if all goes well, I could teach you to play. There really isn't that much to do around here, but I'm getting older and some of the simplest chores...well, I don't believe in complaining. Come, I'll show you around."

The tour of the mansion didn't take as long as Elizabeth expected. Many of the rooms were uninhabited or empty. It appeared Avram and Julian spent most of their time in separate areas—she loved her sunlit open spaces, while he hid from the sun in his study or the cellar. Elizabeth also noticed they slept apart.

"You can use this room," Julian suggested, showing Elizabeth a room near the kitchen.

Elizabeth nodded, slung her backpack over her shoulder, and entered the space—a storeroom with various crates and barrels dumped haphazardly just inside the entrance that blocked her view and access to the rest of the room. Disappointment must have shown on her face. They had passed several bedrooms she thought Julian might have offered instead. All of them were spacious and clean.

"Is anything wrong?" asked Julian.

"No, no...just, I want to thank you for giving me a chance. I won't disappoint you."

"Why don't you take the rest of the day to settle in. Perhaps later you could prepare a light dinner before dimness?" Julian turned before Elizabeth could answer.

"Of course," Elizabeth replied to Julian's retreating back.

Although still early, she was tired. It had been a long couple of days on the trail. She thought about closing her eyes for a few hours, but there was nowhere she felt comfortable enough, certainly not in this mess. There wasn't even a mattress, much less a bed here. She eyed the barrier of crates and barrels. Maybe there was someplace she could take a short nap on the other side of the room. She lifted one of the crates and realized why they hadn't been moved before. Julian or a small towa would not have been able to manage the heavy boxes, nor was it the type of chore she thought Avram would have performed.

After thirty minutes of backbreaking work, a narrow path had been cleared and Elizabeth squeezed through, gaining a complete view of the room. Her earlier disappointment was replaced by excitement as the potential of what she had been given revealed itself.

Hidden behind the old crates was a space larger than the entire Wynosk home. There were real mineral windows, filthy, of course, from decades of neglect; a small table and reading chair; a built-in basin and a large tub that appeared to be tiled; and a raised platform holding the remains of a mattress that had become home to several small field diggers. Off to the side was a separate doorway and although it was difficult to see through the grimy windows, it apparently led to a small private garden.

This neglected room was a treasure to be earned. Elizabeth smiled to herself; she was beginning to understand Julian. Tests, questions, and challenges—Julian was taking her measure, seeing what she was made of. What would Julian have learned giving her a clean bedroom?

There was plenty of space to move the entire barricade of boxes and barrels to one side of the room and still leave more personal living space than she had ever had. Using the few hours she had before beginning dinner, Elizabeth managed to move most of them. A few of the larger ones needed to be unpacked, or perhaps she could get help moving them. Finally, she turned her attention to remnants of the mattress. It would be best to sweep the decayed straw and droppings directly outside. Elizabeth tried to open the door leading to the garden, but found it stuck or possibly locked. Rest would have to wait.

Dinner was a simple affair, just Jasin and his parents. A variety of vegetables, mangled by the dullest knives

Elizabeth had ever used, but enhanced by a few random seasonings became a passable soup. She sat alone in the kitchen eating her own meal and eavesdropped on the spirited conversation from the other room.

"He must be punished," Avram was saying. "A murder has been committed. There must be justice or the peace between us will eventually crumble. It's just a matter of time. Sy Lang said he'd help, if we could prove it was Loeton, but without proof, he and the Council would just as soon let it be."

"I doubt it can be proven." Jasin was saying. "There were no witnesses. Only the injuries indicate it was probably native. Impossible to prove it was Sy Loeton, although I have little reservation."

"I still have trouble believing it was a towan," Avram muttered.

"Someone or something attacked that girl. What other possibilities exist?" Julian asked.

"You know what really upsets me?" Avram continued, "Even if he admitted doing it, there isn't a law or agreement to punish him. All Lang said was that he'd support such a law between our races afterwards. As it stands today, Sy Loeton could actually brag about it and escape punishment. It isn't any secret that he hates humans. He continually votes to restrict our rights and there are probably a lot who agree with him."

"Wouldn't he loose respect and his place on the Council?" Julian asked.

"There's a good chance, but the Council has to be convinced. He'd have to admit it to them, or in front of them. Our hearsay won't persuade them. Still, it is a small punishment for murder."

"Maybe the murder was a new form of towdom initiation," Jasin interjected.

Towdoms? Was Jasin implying that the murder was purposeful, some form of human sacrifice?

"That's a sickening thought," Avram replied to Jasin's suggestion. "I doubt it's anything like that. I still believe we're dealing with a peaceful race. The towdoms are no more than brotherhoods, a form of local government," said Avram. "No, as impossible as it sounds, we've got to get Sy Loeton to admit to the act, to brag about it while other Council members are present. He's got to believe he's invulnerable, and then let his hatred and arrogance toward us humans take over."

"How can he be manipulated like that at a Council meeting?" asked Jasin.

"Never happen," Julian declared. "I'm afraid Sy Lang might be right. Sy Loeton or whoever did this is probably safe. We are legally defenseless. Our agreements with this race are incomplete and one-sided."

"Of course they're one-sided!" Avram shouted. "Do you think I was in position to demand equality from the Sytonians? We were lucky just to be allowed to live here."

"No one's blaming you, Avram," Julian said calmly, "I was just stating the obvious."

"Well, what's obvious is that unless someone cares enough, this incident will go unpunished, the injustice of our situation will be exposed, and this will be the beginning of the end. If we can't get Loeton to admit it in a Council meeting in T'Matte...well, maybe we can get him to admit it here."

"What are you talking about?" asked Jasin. Elizabeth felt lost as well.

"I've been thinking about this all day. Sy Loeton didn't want humans to settle in the gorge in the first place. He was terribly outspoken about it. What would happen if we invited the entire Council to a party, a truly spectacular, extravagant affair, with beautiful food, lots of keetah, music, fine clothing...you know, do it up right. Invite the Human Caucus as well, and tell them to really push the glamour envelope. Let the Sytonians, especially Sy Loeton, see how successful we've become and how powerless he is when it comes to controlling human affairs. Make his worst fears a reality. Make him resent our lifestyle. Maybe we can push some of his emotional buttons, get him mad or upset, and goad him into making some kind of unguarded admission."

"You're describing a lifestyle that doesn't exist," reminded Julian.

"He doesn't have to know that. He has never seen where or how we live. There can't be many homes as beautiful as this. All we have to do is clean up, put on a little show. If we let the Caucus in on the plan, they can help bring in food and furnishings. We can fake it for just a night."

Elizabeth groaned. She really wanted this job to work out; she needed this job. But her first day here and all of a sudden Avram is talking about throwing a spectacular affair. She still hadn't mentally recovered from Hyland's funeral, and this was much more difficult, involving weeks of hard work. Any thought of easing into this new life and quietly enjoying her new surroundings suddenly evaporated. She rose, lit a few of the lanterns in the kitchen, and began cleaning the pots and dishes from dinner.

Avram stuck his head into the kitchen as she was finishing. "I wonder if you might bring a pot of boiling water to the study later?"

"Of course, sir. It won't take but a minute."

"No rush. And Elisabeth...?"

"Yes sir?"

"Please call me Avram. We're not especially formal around here." He smiled.

Elizabeth lowered her eyes. "Thank you...sir. I'll try to remember. It's just not..."

"Not what?"

"Just not the way I was raised, I guess. You're my employer."

"Try to remember our first meeting when you scolded me for wearing my boots inside."

Elizabeth blushed.

"Relax, everything will be fine. I understand Julian suggested you use the storeroom."

"Yes sir, it will actually be quite nice once I get it clean. I was wondering...do you know where Jasin went off to? There are a few crates I could use his help moving."

"He headed back to his cabin out back." Avram turned to leave. "I'm sure he'd be happy to help."

Elizabeth watched Avram depart, suddenly having second thoughts about asking Jasin to her room to help. Was that smart? She wasn't that interested in him, didn't want him to get the wrong idea. She couldn't afford getting involved with the boss's son, but before she could sleep, that mattress had to go. She filled a pot and set it over the fire to warm.

Ten minutes later, Elizabeth entered Avram's study with the hot water. The new map of the Kaysop range still lay open on the desk. She stole a glance. She had never been lower in the gorge than Lake Chook, so the mountain range was unknown to her. While Avram mixed an evening cup of keetah, she took a moment to study the map.

"Are you interested in maps?" asked Avram, letting the keetah cool.

"I've only seen a few in school. They were never this beautiful. I don't recognize the area."

"It's the mountain range beyond the Kull, separating the bigger Sytonian cities from our cooler lands. You don't recognize it because most of our maps go no lower than the Andoree River. Sometimes they show Bistoun, or perhaps the Kull, but we rarely have any reason to travel through these mountains since the Kull which lies before it is prohibited."

Elizabeth wasn't interested in a long geography lesson, but politely listened as Avram pointed out Mount Doerr and Mount Kaysop. When he paused, she quickly seized the opportunity to change the subject. "I wanted to thank you for allowing me to stay here. It's a beautiful home and I'll make sure you won't be disappointed in me."

"I'm sure everything will work out fine, but we have much to do in the next few weeks." Elizabeth cocked her head, pretending to be confused. Admitting to eavesdropping on their dinner conversation probably wasn't the best way to start her employment.

Avram explained his plan for the party.

"Well, you can count on me, but I have to be honest: the funeral was the largest event I've ever planned."

"Don't worry; you'll have lots of help."

"Yes sir. Thank you again, but if there isn't anything else this evening…"

"Not this evening, but bring another pot here in the morning. I'm up early."

"Thank you, sir. See you in the morning."

Elizabeth left and walked back through the empty hallways to her room. She stared at the few heavy crates that she needed help moving then walked to the stuck door. She braced herself and gave it a strong push.

Nothing.

She looked at the decayed mattress. There was no way she would be able to sleep here. She peered out into the dimness, suddenly trapped between the need to find help and her fear of the darkness. Pushing that fear to the back of her mind, she grabbed a torch and went in search of Jasin's cabin. Luckily there were only two outbuildings on the property used by the Elstradas and one was a gardening shed. She stopped several feet from what she assumed was Jasin's door. A rustling in the bushes raised the hairs on her neck. She called out his name in almost a whisper. No one answered. She moved cautiously towards the door, her torch flickering. Maybe he was sleeping. She should probably go. Suddenly, footsteps from behind startled her. She turned to find Jasin.

"You're always sneaking up on me." She could feel her heart beating.

"I wasn't expecting a visitor. I was…ah, out for a short walk."

Elizabeth understood. She, herself, had never been comfortable squatting in the bushes at night. During the day she had no problems, but exposing herself like that at night…well she preferred the pot. "I was hoping to get your help moving a few things in my room…I mean, if you weren't going to bed. Would you mind?"

The two of them went to Elizabeth's room and managed to slide the last few crates to the side. Jasin surveyed the room and noticed the dilapidated mattress. "Where were you planning to sleep tonight?"

"I thought you might be able to open this door and I could toss that disgusting thing outside."

Jasin walked over to the door and leaned into it. The door didn't budge.

"I tried that. It's probably sealed outside."

"Why seal a door from the outside? That doesn't seem to make sense."

Elizabeth shrugged. "I can't see anything from inside. I just assumed."

They went outside. Fighting through overgrown shrubs and thorny popper plants, they arrived at the back of the house. Elizabeth had been right. The doorway led to what had been a small private sitting area surrounded by the remains of an old garden, barely discernable except for the unusual assortment of flora growing out of control. They made their way to the stuck door where the cause became immediately apparent. The ground had heaved and held the door firmly in place. Elizabeth sat down, burying her chin in her hand.

"Well it doesn't look like you're going to get rid of that rodent nursery tonight. You could sleep in my cabin if you'd like." Jasin felt awkward making the offer. She hadn't given him the slightest encouragement. What he was beginning to feel was surely one sided, but perhaps....

"I'm not sure that would be wise. I don't want to put anyone out," Elizabeth said.

"It's no bother."

"I don't think it would be proper. It's my first night. Hardly appropriate for the help—"

"If you're uncomfortable being with me... I just thought...well I could sleep at Mas's."

"I'm not uncomfortable, Jasin. Truthfully, I am so tired I could sleep anywhere tonight. Don't take this wrong, Jasin, but I doubt whether you being there will make the least little difference. It's been a long day and I haven't slept well on the trail. By the time my head hits a pillow, I'll be out."

A single candle lantern lit the interior of Jasin's cabin. Elizabeth removed her shoes and made herself comfortable on the proffered bed. Jasin slumped into an oversized chair. They talked awhile until sleep overwhelmed her. Jasin, however, wasn't able to fall asleep so easily. He had never shared a room with a woman as captivating as Elizabeth without paying for the privilege. He'd had a few girl friends while in Advanced Studies; had sex with several of them, but they all seemed like, well, like girls. He'd never been as totally enchanted by a woman before. He felt foolish; he hardly knew her, but wished she would wake up so they could continue talking. His heart raced as he looked at her sleeping. Her delicate nose and left cheekbone were smudged with dirt, and the memorial mark for her brother peaked out between auburn strands. He felt himself drawn to her, wanting to gently caress her soft hair, to brush it from where it fell across her face. He watched her chest rise and fall, and stared at the graceful curve of her hip and those impossibly long legs that stretched beyond the light of the dim candle lantern.

The Knife

Morning light streamed through the small openings that served as windows in Jasin's cabin and crept slowly along the floor's stone pavers. Moving hesitantly up Elizabeth's legs, the sunlight gently warmed her before finally falling across her eyes to wake her. Disoriented and attempting to regain her bearings, she surveyed the room.

Jasin's cabin was sparsely furnished—a rough table, a straight back chair, a travel backpack, stuffed full, rested against a stucco wall awaiting his next trip. The tiny utility kitchen was tidy except for where several breathing scarves were haphazardly draped over the sides a meita pot. Red stains spread from its base like veins. A wooden chest held his neatly arranged clothes; a small looking glass perched on top. Elizabeth smiled; he had a bit of vanity, but few if any hobbies, at least from what she could see.

Where had he gone? Last night he had mentioned jogging in the foothills with Mas. Perhaps Jasin had already left for his morning run. Her eyes wandered back to the backpack. He had talked freely about so many things, but she didn't recall anything about him leaving town.

She yawned; considered turning over, but there was something Avram said…something he wanted early. She bolted upright. What time was it? The old man wanted hot water for his habit. Was he so completely useless that he couldn't boil water? She quickly rose, checked herself in the small mirror, ran fingers through her hair, and headed for the door. She paused and turned back to see if there were any dirty clothes that might need cleaning. Did her duties extend to taking care of Jasin and his cabin? It would be the least she could do for his help last night, but she could find nothing, not a single article of clothing lay tossed about, everything had its place.

As she hurried back to the main house, Elizabeth sorted through her first day with the Elstrada family. Avram, the politician: All smiles on the outside, plots and intrigue laced through his soul. Obviously, he was used to being served. Was his keetah use hiding some personal failing? Julian: Testing, sharp, very intuitive, undemanding, as shy and reserved as Avram was verbose and social. And Jasin: Organized, neat, a bit shy, attentive—Jasin had asked as many more questions of her, than she had of him. Pleasant enough. She hadn't felt awkward. She hadn't felt much of anything. It must have been how tired she was last night.

Avram, hunched over his writing table, surrounded by stacks of invitations, glanced up as she entered with the hot water.

"Late night?" he asked raising an eyebrow.

A scolding or just misplaced curiosity, Elizabeth couldn't read him. She decided to play it safe. "I'm sorry, it was a long day yesterday and I must have overslept a bit. Where would you like this?" Did Avram know she had slept in Jasin's cabin? Of course he knew. Elizabeth bit her lip. A bad decision, just like she had feared. Now they think she's interested in their son.

Avram gestured towards a collection of cups. "I like it strong, but cool. You know the water has to be extremely hot, especially with the superior grades."

"Yes sir, it's pretty hot. I'm sure it will do nicely." She set to making his keetah. As she stirred the powder she glanced about the study. Her gaze fell on an ancient book. "That old book reminds me of something I've always wondered about."

Avram stopped writing and look over to her.

"Where are the things from the ship? I mean, in all my years—"

"All your *many* years…" Avram interrupted. He smiled. "How old are you? Twenty? Twenty-five?"

"Twenty-six sir. Twenty-seven on the 43rd of the second," She shook her head. Why did she add her birth date? That's what young kids do. "It's rare to see anything from the ship. There had to be other books."

"Very few. Most information including our literature was stored electronically. Even the simplest readers used technology we're prohibited from using now."

"Then it was all lost."

"It was the price we paid to survive." Avram's eyes twinkled and a smile bloomed on his face. "You aren't one of those that wish me harm are you?"

"No sir, of course not. I'm not particularly political and I've got enough faults of my own to start finding them in others. I don't mean any offense at all. It's more of a curiosity. It's like human existence started only thirty years ago. There had to be so many interesting stories and discoveries and, well, I mean our whole history, what's come before. You know what I mean don't you?"

Avram's voice was subdued, "Of course. I am tormented every day by the loss, especially for the planet-born." He walked over to the ancient book and carefully picked it up. He ran his fingers gently along the frail cover. "That's one of the reasons I protect this one. Not because of what it contains, but for what it represents." He eyed the keetah Elizabeth was absently stirring. "Done yet?"

"I think so, but be careful. It's still kind of hot."

With care, Avram replaced the book and took the steaming cup.

"Was there anything you wanted me to pick up at the market for dinner? Anything special you would like me to prepare?" asked Elizabeth.

"I'm sure whatever you make will be fine. Neither of us is too particular, but you should ask Julian"

Elizabeth nodded and started to retreat, but hesitated. She had to say something about last night; she couldn't leave having him think she was getting involved with Jasin. Turning back to Avram she said, "Last night…the mattress in my room…" She made a face. "It was really nasty. Jasin offered to help, but we couldn't remove it. Really, I have no intention…you needn't worry about anything." Before Avram could comment she turned away.

Elizabeth retreated to the kitchen and took an inventory of the cupboards, pantry, and cellar. Some of the dusty jars contained moldy mysteries she refused to investigate for fear of becoming sick. She made mental note of what she could make use of. Aside from last night's leftovers, there were a few pieces of spoiling fruit, a container of grass tea, some gilia pudding growing hair, and several salted paddlefish that had become leathery. A trip to the market was certainly in order. But first, breakfast. Paring away the worst sections of the mushy fruit, made even more difficult with the dull knives, she salvaged enough for a modest first meal, and set the table.

Julian arrived and stuck her head into the kitchen.

Elizabeth looked up from the toast she was preparing from the ends of yesterday's bread and asked. "Do you think Avram will be joining you for breakfast?"

"You saw him this morning, not I. What do you think?"

Elizabeth blushed, another test? "He asked for hot water. He looked busy."

"Of course he did." Julian sat down at the table in the kitchen. The massive Sytonian furniture nearly swallowed her petite form.

"Wouldn't you be more comfortable in the dining room?"

"This is fine. I find it awkward being served and eating alone. Would you do me the favor of sitting with me?"

"Would you like tea with your fruit and toast this morning?" Elizabeth deflected Julian's question. What would be the proper response?

"Thank you that would be nice. You don't have to fuss so. You'll find our eating habits quite basic. Come sit. Keep me company."

Elizabeth served the hot tea, along with the fruit and toast, and then with some hesitation, she sat.

"Are you not eating?" asked Julian between mouthfuls.

"I nibbled a little while I worked. You know how it is in the kitchen." Elizabeth doubted she did. "I would like to go to the market today. The knives need sharpening and I'd like to pick up some supplies. Is there anything you'd like me to make you? Any special requests?"

Julian shrugged and smiled. "Why don't you decide? I appreciate the thought, but as I already said, when it comes to food we're quite simple."

As I *already* said. Elizabeth made the mental note— Julian didn't like repeating herself. To Julian, eating was an inconvenience. Elizabeth reached for a bit of toast.

Julian smiled. "Thank you," she said.

Elizabeth was surprised at her sincerity. Julian was a lonely woman.

After breakfast, Elizabeth quickly straightened the house. Avram and Julian each had their own rooms. Whether this was a reflection on their marriage or simply a matter of privilege, Elizabeth wasn't sure. She refreshed the meita pot, gathered used breathing scarves and dirty laundry, and filled the washtub. While the clothes soaked, she grabbed a handful of rags and went to work on the windows of her new room. How she wished she could open her private door. Stale air permeated the room and the disgusting remains of the tattered mattress gave off a fetid smell, but disposing of it would have to wait until after she returned from town. She didn't plan on spending another night with Jasin, even if it wasn't entirely unpleasant.

Definitely the strongest memory of the night was how tired she had been…that, and how eager he was to talk, as if he'd never have another chance. It was a little unnerving; his dark eyes had never drifted from hers. Details of what they had discussed eluded her, yet his obvious desire to share, to find some connection with her, was still vivid.

By noon, she had clean windows and clean clothes. Not a bad morning, she thought as she gathered the dull knives from the kitchen, wrapping them in rough cloth before dropping them in her daypack. If she had a stone, she could have sharpened them herself, but saving a few meita didn't seem to matter in this privileged household. She'd just drop them off at the cutlery while she went to the market. Elizabeth took a few minutes to see if either Avram or Julian needed anything before she left.

"If you would deliver these invitations for the party to a few Caucus members who live in town, I'd be most appreciative," Avram handed Elizabeth the bundle.

She hesitated, but reached out and took them. "I really don't know anyone in Nova Gaia."

"Don't worry. It's not as hard as it sounds. At this time of day most of them can be found either at the market or in their homes off Main Street. Just ask Janess; she practically lives in the market. She'll be the one selling tiela gourd. You can trust her. She's from a good family. I'm sure she'll be glad to point you in the right direction."

Being careful not to crumple them, she placed them in her pack and headed out through the wide courtyard to begin the fifteen-minute walk to town.

Nova Gaia had grown at the base of rolling hills beneath imposing Mount Trinity, a ragged peak that blocked the view to the gorge rim. The Elstrada complex sat nestled in the foothills, so after just a few twists in the road, she was looking down into the center of town where dozens of empty buildings lined the main street. Only about 300 humans lived in the immediate area, yet strangely, the city had been built for a population ten times that. With the exception of her own town of Panvera, which was built entirely by and for humans, Elizabeth knew this oddity to be true throughout the cold region. Most humans believed the Sytonians who had inhabited these cities had been relocated to the warm side of the Kaysop range, or they moved willingly after the Council had informed them of the settlement agreement. Nobody knew for sure. A few months after the humans reoccupied the empty cities, the extra space became normal and no one gave it much thought. The ship-born often commented that coming from the tight quarters of Tanis, normal living space took on new meaning.

She found the cutlery and approached the proprietor, an older, ship-born gentleman. After receiving assurance that they'd be worked on immediately, she continued on to the market. Without difficulty, she found Avram's friend, Janess, a young woman, with curly dark hair. Elizabeth estimated her age at twenty-one or so.

"What's they say?" Janess asked without a hint of propriety. "Don't believe you haven't took a peek." The scruffy, thin youth snatched one of the invitations and smiled, revealing more than a few missing teeth.

Elizabeth reached for the invitation, uncomfortable at the breach of etiquette, but Janess turned away.

"You wants my help or not?" With tiela stained fingers, the young merchant opened the folded paper and peered at it for the longest time. She turned it this way and that, leaving purple fingerprints upon the fine handmade paper. "It ain't good writing...not that I can make out anyway." She held the invitation open for Elizabeth to see.

The invitation was written in elegant sweeping script. Only the ship-born, and perhaps the daughters of professors, such as she, were taught the novelty of the ancient hand. Elizabeth couldn't help notice the date of the party—fortieth of the fifth, not even two septets from today. She refolded the invitation.

"You're right," Elizabeth said. "It's impossible to make out. Besides, it's just Caucus business. So where do I find..." She sorted through the invitations. "Sandist Lee, Findley, and this Yarrow fellow." The fact that she could read the names somehow failed to register on poor Janess.

"Them old folks be by soon enough. Everyday I sees them," Janess said. "You want me to give um to them?"

"That would be nice. Are you sure? It's important."

"Just two meita. I'll make it my top pree-or-a-tee," she said with another toothless grin.

Elizabeth couldn't help but smile. "Or maybe I'll just buy a few of your gourds and we'll call it even." Somehow Elizabeth trusted her; Avram had, so she bought several ripe gourds, paying more than a fair price just to make certain Janess would do as she said.

"This one is for Lee, this one's for Findley, and the last is—"

"Yarrow, yous already told me."

"Thank you Janess." She entrusted the invitations to the waif's filthy, but seemingly capable hands.

Elizabeth continued to explore the market for several hours, getting to know where the best food could be had at the best prices. Finally, with a full bag of groceries, she made her way back through a street of deserted buildings to the cutlery. The older gentleman who had taken them was no longer there, but a younger boy, about sixteen, eagerly ran into the back of the shop to retrieve them.

"Here they are. Like new if you ask me." He handed the package of knives to Elizabeth who unwrapped them to make sure they were all there.

"If you don't mind me asking…it's just that I know almost everyone in the area…well, my name is Joey." The boy stuck out his hand and Elizabeth shook it. The boy smiled broadly and held her hand a trifle longer than good manners might dictate. His gaze wandered over her.

"Elizabeth," she stated without hint of emotion so as not to encourage him. She spread the knives out and tested the edges of several of them against a fingernail. They slid across with biting. "Did you sharpen these?"

"Yes, one of my better jobs if I must say."

"Well, you'll just have to do them again or get someone else who knows what they're doing. These are worse than when I dropped them off."

The boy's face fell. "There wasn't enough time and…and you had too many of them to do well. Seriously, I can usually do a really good job."

"You can't tell it from these." Elizabeth took a few of the sharper ones she knew she would need and pushed the rest back towards the boy. "I'll take these now and pick up the others tomorrow. They'd better be sharp, really sharp. Do you understand?" She made it sound more important than it really was. There was just something about the boy she immediately disliked— inept and a trifle too friendly, a bit like Jorge Wynosk with his creepy staring.

Elizabeth left the shop and headed up the road, back toward her new home. It was a rare clear day. The sun shone brightly and she could easily make out all the distant peaks including Mount Schtolin. Beyond it and further up lay Panvera. She hadn't been back in over a year and while she missed her father, the thought of her childhood home, now filled with haunting memories of her mother and brother, only brought back sadness.

Approaching the Elstrada gate, she met Mas, just leaving the house. His clothes were covered with grime and he greeted her with a broad smile and laughter. "Going to cook me dinner? How sweet! And we've only just met."

Elizabeth grinned. Mas was so easy going. It was a pleasure seeing him again. "I couldn't wait to impress you. I was hoping you'd propose after sampling my soup."

His eyes glistened and he swept an errant lock of blond hair from his eye. "What's the rush? Mark my words; we'll fall in love by the end of the week. Do you need help with your sack?"

"No thanks. I didn't buy much."

"I saw what you've done to that old store room. Looks great."

"Snooping around in my room? Should I be worried about you?"

"No, just helping out a bit." He flashed another of his endearing smiles and started down the road, but stopped and shouted back, "Tell Jasin, I'll be at Suzy's tonight. You should join us."

She watched him walk away, feeling a little guilty for checking out his tight backside. It had been a long time since she even let herself consider an offer like that.

While dinner baked, Elizabeth retreated to her room. Kicking off her shoes, she headed to the washbasin. It had already been a full day and as tempting as Mas's offer to go out had been, she knew she would probably pass on it. She dipped a cloth into the cool water and scrubbed her face. A shadow passed by the freshly cleaned windows and she jumped. If she were to have any privacy she'd have to make some drapes. Then there was a knock on the outside door.

"Who's there?" she yelled. When no one answered, she asked again.

Suddenly, she understood and ran to the door, throwing it open to find Jasin standing next to a pile of dirt. "It's great! Thank you so much," she said swinging the door from side to side.

"At your service." Jasin beamed.

"I should have guessed what you were up to when I saw Mas."

"He didn't tell you did he? I'll kill him."

"No, I just should have figured it out…He wanted me to tell you he was going to a girl's place tonight. A Sue somebody.

"Suzy's? That's a tavern we like to hang out at."

"Are you going?"

"Probably, unless something comes up."

Elizabeth nodded. "I suspected that something was wrong. I saw your backpack. Are you going back to Bistoun?"

"No. There are no plans whatsoever, at least that I am aware off. I always have a few things ready. You never know when Beloit might call. It pays to be prepared. You should join us at Suzy's after you're done with dinner," he said.

"Aren't you having dinner with your folks?"

"Two nights in a row? That's a bit much. Join us after you're done. I'd like to spend some time with you when your eyes are open."

"Two nights in a row?" She repeated with a smile, and a shake of her head. "That's a bit much." She grew somber. "It'll be dark soon. Conboet and Eian have been setting early. I think I'll just stay here."

"That's ridiculous. I'll come get you. Don't worry. I'll have you back before breakfast." Jasin didn't wait for another objection, but turned and headed for his cabin. It wouldn't have mattered what excuse she had. He was going to spend time with her tonight even if he had to help her clean his parent's dishes.

Smoke filled Suzy's, a crowded inn just big enough for five small tables, a native grill pit, a dozen loud people, and Rahfi, the most obese human Elizabeth had ever seen. She couldn't help but stare as he moved around the grill adjusting cuts of turbak to keep them from burning. Sweat poured from the man, dripping onto the hot metal and, although the room was loud, Elizabeth was sure she could hear the droplets sizzle as they danced off the cooking surface. The crowd was almost entirely planet-born. To most that grew up aboard Tanis, dining on animal meat was a difficult concept to accept.

Jasin introduced Elizabeth to a few friends, but never moved far from her side. They watched Mas float through the crowd, enchanting and entertaining friends and strangers alike. His blond curls stood out among the sea of darker heads.

"He's been able to do that since we were kids," Jasin said leaning close to Elizabeth so he could be heard.

"Do what?"

"Talk to strangers... I can't do it. How do you know if they're interested in what you have to say? How do you not know you're not interrupting or being a pest?"

"You don't seem to have difficulty talking to me."

"That's different," he said, nervously running a hand across the rough stubble on his cheek. He couldn't explain why, but his desire to be with Elizabeth, to talk to her, was so great, that it had never occurred to him that she might be offended by his ramblings, but the thought stopped him cold. Why did she bring it up just then? Was he just babbling? Was she bored with him already? He should have shaved. His brain refused to move beyond the nagging thought that he was making a fool of himself. The next few seconds crawled; she had to say something first.

Elizabeth could sense his anxiety. "I'm glad you feel like you can talk to me." She briefly touched his hand, and then feared he would take it wrong, but it was too late. She was enjoying both men's company and there was no reason to lead either of them on.

Mas eventually made it back to their table. "There's a lot of talk about Bistoun," he said. "You should go out there, Jasin, and impress a few ladies with your first hand knowledge."

"You know I can't talk about that."

"Too bad. You wouldn't have to coerce bedless women to your cabin tonight." Mas winked at Elizabeth. "Come Elizabeth, leave this loner. There are a dozen lovelies that are dying to meet their new competition."

She laughed, but made no effort to move.

"Perhaps you'd rather just get out of here and give my bed a whorl." His toothy smile lit up the room. "Come on Jasin, give a brother a chance. Let her free."

It was easy to be attracted to Mas's natural charisma. He was handsome and exciting, but Elizabeth felt a bit out of her class. It was difficult keeping up with his energy and flamboyance. Mas flew just beyond her, just out of reach.

On the other hand, Jasin's relaxed quiet nature, his reserve and undivided attention towards her was much more comfortable, more grounded. Together, they watched Mas flit about, never quite landing until it was time for dinner.

Rahfi grilled them one of his specialties—marinated splayed turbak—and they ate the delicacy along with fermented fruit drinks as if they were starving barbarians unsure where their next meal would come from. Jasin and Elizabeth soon tired, but for Mas, the evening was just starting. They both gave him good-natured hugs goodnight, made plans to meet him tomorrow, and then together headed for the door. However, before they had taken a dozen steps, Elizabeth stopped.

"Just give me a minute," she said running back to Mas.

Jasin watched as she took Mas by the arm. He swayed unsteadily as she pulled him aside. After a few words, she leaned forward and spoke intimately into his ear. When she had finished, he leaned forward, his lips puckered and his eyes closed. Elizabeth laughed, then kissed him, and ran back to rejoin Jasin.

As they began slowly walking home, the distance between them widened ever so slightly and the cold of the darkness descended into the space between. Jasin couldn't get the scene out of his mind. He couldn't believe the two of them. Right in front of him. They didn't even have the decency to hide their desires. Finally, he stopped, unable to continue any farther.

"What was that all about?"

"What are you talking about?" said Elizabeth, truly confused.

"That last little thing with Mas."

"I made a date with him for later," she said, with as much seriousness as she could muster.

He was speechless. How could his best friend do this to him? He had read Elizabeth all wrong. She was like all the others—easy prey for Mas. Suddenly, he erupted. "What is this then? Why are you here now? What kind of game—"

"Oh, stop it! You've got to relax. It's nothing. I only asked him to pick up some knives for me. He said he wouldn't unless I gave him a little kiss. Don't spoil a perfect night."

Jasin looked away for an instant hiding embarrassment so strong he was sure she could see it in the dark. What should he do now? The wind picked up and cooled his blushing cheek. A popper bush rustled in the breeze.

She stepped closer and held out her hand, "Don't you think it's time we get back?"

They held hands and walked through the town in silence. The few torches and lanterns that had illuminated their way earlier that evening were now extinguished and insignificant sounds caused Elizabeth to jump. She drew closer. Sensing her discomfort, Jasin quickened their pace. A hundred paces on a distant cylith howl froze her.

"Everything's fine," Jasin said calmly. "No one has ever seen a pup in town."

"We're no longer in town," she pointed out.

"Let's just keep moving." He coaxed her forward, but by the time they arrived at her bedroom door, she was trembling. Shyly, he embraced her, hoping to comfort her. Elizabeth's arms lay limp along her side. He looked at her, wanting to kiss her, but in the darkness of the night, found only an empty mask where he had seen such joyful animation earlier. He opened her door and helped her light a few candles. Once inside, Elizabeth calmed down. Color returned to her face, but Jasin couldn't detect even a trace of interest or desire. He wanted to approach her, but whatever intimacy they had begun to share had vanished. She coolly thanked him for the evening and they parted awkwardly.

Jasin wandered slowly back to his empty cabin. What must it have been like for Elizabeth that dreadful night, watching Michael mauled to death in front of her? He shuddered and opened his cabin's door. Stepping inside, he shut the unknown out and settled in. Yesterday had been much nicer. He looked at where she had slept the night before, picturing her long beautiful legs in the candlelight. Tonight hadn't ended as he had hoped. There were a few brief smiles, a tender touch, and unspoken moments that held promise. But had she held his hand out of fear of the dark? Perhaps, he was rushing her. He would slow down. Elizabeth was worth whatever effort or time that was necessary. He just hoped she thought the same of him.

For Elizabeth, sleep was impossible. At first, she blamed the cold blankets, then the mysterious sounds she heard outside her window. She tossed about in frustration thinking of how she had ended the night. She found an endless stream of excuses for her lack of sexual desire. There were times that from deep within, she would feel a slight familiar twinge, but it never grew strong. Something always dampened it. She rolled onto her back, and pulled the blanket tighter around her neck to keep the cold draft out. How long had it been since she made love or had sex of any kind? After her mother died, she had enjoyed the company of a few boys, and sharing her bed and body always felt like part of the package. But then Michael died and she found that feeling anything hurt too much. The horrible year she spent taking care of Hyland hadn't helped. Jorge was so awful that she had done everything in her power not to encourage him. She had suppressed her sexual feelings, buried them to such a point that the sensual part of her now seemed dead. She let her hand drift slowly down from her neck and delicately across her breasts, trying to tease her flesh into remembering the sensation. Rolling to her side, she gathered the blanket tightly between her legs and squeezed her thighs together. This is silly, she thought, and rolled back, embarrassed at the futility. A few minutes ago, she had a handsome and willing man that had clearly shown affection. And now...and now she had probably alienated him. She wouldn't blame him if he didn't want to have anything to do with her—a hopeless tease with ice water for blood.

* * *

Mas didn't care to argue with the old man. Last night's excesses still plagued him. His head ached, his stomach felt queasy, and his tongue was having a difficult time finding a comfortable position in his mouth. He asked again, "Do you have them or not? It's an easy question."

"They're not here," said the old man. "Joey said the lady had been in to pick them up. But even if we still had them, why would we give them to you?"

"She asked me to pick them up, that's why. Listen, you know me, you know I'm Jasin Elstrada's friend...well Elizabeth is living with them now. She's their new housekeeper. I promised to get them for her."

The old man shrugged. "They're not here. I can't give you what I don't have."

"Then, you'd better find them. I'll be back this afternoon."

Mas left the cutlery and turned to head back home. He had decided that it would be better to be sick at home than on the street. He hadn't taken more than a dozen steps when a hand grabbed his arm him from behind. Reacting, Mas twirled around and sent a teenage boy flying with a powerful swipe of his arm.

"Are you trying to kill me?" complained the kid. He rose slowly from his crumpled position.

"Don't you know better than to sneak up on someone, Joey? Why'd you lie about giving the knives to Elizabeth?"

"You're a moron, you know that Mas? A total moron. I'm trying to help you and you nearly kill me."

"Kill you? You aren't hurt a bit, but if you don't come up with Elizabeth's knives in the next few seconds, I'll see what I can do to remedy that."

"I don't have them."

"Try again."

"Listen, I don't have them, but I have something better. Come here." Joey backed up into the small alley between the knife shop and the building next door. Mas hesitated, but Joey pleaded, "Come on, what do you think I'm going to do. Let me show you."

Mas looked around. There were only a few people in the street, but no one within a block. He tried to look nonchalant as he stepped into the narrow space, but as he did, the boy reached into his jacket and pulled out a knife. Before the boy could say another word, Mas had grabbed him by the neck and twisted the knife from his hand.

"You're dumber than you look," Mas exclaimed. The youngster's eyes bulged out and he gasped for air.

"You're the idiot," he wheezed. "Let me go!"

Mas tossed him to the ground and kneeled on his chest. He leaned close to Joey's face and hissed, "If you ever pull a knife on me again I'll use it to make you a girl, understand? What were you thinking?"

"Get off me and I'll tell you."

Mas straightened, allowing the boy to rise. Joey's eyes found the knife lying in the dirt, but as he reached for it, Mas pinned his hand to the ground with a muddy boot. Mas leaned down and removed the weapon. It was a very thin stiletto with a blade a couple centimeters across and fifteen centimeters long. It weighed practically nothing, and the edge was perfectly honed. "Where'd you find this?" Mas asked, continuing to examine the greenish-blue instrument. The handle was gracefully wrapped in black leather that had been tooled with an unusual intricate design.

"Elizabeth said she liked her knives sharp...I thought she might appreciate it. I thought..."

"You thought you might impress her. Listen to me you rodent, she's way out of your league, and there's a city full of better men in line before you. Where'd you get this?"

"No reason she and I couldn't—"

"Where did you get this?" Mas asked again, punctuating each word.

"None of your business."

"I'm making it my business. Now, answer me. Where did you get this knife?"

"I traded her knives for it. Had to throw in a little extra on the side too. It's special. Never needs to be sharpened. Probably put us out of business if there were more of them, but I haven't seen another like it."

"Because it's probably illegal. It's a weapon."

"Says who?"

"It's certainly no kitchen knife."

Joey shrugged, "When does a kitchen knife become a weapon? Who's to say?"

Mas hefted it. "That would be up to Jasin or Beloit. You could get in trouble for just having this on you. You know the Prohibitions. The Sytonians could kill you for dealing in this sort of thing. Trust me. If you don't want to get Elizabeth into trouble, you won't be giving it to her or selling knives like this to anyone else." Mas grabbed Joey's shirt, and with a single slash, cut off a large piece of cloth, which he used to wrap the knife.

"Mas...I'm out a lot for that thing. I need it back or you'll have to cover me."

"Listen, I'm not feeling well enough to deal with your nonsense."

"Two green...I'm out two green."

"You paid with crystals?"

"That's what the trader wanted—two plus all her knives."

"You are a fool. All that just to get yourself into trouble." Mas shook his head. "Isn't love grand?" He pulled his pouch from his pants and dug out two green and a couple of larger meita. "I'll figure out how to get rid of it. Now go inside and get me a bunch of new kitchen knives—enough to replace what Elizabeth left here. I'll tell her that hers wouldn't take an edge any longer."

Joey ran into the shop and returned with the new knives. "These are the best we have."

Mas rubbed his forehead as if that would lift the dull ache from his pickled brain. Mas took the knives. "Don't ever talk about this to anyone, understand?"

Joey nodded weakly.

* * *

A day on Syton was approximately twenty-eight shipboard hours, but the erratic cycle of brightening and returning dimness in the Syton gorge was dictated by several confusing factors—Syton's own rotation, the presentation of the chasm to the sun, and the reflected light from the planet Conboet and sister moon, Eian. Conboet dragged its two moons about the sun creating a year of three hundred and twenty-nine of these extended days, making a Sytonian year about five percent longer than a year as it had been measured on Tanis. The natives divided their year into septets or months of forty-seven days, and while the natives never developed the concept of a week; humans had difficulty leaving the seven-day period behind. By the Sytonian calendar, Avram's party was planned for the twentieth day of the Sixth septet, or sixty-seven days away.

It was a time of constant activity for Elizabeth. Everyone tried to help, but Avram was useless, Julian kept to herself and her music and Beloit McMaster kept Jasin busy away from home. The incident in Bistoun had traveled widely, causing unrest and more civil disobedience than normal. Covering the territory between four widely spaced major human settlements was nearly impossible for only two Enforcers, but they were unable to recruit anyone else to the thankless job. When Jasin *was* home, he tried aiding Elizabeth, but their relationship was awkward. Forced conversation or uncomfortable silence too often accompanied their times together. Jasin, figuring that he had been rushing things a little too fast had pulled back to a comfortable emotional distance.

Elizabeth, however, was convinced that he had lost interest, and that it was her fault. She tried to tell herself that it was better this way. An affair with her boss's son probably wasn't wise or what she needed right now.

In preparation for the party, Avram met with the Human Caucus to convince them that it was important to try to persuade the Sytonians to grant them equal protection from violence, even if they had to resort to the entrapment of Sy Loeton. Avram had asked Sy Toberry for help delivering personal invitations to the entire Council of Seventeen. While the towan was gone, cart after cart arrived at the mansion bringing the settler's best furnishings. Elizabeth cleaned, and continually rearranged all the new furniture and expensive trappings, keeping a careful record of who had loaned what.

One day after receiving a particularly cumbersome cabinet, meticulously carved from dense ironroot, she sought Jasin's assistance to rearrange, for the umpteenth time, the main living salon where the party was planned. Positioning each new piece usually involved moving several others.

She walked along the path that separated her small private garden from his cabin and found him sitting on the ground leaning against a large boulder, reading from Avram's ancient book.

"I didn't think Avram liked anyone touching it," she said.

"He doesn't," he said, closing it carefully. "But there isn't much else to read that I haven't read a dozen times."

"I would be afraid to touch it. The pages look like they could fall apart just looking at them. Why do you take the chance?"

"What's the sense of having it disintegrate with no one having read it?"

"Interesting?"

"I don't know. I don't understand many of the ancient words and the phrasing is pretty convoluted, but you can make out the gist of the stories: a creation myth, brothers who fight each other, an enslaved people, things like that. I'm not very far into it. If there was anything else..."

Elizabeth understood. She too had often wished there was more to read. "I was hoping you could help me move a new piece that just arrived."

"Just one piece?" He smiled. They had been through this before. "Help me up." He held out his hand.

She grinned, "Yeah, just one, like all the other times." She reached out and took his hand to pull him to his feet.

It was a simple touch—Jasin didn't mean anything by it, and Elizabeth certainly hadn't expected the feeling that spread through her body from the hand he continued to hold so gently. They made eye contact, but let their hands fall apart, their discomfort with each other returning.

"Do you ever run," asked Jasin, as they made their way towards the house.

Run! He is certainly a strange one, she thought. "It hurts my lungs."

"You just need more meita. Tomorrow morning, there's a place I want to show you."

"We'll see," she said. Why lead him on when she felt no desire to get involved? Why hadn't she just turned him down flat?

The next brightening brought a bone chilling mist, a penetrating fog that refused to lift. Stones crunched beneath their feet and the thick atmosphere condensed, then froze across their scarves as they ran. Elizabeth shifted a fresh, porous section of her meita soaked cloth over her mouth and nose and struggled to keep up with Jasin, who was totally focused on the terrain ahead. She didn't think he had even glanced in her direction. Maybe she was wrong about him. She admired his focus and drive to succeed, shown as much by the way he attacked this broken mountainside as his dedication for his job. How could he possibly believe there was room beside his ambition for her in his busy life? Why after ignoring each other for weeks did he suddenly think there was a place for her? That she was the least bit interested? She wasn't...was she?

Occasionally wisps of snow, falling from the gorge rim high overhead, blew across their path, refreshing their sweaty faces. As the incline increased, Elizabeth's knees began to ache. She couldn't remember the last time she had run or been so physically challenged, but she wasn't going to let him get the better of her.

Jasin heard her grunt and turned to check. All he could see were her eyes peering out from above her breathing scarf. "You okay?" he asked, breathlessly.

She nodded, so he turned to concentrate once more on the path. She was remarkable, he thought. This had to be the toughest section of the run. If he had been with Mas, they would have rested by now, but her courage and strength invigorated him. Finally, they rounded a curve and found themselves perched on an outcropping jutting out into open space. On one side of the promontory, the steep terrain fell off into a craggy ravine before rising again into the clouds surrounding the gorge rim. Looking in the opposite direction, a vast section of the inhabitable lands lay revealed. Jasin stopped. They were both panting. Neither said anything until they caught their breath.

"How's your throat...burning?" he asked.

"The extra layer of meita cloth helps a lot," she replied a bit hoarse, unwilling to admit how much pain she really was in.

"For the record," he admitted, "that was the fastest ascent I ever made. For someone who claims they don't run, you're terrific."

"For the record, *we* just made the fastest ascent."

Jasin smiled. "I spend too much time inside my own head. Sometimes, I get a little self-centered, but that's why I wanted to share this. Look." He pointed off into the distance, away from the mountain wall and down into the vast gorge.

The view was unlike any Elizabeth had never experienced. She could follow the road out of Nova Gaia and down towards the billowing waterfall that marked the halfway point to Lake Chook. In the direction of Soto Harbor dense clouds rolled in from the distant Great Lake, obscuring whatever secrets the natives hid from them there.

"Do you know why they have prohibited travel to Soto Harbor?" she asked.

"No, and I don't know what the Kull Prohibition is for either. Neither does Beloit, although he claims to have been there once."

"The Kull?"

"No, Soto. From what I can gather, he wasn't always such a straight arrow. He says the harbor didn't seem special…just boats. He thought it was probably a short cut to the warmer lands beyond the Kaysop range. Fistulee is also a harbor town. That's where that bastard, Sy Loeton, lives now."

"You think he killed that woman, don't you."

"If he didn't, then we haven't the faintest idea who did. Avram's plan to get him to brag about it at the party might be the only way we have to get an answer. Are you sure you don't run?"

"No, and now I remember why," she said rubbing her knees.

"It is such a wonderful release. When I'm up here it feels like I'm half way to the top. Like I could almost escape."

"Escape…to where?"

He shrugged, but looked up towards the rim. Huge clouds flew just beyond the cavern's edge driven by the fierce surface winds.

Elizabeth raised her eyebrows. "You'd freeze before you got within five kilometers of the surface. I didn't take you for a dreamer."

"I'm just curious. I know it's unreasonable, but when you look down from up here our settlement appears so insignificant. Makes you wonder what's outside."

She stared at him. Nothing had led her to believe that Jasin was a hapless explorer, a daredevil capable of throwing caution to the wind. "You said escape. Escape from what?"

"Poor choice of words I suppose."

But it wasn't. Elizabeth felt like a bright light had broken through the clouds above to illuminate his soul. It was suddenly obvious. He felt trapped; his life as one of only two Enforcers was a series of expectations and duties. He lived in the shadow of his parents, both figuratively and in reality. He lived in Beloit McMaster's shadow as well.

"You should move away," she said. "Make a new life just for you. No obligations to anyone."

"You think you know me well enough to make that suggestion?" he retorted, but his gentle smile revealed she had struck close to the truth.

"No...but I'd like to." Her unguarded admission surprised her; it was as if someone else had spoken. Jasin was not only kind and sensitive, but complex as well. He was attentive, supportive, and reliable. Her unconscious mind must have understood all this, forcing itself to be heard. Quickly, she tried to break the silence and embarrassment her revelation had brought.

"Panvera is high like this, just on the other side of Mount Schtolin. Sometimes the temperature is pretty brutal. Have you been there?"

Jasin shook his head.

"Well, maybe someday you could come with me and meet my father. Panvera is unique."

"So is this," he declared softly.

They spent nearly an hour sitting and talking, taking in the views Jasin's special spot afforded until they became chilled from their sweaty clothes. Jasin helped her stand and once again they both could sense something pass between them as they touched. This time Jasin didn't let go.

It was an awkward first kiss, uncomfortable, as much from the differences in their heights, as their unfamiliarity with each other. They each backed away slightly, unsure. She brushed Jasin's shaggy locks aside to see his eyes.

"I need a haircut," he said lamely. "I usually wear it shorter."

"I'm pretty good with a blade." She smiled.

"We'd better be getting down," he said, his heart beating so loudly he was afraid she'd hear it.

"I promised Julian I would help her with the hem of her dress," she said, lifting the edge of her scarf self-consciously over her mouth and nose, leaving only her sparkling eyes to reveal the feelings he had awoken.

"Did you enjoy your run this morning, Elizabeth?" Julian inquired. "Lucky you got it in before the storm. I haven't seen the two of you together much. Not that it's any of my business…just a mother's curiosity."

Elizabeth tried to ignore the opening that Julian had created. She was unsure and uncomfortable even thinking about their relationship, if that's even what you would call it. She asked Julian if she thought the rain would continue much longer.

But Julian ignored her parry and continued, "You know…I believe he has deep feelings for you."

Elizabeth looked up from the hem she was attempting to level and stared at Julian. "Your son is a wonderful man. He has gone out of his way to make me feel welcome here, but I'm afraid there's little chance of any…romantic involvement." She wondered if Julian could detect her hesitation, but disliked Julian's prying.

"What do you mean, *you're afraid*?"

Elizabeth took a deep breath and sighed.

"Do you have another boyfriend? Is it Mas? All the girls like him."

"Oh no! Mas and I are just friends. It's nothing like that."

"I'm sorry. I'll keep my mouth shut. It's just that you should try to be clear with Jasin. He's inexperienced at reading emotions…not much practice in a family like ours. But I know my son thinks you're one of the most intriguing and intelligent young women he's met."

Elizabeth looked away, her face turning red. How does she know what her son thinks? Whose business was it? Certainly not Julian's.

Julian knelt down beside her and gently turned Elizabeth's head so she could look into her eyes. "If it's the job you're worried about, you needn't be afraid. You don't work for Jasin; you work for us, and as long as you continue to perform your duties here, we don't care what you do in your spare time, but if it involves our son...well, just don't avoid a relationship because of what Avram or I might think." Julian stood up and unfastened the gown, letting it fall to the floor. She put on her robe. "Avram and I will fix dinner for ourselves tonight. Why don't you take the night off." It wasn't a question.

Avoiding a relationship? Is that what she was doing? That's definitely what she *should* be doing. Julian should only know what happened on the mountain. Elizabeth's head was spinning. It would affect her job. There was no doubt about it. Perhaps Julian believed that any woman that would reject her son would need some really outlandish reason like being afraid for her job. But no, Elizabeth knew that Julian had a pretty honest appraisal of her son. She had heard them talking at the dinner table about his stiffness and difficulty in letting go. Elizabeth recognized those attributes too, but she also saw sides of Jasin they probably never knew existed.

After finishing her chores for the day, Elizabeth warmed some water and filled the tub in her room. She still couldn't believe the luxury she had been provided. Even Avram and Julian didn't have a bath in their room. True, she had to spend hours cleaning the ceramic monster when she first arrived, but now it was a welcome treat, when she found the time to fill it, which today Julian had provided. She shed her clothes and stepped into the bath, letting the warm water relax her. She hadn't stopped thinking about Jasin since they kissed. She had to see him again if only to prove that the feelings on the mountain had been real.

Before the water cooled, she washed her hair and made sure she was clean head to toe. She stepped out and dried herself, and then sorted through her few clothes, putting on a blouse and simple skirt that made her feel pretty. As she brushed her hair, feelings of anticipation and excitement began to simmer, feelings that she thought had died were awake and it frightened her. Was she being too forward thinking Jasin might be feeling the same?

Suddenly a blinding flash of lightning cut the dimness outside and it began to pour. She peered through her windows. Blackness and rain filled her small garden. Elizabeth took the small candle from her table and brought it closer to her bed. Her first night off and she was trapped inside her bedroom. She put the candle down and rolled onto the bed. All the exhilaration she had felt was melting into despair, and she desperately fought to control the heaviness in her heart. Listening to the storm, she fell asleep.

She slept for over an hour. Her room was dark, but clearly from the emerging stillness, the rain must have abated. Rising, she peered out the window. The sky above Jasin's cabin was speckled with small pinpoints of moving light. It took a moment before realizing that she was seeing burning embers escape from Jasin's chimney.

As she watched the tiny glowing bits, Elizabeth's desire returned. Jasin was just a short walk away…a short walk through the darkness. The path would be a mess and she only had a small lantern. It would be enough she told herself. She could do it. Before fear could change her mind, she quickly brushed her sleep-tossed hair, threw on a coat, lit the small lantern, and opened her outside door.

There she froze. Deep puddles, visible from the light of her lantern, dotted the path and revealed a light rain. Five meters beyond the doorway, at the edge of her circle of light, heavy blackness barred the way. She took a hesitant step outside and closed her door. Carefully, she made her way across her small garden terrace, and moved toward the cabin. The wind blew rain into her face and swept her long hair aside. She forced herself to keep her mind clear of any thought other than seeing Jasin, but the darkness closed in around her. Just take one step after another, she told herself. Doubt invaded. She turned to look at her room. Through the window, she could make out the tiny glow of the candle she had left burning. It was reassuring. All she had to do is take a few steps and she'd be safely back in her room. She steeled herself. Taking a deep breath she turned to go on, but the path had disappeared. Everything had disappeared. The lantern's flame had gone out.

Her breathing became shallow and rushed. Disoriented, she took a few hesitant steps forward. Blinding light flashed, flooding the surrounding area, then immediately a deafening clap of thunder and darkness. Rain pummeled her.

The first thing she saw when her sight returned was the plume of sparks from Jasin's flue. They were actually much brighter than her lantern. She hadn't seen them before. Her focus had been down on the path, not looking up into the sky, but there they were, beckoning her. She would follow the column of burning embers. Anything would be better than standing in the rain. Slowly, no longer following the path, she made her way straight towards the cabin.

Occasionally, she imagined scratching sounds or footsteps near her and she would stop and hold her breath unwittingly. She could smell wet musky cylith fur. They were hiding in the dark, waiting for her to stumble, waiting to attack. She squeezed the lantern handle prepared to swing it into the lunging beasts. She knew it was irrational, but she listened for their movement nonetheless.

By the time she made it to the cabin, she was wet, muddy, and totally frazzled. Not exactly the in the condition she had hoped, but extremely proud of herself. She knocked on the door.

"Come in, come in. You're crazy to be out in that weather. Do you know that? Here, let me take that wet coat" Jasin placed it carefully over a chair and hurried over to the corner to find a towel.

Elizabeth exchanged the useless lantern for the towel and started drying her hair. "The lantern went out..." she began lamely. "I wanted...I want..." Elizabeth shook her head in frustration. The words stuck in her dry mouth. "Do you have any water?" she finally asked.

"Of course. Come sit down next to the fire and I'll get you some."

Elizabeth looked down at her muddy shoes. "I'm filthy, and I wasn't going to stay long."

"Don't be silly." He knelt down and untied her shoes, removing them gently, using one hand to hold her ankle steady so as not to make her fall.

They walked over to the fireplace and she collapsed into his only chair. He handed her some water, which she sipped slowly, taking a few moments to warm-up and relax.

"Jasin..." she finally broke the silence, "I came over to—"

He leaned over and kissed her. She wasn't prepared for the passion in his kiss, but it was her intense desire that surprised them both. With tender intimacy, they took time exploring. Initial nervousness melted away as they teased and excited each other, finding little hot spots and secrets that hid beneath their clothes. Jasin, delighted in discovering Elizabeth's body— the beauty of her large brown eyes, her delicate nose and slender neck, the perfect curve of her full breasts. He caressed them until Elizabeth coyly covered their aroused firmness. She rolled over, pulling Jasin beneath her, and swirled her silky hair sensually across his handsome face and broad, hairless chest. Their love play continued until Jasin, unable to restrain himself any longer, entered her.

She took him willingly, moving against his motion, wrapping her long legs around his muscular body, pulling him into her, until his deep thrusting brought him to a breathless climax. She held his shaking body, stroking his thick, black hair, until he rolled to her side. She turned to face him and asked, "Why did we wait so long?"

They cuddled for nearly an hour, listening to the storm, whispering, and touching, until Jasin, newly aroused, resumed their lovemaking. Wanting to please Elizabeth, he concentrated on her pleasure. She lay still, passively trying to enjoy his efforts, but soon her mind began to wander. She needed more.

Exchanging places, she immediately began to feel empowered and the control excited her, making her feel more lustful. She straddled him, tilting her hips forward, and rocked gently, finding just the right rhythm, the proper pressure. From deep within, her passion grew and spread throughout her body, enveloping her, the warm glow...and then, violent spasms took her, along with Jasin, over the edge, and into that long awaited bliss she had nearly forgotten.

Soiree

Frosted mist often enveloped the gnarled foothills behind the Elstrada compound. On other occasions, a warm breath of fog obscured the roll and tumble. Seasons had no place in the Syton gorge, especially at the base of Mount Trinity where the fickle climate continually transformed the hidden valleys and enchanting vistas that became Jasin and Elizabeth's private playground. They spent most of their free time during the next half-septet exploring the ever-novel terrain and equally convoluted corners of each other's lives. Running together, they would ascend the tumultuous landscape before the brightness became full and duty and obligation called them to their respective jobs.

Mas joined them occasionally, but he never truly enjoyed rising early, and complained of being the odd man out, which in truth he was. Jasin and Elizabeth were deeply in love and nearly all their attention was lavished on each other. Avram delighted in watching the blossoming relationship, taking credit for the fine match. Julian, more restrained, never missed an opportunity to test Elizabeth's sincerity or resolve.

As the days of the fifth septet passed and the party approached, Elizabeth's duties increased. Snuggled in Jasin's arms one night, she confessed her fear that it would become more difficult to find time for each other. The next day, Jasin told Beloit that until Avram's party, he would be staying in Nova Gaia to help Elizabeth with the preparations.

"She's already got the ring through your nose, boy. You're going to regret ever falling in love," the elder Enforcer groused. "It leads nowhere. Keep your distance."

"I don't think so, Beloit. This is special," argued Jasin.

Beloit McMaster nodded knowingly, but his gesture turned into a sorrowful shake as he turned away.

A week before the party, Jasin approached Avram. "Father, Beloit and I will be the only men without wives or companions. It might be construed that we have been invited in an official capacity and ruin the festive nature of the event. I don't believe Sy Loeton will let down his guard knowing that we, who have been investigating him, seem to be standing guard."

"That's not true. I can think of several members of the Human Caucus that will not be accompanied. Jorge Wynosk for one."

"You don't think Nanc will come?"

"I've heard she's gone back to the Women's Colony. Unless Jorge finds someone else…"

"Still, there's no reason for me to attend alone. Would you mind if I invite Elizabeth?"

Avram tilted his head. "I don't understand…Elizabeth will be there."

"I don't mean in the kitchen. We could find someone else to help out."

"You know how important this party is to me, Jasin. Elizabeth has control of everything. She's indispensable. Without her—"

"Father, this is going to be the most extravagant party in thirty years, probably the best party in the next thirty as well. I don't want Elizabeth to remember it by a few stolen glimpses from the kitchen. She's worked hard to make it successful. Don't you think she has a right to experience it as we will?"

"A right? She was hired to serve, not to party."

"I'll find a dozen to help serve," Jasin pleaded. "You know Elizabeth's more to me than just a maid or kitchen servant."

"I don't think of her as just a servant; she's critical to the success of this event. Are you asking for her...or yourself?"

Jasin paused. "Elizabeth doesn't know I'm here. She would never presume..."

"Then you're asking for yourself, not on her behalf."

"I guess that's true." Unmasked, he felt embarrassed for asking. He wasn't accustomed to talking about his romantic interests with his father. His personal relationships had always been private, his own intimate business, and not a subject for family discussion. His parents would pry, asking little sneaky questions to see if in a moment of unguarded weakness, he would admit to seeing this girl or liking that one, but he had always avoided going into detail, hardly ever even revealing a name. And now...

Avram stared at his son. Jasin, lost for words, was nervous and confused. They stood silently until Avram smiled, breaking the stalemate. "I'll let you in on a secret. Although your mother doesn't show it, she is also quite impressed by Elizabeth. Perhaps Elizabeth could act as her attendant...if you can actually find sufficient help for the kitchen."

"An attendant!" Jasin felt the anger rising within. "I'm asking you to allow her to be my companion for the evening and you're still thinking of her as a servant."

"She does us no good hanging on your arm. Need I remind you that the purpose of this little soiree is to infuriate Sy Loeton? He must be dismayed at our supposed wealth and success. I want him angry, emboldened and careless. According to Sy Toberry, he believes females are nothing less than the dirt between his toes. I think seeing Julian with a servant of her own would upset him. And their size difference! I can't imagine what that barbarian would think of a tiny female given status by a magnificently tall, personal handmaiden."

"You're twisting my request to suit your own purposes."

"My purposes? Gaining our rights as full citizens isn't just for me. I'm an old man. You're going to be living here long after I'm gone. Do you want to be a second-class citizen? Do you want the likes of Sy Loeton to be able to kill whomever he pleases and have no legal recourse? You're right about the importance of this party, but not because it's going to be a glamorous affair with great food, but because Sy Loeton, knowing that he can't be hurt, is going to foolishly brag about his involvement with our women. And possibly, with enough keetah and subtle manipulation, he's going to admit using that woman and throwing her away like some piece of garbage."

"I only wanted Elizabeth to be able to enjoy the party," Jasin said meekly.

"And you're right. You have changed my mind. She's much too valuable to be hidden away. Tell her to get sewing on a dress for the evening—nothing too fancy, it shouldn't detract from Julian."

Jasin turned away without saying another word, without saying what swelled and filled his heart. It wouldn't matter what Elizabeth wore. Next to his mother, next to any woman he'd ever seen, she would draw attention.

The rest of the week flew by. Elizabeth barely completed one chore before another three appeared, demanding immediate attention. At night, she sewed her dress by candlelight, fussing over each seam and stitch. She obsessed over minor details, telling herself it had to fit perfect. Any minor gap or fold of excess material taunted her and she'd work on it until, satisfied or exhausted, she'd collapse into bed. When morning came, she would slip into the gown and check her work in the brightness, mentally making a list on what needed to be adjusted when her household duties were done. On the day of the party, Jasin pulled Elizabeth aside.

"This had better be important. I've got a million chores to complete before the guests arrive," Elizabeth said.

"It will just take a minute. There's something I want you to have." Jasin held out a small linen pouch that was bound with delicate purple string. Elizabeth untied the package and withdrew a sparkling azure crystal that hung from an intricately woven cord.

"It's beautiful, but you shouldn't have. It must have cost you—"

"Shush... just put it on."

Elizabeth slipped the pendant over her head, then leaned over and kissed him. "Does it have to be returned after the party, like the furniture?" she teased.

"Of course, so don't lose it or it will come out of your salary." He was proficient now at reading her sarcasm, so he was surprised when she wiped a tear from the corner of her eye and carefully replaced the necklace into the small pouch.

"I was just teasing. You know that. Aren't you going to wear it?"

"Of course, but it's not the sort of thing you wear cleaning. I love it, but go now, let me finish."

As soon as she was alone, she sat down and pulled out the necklace, letting it twist at the end of the fancy cord where it caught the sunlight and sent out little shafts of blue to dance on the floor. He had no way of knowing what this meant to her. She was twenty-six and this was her first piece of real jewelry.

As requested, the five members of the Human Caucus arrived an hour before the towans from the Sytonian Council. Avram wanted everyone to be at ease with the staged improvements so they would be able to act naturally, as if this level of wealth and success was normal—a wise idea since the human visitors wandered through the mansion ogling the lavish furnishings, trying to guess from whose home this or that item was borrowed. All brought their spouses, except Jorge Wynosk, who in a typical breach of etiquette managed to surprise everyone by bringing little Wilem. The boy, according to Jorge, insisted on coming in order to see Elizabeth again.

Avram mingled, enthusiastically complimenting everyone on their handsome dress. He scurried from one group to another, speaking rapidly and with great emotion, reminding them of his plan to goad Sy Loeton into bragging about his dalliance with the young woman from Bistoun, warning them not to be surprised or to interfere with his provocative manner directed towards his target. When asked about his excitement, he explained how important he felt this event was; how it could lead to great improvements, even the granting of rights to the Human settlement. Avram offered everyone keetah, but other than himself, no one showed interest in the bitter drink, especially without cause and appropriate ceremony. His capacity to partake in the intoxicating beverage, however, appeared unlimited and he hadn't stopped drinking since first brightening.

Music filled the great room. Julian had arranged with several of her musical friends to play for the evening. She often led these same musicians and was by far the most skilled. Avram had begged her to play, believing that the resulting attention and adoration focused on his petite wife would further irritate his mark, but she refused to be exposed to such attention, preferring, as usual, to remain unobtrusive in the shadows.

Julian, however, had difficulty hiding with Elizabeth by her side. As Jasin had predicted, Elizabeth was absolutely stunning. The nights she had spent sewing by candlelight produced, a simple, yet exquisite, unadorned gown of unpretentious dark fabric. The careful tailoring accentuated her statuesque figure, allowing expression of every curve. She had artfully arranged her hair exposing her graceful neck around which she proudly showed off her new crystal pendant. Perhaps it was Elizabeth's elegant simplicity, which stood out against the sea of intricate fabric and overdone jewelry on display, or perhaps it was just the fact that she stood a least a head taller than any other woman, but whichever, she drew appreciative looks from all the men, and quite a few jealous glances from the women. Elizabeth appeared oblivious to the attention, but Jasin enjoyed watching her as she attended to Julian's wishes, confident that she was his love alone, and no one else would turn her head tonight.

Before the natives arrived, Julian asked Elizabeth to put Wilem to sleep in her back bedroom. With Jorge's permission, they hurried through the kitchen, where Rahfi had been recruited to prepare his grilled delicacies. Wilem stopped to look at the raw meat and wrinkled his nose. The huge chef approached, pretending to size up the young lad for appetizers. With a playful shriek, they quickly escaped laughing into Elizabeth's bedroom.

"How have you been?" she signed. Her unpracticed fingers found it more difficult than she expected.

"It's boring at home without you. When are you coming back?"

What could she say? She offered a hug and he practically flew into her arms. For the second time today tears began to well up. She hadn't thought about Wilem much, but it was evident the little boy still loved her, and suddenly she felt that she had betrayed him. "Time to get undressed," she signed and began to unbutton his shirt.

Wilem pulled away. He shook his head forcefully and pushed her outstretched arms aside. "You're a girl," he signed. "I will undress myself, but not in front of you."

"My, my," she muttered under her breath, "such a little man." Elizabeth smiled and told him to lie down and get some sleep, explaining that the party was bound to be long, with lots of speeches.

"Just like the funeral?" he asked.

"Just like the funeral. I'll come get you when it's time to leave."

Sy Toberry was the first native to arrive. Once inside the house, the honored and respected towan quickly shed his dark cloak. Such protection from the colder climate—in fact clothing of any sort—was unusual for a towan, but his status allowed him to wear protection that other towans generally shunned. The female towa were occasionally seen with temporary wrappings for uncomfortable weather. One might see protective clothing at a work site, but native skin was much tougher, and a pelvic fold encased their reproductive organs making clothing a minor issue. Modesty, it had been discovered, was decidedly human. For a towan, displaying their scars of prestige was eminently more telling than mere cloth decoration. Sy Toberry immediately sought out Avram's company.

"Sy Toberry! I'm so glad you are honoring us tonight," Avram proclaimed in his best Sytonian. "Would you care for a glass of refreshment, or perhaps you're hungry. You must try these." Avram indicated an untouched plate of sliced, grilled meats, arranged on rough native bread. "I understand they're wonderful."

"Avram, your home is much different. So many more things."

"A few presents from friends. Nothing important."

Toberry nodded and reached for a piece of the cooked meat, giving it a sniff before swallowing it whole. His neck folds fluttered momentarily. "Thank you for preparing this gathering. It has been too long since both our councils have been together." He took another slice and performed the same routine.

"Come share keetah with me before the others arrive," Avram suggested.

Sy Toberry leaned forward off his middle leg. "I have warned you too many times not to drink the keetah cold."

"But it isn't. Actually it's quite hot tonight," Avram protested.

"Perhaps later, for ceremony."

"Well, suit yourself. My cup is nearly empty."

But before Avram could refill it, several more towan Council members entered the room. They were not as blasé about the surroundings as Toberry. Sy Lang brought up the rear of this group.

"Avram!" he exclaimed. "This is magnificent. You've even prepared native food. How thoughtful." Then gently, he pulled Avram aside for a word in private. "I have talked to several of the Council members. They agree that if Sy Loeton has harmed your people, he will be dealt with, but they warn you to be careful. Sy Loeton will not like being tricked. Traditionally, it is a sign of weakness not to confront your enemies honestly and if Sy Loeton is anything, he is a traditionalist." This Sy Lang said with great conviction.

"You promised that if Sy Loeton were proven guilty of the murder you would support granting humans full rights of citizenship. Has that changed?"

"I will keep my word. But it is only *my* word. I will support the concept, but there isn't a clear consensus among the Council. Sy Loeton is highly respected. He might be the most outspoken concerning his position on Human settlement, but there are others that silently agree with him. This gathering is a perfect opportunity to restate his feelings. It is the first such meeting in almost thirty years. Most of the members who will come tonight are here to support him. You must be careful how you act and what you say."

"That's all the better," said Avram, "then he'll be at ease and overconfident. My plan here isn't trickery. I imagine between you and Toberry most of the Council know what I'm up to. It doesn't matter really. All that matters is that Loeton thinks so little of us humans that he is willing to admit, without fear of retribution, that he harmed that girl. It isn't much of a plan. Just get him to boast a little, to brag about his sexual interest in human females. I wonder how the traditionalists will feel about that."

Avram and Sy Lang walked over to a small table where the keetah makings were laid out. Avram fixed himself yet another cup while the other natives watched with disapproval.

"They're not very understanding of your addiction," observed Sy Lang, indicating his fellow council members.

"My addiction! When did my enjoyment of your native drink become an addiction?"

"Let's just say it's unusual." Sy Lang distanced himself by finding the table of grilled meats. What was once a full plate was now nearly empty.

Jasin joined his father at the keetah table. "Do you think he'll show?"

"Of course. From what I understand, the egotist probably thinks we're throwing this affair to allow him to make speeches."

"Aren't we?" Jasin raised an eyebrow and left to find Elizabeth.

Food flowed from the kitchen and music filled the air. The party was now in full swing. Most had arrived, except Sy Loeton. Whispered concerns that the towan wouldn't show percolated in the corners of the room. Without Loeton, the party was meaningless.

Elizabeth was surprised at the constant attention the humans paid Julian. Everyone made a point to pay their respects. She greeted them all and, without missing a name, introduced them to Elizabeth, who stood dutifully by her side. In the beginning, Elizabeth was quite honored by Julian's unnecessary kindness, but eventually realized that all the attention was making Julian uncomfortable and she was purposely diverting it. The extent of her shyness amazed Elizabeth. It didn't quite fit with the private persona revealed to her these past months.

Jasin joined them and for a few minutes the three enjoyed watching several couples try to dance to the music, but it lacked a strong beat and their attempts resulted in embarrassed laughter; the loudest coming from the would-be dancers themselves. The towans looked on with blank stares, not knowing what to make of it. Jasin counted heads. The crowd numbered almost thirty.

Then, almost hidden beneath the cacophony of the party, Jasin detected faint barking and looked over at Elizabeth to see if she had heard it as well. The answer was evident in her blanched and terrified face. It was the sound of a cylith, and by the depth of the sound, it wasn't a young pup. Others began to notice as the barking neared. The musicians stopped and silence filled the great room. A knock on the door broke the suspense. Avram walked over and opened the door himself.

Sy Loeton, naked except for a dusting of snow on his shoulders, stood surrounded by two cloaked shivering bodyguards, at his side, an aged cylith. Shimmering flakes from the light snow that had begun to fall clung to the creature's fur. Avram seized the opportunity to deflate Sy Loeton's impressive entrance.

"Your animal stays outside with one of your pytors. You're most welcome, as is your other pytor if you feel the need for protection from our fierce little group," Avram proclaimed in a voice guaranteed to carry.

"Your language skills have improved," Loeton responded, "but not your understanding. A towan has but one pytor. A second would be an insult to the first." Sy Loeton stepped inside followed by one of his two companions. "This is Sy Hone."

Avram acknowledged the pytor, then turned his attention back to Sy Loeton. "It has been a long time, nearly thirty years. I see you've been productive." Avram reached out and traced Loeton's scars. "Except for Sy Toberry, I have never known a towan so honored." Sy Loeton's chest held record to over fifteen initiates. The last was quite fresh.

Loeton ignored the compliment, looking around instead. "And while I've been busy training towan, you've been busy collecting...trinkets." He fixed his eyes on Avram daring him to counter the insult.

Instead, Avram broke the tension with a good hearty laugh. "The rumors that you've lost your fire aren't true after all. I've been misinformed. Please join us before the food is gone." Avram led Sy Loeton and his pytor back to the party and introduced his family. Sy Loeton ignored Jasin and Julian, who barely reached his shoulder patches. Elizabeth was a different matter entirely. She was able to look him in the eye and didn't blink during her introduction. Loeton asked Avram to repeat her name so he would remember it.

The towan sniffed the air in front of Elizabeth and spoke to her. "Elizabeth Tournell. It is a big name for a big woman."

She didn't understand.

"He says your name is long, appropriate for a tall woman," translated Jasin. "I think it's a compliment."

The huge towan continued his overt inspection of Elizabeth until Avram, sensing her discomfort, suggested they continue into the heart of the party. Avram guided Sy Loeton and his companion over to the refreshments where Beloit joined them. Sy Lang, along with Sy Toberry, watched intently and listened from a distance.

"Beloit, may I introduce Sy Loeton and his pytor, Sy Hone," Avram then easily changed to Sytonian for his guests' benefit, "Sy Loeton, this is my good friend Beloit

McMaster. Beloit is responsible for enforcing our adherence to the Prohibitions."

They silently took measure of the other.

Beloit was the first to speak. "Avram, please tell our guest that I am pleased to finally meet him."

Loeton responded directly to Beloit, and in Human. "Am I the monster you expected?"

Avram and Beloit's surprise was clear, but each for a different reason. "I wasn't aware you spoke Human," said Avram. "You have my admiration."

"Did you think it such a feat to learn another's language in thirty years? Even you managed to learn ours. And you, McMaster..." Loeton shifted his attention to Beloit. "If you have questions concerning my activities, which are none of your business, honor dictates you should speak to me directly instead of questioning my friends. They shouldn't be bothered."

"I'll decide what my business is," replied Beloit strongly.

"You have no reason to look into the affairs of any Sytonian. As I understand your job, it is to police your own people; to insure *your* compliance with the Prohibitions."

"Gentlemen, please—" Avram began.

Stung by the use of the word, Sy Loeton responded vehemently in his native tongue. "I am not any sort of *man*. I am Sytonian. I am towan. You will remember that. We have foolishly granted you permission to settle here, but you are only guests. You will not insult me again."

"Respectfully, sir," Avram now spoke Sytonian as well, "Beloit is only trying to keep the peace. He is acting on my suggestions. We are most troubled by the death of a woman in Bistoun—"

Avram was interrupted by Sy Lang's arrival. "Sy Loeton, greetings." He traced the fresh initiate scar. "You have mentored again I see. You are an inspiration to us all. Come, Sy Toberry wishes to see you." The three natives left the humans.

"I'm always amazed at Toberry's status among them," observed Beloit, whispering. "One mention of his name and the mighty Loeton follows like a cylith puppy."

"I have a feeling several of Toberry's initiates are here tonight," Avram replied. Then taking a deep breath he said, "Well, since we've lit the fire, let's not let it cool down." Avram walked over to the steaming keetah kettle and waved Elizabeth and Jasin over to help him prepare the first round of cups. While they filled them, Avram called for attention.

"Now that all our honored guests have arrived, I would like to say a few words and offer the first keetah. Everyone in this room has worked hard on our behalf." Avram looked directly at Sy Loeton to see if the lie registered. "And we are thankful. When we landed, we were barely four hundred. Now we number well over a thousand. Most of our people, like our children here…" he gestured towards Jasin and Elizabeth "…have never known any place other than this beautiful moon. This is now *our* home. Please join me in drinking keetah."

Steaming cups were handed out to many. When Elizabeth handed Loeton his, he placed the steaming cup firmly on his open palm, and sniffed the air again. She couldn't tell if he was trying to smell the keetah or her. It struck her as rude and unnerving.

Avram continued, "To all of you who have supported us…and to those willing to continue trusting us in the future as we join you in becoming *full citizens* of this world. Tyhinga!" Avram took a full swallow of the boiling liquid. Many of the humans repeated the salute, however, not one of the towans lifted their cup.

An awkward pause followed. It was quiet except for the distant barking of the cylith outside. The natives continued to stare at Avram, who shifted nervously under their gaze. Normally, the remainder of the keetah was spilled on the ground, but the humans were unsure about soiling the fancy rugs they were standing on, and no one had ever dared perform the ceremony over such a controversial toast. Once the keetah was poured, tradition demanded it be drunk.

Once again Sy Lang defused the situation. "To Avram and his family, for providing good food and shelter from the cold. Tyhinga!"

"Tyhinga!" everyone proclaimed loudly as if to erase Avram's first, inappropriate salute. Following Sy Loeton's lead, the natives poured the remaining keetah ceremoniously onto the elegant rugs. The humans uncomfortably followed suit, watching the brown stains slowly grow. Only Avram continued to hold his full cup, but it didn't matter. No one noticed this additional breach of conduct. No one even looked in his direction. He had embarrassed everyone with his presumptuous toast.

Avram moved despondently to the edge of the room and leaned against the wall. Julian tried to console him but he seemed to have trouble concentrating on her words. His face was flushed and perspired. His hands trembled as he continued drinking the cooling keetah. Jasin and Elizabeth joined them and stood nervously by Avram's side.

"Father?" When Jasin got no reply, he turned to Julian. "Is he sick? Why is he sweating so?"

"He's upset," Julian replied. "Just give him some time. The party isn't going as he had hoped."

"Avram, come sit," Elizabeth suggested. Avram looked up at her, his eyes glazed. Elizabeth felt a pang of recognition. Hyland had looked at her like that in his final days. After a few moments however, Avram began to return to normal, except that his breathing was shallow.

"I'm fine now, thanks, but there isn't any cause, for concern. I'm sorry, if I scared you. I'm fine now...really, just fine now. I don't know what came over me. That was so stupid, so stupid...but I'm fine now." Avram tried to take a deep breath, but it gave him pain. "Just give me some air." He straightened up and pushed himself from the wall. "That insolent bastard...thinks he can walk, into our home, embarrass me...He's nothing but a savage murderer."

Avram collected himself and rejoined the party. The family watched him with concern, but he put on a smile and plunged back into his role as host, making sure everyone was fed and making small talk among the humans. A large native group surrounded Sy Loeton and the meat platter, which Rahfi kept refilling.

Once again, Loeton's cylith howled. It was a haunting sound. Most of the human guests either didn't hear or were ignoring it, but several of the towans became concerned, especially as the sound grew closer. Among the few humans obviously troubled were Elizabeth, and young Wilem, whose frightened cries from the bedroom demanded attention. Elizabeth, trying to hide her own fear, scurried off to look after the boy. Jasin recognized her anxiety and followed her out of the room. The gruesome noise intensified. Finally, Avram, unable to stand it any longer, hurried out to see what could be done. Loeton, his pytor, and several curious towans, including Lang and Toberry, followed behind him. Most of the other guests continued to be unconcerned.

Avram threw open the door to find Loeton's companion struggling to control the powerful animal, which appeared intent on finding its master. The towan had tied a makeshift slipknot around the cylith's neck and was trying to drag the choking beast away from the house. A ring of blood was evident where the rope had torn away fur and flesh. Loeton hastily pushed past Avram and immediately the barking stopped. Loeton tore off the leash and examined the wounded creature, which became docile in his presence. The towan who had tried to control the animal approached. He still held the bloody rope. Loeton looked up at him with anger. "You fool! You would have killed him." Then Loeton rose and struck the towan who toppled over.

"Is that how you deal with everything?" Avram asked. "Beloit was right, you're a violent *man*."

Loeton stepped into Avram's space. "I told you not to refer to me in that way. I'm a towan, but you...you're a pathetic old man." Sy Loeton's voice was growing more intense.

"What you don't like, you try to destroy," continued Avram, sensing an opportunity to goad Loeton, now that the native's temper had surfaced. "You don't like me, what are going to do about it? Strike me down? You don't like humans. What are you going to do about us? Kill us off?

You can't do a thing. We're here to stay. And you're powerless to stop it," shouted Avram, his breath condensing in the cold air, his face flushed.

The small group of towans, who had followed them from the party, gathered near the door watching the encounter. Julian and Beloit, hearing Avram's raised voice, rushed from the party to locate the trouble. They found the small group of natives blocking the doorway and tried forcing their way through the alien crowd.

"No one has ever talked to me in this way. Why do you risk it?" Loeton asked Avram.

"Because you're a hypocrite, hiding in the shadows. You pretend not to like humans while secretly having intercourse with our women." Avram glanced over his shoulder at the natives. "But you won't admit it because you're frightened that they will think less of you." Avram raised his arm and repeatedly pointed his finger at Loeton while shouting, "You fear us, you're afraid. That's why, you won't admit, harming that girl, you…" Avram stumbled and fell towards Loeton, who instinctively thrust out his arm striking Avram sharply in the chest to prevent him from falling into him. Avram dropped to his knees before collapsing to the cold ground where he lay lifeless on his side.

To the crowd, who had only seen Avram from behind, it appeared as if Avram had yelled and lunged for Loeton. The aliens surged forward, the shifting bodies allowed Julian and Beloit to sneak through. They ran to Avram's side and Julian tried frantically to breathe life back into him. Beloit pumped his chest attempting to get his heart started, but it was futile. They looked up into the crowd, searching for human help, but only indifferent native faces stared back. The cylith rose from Loeton's side, silently moving over to the dead body, and began to sniff.

In despair, Julian swung to hit the animal, but Loeton swiftly intervened. "He would kill you before you took your next breath," he warned, slipping the rope loosely around the animal's neck.

Sy Toberry stepped out of the crowd and squatted beside Avram. He put his hand on Avram's face and solemnly looked to the sky. Sy Lang also lowered himself, and for a brief moment, the entire native crowd followed their lead, lifting their heads as if following some unseen spirit.

"Sy Loeton, it is time for you all to go," said Toberry. He turned to Julian. Loeton's two companions stepped forward taking their place on either side of her. "Take good care of your new wife as duty, honor, and tradition decrees," added Toberry.

Neither Julian nor Beloit, who were still numb from Avram's sudden death, comprehended what was happening until Loeton's companions lifted her from her feet. She swore loudly and struggled as her abductors carried her briskly away.

"What do you think you're doing!" screamed Beloit, as he lunged for them. Without breaking stride, the pytor delivered a vicious blow to the Enforcer's head. Stunned and momentarily blinded, Beloit took a few faltering steps towards Julian's fading voice, and then fell unconscious to the snow covered ground.

Betrayal

Sy Loeton traveled quickly, but Jasin easily followed the trail left in the snow. Reacting more on instinct than forethought, his ill-prepared rescue attempt quickly turned into a beating. Sy Hone, Loeton's pytor, hearing Jasin's approach, simply hung back and ambushed the inexperienced boy. Jasin saw neither his mother nor her new master before being dispatched. By the time Jasin returned bruised and humiliated, the great house stood empty of guests, the festive remains of the party a hideous mockery to the fate of the Elstrada family.

Elizabeth had remained behind to focus on Beloit, bandaging his head injury, and forcing him to stay still. Upon Jasin's return, her attention turned to his injuries, both physical and emotional. She caught what sleep her anxiety allowed in a chair between the two injured Enforcers. Waking them both every few hours, she looked for signs of concussions. When sleep evaded her, she walked the cold, dark house still haunted with smells of Rahfi's grilled meats and spilled keetah.

Both men rose with the brightness and by midday Beloit, arms limp at his side, stood next to Elizabeth and apart from the small crowd that had gathered to watch Jasin and Mas cover Avram's linen shrouded body one solemn shovelful at a time. Tears stained the senior Enforcer's gray bristled cheeks above the breathing scarf that poorly hid his emotions. Despite their arguments, Beloit had been devoted to Avram and shared his dream of peaceful co-existence. He had sacrificed much acting as the diplomat's hammer. Now his inspiration lay dead in a shallow grave.

Jasin had refused a service appropriate to Avram's legacy, insisting on a quick, simple affair. "My father's dead, my mother is not," he had argued. "Our thoughts must be focused on her safe return and not on celebrating Avram's life. There will be time later for a proper memorial."

Elizabeth knew he was right, but the haste and lack of tribute for a man who had dedicated his life to the safety of his fellow humans and died trying to secure their rights as a people hardly seemed fitting. She wondered what might have happened to the Tanis crew had Avram not been able to decipher and learn the native language, if he hadn't agreed to the Prohibitions. Some people rise to the challenges before them and make difficult decisions, and some hide in silence. She looked over to Jasin. What kind of man was she getting involved with? Jasin lifted his head and returned the gaze. Sweat glistened on his forehead. Suddenly his focus shifted to the horizon behind her. She turned. Two native figures, their multiple legs hidden in the ground fog, watched the proceedings from a distance.

Jasin threw down his shovel and stormed off in their direction. Mas grabbed his arm and Elizabeth ran over to help control him.

"Jasin, let it be." Elizabeth advised.

"She's right Jasin; they're here to pay their respects...not to fight."

"How do you know why they're here?" He shook off his friend's grasp. "That's the mistake we've been making—assuming they have human feelings, pretending that we understand them. They're alien! We mustn't forget that again."

Beloit walked unsteadily to join them. "Calm down Jasin...It's Toberry. You've known him, all your life," he said. His voice was strained and tired. Blood seeped from beneath his bandage.

"I thought I did," Jasin muttered.

Elizabeth reached over and tightened Beloit's dressing. It had shifted and blood was now dripping down the side of his face, first traveling along the edge of his breathing scarf, then seeping deeper, becoming indistinguishable from the meita-stained cloth. "You really should be resting," she scolded.

The two natives approached under the scrutiny of the entire human assembly.

Sy Lang spoke first. "We are here for Avram. He was a good man and we honor him on this sad day. We will leave shortly."

Sy Toberry said nothing. He refused to look at Jasin, who before rushing to his mother's rescue had publicly berated the native for not protecting his mother.

"Tell me again…" Jasin nearly spat the words out into Toberry's face, "why you thought it perfectly all right to encourage Loeton to abduct my Mother. Tell me again because I don't understand, because…" Jasin pointed at the grave. "Because *he* trusted you. You were practically a member of our family. Make me understand."

It was Sy Lang that answered. "Sy Toberry did nothing wrong. It is our way. Sy Loeton was honor-bound. It was his duty and responsibility to take care of the wife whose adversary fell at his hand, whether it was an accident or not. It is one of our oldest and most sacred traditions. He did not want or need your mother, but no other course of action would have been acceptable."

"And now he can just send her back—honor fulfilled," suggested Jasin.

"He must take care of her."

"She doesn't want to be taken care of, whatever that means in your twisted society. She's not one of your females. You don't have the right—"

"No, young Elstrada, it is *you* that don't have the right," Sy Toberry interjected, finally breaking his silence. "You have no rights whatsoever. Don't you understand? That is exactly what your father was trying to accomplish when he died. On this world, you are the visitors, the guests. You have only the rights that have been granted by the Council of Seventeen and since Sy Loeton sits on that council—"

"Not for long," Jasin interrupted, and turned to face Sy Lang. "Sy Loeton must be called to stand trial for his actions here and in Bistoun."

"Sy Loeton did not kill that female," stated Sy Toberry emphatically. "You disgraced him last night. I know him." The towan touched one of the scars on his chest.

"You only think you know him. He may have been one of your Initiates, but I have seen the results of his actions here and in Bistoun." Jasin turned to point at the half-filled grave. "He leaves death in his wake. You have a rogue on your sacred council. He is not fit to represent anyone."

"We don't represent anyone," argued Lang. "That is a human conceit, one of your fantasies. We serve on the Council because we are trusted and honored. Our opinions are valued. Loeton *is* honorable."

"Is mutilation honorable now? Is the murder of my father honorable? Is kidnapping the wife of the Human Caucus Leader, then running away, honorable? You have a monster on your Council. You say you come here out of respect for my father...then do more than just come and look at a pile of dirt; do more than tell me of your traditions. Call for an explanation; call for some answers. My father was right. If this conflict isn't solved, it will put our races at each others throats."

"And then you shall all die," stated Sy Toberry calmly, who turned and walked away.

"Well, that's a cheerful thought," said Mas.

"Jasin, your father was a special man," Sy Lang continued. "For him, and for the peace between our people, I will see that the Council asks these questions of Sy Loeton. But you must be patient. Sy Toberry believes the Rhan-da-lith will occur in about twenty days. The Council does not reconvene until after that." Lang turned and followed Toberry from the graveside.

* * *

If Rhan-da-lith were tomorrow, it would not be soon enough, thought Elizabeth as she pulled the sweetberry pie from the oven. It was Jasin's favorite dessert and her last resort. He hadn't eaten a reasonable meal since the party, now nearly a week ago. Having experienced the loss of loved ones she knew all too well the grief Jasin was dealing with. She knew how difficult it would be returning to work, finding normal again when normal would never be the same. But he must try to start picking up the pieces of his life. She sighed; he showed no interest in anything. Although he moved out of his cabin and back into the house, it felt like he had moved farther away, out of her life. Their relationship had become a hollow fragile shell, barely holding the memory of their previous love. Jasin hadn't spoken of the pain she knew he must be experiencing, hadn't shared a single emotion, thought, or tender touch.

One evening, she dragged him into her bedroom where she had prepared a luxurious bath of scented hot water. Candles flickered as she undressed him, and made him lie still as she sensually bathed him. She lathered his face and with exquisite tenderness drew a razor, one careful stoke at a time, across his cheeks. When she was finished, she took him to her bed and made love—all this in perfect silence, and all one-sided. Afterward, he rolled to his side and wept.

In the middle of the night, she would often find him walking through the mansion muttering to himself, or sitting in his old room rummaging through his childhood toys. Sometimes he would go to Avram's study, or she would catch him standing by the door of his mother's room, never daring to enter. He slept even less than he ate. There were days Elizabeth wanted to leave him, to be done with the whole affair, yet she loved him deeply and knew he needed her. Today she would tempt him with pie, tomorrow...she would think of something else. Take just one day at a time; it would get better, she promised herself.

Jasin couldn't explain his feelings even to himself, much less to Elizabeth. He knew he was being unfair to her, but somehow fairness seemed irrelevant, a meaningless concept in his life on this world. Depression had gotten hold of him, but there was something more—a battle raged inside— action or inaction, patience or retaliation, obey the

Prohibitions or just kill the bastard. Every day that Julian's rescue was delayed Jasin knew it was more unlikely he would ever see his mother again. And yet, he was the son of a diplomat and had chosen to be a peacekeeper, an Enforcer of the Prohibitions that he now considered breaking. How could he dare think of just marching into Loeton's home and taking his mother back? It wasn't only figurative political suicide he was considering. Deeper and deeper, he sank under the weight of his despair and indecision. The lack of sleep and nourishment hid any answer behind a murky veil that stubbornly refused to lift.

One morning, nearly three weeks from the day they buried Avram, Elizabeth awoke to the clanging of pots and pans. Throwing on a robe, she ran to the kitchen. Jasin had decided to fix himself breakfast. At least it looked something like breakfast. Elizabeth wasn't sure.

"Ah, did I wake you? Sorry. Just woke up famished and had to eat. Want some?"

She yawned and tried to control her tangled hair. She looked at his handiwork. "What is it?"

"It's going to be…it's just…I'm not sure." He laughed as he realized he didn't really know what he was hard at work preparing. "It's food…definitely…definitely food." He thought that was funny and laughed again.

There hadn't been laughter in the house for weeks and Elizabeth welcomed the sound. "Well, make enough for both of us and I'll be right back after I dress." She scampered back to her room like an excited little girl celebrating her birthday and a few minutes later joined Jasin for breakfast.

He didn't talk about politics, the council, the death of Avram, or even his mother's plight. It was just mindless banter, but Elizabeth knew that his internal struggle was over. A decision had been made. She hadn't the faintest idea what he had decided, or if he even knew, but the war was finished and they were enjoying the peace.

When they finished eating, Jasin asked if she would like to run in the foothills. "I've just got to get out of this house," he explained.

Elizabeth looked around the messy kitchen, about to suggest they clean up first, but realized how unimportant that really was. Maybe he'd talk after their run. They had some of their best conversations in the low rocky hills or sitting on the promontory. Besides, she thought, she could use the exercise as well.

Even when the rough terrain finally prevented further running, Jasin refused to rest. He continued climbing over the immense boulders until he couldn't go any higher. Then he sat, breathing through his scarf to soothe the burn in his lungs, and watched Elizabeth carefully pick her way through loose, snow-covered rocks to join him. She lifted her own scarf over her nose and sat quietly beside him, waiting for him to speak, but Jasin was content with the silence. So they sat. A chill air blew through their rough-cloth. Neither had dressed for this altitude.

Finally, she lowered her scarf. "You seem like a new man this morning. Did you sleep well?"

"Hardly slept a wink," Jasin replied.

"Well, you seem to have more energy than usual. We've never climbed this high before."

Jasin merely nodded his head in agreement.

Frustrated that he wasn't taking her bait, she tried a different approach. "Several of the neighbors have come over to retrieve their furniture and other belongings they lent us, but many haven't. Do you think they're waiting for us to bring their stuff back?"

"Who knows what they're thinking? I imagine they'll be along soon enough."

This time it was she who simply nodded, hoping that he'd pick up the conversation. Again they sat in silence. To Elizabeth, it felt like an eternity.

Finally, Jasin looked over at her and for a brief moment it appeared he was about to say something. Instead he stood up and stretched. "My legs are cramping. Let's head back." Then without offering her a helping hand or even waiting for her to rise, he started down.

Angered at his abruptness, she just watched him, sure that he'd eventually realize she wasn't rushing to his side and was upset. But, oblivious to whether she was there or not, he never turned to find her. Never had he cast her off or been so inattentive or rude to her before.

Well, at least he was making progress. She tried to concentrate on the positive. Compared to yesterday, he was nearly normal. She'd seen him through the worst of it, and now each day, she was confident he would take another step back. A little discourteous behavior could be tolerated, knowing in her heart what kind of man he really was.

Once she made it off the awkward boulders, she caught up quickly. Her longer strides allowed her to easily pull even with him. Keeping pace now, she half expected him to glance over, as he usually did, with one of his, "You want to race?" smirks, but he merely jogged on until they reached the cut-off into town. There, he unexpectedly turned away from the road leading back to the house. Elizabeth stopped, unsure.

"I've got to talk to Mas," he yelled back over his shoulder.

"When are you coming back?" she shouted. Jasin, however, continued on without another word.

Elizabeth spent the rest of the day alone, one eye on her chores, the other looking for Jasin's return. Perhaps she'd made a habit of worrying. The tide had turned. He had seemed better this morning. She had seen him through the worst of it and could begin to relax. It would be all right.

After preparing a vegetable casserole and putting it in the stone oven to bake, she went outside to gather nutgrass. Later, she would grind its seeds into tasty flour for dessert cookies. She glanced over at Trinity Peak. Feathery yellow clouds hung motionless over the jagged mount. This afternoon, the setting sun's rays revealed only a long sliver of Conboet, but Eian's position allowed it to be fully illuminated, reflecting a strong saffron moonlight that bathed the clouds. She always enjoyed the ever-changing celestial show—the fantastic lighting effects caused by Syton's sister moon and the giant planet's intricate dance. Sometimes the eerie bluish sunlight, yellow moonlight, and the green light from the planet combined to cast wonderfully surreal illumination on the high mountain formations. She scanned the ragged range, enjoying the oddly colored clouds that hid the three highest peaks, then gathered the nutgrass and went inside.

After stoking the oven and baking cookies, she placed the casserole in the oven and snuggled into a huge overstuffed armchair that had become her favorite. It was one of the borrowed pieces and Elizabeth held out hope that its owner would never return for it. For once she had found a chair that comfortably fit her, that wrapped her in exquisite softness and provided refuge where she usually found a most restful nap.

Distant voices woke her. Jasin and Mas were arguing and while she could tell they were agitated, the subject was unintelligible. The oven's aroma drifted in, demanding attention, and interrupting Elizabeth's efforts to eavesdrop on their heated conversation. In the kitchen, she removed the casserole and placed it on the oven top to keep warm. She was glad Mas was here. His hearty appetite and carefree spirit could only support Jasin's brighter mood, unless of course their heated discussion was serious. She found them in the second floor study, huddled over one of Avram's maps, and totally oblivious to her approach.

"No way! I've never heard of a high pass through them," Mas was saying.

"Right there," said Jasin pointing to an area of the map. "See how the two high peaks are widely separated. There's a pass through there. I'll bet on it."

Elizabeth interrupted, "Dinner's ready. Let's eat before it becomes cold."

Surprised, the two men turned. "Didn't hear you come in," Jasin said.

"Hey, beautiful," Mas smiled, "It smells great. What's cooking?"

"Does it matter?" she replied.

"Not a bit!"

"We'll join you in a minute," Jasin said. He paused to see if she would take the hint.

"In one of your minutes, it will be ice cold. You can talk over dinner." She reached out towards Mas and he took her hand. "Come and he will follow. He wouldn't dare leave us alone in the same room."

"I'm really not hungry," Jasin complained, but reluctantly, he fell in behind them.

Over dinner, which he wolfed down despite his claim, Jasin's plan became clear. The details needed to be worked out, but there was no mistaking his intent to mount a rescue.

"We just can't wait and see what the Council of Seventeen will do," he explained. "At best they might ask Loeton a few questions concerning the Bistoun matter, but neither Toberry nor Lang cared to discuss Mother's situation. To them it isn't even an issue. Their view of females is barbaric."

"I don't understand," said Elizabeth, "Loeton's not going to give up Julian just because we ask him nicely."

Mas looked over at Jasin, curious as to how he was going to answer. After an awkward pause Jasin said quietly, "Then we won't ask him."

"You're going to travel all the way to Fistulee, walk into his house, and just take her? That's your great plan?"

"We weren't planning to simply walk into his house," Jasin explained, "more like sneak into it."

Elizabeth shook her head. "You won't get one day from here before Loeton will know you're coming."

"That's what I've been telling him," said Mas.

Elizabeth nodded. "You should listen to your friend. You can't cross over at Bistoun. From what you've told me, Loeton practically owns the city and if you go around the Lake, you'll be seen passing the logging camp. Even if you avoid being seen, there's too much traffic through the pass, and on the road to Fistulee. Once you're on the other side of the mountain range, you'll be noticed for sure."

"There's another way to get into Fistulee," Jasin said softly.

"You can't be serious!" Elizabeth exploded. "By sea? You're the Enforcer. No human has ever been allowed aboard any ship leaving Soto Harbor for Fistulee. No I take that back. No human has ever been allowed to leave Soto by ship to anywhere. Period. It's like the Kull—strictly prohibited. You know that."

"It's not exactly like the Kull," Jasin corrected.

"He thinks you can cross the Kull undetected," explained Mas.

"You've lost your mind."

"I agree," said Mas.

"You're both basically right," Jasin said. "You can't use Soto, or cross the Andoree River at Bistoun; and going around the end of Lake Chook and through the pass to Fistulee would take weeks, and the chance of detection would be too great. I agree with you, but crossing the Kull isn't impossible. I believe it's merely prohibited, but it isn't enforced; it can't be enforced it's too huge an area. They are relying on the fact that it's naturally inhospitable and already protected on three sides by the Andoree, the sea, and the Kaysop Mountains. The remaining side is next to Bistoun and the heavily traveled road to the pass. By the time you're there, you've been detected. But that's the only side of the Kull where you'd be noticed. They couldn't possibly protect all the borders surrounding an area the size of the Kull."

"So if you could enter and cross the Kull...then what?" Elizabeth couldn't believe what she was listening to. Jasin's entire life was dedicated to enforcing the Prohibitions and now he just wanted to ignore one of them.

"I still say there's no high pass through the Kaysop," said Mas, taking another nutgrass cookie.

"Sure there is. That was what I was showing you." Jasin jumped out of his seat and rushed back to the study. "I just thought of something," he yelled back.

Mas and Elizabeth followed and found him scrutinizing the map he had laid out earlier. "Avram showed this map to me years ago. It was one of the first that was given to us in the beginning." The others leaned over to take a closer look. "All these years we've called this passage through the mountains, 'the pass'. See it here? Look what the map calls it—'the Low Pass'." Mas looked up puzzled. He couldn't read the alien symbols. Jasin continued, "Don't you see? If there is a Low Pass doesn't that imply the existence of a 'High Pass' through the mountains at some higher altitude?"

Mas shook his head. "Maybe your translation is faulty. Maybe it's just another way of saying easy or swampy or..."

"No, it means low or not high," argued Jasin.

"Well, not high pass can still be descriptive of its difficulty or elevation without implying another one," countered Mas.

"Why are you using this particular map?" asked Elizabeth.

"Because it's the best one covering the area into Fistulee," replied Jasin.

"Maybe...but it's not the best one of the mountains."

Jasin stared at her. "I looked through all of Avram's old maps."

"Avram had a new map. He showed it to me; it detailed the Kaysop range and was more a piece of artwork than this. I think Sy Lang gave it to him." Elizabeth glanced about the room.

After a quick search, they discovered that Avram had been pressing the new map underneath a cloth and a couple of mud bricks in a corner of the study. Jasin freed the flattened map and examined the beautiful artwork. "I'll bet he was going to frame this." Then excitedly, he brought it to the desk and placed it over the other map. "See! What did I tell you?"

Mas and Elizabeth peered at it. Jasin was right. This map definitely showed another pass in the mountains above Fistulee. The artist didn't label any of the features of the map, preferring instead to have created a work of art rather than a reference. In fact, the mountains were so well drawn, painted so realistically using shading and textures, that one could almost picture the approach to this "High Pass" from the cold desert plain of the Kull.

"It still doesn't matter," said Mas. "We'll never even get to the Kull undetected, much less cross it, even if it is unguarded."

"Look," Jasin switched the maps to show the first one with the wider view. "We leave at night, during Rhan-da-lith. We head towards Canyon Road as if we were going to Lake Chook or up to Panvera. We get into this wooded area along the rim of the canyon, but instead of following the normal trail down to the waterfall, we cut off into this small area of trees and follow the rim of the canyon until we find a way down to the Canyon River. If anyone was following us they'll assume we are either on the standard trails, or if they do figure out where we're heading, there'll be no way for them to follow us without being heard. It's too hard to move through the brush without making a racket, especially during the darkness."

"So...we cut through the wooded area and just slide down the canyon wall?" Mas asked sarcastically.

"There will be trails."

"And how do you know that?" Elizabeth asked.

"Do you see this little village? It's Cernai. It's right on the canyon rim, at the edge of the forest. They're a weird bunch of assorted misfits and recluses. Half the cases Beloit and I investigate end up having some connection with these people."

"And the trails into the canyon?" reminded Elizabeth.

"You can bet they have some backdoor in and out of the village."

"But you don't know for sure?"

"Well, I've never actually seen them, but Beloit and I have talked about it often. We figure they must have a shortcut to Bistoun or Lake Chook, so they don't have to backtrack along the canyon rim and follow the normal Canyon Trail."

Mas leaned over checked the map again. "So, do we end up on the Canyon River or the Andoree?"

"Doesn't matter. We'd be near where the Canyon River empties into the Andoree—right across from the Kull."

Mas couldn't help smiling. "Ok, so if I understand all this…we cut through these woods; take some mystery trail down into the canyon; somehow get across the Andoree; simply walk across the restricted Kull where no human has ever been; climb through an unknown high pass; and roll down the mountains into Fistulee, where we sneak into Loeton's house and take Julian back without his noticing, and all this during the darkness of Rhan-da-lith. Do I understand the plan?"

"Basically."

"Basically? You mean it's actually more complicated than that? Jasin, you're out of your mind. Even if we could accomplish it, what happens when she's back? How do we explain it? Loeton will be embarrassed. He will just send his pytor here to retrieve her. Nothing's solved."

Elizabeth agreed. "Won't he simply pursue? There's got to be a better way."

Mas nodded. "Why not find one of their females and make a trade? Why not kidnap Toberry and exchange him for Julian? Why not go directly up to Loeton's front door and beg on your hands and knees for him to return her? Maybe, by this time, he would like to get rid of her. He's probably not used to anyone like Julian."

Elizabeth could not hide her smile and Mas grinned at her before continuing.

"Maybe you can buy her back. Why not challenge him to some contest? Winner takes Julian. Wait, I've still got a better idea. Why not get him alone somewhere without witnesses and just kill him. Claim it was a fair fight or an accident or that he lost his temper and you were defending yourself. You'd inherit all his wives, including Julian, and the Council probably won't say anything. They'll just be glad that all the troubles between our races are over—girl murdered; suspect dies; justice served, and everyone's happy. Back to business as usual."

Jasin raised an eyebrow. "I said that you basically understood the plan. I didn't say you knew all of it, although it appears you understand that just freeing my mother isn't enough."

"What are you saying?" Elizabeth asked.

But Mas understood. He took a deep breath. "He's saying that he likes my final solution best."

"Jasin...is Mas right?"

"If Loeton dies, the tension caused by the incident in Bistoun will all but disappear and Julian is free to come home, but...it's important that no human be blamed. Loeton's death would solve a lot of our problems."

"So that's why it's important that our little field trip is secret. No one must suspect or be able to prove anything," Mas continued.

Jasin nodded.

Elizabeth couldn't believe this was the Jasin she had grown to love. She shook her head and spoke directly to him. "You've told me how important it is to keep the peace between the races. You've spent the last few years enforcing their Prohibitions. Are you telling me now that the best chance for peace is murder?"

"The best chance for peace is for Loeton to mysteriously die. He must die alone, without witnesses and he must die soon. For humans, he represents a monster; for the Sytonians his interest in women and probable involvement in the murder in Bistoun are embarrassing."

Elizabeth was having trouble understanding how a rescue mission had suddenly turned into a murder. She felt trapped, cornered. One minute she was preparing a wonderful dinner and the next she was involved in plans to kill someone. Common sense told her to distance herself from this crazy idea, get away, and don't look back. It was insane. It was time to leave. Shaking, she turned and walked toward the door.

Then she hesitated, realizing why Jasin had spent the last few days in inner turmoil. It was a solution he hadn't desired. He had fought it for days, just as she was fighting it now, but it had been forced upon him. She knew him intimately. He was the ultimate peacekeeper, tender and kind, yet it appeared the best chance for a far-reaching and enduring peace was quick personal violence at great risk. How could she let him face it alone? Was walking out a true reflection of her love? Go ahead, turn your back on him now and try to live with it the rest of your life, she told herself. How could she do that? What if he got hurt? What if he died trying to sustain peace and rescue Julian and she weren't there to help? She had to stand by him.

She turned around to face her friend and her love, feeling as if she were floating above the scene, looking down at a stranger. Never having done a violent thing in her life, she was about to agree to help kill someone. She took a deep breath, "O.K. Let's do it."

"You're not going," said Jasin coldly. "You'll only get in the way."

Elizabeth's breath caught in her lungs. Her heart skipped a beat.

"You'll put us in danger. You can't help. Stay here if you like or go home to Panvera. You're not coming with us," he repeated coldly.

She tried to move, to say something but she was frozen. Her mind couldn't focus; her muscles didn't work. She knew she looked ridiculous standing with her mouth open. Slowly the shock lessened and she could breathe. If she doubted her capacity for violence before, she now was feeling the level she was capable of. All she wanted to do was strike Jasin and toss him across the room. She had been willing to kill for him and he rejected her. She clenched her fists and stepped forward, but anger suddenly gave way to a wild mix of emotions. Unwanted tears welled up, but before she allowed them to be seen, she turned and ran out.

Mas looked dumbfounded. "How could you say that to her? She loves you, she would give up her life for you, commit murder for you, and you tell her she'd get in the way?"

"We don't need her. Three cannot travel as fast or as quietly as two. She's always attracting attention."

"I'm not talking about logic here. How could you be so cold and heartless? You've just destroyed a precious relationship. Something I can only dream about."

"Don't lecture me about love, you idiot. Don't you realize how dangerous this is? I'm probably saving her life."

"I'm an idiot? She wasn't asking to be saved; she was standing beside you in a time of need, willing to risk everything, willing to die…like I am. Listen, she's twice as smart and probably twice as strong as either of us. If you don't think she understands the danger…then you're the moron."

"It's a moot point. It's over."

"No it's not. Go to her. Apologize. Explain you were just trying to keep her safe."

"I'm trying to keep all of us safe."

"Doesn't matter. If you have any chance of salvaging your relationship—"

"I can't afford the relationship. What happens if she is captured or hurt? I couldn't live with that. Knowing she is safe frees me; it makes me stronger. If she's with me…listen…her love…our love handicaps me. It weakens us and puts us at greater risk."

"What about her strengths? Ever think that her skills and qualities would be assets?"

Jasin sadly shook his head. "You don't know…she's scared of the dark."

Stunned, Mas paused. "What are you saying?"

"Just that. She's nearly paralyzed by darkness and evening sounds."

"Well…we all have our little—"

"Mas…we're going during the Rhan-da-lith, the darkness."

"You were still a boor."

"Maybe so, but I'd rather be a unhappy boor knowing she's alive and well, than a sorry gentleman mourning his dead love. She'll probably head back to Panvera. I can't think of a safer place. You can't get any farther from the natives…or from Fistulee."

Jasin looked down at the maps pretending to study them, attempting to hide his true pain from his friend. Damn it! He knew he hadn't handled the situation well. The last thing in the world he had wanted to do was hurt her, but he had been afraid he would weaken, lose his resolve and allow her to join them in the most dangerous gamble he could imagine.

He wasn't about to lose another loved one, even if it meant she would never speak to him again. If they all survived, there was always hope.

Mas left Jasin with the maps and walked downstairs. He needed some fresh air and the walk home would help him put this disturbing day in perspective. As he passed the kitchen, he could hear sounds from Elizabeth's room. This might be the last time he would see her, he thought. But should he intrude? He could hear Elizabeth's sniffling and other sounds of rummaging around in her room. She was packing. This wouldn't be a good time and what would he say? He hated how Jasin had dealt with the situation. It wasn't fair. If he had a woman like Elizabeth he wouldn't have been so harsh. He wanted her to know that. Maybe they would see each other again. He went to her room.

"Go away!" she responded to the knock on her door.

"It's Mas. I was leaving." He waited a few moments for a reply, but there was none. He walked away, his loud boot steps punctuating the uncomfortable silence.

He crossed through the messy kitchen, never having been cleaned in their haste to follow Jasin to the study. Maybe he should clean it up. He looked around; his gaze fell on the knife she had used to cut the rough bread. It was one of the new knives. He turned back to Elizabeth's door. "Elizabeth...I need to talk to you."

"Say what you need and please go." Her voice sounded distant, as if she were across the room.

"No, I mean I need to see you."

"Go away! I don't feel like seeing anyone right now."

"I've got something for you."

"Just leave it next to the door."

"I can't do that."

He heard her footsteps approach. She whispered softly from the other side of the door. "Please Mas, just go away."

"I won't go until I can give it to you personally."

Elizabeth opened the door slowly. "Ok, give it to me and then go. I have lots to do." Her eyes were swollen and she held a rag to her runny nose. Her clothes were laid out on the bed.

"Can I come in?"

She motioned him in and he closed the door.

The reality of her packing struck him hard. "You're leaving?"

"What is it you want?" she said.

"You know he loves…"

"Don't even start! Get out!" She flew past him and threw the door open. She was furious at his deception.

"No, really…I'm sorry…I really do have something for you." He closed the door again and retreated further into her room, closer to one of the bright lanterns. "Come here."

She approached hesitantly, looking him over. He wasn't carrying anything. Then she thought she understood and held out her arms and the tears rolled down her cheeks. "I'm going to miss you." They hugged each other tightly and shared a brief, innocent kiss before letting go.

"I'm sorry things turned out this way…I have something of yours." Mas reached down into his boot and from between two pieces of leather pulled out the small alien blade that Joey had purchased for her. "Be very, very careful with it. I've ruined quite a few items with it before I found a way to safely hide it. The blade is razor sharp."

She took the stiletto and examined the thin black leather handle. "What are these strange markings?"

Mas shrugged.

"You said it was mine?"

"From a couple of secret admirers."

She smiled coyly. "You must thank them for me."

He lowered his head, silently accepting her recognition. "Just don't let Jasin or Beloit see it. I've carried it since Avram died. I don't feel comfortable like I used to. Now, I want you to have it. Hide it, but don't hesitate to protect yourself. We want you to be safe."

In her heart, she knew he spoke the truth. "I'll be careful."

"Where are you going?" Mas asked.

"I don't know, but I can't stay here any longer."

"Go home. Go to Panvera. When it's all over we'll come find you."

She bit her lower lip and fought back a new wave of tears. She shook her head. "Don't bother. It's all over now."

Mas reached over and touched her tenderly. "I think it's just beginning."

Elizabeth

Once again Elizabeth glanced back in the direction of the Trinity peaks trying to measure her progress, and again, as they had been for most of her flight from Nova Gaia, the distinctive peaks lay hidden behind dark storm clouds. She wrapped her tattered shawl tighter about her shoulders and adjusted her breathing scarf to provide a fresher, more potent swatch of medicated fabric. At least another four tedious hours before she would arrive at the Valley Trail, she guessed. There, she could cut between the two mountain ranges that separated Panvera and all the other human settlements. Four hours if the snow held off, longer if the weather turned.

Mas was probably right—going home to Panvera made the most sense. She had no desire to remain in Nova Gaia, and except for little Wilem, there was nothing in Lake Chook. The thought of dealing with Jorge again repulsed her. Bistoun had briefly entered her thoughts, but with the tension building there, avoiding it was probably smart. So that left Panvera...and home...and Father. She loved him dearly, but could she live with him for any length of time? If she changed her mind she didn't have to stay, but at least she was heading somewhere. She had a destination. In only two long days and one sleepless night—actually two, if she counted her last—she could be home.

How could she have been so wrong about Jasin? To be so cruel, so cold. She tried unsuccessfully to shake off the thought, to concentrate on something else. Didn't he feel anything towards her? Couldn't he have shown a trace of sensitivity, instead of making her feel worthless? Less than worthless—a danger to them! Maybe he thought he was protecting her, unsure of his plan, but he could have admitted that, held her tightly, and told her how much he loved her and didn't want to expose her to danger. He could have, but he didn't.

Elizabeth stopped and shifted the painful leather straps of the bulky backpack. It was a bit heavier than the last time she had traveled this road. So much had changed. Two septets ago, she had nothing to lose; now she felt as if she had lost everything.

The sun hid behind an overcast sky, revealing its position by a hazy glow. Dejected, she realized it would be trapped behind that gray curtain for the rest of the day. A cool breeze penetrated her thin shawl, sending a shiver through her and she dug a warm jacket out of her pack before continuing. That was another thing that had changed. She remembered being soaked with sweat when she first arrived. Day to day, weather in the gorge was never predictable; there were no seasons, only one's elevation within the chasm, whether you were closer to the frozen rim or the inferno below mattered at all. There was a fairly good chance that once she reached the high plateau beyond the mountains the temperature would drop even further, and by this time tomorrow, she would be wearing just about everything she carried with her. Elizabeth trudged on. It would be a dismal march—dark sky, dark mood.

With a sigh, she accepted the reality that she was running away and blamed Jasin for practically throwing her out, but her unquiet mind refused to focus solely on him. Her self-respect and sense of dignity had been damaged as well. She wasn't comfortable having Jasin believe she was a liability or burden so easily dismissed. Did being the family's housekeeper and Julian's handmaiden distort his image of her? Why couldn't he realize how resourceful and strong she could be? Didn't he see the depth of her resolve?

She wished she had gotten to know him under better circumstances, as equals.

She walked on, deep in thought, moving instinctively, not really aware of the hours that drifted by or the terrain. Even if Jasin and Mas survived their suicide plan and joined her in Panvera, she would always be the one who ran away, who didn't risk a thing, the coward who played it safe. She knew it wasn't her fault, but it bothered her just the same.

Of course, she blamed Loeton most of all. Without his perversity and hostility towards humans, the problem wouldn't exist. She remembered his unblinking eyes examining her like a piece of meat to be eaten, his sniffing the air, attempting to smell her. Even her brief exposure to that formidable creature convinced her that Jasin's plan to kill Loeton would likely fail. Her growing despair and exhaustion gnawed away what spirit she had left until finally, she sat dazed beside the cut-off that would bring her home.

Thinking about the disgusting towan brought to mind Mas's alternate rescue plans—particularly the ones involving direct confrontation. How did Mas put it? "Why don't we just walk up to Loeton's front door and ask him to return Julian?" Mas was only half-serious, but the idea did contain an element of genius. It was too simple, too naïve to actually work, and two hostile men probably wouldn't be accepted warmly, but…what about a servant? What about a servant that had already attracted the master's attention? Would Loeton turn *her* away? Probably not before raping her like the woman in Bistoun, she thought morbidly. Jasin couldn't talk about the incident without emotion. He would shake his head; change the subject. But that didn't stop McMaster. She had overheard him graphically describe the horrid brutality to a member of the Human Caucus. "No woman could survive what that animal did," he concluded.

Whenever she thought of it her whole body would involuntarily clench up. Elizabeth's hand dropped to her boot where she ran her fingers lightly across the hilt of the hidden knife. It made her feel safer even though she was afraid of it. Just having it was against the Prohibitions.

No, she shook her head. She would avoid tempting him, but maybe he would allow Julian the services of her handmaiden. If she were there when Jasin and Mas arrived, she was certain she could help. Who was she kidding? What could she really do, a woman who was even scared of the darkness, especially the total darkness of Rhan-da-lith?

No one actually knew when the darkness of Rhan-da-lith would begin, but Sy Toberry had said twenty days, and most believed he had an uncanny intuition about that sort of thing. If he was right, Jasin and Mas would begin their secret rescue in about a week, and then they would have to negotiate the Kull and cross the Kaysop range before arriving in Fistulee.

Elizabeth's mind wouldn't let it go. If she took the direct public route, Elizabeth figured she could be in place, in Loeton's home, for at least two weeks before they arrived. Having someone on the inside, even someone Jasin hadn't planned on could be the difference between success and failure. She could inform Julian of the plan and keep her from trying anything foolish...if she hadn't already.

Silly dreams. Here she sat exhausted from just the morning's walk. Fistulee was at least six long days away if she had enough crystals to cross the Andoree by ferry— which she didn't—and even longer if she were to go through Lake Chook and around the logging camp. Six days meant five nights in the open. She hadn't planned on camping, had no extra food, no extra meita tablets, and knowing that Panvera was so close, she hadn't even packed a blanket. Just sitting for these few moments, she could sense the cold ground sucking the heat and feeling out of her bottom. There was really only one intelligent choice, she told herself. She stood and stepped off the main trail and toward Panvera and her father. Having made the decision, she relaxed and focused on the trail in front of her.

The night came. A faint glow from Eian kept her from stumbling over any of the larger rocks, but after the moon set, the dimness thickened and the ground fog rose. She hesitated, dreading the thought of stopping, fearing what must certainly lay hidden in the darkness. Rational or not, ever since that last night with Michael, and the cyliths, and the darkness, and the sounds of a gruesome death, she could never again be comfortable when the brightness left and memories invaded. Conboet would soon rise again, but in the meantime, she bravely made her way by what little starlight penetrated the dense clouds. If she didn't stop, they couldn't find her. It was a comforting lie.

The dimness seemed to last forever and she trudged on barely able to see her feet. When her throat hurt, she would rotate or refold her scarf. She stumbled only once and the awkward weight of her backpack drove her crashing into the ground, scraping her knee on the sharp stones. The bleeding quickly stopped, and the gnawing pain actually sharpened her senses. By first brightening, she was on the high plateau. The massive hulk of the Schtolin range was behind her right shoulder and Trinity made an appearance over her left. In ten hours, she would be having dinner with her father.

As she had predicted, the temperature dropped, but the overcast sky cleared and the radiant sunlight warmed her face. She decided to rest and emptied most of her clothing from her backpack to create an inviting bed behind a huge boulder that would shield the cool wind. Ever mindful of cyliths, she lay back and let the sun warm her tired body. She fought the waves of sleep that tried to overwhelm her, knowing that to lose consciousness could still be dangerous. Just rest, she reminded herself…just rest. Then, whether she wanted it or not, her body stole the sleep it needed.

She awoke in pain. Before, when she was moving, her knee felt fine, but now she realized, it must have been more than a simple scrape. While she slept, it had swollen and she was having trouble straightening it. Trying to ignore the pain, she donned a few more layers and tried to stand. Slowly she was able to extend her leg and put weight on it. I'll be fine, she convinced herself, and she resumed her journey with only a slight limp that diminished as her knee warmed up.

She noticed the approaching caravan while it was still an hour away. The dust cloud that the blaythons and carts created was easy to spot, but she doubted that they could see her, a single person. As it drew closer, the distinctive clatter from the traders' hoard made her smile. She fondly remembered scavenging through their junk piles when she was a child, their rapid-fire banter begging you to buy or trade a worthless trinket or two. They probably left Panvera early this morning, she thought.

"Here's a customer," shouted the blond man in the first blaython cart. Elizabeth suspected he was the leader. "Looks like she needs a new leg." Then turning to the small boy walking next to him, "Hey! Check under the pots there…see if there's one that'll fit."

"Looks like she'll need a long one," answered the flaxen haired boy, without missing a beat. "Want to take a look-see lady? Never can tell what's stashed underneath."

The caravan came to a halt beside Elizabeth, who grinned broadly. There were two other blaython carts, about six children on foot, and two older women on their own animals: eleven humans, three carts, and five blaythons in all.

"Trying to sneak up on me?" Elizabeth asked jokingly. "I almost walked right by without noticing you."

"Can't have that, nope, bad for business," replied the ill-shaven leader with a nose reshaped by too many disgruntled customers. "Name's Simon, young lady. You need something, ask Simon. What do you need?"

"Well, you might as well get on your way. I haven't a decent meita or crystal; not a thing to trade."

"Heard that lie before, but we have what you need, you can be sure."

"What I need is to get home before the dimness." Elizabeth glanced at the gathering traders and their families. She recognized one of them—a slender man with shaggy, dirty hair falling out of a floppy hat and ending at his shoulders. "You there, in the red hat...still selling keetah from T'Matte?"

The man stepped forward to take a better look at her. "You want keetah?"

"You sold me keetah when I lived in Lake Chook...for the funeral, remember?"

Recognition spread across his face. He tossed a handful of hair behind an ear. "You're the lady who smoked Hyland, aren't you?"

"I had a friend who said it was the best keetah he ever had."

"You want more? We have plenty of keetah...good stuff from Bistoun. Won't have more T'Matte keetah for awhile, but I'll save you some." He drew closer and whispered, "If you're partial to keets though, we still have some from Fistulee."

Elizabeth wasn't sure what he was referring to, but the mention of Fistulee perked her interest. "You get down there often? To Fistulee?"

"Hey there! Stop hogging the customer," yelled Simon.

"She's just interested in our travels, that's all," replied the man in the red hat.

"What she's interested in is getting home before dark...say lady, you wouldn't be interested in a lantern just in case you don't make it before the dimness returns? Got a good one...won't cost you much."

"No, just want some information. Do you plan to go to Fistulee?"

The caravan leader scrutinized her. "You really don't have a yellow crystal to your name, do you?"

Elizabeth shook her head.

Simon turned to his small band. "Let's get moving, there's nothing here...don't mean to offend miss, it's just that we've got to get on." As the others got back to their carts and blaythons, he added, "We're not going to Fistulee this leg. Bistoun, then T'Matte."

He turned away. What a strange assortment, she thought as the caravan started moving past her. They must join and split up at will. The trader with the red hat was alone when he sold the keetah to her. His junk filled cart brought up the rear and although he was now part of the larger caravan, she sensed he was a newcomer. He still appeared a little detached, still alone. "Hey! You with the red hat," she yelled. "Where after T'Matte?"

"Fistulee, then back to Lake Chook. Round and around."

She watched them leave. Her father and a comfortable bed were just a few hours away, but they were heading to Fistulee. Forget it, she told herself. What could you do except get yourself hurt again? Without realizing it, however, she moved to follow the last cart. She could help Julian; that's what she could do. She could help Mas. She might even keep Jasin from getting killed. The bastard didn't deserve to die at Loeton's hands. She laughed to herself, no...if anyone was going to kill Jasin it would be her. She walked as fast as her knee allowed until she was even with the last cart carrying the man with the red hat. She smiled at him. "You want company?" she asked.

The man stopped the cart and helped Elizabeth onto the seat beside him. "I thought you were going home."

As the cart rattled forward, she turned and looked over her shoulder toward Panvera. "I thought so too."

Over the next few hours, barely a word passed between them. The trader stole a few glances in her direction, but Elizabeth pretended not to notice. Finally, he mumbled something that Elizabeth couldn't make out over the clanking. "What?" she asked.

"I said, 'you're not much company.'"

Elizabeth realized he had a point. These traders didn't give anything away and she supposed conversation was a small price for the ride. "My name's Elizabeth. Thanks for the ride."

"You're welcome."

She sat waiting for him to tell her his name, but instead he began to hum to himself. He was happier now. That was easy! After a few minutes, she began to laugh.

"What's with you?" complained the trader.

"Nothing...have you got a name?"

"Does it matter?"

"I guess not." He was obviously a brilliant conversationalist. She couldn't help a small giggle.

"Eddie, my name's Eddie. Why you laughing at me? Want to get off and walk."

"No offense, Eddie...I like your hat," she said with a grin.

"Can't have it." He pulled the hat tighter. His greasy hair flared out beneath the brim.

"I don't want it."

"Good!"

They rode on in silence. Elizabeth thought about the caravan's itinerary. Panvera to Bistoun to T'Matte. If they weren't going to Nova Gaia, why come through the valley? Why didn't they skirt around the Schtolin range? It would have been more direct and they wouldn't have to take the carts down the steep and rocky canyon trails. It didn't make sense.

"Eddie, why come this way if we're going to Bistoun? Isn't it easier to go around Schtolin?"

"Went that way from Lake Chook. Got a stop to make tomorrow."

"In Nova Gaia?"

Eddie shook his head, but offered nothing more.

"You might as well tell me. I'll find out tomorrow."

"Not if you keep nagging me you won't."

It was her turn to shake her head. Now she knew why he traveled alone. "No family?" she asked.

"I got family...a boy in Bistoun."

"Yeah?"

"Hey, just cause he ain't here doesn't mean nothing. Sami gets along fine. I check in whenever I pass through. Who are you to make judgments?"

"I wasn't saying anything." And she thought that was probably the best way to keep it.

The next day the caravan left the valley trail and turned onto the road that led away from Nova Gaia and toward the canyon. Within an hour, they entered the thick stand of skinny trees that skirted the canyon rim, exactly where Jasin and Mas planned to leave the road to find an alternate path down to the river. Suddenly, the lead cart headed into the woods and, for a brief moment, she wondered if the caravan planned to descend the same way. Eddie maneuvered their cart to join the rest of the group, who had already stopped in a clearing just out of sight of the main road. He got down off the cart, opened his tousers, and pissed against a nearby tree. The women scurried into the bushes to find slightly more private spots. All of this had a sense of practiced routine. They had been here before. Eddie walked back to his cart, closing up as he approached. "It would be best if you didn't show much interest in what happens here."

Elizabeth nodded and gingerly stepped off the cart. Her knee was stiff and still hurt when she tried to fully extend it. She followed the women but headed deeper, just beyond the brush to the edge of the woods. They hadn't stopped since breakfast and she was about to burst. There's probably no other position that feels so defenseless, she thought as she squatted. Looking around, she hoped there were no curious animals. She tried to finish quickly, but a rustling sound interrupted her.

"Damn!" she swore under her breath. Moving easily between the thin trees, she could see five humans carrying bundles, heading for the caravan. She crouched low allowing them to pass before resuming, then nonchalantly made her way back to sit among the playing children and listen to the visitors begin to barter.

The trading session proceeded smoothly. Goods changed hands and occasionally a visitor would lean over and dig into one of the carts. Elizabeth figured the strangers were from the village Jasin had mentioned.

While the others finished their exchanges, Eddie and a short, scrawny man, who carried a small sack, separated from the group and a private negotiation began for the contents. Elizabeth couldn't tell what the bag held, but Eddie kept peering into it and shaking his head. The conversation became quite animated.

"Do I look stupid?" she could hear Eddie saying.

The anemic looking fellow shook his head and quietly explained something she couldn't quite hear. Eventually, he dragged Eddie by the sleeve into the woods. They were gone about five minutes when Elizabeth was surprised by a muffled explosion. She jumped and turned towards the sound just in time to see one of the taller trees come crashing down. Most of the assembled group turned and laughed; no one else appeared shocked or as amazed as she. To them it appeared commonplace, but to her it was totally inexplicable. She had never seen anything powerful enough to topple a tree. It had to be prohibited. A minute later Eddie emerged alone from the woods and walked straight to his cart where he stashed his newly acquired bag beneath several heavy bundles. He looked around to check who might have seen him. Elizabeth turned away, pretending she hadn't noticed.

Done with their business the caravan left the clearing. After they had been on the road for several minutes, Eddie confronted Elizabeth. "I don't need you getting curious. Be bad for everyone. You too. Understand?"

Elizabeth nodded. Clearly, she had a lot to learn. Jasin had mentioned that much of his work involved the Village of Cernai and she was sure she had just witnessed a sample of their prohibited handiwork. Courtesy of the traders, the entire human domain was able to gain access to it—if one knew what to ask for. She thought about the unusual greenish-blue knife hidden in her boot and wondered if it too came from Cernai. After what she saw today, and Eddie's overt threat, she was smart to keep the weapon close at hand.

The next few days passed without incident and Elizabeth enjoyed the beautiful passage through the canyon, past the thundering waterfall, and over the precarious bridge, spanning the wild upper branch of the Canyon River. The weather became balmy once they left the highlands and neared the Andoree. Elizabeth continued to shed her bulky outer clothing and warm sweaters, emerging like a pretty butterfly from her insulated cocoon. Lewd glances from the men of the caravan, and scathing looks by their women gave

Elizabeth notice that she had upset the group's sexual balance. Eddie, knowing he was gaining significant stature by being in the company of such an attractive young lady, sat next to her beaming, his head held high.

After the caravan used the ferry to cross into Bistoun, Eddie made a point of reminding her that she owed him her share of the toll. "You know, there're other ways of making payment. A man gets lonesome on the road. I have given you transportation, food, a place to sleep. I've paid your toll... and what I'm asking for now you can give away and still keep."

Elizabeth played dumb. "I don't understand. It was only a few little crystals. Haven't I been good company? I should see if anyone else is willing to let me ride with them." She felt guilty taking advantage of his loneliness and generosity, but she really didn't have anything to give except some clothing, her body, or the knife Mas had given her. He wouldn't want the clothes, and parting with the other two was out of the question. The issue smoldered just below the surface. Eddie never pushed exceedingly hard, but it was obvious to Elizabeth she had a kindness, if not a debt to settle.

Their last night in Bistoun brought a warm muggy night. Air plankton displayed their mating colors. Sounds of laughter spilled out of the nearby inn. Elizabeth watched Eddie and his son, Sami, sort through the cart's inventory, arguing over what should be kept and what they could afford to trade. Once in a while they'd turn and give Elizabeth the evil eye as if to say this was none of her business. She wandered over to the fire where Simon, the caravan's leader, had decided to get drunk. He offered her a swig.

"Well, girly, you the kind that likes showing merchandise not for sale? You've been doing a good job of it. Got the other women talking, that's for sure."

She took a long draw from the bottle and handed it back. "Don't be disgusting. You've been a proper gentleman all these days. Don't let the drink talk for you."

"Ain't the drink. Comes from here." Simon grabbed his crotch. "Human nature. You're too young and pretty to be hanging in a traders' caravan without eventually turning. Seen it before. You're one of the lost ones. Not too long before people going to think you're trading your wares too. Pretty soon you'll be considering it. Fast, easy money."

"You think that? You think I'm a whore."

"I don't think you know what you are yet. But we could make a lot of meita with a fine ass like yours."

Before Elizabeth could respond, they both turned at the sound of footsteps on the gravel. Eddie approached. There was no sign of the boy.

"Ah, Eddie my good man. Join us. Tell me straight. All these days this fine woman is sitting next to you, you ever think—"

"Come on, boss. She don't deserve this. You horny, you want to get laid? There are a dozen ladies happy to take care of you in this town. Hardly cost what you've already drunk. Let her be."

Simon squinted and leaned in towards Eddie. "My, my Eddie, protective aren't we?"

Eddie said nothing.

"Well Eddie," Simon continued. "I've been thinking. I'm cutting the troop down. You been square with me as the leader and all, but the rest...they ain't coming. You know how it is out here. If they travel with me, I get a share." Lifting his head and looking directly at Elizabeth he continued. "You can pay her cut if you're so inclined."

"My cut?" Elizabeth faked an innocent frown. "I haven't made any trades. How can I owe you anything?"

"From what I have seen, you haven't done much of anything around here since you began riding with us, except maybe eat our food. We don't cater to freeloaders. This is a pay as you go situation. Either you pay or you go."

Eddie shook his head. "There's no reason to be pressing her for what she ain't got."

"She ain't got nothing but that fine body far as I see. Peoples pay their way. You know it. Time she learns it."

Eddie nodded. "Can't be arguing that, but...but she's paying in private if you know what I mean." Elizabeth was about to object, but caught herself and remained silent.

"Ha, I knew it." He stared at Elizabeth. "I ain't dumb. Remember what I said, human nature…but," Simon turned to Eddie and shrugged. "That don't fill my poke any."

"Boss, I'll make sure you're happy by circuit's end. Trust me."

Grousing to himself, Simon teetered to his feet and staggered off.

"Thank you. I'll make it up to you," Elizabeth promised Eddie. "Someday, I'll find a way to pay you back."

"Someday," he replied dolefully, "I'll be dead."

By first brightening the two remaining carts were already outside Bistoun and skirting the short inland border of the Kull. The caravan leader had been true to his word. All that was left of the group were his wife and kid, and the two of them. She felt lucky to have caught Eddie's fancy, but despite what slimy Simon had said, and Eddie had intimated, she had definite boundaries she wouldn't cross. She could see how easily a young woman could slip. Other women, perhaps; not her.

"Hey, Eddie. What do you know about the Kull?" she asked, trying to make conversation.

But Eddie didn't know much and cared to discuss it even less. "It's just a desert without roads, and more importantly, without customers. Not much use to a trader," he said.

"You've been there, in the Kull?"

"Don't want to see what I don't need."

Elizabeth nodded, pretending to agree and sat quietly.

The road to the native capital, T'Matte, was fairly straight and well travelled. They made good time. By midday they approached the so-called Low Pass. Compared to the deep valley between the colder ranges leading to Panvera, this cut through the range seemed barely elevated, yet when Elizabeth looked back towards the Andoree, the entire course of their trip could easily be traced.

Turning to Eddie she asked, "I was wondering, you know whether there is any other way through these mountains, other than this pass?"

"Never heard of anything but the pass here. I was told once that you could go around the mountains but far as I know, this is the only way through them."

Since joining the traders, this was the first time Elizabeth knew better. As they made their way through the pass, Elizabeth scanned the high, inhospitable mountain range to the right. If there was a "High Pass", she couldn't see it. She thought of Jasin's plans, and found it difficult to imagine how they were going to make it over or through, even if they survived the Kull. From her perspective, the maps in the study poorly represented the journey.

They continued down into the warmer region, through vast expanses of humid grazing land. The two women had stripped down to their thinnest shirts and the men wore nothing but shorts. Still, everyone was red faced and dripping. Elizabeth packed her boots along with the thin blade. The traders had their own code of honor, and if they hadn't threatened her to this point she felt safe, she could trust them. On the third day out from Bistoun, they came to a fork in the trail and took the left branch. "Where does the other road lead?" Elizabeth asked Eddie.

"Fistulee."

"How far away is it?"

"A full day's walk. Not thinking about deserting me are you?" His gaze drifted to her chest. Elizabeth's face reddened, realizing how her sweat-soaked blouse stuck to her breasts.

"And how far is it to T'Matte?" she asked, ignoring his stares.

"Full of questions, now aren't you."

Elizabeth turned and looked over her shoulder at the cut-off receding into the distance. "How far?"

"Another day, but T'Matte is much nicer. You'll like it. We'll stay a few days and then, drop you off on the way back."

"But that would be four or five days from now."

"Five at least."

Elizabeth knew the timing of that wouldn't work. "Can't you drop me off first—"

"Listen, woman! Don't be asking me to do you no favors...what with all your goods hanging out and teasing me without so much as letting me have a little—"

"Quit it, Eddie, and stop the cart. I want to get down." Elizabeth reached behind her and grabbed her pack. "I can't wait five days."

"I ain't stopping."

"Come on, I've got to get off."

He ignored her and kept the blaython cart rolling, encouraging the animal to speed up. Elizabeth considered jumping, but her knee had just begun to feel better and was afraid of hurting it again. If she didn't get off now she would waste at least two days walking back. Every minute took her further from Julian and Fistulee. Finally out of despair, she said, "I'll let you kiss me." Her stomach turned just to say the words.

"What?"

"You heard me. Don't make me say it again. Stop now or I'll jump off," she bluffed.

"No little peck on the cheek," Eddie warned. "And you kiss back or no deal." He pulled back on the reins and the blaython came to a halt. Before she lost her nerve, she leaned over and gave him a kiss on the lips and suddenly felt his hands cup her breasts through the thin fabric.

"Hey, that wasn't part of the deal!" she complained. He was grinning broadly. She thought about slapping him...but what good would it do? Instead she gathered her belongings and climbed down the blaython's middle leg.

"You got off cheap," remarked Eddie, who was still smiling.

She wasn't really angry. In fact, she secretly agreed with him; if a kiss and stolen touch were all it cost her to get to Fistulee, it was a bargain. "Good luck in T'Matte, Eddie. Maybe I'll see you in a few days."

Eddie lost his smile. "Do you know what you're doing? Some of the natives haven't ever seen a human female before. It's really not safe. Haven't you heard about the woman in Bistoun? Won't be any other humans in Fistulee 'til we get back."

Elizabeth knew there was at least one other. "I'll be all right, but thanks for the warning...thanks for everything." Eddie shook his head and frowned. "Put your boots on you fool woman." Without another word, he shook the reins, urging the blaython forward to rejoin the others.

Eddie had lied. Elizabeth discovered Fistulee was actually much closer. By mid-afternoon, she stood on the crest of a hillock and was able to look down at the town. A wide road switched back and forth from where she stood, descending the steep grade before ending at a busy harbor. Squat, reddish-brown, mud homes lined the edge of the water except near the dock, where the usual assortment of warehouses, taverns, and shipyards catered to the fishing trade. The town expanded along a series of nearly concentric roads, which roughly followed the curve of the irregular bay. The largest homes were the farthest from the water's edge and she figured Loeton's had to be one of them. Off in the distance to her right, she could see the backside of the Kaysop range. Elizabeth strained to make out a high pass. Heat roiled the atmosphere making the mountains shimmer and distort. If a high pass existed, she couldn't make it out. She felt faint and a little dizzy; the combination of heat, exertion, and the lack of water were exacting their toll. A scorching exhalation of wind off the plain coaxed her onward.

Instead of following the twisting road, Elizabeth discovered a more direct footpath down through the brush. Fifteen minutes later, she emerged at the edge of town, bleeding just above her boot tops where thorny foliage had scratched her. She found a large boulder to rest on while she dabbed the blood with a strip of cloth cut from an old sock.

What now? How would the natives react to her just walking alone into town? Eddie might be right about the danger. She thought of the sharp little knife hidden in boot. Would she ever have the nerve to use it?

She was hungry, hot and tired. Her head ached and she needed something to drink. Should she try to get some rest and water before finding Loeton? She couldn't imagine what she looked like after five days on the trail without washing, but she already knew how awful she smelled. If she was hoping to persuade Loeton, with his sense of smell...she started to laugh. What did she know about the native's tolerance or for that matter attraction to what she considered offensive? She recalled Jasin's admonition not to forget that they aren't human. It didn't matter, she finally decided, she needed to find some water and clean up.

She took stock of what she was wearing—a filthy thin blouse, grimy shorts, and a pair of heavy, cold-weather boots. She looked like a misfit, a vagabond, not exactly the presentation to make a positive impression on Sy Loeton when she asked for refuge, at least not like the last time she had caught his eye. At the party she wore a simple, elegant dress. That had pleased him...at least he took time to look at her, to smell her, but that dress hung in an empty room in Nova Gaia. She forced the image out of her head. That was the past.

She emptied her pack on the ground. It was mostly warm clothing, sweaters, her long coat, pants, a heavy skirt, another smelly shirt, a pair of lighter shoes, dirty socks and underwear. She began stuffing the clothing back into the pack; there was nothing, except the shoes, that she could wear in this climate. The heavy coat was the silliest, but as she jammed it into her pack she realized it had an inner liner of smooth thin fabric. She rolled the white material between her fingers; it was quite soft and because it had always been protected from the elements, it was clean. She used the little knife to effortlessly cut the lining from the coat. If she removed the long sleeves and cut them into long strips, she could use the fabric to lace up the front. It could pass for a makeshift dress. Quickly completing the alterations, she slipped off her clothes to try it on. By adjusting the lacing, her design worked fine. She could tighten the top to hold herself in, and again across her hips for modesty, but the rest of the lacing could remain loose allowing the garment to move comfortably. Finally, she cut a slit where her right hand would lie against her thigh. There, she would hide the knife where she could easily reach it, hidden between loose folds of fabric. Now after she washed up, she would have something to wear and if anyone searched her pack or it were taken or searched, the knife would never be found.

Elizabeth exchanged her boots for the lighter shoes and changed back into her shorts and blouse. She wrapped the thin knife in the blood-soaked rag she had used on her calves, and tucked it into the back of her shorts. Her loose shirt covered the handle, but allowing it to be reached in an emergency. Finally, she headed towards the small harbor.

She hesitated. The waterfront was crawling with towans. What did she expect? Scanning the bank, she realized that she'd be exposed anywhere along the bay, so she cut between a few homes, looking for fresh water. Anything would do; she was desperate. Finally, she found an animal water trough near a stable. If it were clean, it would suffice. Looking around to insure she was alone, she scooped up a little water and brought it to her nose. It smelled putrid and she let it drain through her fingers. Ducking behind the stable, she went to the next bale and stucco home. It looked deserted, but next to the back door flap was a rain barrel. She leaned over and gave the water a good sniff; it smelled fine. She dipped her cupped hand into the water and brought it to her mouth. When she had drunk enough, she stripped off her shirt, and using it as a rag, began to clean herself. Her hair felt like it carried a bucket of dirt from the trail. Holding her breath, she leaned into the rain barrel to rinse it.

As she stood up, intense pain sliced through her skull and darkness closed in around her. She fell back into the water, blood pouring from the back of her head where she'd been struck, turning the rainwater red.

Elizabeth drifted in and out of consciousness for what seemed like hours. Finally, when she could focus, she found that she was lying on her stomach. Someone had dragged her half-naked body a few feet from the rain barrel and dumped her face down in the dirt. Her hair was a snarled mass of mud and she was caked in dried dirt. Any attempt to move her head caused excruciating pain.

A three-toed native foot came into sight. It slipped under her shoulder and forcefully flipped her over onto her back. A sharp sting shot through her buttocks, and through her hazy fog of consciousness, she realized she had cut herself with the little dagger hidden in her shorts. The towan loomed over her and was talking excitedly. Elizabeth couldn't understand a single word. He leaned over her and turned her head from side to side. Elizabeth cried out in pain and he drew back. Blackness filled the edges of her vision and she felt nauseous. He peered down at her bare breasts and reached down to touch the strange creature he had found in his rain barrel. She let out a low animal growl to scare him off, but the towan ignored her and pressed a bony finger into her soft bosom. With as much force as she could muster, she slapped his hand away. Consciousness began to slip away again, but before the darkness completely enveloped her, she pointed to the center of her chest and said the only thing she thought he'd understand. "Loeton...Sy Loeton." Then she passed out.

Phenomenon

Elizabeth struggled to open her eyes, but they wouldn't obey. Frightened, she ran her trembling fingers across her eyelids and felt a thin coating of gritty paste, which she frantically tried to wipe away. Dozens of tiny hands attempted to hold her arms still. She fought them off while again trying to open her eyes, but darkness still enveloped her. Terror crept in and she screamed at the restraining hands, lashing out blindly at anything within her reach.

She was naked, and exposed, without even a thin sheet to cover her. Total blackness magnified her labored breathing. What had happening to her eyes? Her bottom ached and the blackness swirled around her. Then strangely, her fingers began to feel numb, not from making contact—she hadn't struck anyone or anything very hard—her fingers were just losing their sensitivity. She felt herself falling, tumbling farther and farther down.

Elizabeth awoke countless times with the paste on her eyes, and always the tiny hands would come to restrain hers. Sometimes they would tenderly stroke her face. Occasionally, she heard soft singing. It was comforting and she would relax…and sleep.

Her dreams were vivid—distorted, frightening images that assaulted and terrified her. During brief moments of lucidity, Elizabeth struggled in vain to recall what had occurred, where she was, what had happened. Sometimes, her head ached, other times it was her buttocks.

Time had no meaning. Days passed as hours. They fed her, cleaned her as if she were a baby. Beneath her lay a mattress, her head rested on a soft pillow, she felt clean and cared for. There was no need to be afraid, but she was.

One day, she gained consciousness while the paste was being removed from her eyes. She strained to open them, but the lids were still numb. She reached up to touch them, but as always, the hands pulled hers away. Suddenly, she felt something drop on her cheek. They were reapplying the paste to her eyes. Overpowering the restraining hands, she wiped it away and again noticed her fingers became numb. It was some crude local anesthetic and painkiller that relieved her head pain. Was it also paralyzing her eyelids? Perhaps she wasn't blind after all.

Elizabeth held her hands over her eyes, refusing to allow them to apply more paste. She could hear alien jabbering, but it wasn't the low gruff voices of the towans. These must be the voices of their females, the towas Jasin had told her about. She was anxious to see them…anxious to see anything.

Her caregivers relented. Without the numbing paste, her eyesight slowly returned, along with a terrible headache. She lifted her head with difficulty, attempting to focus. It was dark. Her sight was blurred and she could make out very little. The more she strained to see, the more her head throbbed. The price of her sight was difficult to bear. She could feel a huge swollen egg on the back of her head. And then it all came back.

Why did the towan have to hit her so hard? It was only water. Maybe she scared him. That was a funny idea. Maybe he was just angry to find a tall, half-naked woman bathing in his drinking water. With a groan, she lay back down. Sweat dripped from every pore, soaking her mattress. She missed having a blanket or sheet to cover her.

How much time had passed since she was struck? She had vague recollections of strange dreams and of waking often. Perhaps several days had passed. No matter, tomorrow morning she would force herself to get up. Tonight it felt good to lie still, to rest…just to sleep.

It was the singing of the towas that woke Elizabeth. Bright sunlight streamed into the room. The tiny natives moved quickly about the large, undivided room performing chores, singing to themselves and each other. She smiled. Following an individual was confusing, like the tavern game where the object was to follow the movement of the ball as it was shuttled beneath various cups and then to guess under which the ball rested. Several were busy boiling a red liquid over a miniature clay stove. In the center of the room was a shallow pit lined with pillows. She knew the natives didn't sleep, so its purpose was a mystery.

Ignoring the pain radiating from the stab wound on her bottom, she raised herself to a sitting position. The towas gathered around her. Even without standing, she was able to look them in the eyes. She counted seven tiny females. Loeton had seven wives. Pointing to the ground she asked, "Loeton?"

The towas stared at the floor where she had indicated, as if expecting something to materialize there. Finally one of them pointed at a door across the room. "Sy Loeton," the tiny female declared. The others turned quickly to face the door, now anticipating their husband's entrance. Elizabeth laughed and understood. Not exactly as she had hoped for or planned, but she had made it.

The towas turned back to see why she had laughed. They all looked like twins leaning back on their thin middle legs. It was difficult to differentiate between the tiny females. They wore no clothing, and each of their round faces was practically identical; short curly brown hair covered their heads, but they had no eyebrows; their bodies were slender, without breasts, but with protruding nipples; long thin arms ended in delicate three-fingered hands with double opposable thumbs. One striking difference between them was the varying appearance of their groins. One towa hadn't a single hair covering her delicate folds, which looked pink, fresh, and soft. But on another towa, a thick coarse mat of hair protected her reproductive opening. Her vulva also appeared toughened by calluses. In between these extremes, were towas at different stages of growing the thick patch over increasingly callused tissues. At first, Elizabeth thought she was seeing different stages of adult development, but at least half of them were in the process of molting their pubic hair and their calluses were flaking off. A cycle, she guessed.

One of the towas brought Elizabeth a cup of warm liquid from the stove. It tasted awful, like weak keetah, but she drank it and soon the residual pain lifted. She stood, a bit shaky at first, but after the initial dizziness passed, she was able to walk slowly around. In a far corner of the room, under one of the large windows, lay her mud encrusted shorts and, tucked within it, a bloody rag. Perhaps in haste as she was attended to, they were carelessly discarded. If she were lucky, the towas thought the rag had been used to absorb blood from the injury and not to hide the little dagger that she hoped still rested inside. Not wanting to elevate the rag's importance, she turned away quickly and let it be.

The natives watched her intently and she became self-conscious about being naked, even if they all were as well. Hoping to locate her backpack, she glanced about the room. She must make them understand what she was looking for.

Her pantomime must have appeared ridiculous as she pretended to lift an invisible bag and put her arms through phantom straps; with a real backpack, it was awkward enough. The wives didn't budge and just stared at her. Finally, one of them walked forward and tilted her head up to look at Elizabeth towering above her. Reaching out, she delicately brushed the human's soft pubic hair. Elizabeth jumped back in surprise.

Enough of this, I must find some clothes, she thought. Unfortunately, it didn't appear that her pack had made it. Feeling a bit light-headed, she walked to the shallow pit and lay among the pillows, pulling them close to help cover her. In no time, she was asleep.

The towas shook her awake and tried to pull her from the pit. What was their problem now? She heard footsteps outside the door to the room and suddenly Sy Hone, Loeton's pytor, stormed in and confronted Elizabeth.

Embarrassed at her nakedness, she clutched the pillows in front of her. He sniffed the air and said in broken human, "Julian pytor, why Fistulee?" She had seen her standing next to Julian at Avram's party. Evidently he assumed she was Julian's bodyguard.

"Julian is in Fistulee. That is where her servant should be," she answered.

"Servant?"

"Pytor then," Elizabeth corrected herself.

"No! You go Bistoun, You go Gaia. Go."

"Where is Julian? Is she well?" Elizabeth tried to take the offensive, ignoring his demand.

He pointed out of the room. "Julian."

"I must see her."

He grabbed her arm roughly and yanked her out of the pit. She lost her pillows and ended up standing in front of him, trying to cover herself with her arms and hands. He looked her over, finally pointing to her head. "Good. Go home."

"Where are my clothes? My pack...bag..." He obviously didn't have much use for the word "clothes". She searched to find a word he might understand, running her hand over her bare skin. "I need a wrap...something to cover me, to hide me, protect me..."

Finally, he seemed to understand and spoke to one of the females, who ran out and brought back Elizabeth's pack. Elizabeth tore it from the towa's hands and put on her makeshift dress. She was amazed at what a difference clothing made, how much stronger and more secure she felt. Boldly, she approached the towan and demanded to see Julian, but the towan was not impressed. He took her by the arm and began to pull her.

"Wait!" Elizabeth screamed. "Where is Sy Loeton?"

Sy Hone stopped. Once again, Elizabeth marveled at the effect Loeton's name had. "Sy Loeton comes ...after dimness, after brightening."

She understood. Loeton wouldn't be back until tomorrow.

"I will stay and serve Julian and Loeton as you do." She could see he didn't comprehend. Elizabeth looked him in the eye and pointed at his chest. "You are pytor. You serve Loeton." She pointed to herself. "I am pytor. I serve Julian." In desperation, she lowered her head and bowed slightly. "I will serve Loeton as well."

She felt he understood. At least he wasn't dragging her out. She lifted her head, but remained slightly bowed. After an awkward moment, the towan said, "Come. Serve Julian."

He led her out into a hallway and past several large rooms. Turning a corner, they entered a tremendous windowed chamber. Elizabeth gasped. It was the largest indoor space she had ever seen. In the center of the space grew an immense tree surrounded by an explosion of colored flowers. Light filled the room from every direction through dozens of paneled, mineral windows that rose at least eight meters to a vaulted roof. The tree sat by a small stream that entered though one wall and disappeared out another.

Glancing at Sy Hone for permission, Elizabeth walked to the windows to take a better look. The multi-storied house was surrounded by exterior gardens. She tried to grasp the size of this estate. It could have held twenty, maybe thirty homes the size of the Elstrada's.

"Come." Sy Hone finally commanded. Elizabeth followed him until they stood in front of a massive door secured by a system of interlocking blue metal rings. She had pictured Julian's prison cell in her mind countless times—the locked door, dingy interior, and sparse furnishings. The towan twisted the blue rings until they separated, and then swung the door aside.

At first, Elizabeth couldn't locate Julian. She had anticipated a confined space, but the door opened onto another immense, sunlit room, beautifully appointed with colorful woven rugs, carved stone table stands, and a plush mattress resting on a raised platform.

"Elizabeth!" Julian's small voice exclaimed. Elizabeth turned to see Julian, wearing the same dress as the night of the party, enter from a smaller antechamber. The gown looked entirely out of place. They hugged each other awkwardly, then Julian addressed the towan firmly, "Thank you for bringing Elizabeth to me. You may leave us now."

Hone growled a few native words and retreated, closing and locking the door behind him.

"He hates it when I order him around. If it weren't for his fear of Loeton he'd...oh my! Look at you. Come sit down, you look awful." She led Elizabeth to the mattress and fussed about making her comfortable. "This is such a surprise..." she lowered her voice, "but you shouldn't have come."

"Are you all right?" asked Elizabeth weakly.

Julian waved the question off. "Why are you here? Jasin didn't..."

"No, Jasin's not here."

"That's good. Now tell me, what's going on?"

"I came to help...but ran into a little trouble. I'll be fine." Elizabeth took a deep breath and surveyed the room. "This isn't what I expected."

"Loeton raises styke for slaughter. I gather most of the meat eaten in this region comes from his stockyards. He's been quite successful."

"I meant...I expected you to be...I don't know, a prisoner I guess."

Julian shrugged, "The door is still locked."

Elizabeth shut her eyes, fighting back the exhaustion and crushing headache that were closing in. Her breathing was labored. "Do you think Loeton will let me stay?"

"Only if he thinks he can control you, but why would you want to? Tell me, how's Jasin? Is he doing all right?"

"Jasin is..." she leaned forward to whisper in Julian's ear, "he's planning to rescue you."

Julian shook her head and let out a long sigh. "You've got to tell him not to. He has no idea what he's up against."

"I've got no way to contact him."

Julian hesitated only a second. "You've got to leave. Find him. Tell him I'm fine. Go before Loeton returns. Sy Hone isn't very smart. His job is to protect Loeton. He'll want you to leave, but if Sy Loeton sees you here..." Julian paused.

"What?" Elizabeth detected a hint of fear, something she had never sensed in Julian before.

Julian turned cold and unemotional. "You'll leave tomorrow and warn Jasin. Your staying is dangerous. There is no reason there has to be any more deaths."

Elizabeth's mind was a blur. She had traveled all this way to help and now... She was dizzy again. Her head pounded.

Julian continued, "Elizabeth, look around this place. Don't be concerned about me. Tell Jasin I'm fine. Tell him not to do anything foolish. Listen to me..." She sat on the bed beside Elizabeth. "I'm an old lady and this is probably the most luxurious accommodations to be found anywhere on this snowball of a moon. I'm not suffering. Tell him...Elizabeth?"

But Elizabeth had passed out.

Julian's light snoring greeted Elizabeth when she woke the following morning. She felt revived, her mind was clearer, but she was ravenous. How many meals had she missed in the last few days? She didn't have a clue how long she had been in Fistulee, not more than three days she hoped, but she wasn't sure. Had Rhan-da-lith occurred? Should she leave as Julian suggested? How could she warn Jasin? After all she had gone through to get here, the thought of leaving now was ridiculous.

She understood Julian's fear of losing her son, but there was no place she could help more than here. Julian would have to be convinced, because without Julian's support, Loeton would have no reason to allow her pytor, her servant to stay. Elizabeth closed her eyes and listened to Julian beside her. She respected the old woman's intelligence and quiet inner strength, but Julian had that same self-assured ruthless streak that Jasin had shown that last night in Nova Gaia. Julian tried to be kind, but rarely showed any warmth or love.

Sy Hone arrived and took Elizabeth to a kitchen area where six towas were preparing several large platters of food. From the quantity, Elizabeth figured they could feed at least three-dozen towan. If that many actually lived here, Jasin's plan was foolhardy. He would need her help just to survive.

She fixed Julian's breakfast, adding much more than Julian would eat, hoping to partake of the extra. With no one to accompany her, she headed back to Julian's room. Strange. Why didn't they worry about her movements? The answer became apparent as she approached Julian's door. It was now guarded by a stern towan that Elizabeth recognized as the second companion Loeton had brought to the party. As long as they controlled Julian, they controlled her as well. The towan spun the blue metal rings to open Julian's door and Elizabeth slipped inside.

"You must be kidding," Julian said, looking at the heaping tray. Then seeing Elizabeth smile, she understood. "Perhaps you would be so kind as to help me."

"I'd be happy to," replied Elizabeth, a little embarrassed that her desire was so easily read. Julian nibbled at the food and watched Elizabeth eat enough for both of them.

"Do you remember what I said yesterday?" asked Julian.

Elizabeth, her mouth full, nodded.

"If you don't leave soon Loeton will be back, and then you may not be allowed to leave."

"There is absolutely no way for me to find or stop Jasin."

Julian shook her head. "You're going to have to find a way. Staying here could be extremely dangerous for you."

"They've actually been quite nice to me, except Sy Hone."

"You mean, the towas have been nice," Julian corrected. "As you pointed out, the males are different. They couldn't care less about most females, of either race. As far as a towan is concerned, a towa is expendable, worth less than their cyliths. Sy Hone can't comprehend my being treated as an honored guest. He wanted to strip me and throw me in with the other wives. Can you imagine?"

Elizabeth turned red and scanned the room. "But Loeton treats you nicely."

Julian leaned closer. "I doubt he even knows which room they put me in. He has no interest in a tiny, dried up old hag. I'm just another towa in his eyes." Julian pushed her plate back and rose. "But *you're* a different story. You've got to leave before he finds out you're here. Sy Loeton has everything this world can provide. From what I've gathered, from what Avram and Beloit learned, Sy Loeton is eccentric, in search of novelty and excitement. Do you understand what I'm saying?" Julian paused thoughtfully, then moved to Elizabeth's side of the table. "Tell Jasin not to worry about me and please, please, don't be mad." Julian walked to the door and shouted, "Sy Hone! I want Sy Hone."

"What are you doing?" Elizabeth asked.

Julian smiled, "You're so young—"

Sy Hone appeared at the door. Julian pointed at Elizabeth and demanded, "Send this servant away. She is bad. Put her out before Loeton learns you have made me angry. This servant does not please me." Sy Hone jumped into action, escorting Elizabeth from the room, while Julian stood with her back turned.

The towan dragged her down the hallway. Struggling only made Sy Hone tighten his vice-like grip on Elizabeth's arm. Her mind was racing. There had to be a way she could stay. She understood what Julian was trying to do, but the woman didn't understand how worthless she would be outside these walls. She would never find Jasin in time and he wouldn't listen regardless. They turned the corner into the great arboretum and nearly collided into Sy Loeton himself. His cylith surged forward only to be restrained by Loeton's firm grasp.

"Sy Hone, what is this?" Elizabeth could not understand Loeton's words although his agitation was clear.

"A small matter that I am taking care of," Hone answered.

"Sy Loeton, respected sir," Elizabeth blurted out and bowed deeply. She stared down at the cylith, and then with great effort forced herself to ignore the beast and look straight at Sy Loeton.

"Sy Hone misunderstands my purpose here. Let me explain." She straightened and cautiously moved away from Hone and closer to Loeton. The pytor's rough grasp tightened, threatening to break through the skin on her arm. Elizabeth's mind was whirling. What could she say? Forcing a smile and trying to ignore the presence of the cylith, she stepped even closer. The animal growled. "Do you remember me?" she said.

Sy Loeton looked her over and when he took the expected sniff, Elizabeth leaned towards him. "Elizabeth Tournell...a big name for a big woman," he said.

"I am honored you remember." She looked over at Sy Hone. "Sy Hone doesn't understand our language as well as you do and is confused."

Sy Loeton turned to his pytor. "I have no time to deal with humans this morning. You must take care of this." He turned to go, but Elizabeth panicked, reached out with her free hand and touched his arm.

"Please! You don't understand." The cylith bared sharp teeth and lunged at her, but Sy Loeton fended off the attack with a swipe of his hand.

Shaken, Elizabeth pleaded. Without regard for the truth, her words spilled out. "I am Julian's servant. Since Julian belongs to you, by our sacred traditions, I also belong to you. I serve you now. Please do not disgrace me. I will serve you well. I will do anything you require of me. I...I can make you happy."

Loeton tilted his head and scrutinized Elizabeth. She shook off Sy Hone's grasp, squared her shoulders, and defiantly stood as tall as she could. Her breasts pressed against the crude lacing of her makeshift dress. Indifferent, Sy Loeton turned to his pytor, speaking in Sytonian again.

"I have heard from Sy Toberry. The Rhan-da-lith approaches. We should leave today for the hilltop ceremony. Put this human in with the wives. I will deal with this after the darkness." Then he left with his cylith beside him.

Elizabeth didn't understand what Loeton had said, but his abrupt departure wasn't the result she had hoped for.

"You are to stay with the towas," Sy Hone said and reached out to grasp her arm once again.

Elizabeth breathed a sigh of relief, then remembered how Julian was able to intimidate Sy Hone. She drew back. "I know the way," she announced and headed for the wives' quarters.

Sy Hone followed a few steps behind. She resisted the desire to look over her shoulder. Instead, she straightened her back, raised her head, and walked down the corridor as if she owned the entire estate.

When they arrived at the wives' quarters, she turned to the pytor. "Thank you Sy Hone for seeing me safely to my room. You may go."

The towan stood expressionless, then Elizabeth, hiding a slight grin, turned and entered the room.

Seven sets of identical eyes watched her as she retrieved her backpack and carried it over to her makeshift mattress. Her heart beat wildly and she lay down to regain her composure and rest. Elizabeth closed her eyes and pretended to sleep, waiting until the towas lost interest in her. After about ten minutes, she turned quietly and opened her eyes. A few towa jabbered away in the opposite corner, but apparently the rest had left the room. Elizabeth rolled off her mattress and took a few short steps to retrieve her shorts and bloody rags. She returned to her mattress and breathed deeply. Couldn't they hear her heart pounding in her chest? She checked out the towa. No one had paid much notice. She felt the stiff, blood-soaked rag. Her knife still hid inside. She slid it under the mattress. Now she could relax. Both she and Julian were safe…at least for the moment.

Loeton had mentioned Rhan-da-lith. Why would he care about that if it had not yet occurred? So Jasin hadn't left Nova Gaia. Elizabeth figured it could be as many as eight or nine days until Jasin and Mas would arrive. Then what? What could she do to help them? How could she prepare? The more she considered Jasin's plan to kill Loeton without witnesses, the more it seemed like lunacy. But if she was going to help Jasin succeed, she needed to gather more information. Where did Loeton spend his time? Was he ever alone? She would need to get close to him.

The planet Conboet, and her two moons, Syton and Eian, orbit each other and their sun in such a complex dance that no one ever bothered to predict the countless partial eclipses. The shadows that raced across Syton's face were largely ignored, a minor inconvenience now and again. But occasionally, an extended eclipse fell upon the Syton gorge bringing a full day of absolute darkness—the Rhan-da-lith. The orbital geometry was complex and no one was able to predict its occurrence...no one except Sy Toberry. The towan was able to predict its arrival, and to give his people ample warning. When asked how he accomplished this, he simply claimed it was intuition born from experience. Everyone accepted this since Toberry was the oldest towan anyone knew or had ever heard of.

Traditionally, Sytonians gathered with their closest comrades during this celestial phenomenon. It was a time of bonding and mutual comfort. So whenever Toberry predicted a Rhan-da-lith, Loeton left his vast estate, his many wives, children, and servants—none that held his love, trust, or allegiance—and traveled into the hills overlooking Lake Chook, across the lake from the Wynosk cabin. There he experienced the darkness and waited for the brightening with his towdom, a small but fiercely loyal group of fellow towans, who have sworn lasting allegiance to each other. Many in Sy Loeton's towdom were bound together by their initiation, either having been initiated by Loeton, or in Sy Loeton's case, being an initiate of Sy Toberry himself.

"Sy Toberry, it is good to see you," Loeton greeted his mentor. "Let us hope this gathering is somewhat less exciting than the last time we shared food and drink." Loeton's cylith approached the elder towan. Distant thunder rumbled through the pitch-black sky.

"It should be. The closest humans are across the lake." Toberry knelt down to inspect the animal. "How old is he now?"

"This will be our forty-third dark passage together."

"Remarkable. You are lucky."

"He eats well," said Loeton. Toberry nodded and buried his head in the deep fur of the cylith's ruff. They were old friends.

Sy Hone joined them just as a flash of lightning lit up Mount Schtolin's distant peak. "Unusual. I can't remember another ceremony where it stormed. But it should hold off until we're finished," Sy Hone predicted. "Come...let's begin"

Toberry and Loeton followed Hone down a short rocky path, illuminated by a string of torches, to a clearing. The group numbered just less than a dozen, mostly older towans and their cyliths. They acknowledged each other, but their attention was in the direction of the Lake.

"The glow is spectacular tonight," commented one of them.

The normal bioluminescence found along the Andoree had infiltrated Lake Chook, and from this extraordinary vantage point, the full shape of the large bay stood out in sharp relief even in the darkness.

"It's an unusual large bloom this year," added Toberry. Another flash of lightning and accompanying thunderclap struck nearby.

"The rain is coming. We should start," said Sy Hone, who moved to extinguish the torches along the path.

Sy Toberry nodded and gathered the towdom together. "Sons of the day, we gather together once again to endure the darkness and find comfort in companionship. As this darkness descends let our spirits be lifted with the knowledge that light will return, goodness and beauty will—"

Suddenly a massive stroke of lightning split the sky above them. One end of the bolt struck the surface of the lake, stimulating the already bright plankton, and caused it to glow as if it were aflame. The bright eerie light not only illuminated the entire lake but the shore as well. The group turned to look at the phenomenon.

On the surface of the water, as if the lightning had left a scar, was a brilliant spot. As the natives watched, the spot grew even brighter until...a large oblong mass broke through the surface of the water in the direct center of the glow. Billions of glowing organisms spilled off its sides. Rising out of the water was a form that the towans had not seen in over thirty years. Powerful, swirling eddies surrounded it as the dark shape labored to keep itself afloat.

The last symbol of human technical superiority, the flying craft supposedly destroyed, set aflame and discarded forever, had brought itself to the surface. Within minutes, the jets subsided and the shuttle gracefully descended.

And on the opposite shore, illuminated by the fading glow off the lake, the natives could see two humans, an adult and a little boy, turn from the scene and calmly walk back to their cabin.

The Andoree

Mas's sputtering torch cast long shadows through the courtyard. By its amber light, Jasin tied down the last of their provisions to his blaython. He took one last look around the spacious compound. Now, memories alone inhabited the only home he'd ever known. He wondered who'd take it over if he didn't return. If he had only managed the relationship with Elizabeth better, perhaps she could have stayed and watched over the house. He pictured himself returning triumphant with Julian; Elizabeth running to great them. But he knew in his heart, Elizabeth wouldn't have been content house sitting. She would have forced him to take her with. No, this was as it should be. He cinched the leather straps holding their bags tighter. "We're going to be short of biscuits," he said finishing.

Mas extinguished the flame in the dirt. "Better biscuits than water."

They stood in the darkness of Rhan-da-lith with only the starlight shining through holes in the clouds to illuminate the path out of the compound. Lightning flashed in the distance. "Looks like a storm over the canyon."

"Looks farther away than that," said Mas. "Over Lake Chook, maybe."

Jasin nodded and mounted his blaython.

They didn't speak as they followed the trail into town, knowing well what occupied the other's thoughts—death was as reasonable an outcome of their plan as success. Occasionally, clouds obscured the precious starlight and they were forced to halt in fear of losing the trail all together. The streets of Nova Gaia were deserted and they slipped through under the protection of complete darkness. They travelled as quietly as possible afraid that any sound would give them away. Each noisy step seemed like a cannon shot and they hurried to put distance between themselves and the town. An hour passed until finally they felt like they could speak.

"I think it's almost morning, but it's difficult to tell," said Mas. They had fallen into a steady, deliberate cadence, pacing themselves in order to cover as much distance during the darkness as possible.

"At this time of the year, you'll see the Circle constellation set just before dawn." Jasin pointed to the group of partially obscured stars that was still above the horizon. "It looks like we'd normally have at least a couple of hours before brightening."

"Learn that stuff from Avram?"

"My mom. Sometimes when I was young, I'd look out my bedroom window and she'd be standing in the yard studying the stars. I'd climb out of bed and join her. She had names for the star groupings. Avram thought it was a silly waste of time, but I enjoyed it…quiet time…with my mom."

"You were lucky."

"Didn't you and your aunt or uncle do anything special like that?"

"By the time I came to live with them, they had already raised their own kids. I guess they were tired."

It was always hard for Jasin to relate to Mas's childhood—no father that anyone knew of and a mother that died in childbirth. Perhaps that explained why Mas enjoyed being around the Elstrada household—a chance to experience a real family.

They plodded forward. Off to their left, the bulk of the Trinity range hid the lowest stars and storm clouds hid most of the others. They relied heavily on the few pinpricks of light that broke through. Like most in the Syton gorge, they had only experienced the Rhan-da-lith indoors or surrounded by fire. Neither of them had expected the darkness to be so smothering and oppressive.

"We have to try to get back on a normal schedule or we'll be messed up after Rhan-da-lith. We should push through and not stop for sleep until next evening," Jasin suggested.

"Whenever that will be."

"The stars will tell us."

Jasin looked ahead, trying to detect the valley pass Elizabeth would have taken to Panvera. He was glad she was safe. His heart ached every time he thought about the pain he had caused her their last night together. He tried to ignore the guilt that welled up inside him, but it burned in his gut like he had swallowed a smoldering ember.

By mid-morning, stars appeared through the shallow V-shaped notch between the mountain ranges, and they left behind the cut-off that led to Panvera. Several hours later they entered the outskirts of the forest and pulled off the main canyon road and into a clearing where they hoped to find a trail down into the canyon and to the river .

"This area is used by traders and the people of Cernai. Beloit and I have witnessed a dozen exchanges here. Mostly glowsticks, keetah and other drugs," commented Jasin. "Let's have a bit of lunch."

Mas didn't hesitate and pulled out a couple of pieces of dried meat and a container of water. In the dark, Mas felt around for a couple appropriate rocks and put his aching feet up. They ate in silence.

Unlike Mas, Jasin couldn't rest. He walked into the woods a short distance before returning with bad news. "It will be much slower going on from here. The forest trails will be difficult to follow in the dark. The starlight isn't penetrating the tree canopy."

"Then why not rest here until we get a little light?"

Jasin peered up into the sky. The storm clouds were moving rapidly. "I get the impression that the bad weather hasn't dissipated. If anything, it will get darker over the next few hours."

"What do you want to do?" asked Mas.

"If it begins to rain, I'd rather be under cover of the trees. We're not going to start down into the canyon until after Rhan-da-lith, so it's fine to take it slow. I think it's safe to light the lantern and we'll move on."

As soon as they entered the dark forest, they realized they had made a mistake. The travel lantern projected only a small circle of faint light. Without a clear trail, they became lost and confused.

"As long as we're in the woods, we're either traveling towards the canyon or the village of Cernai."

"Or in circles," added Mas.

"Or in circles," agreed Jasin. "All right, let's call it quits. Maybe later there'll be enough light to find a trail."

They made camp. Jasin insisted they take a few minutes to construct a simple lean-to in case it rained. Then extinguishing the lantern, they settled in. Sleep should have come easily—they had been up for thirty hours—but it proved elusive. They passed the time with small talk, avoiding the subject of Elizabeth.

Mas was the first to nod off, leaving Jasin to listen to the rustle of leaves in the treetops. Then along with the distant thunder, almost like a whisper traveling on the wind, a haunting melody rose and fell. Growing in strength, a voice of pure emotion sent forth a message of loneliness and intense desire. He rolled over and woke Mas.

"Shh, just listen…" Jasin whispered.

Captured by the song's spell, they lay still, until the wordless aria drifted away on the same enchanted wind it arrived on. To answer Mas's unspoken question, Jasin whispered, "Towa song." Then, as if they had been sung a lullaby, they turned over and slept, interrupted only once during the night by light drizzle.

Jasin rose first and made a large circle around their camp looking for any trails that might help them. A hazy light filtered through the trees and a slight wind rustled their leaves, releasing captured raindrops that fell refreshingly on his face. Inattentively, he stepped over a fallen but healthy tree; its leaves still green. He stopped short and turned to examine the trunk. It showed no sign of disease. He followed the fallen tree to its base and discovered a shattered stump standing at least a meter off the ground. It showed burn marks—but this tree hadn't been burned down. Some great force had severed this tree in one mighty explosion. Possibly lightning, thought Jasin, or more likely the renegades in Cernai had developed an explosive—more forbidden technology. They were becoming a major problem. When he finished with Sy Loeton, he would deal with these troublemakers. Every time they broke a Prohibition, the peace between the races was threatened.

He laughed to himself as he made his way back to their little camp. He was planning to murder a high-ranking official of the Sytonian Council—probably dying in the process—and he was concerned that some minor invention by a bunch of misfit hermits might harm the peace. Yet, some explosives might be useful in Fistulee. As an Enforcer, he was surprised at the thought. How far had he fallen?

As Jasin approached their campsite, he could see Mas wandering around looking for something.

Mas asked, "Did you put the lantern somewhere? I thought it was next to us when we fell asleep last night."

"I didn't touch it. Maybe you put it back?"

Mas shook his head and walked over to where their blaython was tied. "Damn!" He threw up his arms and grabbed his head. "All the food is gone; the lantern is gone; our spare clothing is gone. Jasin?"

"Don't move about. The ground is damp. We might be able to find footprints."

The area immediately around the blaython was quite trampled, so they widened the search. Unable to find any signs, Jasin concluded, "They must have stolen the stuff before the rain."

"What should we do?" asked Mas

"Only one thing we can do. We've got to make a side visit to Cernai to pick up provisions."

"I thought you wanted to stay out of sight."

Jasin shrugged, "What choice to we have?"

He and Beloit had endured a good deal of professional ridicule concerning the Village of Cernai. For most humans, it was an embarrassment. Cernai didn't attract those that believed in law and order, or clung to the notion of social responsibility. If you found beauty in organization, planning or cleanliness, you simply didn't live there.

After a frustrating morning of dead end trails and backtracking, Jasin and Mas finally led the blaython into the village of Cernai where they wandered among the various houses and craft shops attempting to purchase supplies. Cold shoulders and inhospitable stares greeted them everywhere.

"I think they may recognize you," said Mas.

"I doubt it. Visitors of any sort aren't common here."

They heard the squabbling before finding the crowd gathered around merchandise laid out on the ground, a market of sorts. They pushed their way into the mass to see what was for sale. Among the vegetables and odd trinkets were familiar packages of dried meat, biscuits, bundles of clothing and of course, their lantern.

The wizened salesman looked up at them. "Ah, here we have some interested souls. Would you like to buy a shirt or two? I wouldn't be at all surprised if they were your size."

"Of course they're our size, you thief," exclaimed Mas.

Jasin laid a calming hand on his friend's shoulder. "How much for the whole package?"

Stunned, Mas turned to face his companion. "You're not serious."

"How much for all our gear?" Jasin repeated.

"You can have all your stuff back for two blue or a dozen decent meitas."

"So you admit the merchandise is ours," said Mas.

The salesman shrugged his shoulders, "If you say so…the price is still firm."

Mas reached over and grabbed the man by his shirtfront and lifted him to a standing position. Leaning forward he growled, "Be on your way, thief, and count yourself lucky I don't break your neck."

The old man didn't flinch. Instead he leaned into Mas and whispered, "Fool…pay me and consider yourself lucky I don't kill you." The man drew away slightly and looked down between them. Mas followed his gaze and saw the gray knife held to his gut. Instinctively Mas shoved the man away exposing the weapon. As if by prearranged signal, primitive knives appeared on almost every person in the crowd and they held them towards either Mas or Jasin. Eyes nervously shifted about, waiting for someone to make the first move.

Jasin broke the tension. "Two blue seems like a fair price."

The crowd put away their crude weapons. With nothing left to buy the villagers dispersed. Jasin leaned over and dug through a bundle of his clothing to retrieve a small leather poke. The salesman stepped on Jasin's hand, pinning it to the ground.

"And just what do you think you're doing?" the man asked.

"Getting your money so we can be on our way." Jasin winced as the man applied even more weight.

"What's on the ground is mine until you pay. If you would like to purchase these items you must pay with your own money...or trade." The salesman looked over at the blaython. "You have a fine beast there. Worth two blue easy."

"You're not serious. The animal is worth ten times that." Mas blurted out.

Jasin extracted his arm and said, "My friend is right. The animal is worth much more than what's on the ground. Perhaps you could sweeten the deal a little."

"What do you want?"

"I have a need for something...to clear trees or rocks from my property. Perhaps you might be able to provide something helpful in that regard, shall we say, something powerful."

Mas, confused, looked at his friend.

"What is it...trees or rocks?" The salesman smiled at the awkward lie. Jasin, unmasked, simply smiled back.

"Come on, Jasin. Let's not fool around here. We've wasted the whole morning." said Mas.

"I have no idea what you think we might have." The old man said with a shrug.

"Oh, I think you do. Now, you'd like the blaython and I'd like something that could blow a healthy tree down. I've seen an example just off the trader's clearing. I'll pay double whatever you're getting for it."

"Now who would want to kill a nice tree?" The wrinkled villager laughed, shook his head, and turned away, beckoning for them to follow.

They passed several small huts, receiving dozens of curious looks before coming to a large, fancy multi-room abode. The salesman called out, "Demos, I have a couple of gents here that would like to talk. You in there?"

A younger man, with a hooked nose and darting eyes cautiously came to the doorway. He scrutinized Jasin and Mas, then looked past them to see who else may have been seen them come to his door.

"These gentlemen are in need of some of your new stuff," the salesman said, turning to go, "They're good for double. Just make sure I get my commission. You two come find me when you're done. I'll be checking out my new blaython."

Jasin and Mas followed Demos back inside and sat where they were instructed. "How much do you need?" he growled, opening up a yellow sack with blue trim. It was an unusual bag made of a shiny material neither Jasin or Mas had seen before. Jasin felt awkward. He should be arresting this man instead of purchasing his wares.

"One or two should do. We need to blow through a wall," answered Jasin, trying to sound like he knew what he was asking for.

Demos cocked his head towards them and scowled. "You dimwits don't even know what you're asking for. How'd you find out about it? Never mind, I already know. That idiot trader, am I right? Of course I am. Listen, I'm not going to explain this to you twice. If you don't listen carefully, you'll blow yourself up, understand?

"I'll sell you a full tube, which you can split if you want. I'll give you a couple empties and here are the covers you'll need. They're easy to lose. Just be careful. To set them, you place the smaller tube upside down inside one of these larger tubes where you've combined the detonator mix. Now depending on how long a delay you want, you adjust the mix of these two liquids here. Are you getting this? The more yellow, the longer it takes to heat up. Mostly yellow, you've got maybe half an hour. A nice blue-green is what I recommend. You got it? You understand? Don't ever just use the blue, or you will lose a hand altogether. I don't care mind you. Just don't be coming back here crying. I've never seen you guys. Understand? Once you're gone, you're gone."

He gathered the tubes, covers, and the detonator chemicals, and placed them all in a crude native sack. "Now that will be four blue, or a green if you want a piece of advice."

"What's the advice?" asked Mas.

Demos held out his hand.

"I'll pay you when we retrieve our stuff." Jasin stood up.

"What is this, some kind of trick?" Demos complained.

Mas stood as well and slapped Demos good-naturedly on the back. "Come on, bring the stuff. You'll have your crystals in a minute, and then you can come back and hide."

Unsure of this turn of events, Demos followed them back to where they had left the blaython. The old salesman had collected all their belongings and was now busy inspecting the creature's hooves.

"That didn't take long," he said, straightening up. "Everything settled?"

"Almost," said Jasin. "One last question. We are looking for a path directly down to the river from here. We don't want to backtrack. We were hoping you might know of such a path."

Frustrated, the salesman asked, "Now just to be straight, there are no more hidden terms? I get the blaython and you get this stuff and the location of a path down to the river. Is that the deal?"

Jasin nodded.

"Done!" the salesman said firmly.

"What about my green?" asked Demos.

"You'll get your crystal. Just relax," said Mas.

Jasin gathered their belongings, paying particular attention to the contents of his small leather pouch that contained the crystals. He removed a green and handed it to Demos, who gave him the rough sack and turned to leave.

"Hey, I thought you had some advice for us?" Jasin yelled after him.

Demos stopped and turned. Pointing to the bag he had just given Jasin, he said, "I suggest you leave that here." He waited for some response from Jasin, who merely smiled. Demos shrugged and shuffled back to his fancy hut.

The wrinkled salesman took the blaython's reins and guided them out of the village and on to a well-traveled path. It clearly descended into the canyon. Jasin addressed him coldly. "Listen carefully. If anyone from Cernai attempts to follow us, or talks about our passage, we will return with a dozen friends and burn your stinking town of thieves to the ground. Do you understand?"

"We aren't thieves. You shouldn't be accusing anyone without proof. No one from Cernai stole your things," replied the old man clearly upset. He pulled the blaython around. "Your stuff was found scattered throughout the village at the brightening." The man yelled over his shoulder as he headed back to the village.

"Can you believe the manure that guy was handing out?" exclaimed Mas.

"I think I may believe him. They never opened my poke. I'm carrying enough crystals to buy a dozen blaythons. If they're thieves, they are the worst I've ever encountered. All that was missing was some food. Maybe the real thief was merely hungry."

"So why take our other stuff? No, you're wrong. The real thief just left with our blaython."

Jasin and Mas lost no time in beginning their descent into the canyon. The path was clear, but quite steep, and they'd often slip and slide in the loose gravel. "You knew the blaython would be worthless on this path, didn't you?" asked Mas.

Jasin smiled. "Actually, I had hoped he'd be helpful getting down into the canyon, but I knew that the blaython would never make it across the river."

The trail narrowed and Mas took the lead. At one point, the edge of the path had broken loose and erosion left only a thin ledge, just the width of a foot. Now, Jasin's gamble to trade the blaython seemed like genius. By leaning into the hill, they carefully made their way past this precarious section. Over the next several hours, they made good time. Occasionally, they would carelessly step too close to the edge and dislodge rocks and gravel, causing them to pause and listen as the debris nosily disappeared into the depths below.

Hours passed and the sun eventually sank behind the canyon rim, casting a shadow over the trail. Unable to find sure footholds, they were forced to rest for the night. As evening darkened the entire canyon, they were once again treated to the eerie melody of towa song, but instead of riding the wind, tonight's enchantment reverberated off the surrounding rock walls.

"The singing seems closer than last night," said Jasin.

Mas nodded absently as he fussed over the lantern.

"Something wrong with that?"

"Not a thing. You hungry?" asked Mas.

"A little...mostly thirsty."

Mas sorted through several canteens until he found one with more than a mouthful of water, and tossed it over to Jasin. "Where did you put those leather straps we used to secure the packs to the blaython?" Mas asked.

"They're in the bottom of the large brown pack."

Mas dug out a long strap and tied it between the lantern and his wrist. "Just playing it safe," Mas said quietly. He extinguished the light and settled back on his ground cloth, gathering the packs between them. They lay quietly, listening to the towa song, and soon they were fast asleep.

In the weak light of early morning, Jasin rose to relieve himself. Upon returning, he looked over at his slumbering companion and laughed.

Mas woke. "What's so funny?" he said with a yawn.

"Your prey stole the bait," Jasin answered, referring to the leather strap tied to his friend's wrist. The other end lay unattached in the dirt.

"Damn! Whoever it is must really want that lantern."

"Or it was the easiest thing to steal." Jasin knelt, staring at a small patch of ground near where the lantern had been. Unlike yesterday, here the dirt held footprints. Mas joined Jasin and together they followed the small three-toed impressions for a few minutes until they disappeared off the trail and over the edge into a steep ravine. "It doesn't make any sense," said Jasin thoughtfully.

"A towa? I guess you were right about the villagers."

Jasin carefully checked his footing and leaned far over the edge but he couldn't see any further signs. Why steal the lantern again? Presumably, the same thief had stolen it yesterday and had returned it. The only thing not returned was some of the food. He jolted to attention. "We've got to get back to the camp quickly…and as quietly as possible," he whispered.

But it was too late. The contents of their packs were scattered on the ground and another food packet was missing. The lantern sat on the exact spot it had been stolen from. "Very clever," said Mas, as he repacked their bags. "I've never heard of a rogue towa."

"Especially one who's fertile," added Jasin. "Towa song like that is a mating call. She's hungry, lonely, and wants a towan."

The trail continued to widen, and near the bottom of the canyon, became a series of serpentine vales that emptied into an extensive marsh. A putrid smell from rotting vegetation was their reward for a successful descent. They turned away from the highlands, and skirted the marsh along its muddy perimeter, eventually coming to a shallow river. "Is this the Andoree?" asked Mas.

Jasin looked at the position of the sun and then at the steep cliffs across the water before answering. "I think the Andoree is about an hour's travel from here." He opened one of the packs, took out a biscuit, and unfolded a map he had taken from the study. "My guess is we are about here." He indicated a point on the map with a corner of his biscuit.

Mas nodded, but was too busy taking his boots off to take a look. He walked barefoot to the edge of the water, carefully waded in, and wiggled his toes in the rough sand. He let out a moan of delight as the cool water soothed his travel worn feet.

Jasin walked over and handed Mas the remaining half of his biscuit. He swatted at a flying insect on the back of his neck. "Hopefully, our unseen traveling companion doesn't intend to follow us across the river. We don't have enough food for two of us, much less a third," he said.

"Aren't you curious to see her?" Mas asked.

"All the ones I've seen look alike." Jasin peered across the marsh. A cloud of small black bugs swirled about. Before he could mention it, the swarm was upon them.

"Time to go," Mas declared as he jumped up and shoved the biscuit into his mouth. He grabbed his boots and they hurried off the sandbar.

Over the next few hours, they hiked along the Canyon River until it finally merged with the Andoree. "We were further up the canyon than I thought." said Jasin, looking back. They turned their attention to the wide river flowing strongly before them, the opposite shore where the Kull began appeared a great distance away.

"Weren't there supposed to be islands here?" asked Mas.

Jasin pulled out the map and they huddled over it, comparing real landmarks to what was shown. "Those are the high cliffs across the Canyon River and the gradual sloping ground on this side. All that's missing are the two islands."

"Without those islands we'll never make it across against this current," Mas observed.

Jasin looked at the flowing water. Mas was right. There was a healthy surge coming in from the Great Lake, moving from right to left. Suddenly the answer to the missing islands was clear—water was moving in. "The islands are just below the surface, hidden by the high tide," he explained to Mas.

"If we cross now, will we still be able to use the islands?"

"If the map is accurate, we should be able to find and stand on them to rest."

"And if the map isn't accurate?"

Jasin detected a hint of concern in his friend's question. "Then it will be a long swim," he answered with a laugh.

"Jasin...I haven't done much swimming." Mas turned away.

Embarrassment? Jasin had never seen this from his friend. Mas, who could best him in any activity, couldn't swim. "When were you going to tell me?

"I think we should wait until the water is shallower and we can see the islands," Mas offered.

"When were you going to tell me?" repeated Jasin.

Mas turned to face his friend. "I...I figured that we would find something to float on, or maybe use the canteens. I don't know...put the empties in a bag or something. I was hoping you would figure something out. I wasn't about to spoil the whole plan over it."

Jasin walked to the water's edge and looked at the far shore. All of a sudden, it seemed a lot farther away. He knelt down and tasted the water. As he feared, the Andoree was bitter, filled with accumulated minerals, salts, and waste from towns along its path. They should fill the canteens from the fresh water of the Canyon River before they attempted to cross. He looked around for anything else that would help float his friend across. Finding nothing he walked back to Mas.

"If you do what I say and don't panic, we'll float across without any problem."

Mas looked worried but hid behind brave words. "Don't worry about me. I'll make it."

They filled the canteens from the clear crisp water of the Canyon River, and using the leather straps, bound them together with all the supplies into a single package that Jasin could drag behind him. When the current finally eased, Jasin pointed out the direction they would have to swim in order to reach the closest submerged island. It wasn't the most direct route across the water, but Jasin promised it would be the easiest. "We'll make it in three legs, with two rests. The first island is the biggest. We can't miss it. It fills the mouth of the Canyon River where it joins the main channel of the Andoree. It should be right there." He pointed at the open expanse of water.

"I'll follow you," said Mas doubtfully.

"No. You're going to float on your back in front of me. I'll direct you." Jasin took off his pants and tied tight knots in both cuffs, and after filling the legs with air, he rolled the waist and used his belt to close it off. Mas followed suit. "It won't last forever, but it should give us some buoyancy for a few minutes. Now, you've got to relax and let the water support you. Just worry about moving in the right direction." They waded into the still water and Jasin jammed his air-filled pants under the supplies. "Use yours around your neck," suggested Jasin. "Now, lie back slowly and move out."

Mas obeyed without hesitation and started swimming on his back into deeper water. Jasin got him going in the right direction and soon they were over their heads. He listened to Mas's labored breathing. As long as Mas didn't panic, they would be all right.

They had been swimming for over ten minutes when Jasin felt a pull behind him. The pack had sunk and was pulling him down. Jasin's strong arms dug into the water, pulling his body forward. His legs kicked until they began to cramp. He lifted his head and could see that the air had also escaped from Mas's pants and his head was in danger of submerging. Swim harder, he told himself, but he wasn't moving. The more he struggled the more he was pulled down. He turned onto his back and yanked the strap as hard as he could. He felt it give a little. He tugged again and again, but it wasn't moving and suddenly he felt panic overtake him. He gulped a mouthful of brackish water, coughing as some found its way into his burning lungs.

Strong arms suddenly grabbed his waist and held him. "Put your feet down," Mas suggested. "We're there."

Embarrassed, Jasin stood. They were in about a meter of water. "The pack...it must be caught," Jasin said breathlessly.

Mas ducked under and freed the pack. It had torn and spilled some of its contents. The explosives Jasin had just purchased in Cernai were gone.

"Well that was a waste of a green. Next leg, I should let you drag the pack."

They rested until both of them felt they were ready to attack leg two. Jasin pointed out the direction, and after reinflating their makeshift floats, they walked until the water was nearly over their heads and began swimming. This time at the first tug from the submerged pack Jasin tested the depth and found he could just stand.

The third leg was quite a bit longer, but they didn't have to worry about finding any hidden islands. They could head directly across. Fifteen minutes later, they were standing in their underwear on shore. Everything they owned was soaked, but they were ecstatic. Mas slapped Jasin on the back. "Welcome to the Kull, Enforcer. You want to arrest me now or later?"

Using the last remnant of light, they moved ashore, unpacked their bags, and laid out their soaked bedrolls and clothing, hoping that by morning they could be rolled up dry. The preserved meat and nuts would survive, but the biscuits were mush and they dumped the mess away from their makeshift camp to prevent another insect invasion. Mas tried unsuccessfully to light the wet lantern, while Jasin ate a few mouthfuls of jerky and drank a half-cup of water. Mas joined him and they finished eating in silence.

The temperature had risen substantially over the last few days as they descended into the canyon, but it still wasn't warm enough to remove the chill from two tired, almost naked men. They sat with their backs towards the desert and scanned the hills across the river that they had just left behind. Reflected light from Conboet painted the high cliffs and canyon walls a dull yellow-green. Now, without the warmth from the sun they began to shiver.

"The water sucked the heat right out of us," complained Jasin.

Looking over his shoulder at the mysterious dark expanse they intended to cross, Mas said, "I thought the Kull was supposed to be hot."

"They call it a cold desert."

"Isn't that the truth," said Mas, rising to check whether any of the clothes or blankets might provide some warmth. "It's going to be a rough night." He returned empty-handed to sit beside Jasin, who soon dozed off, but Mas's shivering grew more severe, preventing any chance that he too might find comfort in sleep.

After half an hour of restlessness, Mas once again heard the desperate towa song. He stood and walked slowly towards the river where the sound seemed to emanate. On the opposite shore, stood a tiny towa, silhouetted by Conboet's eerie, dim light. She was a mere speck this far away, but Mas quickly hid amongst a few boulders where he could still watch and listen without being seen. It was warmer among the massive rocks that still retained some of the day's heat and he was able to stop shaking. The towa continued her mournful plea. Her song continued for a long time, and when she was finished, she sat in the sand and stared across the river. Mas watched the alien until sleep overcame him.

He must have slept for several hours, for when he woke, Conboet had set and a bright sliver of Eian had taken its place. The river shimmered in its glow. The islands were now uncovered and Mas noticed that except for two deep cuts they were practically connected. If only they had waited, their passage might have been much easier. In fact, Mas noted, the towa appeared to agree, for she was wading out onto the first island, which now seemed merely a submerged extension of the far shore. When she got to the deep cut between the first and second island, she hesitated.

"I wonder just how hungry she really is," Mas muttered to himself. As if to answer, the towa lunged into the water and began an uncoordinated attempt to swim to the second island. Mas's jaw dropped as the towa struggled against drowning. Her round head bobbed as she gasped for air. Her little arms and legs barely moved her, but after a valiant effort she pulled herself up on the second island. "Now she's trapped," Mas thought out loud.

The little towa paced back and forth, first looking at the far shore and then back at where she had come from.

"Turn around…go back," coaxed Mas under his breath. The towa looked up towards the boulders, as if she heard him, and without another moment of hesitation, launched herself towards him. Mas groaned and shrunk back behind the boulders.

The towa struggled to make headway. She thrust both her arms forward while making a jumping motion with her legs. When she became tired, she would roll on her back and kick her legs. Her progress was slow and noisy.

Mas peeked over the top of the rock. The small swimmer had barely made it a quarter of the way across. Soon it became clear that her energy was fading. More and more of her effort seemed to be spent keeping her head above water. "Float…just relax and float," Mas pleaded quietly. She seemed to get a second wind, and for a few minutes, resumed her awkward swimming, before quickly tiring again. The slight current slowly carried her down the river with the outgoing tide.

Mas stepped out from behind the rock and kept pace along the riverbank. He looked back toward Jasin and screamed, "Jasin!" But his friend didn't move. He screamed again and then turned to find the small dark head.

Mas ran down the bank until he was even with her. He scanned the shore, looking for some way to help her. She was still alive, but hardly swimming. Occasionally she'd tilt her head back for air, but she was exhausted and the tide moved her swiftly away. Again, running along the shore he got ahead of her and waded into the water. It was almost low tide and he walked out as far as he could, but he could tell that the towa would pass him with several meters of deep water between them. "Swim you stupid creature!" he yelled. "Come on, I can't help you if you don't swim."

The Kull

The towa rocked back and forth on her middle leg watching intently as Jasin and Mas struggled into their damp clothes. She called herself Li Sy. Her name was all the little towa was willing to disclose and Jasin quickly lost interest in attempting further communications. Mas, however, wouldn't give up and continued to engage Li Sy while they gathered their belongings and repacked their bags.

"Li Sy, trying to cross the river if you can't swim was really quite dangerous," Mas scolded. "I know what I'm talking about, believe me."

"I'm sure the dumb little creature doesn't understand a word you're saying."

"Well, she'd better learn, because there's no way that I will ever speak her language." Mas dug out a handful of nuts and a few pieces of dried fruit, and split the meager breakfast between them. Li Sy wasted no time devouring her share.

Jasin eyed the towa with disdain. Li Sy had complicated matters. If they abandoned the small creature, she might tell others about their entry into the Kull. On the other hand, if she came along they would run out of food and water long before reaching the mountains. "With what she already stole from us and the ruined biscuits, we won't have enough food for all three of us," said Jasin.

"You didn't think there would be enough food for the two of us to begin with."

Jasin nodded thoughtfully, "What do you think we should do with her?"

"Kill her, I guess," Mas answered with a smirk. "Come on Jasin, relax. She risked her life to join us, are you suggesting that we might leave her here?"

"That wouldn't be my first choice. She's a liability either way. Let's get going and see whether she'll follow. Maybe she's done with us. Maybe she just wanted a little sack time with you and found you a bit deficient in that department." It was Jasin's turn to crack a smile.

The two men grabbed their packs and struck off toward the mountains. Li Sy showed no sign she cared to follow, but before they had taken a half dozen steps the naked towa ran to them and yanked at their arms to stop.

"I guess she doesn't want us to go," said Jasin.

Getting their attention, Li Sy ran back to where they had discarded the soggy biscuits and motioned them to come over. Reluctantly, they joined her. She squatted over the sodden mess. Small insects infested what remained of the ruined food. She picked up a piece and stuffed it into her mouth, bugs and all.

"Oh…" Jasin turned his head away in disgust.

"Maybe she's not as dumb as you believe," said Mas, who knelt down, brushed the insects aside and began scooping the mess into one of their now empty food pouches. "If she's willing to eat this, there will be more of the other food for us."

"Maybe you should leave the bugs in," Jasin said half seriously.

The towa appeared to agree as she helped Mas top off the pouches with the protein enriched biscuit mash.

Jasin took the lead and the three trekked into the Kull. Flat terrain with scattered patches of stubby sparse vegetation stretched out in front of them. An occasional dusty ridge crossed their path and once, in mid-afternoon, they followed a gully that looked like an ancient dried up riverbed. So far, they hadn't found any large expanse of sand. From what they'd seen, the Kull was less a desert and more like a dry savanna. Since no human had ever been allowed into the area, or at least admitted to knowing about the terrain, the description of it being a desert had come exclusively from the natives and their understanding of the human word. Mas filled the hours teaching Li Sy to speak and understand a few words. By nightfall she knew a dozen or so. "She's really quite bright," said Mas.

"I'll take your word for it."

"No, really."

"Then why is she without a home? Why is she following us through this desolation, eating rotten scraps?" Jasin turned to Li Sy and spoke to her in Sytonian. "Li Sy, where is your home? Do you have a family?" It was absurd that she wouldn't understand her own language. On a whim, Jasin asked in human, "Is the Kull a good place or bad?"

Li Sy's eyes brightened. "Kull no good. Kull bad," she replied.

"See, I told you she was smart."

Jasin ignored him. "Why is the Kull bad?" he asked Li Sy. When she didn't answer, Jasin turned to Mas and complained, "I don't know whether she's very bright, but she *is* very stubborn. It would be easier if she just spoke Sytonian."

"She just doesn't want to."

"Really?" Jasin's patience was wearing thin. He pulled his collar up to protect himself from a stiff breeze that had begun to pick up. They trudged on.

As dimness fell over the Kull, they made camp in the hollow of a tall ridge where they'd be protected from the wind. Mas protected the wick as he lit the lantern. "At least we don't have to worry that she'll steal it," he said.

"Now that she knows where we keep the food, she needn't bother with the lantern trick." Jasin laid out the sleeping blankets. With a grin he placed two blankets together and his separated a bit. "Just in case you two want some privacy," Jasin joked.

Mas turned to look at the sleeping arrangements. "Not very funny."

"I think she's found a mate."

"I hope not…" then under his breath, as if she would be offended, "…she's hard and prickly down there."

"How would you know? You didn't…"

"Of course not, but she was up against me all last night. It was impossible not to notice." He paused thoughtfully. "I don't think she would mind though."

"It's her time."

"Well, she'll have to find someone else. Even if I were interested, I would be torn to a bloody mess. Their males must be…well, they must have special armored equipment."

Whether Mas wanted her or not it didn't seem to matter to Li Sy, for when it was time for the humans to sleep, she crawled next to him and rubbed up against Mas. He shifted his position to avoid her. Jasin heard the rustling. "Be careful there Mas. You don't want to hurt yourself." He chuckled and turned his back to them.

After several more attempts to interest Mas, Li Sy rose and left the humans to their sleep. She wandered off into the Kull, found a knoll, and began to sing. Mas and Jasin listened to the melody, mesmerized by its overtones of longing and desire. The longer her song went on, the more it expressed other more desperate needs. Fear and pain became interwoven with yearning, and panic replaced her earlier enchanting melodies. And then suddenly there was silence, her last notes of agony hung in the air until a scream finally shattered the stillness.

Jasin bolted upright and turned to where Mas was supposed to be lying. Both blankets were empty.

"Damn it," swore Jasin, peering out into the dimness, turning slowly, listening for any telltale sound. He hadn't the vaguest idea which direction the scream had come from. He yelled for his friend. Finally, after a few long minutes, Mas returned alone.

"I couldn't find her," he reported. "The song…I thought she was in pain, but before I got close to finding her the singing stopped and she screamed. I got turned around until I heard you."

"Well, let's hope she's all right. It's probably not a great idea to wander off. We'll try to find her when the light returns. Until then let's try to get some rest."

"How do you expect to sleep now?" Mas complained. "She could be dead. Something or someone may be out there. We don't have a clue what else is out here."

Jasin didn't want to admit it, but the incident had unnerved him as well. Mas was right. No one knew what to expect in the Kull or why it was prohibited territory. "Let's not let our imaginations get the best of us," said Jasin. Let's just focus on getting across the Kull in one piece." Hours crawled by as they tossed and turned. Their thoughts haunted by Li Sy's last scream. Mercifully, the brightness arrived. Neither had gotten more than a fleeting few minutes of shuteye worrying about her fate.

Jasin began rolling up the blankets while Mas rummaging through one of their packs for breakfast. "I swear there were more biscuits than this," Mas grumbled.

Jasin looked over at Mas. Then suddenly he backed away from the base of the tall ridge that had protected them. Li Sy sat on top looking down at them. She held one of the biscuits. "Looks like we *all* survived." Jasin observed.

Mas looked up at the towa. "I wonder if she'll talk about what happened."

"You'll have the rest of the day to try to find out."

Li Sy stuffed the entire biscuit into her mouth, storing it in her food sack, and slid down the incline to face Jasin. Searching for the right word, she finally said, "Hello".

"Good morning," said Jasin.

"Good morning," she repeated, then regurgitated the biscuit into her hands and offered it to him. "Food?"

Jasin shook his head, which the towa found peculiar. "Food?" she asked again, shaking her head from side to side mimicking Jasin.

Again Jasin shook his head, this time smiling. "No, thank you. I don't eat someone else's food," then under his breath, "especially once it's been eaten."

Mas continued to dig through their packs until he found a little dried styke and a small piece of crystallized sweet melon, which they munched on. They each took a swig from the water gourd, and then Jasin pointed to a distant peak, which stood silhouetted in front of a rising cloud of warm moisture, emanating from the gorge's depths.

"That's Mt. Doerr. The high pass should be just off its right shoulder. That's where we're heading. If all goes well, we should make the mountains in three days." The little troop shouldered their packs and headed off, deeper into the Kull.

It was noon when they came upon the first skeleton. They gathered around it. Mas poked at the bones looking for some apparent reason for its death. "Nothing broken…skull's intact…looks like it's been here awhile."

Li Sy studied the long arm and leg bones, then stated the obvious, "Towan".

They surveyed the area around the spot and found nothing out of the ordinary. Whoever it had been appeared to have just walked to this spot alone and died. "Could have died of hunger for all we can tell," said Jasin.

Leaving the remains, they walked on. An hour later, they came upon what was left of two more towans. "We're not on any particular path. I wonder how we can just stumble upon three dead towans in an hour?" Mas asked.

Ignoring the skeletons at their feet, Jasin surveyed the area. "That's a good question. Stay here a minute." He left the group and walked a wide circle around the new bones. A few minutes later he called for the others to join him. At his feet, was an even larger pile of bones.

"I would estimate there are at least five bodies here. From what I've seen, I'd wager there are hundreds of dead towans around here. Maybe this is a cemetery or sanctuary for their dead." He spoke Sytonian to Li Sy trying to confirm that, but she refused to engage.

Mas agreed. "Maybe that's why it's forbidden land—the Prohibition is protecting the Kull from desecration."

"No towa," added Li Sy.

"She's right," said Mas. "We've found only males."

"With their sexist society, it wouldn't surprise me if the women were also treated differently in death. Maybe there's a separate area of the Kull for them. Let's move on."

Much of Mt. Doerr hid beneath clouds, but they had become so familiar with the mountain's form even the smallest hint of its massive facade provided adequate guidance. The hard-packed ground flattened and the vegetation thinned out considerably. Mas kicked at the parched soil, but barely broke the surface.

"Now we know why they just leave the bodies. It would be crazy to dig graves in this," said Mas.

"Maybe when it's time to die, they walk into the Kull and wherever they happen to collapse—"

"In groups?" Mas cut Jasin off and shook his head. "I don't think so. Look…there's more."

Jasin and Li Sy followed Mas. This bone yard was different, and not just for the number of individuals present—which numbered more than fifty—but running through the field of bodies was a perfectly straight ridge of dirt a half-meter high extending left and right across their path. Dispersed throughout the carnage, were crude weapons. Jasin picked up a spear with a gray metal point. "I guess this disproves the cemetery idea." He threw the spear to the ground and lifted a massive club.

Mas picked up a serrated curved sword. "I wouldn't want to be on the receiving end of this."

Jasin looked up at the massive blade his friend was holding, then started rummaging through the bones looking for something. He continued for several minutes, widening his search through the mass of slaughtered bodies, before rejoining the group.

"Quite a battle, wouldn't you say?" said Mas.

"That's just the puzzle."

"What puzzle?" Mas threw the sword to the ground, and retrieved a sturdy spear to lean on.

"Not one bone has a single scratch. Not one nick or cut, not a single smashed skull."

"What about that one?" Mas pointed at a damaged skull partially hidden by the larger skeleton that lay on it. Jasin cleared the bigger bones away revealing a smaller skeleton whose skull had evidently been caved in. Li Sy leaned over the exposed remains.

Jasin turned to Mas. "Our first towa."

"Our first and *only* towa," corrected Mas.

"No towa," said Li Sy.

"She could be right…maybe it's just a younger towan," said Mas.

"No towan." Li Sy said quietly.

Jasin turned angrily to the native and yelled at her in Sytonian. "What are you talking about? No more games! I understand your language well, so there is no reason for you not to explain yourself clearly. What do you mean? What are these bodies doing here? Why are humans prohibited from being in the Kull? Do not speak in riddles if you don't have to."

Li Sy stood as tall as she could, and without a single word, stepped over the dirt ridge and walked off, leaving the men stunned by her insolence.

"That was good. What did you say to her?"

"I just asked her to tell us what she knew."

"Asked her? Sounded more like yelling to me?"

"I didn't—"

"I don't even speak the language and could tell that you were yelling at her."

Jasin looked at the retreating towa. "Sensitive, isn't she?"

Mas shook his head angrily. "You sure have a magic touch with females. Are you going to let this one just walk off like the last one?"

It felt as if Mas had actually impaled him with the spear he held in his hand. Jasin exploded and lashed out at Mas, knocking the spear out of his hands. It flew into the raised seam of dirt. How could he compare Elizabeth to this insignificant towa? Li Sy was a thief and a parasite…but she knew something important about this place. "We've got to stop fooling around here. I'll get her. Then we've got to get moving." Jasin sprinted to catch up with the towa. When he grabbed her arm, she swung around and furiously swatted his hand away.

In Sytonian, she screamed at him. "Don't touch me and don't ever yell at me again. I've had enough of both in my life. I am not your slave. I don't have to do as you say. If I don't want to speak Sytonian, that's for me to decide, not you. If you don't want to share your food that's fine, but your food doesn't grant you power over me. I am not property."

Jasin stood dumbfounded. Towas didn't speak like that. In their society, females *were* slaves; they *were* property. In his experience, these feelings and thoughts could not be coming from the mouth of a towa. He looked deeply into Li Sy's dark eyes trying to comprehend. Finally he apologized. "I'm sorry, I yelled at you," he said weakly.

"Say that in human," she demanded.

"I am sorry."

"I am sorry," she repeated the words slowly and carefully. "I am sorry. Good words," she declared.

Jasin smiled at her and nodded. "Yes, they're very good words. Good words that I don't use often enough. I promise not to raise my voice again. Will you please come back?"

"Please?"

"Another good word I need to use more"

They walked back to rejoin Mas, who was on his knees, using the spear to scrape at the curious seam of raised earth.

"Find something?"

"The spear knocked away some of the dirt. Take a look." Revealed beneath the dirt in the small cleared section was a hint of greenish-blue metal. Using other weapons as tools, Jasin and Li Sy helped Mas excavate a meter of the buried mystery. The ridge was evidently a long metal rail having a triangular cross-section pointing upward.

"I've seen this type of metal before," said Mas.

Jasin ran his hand along the smooth surface and nodded. He'd seen this before as well. He took a few steps and picked up a massive sword from underneath one of the skeletons and brought it back to the rail. The absolute perfection of the buried form stood in stark contrast to the crude hammered metal. Jasin raised the sword over his head and brought it crashing down on the top fragile edge of the rail. Li Sy recoiled and Mas ducked his head as a small chunk of blue metal flew off towards them.

"Have you gone crazy?" Mas shouted.

"Sorry...come take a look." They gathered around the gouge. Slowly the deep notch filled in, and within minutes there was no sign that there had ever been any damage. Jasin went to look for the piece that had been chipped off.

"How did you know?" asked Mas.

"I've also seen this stuff before." He bent over and picked up the fragment. It had the consistency of soft putty. "Feel this," he offered it to Mas, who held it in the palm of his hand and prodded it as if he thought it might come alive. Li Sy stood on her toes to get a look. He took her hand and dumped the glob into it. She sniffed it, then tried to give it back, but they declined. She looked around deciding where to put it. Finally, she walked over to the exposed rail and scraped it onto the surface. The material appeared to melt, and in a few seconds it disappeared, completely absorbed back into the rail. Li Sy cocked her head and tested the surface with a finger. It was hard.

Jasin turned to Li Sy and pointed at the rail. He asked in Sytonian, "Do you know what this is and where it leads?"

She looked up and down its length. It seemed clear she hadn't a clue. After a short discussion, they decided to allow themselves an hour to follow the dirt-encased rail towards Bistoun. It was a disturbing detour.

Countless towan bodies littered the landscape. Occasionally, they would notice a smaller skeleton, but primarily the Kull was proving to be the site of a massive war that killed thousands, perhaps tens of thousands of towans. As they continued the skeletons became denser. Finally, they were forced to stop. A compact field of bodies completely blocked their path. If they were to continue, they would have to step on the bones. There was simply no way to pick their way through. Li Sy refused to go further and they were just about to turn around when Mas pointed out a low structure in the distance.

"That's the first building we've seen since entering the Kull. Aren't you curious?" Mas asked.

The two men moved forward, pushing the skeletons aside to clear a path for Li Sy. Soon their faces were flush and sweat dripped off their chins. The rail beside them gradually descended into an artificial valley before disappearing into a dark tunnel clogged with bent and twisted rusted poles, wire mesh, and piles of desiccated bones. They struggled on through the field of dead towans until they stood in a circular clearing surrounding the low building. It was completely devoid of bodies.

"Why remove the dead? What's so special about this place?" asked Mas.

Jasin surveyed the scene and turned back to ask Li Sy what she knew. She had stopped at the border of the empty circle and had curled herself into a ball. "Maybe they didn't have to move them," he said pointing to their companion. They walked over to assist her.

"Bad...much bad...here," she stammered, holding her head.

"Do you feel anything?" Jasin asked Mas. Mas shook his head. "Me neither. We need to take her away from here," said Jasin.

"What's the matter with her?" asked Mas. With a grunt, he lifted Li Sy to his shoulder.

"Nothing, I would guess. I think she just needs to be moved from the edge of the clearing."

Mas carried her a dozen paces before setting her down. Slowly, she regained her strength. Jasin's conjecture was confirmed. "The area around the building is somehow poisonous to natives. That's why it's clear of bodies. They can't...they couldn't get near the building, It's protected." He turned to Li Sy. "Rest here while we look around,"

They walked slowly along the perimeter of the cleared space. "What are we looking for?" asked Mas.

"Something."

"That's a lot of help."

Jasin smiled. A minute later he stopped in front of a depression in the ground. A mound of dirt and several towan skeletons lay next to it. Among the bones were weapons of various sizes and what looked like shovels. Jasin took a couple and handed one to Mas. "Let's see what they were looking for."

"What makes you think we can succeed where they failed?"

"We're not doubled over in pain. If we don't find anything in a few minutes we'll explore the building without her." They turned to see the towa standing, watching them from a distance.

Barely thirty seconds later, a section of greenish-blue tube lie exposed. It was the diameter of one of their arms. Jasin stepped into the sea of bones and retrieved the largest weapon he could carry.

"My turn," said Mas, who took the battle ax and swung it high over his head. The massive blade came crashing down, severing the blue metal. Li Sy screamed in anguish. They turned to see her collapse and rushed to her aid. She was unconscious, lying amid a jumble of rib bones; her mouth open and distorted, frozen in a grimace of horrible suffering. Mas lifted her head, and with his free arm, swept the parched bones from beneath her, then laid her back gently. The muscles in her face relaxed and she opened her eyes. After resting a moment and taking a sip of water, she was able to stand.

Cautiously, they approached the edge of the clearing. The men kept an eye on Li Sy, who paused every few steps to sense any return of the mysterious headache. Crossing the invisible perimeter of the clearing, she relaxed and led them to a short blue-metal door. Mas gained entry by demolishing it with the battle-ax. Bits of blue metal flew in every direction. "I'm beginning to like this delicate instrument," he joked.

"You're the picture of style and finesse," agreed Jasin.

They unpacked the lantern, and then leaving their packs in the doorway, they ducked their head and entered through the low doorway. Their long shadows stretched out in front of them on the stone floor as the men stepped deeper into the musty room. Light from the doorway defined their narrow path, and they strained to resolve the details hidden in the dark corners. Li Sy moved easily through the darkness continuously sniffing the air. Benches, lined up in neat rows, occupied most of the space.

"Might have been a school room or shelter," said Mas. "This place was built to hold a lot of people."

"A lot of towa, by the size of the door and these benches. But why attack a school?" Jasin countered. "They went through a lot of trouble to protect this building. It was important enough that thousands of others died attacking it."

The thin wedge of light failed to illuminate the depths of a wide stairway, forcing them to light their lantern before descending. Carefully, they negotiated several dozen mold-encrusted stairs, emerging in a cavernous space with a vaulted ceiling that their lamp barely illuminated. In the center, ten tubular pods, each six meters long and half as tall, balanced on the rail of blue metal. They slowly approached. Dust and dirt covered indents in the sides that appeared to be windows. Sloping ramps led to larger openings in the center of each pod. They cautiously stepped into the nearest one. The interior instantly brightened. A sophisticated control panel on a far wall flashed cryptic messages.

Jasin and Mas exchanged glances. "Our friends have been holding out on us," Mas said, finally breaking the long silence. They sat in the comfortable seats and took a few minutes to digest their discovery.

"Must have been some kind of transportation system," offered Jasin.

Li Sy sniffed the interior briefly. "No food," she said, before leaving the cabin.

Jasin stared at the departing Li Sy trying to determine whether she had been surprised or knew about what they had discovered. "Food is all she ever seems to be interested in," said Jasin He blew out the weak, unneeded flame of their crude lantern.

Mas shook his head. "Incredible...the bastards force us to dispose of our technology, prohibit us from teaching or developing anything new and all the while they're hiding evidence of their advanced science and engineering. We've been living a charade."

"In another generation, humans will be as backward as we thought they were," added Jasin, dazed. "Then we could fall victim to their total control."

"In another generation?" Mas used the crude battle-ax to point to the dials and multi-colored readouts on the control panel. "That's way over my head."

"Li Sy is right about one thing—if we don't find food or water it won't matter to us." Jasin said. They stepped from the confines of the vehicle and the interior lights shut off leaving them in total darkness. They returned to the cabin and the artificial lamps once again illuminated, allowing them to light their lantern before once again stepping outside. "Let's see where she went."

"I wonder whether they all can see so well in the dark, or whether it's just the towa?" Mas thought out loud.

Jasin shrugged, and they slowly continued past the pods calling out her name.

The uniform blue rail stretched out in front of them, disappearing in the darkness beyond the glow of the lantern. After walking for ten minutes, they turned around and headed back towards the cars. Suddenly, an excited Li Sy appeared out of the darkness claiming she had found food. They followed her into the darkness, trusting her keen senses to guide them, until they stood before a door at the end of a narrow corridor. It yielded to Mas's axe.

This time the lights didn't turn on when they entered. "These rooms and the rest of the building must be on the same dysfunctional power source, where the pods, and the defense system, must each have their own," guessed Mas.

Li Sy sniffed the air and led them to yet another door. Mas raised his ax, but Li Sy stepped in front of him and simply pulled the door open. Inside there were stacks of tightly covered blue metal cubes. "How in the world can she smell food in sealed containers behind two doors?" asked Mas.

Li Sy reached down along the back of the storage closet and brought her three fingers to her nose. She closed her eyes and breathed deeply. An intense shudder ran through her body. Jasin knelt beside her bringing the lantern low. Along the back of the closet and covering one of the bottom cubes were crawling insects. "Maybe she's smelling the insects and not the food," Jasin suggested. Li Sy brought her hand to his nose He sniffed carefully but was unable to smell anything. He looked in her hand. She had squashed a few of the bugs between her fingers. She offered her treasure to Mas who was also unable to detect the faintest odor. She sniffed her fingers again with the same result.

"I hope there's more than bugs here," said Mas.

Li Sy pointed at the insects. "Forn."

"Well, whatever you call them, let's see what they find so interesting," said Jasin. He took a container from the top, and after a few awkward moments of trying to pry the lid open, he discovered that it pivoted from one corner if you applied pressure in the right spot. The cube contained a golden syrup. He held it out for Li Sy, who smelled it. She dipped her bug-covered fingers into the thick liquid and tasted it.

"That's hers now," stated Mas wrinkling his nose. He put the ax down and opened another cube. "Tastes slightly sweet," he said after sampling the goo.

"Sweet's good," said Jasin, as he took a cube of his own. They each slurped down about a third of their container. "Grab as much as we can carry and let's get to the surface."

Dimness had begun to engulf the Kull, but since none of them felt like sleeping among thousands of skeletons and there was still sufficient light to travel by, they left the vicinity of the transport station and headed towards Mt Doerr. After an hour of fading light, they cleared the sea of bones. When it became too dark to travel, they unrolled their blankets and settled down. Not even the towa felt the least bit hungry or thirsty even after an hour of walking. The golden syrup had satisfied them completely. Soon they heard Li Sy wander off. They lay awake and struggled to find comfortable positions, half expecting to hear towa song again.

Mas rolled over to face Jasin. "Do you think they've abandoned their technology or simply hiding it? I don't get it."

"It's massive deceit either way."

"Massive hypocrisy," Mas declared.

Jasin listened to the wind blow across the open plain. "Where do you think she has gone off to?"

"Who knows? Maybe looking for more bugs."

"Forn. You should learn a few of their words."

They talked a bit longer, pausing now and again to listen for the towa, but only the wind and their yawning broke the silence of the Kull. Jasin stared up at the stars and thought about what Beloit had told him of vast numbers that could be seen from space. What wonders his parents must have observed. Just the idea that you could see more than a small section of the sky befuddled him. If you were floating in space, he thought, you would see stars all around you, in any direction. Sleep came surprisingly easy.

In his dreams, Elizabeth was crying tears of liquid gold. He reached out and brought an amber teardrop to his mouth, expecting it to taste sweet. Its bitterness surprised him. His stomach churned and he turned away from her, afraid he would be sick. When he turned back, she was gone, and there was nothing but the Kull. He had to find her and peered into the barren landscape, straining to see her, to hear her, but all he could detect was the faint sound of the alien transport rolling along the buried track. Sh, sh, sh, it was a faint sound and it continued repeatedly. Sh, sh, sh. The sound filled his head and something made him open his eyes. He rolled over to see Mas standing.

"What's wrong?" Jasin asked sleepily. But Mas just held up his finger to silence him. Jasin stared at his friend, standing frozen against the starry sky, and then off in the distance, riding along with the blowing wind and quickly fading away, Jasin barely made out the faintest of sounds— Sh, sh, sh.

Seduction

Rage boiled inside her, yet Elizabeth stood helpless, fists clenched at her side. Blood from her split lip trickled down her chin as she watched Sy Loeton tear Julian's clothing off and drag the frail seventy-year old from her comfortable quarters and throw her into a cramped, dark, storage room. Something had occurred during the towan's Rhan-da-lith celebration that had changed his attitude towards them. They were no longer a mere nuisance. Fighting through pain, she flexed her jaw. Sy Loeton's crushing blow had caught her by surprise. His anger filled the residence.

Loeton's cruelty toward Julian, a defenseless and benign old lady, only reinforced the hatred and disgust she felt towards him. His fascination with human females obviously had its limits, and now she feared her ruse and promise to serve him would likely result in her joining Julian or even worse.

Her hand drifted through the slit in her thin dress and felt the hilt of the blade she had tied to her thigh. So far, the only blood it had drawn was her own, but she swore to change that. How could she just stand by and do nothing?

Suddenly, she was grabbed from behind. Sy Hone lifted her from the floor and brought to stand before Loeton. He looked at her busted lip. Her blood hadn't stopped flowing and a fresh drop hung from her jaw. Sy Loeton reached over, took the drop, and brought it to his mouth.

"I have no use for you and neither does your master," he began. "The old woman has sent you away once. Now I insist, go back to your people."

Elizabeth hesitated. In just a few days, Jasin might arrive, but this was no time to argue. "I will leave in the morning...after...." Her mind raced to find an excuse. "I need to thank you properly for your hospitality."

"My hos-pi-tally? What is this?"

Elizabeth stepped forward and lowered her head. "You have given me food and shelter. You have helped me recover from my earlier injuries. Honor demands that I must repay you. I must do something in return." Talking had increased the flow of blood from her lip. Her tongue explored the cut, tasting the metallic drops.

"You are free to go. You owe me nothing."

Moving closer to him, she brushed a finger along her blood smeared lip and brought it to the native's mouth. "Perhaps tonight I could serve you dinner...just you and I alone..." she glanced at the pytor, "without your animals." Sy Hone stepped forward to slap her again, but Loeton caught his arm before it struck.

"Sy Hone, do you think I need protection from this female?" he asked in Sytonian. "Her boldness amuses me. I will spend a few moments with her before we leave for the council meeting tonight." He reached down and grabbed the cylith's leash and handed it to his pytor. "Feed him, we will travel far before the brightness." Sy Hone led the animal away, but not before giving Elizabeth a withering look.

"You may repay your debt by helping me practice your language," suggested Loeton.

"You speak Human very well, are you sure there isn't anything else that I could do?" She turned coyly and slowly inspected the room. What did she think she was doing? Her hand brushed the slender hidden weapon. If she got close enough did she have the nerve to use it? Wait for Jasin she told herself. Let him initiate the plan.

"Do you know the humans that live on the cold shore of the lake? A man and a small boy."

Startled, she turned to face him.

"I see that you know who I am talking about. What are their names?"

"Why do you ask about them?" She felt tightness in her chest and the room suddenly felt cold. Forcing herself to smile, she approached him, playing with the ends of the lace that held her dress together. "Aren't I more interesting than some man and his son?"

"So...the small boy is his son. That should help us find them."

Find them. Why would he be interested in Jorge and Wilem? Maybe she should finish this now. They were alone just as Jasin had planned. Kill him, rescue Julian, and get as far from here as possible. She was very close to him now and he leaned into her sniffing the air. In turn she took a deep breath, filling her nose with his musk and traced the scars on his chest with her thumb as she had seen others do. His neck riffled slightly as she let her left hand drop to his pelvic folds and lightly ran her fingers along the ridges. She stared onto his unblinking eyes and wondered whether he would close them. Her right hand fell to her thigh and slipped through the slit in her dress, inching toward the knife.

He pushed her away.

"I am not due for several days, and my new fifth is in need, but perhaps you can join us when I return from T'Matte. It might be interesting. Be waiting for me in the hardel, the sitting area I'm told you are so fond of. There, among the wives, we will see if you can repay me."

Elizabeth left the private room in a daze and wandered back to the atrium, collapsing beneath the giant tree, nauseous and emotionally drained. She had bought herself a few more days, but at what cost. Completing the seduction would be suicide. She remembered Jasin's description of the mutilated girl. Loeton was immensely strong, and his actions were unpredictable. How could she ever think that she would be able to get close enough to help Jasin kill him? But if she was careful, and the towan's response to sex was similar to other males, a little foreplay might present an opportunity to catch him in a vulnerable moment.

What about Loeton's fifth? Would the plan work if she were present? The wives would have to leave them alone, or she would have to convince him to find a more private spot. It was getting complicated At first it had seemed easy...excite him, and then kill him. Kill him before...before he killed her.

Sy Lang gave the traditional keetah toast to the gathered Council of Seventeen. "We can wait no longer for our brother to join us. Let us begin deliberations, and hope our wisdom is sufficient to guide our people. Tyhinga!" The assemblage repeated the salute and burnt their throats with a gulp of steaming liquid. A chorus of spirited howls accompanied the spilling of the excess liquid onto the rough stone pavers. Lang walked past the first set of junior sentinel guards and sidled up to Loeton, "Have you seen or spoken to our teacher?"

"We observed the Rhan-da-lith together. It was quite a show. You should join us next year."

"A show?" asked Sy Lang.

"I'll explain, but I need the privilege of Durougia," Loeton replied earnestly, asking for the right to change the council's agenda.

"We have much to discuss tonight. If there is time you may request the privilege."

Their cyliths playfully circling each other, nose to rump, as their masters walked together from the sacred stone circle and through the sculpture garden where they passed rows of moss-covered bas-reliefs and busts. Sy Lang stopped in front of one. Loeton's cylith chose its base to urinate upon. "Not much regard for his master," reflected Lang, gazing at the likeness of Sy Loeton.

"You only amuse yourself, Lang," said Loeton.

"It would benefit you to relax tonight."

Loeton looked at his fellow council member for clarification, but Lang offered nothing. They continued walking and passed between the second set of young towan sentinels and their unruly pups. The young natives were being honored with the symbolic guarding of the entrance of the immense stone cavity that served to house and protect the business of the assembly. Others had already taken their designated positions on the elevated concentric terraces surrounding the leader's pit. Sy Lang stepped down into the center of the depression while Loeton joined the highly respected members in the inner ring.

For the next few hours, Sytonian issues and concerns were debated. Most involved territorial disputes and trading conflicts. As dimness spread, torches were lit. Eerie shadows danced against the steep natural stone faces of the chamber. Sy Loeton endured the tedious agenda patiently until there was an extended pause in the proceedings.

"I ask the indulgence of my fellow council members. I know the hour is late, but I bring an issue of great importance," he began. "I request the privilege of Durougia." All eyes turned to Sy Lang, who would have to grant the privilege.

"I assure you if there is sufficient time after one last matter is discussed, the privilege will be granted." Loeton spread his arms in acquiescence. Sy Lang continued, "On behalf of this council, I have promised the humans to ask you, Sy Loeton, a few questions concerning the death of one of their women."

Loeton raised his head in surprise and glowered at Sy Lang.

"With great respect, we ask you to enlighten the council on anything you might know. For whatever reason, the humans seem upset over the inconsequential death of this female. I believe she lived in Bistoun and worked in one of the eating establishments along the river," added Lang.

Now, all attention turned to Sy Loeton who held his head high and replied, "I have eaten in Sy Fask's establishment for many years. The woman you refer to worked there. It is my understanding that she was injured and eventually died. Now...if we are finished exploring trivial matters, I have an important discovery to bring to the council's attention. I request Durougia."

"Perhaps, in a minute. There is more that I must ask you, my friend."

"Friend! You have the disrespect to interrogate me here, in this sacred chamber, and call yourself a friend?"

It was Sy Lang's turn to spread his arms, but he continued, "It has been said that you have had lengthy talks with this girl and that you may have seen her...outside of Sy Fask's. Others have mentioned that her services were available to many men."

"You use that term to insult me?"

"Never, respected sir."

"Then your insinuation is meant to imply?" His tone clearly indicating a question.

"Sy, Loeton, please help us put this matter to rest," begged Lang.

Loeton looked around at the other members. They had been on their feet for hours and it was obvious they wished to put an end to this session. "My personal behavior is really none of this bodies concern," he stated flatly.

"On the contrary," replied Lang, "all of our behaviors reflect on the stature of this body. Our suggestions are followed because we are respected, and we earn that respect by living by the highest code of conduct. You are known as a towan of great moral integrity, but that has been challenged by the humans, and I have promised to resolve this problem."

"Why do we care about what the humans believe?" roared Loeton. "We set the standards by which they must live, not the other way around. They have no right to question our behavior. You waste the council's time worrying about human concerns and questioning my moral integrity, when we should be discussing the fact that humans have been deceiving us for decades and pose a serious threat. Why should we care about what happened to one of them, especially a female?"

"Sy Loeton...some of the girl's injuries could have been caused by sexual congress with a towan." A murmur of confusion swept through the council as members sought to picture the unlikely act.

Enraged, Sy Loeton left his alcove and approached Sy Lang. His cylith followed growling, sensing his master's anger. "How dare you suggest I might be involved? It is no secret that I find human females intriguing and that I have recently taken Avram Elstrada's widow as a wife. But how dare you suggest that I, or any towan, would be capable of the intentional mutilation and murder of another species for sexual gratification? That is a sickness, not an interest. I do find their females stimulating and yes, I enjoyed talking to the girl in Bistoun, but I can assure you that her death had nothing to do with me."

"Your interest in human females doesn't help matters," said Lang. "Is there any proof you were not involved."

"Proof that I wasn't involved? I need proof? My word has always been enough and it should be enough now. I didn't harm that girl, I...I couldn't have." The last few words were spoken under his breath.

Sy Lang leaned over and quietly asked him to explain.

"It's actually quite simple," whispered Loeton. "It was not my time. I was not due for a week."

"There is no need for secrecy, Sy Loeton. Your personal schedule is clear evidence of your innocence. It has just never been needed as a matter of defense before. Please, go back to your alcove." As Loeton walked back to his space, Lang announced, "Sy Loeton, while not required, has graciously provided proof of his innocence—his personal cycle. This body offers its apology and grants him the privilege of Durougia."

Sy Loeton paused, allowing the first matter to fade a bit before continuing. "A group of us, including our respected teacher, Sy Toberry, have witnessed a disturbing event during the last Rhan-da-lith. Our towdom traditionally celebrates the darkness in the hills overlooking the lake. This year, as many here must know, there was a terrific lightning storm." A smattering of heads nodded, remembering. "And the glow from the lake has been naturally brilliant, unusually so." Heads once again nodded in agreement. "During the storm, the surface of the water was struck by a lightning bolt; the entire lake and shoreline were illuminated. That's when we saw it. The humans have hidden it beneath the water for thirty years and now they are going to raise it and use its power against us."

"Excuse me Sy Loeton," said a small, weak voice from the outer circle. "If I may? What exactly did you observe?"

"I am sorry Eidorf, let me explain. Thirty years ago, a ceremony was held at the lake where the humans supposedly destroyed the last of their flying vehicles...but a few days ago we saw it rise under its own power. It was working, and what is just as important, we saw a man and his son watching the machine. Either they were controlling it or they knew when to expect it. Either way they have deceived us."

"Sy Loeton, this is indeed serious," remarked Lang. "I can assume that Sy Toberry saw this event as well?"

"Of course. I told you we were together."

"And there is no possibility that what you saw could have been anything other than what you have described? You said you were high on a hill. It was the darkest day of the year."

"Sy Lang, there is no possibility it was anything else. I remember their flying craft clearly, as should you. We sat together with Sy Toberry, and we saw them set it on fire and pretend to sink it. It was the same machine."

Lang nodded, remembering. "Do you believe all the humans know of its existence, or just the few at the lake?" asked Lang. "We must find out who was responsible."

"Respectfully sir, it is irrelevant. As far as I can see, the issue is how to find and destroy it before they use its terrible power against us. This proves what I have always believed— that humans cannot be trusted to abandon their technology. They are a dishonest and dangerous race. It was a mistake to grant them settlement rights as I have insisted continuously. We must take the necessary steps to punish and control them. I have already taken the precaution of securing one of their elders, who by chance was under my care before Rhanda-lith."

A murmur spread through the council. Loeton surveyed the assembly trying to detect any dissention.

Sy Lang voice quieted the crowd. "You were right to bring this to the council's attention, but the hour is late and we must have clear minds and more information to deal with a problem of this magnitude. I suggest we all investigate the human activities within our territories to determine the extent to which the humans have disobeyed the Prohibitions. If they have broken their promise they must be dealt with. The machine in the lake poses a serious peril and we must find out who controls it, and how we can eliminate its threat forever. Due to the seriousness of the situation, we will meet again in ten days to continue discussion of this matter."

* * *

Just as she had done a dozen times during the last few days, Elizabeth approached the guard who controlled entrance to Julian's prison room. She needed him to become relaxed in her presence and trust her. Usually, she just brought Julian her meals, but this time she carried a cloth bundle. If her rendezvous with Loeton tonight was successful, she would return here to free Julian and escape would be much easier if this towan felt at ease and complacent.

"Dearest imbecile," she said sweetly, knowing the towan didn't understand a word she spoke. "Loeton has asked me to bring the lady a blanket. Loeton says this and Loeton commands that and if you understand anything, it's the word Loeton. So be a nice servant and move your ugly body away from Loeton's door and open it so I can care for Loeton's wife."

Elizabeth waited with her head deeply bowed as he opened the unlocked door. Julian sat dejected, naked on a barrel, her thin arms crossed in front of her old shriveled body. The stench of her chamber pot filled the cramped room. Elizabeth entered and pulled the door closed behind her.

"Bless you, darling," Julian muttered, as she donned the makeshift cloak that Elizabeth had fashioned from a blanket. Julian had finally accepted her presence after Elizabeth lied to her, saying that Loeton would kill her if she didn't serve his new wife as she had before. The small deceit had worked, or at least Julian had the good sense to realize her pampered days were over and she might need a friend.

Julian's confident demeanor returned and she spun around pretending it was a beautiful gown. "What do you think? Is it me?"

"It's probably pretty itchy, but it was all I could find." She paused, she wanted to confide in Julian and tell her to be prepared tonight, but she knew that was foolish.

"What is it?" asked Julian. "What's troubling you?"

"Nothing...just thinking about Jasin," she lied. "Listen..." She walked over and took Julian's tiny hands in hers. "I wanted to tell you that..." Elizabeth struggled to find the right words, "I wanted to tell you that I wished we had had more time together before all this." She glanced around the barren cold interior.

Julian stood on tiptoes and hugged her. "It will be all right."

Tears flooded Elizabeth's eyes as a wave of sadness overtook her. She tried to take a deep breath, but it became a small cry. Her loneliness and memories of her own mother weren't as deeply buried as she had thought. She held Julian tightly. There was a fair chance this would be the last human she would ever see, ever hold. If she didn't slay Loeton in a single stroke, if she wasn't able to kill him before...before he used her, well...if the act didn't kill her, she knew he wouldn't hesitate to kill her.

"Everything will be just fine." Julian reached up and wiped Elizabeth's runny nose on her sleeve. "We'll find a way out of here."

Elizabeth nodded weakly and turned to leave, but hesitated and turned back to face Julian. "There's a chance I might find a way to...to leave...maybe find some help," she lied. "If Jasin makes it here would you tell him something?" Julian nodded. "Please tell him I couldn't wait. That waiting was too dangerous. Tell him, I thought I had a better way. Can you tell him that, if I don't have a chance to speak to him first? And…can you tell him, I'm sorry that I didn't listen to him."

Julian walked up to Elizabeth and gave her another hug. "You'll tell him yourself when you see him." Elizabeth turned away, hiding the tears streaming down her cheeks and rushed out the door.

She ran to the wives' quarters, where she lay down in the hardel. She didn't care that the little towas stared at her. What could they do to her that would mean anything? Since the last time she stood in front of Sy Loeton, her half backed plan had crystallized. If she waited until Jasin arrived, she would have to watch him die at Loeton's hands. There was absolutely no way for Jasin to secretly penetrate this huge compound and he wouldn't have the slightest clue where to find Loeton. After nearly ten days here, she still didn't know where he spent his time.

And if they succeeded, how would Jasin and Mas escape unseen? How could they possibly avoid Loeton's numerous guards? No…she had the best chance of getting a blade close to Loeton's neck, the best chance of walking the halls unnoticed, the best chance of freeing Julia. If she didn't want to lose either Jasin or Mas, she had to take the gamble and attempt to carry out Jasin's plan herself.

In a few hours, she would kill Loeton in this very spot. He would find her willing; there would be no reason for violence until…Hopefully she would be able to excite him quickly, but she really had no idea how long or what it took. Maybe he would be quick like an animal, or because she wasn't a towa, he might never respond. Regardless, she had to be ready to act. Her hand slid through the slit in her dress, making sure the knife would easily come free. Should she hide it in the cushions, or keep it on her? Would he detect it? The thought of him running his hands over her body made her stomach turn. She didn't want to think about any of it anymore and she laid her head down to rest, trying to picture where Jasin and Mas might be. She had a picture in her mind of the two of them coming down from the Kaysop Range. That's where she and Julian must head for. Hopefully they would meet them before they entered Fistulee.

Suddenly, Elizabeth sat up. If she was successful, they would be leaving hastily and not stopping until they reached the safety of the mountains, but she didn't have a thing prepared for the flight. They'd need food and water. Julian would need shoes. A lantern and blankets would be essential. Her backpack would be *very* nice. She pulled herself from the hardel and headed for the kitchen, where she gathered a large quantity of food. Glancing about the kitchen, she was relieved that no one had taken notice of her activities. Why should they? She had prepared a tray for Julian several times a day for the last few days. Maybe this was more food than usual, but no one appeared to care. Just before she left, she grabbed two water skins and cloth sack from the pantry and hurried out of the kitchen nearly running over a lone towa who was scurrying down the hallway herself.

"Sorry," Elizabeth blurted out, trying to regain her balance and not spill the overloaded tray. The little female caught one of the small vegetables as it tumbled towards the ground, and before Elizabeth could say a word, she shoved it whole into her dirty mouth. "Nice catch..." Elizabeth was about to say, but before she got it out the towa darted into the kitchen.

Continuing on, Elizabeth found a quiet corner and stuffed the food into the sack, then stashed the supplies in a storeroom where she could quickly retrieve them. Not knowing when Loeton might show up at the hardel, she hurried back and plopped back into the soft cushions.

All the wives, except one, sat huddled together finishing their meal. The lone wife, Elizabeth assumed was Loeton's new fifth, stood rocking side to side in the corner, singing a haunting melody. The song was mesmerizing and Elizabeth lost herself in its yearning. Suddenly Loeton was standing next to her. The wives turned to look at Elizabeth.

"Why do they look at me whenever I rest here?" asked Elizabeth, pretending to be calm.

"The hardel isn't for resting," Loeton replied.

Elizabeth blushed. "Well it's a shame that the most comfortable place in the entire estate is used so seldom."

"I am glad you have found an additional use for the hardel, as unconventional as it is. I'm afraid the wives are ignorant and... what is your word for a belief not based on reason?"

"They are superstitious."

"Superstitious. It is a difficult word to say."

Elizabeth looked at the six wives who continued to stare at them. The seventh continued to sing softly, oblivious to anything but her desires. "What are the others afraid of?"

Loeton stared back at the cluster of petite females. "Ignore them. Who know what goes through their tiny heads. It can't be much." He turned back to look at Elizabeth. "But you human females are different. I have always enjoyed your company. Talk to me."

She turned away from the towas and sat down. Loeton stepped into the hardel, gathered a couple of pillows behind him, and reclined. "It is my time," he began, "and my fifth's. I suppose they are curious about you." He waved his hand towards several of the wives who had positioned themselves around the hardel. "As I am," he added.

"Curious?"

"Am I using the word incorrectly? We wonder what your reason is for entering the hardel tonight."

"Curious is the right word, I guess." She hadn't thought about this from their point of view. "There are many reasons. I have told you that I need to repay you in some way...and I am curious as well."

"I don't believe you," he stated flatly.

It was as if her heart stopped beating. Tiny beads of sweat formed on her upper lip, which she tried to nonchalantly wipe away.

Sy Loeton's eyes grew stern, his voice strong. "You work for the Elstrada family. You believe I murdered the female in Bistoun, like the rest of the humans. But I didn't...I liked that woman. She wasn't afraid like you are."

"I'm not afraid," Elizabeth stated boldly.

Loeton shifted and moved closer to her. He leaned into her and took a deep whiff. "Yes you are."

"I am merely nervous, there's a difference." Elizabeth turned away to hide her face and found herself looking at one of the towas, just a few feet away. "I don't like being on display. Is there any reason why they have to be here? They are making me uncomfortable."

"Ignore them, they are insignificant."

"Then send them away. I can't relax with them here." Loeton barked a few words in Sytonian and six of the seven wives quickly fled the room. The last continued rocking back and forth, already seemingly elsewhere. "It appears that your wives are the ones that are afraid of you."

"Most of them anyway." Loeton glanced at the last towa.

Elizabeth remembered what he had said about this fifth wife. "This is a new wife. Did your last fifth die or leave you?"

Loeton turned back to face Elizabeth. "She was unusual." Elizabeth thought she detected something different in his voice.

"Unusual?"

"A bit unorthodox."

"So, you didn't answer my question. You seem to enjoy unusual females."

He thought before answering, "They can be more trouble than they're worth."

"And this one?" Elizabeth indicated the remaining towa. "What about her?

He looked over at the little female. "She appears to be common. It is her time. I must help release her water. Would you like to watch?"

He had softened a bit and she moved closer. "I am curious. If you help her, will you be finished? I mean…how many times…can you help?"

"I don't understand."

This towa had complicated things for her. Little did she expect competition for his attention, but maybe she could use it. "Have you…I mean can you have more than one wife during your time. Can you have two fifth wives?" She paused, "Because, I haven't told anyone this before but I think you might understand. I am taller...larger than most human males."

"That is hardly a secret. It is what has attracted my attention."

"No, that's not the secret." She leaned over, placing one hand gently on his pelvic folds, she whispered, "They don't excite me." As she leaned back, she stroked the rough covering and looked deeply into his unblinking eyes.

She had no idea what she was doing. For all she knew she was supposed to scratch at the covering, knock on it, spit on it. Perhaps treating him like a human male was a turn off, but she had nothing to go by.

Loeton was unmoved. He sat silently, staring at her. "I believe I can have only one fifth wife. Do you understand that if her water isn't released she can die?" His gaze tilted down to her breasts, barely visible through the crisscrossed laces holding her dress together. She took a deep breath and they swelled against the fabric. She looked down at her chest and back to him. "Would you like to see them," she asked.

"Your body is of no interest to me." But his shoulder patches took on a vibrancy she had never seen. Elizabeth guessed that was not exactly the case. She remembered the towan who had pressed his finger into her breasts as she lay naked and untied the laces letting the top of her makeshift dress fall open. Exposed to his stare, her nipples hardened. Loeton reached over and pushed the nipple inward. She laughed and took his hand and showed him how to caress her breasts. His hands were like rough tree bark.

"Now it's your turn to teach me," she said, and again rubbed his pelvis. "Do you like to be touched?"

The towan shook his head, but lay back against the pillows allowing her to continue. "There is nothing for me to teach you yet." He tilted his head back and stared at the ceiling. This was what Elizabeth had waited for. She continued to massage his folds, but he acted as if she wasn't there. His shoulder patches were turning a bright orange and she looked down to see that the edges of his folds were beginning to contract, creating a slit that slowly widened. She was mesmerized watching the metamorphosis, but she forced herself to look at his face. Watch his eyes, she told herself as she freed her knife. She would have to keep it close to his body and bring it up under his chin or he'd see it. One quick slice, she reminded herself, can't take the chance of a non-fatal injury.

Suddenly there was a sharp pop and a fine mist sprayed over her. An overwhelming stench enveloped her. Dizzy and numb, she fought to retain consciousness, but had the presence of mind to stash the knife between the cushions before collapsing almost paralyzed against his thigh.

His organ had been released. It was fairly long, but thinner than she expected and it was tapered. It had a bump about midway down its length where it bent at a slight angle. The entire surface appeared exceedingly rough, especially the knobbed tip. Along one edge of the contracted pelvic folds lay a burst yellow membrane. She suspected it had released some type of narcotic pheromone. Elizabeth took a deep cleansing breath and forced herself to sit up. Loeton was looking at her. There was an air of intensity about him.

"Now I can teach you something," he growled, and then left the hardel and lifted the little towa around the waist and impaled her with a single stroke. Amber fluid tinged with orange towa blood gushed from the female, but then, with visible effort, he forced himself to stop, discarded the towa, and bound back into the hardel. His shoulder patches still glowed brightly.

Aghast, Elizabeth considered fleeing, but before she could move his strong hands squeezed her waist tightly. He lifted her as he had done to the towa. The remains of her dress fell aside. She squirmed and attempted to pry off the iron grip that imprisoned her. He drew back preparing to thrust. She dropped her hands over her groin, pushing the rough organ aside where it scraped the skin along her thigh. She bit her lip to keep from crying out and tried to twist free of his grasp. Warm blood trickled down her leg from the gash a mere brush had inflicted.

"Wait. There's no need to be rough," she pleaded. "You don't want to hurt me." Elizabeth looked into his eyes, but the intelligence was gone. What remained was entirely animal. She reached down searching for the knife, trying to ward off his member at the same time. The penis was slick from the towa's fluid and her own blood. She tried to give him pleasure, but ended up tearing the skin on her palm releasing even more blood. Wincing with pain, she grabbed at the phallus trying to maintain some contact and at the same time deflect his jabbing. It bent easily at the bump.

Loeton gasped in delight. She bent it again and Loeton began to moan. He released his grip on her. This was the way, she thought. Now she might be able to control him, but with a powerful hand to her chest he knocked her onto her back. He bent his head into her crotch and sniffed, then forced her hands aside to feel her, to open her. His hand touched her alien softness and for a moment he paused.

Elizabeth took advantage of his hesitation and with all her strength she twisted, pushing him over. Then, with one hand, she grabbed him again and resumed bending. With her free hand she searched between the cushions for the knife. Her fingers closed around the hilt. Suddenly, he grabbed her hips and once again lifted her above him, preparing to penetrate her. She clenched her thighs together tightly. She had to kill him now before she lost the struggle, but his eyes were wide open and he stared at her coldly. Only a single quick slice across the monster's neck would guarantee his immediate death, but from this angle, with those thick arms in the way, he would see the knife coming. She hid the knife low at her side avoiding his thrusts, staring at those eyes, waiting. With each movement his tapered member tore a new gash into her flesh. Suddenly his eyes closed and he convulsed violently. She lost her balance and fell across him. The tip of his organ raked across her outer lips and she screamed in pain as he exploded onto her stomach. She looked up at his face. His eyes were pinched shut.

Now, he's going to die, she thought and raised herself from his chest. His seed dripped into her bleeding crotch. She began to lift the blade just as Sy Hone burst through the door. In the distance, a loud alarm bell was tolling.

Mas

The knife had barely risen past her thigh when Elizabeth let it drop unseen between the pillows at her side. Sy Hone froze, staring at Elizabeth's naked body straddling his spent master. Suddenly modest in the pytor's presence, she crossed her arms over her breasts, and slid off, making sure the bodyguard did not regard her as a danger to the defenseless figure it was his duty to protect. The sounds of clashing metal mixed with the alarm drifted through the open doorway. There could only be one explanation and Elizabeth's heart sank. Jasin and Mas were now fighting for their lives.

Confused as to where his duty lay, Sy Hone spun around to leave, but then hesitated, turned, and took a step back toward the hardel, shifting his gaze between Loeton to Elizabeth. Blood dripped down her legs from various scrapes and gashes. Her groin burned, but she had survived, unfortunately, so had Loeton. Suddenly, the sound of battle stopped and she grew terrified. As long as she heard the clash of weapons, she knew Jasin was still alive.

It took only seconds for the alarm to roust Sy Loeton from the nest of cushions. His closed pelvic folds revealed no sign of his recent activities. Without even a glance in her direction he and Sy Hone rushed into the corridor. Elizabeth hurried to retrieve her crumpled dress, and with a wince, tied her knife against her bleeding thigh.

Beneath the giant tree in the arboretum, a towan lunged, trying to impale Jasin, but he easily avoided the sharp tip of the crude sword and escaped to the other side of the thick trunk, using it as a shield. The native circled the tree in pursuit and Jasin bolted towards the wide hallway nearby, easily outdistancing the slower towan. His legs and arms felt heavy. This had been Loeton's third servant he had encountered, and by far the least skilled. The first had sliced a long cut across his abdomen before Jasin had subdued him, and while it didn't hurt terribly, it bled profusely. Now that the alarm had been sounded, he was sure he didn't have much time left to find and dispatch Loeton. Li Sy hadn't been clear about the distance between the large atrium and wives' quarters where her surveillance told them he would be found.

He ran as fast as he could with the clumsy, heavy sword he had carried from the Kull. There wasn't any reason to save his strength. This was a one-way trip; he was just hoping to take Loeton with him. The peace would still be restored. Humans would figure that Avram's crazy son had avenged his father's death, his mother's abduction, and the murder of the Bistounian woman. The Sytonians would have Jasin's death as payment for Loeton's murder...if he were successful. Without the need to think beyond the next few minutes, clarity and peace pervaded his being.

Two more towans emerged from a room just ahead. He raised the sword over his head and ran towards them, hoping they would scatter, leaving him to find Loeton. Then, he recognized the imposing towan. It was Loeton, and his brainless pytor.

Sy Hone pushed Loeton aside and stepped forward. Jasin wanted no part of the pytor. Unwilling to waste his life killing a mere bodyguard, he extended his weapon and lunged forward, trying to pass. Sy Hone feigned leaning away, bending his two far legs, but thrust out his third leg out for the reckless human to trip over. Jasin fell, driving his face into the floor; his crude weapon slid out of reach. Instantly, Loeton knelt down on the back of Jasin's neck to kill him.

"Wait!" Sy Hone yelled. Loeton looked up at his pytor bewildered. "We need him alive to answer a few questions. Then we'll kill him."

"Kill me now," Jasin rasped in Sytonian. "I won't answer any of your foolish questions."

"What questions?" asked Loeton.

"The others have stolen the old human female. He probably knows where they have taken her," explained Hone, picking up Jasin's weapon.

"What others?" When Sy Hone wasn't able to answer, Loeton repeated his query, but obviously Sy Hone didn't have an answer. Loeton stood and kicked Jasin in the ribs. "You answer. Where is my wife?"

"Your wife!" exploded Jasin. "How dare you abduct a woman without consent and call her your wife."

Although Elizabeth couldn't understand, she listened to Jasin's brave outburst from the wives' chamber, ready to join the fight if needed. Her heart swelled with gladness that he still lived. She pulled the tiny stiletto from beneath her shift and peeked out. Thankfully, it didn't look like they were about to kill him, and then seeing Sy Hone holding a tremendous sword, she suddenly felt silly. She drew back and hid the small knife. One day she'll use it to cut their throats, she promised herself, but not now. Her time would come.

"Bind and lock him up," demanded Loeton. "Then I want you to go and find the old woman. There are still questions about the machine in the lake that she may be able to answer. She was there from the beginning, when their deception began."

"What machine?" asked Jasin, attempting to rise.

In reply Loeton kicked him again. "You're the last one I need to give answers to. You have violated enough Prohibitions to warrant death, and when we find your mother, she will watch you die." He walked off leaving Sy Hone alone with Jasin.

Instinctively Elizabeth began to move into the hallway. Two against one, these were probably the best odds they'd have. Neither Hone nor Jasin were looking in her direction.

She inched forward. The towan squatted next to Jasin, flipped him over and laid the massive blade across Jasin's neck immobilizing him. Blood flowed from the slice across his abdomen as the towan examined the parted flesh, running the double thumbs of his left hand along the weeping edges. Jasin groaned. With increasing pressure the pytor spread the wound and then violently thrust his fingers into the gash. Jasin screamed and passed out. Elizabeth froze. Sy Hone raised his blood soaked hand to his nostrils, and at the same time sensing Elizabeth's presence, he turned to stare at her, daring her to attack.

The odds were no longer in their favor. Elizabeth stepped back. Seemingly disappointed, Sy Hone wiped his bloody fingers on Jasin's cheek, then dragged the unconscious human to his feet and heaved him over his shoulder. Without even a glance towards Elizabeth, the towan carried Jasin away.

A few minutes later, his arms tied behind his back and ankles bound, Jasin was thrown into a reeking cylith pen, where he fell among freshly severed styke limbs, his mouth and nose barely above the animal remains and other kitchen scraps.

Several cyliths stood silently gnawing and crunching bones not three meters away. Jasin groaned and rolled to his back. Disoriented and nauseous, it took several minutes before he fully came to. Failure inundated his spirit. All he could hope for now was a merciful death, but he knew Sy Loeton and his bastard pytor would keep him alive if they thought he could answer their questions. What were they asking? Did he know about the machine in the lake? No...but he knew of the machines in the Kull. He had a few questions about that himself.

Jasin struggled to slip his hands under his legs. Searing waves of pain tore through his abdomen forcing him to pause several times in order to catch his breath. The leather straps dug into his wrists, turning his fingers numb, but he soon managed to bring his bloodied wrists to his mouth where he chewed at the filthy knots until his hands were free. The cyliths approached cautiously, smelling his alien blood.

Jasin found a severed leg and tossed it to them. Satisfied, they attacked it instead. While he unbound his ankles, Jasin searched the pen for an escape. Should he try for Loeton again? Without the element of surprise, he doubted another attempt would be any more successful. He surveyed the cylith enclosure. He wasn't going anywhere.

At least Mas and Li Sy had gotten Julian out, and by now, they should have left Fistulee. Without provisions, returning through the Kull was unthinkable. Jasin figured the only route left was towards the logging camps at the head end of the lake near the black rocks where the steepest wall of the gorge nearly touched the shore. They had planned to head towards Mt. Kaysop first to avoid the heavily traveled Low Pass, but now that was up to Mas.

He looked at the cyliths and the raw meat. He was embarrassed to feel hunger instead of revulsion. His empty stomach ached from days of neglect, but would the animals allow him to eat any of their food? With a winch he brushed grime from his stomach. Blood oozed from the wound. The cyliths looked up from their feast, and prudently, he covered the damage with his tattered shirt. It probably wasn't wise to challenge the animals for their food. It was best if they were sated.

Elizabeth walked over to the atrium's miniature creek that wound its way past the immense tree and let the cool water soothe her sore feet. She had already looked for Jasin nearly everywhere she was allowed. A different approach would be necessary. Wading in deeper, she lifted her soiled skirt and squatted to relieve the burning and gently wash herself. What she wouldn't give for a bath and a bar of soap. Her hair was a tangled mess. The oppressive heat of Fistulee was causing her to perspire constantly. It hadn't bothered Loeton, who appeared to enjoy her pungent smell, but she couldn't stand herself. She left the refreshing stream to search for Loeton. Following behind several young towan, she found him surrounded and talking to over a dozen males. She waited patiently until they dispersed.

"You left me so suddenly," Elizabeth began. "Didn't I please you?"

Loeton pretended to ignore her and walked briskly away.

Elizabeth kept pace. "What's wrong? Did I hurt you?"

Loeton whirled around. "Hurt me! While I wasted my fifth seed, your master's son stole my wife. Whatever you felt you owed me is repaid. Leave now and do not speak of the hardel to anyone. It was...unfortunate."

"How do you know it was Jasin who stole Julian away, did you see him? Is he here?" She took the chance that Loeton would accept her apparent ignorance.

"Jasin Elstrada was captured. He will be executed tomorrow, when Julian is returned." Loeton impatiently turned to go.

Elizabeth struggled to keep the conversation alive. "He was once a friend of mine. May I speak to him before you kill him?"

The native turned back and stared at her. "You say a friend? You shared a hardel with him?"

Elizabeth blushed. "He was not that kind of friend," she lied, hoping to minimize the importance of the meeting.

"That is too bad," said Loeton, "because if you were a true friend you might be able to convince him to tell us where his companions have taken your master."

"I know him well enough to tell you he would rather die than help you re-capture his mother."

"Then he will die."

The conversation had taken a poor turn. "You are right, but before I leave...before he dies, I would like to say goodbye. It is one of our traditions."

"Tomorrow I will allow it, but only if you promise not to ever speak of the hardel we shared."

The bold Loeton seemed almost intimidated by their illicit tryst. "Why, does it cause you embarrassment?"

"What is *embarrassment?*" he asked.

"Are you sorry that you have been in the hardel with me? Do you feel ashamed?"

"I do not understand these words...*embarrassment, ashamed*...they have no meaning."

Elizabeth struggled to explain the concept. "Haven't you ever done something that you regret later?"

"Again a nonsense word...*regret*...Why do anything you do not want to do?"

"Then tell me why you don't want me to speak of the hardel."

"Others will not understand. It is not customary to share your seed with another species," he tried to explain.

"You did not share your seed with me. The spilling of your seed was incidental, of little importance. I tried to bring you enjoyment. Pleasure also has value."

"Some would find it perverse."

"It harmed no one." The ache in her groin, however, screamed in opposition. "But some humans would also find it hard to accept. I will honor your request. I promise, it will remain between us."

Elizabeth walked back to the wives' quarters. Why had she defended their actions? Sexual gratification between species was perverse...wasn't it? But there had been mutual consent. Sex without consent was unacceptable no matter what the mix of species, so wouldn't the opposite, sex with mutual consent, no matter the mix, be acceptable?

But she was really just trying to kill him, to punish him for killing the girl, for killing Avram, to protect the ones she loved. Was killing under those circumstances also acceptable? She had a duty to protect them, to seek retribution. It was just strange—they could each rationalize killing each other, but their experience in the hardel was somehow an unspeakable sin. The other wives refused to look at her as she entered the large room. Obviously they thought so as well.

The next day, Elizabeth kept busy helping the kitchen towas prepare meals for Loeton's compound. It was easy, mindless work, and it helped pass the time. What would she say to Jasin? How he would react? At one point she had convinced herself that it would be better if he thought she were in Panvera, but if Julian had remembered to relay her message, he already knew she was here and wondering why she hadn't attempted to speak to him. Just before dimness closed in, Loeton finally sent for her.

"You will say your farewell and leave at the brightening," he instructed. He led her through an area of the estate that she had never seen. The compound's vastness struck her once again.

"How many live here?" she asked.

"My family numbers twenty-three towans," he replied.

"How many including the females and children?"

"I have never counted."

They left the building and entered an exterior courtyard filled with blooming flowers. They followed a winding path before coming to a locked animal stockade. A putrid stench assaulted them as Loeton opened the gate. Elizabeth froze. The cyliths growled at her and she instinctively stepped closer to Loeton.

Jasin looked up, but he couldn't believe what he was seeing. His heart seemed to stop and time slowed to a crawl. Elizabeth...here? And seeking protection from the one creature he hated most! He forced himself to breathe. This was absurd. Elizabeth was supposed to be safe in Panvera. He had been content to die, but now?

Elizabeth forced herself to ignore the animals and focused on Jasin. He was gaunt and filthy. His eyes were sunken with dark shadows beneath. His stomach and swollen lip were crusted in dried blood. She took a deep breath and ran to him.

"You look awful," she cried.

"What are you doing here," he whispered. "I don't understand..." He looked at her tattered, revealing dress and at the bloody stains. "Why?"

"Shhh..." She leaned closer and spoke so Loeton wouldn't overhear. "I can help. Follow my lead." She confronted Loeton bravely. "Why do you treat my master's son, your wife's son with such disrespect?"

Loeton snarled back, "He attempted to kill me. Would you have me bath him? He will die the same, clean or dirty. Say goodbye and then you may leave."

"You are afraid of this scrawny human?" said Elizabeth. Jasin scowled at her.

"Of course not. Nor am I afraid of the tiny insect that bites me, but they both will die."

Jasin couldn't contain himself, "Spoken like the murderer that you are."

"This is tiresome. I have answered to the Council, I don't have to answer to a human."

Jasin stood up and approached his enemy. "Yes you do! You murdered my father, murdered the girl in Bistoun, kidnapped my mother and..." he glanced at Elizabeth..." it looks like you've—"

"It looks like you should be more respectful." Elizabeth turned and slapped Jasin cheek hard, stopping him cold. "Loeton, you say you've answered to the Council? Did Sy Lang ask you about Bistoun?"

"It is none of your concern."

"This man accuses you of murder and you refuse to answer. If you have a defense he deserves to hear it before he dies."

"He deserves nothing."

Jasin backed off a step. "There is much trouble brewing between our races, Loeton. We believe you murder humans at will and will never be punished."

"I have killed no human. You will be the first. Your crimes and the crimes of your race are deliberate and are clearly in violation of the Prohibitions. You shall all be punished."

"Sy Loeton...respected sir," pleaded Elizabeth, "how have you answered the Council?"

"This is over," Loeton stated, and turned to go. "Come, you have had your opportunity to say goodbye."

Elizabeth grabbed his arm to try to hold him from leaving. He swatted at her face, but she recoiled. Losing her balance, she fell backward. Jasin lunged forward. "No!" she screamed, but Jasin jumped at Loeton, knocking the surprised towan to the ground, then fell on top of him, shoving his hands into the folds of Loeton's thick neck, searching for some way to strangle him. Loeton grabbed

Jasin's wrists and twisted them off his neck, then still holding them, he stood, lifting Jasin, and threw him towards the growling cylith who was coming to protect his master.

Had the beast been truly hungry, Jasin would have been mauled, but he had seen to it that they had all eaten well and the animal simply stood over him drooling thick, gooey saliva. Jasin rolled to his feet and helped Elizabeth up. Knowing he was defeated physically, he attacked by shouting in Sytonian.

"The reason you don't explain yourself is you can't. You are a guilty coward who hides behind the Council. Your entire race hides behind lies and deceptions. I have been in the Kull. I have seen the technology you pretend doesn't exist. I have seen thousands of your dead that you have left to rot.

"I acknowledge my crimes. I come here carrying weapons. I have tried to kill you. This is true. At least I have the courage to admit it and I'm willing to die defending the right of my people to seek justice for your crimes against us. You…you have no honor."

With that, Jasin turned his back to Loeton and walked to the cyliths and scratched them roughly behind the ears.

Elizabeth watched Loeton carefully. She wasn't sure what Jasin had said, but his final act appeared to shock the native.

"You accuse us of deception? It is you that have hidden technology. Humans have lied to us for thirty years."

Jasin ignored him, refusing to face him.

Elizabeth thought she knew Loeton's every mood, but she had never seen Loeton so confused and hesitant. He turned to Elizabeth and repeated his claim in Human. "It is you humans who are dishonorable. I have never lied. I didn't kill that girl. You must know that I couldn't have."

"And how am I to know that?"

"Are you not aware of how many septets have passed? Are you unable to do the simplest addition? How could I have assaulted the girl in the way you human's say? You must now be aware that the girl died between my cycles."

Elizabeth tried to figure the septets since the girl's murder.

"Two and a half," muttered Jasin, who turned to face Elizabeth. "How are you supposed to know his cycles?"

Elizabeth ignored him and faced Loeton. "That...that may the case, but everyone saw you kill Avram."

"Did you see?" Loeton asked Elizabeth, then to Jasin "Or you?"

Silence

"Your father's heart was sick. Everyone knew he was dying. Sy Toberry tried to warn him. Sy Lang tried to tell him. It was the keetah that killed your father. He fell into me and I struck his chest. His heart stopped. It might have stopped even before he stumbled. It would have happened eventually...if not that night, the next. There was nothing left of his heart."

Jasin's head swam in confusion. This couldn't be. Loeton was a monster and that was that. Loeton killed his father...

Suddenly a loud voice called out and Loeton bolted from the pen. "It's Sy Hone," said Elizabeth running after him. Jasin followed, hopeful that the towan had returned empty handed. A small crowd had gathered around Sy Hone and a long wooden cart. They pushed through. On the cart, the broken body of their friend Mas lay still. A few of the towa were touching his body.

"Stay away from him," cried Jasin, pushing them aside.

Elizabeth stopped him. "If anyone can help..."

"Can't you see? He's dead."

Elizabeth leaned over the limp body and put her ear close to his nose and mouth. "Not yet," she muttered.

Jasin began to tenderly lift him off the cart. Sy Hone stepped forward to help, and for a moment, their eyes made contact as they carried Mas inside where the little females began cleaning and caring for his wounds.

Sy Hone claimed to have found him nearly beaten to death on the foothills of the Kaysop range. Julian was missing. Sy Hone believed that whoever had attacked Mas had taken her and headed towards Bistoun along the edge of the Kull. He had returned alone with Mas while the rest of his team went on to see if they could find Julian.

"If he survives," said Jasin, "you will have saved his life. For that I thank you." He bowed his head in respect.

Sy Hone answered, "We are not without compassion. We are not killers."

"So I've been told," mumbled Jasin, turning away. There was nothing more he could do for his best friend. He left the huddle of busy towa and found a quiet spot to collapse. Sy Loeton assigned a towan to guard him. Jasin tried to focus, to think...who could have attacked Mas so viciously and what did they want with Julian? Was Loeton telling the truth? What was that nonsense about a machine in the lake? No single question stayed in his thoughts very long before another pushed it out. How many days had it been since he'd slept ...since he'd eaten? He couldn't remember. Like a sand pile in the rain, his mind was breaking down from exhaustion. He was supposed to be the one to die not Mas. Why was Elizabeth here? She should have listened...they were in trouble. Stay awake...think. But there was nothing left. Nothing. Then he slept.

Elizabeth watched the towas skillfully care for Mas. They spread their thick gritty paste—they called it keets— liberally over his jaw, as well as the bones in his left forearm, which appeared shattered. Swelling had caused his skull to become misshapen, indicating a massive concussion, so patches of the numbing mixture were applied to his eyes, just as they had done for her. They tore off what was left of his shirt revealing a puncture wound in his side. The attack had been violent and merciless. His assailants had meant to kill him.

Who could have wanted Julian so badly? Mas must have fought bravely, but even if he survived, it would be days, possibly weeks, before he would be able to tell them who had done this. She stared at his once handsome face, now bruised and broken almost beyond recognition. She kissed his forehead gently. "Be strong, don't give up," she whispered.

Elizabeth sat with Jasin, holding his sleeping head in her lap. Loeton and Hone stood apart, speaking quietly, occasionally glancing in the humans' direction. It was a disagreement, thought Elizabeth, as the intensity rose. Finally Loeton approached. He towered above them and demanded her attention. "Wake him. There is much to discuss."

She raised her head. "Not tonight, not here," she replied defiantly.

"Tomorrow he dies. Tonight we need him to answer questions."

"No, not tonight...tomorrow we will try to answer your questions, then together we will leave to find Julian. But tonight we rest."

Loeton knelt down and leaned forward until his face was nearly touching hers.

Locking eyes with the towan, she didn't flinch. With a strength that surprised her, she spoke with conviction. "He has lost his father, his mother, and now his best friend lies dying. All he wanted, all he wants is to keep the peace between our races. His attempt to kill you was a foolish mistake, but you haven't been harmed in anyway. If, as you claim, no human has died by your hand then why begin now? What do you gain with Jasin's death?"

When Loeton failed to answer, she pushed on. "You claim there is something important in the lake which proves humans have deceived you. Jasin claims you have hidden your advanced technology in the Kull. You are right. There are many questions that need answers, but we won't get those answers by killing him." She broke her stare to look down at Jasin's thin body. Compared to Loeton, even to herself, he appeared so small and fragile. She tenderly brushed a long lock of hair from his gaunt face before looking up into the alien's stern eyes. "Must every insect that bites you die? Respectfully sir, I beg you, let this insect live."

Loeton stood, and uncharacteristically looked over at Sy Hone before answering, "I will consider your request. We will talk in the morning."

The towas covered the bowls of water and keets, then gathered the torches and departed with Loeton, leaving Sy Hone, and one small candle, to watch over the humans. For a few minutes, Elizabeth and Hone exchanged frigid stares. It was clear that Hone wanted the threat to his master eliminated immediately and couldn't understand Loeton's hesitation to cleanse the compound. Finally, Elizabeth decided that sleep would be more productive and she closed her eyes.

In the morning, she checked on Mas and then made a trip to the kitchen, returning with a tray of food. Before waking Jasin, who was snoring softly, she offered Sy Hone his choice. The pytor took several handfuls without a word. She took the remainder, sat next to Jasin, and began munching sweet melon. Jasin rolled to a different position and his snoring stopped. Elizabeth reached for another piece of fruit.

"Aren't you going to save any for me?" Jasin asked with a yawn.

"There's enough here to feed five, if Hone will allow you to have any," she replied.

"Let's not ask him then."

Elizabeth handed him a piece, which he devoured in a few bites. "Last night was like a bad dream," he said, reaching for more food. "I can't believe you're here. Why? What were you thinking? You must be crazy."

"No crazier than you." She smiled and moved closer. "I hitched a ride with some traders. You'd be dead if I hadn't."

"There's still time," Jasin smiled weakly, taking a couple quick bites. "How's Mas this morning?"

"The same. I doubt whether we'll know anything for a couple of days."

"He hasn't had anything to eat for nearly a week. We ran out of supplies long before reaching the mountains."

She glanced over at their friend's motionless form. "His jaw's busted up. He's not going to eat for awhile longer."

They sat looking at each other in silence until Jasin finally broke the silence. "I never thought I would be able to tell you how sorry I was for how I acted. I was sure—"

"You were awful."

"I was trying to—"

"I hated you." Elizabeth was shocked at how easily she could say that. She *had* hated him more than anything or anyone, still....

"And now?"

But before she could answer, Loeton's return interrupted them.

"Just let me talk to him, Jasin, or your death wish will be fulfilled," she whispered.

Loeton walked over to Hone and they exchanged a few words before approaching them. He spoke directly to Jasin. "There are many things you must tell us. Who is the man with the little boy on the cold shore of the lake?"

"He doesn't know them," Elizabeth began. "But I know them well, and I assure you, they will never talk to you. Take us there if you must, and I'll get some answers." Then Elizabeth paused, then asked, "If you didn't kill the girl in Bistoun, who do you think might have wanted it to look like you did?"

Loeton ignored her question. "Tell me about the machine in the lake. Who controls it? Why have you humans hidden it from us?"

Jasin butted in. "We know of no machine in any lake. Tell us about the vehicles in the Kull. Why did so many of you die there? Why do you pretend not to have advanced technology? Your Prohibitions demand that we have no technology beyond yours. Is it to keep us humans from developing? To keep us primitive until the old knowledge dies with our elders?"

Elizabeth shot Jasin a perturbed look, which he ignored.

"You may not know of the machine in the lake, but there are humans that do," replied Loeton.

"You may not want to speak about what we found in the Kull, but we now know the truth," Jasin countered.

Elizabeth tried to regain control. "There are many questions here. Some you can not, or do not want to address, but there are matters we can agree on."

Their silence gave her license to continue.

"Someone murdered a girl in Bistoun and made it look like you did it, Sy Loeton—someone that must be your enemy. Second, we don't know why Avram died. It could be that his heart gave out, as you believe. I agree. He wasn't feeling well the night of the party. But it is irrelevant; nothing can be done now. And finally, we all want to find Julian. Whoever took her from Mas must be our mutual enemy and they're either headed towards Bistoun, where the girl was killed or towards Lake Chook where you claim there's this machine. The answers to our questions are there, not here. We must leave immediately."

"And what of this...this *forn* that has tried to kill me, who carries weapons and trespasses in the Kull," said Loeton, addressing Elizabeth directly.

"This what?" she asked.

"Forn, it's a bug or insect," explained Jasin, irritated by the comparison.

Elizabeth smiled. The danger had passed. "You may have opportunity yet to swat the little forn, but for now he will be helpful. No one is more motivated to find our mutual enemy than he is."

Jasin was impressed at how well she handled the towan. She had been correct. Left on his own, he would most likely be dead already. "Then we should head for Bistoun as quickly as we can," he said.

"We will head for the lake," corrected Loeton.

Elizabeth quickly agreed, "Yes, of course...the lake." She looked firmly at Jasin to make sure he kept his mouth shut.

Sy Loeton

Sy Hone set a swift pace. His protective gaze never stopped sweeping the hot dusty landscape. He glanced behind at his master riding the largest of their blaythons and then beyond to the humans that sat in the blaython drawn cart bringing up the rear. By habit the pytor checked for his cylith that should have been keeping pace beside him, but all that accompanied either towan was their apprehension over leaving their beasts in Fistulee. The bodyguard did not like the level of control Elizabeth had over his master. The woman apparently feared the animals, but what did that matter? Sy Loeton was wrong to acquiesce to Elizabeth's demand that they travel without their cyliths. He put too much value in her supposed knowledge of the man and boy. Withholding the identity of the humans on the shore of the lake, gave Elizabeth and Jasin power they should not have. He would have forced them to give up the names. A few broken bones would have been sufficient.

The cart that carried Elizabeth and Jasin lurched relentlessly. Wedged between supplies, they leaned against each other for support. As the morning progressed, they fell farther and farther behind the two towans, hardly noticing as they shared their adventures of the last few weeks.

"This towa…it was her time?" asked Elizabeth, thoughtfully.

"By her song and according to Mas. Why?"

"Just interesting."

"If it wasn't for her, we'd never have made it through the mountains. After we found the golden syrup in the transportation depot, we thought our troubles were behind us. It fed her well enough, but the stuff made us both sick. She doctored the syrup with a plant tuber she found and mashed up. That settled our stomachs."

Elizabeth nodded. She had also gained an appreciation for the towa's medicinal expertise. "Where do you suppose...what was her name?"

"Li Sy"

"Where do you think this Li Sy is now?"

"No telling. I suspect she was with them during the attack. I think she's actually fond of Mas, so maybe she followed Hone back to Loeton's. Maybe she followed Julian. She's quite a free spirit."

"Unusual."

"Very," replied Jasin, who searched the terrain almost expecting to find the little towa. "We are falling behind."

Elizabeth shifted uncomfortably. Her groin still hurt and the bumpy cart ride was not helping. It was hard to believe the Sytonians gave up their rail system for carts and donkeys. "Why do you think they abandoned their technology?"

"I don't think they have. We have access to only a small part of this gorge. Maybe they use their technology lower down, past T'Matte where it is too hot for us. That's probably what makes Sy Loeton and the other local natives so angry. Their life here is a sham meant to deceive us into abandoning our own technology. When our parents take their scientific knowledge to their graves, the Sytonians will have nothing to fear from us and I'll bet we see a return of their own advanced way of life. The discomfort of one generation isn't a high price to eliminate the threat of domination by a more advanced race. Knowledge is perishable. If it isn't used, it's lost."

"That's quite a theory. Don't you think Avram, Hyland, and the others would have detected signs of their advanced technology from the ship? It's hard to believe they could have missed it."

Jasin thought about his father's continual efforts towards peaceful integration of their races; his insistence that we accept the Prohibitions; that his son become an Enforcer of those restrictions. If Avram knew, wouldn't he have negotiated differently? Probably not, Jasin realized. From what little he had been told, the technology from the ship was much more advanced than what they had discovered in the Kull. Avram must have understood that utilizing human technology would still have upset the balance of power. Humans would become feared and hated. If he was aware of their ruse, he accepted it as a necessary evil. Maybe it was even his idea to begin with.

Jasin finally answered, "If any of the ship-born were aware or afraid, they never showed any sign."

"Until now…"

"The machine in the lake."

Elizabeth nodded and wiped perspiration from her forehead. "It seems to be getting awfully warm. Aren't we heading up?"

Jasin nodded. "It's no warmer than it was this morning and in a few hours it will be much cooler. You know…my father told me that dozens of people saw Hyland destroy the last shuttle. It burned and sank. I've heard the story from other people who were there."

"But now it suddenly appears and they immediately start asking questions about Jorge and the boy." Anxiety churned inside her. Elizabeth turned to look away, not wanting Jasin to see her fear. She took a deep breath burying the anxiety she felt, steeling herself. She'd protect the boy, even if that dimwit of a father couldn't.

"We don't know what they saw," said Jasin.

"What else could it have been?"

They made camp at the Low Pass, at the very spot Hone had found Mas. Perhaps in their haste to return to Fistulee, he had missed something the pytor explained then set off with Sy Loeton to scour the area for clues. A moment later their excited voices could be heard.

"Sounds like they found something," Jasin said. "What do you say we lay out our bedrolls away from the center of camp?"

With a weak smile she declined the veiled invitation. "If you don't mind, I think it's best...safer if we stay close together. You don't mind, do you?"

"Mind? The first night we have a chance to sleep together and you prefer a chaperone," Jasin complained weakly.

"I still don't know if I like you," she said with a smile. "I'm not feeling well and it's better if they don't know the extent of our relationship," Elizabeth tried to explain.

"Why?" His attention now totally focused on her. Was she punishing him or was there something else he was missing?

It was a simple question, but she wasn't going to answer. She walked away towards a secluded spot behind a group of boulders that the natives had used earlier to squat. Only human males, it appeared, could stand. Her urine smelled peculiar and she burned. Finished, she turned and noticed a small patch of fragrant, purple flowers that had broken through the infertile soil to blossom in the protection of the rocks. She stooped down to take in their wonderful bouquet and admire the delicate filigree. A few of the thin stems had been broken and the heads were missing. Someone...or something had already picked several of the small buds. She followed suit putting an aromatic sprig in her hair. After a day on the trail behind a repulsive beast, the blossom's perfume was heavenly. Suddenly she felt watched. She spun around to find the two towan. They were sniffing the air.

"They're beautiful, don't you think?" she asked, indicating the flowers.

Hone walked over to where she had urinated and bent over to smell. After a few unintelligible words to Loeton, he wandered away.

"You are with child?" Loeton asked.

"Of course not," Elizabeth exclaimed.

"Are you sure? You have the smell." He stared at the flower in her hair.

"I might have an infection. It is a small matter."

"What is infection?"

"I am hurt down where you rubbed me." She felt blood flow to her checks.

Unconcerned, he removed the flower from her hair and handed it to her, then he walked off to join Hone who was busy looking among the rocks and outcroppings.

Rejoining Jasin, Elizabeth plopped down.

"Where are our friends," he asked.

"Looking for something in the boulders."

"Li Sy. They won't find her." He noticed the flower she was holding.

"How do you know?"

"That they won't find her?"

"That that's what they're searching for. That she's even here." Elizabeth surveyed the surrounding terrain.

"They smelled her the minute we got here. That's what all the excitement was about earlier."

"Maybe they just smelled me. All us women smell alike to you men," she teased him. "Why won't they find her?" unsure of the source of his conviction.

"She's too smart and too fast, and she's not about to be caught by Loeton again."

"Again?"

"I'm not sure, but I believe Li Sy was his fifth wife," explained Jasin.

Elizabeth blushed at the thought, although she had begun to suspect it herself. "How do you know?"

"She seemed to imply as much in the Kull. All I know for sure is that she fears him. It is an insult to leave your towan and she's afraid to be punished."

Elizabeth thought for a moment. "Then why would she stick around here to be caught?"

"This is where Mas was hurt, where Julian was taken, and where we were sure to return. Li Sy is smart."

"So why is she still here?"

"In her own strange way, I think she's loyal to us, or at least to Mas, and she's most likely hungry. And maybe…Mas wasn't the only one injured during the attack."

Elizabeth raised the flower she was holding to her nose, taking in the pleasing aroma. A milky sap oozed from the broken stem and she put the bud aside. Remembering the other broken flowers, she was now sure that Li Sy had been the one to pick them. Loeton may have noticed them as well.

The next morning, Loeton informed them that after passing through the Low Pass they would head immediately for the logging camps, and then around the lake to find and interrogate the man and the little boy he had seen watching the shuttle rise from the water. Although Elizabeth and Jasin tried, no amount of arguing or pleading could persuade him to follow the path to Bistoun, the direction Jasin and Elizabeth were convinced Julian had been taken. It made no sense to them that Julian would be abducted and taken towards the human enclave of Lake Chook, but Loeton, having different priorities, all but ignored their suggestions. So, after a small snack of salted styke meat and fantale, they resumed their trip. Once again the towans took the lead, leaving the cart to bring up the rear. This time Jasin purposely held their blaython back until some distance separated them from the towan.

Elizabeth scanned the boulders and rocks bordering the passage through the mountains, sure that Jasin was slowing to allow the towa time to track them. "Doesn't look like she's going to join us."

"No?" Jasin leaned back and lifted the cloth protecting the supplies. Out popped a little round face covered in grime. Elizabeth was sure it was the same dirty face she had almost collided into outside Loeton's kitchen. "Elizabeth, this is Li Sy."

"I believe we've already met. It is good to make your acquaintance."

Li Sy ignored her completely and immediately asked Jasin, "Mas lives?"

"Mas lives, but he's very hurt and unable to travel. Tell us what happened," he replied.

The towa reached underneath the tarp and took a large sweet melon from the pack. She took several incredibly large mouthfuls, while Jasin and Elizabeth waited patiently. In-between bites she glared at Elizabeth.

"I don't think she likes me," Elizabeth observed.

"She doesn't even know you," Jasin said.

"You are fifth wife," blurted out Li Sy.

"You mean to say, 'Li Sy is fifth wife,'" corrected Jasin.

"No!" Li Sy stated firmly, then pointed at Elizabeth, "This human is Loeton's fifth. She shared the hardel. All towas know. They will never say, but Li Sy will say...this is Loeton's wife."

Jasin's mouth hung open. He couldn't believe what he was hearing—Elizabeth in Loeton's hardel. Li Sy couldn't be mistaken. It wasn't as if Elizabeth could be confused with any other female in Loeton's compound. He turned to Elizabeth. "What does she mean?"

Elizabeth was furious. They were well on the way towards repairing their relationship and in a single blow this...this small piece of... "How dare you suggest I acted as Loeton's fifth wife, you little—"

"You were his fifth."

"Is she saying you...you slept with Loeton? You acted as his wife?" asked Jasin in a stunned whisper.

Elizabeth ignored Jasin and grabbed the towa's arm. "You don't—"

Li Sy raked the nails of her free hand across the offending arm and Elizabeth let go. Blood dripped from the three slashes. "Never grab Li Sy. Never hold Li Sy. Li Sy is free towa," She snarled.

"I'm sorry," croaked Elizabeth, holding her bleeding arm. "I didn't mean to harm you, but you don't understand what you are saying."

"Maybe you don't understand," countered Li Sy.

"Well, I'm sure I don't," added Jasin. "Why were you in the hardel with Loeton?"

Elizabeth hesitated, but Li Sy was quick to answer. "To receive Loeton's seed. It is the only reason to be in the hardel."

Jasin shook his head in disbelief, but he remembered the first time he saw them together, how she stood close to him...her ripped and stained dress. Why didn't she want to sleep with him last night? Li Sy had no reason to lie...yet how could any of this be true?

Elizabeth turned to Jasin and pleaded. "You have to understand and believe me. I was in the hardel to kill him. I seduced him to make him vulnerable, so I could kill him."

Jasin was repulsed. "You let him touch you? What were you thinking? How in the world were you going to kill him? With sex?"

Rage ignited within her. "No...with this." And in one fluid movement, she grabbed the hidden knife and brought it to within a whisker of Jasin's throat. Jasin fell backward into the cart, nearly on top of the little towa. "And I got a lot closer than you did." She spat the words out in anger, grabbed the reins Jasin had dropped, and turned her back on them both.

For several minutes, there was silence. Jasin stayed in the back of the cart gathering his thoughts, while Li Sy stared at Elizabeth's strong back in shocked respect. Eventually, Jasin meekly climbed next to Elizabeth. Tears were rolling down her cheeks and she refused to look at him. She had hoped he would never learn of the hardel. Handling his normal jealousy was difficult enough, but giving pleasure to his enemy was probably unforgivable, no matter what the reason. It was Li Sy who finally broke the silence.

"You are brave...stupid and brave. Loeton is unlucky with fifth wives." Then she made a light gurgling sound as if something were caught in her gullet. Both Jasin and Elizabeth turned back, afraid that she was choking, but found Li Sy flapping her arms. She was obviously fine and they laughed with her.

It took two days for the small band to travel around the lake and each time as they prepared to stop, Li Sy would scurry away and hide until they once again broke camp and departed. Then she would find a spot to slip back onto the cart. The first time Li Sy was forced to leave, she had brought back a handful of the fragrant rock flowers and squeezed the milky juice from their stems over the inflamed slashes on Elizabeth forearm. Within hours the redness was gone and the slight swelling reduced. Elizabeth thanked her profusely and asked that she bring back more next time, secretly hoping it would have a similar therapeutic effect elsewhere. Li Sy seemed to understand, bringing not only the milky stems, but also a foul tasting root she insisted that Elizabeth chew. Both brought relief.

Finally upon arriving in Lake Chook, Loeton turned to Elizabeth and demanded, "You know of this man and boy. You will find them for me."

Elizabeth hesitated. She dreaded the confrontation between Jorge and Loeton. "There are many little boys in Lake Chook, and most of them have fathers or uncles. How can you possibly expect me to know which you saw from across the bay?"

"We're all wasting time here," said Jasin. "If there is a machine in the lake as you claim, it is not going anywhere. Meanwhile, my mother's abductors are getting away. If it will hasten our departure for Bistoun, I'll tell you where to find a man with a young boy myself."

Elizabeth shot him a disgusted look. "What difference does it make?" Jasin asked her. "They can be found easily enough without our help." She had to admit Jasin was right. Stalling would only have delayed the inevitable and aggravated Loeton. Perhaps it was safer for Jorge and the boy if they accommodated Loeton.

It was late afternoon when they arrived at the Wynosk's home. She looked forward to giving Wilem a hug and retrieving fresh, warmer clothes from the chest in her old room. She looked down at the frayed dress she had made from the coat lining weeks ago. It had sufficed, but a few more days on the trail and she was sure it would disintegrate.

They tied the animals in the field across from the home where months earlier Jasin, Sy Toberry, and Beloit had camped. Elizabeth looked for signs of Wilem, but there was no sign of life anywhere.

They crossed the path that led down to the water, and headed for the small house. "Perhaps they're down near the water?" suggested Jasin. Loeton sent Hone to check.

"Probably preparing a meal," offered Elizabeth, as they got closer. "I think I can hear activity inside."

Suddenly from inside the cabin, a terrifying cry surprised them. Elizabeth reacted fastest and leapt up the steps and charged through the doorway. Strapped to a chair by bands of blue-green metal sat Jorge, his face contorted in hideous pain. A glowing energy halo emanated from a wire band that enveloped his forehead. Sweat poured down his cheeks, mixing with the blood that dripped from his ears. Behind him stood an abnormally diminutive towan, busy adjusting a complex machine that hummed with power. Seconds later Jasin entered the room, followed by Sy Loeton.

"Stop that!" screamed Elizabeth. The little native quickly scooped up a fat rod from beside the device and pointed it at Elizabeth who drew her knife from her inner thigh. Loeton jumped in front of her just as a flash of purple energy burst from its tip. The blast knocked the native back against Elizabeth, sending them both to the floor. Jasin froze as the rod was pointed at him. The strange towan reached over and made a quick adjustment to his machine. Jorge screamed. His jaw twisted as his facial muscles contracted in a spasm. His eyes bulged, threatening to pop from their sockets.

"Daddy!" screamed Wilem emerging from behind the curtain of Elizabeth's old room where he had been watching and hiding. He ran to his father.

Startled, the assailant spun and leveled his weapon at the little boy. Jasin jumped, smashing the small towan against his machine. The alien rolled to his feet and dashed out the door past Elizabeth who, in shock, cradled Loeton's head in her lap. His chest was blown open. Elizabeth and Jasin turned to Wilem and his father. The little boy was sobbing, clawing at the bands that bound his daddy's arms.

Jorge's breathing had become labored. Garbled sounds emerged from a twisted mouth struggling to speak one last time to his beloved son. Tears rolled down both their cheeks. Jasin turned to the machine, desperate to find some way to turn it off. Jorge struggled to touch his son. Violent spasms jerked his arms about like a berserk marionette, but he finally managed to grab hold of his son's tiny hands.

"Do something," Elizabeth pleaded, trying to free herself from Loeton's weight.

Not knowing what else to do, Jasin lifted the hateful machine above his head and sent it crashing to the ground. The halo of light around Jorge's head faded, the low hum ceased. He turned to find Jorge's lifeless eyes staring at him, and Wilem crying in his father's lap.

Sy Hone

Sy Hone squatted next to Loeton's body, eyes fixed on the charred remains of his master's highly decorated chest. The pytor recited a short phrase that Jasin, busy removing the restraints from Jorge's arms, could not understand. Elizabeth held Wilem, gently diverting his eyes from his father's distorted face. Wilem began to shake and Elizabeth realized she too was starting to tremble.

"Let's go outside," she signed, and led him past Loeton's corpse and Sy Hone, who continued to mumble unintelligibly. They sat on the porch; Wilem nestled between Elizabeth's knees. A lake breeze played with her long hair, blowing it into the boy's face. The boy moved away and turned to face her. "You look different," his hands moving between sniffles.

She replied, her hands stiff and clumsy from lack of practice, "So do you. You're getting big." She tied her hair into a knot.

"Daddy didn't do anything wrong." He rubbed his nose on the back of his wrist. "That…that thing on his head. It hurt him so bad, but he didn't tell. My daddy wouldn't tell that little guy anything. I don't understand."

She hugged him. How could she explain something she didn't understand herself? It had all happened so fast. What was that machine? It certainly confirmed what Jasin had been saying about hidden technology.

Wilem hesitantly approached the door of the house and looked back inside. Jasin had finished freeing Jorge from his restraints, but the boy wasn't looking at his father's body. "Their guts ain't red like ours," he said, his hands mechanically echoing his strange little voice.

"Come, let's let them finish. They don't need a..." Elizabeth's struggled to remember the sign for "audience". She settled for finger spelling "crowd" into the palm of the boy's hand. "Do you understand?" she asked. The boy nodded.

They walked down the path until they came to the shore. Sunlight glimmered off the crests of the waves. Wilem stood quietly next to Elizabeth. She played with his unkempt hair. It hadn't been cut in months; it wasn't something Jorge would have thought to do.

"It was strange looking," he said, moving away from her touch. "I've never seen a towan that small. Maybe it was one of their girls. I hear they're little."

"No, it wasn't a towa."

"How'd you know?"

"I know."

Nor was it a young towan, she thought. Its collar ridge and shoulder patches were mature and well developed. But it wasn't a normal towan either—a midget then. She had been taught about human midgets and dwarfs in school. Loeton's blood had dried on her arms, and she knelt at the water's edge and washed. She stood and shook the water from her arms, then crouched down and faced Wilem so he could read her lips. "Wilem...did you and your Daddy ever just stand here, along the shore, and look at stuff out in the water?

"Looked at Grandpa, remember? Grandpa always said this was a special spot."

"Of course, but I mean afterward, a few weeks ago, during the long darkness, during Rhan-da-lith."

The boy was silent. He looked down at his feet. "Look! It made tracks. Maybe we can hunt it down?"

Avoiding the question, she thought, but she looked down, and saw what Wilem had discovered—a trail of clearly defined tracks leading directly from the end of the path straight into the water. Actually, there were two sets, she observed. The other, a much deeper set, about ten meters farther down, led from the water. She scanned the horizon unsuccessfully for a boat. Only a random gilia head floated nearby. She turned back to the boy. It would be the perfect time to raise the subject of the machine in the lake, "The footprints lead into the water. Do you know what's down there?"

Wilem shook his head.

"Wilem?" She looked at him sternly.

"I'm not allowed to say. Daddy said it is a secret."

"Well then, you don't have to tell me what the secret is, but can you tell me whose secret it is? How many people know the secret?"

He hesitated, eyes in constant motion, as if he would discover the answer there on the shore. "It's my secret now," he whispered, barely able to speak.

"Maybe the little towan knew about your secret. Maybe that's where he swam to."

He walked towards the water's edge and looked out over the waves. "No one knows, 'cept me."

How she wished that was true. The waves splashed at their dirty feet. She tried a different tack. "Does the machine in the lake work?"

"I'm not supposed to talk about it," he said defiantly.

"A secret is sometimes best if you share it with a friend, like your Dad did with you." She hoped that mentioning Jorge would open him up and was surprised when Wilem turned and yelled at her.

"Why should I tell you? You're not really part of the family. You don't get to know about it. You'll just leave again. Women always leave. They can't be trusted."

It was Jorge talking; something she was sure the boy had picked up, but it was true. Poor Wilem, from his perspective, women *were* always leaving. "I won't leave you. You'll have to come with us and we'll take you to find your mother?"

"Then you'll leave…" When she didn't deny it, he ran back up the path.

Elizabeth turned to follow him, watching his little behind scoot up the path. That didn't go so well, she thought. He used to tell me everything. Then she paused...and turned back to gaze at the water. This *was* a special spot. The ship-born had gathered here to watch Hyland destroy the shuttle; they gathered here to witness his cremation; and that night, Jasin had joined her here, igniting a flame that she feared was now in danger of being extinguished. A week ago, natives claimed to see the shuttle reappear here. Today, some dwarf towan, killing twice and using technology unlike anything she had ever seen, had disappeared beneath this same cold water, colored now by the yellow-green light of Conboet. Bright multi-colored sparks reflected off the ripples and waves that rolled across the surface of the lake; a surface that hid the answers to Loeton's questions...her questions now.

Sy Loeton—an enigma to be sure. Cruel and arrogant, but he had saved her life, a chivalrous act from one who despised humans. I just hope Jasin doesn't make a big deal about it, she thought, as she followed Wilem back up the narrow path to the small, mud-brick dwelling that had seen so many deaths the last few months.

Dimness had settled in by the time they finished burying Jorge. Jasin and Elizabeth left Wilem sitting by the grave and helped Sy Hone carry Loeton's heavy body to the cart, laying it alongside the supplies with his three feet dangling off the end. Jasin retrieved the machine that had killed Jorge and lashed it to the side of the cart. The pytor refused to help, preferring to squat and stare off intently off into the surrounding brush.

Elizabeth returned to the house and entered what had been her space behind the curtains. She was overwhelmed with the desire to draw them closed, lie down, and sleep. The thought of shutting off the outside world for a few hours was delicious, but she was sure her sleep would be troubled by the haunting scene she had just left—of Wilem, tears staining his dirty cheeks, separated from his beloved father by a meter of dirt.

They would need to leave this troubled house tonight. She knelt down and pulled from her chest several pairs of pants, a couple of blouses, some undergarments, and quickly changed. From outside, she could hear Sy Hone bellowing and Jasin trying to talk to him. She silently chided herself for not taking the time to learn Sytonian, and gathered her remaining clothes and tossed them into a drawstring bag. Before leaving, she tried brushing her tangled hair. Realizing that it would take longer than a few minutes to unsnarl all the knots, she threw the brush into the bag, and with one last look around to insure she wasn't forgetting something she might need, turned, and joined the others.

"He wants to know where Li Sy is," Jasin informed her as she approached. "Her scent is all over the cart and he is demanding she show herself."

Elizabeth shrugged, then whispered, "Why should she? I wouldn't."

But just then, the little towa peeked her head out from her hiding place in the brush, and never taking her eyes off the pytor, quickly made her way across the field and cowered between the two humans. Sy Hone lumbered over and soon the air was filled with deafening argument.

Wilem came running, but when he saw the small native he froze.

"It's ok," yelled Elizabeth, knowing he had mistaken Li Sy for the midget towan that had murdered his father. "She's a friend." Wilem joined them cautiously.

"What are they saying," he asked.

"She's glad Loeton's dead. I don't think Sy Hone agrees," reported Jasin. He turned and confronted Hone. "I think it's time you explained a few things. What or who was that creature and what in the world was he doing with that thing?" Jasin pointed at the broken machine he had fastened to the side of the cart.

"I saw no creature. I came back up the path when I heard the loud blast," Sy Hone replied.

Li Sy stepped out from between their legs and jabbered at Hone. When Hone didn't reply, she turned to Jasin and spoke in Human. "Sy Hone saw. It almost ran into him on the path. Li Sy saw."

"Then you answer the questions," Jasin demanded of Li Sy.

Li Sy struggled with how to answer. She turned to Hone, who ended the conversation, "No, it is not possible for us to answer." He turned and began to walk away.

"That's not good enough," shouted Jasin, stepping forward to grab the retreating towan's arm. Hone spun and struck out, but Jasin was ready for the reaction and avoided a blow that would have surely broken his arm.

"It is finished. We will not speak of this. It is not allowed," the native declared.

"Not allowed by whom?" Jasin shot back.

"Only the Council may answer questions such as these. We will return Loeton to his family and his cylith, and then, if you still desire, I will ask Sy Lang to decide what is appropriate.

The narrow path around the lake squeezed between the shore and the nearly vertical cliffs that fell thousands of meters from the lip of the frozen surface of Syton. Travel was treacherous and the footing slick from the torrents that splashed off the intermediate rocky shelves and tumbled from the stone ledges. Here, more than any other spot in the gorge, you could feel the fierce storms on the tortured surface.

As the small party approached a black rock formation on the far side of the narrow trail, a blanket of snow and ice crystals momentarily enveloped them before a blast of warmer air transformed the miniature blizzard into a cold shower.

Sy Hone complained, speaking fondly of his warmer childhood village on the outskirts of T'Matte, where he and Loeton were raised.

With Jasin translating, Sy Hone continued. Living in the shadow of the Great Council, tradition and honor were held in high regard. Becoming Loeton's pytor was his greatest accomplishment and he now worried that his failure to protect him would lead to disgrace, not just for him, but for his entire clan. As the towan reminisced, his normal gruff manner warmed and he became quite loquacious.

One evening, while they camped to accommodate the human's need for sleep, Sy Hone showed them ragged scars on his middle haunch. Wilem, who had lost most of his fear of the Sytonians, approached the towan for a better look. With difficulty, Sy Hone related how, in his fifteenth year, as an initiate, he and his mentor, Sy Toberry, traveled to the cold high country and almost lost his life stealing his cylith pup from under the watchful eyes of its ferocious parents. If it weren't for Toberry, he would have bled to death.

Disturbed, Elizabeth excused herself and moved away. Jasin didn't even seem to notice. Sometimes he could be most uncaring, she thought. It was Li Sy that joined her.

"Bad?" asked the towa.

"What is bad?"

"Hone's leg...it is bad to see...yes?"

Elizabeth smiled. "Yes, it is ugly."

"Ugly...this word sounds like the leg looks. UG...ly." She accentuated the first syllable. "Ugly is ugly word."

Elizabeth turned away from the group and tried unsuccessfully to shut out the sound of Hone's voice. He was explaining that the Initiate is duty bound to provide for his cylith for the rest of its life. It is unusual for a cylith to outlive its master—like Loeton's beast— but in those rare circumstances, traditionally, a towan's last act would be to provide a feast for his animal.

"But he's dead," complained Wilem.

There was a brief silence, then Jasin asked Hone in the native's language, "Are you saying that we are returning Loeton's body so it may be eaten by his cylith?"

"As a reward for being faithful," confirmed Hone.

Disgusted, Jasin turned, finally realizing Elizabeth had left them...and then why. What a cad I am, he thought, and walked over to where Elizabeth lay scrunched up with her back to them. Wilem followed him.

"What did he say? How can Loeton feed his cylith when he's dead?" the young boy asked innocently.

"Go to sleep, Wilem," Jasin ordered, throwing him a bedroll. "It's just towan nonsense. We have a long way to travel tomorrow and Hone will wake us at first light"

Jasin lay next to Elizabeth, holding her close. "I'm sorry," he whispered."

"It's not your fault."

He leaned over and kissed her ear. "Of course it is. This is all my fault." She rolled over to face him. Jasin continued, "We should be back in Nova Gaia sleeping on mattresses and eating at Suzy's, watching fat Rahfi sweat on our meals."

She wrinkled her nose, then reached up and touched his whiskered cheek. "You need a shave."

"What I need is a kiss."

She smiled and kissed his forehead.

"Is that the best you can do?"

"We have an audience," she said, lifting her head towards the towa.

"It's ok," Jasin replied with a smirk, "she already thinks you're a tramp."

In her heart Elizabeth knew he meant it as a joke, but it hurt to hear him say it aloud. She turned away so he didn't see the pain it caused.

"I didn't mean that seriously. It was just a joke." He stroked her hair. "I'm sorry. Again, I'm sorry. I can't seem to say the right things." He cuddled closer, touching her lightly with his arm on her hip, and was relieved when she took his hand from her thigh and held it tightly, drawing it close to her heart, wrapping his arm around her. They lay quietly, finding a precious moment of peace, and tried to shut out the rest of the world. But it was impossible and they each lay there lost in their own inner turmoil.

"Do you think they're still alive?" Elizabeth finally asked in a whisper.

"I don't know about Mas…he's pretty strong, but…I just don't know. I'm pretty sure they'll keep Mom alive until they get what they want."

"What's that?"

He shook his head slightly. "I keep coming back to the shuttle and the little towan. He was trying to get something from Jorge—probably something about the old machine. Maybe they think, because of her age, that Julian knows something about it. She was there when it was supposedly destroyed."

"According to Wilem, its existence is something of a family secret"

Jasin nodded in the darkness. "That makes sense. I don't think either Mom or Dad knew anything about it. Avram wouldn't have allowed the ruse and Mom usually agreed with him on things like that. I think that's probably good for her now—she can't tell what she doesn't know. If she did know something and was forced to tell, she wouldn't be worth keeping alive." He paused, then asked, "What do you make of the dwarf?"

Elizabeth shifted her weight and rolled onto her back. "Midget, I think. The head looked almost normal for the body's size...but it's peculiar."

"What?"

"How they won't talk about it...if they are as susceptible to mutation as any race, why be so protective?"

"Maybe they're embarrassed about it, but I had the impression it was the technology they couldn't talk about."

Elizabeth rolled to face Jasin. "Maybe we shouldn't talk about it either." Looking past his shoulder to insure that Hone couldn't hear, she leaned close and spoke so quietly that even Jasin strained to hear. "We are the only human's that have proof of their advanced technology. It wouldn't be hard for them to eliminate that threat."

"Mas knows"

"Mas could already be dead," she replied. "We left his fate in their hands."

The horrible idea hung in the air between them. Jasin felt his stomach twist. "Then it's good you're fast with that little knife of yours," Jasin said with a feeble grin, only half kidding. "I don't think we have to worry. I get the impression Hone won't take any drastic action without the

Council's approval, and besides...I don't think Li Sy would let him do anything like that."

Elizabeth looked up and over at the towa who had taken a position not far from the resting humans, and then glanced at Sy Hone just beyond. Li Sy didn't look like she could stand in the large towan's way if he decided to take matters into his own hands. Elizabeth still didn't trust her completely, but maybe Jasin was right. He knew her better.

They slept poorly and were glad to break camp at first planet rising so they could be on their way. Moist ground fog obscured the lower half of the cart's wheels, making it look like they were rolling through clouds. When Jasin suggested they ride through the night without stopping, the natives, who didn't understand the human's need for sleep, quickly agreed. Sixteen hours later they arrived sore and exhausted, barely able to drag themselves across Loeton's immense compound to stare at the emaciated face of their friend. Torchlight illuminated the deep cavities where his crusty, vacant eyes lay like dark water at the bottom of a well.

"We shouldn't have left him," Jasin muttered.

At the sound of Jasin's voice, Mas turned his head slightly. His cracked lips opened slightly and a thin wispy sound escaped. They moved closer. "Shh...don't try to talk," Elizabeth said. "Conserve your strength."

Mas tried to moisten his lips with his tongue, but a thin line of blood formed on his upper lip as the skin split. He moved his mouth slowly, using the few drops of blood to lubricate the painful action. "Did...did you...find her?" he asked softly.

Elizabeth looked up at Jasin who shook his head. "There was no clear trail. We went to Lake Chook instead. Loeton's dead, and Jorge Wynosk was killed."

Mas struggled to keep his eyes open, but they fluttered closed. His blond unkempt head shifted from side to side imperceptibly. The torch flared for a few seconds revealing Li Sy crouching a couple meters away.

"Li Sy, go watch the boy. He is under the big tree. I will care for Mas," Elizabeth said.

But the towa didn't budge. "Then come here," Elizabeth suggested.

When the towa joined them, Elizabeth showed her how to dip a corner of a cloth into a shallow bowl of water and hold it dripping into Mas's parched mouth. "Until it is all gone," she instructed. "We will be back in the morning."

But they didn't wake until strong, noon light filtered through the thick leaves and branches of the giant tree under which they slept. Thankfully, sleeping late had provided a reasonable excuse for missing Loeton's last act of kindness earlier that morning. Sy Hone assured them the cyliths were honored and both Jasin and Elizabeth were happy to take his word for it.

During the next few weeks, the humans were largely ignored as Loeton's household vacated the compound and Sy Lang, in turn, moved his family into the vast estate. By virtue of being the region's next most honored elder, Sy Lang had inherited the right to use the house, and more importantly, Sy Hone. Lang had requested that he stay on as his pytor. Sy Hone kept his promise and requested that Sy Lang allow Jasin to attend a Council meeting in order to answer the human's questions and accusations. Sy Lang, while personally inclined to grant the request, would not take that action without first gathering support. It would be several weeks before he would be able to let the humans know whether they would be invited.

While they waited, Elizabeth and Li Sy rarely left Mas's side. Combining the towa's knowledge of native herbal medicine and the simple medical knowledge Elizabeth had learned in school, they nursed Mas back from the brink of death. His injuries normally would have healed quicker, but they had been inflicted on an already weakened body and with the broken jaw, it was extremely difficult to provide even basic nourishment.

Jasin dutifully looked in on their slow progress several times a day, but admitted to having difficulty seeing the frail broken shadow that had once been his robust friend. He tried running to calm his nerves, but the intense heat made that impossible. Instead, he and Wilem would often walk the perimeter of the compound. Some days they packed a lunch and walked down to the bay to watch the short, fat fishing boats come and go. The towans that worked along the docks let them know they were not welcome there and it became something of a game to see how close they could get to the boats before being forced to leave.

Once, Wilem managed to sneak aboard one of the deepfish barges, sending the natives into a frightful tizzy. With much consternation, he was carried from his hiding place and delivered to Jasin who stood laughing at their obvious misplaced alarm.

"What's the big deal anyway?" Wilem once asked.

"It's one of the Prohibitions, one of the things humans are not allowed to do. We aren't supposed to own a boat or travel by ship. They get really upset about it. I think they don't want us spreading out."

"That's not fair," Wilem complained. "It's our world too."

Jasin was about to argue, to teach the young boy about the price of their settlement, until he realized the boy had a point. How many human generations would have to pass before those born on Syton would be allowed to consider it their home too and be afforded the same rights as other beings here? Those that were ship-born, who pleaded to be allowed to settle, might accept that they were immigrants, that they were second class without full rights, but how about the second or third or hundredth generation born on Syton?

One evening after Wilem had fallen asleep in the soft moss underneath the huge tree where they often rested to let their dinner settle, Lang approached the humans with the news they had been waiting for. Jasin would accompany him to the Council of Seventeen in T'Matte where he would formally ask the Council for permission to allow Jasin the privilege of addressing them. This, he assured them, would be granted.

"What about Elizabeth?" Jasin asked, suddenly afraid that once again they could become separated. He would never make the same mistake he had made in Nova Gaia. Now, and especially after he confronts the Council, it may not be safe for any of them to be apart.

Elizabeth eyed Lang and felt his hesitation. "It's probably more important that I stay with Mas," she said. "You don't need me...he does. Besides, I don't think the Council is ready for a female quite yet."

"But..."

"She is right," stated Lang abruptly. A female would be a needless complication."

"I would like her to come," he stated firmly.

"It will be impossible," the towan said.

Li Sy had been listening intently, trying to understand all the Human words. Finally she spoke up. "No female has ever entered the Council."

"Then she will wait outside. One way or another...she will be there," Jasin demanded.

"And Li Sy," added the towa. "Li Sy will go to Council with Jasin and Elizabeth."

Sy Lang ignored her completely. "We will leave in three days. Be prepared for the heat." Then he turned to Li Sy and berated her in Sytonian and strode off.

"What was that?" Elizabeth asked Jasin, watching Li Sy for a reaction.

"He said, the Council would rather eat her then allow her to enter the Council grounds."

"Was he serious?"

Jasin shrugged. "Maybe it would be best if she stays for Mas."

The Council

They had been warned, but they couldn't possibly have prepared for the oven called T'Matte, or the even more intense inferno of the Council grounds. Wilem, who would not be left behind, handled the heat better than either of the human adults. They were not far from the billowing clouds of steam rising from the hell below and all carried large gourds of water, often drinking deeply from them. Yet, no matter how much they drank, they never felt the need to relieve themselves. Moisture streamed from their pores soaking everything they wore.

Sitting as far from the fumaroles as possible, in what little shade they could find among the towering stone spires, the humans waited for Lang to return. Their breathing scarves had become useless. The hot air was difficult to breath and the gases belching from the rocks burnt their lungs. They watched the young towan honor guard positioned on either side of the entrance to the Council itself. The immature cylith pups at their side fidgeted, catching the strange human scent.

After thirty minutes, Sy Lang approached. "As expected, you have been granted permission to enter and address the Council. Watch me. I will try to help you, but be careful what you say. Do not offend anyone. Pay attention to what is not said as much as what is. There are many inside who were Loeton's friends, and blame you and your kind for his death. Be careful." He looked at Elizabeth and the boy. "Don't wander away, but don't come any closer. You should be safe here."

Jasin gave Elizabeth a hug and followed Sy Lang past the juveniles at the entrance, pausing at the first step of the outer tier. It was difficult not to be impressed. Council members and their cyliths were spread along three descending circular rings surrounding a small platform in the center, occupied by a lone cylith that Jasin surmised belonged to Sy Lang. He counted silently; the outer ring had clearings for eight, but only seven were being used. Loeton's position must not have been filled, Jasin guessed. Trying not to look too awkward, he carefully negotiated the immense span between each of the massive stone steps. He made his way past the middle tier of four towans, and eventually stood beside Sy Lang on the platform, looking up at the two elder council members on the lowest inner tier. Each successive tier held half the number as the ring above. Jasin turned slowly, peering up at their stern faces.

Sy Lang began. "Respected council members, I thank you once again for allowing the human Jasin Elstrada to come before you. He is the son of Avram, the first and last human to speak with us here. It is my understanding that he seeks our guidance."

Jasin stood as tall as his small frame would allow. He knew he still must look tiny next to Lang and hoped his voice wouldn't also seem small today. He took a deep breath resolved to speak with strength.

"Respected sirs," he spoke loudly in their native language, only to find that this chamber naturally amplified his voice. Suddenly embarrassed, he glanced towards Lang, but the towan was leaving center stage and to take position in an empty position between two others in the inner circle. Jasin blotted his moist upper lip with the back of his hand. "On behalf of my people, I thank you for allowing me to ask a few questions. I am sorry that Sy Loeton isn't here today. I have learned too late of his bravery and valor. He died protecting one of us. Knowing his views concerning the human settlement on Syton, this action was particularly noble and I will always try to honor his memory."

"Like my father before me, I seek to maintain the peace and good will between us, but in the past weeks, several troubling events have occurred and we have become aware of many new facts, which we need help to understand. A rogue group has taken Julian Elstrada, my mother. No one seems to know why. Does anyone know where she is or why she was taken?"

He paused to catch his breath and see if any one would answer. Speaking Sytonian to individuals wasn't difficult, but trying to project strength for any length was difficult for him and he knew this would take some time. A rivulet of sweat dripped into his left eye, the stinging salt momentarily blinding him. Wiping his eyes clear, he surveyed the crowd, seeing if anyone was interested in speaking. Out of seventeen...no, sixteen, surely someone might be willing to...wait. He made a second turn. There were only fourteen natives present. When none of them answered, he continued....

"Two humans have been murdered. The latest, Jorge Wynosk was killed while connected to a sophisticated device using advanced technology. We brought this machine back; it is not of human design. And this is not the only device we have discovered. While in Bistoun, I came upon a shaving knife, which was exceedingly sharp and repaired itself as if by magic. We have never had metals with this ability. I have become aware of other examples of advanced technology, technology that you claim not to possess. If we are to obey the Prohibition against exceeding your science and technology we must know what that level is. We believe you have technology more advanced than you profess." Suddenly there was a murmur from the outer ring. Jasin strained to see who it was.

"It is you, not we who retain technology more advanced than you admit to," someone sang out.

Sy Lang turned to see who spoke, and then addressed Jasin. "Sy Tanger, refers to the flying machine that was supposedly destroyed. We all know, from what your father told us, that it contains powerful weapons and vast technology. Avram said destroying your technology was the sacrifice you would be willing to make in order to be allowed to live here and we believed him. But we were deceived. It was never destroyed. Now it surfaces and threatens the peace between our people. You must turn over this machine to us immediately or how else can we trust you?"

Jasin bowed his head humbly. Perspiration dripped off his nose. "We have heard that the shuttle has surfaced in the lake. This was as much a surprise to us as to you. It is unsettling and of great concern, but I believe it was a deception by just one family. Our entire race should not be condemned. I believe all those who were responsible are now dead. But you also have powerful weapons. One of these killed Jorge Wynosk without even making a hole in his body. Was this retribution? Did you kill him because his family was responsible for hiding the machine in the lake? We ourselves have killed no one, while two of our people are dead, my best friend severely injured, and my mother taken.

"Why would you take an old woman?" Jasin continued. "What is to be gained? I do not believe she even knows of the machine. If destroying the shuttle would return her and restore the trust between us, I would do it myself." He paused to let that sink in. "But why would I destroy it when you lie about the machines you have? According to your own Prohibitions, we might be able to possess the shuttle's technology."

Sy Lang stepped forward. "Surely you're not saying that your flying machine compares to a knife or the device that killed Jorge Wynosk."

He's being political, thought Jasin. How should he respond? What could he say without revealing the trespass into the Kull? Taking a deep breath of the burning air he decided there would never be a better chance to get answers than today.

"Respected sirs, we all know that we are speaking about issues far greater than a mere knife. We all know that you possess sophisticated technology—technology capable of killing thousands of your kind, technology to transport vast numbers across the Kull, of illuminating the darkness without fire, of feeding yourselves without having to grow food or kill animals."

A wave of blistering air mixed with noxious fumes wafted into the council. Jasin struggled to catch his breath. Stay calm he told himself. Try to maintain control. He was treading on dangerous ground revealing what he knew. If they felt justified in killing Jorge for merely watching the shuttle, they wouldn't need any further excuse to kill him now as well. He had all but admitted to entering the Kull, and thereby breaking one of their main Prohibitions. He lifted his head and stared at the council members, coming to rest on Sy Lang. What was he thinking?

Jasin waited patiently for someone else to speak. Finally, Sy Lang asked softly, "It is our understanding you saw one of them. Is this true?"

Should he lie? He already admitted to knowledge he could only have gotten from travelling in the Kull. "Yes, I saw your transport."

"No, that is not what I am asking. Sy Hone has reported that one of them killed the man who lived on the lake. You witnessed this?"

Jasin was flabbergasted. What was the crime here? Seeing a deformed towan or trespassing through the Kull? Hiding technology, killing thousands, or knowing that their race could occasionally throw off a mutation? What vanity! What was their concern? He remembered the aborted conversation with Sy Hone. He had said that only the Council could explain.

He straightened and squared his shoulders. "Yes, I did. Would you care to explain?" he asked boldly, more from instinct than for any concrete reason. In all the years that Jasin had known Lang he had never sensed such uncertainty.

Lang turned to the other two natives by his side. They talked quietly to each other then together they ascended to the middle tier. The seven members of the highest tier joined them, and they naturally separated into three groups. After a few minutes they returned to their places.

Lang introduced the towan on his left. "Jasin, this is Sy Loyritz. He is our spreewell, our storykeeper. He will explain what you saw, if you keep your promise."

"My promise?"

"You said you would destroy the flying machine to return the trust between us."

"If it would return my mother…yes, I would destroy it."

"It must be destroyed. If it is true that other humans are not aware of its existence, if you value peace between our races, if you want our help in returning your mother, then you must be the one to destroy it. Its continuing presence is a danger to both of our races. Sy Loyritz will explain."

Sy Loyritz was much older than Lang, but his chest showed fewer crosshatches. He moved with difficulty, his six knees afflicted with the muscle bulge. "You will be the first human to be told this," His voice was strong and pleasant to listen to. "Perhaps your mother, if she is still alive, also knows what I will tell you now. We need your help to prevent your powerful technology from falling into the wrong hands.

"You Humans are not the first to join us on Syton. The small creature you saw is not from this moon. Over two hundred years ago, thousands of them came from Eian, Conboet's second moon. Physically, both male and female Eian are small, the size of our towa. When they arrived, they told us that their land had moved and cracked. Heat and steam had escaped from below. Large fissures had appeared throughout Eian, and the steam…the gas made them sick. Most of the plants and animals on Eian died, so they decided to send as many Eians as they could to Syton. We were simple and naïve, but they brought amazing machines and built wonderful cities. Their technology made water from the air and created food from the oceans. They could cross the Kull in minutes using vehicles that floated along blue ribbons. They could make the light shine at night without candles and used intelligent metal that knew how to form. They transformed the Kull into a paradise.

"With their advanced technology and comparatively comfortable life style, Eians soon became admired and powerful. Our people gave up their homes all across the land in order to live with the Eians in the Kull. We wanted to share and enjoy the conveniences that their machines provided. But we did not understand their technology and they wouldn't teach us. They never shared control or access to the machinery that drove their society, claiming we didn't have the intelligence to build, operate, or repair the machines. Many Sytonians found work within Eian households as personal servants.

"As time went on, Eians began to dominate the combined society, never allowing their advanced technological knowledge to spread into Sytonian hands. They began taking over everything and formed a powerful government. A hundred years after the Eians landed, they controlled all the important aspects of our life on Syton. The average Sytonian felt dominated; they felt second-class. Towan met with other towan complaining of the lack of control, the lack of influence in our own affairs. We formed secret groups in order to discuss the situation. Eventually, sixteen of these towdoms each sent a leader to meet…here.

Sy Loyritz paused and looked around. "This spot was well known by all towan because of its unusual formations. They created the Council of Sixteen and discussed what needed to be done. The Council spoke to the Eian leadership on behalf of the Sytonian people. They demanded equal access to the technology or if that were not possible, a prohibition of its use on Syton. Eians found neither demand acceptable and continued as if no request had been made. Word spread rapidly throughout the Syton communities and our people became inflamed. We opened our land, our entire moon to the Eians, and they did as they pleased without so much as the courtesy of a reply.

"At first, there were minor riots, then we began tearing down their power plants and industrial installations. Eians fought to protect what they thought was their property. Using powerful weapons they killed dozens of us, but immediately behind those were hundreds more willing to die to regain control of our native land. Soon the conflict grew into war. Unfortunately the Eians had great weapons, while we had nothing except crude swords and axes. But we had one thing they did not—numbers. We attacked the Eian strongholds with thousands of bodies. The Eians felt that they had no choice and emptied their huge energy weapons into the crowds. Ten thousand died in a single day...but it still didn't matter. Thousands more came.

"Over thirty-thousand towans died before the balance of power started to shift. Now it was the Eians that started to feel overwhelmed. Twenty Eian military complexes were captured in a single week. Countless towans, seeking revenge for the slaughter, gained control of the powerful Eian weapons. The Eians were faced with a difficult dilemma—continue fighting and risk being eliminated as a race, or surrender and face the consequences. Most of them fought on blindly until finally, an Eian named Baseel capitulated. He promised to show us how to locate and disarm the remaining Eian forces. For his services, he demanded assurance that his family and the remaining thousand members of his race would survive. He also demanded a perpetual seat for an Eian representative on the Council. The Council agreed, except they imposed additional conditions of their own. The Eians would only be permitted to live in a specific location. Travel outside their territory would not be allowed. Advanced technology could not be developed. Today, two thousand Eians live under many of the same Prohibitions as do you Humans. The penalty for their disobedience is death without consideration."

Jasin knew he was hearing the truth. Like pieces of a shattered jar coming together to reveal its original shape, the words combined perfectly with the images he carried from the Kull, easily explained the events of the last months, and answered nagging questions about their settlement on Syton that had always bothered him. But as the pieces all fell into place, he became frightened.

Sy Lang stepped forward to continue. "We believe Jorge Wynosk was killed and your mother abducted by the Eians. They are aware of the flying machine and its advanced technology and powerful weapons. We believe they want Julian to help them gain control of it, using force if necessary. She was one of the last humans to leave the machine and is still alive. You must help us to destroy it before it falls into their hands. If they gain possession and learn to operate your machine, they might use its technology to regain their dominance over both our societies."

I'm a dead man, thought Jasin. This knowledge had been one of their most guarded secrets. But his clear understanding of the situation began to cloud over. They could have just forced him, under fear of death, to destroy the shuttle without revealing the Eian's existence. They could have killed all of them weeks earlier after he had attempted to kill Loeton. Why tell him now?

They're afraid! They knew it had been Eians that kidnapped Julian and killed Jorge. They feared unwarranted retaliation by the humans that controlled the shuttle. They didn't understand the shuttle's technology and were scared that it might be used against them. With good reason, they were even more afraid that it would fall into Eian hands. He thanked Hyland silently. After all he had done or attempted, he would most likely be dead if the shuttle hadn't surfaced and put the Sytonians on guard. But even if he knew how, why would they think he would destroy it now? He tested their fear.

Where do the Eians live?" Jasin demanded.

"That, we will not tell you," answered Sy Lang.

"Where is my mother being held?

"We don't know. But if you are successful in destroying the flying machine, we will search their city for Julian."

"Find her now, and I will try to destroy it," he stated firmly.

Sy Tanger spoke from the upper tier. "Young Jasin, even with the flying machine, you few humans are much weaker than the tens of thousands of Eians we were able to defeat. We are trying to be reasonable, but you are not in a position to demand anything. We don't believe those few who know of the machine's existence are able to operate it. Your life means nothing to me. The survival of your race means nothing to me. I believe, as did Sy Loeton, that your settlement here was a mistake."

Obviously, their fear of the shuttle's power was limited. The fact that they wouldn't reveal the Eian's location meant they feared the two advanced races might form a coalition against them. Jasin knew that the shuttle would always prevent peace on Syton and that eventually it would have to be destroyed. Besides, Sy Tanger was right. Neither he nor Elizabeth was capable of using the shuttle. He turned to Sy Lang. "I do not know how long it will take to destroy the shuttle. I fear it only surfaces during Rhan-di-lith. By that time, Julian could be dead. Respectfully, Sy Lang, you were my father's friend. You trusted him. Now, you must trust me. I promise to try to destroy the machine in the lake, but couldn't you begin searching for Julian immediately?"

Sy Lang glanced about the Council chamber. Finally he said, "We will consider it. I personally have no objection."

"There is one last question that I have," Jasin hesitated, looking to Lang for permission to continue. Sy Lang spread his arms in assent. "It isn't that important…but I'm curious. I count only fourteen council members. Sy Loeton and the Eian representative, who has apparently been excluded today, would make sixteen not seventeen. Is someone else missing?"

"Someone is always missing," Sy Loyritz answered solemnly. "It is recorded that originally sixteen leaders set out to form the Council, but only fifteen of the leaders made it to the meeting. The sixteenth, the oldest and most highly respected, never arrived, most likely murdered by the Eians. Out of respect and to honor this absent representative, the original members still called themselves the Council of Sixteen." Loyritz indicated an empty position on the middle tier. "They left space to honor the missing member, just as we do now even though we added the Eian representative. Our ranks will never be closed; another wise voice will always be welcome."

"Perhaps someday a human might be asked to join," mused Jasin, loud enough to be heard, but his comment hung dead in the air.

The Council adjourned and Lang led Jasin from the chamber to rejoin Elizabeth and Wilem. They made their way past the statues and stopped to look at Loeton's likeness. Wilem squirmed. His only memory of Loeton was with his chest blown open. The boy moved on weaving among the other statues.

Suddenly he screamed. Jasin and Elizabeth ran to join him. Wilem stood gaping at a small statue. It was a perfect likeness of the small creature, the Eian that had killed his father.

Jasin and Elizabeth both gasped. As Lang joined them, Elizabeth demanded, "Who is this?"

"Are all the Eians identical like the towa?" Jasin asked. Elizabeth turned to Jasin, puzzled.

"No, Eians are not identical. His name is Eidorf. He is the current Eian representative to the Council."

Samson

Leaving the intolerable furnace of T'Matte, they traveled to Fistulee through a marginally cooler dimness. Comfort, the travelers agreed, was relative as oppressive heat still sapped their energy and they were forced to stop and rest often. Sy Lang accompanied the humans, helping Jasin clarify and explain what he had been told inside the Council rings. Elizabeth, feeling it important to keep Wilem informed, translated the conversation into sign language. Occasionally, Wilem would ask her to repeat sections lost in the darkness. Once explained, the mysteries they had struggled with and the Prohibitions that had been imposed suddenly all made sense to Elizabeth.

"If there is ever to be peace, the temptation of controlling the shuttle's power must be removed," Jasin explained. "I promised to destroy it in return for their help in finding Julian."

Wilem thoughtfully considered Jasin's promise, then breaking his long silence, spoke out. "Daddy said there's nothing to be afraid of. When I was real little, and the machine would come up, I would be afraid, but he would say, 'It can't hurt you, don't be scared.'"

Jasin stopped walking and held Wilem close so the boy could see and read his lips. "There are powerful weapons and a great store of knowledge in it. Your father and grandpa thought they were doing the right thing by hiding the machine, but they didn't know about the Eians. We humans would never use its power against the natives, but the Eians have shown that they might. They have already kidnapped my mother and killed your father trying to recover the machine. It has already caused much pain and suffering. Nothing in the craft is more important than maintaining the peace. If one race has the technology, it threatens the others that don't have it. We have to live together. This is home to all of us now."

Frowning, Wilem left Jasin's side and joined Elizabeth. Reaching out to hold her hand he asked her, "Do you like him? I think he's stupid."

Elizabeth took the boy's hand, looked over at Jasin and grinned. "He's not stupid," she said, loud enough for Jasin to hear. "He's just insensitive at times. He doesn't consider how his words might hurt others."

"I think he's stupid. My grandpa...he was the smartest man ever. He said the machine was important."

"Maybe at one time it was. What do you think Grandpa would do now?"

"He would rest. We have been walking for hours."

She smiled. Wilem rarely disappointed her. "Fistulee is not far. We can sleep when we get there."

"And then?"

"Then we'll take you to your mother."

"She's far away."

Elizabeth tried a quick mental calculation of the distances involved, but her exhausted mind failed. "Yes," she finally replied, "very far away."

The next morning, under the scrutiny of Sy Lang's kitchen help, Elizabeth gathered the supplies she thought they would need. If the towas' disapproved of the kind or quantity of food she took they would simply reach into her basket and remove the item in question. Occasionally, Li Sy would have to argue with them and Elizabeth noticed that at least once, while they followed her, Li Sy returned to help herself to a forbidden item, scurrying out the door before anyone could stop her. Water would be a problem, but she assumed they'd stop in Bistoun or at the Lake to replenish. When they finished in the kitchen, Elizabeth and Jasin packed the groceries in one of the two carts holding their belongings, leaving space for a comfortable bed for Mas. Li Sy joined them carrying a large pouch of native pharmaceuticals that she packed away carefully while Jasin went to get his friend.

"Ready to go," Jasin asked Mas, lifting him from the bed where he had lain for weeks.

"This is embarrassing," he mumbled as Jasin laid him in the cart. "Like a sack of vegetables." His thin, emaciated face was flushed and he collapsed against the sacks of produce, soaked from the exertion.

"Just help yourself to the food whenever you're hungry," kidded Jasin moving to the front of the cart to check the animal's harness. "You need to gain at least ten kilos by the time we get back home."

"Get me out of this heat and I'll be able to stop dripping. Then I'll gain some weight."

"He needs to gain twice that," Elizabeth corrected Jasin under her breath.

"We'll have none of that whispering in my presence. If you are going to pronounce me dead have the courtesy to do so loudly enough for the corpse to hear."

"She said you need to gain twice that," Wilem said helpfully, approaching the cart from where he had been watching them pack.

"There should be a law against that," complained Jasin of Wilem's lip reading skills. "Make sure the water is well lashed to the side, Wilem. I don't want it shifting at the first rut. We'll be leaving as soon as we pay our respects to Sy Lang."

Sy Lang saw Jasin and Elizabeth approach down one of the long corridors that radiated from the arboretum and abruptly halted the conversation he was having. Leaning forward, taking weight off his middle leg, he walked forward to meet them. His cylith shadowed him for several steps until his master commanded him to stay.

"Thank you," Elizabeth said, visibly relieved not to have to stand close to the animal.

"He would not have harmed you, but I know of your fear. How is Mas today?" asked Sy Lang, turning to Jasin.

"Elizabeth believes he is well enough to travel. You have been very kind to let us stay with you, but it is time. We need to take the boy to his mother and there is much we must do before the next Rhan-da-lith when I believe the shuttle will rise again. It would make sense that Hyland would use the darkness to cover its appearance."

"The old man's deception has caused much suffering," Sy Lang said.

Elizabeth nodded. "I'm sure he did not foresee his son's death."

"Nor that of Sy Loeton's," Sy Lang added.

"No, of course, I'm sorry." Elizabeth chided herself. She would never be a politician.

"You know...he died saving Elizabeth. I didn't expect that." Jasin added.

"Then you didn't know him very well. He risked his life often, for many of us."

"But for a human?"

Sy Lang paused before answering. "Perhaps his hatred did not run as deep as he professed."

The young couple bowed their heads showing their gratitude, then Jasin took out his poke and handed it to Sy Lang. "Please take this. It isn't much. You've been so kind to us."

"Kindness isn't repaid with crystals," said Sy Lang.

"We took a fair amount of supplies. I'd feel better if you keep it."

Sy Lang spread his arms in assent and took the small leather bag. "Just remember your promise, Jasin. The shuttle must be destroyed."

Jasin nodded. "And you will continue to look for Julian."

As they turned to leave, Jasin noticed a tall familiar form off in the distance almost hidden in the shadows of the large tree. Walking on, he asked Elizabeth quietly, "Did you notice whom Lang was talking to before we showed up?"

"I saw no one."

"Under the tree...it looked like Toberry."

Elizabeth looked over her shoulder. "Are you sure? We haven't seen him down here. I assumed he was in Nova Gaia with his family. Why wouldn't he have said something to you?"

Jasin shrugged. "He must be keeping an eye on us, just like he did with Avram. Besides, he hates the cold of Nova Gaia."

"And yet he has lived near your family for years."

"Toberry's an anomaly. There's only one reason a native would tolerate the weather in the highlands of Nova Gaia. We think he kept an eye on Avram for the Council, but I haven't seen him since we buried Avram."

Upon reaching the two carts they split up. Elizabeth and Li Sy occupied the cart with Mas, while Jasin and Wilem rode in the other supply cart together. No one had watched them leave, yet Jasin could swear they were being observed. He fidgeted, uncomfortable with the knowledge they held, troubled by the promises he had made, and confused at the change in his role. It had been forty-five days, nearly a full septet, since Mas and he had ventured down into Fistulee to find Julian and attempt to reestablish his Father's peace by murdering one of their leaders. But he had failed. There was still no peace. Julian was still missing. Nothing had been accomplished.

Tension and mistrust between all the races had grown. One of their most respected leaders was dead, and he had broken most of their important prohibitions, nearly killing Mas in the process. He didn't understand. Why was he being allowed to leave without punishment? He felt guilty and unclean, but most of all, confused. Now that the Sytonians knew about the shuttle, why did they need him? What did they think he would be able to do that they could not?

He looked over at Elizabeth, who hadn't stopped talking to Li Sy since they set off. The two of them had come a long way since the towa had accused her of being Loeton's fifth wife. They were a study in contrasts. Uniquely beautiful Elizabeth towered over the minute Li Sy, but beneath their skin, Jasin knew them both to be brave and strong-willed.

The two had become closer, drawn together by the common goal of nursing Mas back to health.

His thoughts returned to the few precious weeks before the party when he and Elizabeth were first discovering each other—memories that lightened his heart and blocked out the heavy burden that had befallen them. Duty and responsibility had gotten in the way and he longed for the day when they could resume the simple task of just being in love…if, of course, she ever forgave him. She still maintained some barrier, a thin protective shield that prevented them from enjoying the same level of intimacy they had shared. He blamed himself.

Elizabeth swiveled, looking behind her. They had taken the lead after Mas had complained that the dust being stirred up by Jasin's cart was making it difficult to breath. Jasin was so deep in thought it didn't appear that he was even aware of little Wilem beside him. Men are so strange, she thought. They probably hadn't said a word to each other since leaving the sprawling complex. Jasin and the boy had much in common, yet they each preferred to deal with it in solitude.

Li Sy, on the other hand, hadn't stopped talking, jabbering away, practicing her Human without a break. When Elizabeth didn't respond, the towa would rephrase the comment or question, trying different intonations. Elizabeth had found it easier just to think of her as a girlfriend from school and converse naturally, regardless of whether the native was making sense or understood anything Elizabeth was saying. Perhaps it was just the attention, but Li Sy appeared to enjoy the exchange.

"Li Sy?" she began awkwardly. "Do you remember those delicate purple flowers you found for me?"

"Conketal," Li Sy answered.

"Do you have any more with you?"

The little towa pulled her bag of medicines from the back of the cart and pulled out a stalk of the flower. Elizabeth looked at the dried petals and shook her head.

"The milky juice was very soothing. I don't see how the dried flower can help." With the heat, and days of walking, she had chafed and feared her infection had returned. It had been a long shot, but she had hoped.

Li Sy seemed to understand and bit off the stem of the conketal, chewed it vigorously, and then appeared to swallow it. Her neck folds bulged then pulsed, continuing to mash the stem. After a minute, she regurgitated a pulpy mess into her hand and offered it to Elizabeth who shook her head in disgust. Li Sy must have misunderstood.

But apparently Li Sy knew all too well what she was thinking. The towa applied the paste to her own pubis where, Elizabeth noticed, the native's rough calluses were sloughing off. Embarrassed to be staring, Elizabeth turned away, blushing.

Li Sy wiped the paste from her crotch, and offered it again to Elizabeth. She was speechless. Obviously Li Sy was trying to help but....

"Thank you, but...maybe later," Elizabeth stammered.

Li Sy reapplied the conketal, and then reached back into her bag and brought out another of the purple flowers, and stuck it in Elizabeth's hair. Elizabeth breathed a sigh of relief, happy that the entire episode was over and wondered whether she would ever attempt to use the dried flower. Well maybe, she was still uncomfortable, still burned down there. Damn that Loeton, she thought, then became ashamed of her selfishness.

The long dusty road climbed out of the valley and by mid-morning they could see Mount Kaysop off in the distance to their right. The oppressive temperature refused to drop. When they stopped to stretch and have a snack, they compared their sweat-streaked faces, laughing at the interesting patterns. Even stoic Jasin grinned when he saw Elizabeth's crisscrossed streaks running down her checks and neck, disappearing into her cleavage.

"I'd be happy to help you wash," he offered mischievously, holding out a water gourd.

"I'll bet you would," Elizabeth said, snatching the water from his hands. "But it would be a waste of precious water."

"He can have my share if you let me watch," Mas volunteered weakly.

"It will do you more good to drink it." Elizabeth put a hand on his burning forehead and helped Mas take a few sips from the container. "I want you to drink as much of this as you possibly can. No arguments." She looked over and caught Jasin's eye. "I think we need to keep going."

For five hours, the small group traveled towards the Low Pass, slowly gaining elevation. Jasin began to feel a cooler breeze on his face, growing more forceful as it squeezed between the mountains. They stopped at the apex of the pass to rest the animals, not more than a couple hundred meters from where Julian had been taken. Jasin, still uneasy, turned and searched the scorched, barren land behind them. Intense heat distorted the view, making him see movement where there was none. His heart raced as he rescanned vacant rock formations that an instant before appeared to hide danger.

Elizabeth walked over, took his hand, and gently pulled him away. "You're looking in the wrong direction," she said quietly, leading him to a vantage point where they could look ahead over the distant river valley and Mount Schtolin. "Our future is there," she said.

Jasin forced a smile, and gave her a hug, but his gaze continued to sweep the nearby foothills.

"Let's get moving," said Mas weakly from the back of his cart. "This is not a great place to stop. Trust me."

"I agree," said Jasin. He surveyed the lava plain ahead and pointed out a camping spot several hours ahead where they could easily see or hear anyone approaching. Elizabeth nodded.

That night the human's slept soundly, knowing Li Sy watched over them.

Two additional days travel brought them to Bistoun. They could have headed around the lake, through the logging camp, and past the waterfalls and black rocks as they had before, but Mas's condition had worsened and everyone agreed that the time saved using the ferry was important. Jasin led them to *The Blue Leaf Inn,* and left them under the huge tree, while he searched for Samson.

The young stable boy was attempting to hustle a towan for an extra crystal chip or two. His grasp of Sytonian grammar was excellent, thought Jasin. The boy spoke the native language far better than Human. When Samson finally noticed Jasin, he ran up to greet him.

"Been to the kitchen yet? Heard they was cooking up your favorite dish." His eyes twinkled at the inside joke and offered his skinny filthy hand, which Jasin shook. "You're in trouble around here," the young boy said.

"Always," Jasin replied.

"There's a rumor you got Sy Loeton killed."

"Beware of Bistounian rumors. Listen, could you help us with water and a few supplies. I'm hoping to get across at the next slack tide."

"Who's us?"

"A few friends. They're resting under the big tree by the river. I thought you might help an old pal."

"An old pal with crystals?"

Jasin glared at the little boy. "No…just an old pal with sick and homeless trying to get across the river and looking for help"

Samson seemed unmoved.

"Forget it," Jasin said abruptly. He turned and began to walk away.

"Now don't be huffing away. At least the water here is free." Samson hurried to catch up. "Hey…what's the story with Loeton. Got killed up river and word around here was you were involved. Truth is worth my help."

Jasin stopped and peered down, locking his eyes on Samson's, trying to frighten the boy. "Truth is I got to him…and now he's dead."

Jasin could tell the boy was awed. "So it's true. You killed him?"

"You can't go around killing Humans and not pay." Jasin felt guilty deceiving the young boy, but it felt good to have his admiration, if only for a brief moment. "Loeton died, but I didn't kill him. You know the Prohibitions."

Samson looked up at him. "Yeh, I know them all," he said with a wink. Apparently the young boy was more impressed believing Jasin had gotten revenge for the murdered woman.

"You know, Jorge Wynosk died as well."

Samson shrugged. "No one cares. He was just a man. Doesn't count around here."

"Well, I know a few people who do care. You should too."

"Only human," the boy said under his breath. "Jasin, you got to wise up. This is their town, their world. We are only trespassers here. Forn is what they call us, bugs, eating off their land. We're nothing."

Jasin found himself breathing heavily, resisting the urge to grab the kid's scrawny shoulders and shake him. He took a deep breath. "You're human; I don't think you're nothing."

The boy stepped back from Jasin and held out his skinny arms begging him to look closely. "Me? I'm 'specially nothing. That's why I work the biz so hard. If you got a pocket full of crystals you might be something. At least that's what my old man says."

"Who's your dad? I'd like to meet him."

"He traveling, trading stuff. Besides, what's it matter to you?"

"Why aren't you with him?"

"Tell me why it matters so much."

"Family matters that's all. We all matter. You matter. Everyone is important, especially we Humans. We have to believe that or else we *will* be forn. At the end of the day, that belief is all that is important. There's so few of us. Our actions are important. What we think is important. What we are inside, in our heart, that's important too, not just what we got in our pockets."

"Says someone with empty pockets."

Jasin grinned and agreed. "Says someone with empty pockets."

They walked over to join the others and introductions were made. Samson greeted Li Sy in her native tongue, which impressed everyone.

"Your friend there doesn't look so good," said Samson. The others had become accustomed to Mas's shallow breathing, but it was clear Samson was concerned. "Ok, let's find some water and get you on your way."

By the time Elizabeth, Wilem and Li Sy finished filling their water jugs, Samson had returned with a sack of fresh biscuits, a couple of recharged breathing scarves, and an arm full of fruits and vegetables he had appropriated from the inn's kitchen. "Where's the boss?"

Wilem pointed towards the ferry. Jasin was talking to the crippled driver. In a few minutes, he returned with a frown.

Samson shook his head knowingly. "Let me guess. He didn't buy the 'it only matters what you have in your heart' speech. I could've told you. He isn't known for his generosity."

"There's more to it than that. Loeton was evidently a friend of his."

Samson agreed, but before anyone else could comment, Li Sy scurried over to have a few words with the towan. "She won't have any more luck than you did, you'll see," said Samson.

Neither Jasin nor Samson could follow the rapid-fire negotiations. The exchange intensified and Li Sy became quite animated.

"Where'd you find that one?" asked Samson. "Never heard one of the girls give it that good."

"She's special," explained Wilem. Samson nodded silently and they all continued to watch. Finally, Li Sy rejoined the group.

"He say's no."

It wasn't what they had expected to hear.

"What now?" asked Mas.

Samson reached back into the pile of vegetables he had just pilfered, grabbed an overripe sweet melon and jumped off the cart. With his free hand, he reached into his pocket and took out a few crystals. He smiled at Jasin. "Now we try it my way."

After a brief exchange, Samson returned, leaving the old native chewing on the piece of fruit. "You're good to go, all except her." He pointed at Li Sy and shrugged. "I guess she insulted him."

"He only helps poor towan. Not Humans in need. He's…" Li Sy searched for the word. Giving up she used her own language, then walked over to see how Mas was doing.

"He doesn't like Humans," Samson translated.

"'He's prejudiced' is closer," corrected Jasin.

Li Sy gently touched Mas. He was feverish and had taken on a yellowish tinge. She looked up at the others. There was an awkward pause. No one moved. She looked back at Mas and mumbled unintelligibly to herself. Finally, she walked back to the ferry operator and, with her head bowed, apologized. When she stood up straight, the old towan hit her viciously, sending her tumbling off the raft and into the frigid water. Jasin lunged forward, but Elizabeth grabbed his arm.

"Let it play out," Samson recommended.

A mud covered Li Sy pulled herself out of the cold river, climbed back on to the raft, and again squatted in front of the ferry operator with her head bowed. The old towan raised his hand again. The humans cringed anticipating another blow. Li Sy reached out and touched his swollen knees and spoke to the towan quietly. Finally, he lowered his hand. Li Sy left his side, and still dripping, walked to the back of the cart where Wilem offered her a blanket. She ignored his gesture grabbing her medicine pouch instead.

"He needs *keets,*" she explained. "Li Sy will apply it before we leave."

"Well, it seems everything's all straightened out," said Samson. "Slack tide's in 'bout an hour."

Jasin knelt down so he could look into the eyes of the frail little boy who had come to their aid. "There's one more thing Samson, if anyone comes asking about us tell them we headed up to Lake Chook."

"Lake Chook?"

"Just tell anyone who asks and thanks for everything. You're a big man in here." Jasin tapped Samson's chest. "We will repay you."

"With interest," the boy added. "I'm not buying the poor is beautiful thing."

"I never said—"

"I know," he waved off any further discussion. "Make sure you're out'a here before dark. No matter what you believe, killing humans isn't a crime and our boat friend there isn't the only towan that doesn't care for Humans."

The Women's Colony

They crossed the muddy Andoree in silence. The crippled towan operator ignored his clients as he wove his ferry between giant bulbous heads of gilia plants, their long tangled fronds gathering the weak rays of the late afternoon light. Upon reaching the far shore, Li Sy fulfilled her promise and massaged the towan's swollen knees with keets, and by dimness, the small group was ensconced at the same clearing that Jasin and Beloit had camped in the first day after leaving Lake Chook. Darkness brought little rest and they were well on their way by the brightening. Three silent hours later the troop arrived at the crossroads of Fork Camp.

Leaving Wilem and Li Sy to watch Mas, Jasin and Elizabeth walked up the trail, holding hands, to the stone bridge that crossed the lower tributary of the Canyon River. They scanned the lush blue-green valley just beyond the bridge, and strained to see into the surrounding mountains. Elizabeth pointed out the spectacular plume of mist rising from the Great Falls, which fed the upper tributary on the far side of the valley.

"Listen," suggested Elizabeth.

Jasin could make the low rumble from the enormous cascade. "This is as close as we'll get this trip."

Elizabeth nodded. They would bypass it this trip and follow the valley between the two rivers to the base of towering Mount Schtolin. There, they would search out the secluded Woman's Colony on its cold northern face—where it was rumored to reside—and return Wilem to his mother before continuing on to Panvera. With her father's help and the resources of Advanced Studies, Elizabeth hoped they would find a cure for whatever still afflicted Mas.

"The open valley should reveal if we're being followed," said Jasin.

"You're getting paranoid," teased Elizabeth, giving his hand a squeeze.

Two days journey bought them to the base of Mount Schtolin, nearly two thousand meters above the Andoree. It had been arduous, mentally as well as physically. Mas, looking more and more haggard, hadn't spoken since leaving Fork Camp. His skin, the color of straw, frightened them and they were convinced he hadn't many more days left. Making camp in the dimness, they lit a cozy fire using the dried thorny bushes that were plentiful in the foothills and nibbled on their dwindling supplies. Jasin paced, unable to settle.

"What's wrong?" Elizabeth asked.

"We haven't the faintest idea where we're going tomorrow. I've got to figure it out. I want to find a better vantage point, away from the base of the mountain."

"Tonight?"

"In the darkness, away from the fire, maybe I can catch a glimpse of light or see something. I'll be right back," Jasin replied, receiving a pout from Elizabeth.

"Come cuddle," she countered, holding out her hand. "Relax. It's been a long day."

He smiled and walked back to Elizabeth and kissed her. "I won't be gone long."

"I'll be asleep."

"I'll wake you up."

"Don't you dare," she said with feigned anger.

Jasin mounted a blaython and moved away from the light of the camp. He stopped often to scan the mountainside, but saw nothing. After an hour, he returned to camp, tied the blaython to a stout branch, and joined Elizabeth beside the fire. Wilem slept soundly in her lap.

"I found another man to keep me company," Elizabeth teased.

"This campfire was the only light I could see," said Jasin, ignoring her taunt. He squatted at the edge of the hot coals and warmed himself.

Elizabeth cocked her head towards Mas and Li Sy. "He's delirious. We've got to get to Panvera tomorrow. I doubt he'll make it another night in the open."

Jasin pursed his lips and breathed deeply through his nose. Frustrated, he shook his head. "I couldn't see anything," he repeated. "Let's get him closer to the fire. He needs to stay as warm as possible tonight."

Elizabeth looked over at the dark mass just beyond the flickering firelight. Li Sy was cuddled up against Mas. "She obviously agrees with you."

They carefully moved Wilem and covered him with a blanket. Then, they carried Mas to the fire and placed him as close as they dared. Li Sy, once again, sidled up next to him. "How can such an unusual pairing look so natural?" Elizabeth wondered out loud, hardly expecting an answer.

"She's had practice," said Jasin without thinking.

Elizabeth shot him a questioning look.

Jasin smiled. Should he keep it to himself? What fun would that be. "Mas said she was rough down there."

"You're kidding!"

"No, I think she *is* rough—"

"You know what I mean. Did they actually…"

Jasin laughed softly.

"I didn't think so," Elizabeth exclaimed. The thought had shaken her more than she cared to admit. Somehow the idea that Mas would have had sex with the towa disturbed her more than the memory of her own experience in the hardel. After all, she had had ulterior motives.

Jasin told her about the night Mas saved Li Sy from drowning and how she tried to warm him. "They were both naked and it was her time. Perhaps she got a little too close, but Mas swears he would have been torn up."

Elizabeth nodded. "No doubt. And when it might be physically possible, without harm, the towa wouldn't accept it…they're quite seasonal," commented Elizabeth.

"How would you know that...Li Sy?" Jasin was surprised that Elizabeth had ventured deeper into the topic, but the answer seemed clear. Li Sy was the only towa that could have communicated with her. The things women will talk about always surprised him.

"Yeah...Li Sy," Elizabeth lied. Jasin never needed to know how she really knew.

Jasin and Elizabeth gathered enough thorny brush to keep the fire burning until first light, and then settled, spooned together for warmth, into a shallow sleep. Lying closely against Elizabeth, Jasin felt his desire growing. He brushed Elizabeth's soft hair out of his eyes and inclined his head to her ear and whispered, "Have I told you lately how much I love you?"

She didn't answer him, but Jasin knew by the rhythm of her breathing that she was still awake. It was unfair that women could suspend their interest in sex so easily. He could become aroused at her slightest touch. Sometimes just watching her was all it took. Well...perhaps in a few days, they'd actually be able to find some privacy and make love in a real bed. How long had it been?

Elizabeth had felt him harden. Men picked the most awkward times. She was no longer sore and the burning had been relieved with regular treatments of the flowers from Li Sy's pouch, but what she had felt earlier that evening was gone. She had led him on, but now...nothing. Searching her feelings, she tried to dig out something sensual, anything. All she felt was exhaustion. Besides, young Wilem wasn't even two meters away. The thought of intimacy here, now, was, frankly, ridiculous. Perhaps they could find some time for each other in Panvera. She wondered what her father would think of him.

Morning made a weak entrance. The black starless night begrudgingly lightened to a dirty gray. They hadn't slept well bundled together. Their muscles were stiff; the cold hard ground had sapped them of their flexibility. Jasin suggested a run to loosen up, but no one else was interested. So after checking that Mas's condition hadn't changed, he took one of the fresh breathing scarves Samson had provided and set off alone.

Stubborn, tight muscles loosened and within minutes he was bounding through the brush and flying around rocks and boulders. It felt wonderful. He couldn't remember the last time he had been able to feel the rush that came as his legs pumped harder and faster and his heart began pounding in his chest. He stopped, gasping to catch his breath, and turned to the mountain before him.

Where were Nanc Wynosk and the other women that made their home here? A women's colony—what an absurd thought. He understood why Nanc might divorce Jorge; he wasn't much to look at and a mere shadow of his father's intellect and personality, but to give up on men all together? To shun the larger villages and towns? Jasin just couldn't understand.

Surveying the mountain for any trail or passage, Jasin began to doubt that they were even in the correct area. Mount Schtolin was immense. Perhaps farther on, he thought. He hadn't a clue where to begin. He turned and jogged back to camp.

But as he approached, he saw that fate had smiled upon them. Their little camp had three visitors—Nanc Wynosk stood nearby holding Wilem's hand. A short, plump woman, in her forties, and a girl, at least twenty-five years younger accompanied her. Except for their ages, they were nearly identical. The "twins" were examining Mas, while Elizabeth leaned over them answering their questions. On a large boulder a few meters away, Li Sy stood apart, leaning back and resting on her middle leg watching carefully. The others turned as he approached. An awkward silence followed.

"Hello, I'm Jasin Elstrada."

"It appears they already know who you are," said Elizabeth apprehensively.

"What's wrong?"

"You're what's wrong," shouted Nanc. She approached him. "Wilem should have been brought here immediately after his father died. Instead, you kidnapped him. You took him with you for weeks. Were you out of your mind? What were you thinking? Elizabeth says you were down in the native lands, in T'Matte for goodness sakes!"

"Unlike you, we've taken care of him," Jasin shot back. "What kind of mother leaves her family?"

Elizabeth quickly stepped in. "This isn't important...what *is* important is we—"

"Don't be telling me what's important," Nanc hissed at Elizabeth. "You both should have known better."

The curious twins who had been questioning Elizabeth approached Nanc and tried to comfort her.

"You have your son back," the younger girl said.

"These people have cared for him and he is fine," said the older woman. She turned to them and continued. "My name is Sheelia, this is Meri. Neighbors in Lake Chook found Jorge's grave, but Wilem was missing. Until you showed up no one was sure about anything. There was no word concerning the boy. I'm sure you can understand why Nanc is upset.

Jasin lowered his head in apology. "We're sorry. There were...things we had to see to. We came as soon as possible."

Nanc began to speak, but Sheelia silenced her with a wave of her hand. "Your friend there is dying. He has a terrible internal infection, and some liver damage for sure. Has he peed lately?"

No one could answer.

Sheelia shook her head. "He must be treated immediately."

"We...how do you know what's wrong with him?"

"Jasin, I think we should listen to them," Elizabeth said quietly. "They've offered to help."

"Listen to what? I thought you said your dad would help him."

Jasin turned at the sound of Mas groaning. Nanc and the young girl were trying to raise Mas to his feet. Li Sy moved about agitated "You're hurting him," Jasin reprimanded.

"If you don't let us help, you'll be killing him," the older woman answered back.

Elizabeth confronted Jasin. "I think it's all right. They seem to know what's wrong." She touched Jasin's check and forced him to look at her. "I don't believe he would make it to Panvera."

Jasin hastened to his friend's side. Mas's breathing was labored and his face twisted in pain. The women were having difficulty holding him up. "He can't walk." Jasin said, struggling to lift Mas. "If you can help, lead on. I'll carry him."

No one moved.

Elizabeth walked over to Jasin. "Put him down for a minute. We have to talk."

Confused, Jasin lowered Mas carefully to the ground and followed Elizabeth away from the rest.

"What's wrong? What's this about?" asked Jasin, feeling foolish. "I agree with you. If they can help, let them."

Elizabeth hesitated, searching for the right words. "Jasin, it's a woman's colony. They don't allow men there. I'll carry Mas. You have to stay here."

"Ridiculous." Jasin exploded, looking deeply into her eyes. They shifted away slightly before returning to his. "They'll accept Wilem. They want to treat Mas, but they won't let me carry him there?"

She pressed her lips together. "They don't want *you* there."

"What have I done to them? It's Nanc, right? She doesn't want me to know where Wilem will be."

Elizabeth shook her head. "No, you don't understand. If you want them to help Mas, you can't go to the village. Do I really have to spell it out for you?"

Suddenly it became clear. He was an Enforcer. It had been so long since he had performed the duties of his job he had forgotten how people could react.

Elizabeth could see he understood. "Stay here. Between the six of us we will be fine carrying him. We'll work in pairs, resting a lot. I'll be back before nightfall," then she smiled, "but make a big fire just in case." She knelt down and with a grunt, lifted Mas.

He knew she was strong, but carrying a full-grown man, even one as emaciated as Mas, would be extremely difficult. "Be careful," he said lamely. His gaze swept up the rugged terrain in the direction he imagined they would take. He should go with them. His brain screamed, "This is wrong!" What if his feeling was correct? What if they were being followed? It was dangerous to separate. Jasin stepped forward to follow, only to stop short. If Mas was to receive their help, if his friend was to survive, he couldn't risk angering them. He turned away, but the feeling in his gut grew stronger. They were being watched.

The small troop started off with Wilem walking next to his mother near the head of the pack, and Li Sy, her medicine pouch tied around her waist, bringing up the rear. In a few minutes, they disappeared into the foothills. Jasin resisted the urge to follow.

After fifteen minutes, Elizabeth lost the feeling in her arms and her back ached. It was no wonder that Jasin hadn't been able to see a trail or path, she thought as they picked their way around stone outcroppings and over scree fields, because...there simply wasn't one. She pushed on through the pain until she stumbled on a patch of loose gravel that had fallen across a large stone ledge they had to traverse.

"I'm sorry," she said, "I have to rest."

"You've done magnificently," said Sheelia, "but you must let us help. You'll never make it the rest of the way."

Elizabeth admitted it was harder going than she expected. Nanc and Sheelia lifted Mas under their arms and they were on their way again. Friendly and open, the women were curious about Li Sy and asked probing questions about Fistulee, particularly about their experiences among the natives. Elizabeth traded information carefully, avoiding telling too much, but Wilem told his mother about his father's death. To skeptical glances, Elizabeth tried to explain about "the other little towans that looked like towas but weren't". In some ways, it was easier the women didn't believe her; it kept them from asking questions she couldn't answer. Breaking an awkward silence she changed subjects, "How much farther is the village?"

Answered only with enigmatic smiles, she turned to the younger girl, Meri. "I seem to have worn out my credibility."

The girl smiled, "You have to admit it is a pretty wild story."

"I suppose...unless you were there. Unless you had it confirmed by their Council."

Meri glanced at her elder twin and Sheelia smiled back. Elizabeth decided to drop the subject. "So, you must be Sheelia's daughter."

She shrugged. "Daughter, sister...however you would like to think about it. Biological labels can get tricky. Sheelia raised me, so she's my mother."

"You seem to know a lot about medicine, nursing, and helping the sick. I went to Advanced Studies in Panvera and couldn't diagnose Mas the way you and your Mom did."

"I'm training to be a doctor someday."

"Where are you studying? Panvera?" The young lady ignored her question. "Well...regardless, it's nice of you to help, Meri."

Elizabeth expected that the colony would be located on the face of Mount Schtolin, so she was surprised an hour later, when they passed single file through a narrow opening in what appeared to be a solid mass of rock and found herself looking into a wide caldera populated with dozens of stone structures of various shapes and sizes. Several active steam vents were belching sulfurous vapor into the air. Before she took another step inside, she turned to admire the sliver of an entrance. If one didn't know of the slit in the stone wall leading into the interior, you would never find the colony. She smiled to herself thinking about Jasin riding out to look for light from the colony. Unless you flew over this colony you'd never see it.

As soon as their small party emerged into the wide volcanic depression, help arrived. Two older age men brought a stretcher and carried Mas quickly into one of the larger structures. Li Sy scampered after them.

"Men?" asked Elizabeth.

All the women smiled and Sheelia tried to explain. "Some misguided souls enjoy their company. We aren't as prejudiced as some think. Ada is nearly sixty. His brother is a few years younger. They and the doctor came here directly from the ship. Come let me show you."

Sheelia led them past several immense shimmering disks that pointed at the sun and into the large stone building where Ada and his brother had carried Mas.

Elizabeth entered the structure and stopped cold. She didn't know where to look first; all around her were wondrous objects of metal and glass. Glistening machines hummed, tiny lights blinked, and dozens of flat screens were filled with small glowing characters in various colors. Twelve rough primitive beds, some with patients, spread out like spokes of a wheel from a central area that held a single body cradle that was bathed in bright artificial light. Mas already lay supported in this adjustable frame, tended by several people who were busy sticking little devices all over his body; all taking orders from the oldest woman Elizabeth had ever seen. She had to be nearly ninety years old. Elizabeth stood agape. After a few minutes the old woman approached her. Her hands were blue.

"Is he yours?" she asked, looking back at Mas.

"A...a friend," Elizabeth stammered, not really able to take her eyes off the old woman's hands.

Noticing Elizabeth's stare, she turned and waved her hands between two disks. When she removed them the blue had vanished. "A good friend, I'd imagine. Well...maybe...if he has a strong heart...I don't know," She looked back again, taking measure of her patient. Finally she shook her head. "I'm sorry. Truth is, he'll probably die, but you can never tell. We'll do our best. Tell me honey...where'd you pick up the little one?" She referred to Li Sy. "I'm afraid she won't be able to leave here. Can't trust her not to talk."

"And just what do you intend to do with her?" asked Elizabeth, annoyed at the woman's brashness.

"I haven't really thought it through. She's the first we've ever had here. First female, in fact, the first native I've seen this high. She must be different. Most of them hide in the shadows. Never saw one so...so bold. You'll have to excuse me. I have others to attend to."

The old woman began to walk away, then turned, suddenly remembering something. "His infection is deep and well established. I expect that you'll grant permission for surgery to clean out if the drugs don't work. You are the closest thing he has to a legal guardian." She waved her hands between the disks and walked off with new blue hands, and without waiting for an answer she already was sure of.

Elizabeth found herself nodding assent to no one in particular, her mind reeling. She had heard about surgery in Advanced Studies. She remembered the hushed secretive tones her professor had used when, contrary to the Prohibitions, he revealed that at one time, humans were routinely cut open, operated upon, and then sewn back together like pieces of cloth.

Sheelia touched her elbow. "Come let's rest our feet and eat something before you return to the Enforcer. There are things we need to talk about."

They walked over to another large building where dozens ate at long tables. Wilem and Nanc were finishing their meal. The little boy appeared happy to be with his mother. Elizabeth smiled and signed hello. Wilem rushed over and gave her a giant hug. Elizabeth reached down to lift him, but realized the morning had taken it's toll on her back, so instead, she held his head between her hands and kissed his forehead. "I'll miss you little fellow." When he looked up, she told him to take care of his mother. He nodded and ran back to Nanc's side.

"I think you will really miss him," Sheelia said, returning with a tray of food.

"I used to be his nanny. We've been through a lot together."

"He clearly loves you."

Elizabeth nodded. Tears formed, which she wiped away before sitting down. She started to shake.

"Eat something, your body's exhausted and I'm sure you have questions."

"Questions? I can't even think straight enough to form questions. I think I'm in shock." Elizabeth accepted a small piece of bread with jam, but before she knew it, she had finished off the entire tray. "I'm sorry, I didn't leave much for you...I didn't realize..."

"Don't be silly." Sheelia dismissed her concerns with a wave of her hand, then stole a look in Wilem's direction. "Did his father ever accept him?" she asked.

Elizabeth was taken aback. "Jorge loved him. What makes you ask that?"

"I know from what Nanc has told me that he never forgave her."

"Indiscretion is often hard to forgive."

"Indiscretion?"

Elizabeth recalled the countless times Jorge tried to gain her sympathy and comfort by complaining about his wife. "Jorge could never get over the betrayal of his love. He became a very bitter man."

Sheelia chewed her lowered lip and nodded thoughtfully. "Are you and Jasin intimate?"

Elizabeth blushed and glanced around to see if anyone else had heard the question.

"I'm sorry. I shouldn't have embarrassed you. It just seemed like you might be. Forget it...just professional curiosity. Perhaps you should rest now, or if you'd like, there's a hot spring bath."

"It's been a long time since my last hot bath," Elizabeth replied wistfully, "but...I'm sorry...what possible *professional* interest do you have in our personal lives?"

"I don't really care about your personal lives, just your genome. Listen...if I was wrong about you two I apologize."

"And if you weren't?" It was awkward to have someone she just met asking personal questions.

Sheelia smiled and placed a hand on hers. "Come with me. It's easier if I show you."

They left the cafeteria and walked across the compound to a smaller stone building. The interior was divided into two rooms. They walked through the center of the first, past a narrow table with a pillow at one end, then Sheelia carefully opened a heavily secured door into a darkened space. Cool air took Elizabeth by surprise. Sheelia turned on a light revealing four cylindrical towers each nearly as tall as Elizabeth. The towers consisted of dozens of gray rings dotted on their periphery by closely spaced holes, some empty, others containing small silver circles with markings on them. Through the center of the rings ran a thick shaft upon which the rings could rotate.

"Would you mind if I sampled you?" Sheelia asked, and then added quickly, "It won't hurt a bit."

Elizabeth shrugged. Sheelia took a tiny bit of Elizabeth's hair and placed it in a small capsule, which was then inserted into a small hand held device. The integrated screen turned on as the sample of her hair disappeared into it.

"Why didn't you tell me you were Di Sidrah's daughter?" Sheelia exclaimed, looking at the readout. Your mother and I were synai partners. She was very good. Do you play?"

Elizabeth shook her head. She never had any interest in the silly table game.

"Now let me see. I don't have Jasin's record, but I have Avram's, Julian's, and her first son...." She entered values into the device and checked the results. "Not bad...not good, I can't really tell for sure, not having Jasin of course, but I am sure I could do better for you. It looks like your lines have mixed three or four times...several common recessives could be a problem if Jasin is carrying them from Avram's side. Not bad if you consider all twenty-five generations or so. You wouldn't have to go as drastic as Nanc did. By the way, Jorge knew about it; he just couldn't accept that his genome wasn't good enough for her. If he told you otherwise he was trying to manipulate you. Nanc did us all a great service, reintroducing the oriental line. It had nearly died out. Believe it or not, your friend Mas has a little too, three generations back. Don't let the blond hair fool you. His line is wonderfully fresh. Have you considered...?"

Again Elizabeth blushed. "You said Julian had another son?"

Sheelia nodded absently. "Look at me going off again. Anyway, this room contains the genetic material from nearly two thousand individuals making up dozens of different races. It's a small sample of the genetic bank Tanis carried from Earth. We couldn't bring it all down. The original planners wanted to make sure the race remained healthy. It takes a lot more than a few hundred humans reproducing on a whim. This small bank was one of the first things Misa saved from the ship. Without it, the human line here on Syton would eventually degenerate."

"Misa?"

"The doctor...the old woman you met. We can trust you not to tell Jasin about all this can't we? At least not until he's ready."

"Ready for what?" In her heart she knew the answer.

"Ready to accept the reality of his father's mistake. Perhaps we should sit." Sheelia indicated a couple of chairs, which Elizabeth happily retreated to. All this information was coming at a dizzying pace.

Shelia continued. "Giving up all our technology meant giving up on the future of our little branch of the human race. Avram thought we were being over cautious, but genetically we are too small a sample to survive...long term anyway. The doctor knew this, as did Hyland. He had discovered this caldera from the air while we were off-loading Tanis. When the doctor refused to ignore her oath, Hyland secretly arranged to have her, Ada, his brother, and the medical equipment flown directly here. They faked their own suicides to avoid questions. Hyland never told anyone, but eventually the doctor got word out to her staff and one by one they found their way here. Over the years, we have continued to adjust the gene pool and help a lot of people who would have died from simple injuries and illness. In return, they keep this place secret."

"The doctor's quite a woman," said Elizabeth.

"Without her stubbornness, this colony wouldn't exist. It's really her doing, it's her colony."

"The woman's colony," Elizabeth said softly, smiling at the unintended joke.

Sheelia reached out and held Elizabeth's hand. "You have such a beautiful smile. I'm glad you enjoy our little pun."

Elizabeth withdrew her hand awkwardly. "We appreciate all that you are doing for Mas. When he can understand, would you tell him Jasin and I will come back in a week or so."

"It is best not to. Every new visit increases the chance we'll be discovered. If Mas makes it, I will tell him you wanted to come, but that we forbade it. And please, honor your promise—Jasin mustn't know the extent of what we are doing."

Elizabeth agreed, and together they left the small building. "I think I should get back before Jasin begins to worry."

"Are you sure you have to go? I'm sure he will be fine for a night. I was hoping to get to know you a little better." Sheelia's eyes sparkled.

"I appreciate the offer...especially the hot bath, but I don't want to try and find my way back in the dark."

"I understand. Just remember my offer when you start thinking about children. Without volunteers and planning we're not going to remain healthy. Keep it in mind."

Elizabeth nodded. "Thank you, I'll remember, but I'm not really at that point." Pausing, she considered whether it was appropriate to ask for a favor after refusing Sheelia's advances, but she had to ask. "You could, however, help me in a different way. The towa's name is Li Sy. She speaks Human well and is a caring nurse. If you must keep her, would you make sure she is accepted?"

"Of course."

"And don't grab her. She doesn't like to be manhandled."

"Who does?" Sheelia answered with a smirk.

Caldera

The old towan was freezing. In all his years—and there were more than anyone knew—he had never dared venture to where the air was so cold and thin. There was nothing but death this far above where the big plants stopped growing, but his human companion was convinced they wouldn't have much farther to climb. They were nearing the ragged summit of Mount Schtolin and even though the cold wind was biting into his thickening skin with increasing ferocity, the native fought on.

In the past, he would have lain with his cylith, protected by its fur and warm body, but his beloved companion was dust, an ancient memory, dead from old age just as he should be, just as he would be if he didn't get lower and return to the river valley. He hadn't expected it so soon—the sluggishness, the familiar numbness that had begun to slow his thoughts. It was the wrong time to be so far away from the black rocks.

He and the Enforcer had followed the humans from the low lands by the river to this frigid mountain. In the beginning, it had only been physically draining to keep up with the carts, secretly tracking the small group, but over the last few days as he had become thickheaded and unable to concentrate, he increasingly relied on the human's judgment. He hadn't wanted to climb up the mountain; he thought it best to stay with Avram's boy, convinced that the male was the only one worth watching. But Beloit had wanted him to track the women and needed his sense of smell. By the time they stopped arguing and began heading up the mountain, they had lost track of the females—a mistake that became more evident the further up they headed into the frozen wilderness.

Convinced that they hadn't missed anyone descending the mountain, they continued to climb until darkness enveloped them. Then at the next light, they climbed even higher, so high that they looked down upon the clouds beneath them. The towan would have turned back if he had been thinking clearly, but now the dying towan simply followed, too weak and feebleminded to make any choices for himself.

Beloit, unaware of his companion's condition, was deep in thought. He hadn't spoken to Jasin since Avram's funeral. How long ago? It seemed like a different age, a different era, when he was sure of himself and what he had to do. He lowered his head and relentlessly drove onward, convinced that they would find the women just over this ridge...or the next. Finding The Women's Colony was something he and Avram had wanted to do since word of its existence surfaced nearly two decades earlier. Ironic that it would be Avram's son and his consort that would lead him there.

He pushed on, unwilling to admit to the towan he was lost. Pride prevented his turning back and heading down the mountain. They had spent too much time, gone too far not to discover where the females had taken their injured friend, where so many had taken their sick and dying. He was finally going to uncover the mystery behind The Women's Colony.

Almost spent, Beloit struggled to pull himself over the last high stony ridge and finally in the failing light, nearly two days since they had started their climb, he gazed down upon the brightly illuminated colony in the bottom of the massive bowl. The mountain was hollow, an ancient volcano eviscerated when its hot guts blew out eons ago leaving an empty cone which now, from all appearances, was a fortress of forbidden technology. He watched people carrying supplies, walking along well-worn paths between buildings and...out through a narrow crack in the side of the caldera's side. Marking its position firmly in his mind, he turned to gloat.

But the towan wasn't to be seen.

Retracing his last few steps, he peered down the mountainside and there, nearly three hundred meters beneath him lay the towan, face down in the snow. He hurried to help, but as he struggled to turn the surprisingly stiff and heavy body over, he realized it didn't matter. Sy Toberry's frozen eyes stared lifelessly back at him. A peculiar smile spread across Beloit's face.

"Well, my mysterious old friend, we all take secrets to our graves, but you're probably taking more than your share." With that, Beloit instinctively looked about, searching for rocks with which to bury the towan, but there were few small enough to carry. The couple he did find held fast in the frozen ground. He gave up and quickly headed down the mountain. Finding and revealing the colony would be his greatest triumph, but he would need help. These fugitives and rebels had remained hidden for over three decades. They wouldn't surrender without a fight.

Panvera

Their breathing scarves hanging unneeded about their necks, Jasin and Elizabeth stood arm in arm enjoying the soothing vapors rising off Lake Meitalyn's crimson surface. Meitalyn, Elizabeth explained, taking a deep breath, was something of an enigma. The water's native name had no meaning so far as anyone was aware, the word itself was unique, so too was its deep red color and near boiling temperature. High in the mountains, Lake Meitalyn stood out like a warm bloody wound surrounded by a frozen wilderness entirely frosted over by its chilled vapor.

Earlier, as they had made their way from Mount Schtolin to Panvera, Elizabeth told Jasin the story of the lake and its importance in the founding of Panvera she had learned as a young girl.

Humans, who had been unwilling to inhabit the proffered native homes, traveled as far as possible from the settled lands, to homestead high into the cold expanse. There they found Lake Meitalyn and channeled its hot water through stone beds beneath their homes to keep themselves from freezing to death.

One entrepreneurial family, the Bartletts, had created a health spa on the shore of the red lake, claiming the water had therapeutic qualities. Indeed, those that visited the scarlet shores always left feeling better. Their neighbors marveled and ridiculed the steady flow of fools who paid for their visit to the spa with precious crystals for what they could have gotten free if they had just walked outside to the edge of the lake. Most of the local residents would readily admit that their derision was simply jealousy that they didn't think of the scam first.

But while bathing in the warm waters had only a minor health benefit, the blood red sediment did. Discovered by accident, breathing through a cloth saturated with the red deposit helped soothe the sore throat caused by the alien blend of atmospheric gases. Within a few years, with the wealth accumulated from the pockets of pilgrims, the Bartletts had created a thriving market for the chemical mixture that brought such relief to the suffering human population, except of course for those in Panvera fortunate enough to live within range of the lake themselves. They called it meita and it wasn't long before humans were exchanging meita tablets as a form of currency. The eldest son of the original owners of the health spa, Stephan Bartlett, perhaps to allay a guilty conscience or out of some form of altruistic philanthropy opened a school for any human child that wished to advance their education beyond what the local schoolhouses were able to teach. Stephan Bartlett paid handsomely for the best teachers to join the hearty discontents at his Institute of Advanced Studies, high in the frozen reaches of the gorge.

Over the last thirty years, the small outpost of Panvera— the only truly human enclave on Syton—had grown to over one hundred families. Still a small village compared to Nova Gaia or Lake Chook, its importance as a symbol of human independence and commitment to learning could not be overstated.

Panvera's abbreviated growing season yielded no surplus; surviving here was a constant struggle against starvation and freezing to death. Jasin tried to picture Elizabeth's childhood here. It was a hard existence and his respect and admiration for her and her family grew. The source of her inner strength and resolve was evident…even more so after he had spent some time with her Father, Dai

Warren Tournell, Professor of Botany and amateur horticulturalist.

"I still can't believe that there is a third race living among us," Warren complained incredulously. He broke off a piece of flat bread and passed the rest to Jasin.

Jasin took a piece and spread a layer of pureed spice vegetables on it. "There is no doubt about it, Dai Warren, but not really living among us. Somewhere else…the natives wouldn't say. Elizabeth and I saw one kill Jorge Wynosk. The Council says they came from the second moon when it became uninhabitable."

"And you think they have kidnapped your mother simply because she flew in on the last shuttle with Hyland, the one he hid in Lake Chook?" he asked, cutting a slice of an oddly shaped fruit. "Here Lizzy…try this. Tell me what you think it tastes like." He handed Elizabeth a piece of the purple melon and cut another for Jasin. They each took a tentative little bite. "Come on… do you think I would poison you?"

"It's…something like tiela gourd, but much sweeter. It's delicious," said Jasin. "Elizabeth said you enjoyed creating hybrids." It was the truth, but he hoped his complement wasn't too blatant. He caught Elizabeth's eye. She smiled at his effort to make a good impression.

Dai Warren was pleased. "Five years…I was beginning to think they would never bear fruit. Wait…" he jumped up from the table. "I've got something else you should try."

"Come sit down. We'll have plenty of time to sample your treats," Elizabeth coaxed her father back to the table.

"You are staying a while aren't you?" Warren asked, "A few days at least?"

Jasin watched Dai Warren fold his long legs under the table. It was abundantly clear where Elizabeth's height came from, but luckily, judging by her father's thin, stringy hair and generous nose, her beauty must have been a gift from her mother—the best of both. How he wished he had been so fortunate! He began to answer Warren's last question, "Well there's a lot—"

"Of course we'll stay a few days." Elizabeth interrupted Jasin, casting him a withering look. "We've been traveling for nearly two months. It will be nice to spend some time with you while we make plans."

"Thank you for being so kind," added Jasin sheepishly, "I've dragged your daughter into some difficult situations looking for Julian."

Warren nodded absently. The nodding became a shake of his head. "I still have trouble accepting it," Warren said. "Another race? Two moons both inhabited by bipedal sentient life forms that except for size look similar, both at approximately the same level of development?" He shook his head. "Not likely."

"Actually, the Eians are much more technically advanced," Jasin corrected.

"Not really, not on an evolutionary timescale. The difference between a stone-age people and space faring civilization is microscopic. The history records aboard Tanis said that for a short period of time, a hundred years or so, Earth had aboriginal stone-age civilizations coexisting with societies that walked on neighboring planets."

"You'll have to forgive Father," Elizabeth apologized, her eyes sparkling with pride. "It's the professor in him coming out." She reached over and squeezed her father's hand. "I've missed you so much. You know…I almost made it home a while back."

"What stopped you?" asked Warren.

Elizabeth looked across the table at Jasin. He answered for her. "Temporary insanity."

It was easy for Elizabeth to kick him playfully under the table.

They finished dinner over more friendly argument and conversation. Jasin found the exchange exhilarating, an open flow of ideas shared with unbridled love—so different than his meals with his parents where he had always felt controlled and surrounded by emotional stiffness.

After helping to clear the table, Elizabeth left Jasin to help Warren with the dishes. They needed time to get to know one another she reasoned selfishly as she wondered off to her old bedroom. It was exactly as she had left it nearly twelve septets ago when she left for her service with Hyland. She affectionately fingered the ceramic cup she had made in primary school; the unfinished embroidery her mother had helped her start; the laskic shell necklace Michael had gotten her for graduation. Each touch triggered memories of an innocent time before death came into her life, before that face of reality introduced itself. Six deaths...seven, if Mas didn't make it. Wasn't it time for that unwelcome caller to leave her alone?

She fought against the gloom and depression that crept in from the edge of her unconscious. Her cold, emotionless shield began to form, defending her from pain and heartache and the despair of futility. Only emptiness stretched out in front of her, a bleak future of death and more death until...until she joined them all in lifeless eternity. What could stand in death's way? Who had the power to fight the inevitable, to push it from the stage? She stood paralyzed, lost in gray dimness for the longest time.

And then she knew. Perhaps she had lied to Sheelia, back at the medical colony. Perhaps she was ready.

After lighting several candles around her room, she went back to the small kitchen and grabbed Jasin by the arm. "Please excuse us father, but it's been a long day and it's time to sleep."

"You can use Michael's bed if you would like, Jasin," Dai Warren offered. A knowing smile spread across his face.

Jasin returned the smile then followed Elizabeth, closing her bedroom door behind them.

"Lizzy?" Jasin repeated playfully after plopping down on her comfortable mattress.

"He's always called me that. Mother claimed that when I was born he promised he wouldn't, but I guess it was just easier. Father always favored old names— Michael...Elizabeth."

"Lizzy...I like that...short and sweet."

"Nothing like the real thing, huh?" Elizabeth kicked off her boots and sat down next to him. "I'm sorry I promised we'd stay...if you want to leave..." she started to remove her shirt, "you shouldn't feel committed," then standing up, she let the rest of her clothes fall to the floor, "in fact, if there's nothing holding you here maybe you should go."

She was beautiful in the candlelight. Jasin, as usual, was spellbound by the sight, unable to respond to her playful challenge except to move the blankets aside, silently asking her to join him.

At long last there was no one else in their universe. They took their time, savoring each kiss, each touch until Jasin, unable to endure any longer, prepared to enter her. Elizabeth stopped breathing. She wanted him badly, ached for his presence inside her, yet the last time she was in this position she was fighting for her life. She looked up into his brown eyes and saw his love and desire. He was being so gentle...too gentle, and without another thought, she surrendered to a primal urge that washed all hesitation, all inhibition aside and pulled him into her.

For Jasin and Elizabeth, the days in Panvera passed quickly. Instead of hiding indoors from the cold temperature, Jasin found that the residents relished the brisk air and were a gregarious bunch. The two of them attended communal dinners with Warren, participated in sporting games, and took long hikes together. Elizabeth renewed acquaintances and introduced Jasin. Typically, upon taking their leave, they were treated to some hushed surreptitious commentary that traveled too easily in the dry air.

"I think most of them think we're engaged," said Jasin, after one such encounter.

"Or should be," Elizabeth hinted. "Actually, I think my Father has been talking."

"Talking? About what?"

Elizabeth raised both hands, making an exaggerated shrug. She couldn't keep from breaking out in a wide smile. They walked on until she broke the silence. "Jasin...I know we've never talked about it but...this is a nice town, don't you think? I mean Nova Gaia is fine but...I like it here. I didn't realize how much, but the last week has been really nice."

Jasin's heart ached. He loved her so much, but he couldn't think beyond finding Julian and destroying the shuttle. But it was *his* obsession and it was unfair and dangerous to drag her into it any further. "I never really thought about settling anywhere. I like it here; don't get me wrong, but I feel...like my life's been knocked off course...like there's a constant cloud hanging over it. Until Julian is safe and the shuttle..."

"Why is the shuttle your responsibility," she said angrily. "I know you promised to do something, but if it bothers the natives, let them get rid of it. You didn't put it there."

"It's because I made a promise. It's my word."

"But they forced you to make that promise. It's not fair."

"What's not fair? That my Father's dead? That my Mother's been kidnapped? That I convinced my best friend to help me and he got hurt? None of it is fair. I'm not being fair to you either and I'm sorry, but I don't know what else to do. Don't you think I would love to settle down and make a life here with you, but how can I just forget everything? The last week has been more than wonderful." He paused afraid of how his next comment would be taken. He lifted her hand to his lips and kissed it. Softly he continued, "You should stay, but I've got to get back. I've got a lot to figure out."

"Get back to where? I thought we were doing this together. Why do you keep trying to push me away? First you say you'd love to make a life with me, then, with your next breath, you say you want to leave alone. Don't push me away like that. I know you think you're protecting me—"

"I *am* protecting you...at least I'm trying to protect you...I'm trying to do...at least something right. We were lucky last time. I couldn't bear to think I ever caused you to get hurt."

"You are not leaving here without me," she said, with a note of finality.

"That's it?"

Elizabeth nodded. The conversation was finished.

Several days later, Jasin woke alone. The smell of fresh baked spice bread filled the air. Usually he could determine the time of day from the color of the light entering the room, but it was gray and overcast. Probably about noon, he guessed. They hadn't gotten to sleep until very late, laughing and talking and planning about where they should go, what they should do next. Of course, they did more than plan. He smiled as he dressed to join the others. It was a wonderful night. She had been right; having someone to share the burden made a tremendous difference. He hadn't felt this close to Elizabeth for many months and the feeling was...well, simply right.

The house was deserted. Grabbing a piece of warm bread, he pulled on the pair of warm boots Dai Warren had loaned him, closed a heavy borrowed parka around himself, and went in search of the Elizabeth. He had no idea where to look and began just wandering about.

Homes in Panvera were packed tightly together. Jasin had assumed it was for mutual protection until Elizabeth reminded him of the underground heating. Red water flowed from house to house like blood keeping the town alive and the farther one lived from a source of the hot water, the longer ditch one had to dig. He followed one line of houses upstream and found Elizabeth and her Father returning from Meitalyn carrying a fairly large multi-legged fish, as red as the lake itself.

"Is it safe to eat that?" he asked.

"Of course. This is a delicacy," Dai Warren answered. "The minerals are held in the skin, which we never eat...unless you'd like to try?"

"The flesh is scrumptious when grilled." teased Elizabeth with theatrical flair. She was in a great mood.

"How did you catch it? I didn't see any boats on the lake."

Elizabeth reached across and wiggled one of the fish's stubby legs. "Land trap," she said as if he had asked the most ridiculous question.

"Don't make fun of me. I'm just an Enforcer. What do I know about catching fish?"

Silence.

"If it wasn't for the smell of that warm sweet bread, I think I'd still be sleeping. It was wonderful...who made it?" Jasin tried desperately to change the subject. The conversation had stopped cold and they walked on in awkward silence despite Jasin's attempts to restart it. When they arrived home, Dai Warren dropped the fish next to the door and went in. Jasin held Elizabeth back. "What's the matter? What did I say?"

"I never told anyone what you did."

"Surely they knew."

Elizabeth shook her head. "You never made it up here before and Beloit always avoided Panvera. My father and Beloit were close friends for years. Dad never particularly liked the idea of Avram asking Beloit to be an Enforcer. According to Mother, Father begged Beloit not to accept the job. When Beloit accepted, well...they've never spoken to each other since. He blames your Dad and he hates the idea that we need Enforcers."

Dai Warren stepped outside carrying a wide flat stone and a sharp knife.

Without hesitating, Jasin asked, "Come for my head?"

The three of them looked at each other and the knife, dumbfounded for a moment before breaking into laughter. Finally, Dai Warren picked up the fish and headed towards a rock pile. "Come on son, let's clean this monster."

Jasin looked at Elizabeth who smiled and silently coaxed him to join her father.

"I'm sorry, Dai Warren, that no one told you I was an Enforcer." Jasin watched as he expertly filleted and skinned the fish.

Warren lifted the skin with the point of his knife and offered it to Jasin with a smile. "Last chance!" He didn't wait for an answer, tossing it among the rocks along with the bones and guts of the large fish. "Listen...you don't have to call me that. Warren will do fine."

"Yes sir, thank you."

Warren smiled at the formality. "So you work with Beloit...is he well?" His voice dropped as if his question carried too much emotional weight.

Jasin thought for a moment. "Actually, I haven't seen him since we buried my dad. He was recovering from a severe blow to the head. Concussion...laceration...."

Warren winced and shook his head. "That's not a surprise. Avram put him in a terrible position. I'm sorry, but your Dad set him up to take the brunt of our hatred. I thought someone would put a knife in him eventually."

"Actually, he was injured by a native...and my dad loved Beloit."

"As did I." Dai Warren sighed and sat down on a clean section of the rocks. "Sidrah and I spent many wonderful nights with Beloit and Marteen, his first wife. We played synai together at least once a week aboard ship. They were quite a team."

"I didn't think Beloit was ever married considering how he sometimes talks about women. He never mentioned her."

Warren nodded thoughtfully. "I never saw a man so destroyed. Marteen had some type of allergic reaction to something in the air. She could never breath right...never quite settled in here—a shame, a real shame. She was a classy lady not like his second wife. Anyway...you think you're doing any good, I mean being an Enforcer?"

"I think it's extremely necessary; now more than ever. The Prohibitions are important to the natives. I've seen what the Eians did to them."

"Lizzy told me you went into the Kull. Disobeyed a prohibition, uh? Where's an Enforcer when you need one!" he said facetiously.

"It was the only way I could rescue my Mother."

"Extenuating circumstances. Is that when it's acceptable? How about to save a life?"

"The Prohibitions are in place to protect thousands of lives."

"You didn't answer my question. Is it ethical to disobey a Prohibition to save lives?"

Jasin didn't have an answer. "What choice did I have?" he said, echoing something he had heard his Dad say a hundred times. "What choice did my Father have? Or any of you on the ship?"

"I'm not sure," Dai Warren admitted, "but…" He looked about his small neighborhood. "Did you know that an average shuttle's equipment inventory is tremendous? Life would be a lot easier with its solar power converter or a couple thousand liters of that shuttle's fuel. It would be a shame to waste it…now that we know where it is. "

Jasin shrugged. "Sacrifices…trade-offs…Why not live where it's warmer?"

"I love Panvera. I wouldn't live anywhere else."

Jasin nodded. The town had a quaint, intimate quality. It was easy to see why its residents were so loyal. "The shuttle's existence now stands as the greatest threat to peace. I made a promise I would destroy it. In return they promised to help find my Mother. It sounded like a good deal, especially since they would have probably killed us if I hadn't agreed. They didn't particularly like that I tried to kill Sy Loeton."

"Yet another Prohibition broken. You've been busy."

Jasin shrugged. "Never said I was perfect."

"You're in good company," said Dai Warren, looking up at the threatening sky, then he picked up the fish, and the two of them walked back to the house accompanied by the distant rumble of thunder.

Hadrious

Under Sy Lang's leadership, two-dozen towans stormed into the rustic Eian city of Hadrious. Over the next week, they searched every corner of the isolated enclave. By tradition, the towans traveled in pairs. History held many stories of single towans falling prey to unfortunate freak "accidents". Not one hint of Julian's existence, or for that matter of Eidorf's, was uncovered. Convinced that all was in order, the small troop left, leaving the unremarkable primitive town and it's simple occupants to their elaborate deception.

The Sytonians had always been pleased by how well the Eians had adapted to sequestered life. The early years of confinement had brought continuous surprise inspections and countless exhaustive searches, and after decades of microscopic scrutiny, the natives were convinced that the Eians had lost their arrogance and desire for advanced technology.

But the constant intrusions had merely taught the Eians how to hide better, and now after almost a hundred years of practice, the Council could have sent a thousand inspectors and the underground caverns would never have been detected. Ventilation shafts were carefully concealed beneath rock piles. Underwater generators spun silently beside water and waste conduits in the riverbeds. Those lucky enough to work underground in the sophisticated manufacturing facilities, schools, or development laboratories enjoyed a perfectly comfortable life with running water, modern communication systems, and a temperature controlled environment unlike anywhere else on Syton—a small oasis of their former life.

On Eian, several billion had died of asphyxiation when the poisonous gases were suddenly released from deep within the bedrock. They barely had the time and resources to send a few thousand across the short distance separating the twin moons, to their outpost in the Syton gorge, before Eian's atmosphere became a death shroud. Over the intervening centuries, the sick mustard colored blanket had not only killed most of the life on Eian, but also the hope of ever returning to their home planet.

But during the last twenty years, the color over Eian had faded. Patches of green and blue had begun to show through, and like a desert seed that sprouts in an unfamiliar rain, the dream of returning home had began to grow again.

During a previous Rhan-da-lith, when Eidorf stumbled upon the shuttle's periodic risings, his imagination was ignited. Here, no matter how tenuous, how miniscule, was a small degree of hope. Could they use this machine or copy its design? What could they learn from the information system he assumed it contained? But most important, did the shuttle have enough fuel to take a small group of them back to Eian to find the remnants of their own space industry? He was obsessed, consumed by the idea, some claimed even fanatical. Could they escape this ironic imprisonment by these defective beings?

This was their reward for being compassionate, Eidorf often complained. The Eians should have destroyed their eugenic mistakes instead of dumping them and their sympathetic creators here on Syton. The genetic scientists had produced such dim-witted monstrosities in their quest for longer life. The towan were too big, too slow, and perversely, they were able to mate each and every month—which they did with great enthusiasm once they overthrew their kindhearted wardens. Scientists could be so near-sighted—create super-charged males without mates, then leave them in a secluded outpost near your wives. Brilliant! Eidorf could just imagine the gene manipulators busy creating giant trees, while their wives were being ravaged. No wonder the original towans took over the gorge. The wild cyliths should have cleaned up the Eian's mess, Eidorf thought wistfully. Instead, the towan made pets of them!

Eidorf never considered the Human's stake in the machine. Why should he? Humans were trapped, their home world countless light years away. This was their new home now, and if they continued to obey the Prohibitions, they would soon find themselves no smarter than the towans. In a few generations, they wouldn't understand the contents of their own information system aboard the shuttle. The vehicle did them little good. For the human's it was a memento, a souvenir, an engineer's keepsake. To Eidorf, it was the future…and he was sure Julian was the key.

"She doesn't know anything about the flying machine." It was foolish for Eiton to question Eidorf, the Council representative, but after days of merciless torture, he was convinced the old human female was telling the truth.

"You question my authority?" Eidorf asked.

Eiton knew he shouldn't have challenged Eidorf. "Not your authority, simply the methodology. Why don't we just use an amplifier?"

"It doesn't seem to work on their kind," said Eidorf, looking down at Julian asleep on the crumpled pile of cloth they had thrown together to approximate a bed. Purple veins spread out like tiny spider webs from her tightly clenched eyes. What remained of her thin gray hair sprouted randomly in clumps from her bloody scalp making her look like an old doll that had lost most of its hair. A stench of sweat and urine rose from her unwashed body.

"Their lobe is probably missing or underdeveloped. I would guess that's also why they spend so much time unconscious every day. After we're done, we'll let the anatomists take this one apart and see."

"She's practically dead already," commented Eiton.

"Let me know when she regains consciousness. I'm going above to eat." Eidorf swept out of the small room, scattering the clumps of loose gray hair that lay in his path.

Eiton sat on the floor next to Julian, gazing at the scabs forming on the old human's scalp. A small rivulet of blood trickled down her forehead. Instinctively, Eiton reached over to daub it off before it flowed into her eye. At his touch, she awoke with a start.

"Leave me alone. There's nothing I can tell you and scarcely little hair left."

"You haven't told us anything."

"Because I don't know anything. You've killed the only one who may have known anything."

"*I* didn't kill anyone," Eiton clarified.

Julian rolled over and scrutinized Eiton. "Maybe not..." With difficulty, she managed a deep breath and rolled onto her back. "Please...just let me rest."

"Eidorf will kill you too before he's done."

"Because I was on the last flight with Hyland? That doesn't mean he told me of his plans."

"That might be the truth...but for you it doesn't matter. It only matters what Eidorf believes."

"And you...is that all that matters to you as well?"

"No, but it is important if you want to live."

Julian gazed at this miniscule copy of a towan. "Are you related to Eidorf? A brother or son?" she asked.

"No, I am not from *that* family. I am a...what is the human word...a maker? I build things and make them work."

Julian thought she detected pride in the small creature's answer.

"I am Eiton," he continued, "...and I do care about many things. The most important is going home. If Eidorf can get us there, I will help anyway I can."

"Including torturing an old lady. How noble!" Julian wiped a drop of blood from the side of her head. "Go away."

Eiton, accustom to taking orders turned to go, but hesitated and turned. "You must have seen our home when you first arrived. Do you remember?"

Confused and in pain, Julian lay down and tried to ignore the new creature, hoping it would get the signal and leave, but Eiton asked again, "Eian was more beautiful than this frigid world. When you arrived, you must have examined the other moon?"

Through the fog of exhaustion, Julian began to understand. But how could the surveyors have missed an entire civilization? Then she remembered. "The long range reports indicated the atmosphere was poisonous to life. We didn't look beyond—"

"But that was thirty years ago," Eiton interrupted. "The color has faded recently. Certainly the poisons have been flushed out by the rains of the last few hundred years."

"Doubtful," Julian murmured to herself.

Eiton drew closer. "Don't you think Eian looks better now?"

Julian hadn't bothered to look closely at the other moon of Conboet for years. But Eiton had. "What happened to your world? How many years have you been here on Syton?"

As Eiton explained everything, Julian found herself forgetting the last few days of torture. Her thoughts drifting among the hundreds of other worlds they had passed by. How many of them had once supported life, but because of some twist of fate or ill conceived action had become unfit?

"You must help us return to Eian," Eiton pleaded. "With just a few of us...makers...we could eventually rebuild our space industry. Then, when we return for the rest of our people, we will take you humans with us. Let the towans have Syton. Just think what you humans are throwing away by following their silly Prohibitions."

"After what you've done, how could we possibly trust you, or for that matter want to live with you? The Sytonians have generally left us alone. As long as we don't take advantage of them, as you did, we will be able to live here in peace. To my knowledge they seem forthright and ethical. You on the other hand, have killed and tortured us. By your own story, it is plain that you have exploited and deceived the very race that opened their world for you."

"Opened their world!" exclaimed Eiton. "Syton isn't theirs. For centuries before the towan were even created, the gorge had been ours. When we deposited a couple hundred of these pathetic creatures in T'Matte, there were already thousands of us running the outpost there, but they weren't content...they rebelled and destroyed everything. In the first year, they ate all the Eian males, and then took our women for mates...at least that's what their legends say. Believe me, if we didn't have to be here, we wouldn't be."

"And now they keep *you* prisoner. Fitting justice if you ask me."

"They weren't prisoners. We let them live free in T'Matte."

"Without females?"

"There were no females. All the experiments were male. It didn't make sense to allow failures to reproduce. Did you know they are capable of mating every month?"

Even with her growing headache, Julian had to smile. She lay back and looked away signaling that the conversation was over. Eiton watched as she tried unsuccessfully to find a comfortable position on the hard floor. When she stopped fidgeting, he started for the door. The small Eian walked with a peculiar gait. His mid-knee on his center leg was stiff, an old scar barely visible at the joint.

"Engineer," said Julian.

Eiton turned. "What?"

"That's the word you're searching for. Engineer— someone who designs and builds things, who knows how things work."

"Then I'm an engineer."

"A word of caution Engineer—if the shuttle in the lake is truly operating and you manage to retrieve it, don't try opening it without the access code."

"And what would that be?"

"I believe Eidorf killed the only one who knew."

Warren

Li Sy hid in the rocks above the Women's Colony and watched as twenty towan, accompanied by their snarling cyliths, demolished the colony's advanced medical equipment and buildings with rough battle-axes. The bright artificial lamps illuminating the medical complex briefly flared as they were smashed and extinguished. Primitive torches took their place. The humans, young and old, healthy and sick, were herded together into the wide courtyard to be surrounded by the towan's cyliths. Those who could not stand or walk were struck down and fed to the snarling beasts.

After destroying the genetic bank, the natives entered the building where Mas was recovering from his emergency surgery. Nanc ran in after them. Li Sy heard her scream, and then Nanc came stumbling out, supporting Mas. Young Wilem ran over to join them. They walked slowly, Mas in bare feet, towards the other Humans. A native tore Nanc from Mas' side and pushed him to the ground. The cyliths closed in slowly.

Mas stared at the cylith's blood stained muzzles and struggled to stand. A few of the animals continued fighting over a human leg.

Nanc strained to free herself from the towan's grasp. "You bastards! Can't you see he needs help?" She yelled to Mas. "Stand up!"

Wilem stood paralyzed. "Stand up," he whispered. "Stand up."

Mas fought to rise on atrophied leg muscles, beads of sweat formed on his upper lip as he strained to force his stubborn muscles to move, but it was clear he wasn't going to be successful. Suddenly, Wilem stepped forward.

"No, Wilem. Stay back," Mas ordered. But the young boy, without hesitation, stepped over the bloody remains in his path to stand between Mas and the creatures. Mas reached out, and using the boy's shoulders for support, struggled to his feet. Under malevolent eyes and with Wilem's help, Mas shuffled, half dragging, half sliding his unresponsive legs to join the captive group. The towan released Nanc and she ran to their side and assumed the burden of support from her son.

Li Sy continued watching in silence as the towan forced the humans out through the narrow passage in the caldera's side. She waited for nearly an hour before leaving the safety of the rocks, cautiously making her way down into the ruins. Digging among the debris she found her medicine pouch and some food. Then wrapping a blanket around herself, she left the broken remains of the colony and ventured into the night.

Spectacular electric ribbons sliced the sky over Panvera and thunder shook the walls of the Tournell house. Sleep was impossible, so Jasin and Elizabeth joined her father in the kitchen where they finished the last of the sweet bread.

"Elizabeth tells me you enjoyed my bread recipe," said Warren.

"Your recipe?" Elizabeth objected. "If it weren't for the spices Mother added it would be quite ordinary."

"Don't fight," mumbled Jasin through a full mouth where just seconds before he had stuffed the last piece. "Actually, I hate it."

"Where'd you pick up this lying scoundrel, Lizzy?" asked Warren.

"It was a mistake...I know that now, but I was impressed by his families huge estate."

Jasin turned red and Elizabeth realized she had embarrassed him. Winking at him, she continued, "Two stories, a courtyard...the kitchen was huge and my own room was larger than any house I'd ever lived in. They even had a servant before she ran off."

"I heard she was sleeping around," Jasin added, sensing an opportunity for revenge.

A deafening crash of thunder interrupted the playful conversation.

"What a relief." said Warren. "For a minute I thought we were going to hear all the scandalous details. Tell me, Jasin, You say you're intent on destroying the shuttle. Have you given any thought on how you might accomplish that?"

"I thought you were against the idea."

"I am...for a lot of reasons, not the least of which is I'd hate to see you get hurt."

"I don't know...burn it, blow it up ...maybe sink it this time for real. I have the feeling the natives would like to be able to see the remains this time. I really haven't thought it through."

Warren shook his head. "Where would you get the explosives? Jasin, you have to be very careful. The shuttle contains an extremely dangerous fuel supply, not to mention the weapons on board."

"Then from what you say, all we have to do is light the fuel supply on fire. It should practically destroy itself."

"And you with it." Warren continued, "You have no idea what you're dealing with."

"And you do?"

"Shuttle maintenance wasn't my specialty," Warren admitted. "I took a couple flights to collect botanical specimens and another when we arrived here," said Warren. "But I know that you can't just paddle up and throw a torch at it."

"I think I know where to get some explosives," Jasin said quietly.

"Are you thinking about the traders?" asked Elizabeth.

Jasin cocked his head "What about the traders? You think they sell explosives?"

"It doesn't matter," said Warren. "No matter what primitive explosives you can get your hands on, they won't even mar the finish on the shuttle's hull. It's built to withstand intense heat and pressure. It's designed to deflect micro-meteors traveling thousands of kilometers per second. You won't be able to damage it from the outside—"

"Then we'll blow it up from the inside."

"You didn't let me finish...I also doubt you will be able to gain access to the inside."

Jasin fell silent.

"Did Hyland or Jorge ever tell either of you anything about the shuttles? Did they even admit to you that the shuttle existed?"

Both Jasin and Elizabeth shook their heads.

"I didn't think so...Jasin, you can't just grab a handle and swing open the door. The hatches are magnetically locked. There's a whole safety protocol to prevent accidental depressurization, environmental contamination, or unauthorized entry. You need the access code."

"So...what is it?"

Warren chuckled, "I'm sorry, you have no way of knowing, but your question is silly. There isn't a single code. Aboard Tanis, we used a standard procedure to assign access codes. It applied to supply cabinets, lockers, room assignments, computer records or for that matter, shuttles. The codes were either assigned as a random sequence by the computer, or set by the controlling authority. It was my understanding that each time a shuttle flight was authorized, the commanding officer was provided with a new access code as part of their mission specifications. I never knew what it was on any of my flights. I was either a mission specialist or a passenger. It could have been anything."

"Are you saying only Hyland knew the code?" asked Elizabeth.

"Or the computer or whoever was the controlling authority. That's right," said Warren.

Jasin sighed and ran his fingers through his hair, massaging his scalp. The storm had begun to move off towards the mountains and the rumble of thunder echoed in the distance. "What you are saying is...the shuttle is impenetrable."

"Without the access code, it will continue to rise and sink as it has for the last thirty years and I don't think there's a force on this world that can change that," said Warren. "I think you made a promise you can't keep."

Jasin sat back in his chair in dismay. "But I've got to try. My mother's life depends on it," he said softly.

Warren moved closer to Jasin and put his hand on his shoulder. "Please, and I don't mean to be insensitive, but...do you think she's still alive?"

Jasin shrugged. "I don't know, but I've got to believe."

"I hope so too, Jules is a special lady," Warren's voice broke, as unexpected emotion surfaced. "I'm sorry, I grew up with your mom, she was more...she was a very special...special friend."

Elizabeth, who had been deep in thought suddenly spoke up, "Dad, you mentioned Hyland *or* Jorge...you asked whether Jorge ever spoke to us about the shuttle. Do you think he knew the code?"

"Most likely. Hyland was sick a long time and knew he was dying. The shuttle was important to him. I would doubt he took the code with him. It's a good assumption that Jorge knew it, but you said he died suddenly and by surprise."

Jasin agreed. "I don't think he revealed anything to Eidorf, nor to any of us. Let me ask you...who was Hyland's controlling authority? Who would have given the code to him?"

Warren smiled. "In the Engineering department, or for that matter almost anywhere else on that ship, he *was* the controlling authority. If it was his plan to save the shuttle, you can bet he set the code himself. You had better come up with a plan to find Julian that doesn't involve the shuttle. But enough talk for tonight. You two should go to bed. Now that the storm has passed, I think you can get some sleep."

Elizabeth looked over at Jasin. He was drained. She knew how he felt about keeping his word. A matter of honor, he had often said. He had to be crushed. "Come on Jasin, we'll solve the world's problems tomorrow after a good night's rest." She took a candle in one hand and Jasin by the other.

She expected Jasin to have difficulty falling asleep, but it was she who tossed and turned. She rolled over and looked at her love. Deep within her soul, she could feel his inner turmoil. They were partners in this, and yet she was helpless. Her father had closed every door they had believed was open to them, without showing even a single new one. She felt like a teenager again when every path to the future was there to be taken, except she hadn't the ability to follow any of them.

What could she do? Unable to find a comfortable position, she sat up, trying not to wake him. It didn't help that he was hogging the bed and snoring softly. She gave him a little nudge and he turned over. The snoring subsided.

She lay back down, trying to relax, to think soothing thoughts. She was home now, safe, surrounded by the ones she loved most, but other more potent images filled her head—Hyland's cremation and the stink of his burning flesh; Loeton, his chest torn open; Jorge's gruesome death; Mas, mangled and barely alive; and Wilem, poor Wilem, too young to have witnessed any of it. Sleep mercifully arrived, but the raw images persisted, surreal memories trapped in her unconscious.

With a startled gasp she woke, her heart beating so fast and strong she thought it was about to burst. She turned to Jasin and woke him. "Jasin! Wake up."

His eyes popped open accompanied by a short gasp.

"We've got to go back. In the morning, we've got to see him. I've got to talk to him."

"What are you talking about…who?"

"Wilem…In the morning we have to return to the mountain. We have to talk to Wilem. He knows! I'm sure of it." She saw that he was still groggy, unable to grasp what to her was so clear. "Wilem knows the code. Jorge told him before he died."

"No he didn't. I was closer to them than anyone. Jorge didn't say a word."

"He didn't have to."

Li Sy

"It's mine. I found it down near the spillway," the young girl tried to explain to her friends why the creature belonged to her. "A bunch of field diggers were nibbling on its arm, but they ran away when I got closer."

"She's a towa, a native female," said Jasin, peering at the body and three bare feet caked in frozen mud dangling lifelessly in Elizabeth's arms.

"Her name is Li Sy and she's a friend," Elizabeth added emphatically, upset with Jasin's detachment. The towa's eyes were glazed, almost frozen; there was no life in them at all.

They covered her with blankets and cleansed the small wound inflicted by the small sharp teeth of the field diggers. From the lack of visible blood or fluids, Jasin guessed she had been frozen before the animals found her. Elizabeth massaged her stiff hands.

"I never seen one before," said one of the boys, who couldn't have been more than six or seven. "My daddy said they were much bigger and he said they can talk."

The youngsters leaned over and stared at her. Finally the older girl proclaimed, "I don't think this one's going to talk." Elizabeth reacted with disdain. Jasin quickly gathered the kids up, thanked them for finding Li Sy and escorted them to the door.

"If she gets better we want to keep her," said the taller boy.

"My sister will be so jealous!" added the little girl.

Jasin shooed them out.

"She's so cold...so gray. I don't even know if she's alive," cried Elizabeth.

Jasin touched Li Sy's face. There was no way to tell. Detecting a pulse was impossible. He didn't think they had a centralized circulatory organ like a heart to pump fluids throughout their body, at least Loeton didn't seem to have such a large single organ. And without lungs there was no chest movement to observe. All he could think of was to get her warm. "Let's soak her in the canal."

They carried her outside and down to the end of the row of houses where the water in the canal, now merely warm, exited from under the last house. They laid her among the warm rocks and red liquid and waited for some sign.

"Mas must have died," Jasin finally said, breaking the silence, his breath visible in the frigid air.

Elizabeth nodded, "I was thinking the same thing. She wouldn't have left him, not while he was still alive." The resumed their vigil. Finally, Elizabeth remarked, "Unbelievable"

"What?"

"Just that she followed us here. Even the towans and their Initiates never come up this far."

Jasin leaned over and felt Li Sy's extremities. "Her feet aren't so hard anymore and her eyes seem less fixed."

"I would have thought she would have stayed in the Women's Colony. It felt right for her. A place where she could help sick people, a place far from the males of her kind."

"Are you talking about Li Sy or the other women there?"

"Both I guess." It was the first smile he had seen that morning.

"You know...while you were out, your father gave me a handful of crystals."

"Let's not talk about it."

"These people..." Jasin looked around at the small houses, many so small they could easily be considered mere huts, "they don't have much."

"*These* people are my people, my family. I would give anything to help them and that's how they feel in return; that's just how we are. You're not from here. You grew up in the biggest house in town. You never learned how to ask for help. It's not a sin to ask for help. It's not a sin to be needy. People with material things are always afraid of not having those things, embarrassed if they don't have them, embarrassed to ask for them. Someday you will ask for help and learn that it can be liberating."

"Maybe it's a woman's thing. I don't know any men that like asking for help."

A soft puttering sound emerged from Li Sy's mouth and they turned to her. After a few more moments, another small sound escaped, and her tightly curled fingers began to loosen.

"She's thawing out," laughed Jasin in morbid relief.

"But is she alive?"

Minutes later she blinked her eyes and tried to move. Thrilled, they quickly carried her back to the house where they laid her on the bed as before and watched her struggle to regain control of her mind and body.

"C...c...cold...Li'..onna cold," the towa muttered, nearly incoherent.

They wrapped her in a blanket and an hour later, she was sitting upright eating her third pickled melon.

"Where does she put it all?" asked Warren smiling.

"She's always had a good appetite," Jasin replied. "I imagine the she burned a lot of calories trying to stay warm. How are you feeling now, Li Sy?"

"Cold. It is cold here. Why do you Humans live here?"

Warren pointed to the pile of blankets and clothing she sat on. "If you'd wear the clothes we gave you, you might be more comfortable."

"If Humans lived lower, Humans wouldn't need clothes," she countered.

Amazed at Li Sy's spunk and apparent intelligence, Warren asked her daughter in a whisper, "Are they all like her?"

Elizabeth shook her head. "But in general I do think the towas are frightfully underestimated. Wouldn't you agree Li Sy?" She was sure the native could hear everything that was being said.

"Most towa are stupid," she declared. "Towa are slaves of the towan. Li Sy is no slave. Li Sy is free."

"Yes, of course. " Elizabeth had heard Li Sy's mantra countless times. "Can you tell us why you came? What has happened to Mas?"

"Mas is gone."

Jasin took a deep breath and looked at Elizabeth. Tear welled up and she lowered her head.

"Wilem and mother are gone. Everyone is gone. Towan destroyed the colony and took the Humans. Li Sy came here to get help—"

"Wait stop! What do you mean? Which Humans? Who took the Humans?" asked Jasin excitedly, his fingers restless at his side.

"All are headed down the valley towards the big river...maybe Bistoun. Li Sy can show you, but all must hurry."

"Li Sy. Stop talking a minute. Tell us who is headed to the big river. Is Mas dead? Is Wilem dead?

"Mas walking. Wilem and Mother walking to big river. The old human opened Mas up, took the bad out, is walking."

"Mas was still alive then? Mas is not dead?" Jasin asked again to be sure.

"Mas walking." Li Sy turned to Elizabeth and nearly screamed, "MAS WALKING. All are walking." Li Sy took another bite of melon. "This is very good."

Jasin was confused. "What do you mean, 'opened Mas up'? Which old human? How many people lived in the colony?" he asked, looking around.

Elizabeth thought about it. "I don't really—"

Warren saved his daughter from having to break her promise. "There were close to fifty permanent residents, maybe eight to ten patients, with Nanc and the boy...maybe about sixty,"

"You've been there, inside the mountain? You know what's there…or what *was* there?" asked Elizabeth.

Warren nodded, but refused to elaborate.

"What do you mean, 'inside the mountain'? What was inside the mountain?"

When no one answered, he asked, "How long ago were they taken, Li Sy?" Jasin continued drumming his fingers against his leg.

Li Sy looked at Jasin, and swallowed a huge mouthful. Everyone, except Jasin, smiled as they watched the awkward lump of food expand the soft folds of her neck as it forced its way down. "All were taken the night of the storm. Li Sy walked here without stopping until—"

"We should leave immediately. They can't be more than two days ahead," said Jasin excitedly.

Warren shook his head. "What do you think you can do?"

"Why do you use that tone?" Jasin exploded. "I'm sorry, but ever since we got here you've questioned our plans, our ideas, without even one constructive suggestion." He looked at Elizabeth for support; not finding any, he got more upset. "I'm going to try and help my friend…" he again glanced at Elizabeth "…alone if no one else wants to help."

"Listen to you. Again with '*I'm* going' and '*my* friend'." Elizabeth blurted out. "Can't you see we all want to help?"

"I just want you to stop and think before you run off and get yourself and my daughter hurt," pleaded Warren. "Like it or not, your actions have become the focus of the Sytonians…and probably the Eians as well. Think about it…the medical facility had been safely hidden for thirty years until you went there."

"What medical facility? What are you talking about?"

Elizabeth didn't know how to keep the truth from him any longer. The colony's secret just didn't seem to matter anymore. After extracting a promise from Jasin not to act against anyone, she explained everything.

Jasin was dumbstruck. Warren shook his head in dismay. "I can't believe you haven't thought about why the Council let you have your freedom after attempting to kill one of their most respected members. They told you secrets no other human ever knew and then even gave you carts and supplies. Doesn't that strike you as a bit generous?"

"They want me to destroy the shuttle," Jasin said meekly.

"They want you to find the Eian that has betrayed them and killed their friend," corrected Warren.

"Sy Loeton," Jasin muttered. Some of the awkward pieces began to fit.

"You and your family have been watched since day one. Surely you knew that."

"Of course, but my father said Toberry was as important to us as he was to them."

"Avram probably used the towan to send the Council whatever information he wanted them to have. Knowing you're being watched and using that knowledge was smart, leading them to the doctor wasn't."

"I didn't know...we didn't have a choice. Mas was dying."

"I didn't realize we were followed either, Jasin. It didn't even cross my mind." Elizabeth said, trying to comfort him.

Jasin moaned, "But...I did. I mean, I thought we were, but I was too stupid to do anything about it."

"I don't think you're stupid...far from it," Warren said. "You just didn't take time to think it through. You believe I'm against taking action; that I'm too negative, but that's not it. I'm cautious because there are consequences to everything you do."

"So what now? What do you suggest?" Jasin asked.

"For one thing, don't rush after them," he warned. "There's no point. If they were going to kill them, they would have done so in the mountain. If you try to free Mas and the others, you will end up captured.

Jasin grew agitated. "Again, you point out what we shouldn't do."

Warren smiled, "I like to stay out of trouble and sometimes if you wait, the way becomes clear."

"How can we wait?"

"What's the hurry? If Mas can travel, he is obviously getting better"

"What about my mother?"

"And Wilem, we have to talk to him," Elizabeth added.

"You're right about Julian," said Warren. "She's been gone a long time. Something's got to be done. But even if the young boy received the code, even if he understood and still remembers...well, that's not important until there's a decision about the shuttle. Rhan-da-lith is probably months away."

"A decision *has* been made concerning the shuttle," argued Jasin, "but I agree, we should concentrate on finding my mother. The Eians have her. Somehow they've kept her from the Sytonians. The last one to see her was Mas at the Low Pass, and Sy Hone thought she was taken towards Bistoun."

"The small human female was taken into the Kull," said the towa between mouthfuls.

Stunned, everyone turned to stare at Li Sy.

"How do you know?" asked Elizabeth. "I thought you stayed with Mas after the attack."

"Li Sy stayed with Mas," the towa agreed. "All others went into the Kull. Li Sy watched their light."

Both Jasin and Elizabeth recalled the vista at the Low Pass and knew it was possible. Li Sy had never told anyone and no one had ever bothered to ask...until now. Julian had never been discussed very much in her presence.

"It makes sense," said Jasin. "People would have noticed if she were brought through Bistoun. The Sytonians practically own that town. If you were hiding from both Human and Sytonian, you wouldn't dare enter Bistoun."

"The Kull is prohibited and guarded. You'll probably end up imprisoned with your friend," reminded Warren.

"It's prohibited, but not guarded," said Jasin thoughtfully. It suddenly became clear where they needed to go.

Discovery

Elizabeth's arm swung tirelessly, using her thin, razor sharp knife to slash and clear the Hackbark that grew thick along the river's edge. Jasin had offered to lead, but she refused to relinquish the alien weapon. Mas had given it to her and, even though they had agreed their first priority would be Julian, holding the delicate yet deadly instrument made her feel closer to their friend, reminding her that until they were all together again, she had to remain sharp and ever vigilant. Already scratched and bleeding from the bushes' nasty thorns, she grimaced as another spiky branch whipped against her thigh setting her nerves on fire. With an angry flip of her wrist, the stiletto severed the offending stalk from its root.

Without a trail, progress was slow. They skirted powerful rapids and passed spectacular rock terraces, sending their torrents crashing down to frothy pools alongside the river. Li Sy didn't have trouble, but Jasin and Elizabeth, continually distracted by the roar and sight of these breathtaking displays, seemed intent on slipping into every hidden stream, tripping on every tangled root, and banging their heads on all the low hanging branches.

When the sun reached its zenith on the second day, pouring light over the edge of the cliff on the opposite side of the river, it revealed a faint meandering line on the steep rugged hillside.

"Can you see the trail?" Jasin asked, tracing the path in the air in front of him. "That's where we descended from Cernai, where Li Sy followed us. Can you see it?"

Elizabeth squinted and cocked her head looking at the steep, twisted trail that often appeared to end at the edge of some broken outcropping. "I'm glad we don't have to mess with that."

"How do you think we're going to get back?" teased Jasin. Actually, he thought, if by any remote chance they were able to rescue Julian and she was able to manage, it was probably a good idea to head back through the Village of Cernai. "It wasn't so bad. It will be safer to climb than it was to descend."

"No bridges," commented Li Sy, pointing downstream. "Ferry." She pointed towards Bistoun.

Elizabeth nodded. "Jasin wants to cross as close to where you swam across the first time."

"Li Sy not swim."

"Don't worry, I'll help you."

The small towa rocked back and forth, shifting her weight between her middle and side legs, clearly agitated. "Li Sy not swim," she repeated.

Elizabeth smiled warmly and held out her hand as she had done for Wilem whenever he got nervous. The towa looked at it strangely and then grabbed onto it.

By mid-afternoon they stood at the conclusion of the Canyon River and peered across the Andoree. Dozens of gigantic gilia heads, some wider than a meter across, floated on its surface. Slender roots reached into the depths and held them to the river bottom. Carried by the outgoing tide still several hours from going slack, their long rubbery fronds trailed out towards the Great Lake. Jasin paced along the shore. The seemingly empty Kull, and the possibility of his mother's rescue beckoned from the far bank.

While they waited for the river to calm, Jasin gathered loose sticks and debris and constructed a fragile raft that he hoped would float their packs. Two hours later, the current had slackened enough to attempt the crossing.

"This is becoming something of a routine," he mumbled to himself before wading into the water.

Jasin swam slowly, carefully pulling the delicate raft. Elizabeth swam behind. Even with Li Sy clinging to her back, her strong strokes propelled her swiftly through the confused water. Little swirls, currents, and counter-currents swung them up-stream and down with little net effect. Only once, on the third leg, did they rest, holding onto slimy *gilia* fronds where they sprouted from the massive buoyant heads.

Curious, Elizabeth thumped the dark burgundy surface. "Hollow," she announced.

Jasin nodded, still trying to catch his breath, was embarrassed to be struggling while she had the capacity to think of anything but getting to the other side. "Ready?" he asked, not sure that he was himself.

They pushed off and ten minutes later dragged themselves out of the water on the opposite shore. Relatively painless, Jasin thought, comparing this crossing to his last. Li Sy scampered up the slightly concave embankment that had been carved out by the tidal action. Elizabeth followed her. Jasin stayed at the river's edge untying their packs from the raft, which he tore apart, scattering the remains to hide their crossing. His careful preparations would afford them dry clothes. Lifting their gear over one shoulder, he climbed the small incline. A loose rock sent him sliding several feet. Swearing, he stood up, brushing the mud off.

"Are you all right?" yelled Elizabeth.

"Yeah," he lied, his dignity bruised most of all. He threw the packs over the edge and climbed up after them.

Elizabeth had shed her wet clothes and was leaning to one side, avoiding the water that trickled out of her hair as she twisted it. "I should have crossed naked. I'd have saved a change of clothes."

"Here," Jasin offered her her pack.

Elizabeth looked up and giggled. "Get out of those muddy clothes and wash up. You're a mess."

"What difference does it make?" He really wasn't in the mood to deal with the trivial.

"Go on, you'll feel better. It might change your mood." Elizabeth threw her head back and turned to face the last warming rays of the day.

He thought to ignore her advice, but realized that dried mud and wet clothing were bound to chafe. He glanced in her direction. She stood chin raised, feet slightly apart, her arms relaxed at her side. Magnificent, he thought, feeling totally undeserving. How could he be so lucky, to be loved by someone of her intelligence, strength, and bravery? Her physical beauty continued to astound him. It was clear by her stance that she was comfortable with her body...even proud. He allowed himself to savor her nakedness—her elegant posture, the firm sensual curve of her rear, the fullness of her breasts, and of course those wonderfully long muscular legs. A red welt colored her right thigh and her calves were scratched raw, but they did little to diminish Jasin's impression of sensual, confident power. The list of her qualities was endless. And pragmatic too, he thought with resignation. He stripped down and walked back to the river to rinse off the mud.

When he returned, she had begun dressing. "My turn," she said smiling.

"For what?"

"Stand there. It's my turn to stare."

"I wasn't..." He felt his face redden. Add sorceress to the list, he thought.

She walked over and hugged his wet body. "I love you Mr. Elstrada. When this is over, " she touched the side of his face tenderly, "we have some serious talking to do." She kissed him, her tongue lightly brushing his lips.

That night while Li Sy watched over them, Jasin and Elizabeth cuddled. He gentle cradled her head in the crook of his arm. They hadn't any torches or candles and Jasin refused to light a fire.

"How are your legs? They were pretty scratched up."

"So you were watching," Elizabeth teased. "They'll be fine, everything will be fine." She felt strangely content considering the circumstances. They lay exposed in the middle of a forbidden wilderness, looking for the secret lair of an alien race whose only activities she knew of were murder and kidnapping. Yet she felt at peace and in love. It had been a good day, a satisfying day, and the only thing that would make it more perfect would be.... She reached down and lightly touched his inner thigh. He turned towards her.

"Do you mind that I worship you?" he asked.

"Worship? That's kind of strong isn't it?"

"It's barely strong enough." He kissed her deeply. Their tongues touched and danced briefly. His hands flowed over her body, caressing her breasts.

She stopped him, holding his hands and kissing his fingertips. "They're too sensitive."

"Anything else off-limits," he teased.

"Nothing else...absolutely nothing." And she spent the next hour proving that.

They woke to the absolute silence of the Kull...and to Li Sy's piercing stare. "Food...it is time to eat." It wasn't a question.

"So eat; you know where the food is," Jasin rolled over and kissed Elizabeth's cheek. "Good morning, how'd you sleep?"

Elizabeth, holding the blanket to her chest, rolled over and was about to answer, but Li Sy's abnormal stare disturbed her. She looked past Jasin and raised her eyebrows. Jasin rolled back and looked up at the motionless towa. "What?"

"She must eat first."

"Since when?" asked Jasin bemused.

"It is her time; she eats first," Li Sy repeated.

At first they merely grinned at the presumption, but finally Elizabeth pacified her by taking the first bite of breakfast, after which Li Sy was all too willing to eat her usual disproportionate share.

Jasin looked at the cloudless sky, then at the distant peak they were using as a guide. "Let's get going," he coaxed, "we can be there in five or six hours."

"Where's there?" asked Elizabeth.

"You know…out there. I'll let you know when we get there," Jasin smiled and pulled her up. "Come on Li Sy, save some for tomorrow."

The mismatched trio grabbed their packs and headed toward the tall volcanic peak. They walked without a word for nearly an hour until Li Sy broke the silence.

"You humans mate with great difficulty and pain." She looked up at Elizabeth for an explanation. "So many different…" the towa searched for a Human word while twisting her hands to mimic various positions, "It hurt. You made sounds of pain."

Elizabeth tried to contain her laughter. "No, it didn't hurt."

"When will there be a small…what do you call it?"

"A baby. There will be no baby, Li Sy." Jasin sidled over to eavesdrop on the conversation.

"It is your time. You made a baby. I saw."

"We made love…we enjoyed each other. It was pleasurable."

"Pleasurable?"

"It felt good."

"Then why did you cry out in pain? If you did not make a baby why do you let Jasin do it?"

Elizabeth directed her answer to Jasin with a smile. "That's a good question. I will have to reconsider."

"Reconsider?" asked Li Sy confused.

"I will have to think about it." She turned back towards Li Sy. "Tell me Li Sy, Do you only do it to make little ones? Is mating painful for you?"

"Towa must mate or die. The water must be released. The pain is before, when you can't bear to carry the water any longer. Towan can release the water. It is good when the water is released."

Elizabeth recalled her experience in the hardel. All that towa needed was to have her water released, then she left them.

Jasin cocked his head. "But you did not die the last time you were here. It was your time then."

"Yes"

"You did not die."

"The water was released. It was good."

Elizabeth shook her head. "But there were no towan…"

Li Sy walked on in silence and for a few moments they attempted to respect her desire not to speak about it further. Finally, Jasin blurted, "It was Mas? Mas released the water?"

More silence.

Elizabeth reached out and held Jasin back. "You don't really think it was Mas?"

Jasin stopped. "I don't know and I suppose it doesn't really matter. I believed Mas when he told me nothing happened, but he might have been too embarrassed or…"

"Or maybe he was telling the truth. Perhaps she got help elsewhere."

"Hey! Don't look at me."

"No, I didn't mean you. Maybe there was another…a native, or even one of them—an Eian. If there was, then she might know where they're hiding out here. You know her. If you don't ask a direct question…"

They quickened their pace and caught up with Li Sy. Elizabeth reached out to grab her arm, but Jasin stopped her, remembering how ill advised that was. "Li Sy, one last question," he asked.

Elizabeth continued, "Li Sy, do you know where the Eians might be? Do you know where they are?"

She did not slacken her pace. "They are out there," she pointed ahead. "Jasin and Mas and Li Sy saw many."

"Live ones?" asked Jasin. "Do you know where any *live* Eians or towans might be in the Kull?"

This time it was Li Sy that came to an abrupt halt. "Why do you think Li Sy knows?"

"We just thought you might. We had to ask," Elizabeth apologized.

Jasin thought about asking Li Sy the questions in her own language, but he doubted her answers would change. In school he struggled to master their language, but that didn't mean he understood them, that he felt what they felt, or knew what they needed. Even among one's own people, one's own family for that matter, true communication was often elusive. Words were exchanged, questions answered, but sometimes they only served to divert and hide the truth, mask feelings, or avoid conflict. Meaning was elusive. Just because you had a conversation didn't mean you said or learned anything.

Jasin leaned in close to Elizabeth and whispered, "She didn't answer the question."

"No, she didn't."

Hours later, after a meager meal of dried fruit and hard biscuits they lay watching giant Conboet slip away, leaving a pale green glow at the horizon. Li Sy squatted, folding her arms and legs against her torso to conserve warmth and rocked gently. She hummed quietly.

"Li Sy, before, when it was your time, you sang a song that Mas and I thought was beautiful. Could you sing it for us tonight?"

Elizabeth wasn't sure Jasin's obvious ploy was well conceived. Attracting "guests" wouldn't necessarily help them find Julian.

"It is not my time," replied Li Sy.

"I understand, but..."

"It is not allowed."

"Who would punish you? Are you afraid?"

"Li Sy is not afraid," she stated emphatically.

Jasin taunted her, "I think you *are* afraid."

The balled up towa unfolded her arms and legs and walked over to where Jasin and Elizabeth lay. She gazed down at them. "We would all die. They would kill you after."

"After?" asked Elizabeth.

"After Li Sy...I am not ready." Suddenly, she turned her head slightly, peering into the darkening landscape, listening.

Jasin jumped to his feet and strained to hear. Elizabeth threw off her blanket and began to rise. "Quiet," commanded Jasin, "Don't move."

It was very soft—sh, sh, sh, sh—extremely faint, but growing louder, traveling left to right. Then the rhythm slowed...and stopped.

"Something's riding the blue rail," said Jasin excitedly. "I just knew—"

"Shh!" This time it was Elizabeth who called for quiet. "It's close," she whispered. Without warning, the sound suddenly started again and a faint rumble rose from deep within the ground to their right, and then faded into the distance.

"Let's go!" Jasin said excitedly, picking up his blanket, "that couldn't have been more than a few minutes from here."

"Tonight?" Elizabeth asked incredulously. It had been an exhausting day and she assumed that whatever lay ahead would still be there in the morning. Julian had been gone months, a few hours wouldn't make any difference.

"Why not? We'll walk to the rail, it should be easy to find, and follow it."

"Follow it where?"

"Wherever it takes us"

Lava Tube

Finding the rail was a simple matter. Even in the dim starlight the half-meter high artificial ridge stood out boldly from the otherwise unremarkable plain. A blind man could have found it, thought Jasin. They turned right and followed it for several minutes until a small rocky gully cut across their path and forced them to stop. The rail continued, however, and bridged the cleft on a narrow strip of land and disappeared into the darkness beyond. Without thought or fear, Li Sy jumped onto the rail and started across. Jasin looked at Elizabeth, but if she had any fear it wasn't evident.

"After you," Jasin offered, tightening the straps on his pack.

Elizabeth nodded, climbed up, and began to cross. Midway she froze and cocked her head as if listening for some signal to continue. Afraid that fear had overcome her, Jasin stopped a few paces behind. "You okay?" he whispered, careful not to startle her.

She nodded, and turned her head to peer into the broken rubble beneath her. There…she felt it again—a slight draft, cooler than the still desert air. She proceeded across and waited for Jasin on the other side. "Did you feel it?"

"What?"

"A cool whiff of air…a slight breeze, rising from the gully."

"So?" Jasin asked. Li Sy returned to their side.

"Why stop here? Dangerous to fall." said Li Sy.

"Perhaps there's water down in the rocks," Jasin suggested. "We're running low."

"Li Sy will get." She took one of their empty water gourds and scampered down the side into the broken chunks of stone and gravel.

A few minutes later she reappeared. "No water. Time to go."

"There was nothing there?" Elizabeth asked.

"No thing. Empty hole," the towa proclaimed.

"Empty hole?" questioned Elizabeth. "Jasin, the sound from the rail stopped somewhere around here."

With Li Sy complaining, they carefully picked their way down over the sharp chunks of stone and into Li Sy's "empty hole", and into absolute darkness. A cool breeze washed over them.

"A cave," guessed Jasin. He backed out and pulled the candle lantern from his pack. A few moments later it's light revealed that it was not a cave as Jasin suspected; instead, they had climbed down through a collapsed stone roof and into a tunnel. The walls curved up and around them to become the roof. A dirt floor held small footprints that led off into the darkness.

"Not good," Li Sy said. "Dark...time to leave." She turned to go.

"I have to agree," Elizabeth said, fearing the thought of staying in the darkness any longer than absolutely necessary.

"This must have taken an enormous amount of digging," Jasin observed.

Elizabeth shook her head, examining the interior walls of the tunnel. "I don't think so, it seems natural...maybe a lava tube."

"A what?"

"A hollow tunnel left when lava flows down a dry riverbed and the outside cools faster than the inside. It forms a crust. The still molten interior empties out eventually or clogs up an end."

Jasin looked at her quizzically.

Elizabeth shrugged. "You'd be surprised at the useless information a daughter of two professors has stored away."

"Well, from the size of these footprints, the Eians must use it. It could lead to Hadrious."

"Why not follow the rail? Isn't it just as likely it leads somewhere important? Couldn't it just as likely lead to Hadrious?" argued Elizabeth.

"But the footprints are here."

"How do you know how old these footprints are? They could have been here for ages."

I'll bet if we follow this, we'll discover where they took Mother."

"Don't you suppose it is guarded somehow?" Elizabeth cautioned, not particularly interested in spending any more time underground. "Now that we know it's here, we could probably follow the tube from the outside in the morning. At least in the brightness we might be able to see any dangers."

"I doubt you can follow this outside. The Sytonians know where Hadrious is and now must suspect the Eians have a secret way into and out it. If you could see this tunnel topside, they would have shut it down already. We should check this out tonight. We know that some thing riding the rail stopped close by, possibly to allow someone to enter this within the last hour so we should be safe from anyone using it again soon and surprising us from behind. If we travel quietly and without light, we ought to see any guards long before they see us. They won't be waiting in the dark."

"Maybe during the day there are cracks or more cave-ins and we won't have to travel in the dark," Elizabeth suggested hopefully.

"The darkness works to our advantage. We're wasting time. This tube is what we've been looking for."

Elizabeth took a deep breath. Her heart was pounding and a chill spread through her body. Jasin was right, but looking into the total darkness.... She took a deep breath. "Let's go then. Li Sy, do you understand what we are doing? Are you with us?"

"It is a mistake. We should leave this place," suggested their little companion.

"Are you coming?" Jasin asked.

"Eat first."

Elizabeth smiled, and in the faint candlelight, she saw Jasin also grinning. As long as there was food, Li Sy was onboard.

Jasin opened his pack and tossed Li Sy a hard biscuit. "You hungry?" he asked Elizabeth. She shook her head. Her stomach was queasy; her breathing shallow and rapid. The thought of spending even a few minutes in the pitch darkness brought on cold sweats.

He nodded in understanding then blew out the candle and repacked it.

They stood silently in the darkness straining to see anything but they might as well been blind. The blackness and silence was absolute. Elizabeth thought she could hear the blood flowing in her ears. Her heartbeat was like a drum. Jasin walked away and she hesitantly followed the sound of his footsteps. No...she was not going to like this at all.

Julian

Peering into super-cooled liquid, Eiton adjusted the rotation angle of the crystal hemisphere slightly. Fine-tuning the basin's refractive index momentarily upset the photonic standing wave, but soon the suspended image congealed again. Then again it was out of focus. Repeating his actions several times yielded the same results. Finally in frustration, Eiton released his head restraint, stepped down off the observation support, and started the long descent along the tapered collecting shaft to the specimen chamber five meters below. He moved slowly as his stiff leg made the climb difficult. The chronic problem of maintaining critical focus was supposedly alleviated in the design of this new magnifier, but the image of Julian's brain cells refused to stabilize.

"Its only a biological construct," he mumbled to himself. The specifications of the viewer far exceeded the demands that this simple molecular mapping required. The construction teams routinely used it to develop new atomic crystallographic lattice designs. Examining biological properties at the cellular level shouldn't be giving him any trouble at all.

He paused to examine the power coupling at the two-meter junction, then again at the four-meter mark. Everything appeared fine. Checking the radiation emitters revealed nothing. Eiton stooped down and removed the specimen cartridge and carefully extracted the biologic tubule. While holding an inspection light to one side, he rotated the thin sample between his two thumbs. It looked perfect and he was just about to place it back in the cartridge when he hesitated and substituted a blood tubule he had taken from the human during the same extraction. He climbed back and secured his head once more. In less than a minute, it was as if he was vicariously swimming among the fantastic alien constituents of human blood—all perfectly clear.

Eiton picked one cell and rotated the crystal hemisphere until the twisted threads of Julian's chromosomes became clear. Another twist—a brief stop at the chemical latticework—an interesting double helix design—then another twist to penetrate and explore the atomic structure. The imager worked flawlessly. There had to be something wrong with the sample of her brain tissues. Either the tubule was defective or there was something strange about the nature of the sample. Perhaps these cells operated differently.

On a hunch, he descended once again, replaced the earlier sample in the chamber, but before climbing back he reduced the output of the focusing field. The modification would only allow low power magnification, maybe a thousand times—enough, however, to test his theory.

This time focused and detailed images formed in the super-cooled liquid—large bloated cell bodies with multiple branches, sprouting fine long extensions all awash in a supportive network of more numerous small glandular cells.

Eiton was jubilant. How he enjoyed solving riddles! The complex focusing field must create a sympathetic electrical reaction in these human brain cells that disturbed the perfect uniformity of the magnification, causing the blurred image. No wonder the first human died using the amplifier, their brain chemistry would never tolerate such intense electromagnetic fields.

He finished mapping the major structures within the human's brain cells before seeking out Eidorf.

"Respectfully sir, I still can't explain what makes them spend so much time unconscious, but I can tell you their cell design and chemistry is vastly different than ours. I would proceed more cautiously. Their brain cells don't seem to have the same regenerative qualities as many of their other cells. We could be damaging her."

Eidorf did not seem to be listening.

"Do you understand what I'm saying? We may have—"

"Just because I am not trained in the scientific arts, doesn't mean I don't comprehend. Can you keep her alive?"

"I am not sure. She seems delirious. We haven't allowed her to obtain her complete rest state for weeks and I'm worried that the sample extractions—"

"See that she survives. One of our teams has just returned. We have finally located the machine in the lake. We must be prepared to seize it during the next Rhan-da-lith, but it appears she was telling you the truth about gaining entry. The human will have to supply the codes."

"She claims not to know them."

"And you believe her?"

"Yes, I think I do."

"Then kill her; she has outlived her usefulness."

This struck Eiton as wasteful. "Perhaps she knows someone who does know the code or maybe she can operate the craft."

"She was only Elstrada's wife. A female. If she doesn't have the code, She's worthless. It would be safer if she were dead. Besides, didn't you claim you would be able to understand the machine's operation?"

"It would be faster to get help. Maybe we could trade her for information."

"I don't care what you do with her. She's your problem now." Eidorf turned and walked away, his voice fading as he left the room. "We've wasted too much time and effort on her already."

Eiton walked back to the chamber where they were keeping the human. The old female lay with her eyes forced open on the dirt floor. A clean white cloth was spread under her head, which was supported in a latticework attached to a control box not unlike the one that had been connected to Jorge Wynosk. A feeding tube led from a cylindrical reservoir of golden jelly into her mouth and then down her throat, all very clinical. Her lower torso, however, had been left to soak in a mud puddle of her waste.

She was his problem now and he was glad. He felt they had mismanaged her interrogation from the beginning and was curious if his ideas and methods might be more fruitful.

He removed the stimulator lattice, being careful not to harm the dried blood that had formed over the extraction site and then tenderly removed the ocular supports that prevented her from closing her eyes. The feeding tube appeared to interfere with her oxygen exchange and he pulled it out. Leaning back on his center leg, he looked the human over. Much better he thought. Clearly, Eidorf's methods had been ineffectual. First get her healthy, clean her up, get her to trust him, and then see what help she might provide.

Darkness

Jasin and Elizabeth discovered the small rail almost immediately. While afraid of being discovered they relit their small candle lantern to reveal a petite version of the blue rail on the surface, leading off into the darkness. In the yellow flickering light, Jasin's eyes sparkled with excitement, sure that the rail guided them toward the hidden Eian enclave and his mother. Extinguishing the flame, Jasin eagerly led them on. To keep oriented in the unbroken darkness, he brushed his left hand along the rail's smooth surface, while never letting go of Elizabeth's hand with the other. Li Sy kept pace across the unseen barrier that effectively divided the tunnel into two lanes.

Any sound they made reverberated loudly against the hard concave walls, and Jasin feared that even the sound of their footsteps would announce their presence to anyone else that might be in the long stone tunnel.

"Sounds in the dark just seem louder," Elizabeth said with feigned calm, sure that if her companions listened carefully enough, they would hear her heart trying to escape her chest. It was her turn to be paranoid, confident that they were being followed; positive she could hear breathing; convinced that every pebble and stone that was put in motion presaged their capture.

Long dormant sounds from her past seeped out of the walls, and crept through the darkness that enveloped them to haunt her anew. Once again she heard the twigs snapping and the rustling of the short undergrowth as the cylith pups approached, the alien shouts of the Initiate as he unknowingly attracted the beasts into their camp, her brother's startled gasps as they shredded his flesh, and the final gurgled breaths that escaped from his torn and bloody windpipe. Gruesome memories flooded her deprived senses. Transported to a time she had fought to suppress she was there again, hidden beneath her blankets, listening to the young towan capture his fierce bloodthirsty prize. The animals, ignorant of the game they were part of, intently gnawed on what was left of Michael, her older brother whom she idolized and loved more than anyone else in this confusing world. Those sounds were all that remained of their last minutes together and they had become burned into her memory as if a red-hot branding iron had seared her brain.

She felt a tug on her arm. "What's wrong?" asked Jasin.

"Nothing," she replied, disoriented.

"Why stop?"

She tried to move forward, but her feet remained immobilized, cemented to the fine dirt beneath her. "I'm fine," she said, more to convince herself, than him.

"Jasin...do you really think this is such a good idea. There's no way to know what we're walking into," she whispered.

Jasin took her into his arms and hugged her tight. "It will be all right. Just relax."

"Aren't you the least bit scared?" she asked. "We might be caught in this tube for days."

"In days we would be back at the river. No, my guess is that in a few hours we'll have found them."

"Or they'll have found us."

"Either way." Jasin didn't really care. He was tired of not knowing, weary of indecision and frustrated of any hesitation. He could deal with imprisonment. Doing nothing, standing still, like this, was no longer an option.

"Just give me a minute," Elizabeth tried to calm herself. "I thought I was through with this," she said speaking to herself. Finally, she felt the muscles in her legs loosen, and although it was difficult, she pushed the vivid memories back. "Jasin...just talk to me, tell me about...about anything. Just talk. The silence is creepy. It's driving me mad."

"I thought it was the darkness?"

"Just talk."

Jasin found the rail again and pulled Elizabeth along reluctantly. He tried to think of something she might be interested in hearing. "I'm not very good at this," he said after a few moments. "At telling stories...just making idle conversation."

"I know. It doesn't matter. Just talk. What do you think will happen to the others from the Women's Colony? Do you think the natives will keep them long?"

"It's really hard to say. I think it's probably temporary. Just a short punishment for hiding and using prohibited technology." It was a lie, which they both knew, but it felt better than speaking the truth. Violating the technology prohibition would not be taken lightly.

"That's something I've never understood. When you or Beloit found someone breaking a prohibition, what did you do to punish them? I mean...there are no prisons or courts for us."

"Until now."

"I mean, we didn't have any courts of our own...that we ran."

"I know what you meant."

"So..."

"Usually just warning offenders was enough. If they were serious and habitual they went underground, disappeared."

"How many?"

"Went underground? Well...there are the traders, and those in the Village of Cernai.

"They're hardly underground."

"I guess the important thing has been to keep it from becoming too overt. Many headed up into the cold; maybe they ended up in the Women's colony. I don't know. For a long time, we suspected Panvera of being a haven."

"But Jasin, don't you think eventually we have to be allowed to grow. If the Sytonians don't loosen up there will be trouble," Elizabeth warned.

"There's already trouble. If we few hundred humans don't respect the tens of thousands of natives, we will be extinguished or forced to live like the Eians—"

"Who have continued to use technology. Progress is inevitable," she said emphatically.

Without replying, Jasin quickened his pace, tugging Elizabeth along. Li Sy scurried to keep up. He had heard it all before. Avram was wrong. The colony on Syton was a bad idea. Jasin and Beloit had sold out. Progress was inevitable. It was a morally wrong to let people suffer when the technology and knowledge existed to help.

Maybe they shouldn't have settled here at all and stayed in space until Tanis fell apart and they all died there? Where was the logic in that? Or maybe they should break Avram's treaty, ignore the Prohibitions, and try to live isolated from the natives. But Jasin knew the towan would never allow that. So, we should just go to war and annihilate the natives, he thought facetiously. Well…it was to late for that. They hadn't the power…but now they could use the shuttle. Its existence was a wild card.

"It's got to be really late," Elizabeth complained. "Don't you think we should catch some sleep?"

"And eat," added Li Sy.

Jasin reluctantly agreed. They gathered together and rested with their backs against the rail, munching on a few hard biscuits, taking turns drinking from the last full water gourd. Sleep came quickly, for they had walked at least an additional twenty-five kilometers since first settling in for the night above ground.

But, just as before, their rest was disturbed by the approaching sound of something riding the rail behind them. Sh, sh, sh, sh, the rhythmic brushing sound grew louder. They backed away from the rail and peered into the darkness straining to see anything, a shadow, a flicker of light, but the darkness was complete. Whatever was using the rail did not use illumination of any kind. If they were quiet their presence would not be detected they thought, but the frequency of the sound slowed as it approached until it stopped nearby. Jasin and Elizabeth held their breath and remained motionless, staring into the black void before them.

"Who is there?" asked a male voice speaking rapidly in a dialect of native tongue. "Why do you not ride?"

Afraid by the stranger's apparent advantage, Jasin and Elizabeth didn't answer, but Li Sy, also able to see farther down the spectrum, stepped toward the faint shimmering image given off by the stranger's heat. "I am Li'onna, these others are humans. They have knowledge of the machine in the lake and seek the old human. Perhaps you can help us?"

"You bring humans here? It is forbidden. You will all be killed."

"No…" Li Sy said with stern conviction, "I have no such limitation." Jasin could barely follow the rapid interchange, but Elizabeth stood totally confused. Slowly, she let her fingers find the hilt of her knife. It gave her little comfort and she wondered whether she would have the nerve to draw it against someone she couldn't even see.

"You are a fool," continued the unseen male.

"If you do not take us to where the old human is, the secret of this tunnel will be revealed to the Council. I warn you not to—"

"It is you that needs to be warned. I do not know anything about an old human. I am merely a supplier, but I know what I've been told to do."

Horrified, they listened as Li Sy suddenly cried out in agony…then there was nothing except the faint persistent howl of the tunnel. Jasin let go of Elizabeth's hand and with arms outstretched waded hesitantly towards where he had last heard them. Without warning, he was struck in the groin. As he doubled, over his nose collided with the top of the stranger's head setting off a retinal flash of intense light and searing pain that sent him reeling backwards to fall over the rail, smashing the back of his head against the hard metallic base on the other side.

"Jasin!" screamed Elizabeth, hearing his pained outburst. But there was no answer. She strained to hear anything…but she only heard the frantic beating of her heart mixed with the hollow murmur of the wind. Then she heard footsteps approaching.

"Li Sy…Jasin?" She reached down along her thigh and awkwardly fumbled to find her knife. Holding the razor sharp blade out in front of her, she threatened, "Stop! Don't move any closer. I have a knife."

The footsteps slowed to a stop.

"Back away," she said waving the thin little knife from side to side in the blackness. "I'll use it if I have to."

The Eian had no experience with the human language, but it made little difference. He could see the shifting heat outline of the tall human swinging her arm defensively and could guess what she held. He spoke softly to calm her and approached cautiously avoiding the knife.

Now it was Elizabeth that couldn't understand a word the stranger spoke. Panic overwhelmed her and she backed away until she felt the cool tunnel wall against her back. The muffled sound of the Eian's footsteps in the soft dirt grew louder. Without waiting, she ran blindly.

After a minute, she stumbled and fell across several large chunks of rock that had broken loose from the ceiling. She felt their contours and, finding several that seemed large enough, hid behind them, crouching low, and tried to quiet her panting in order to hear if the stranger was approaching.

Her knife! Suddenly she realized she no longer held it. Was it worth leaving her hiding place to try and find it? No, she decided and lowered her head even more. As she tried to catch her breath, a retched scent overwhelmed her. Without thinking, she turned away, lifting her head away from the stench, raising her left hand to cover her nose and mouth. A sharp pain stung her bicep. She winced and instinctively jerked her arm away, nearly passing out from the excruciating pain the movement caused. With her good right arm she reached across her body and grasped her elbow. Warm blood flowed through her fingers. Moving her hand higher she felt the hard shaft of her knife protruding from the muscle of her skewered arm. In one fluid motion she yanked the knife free and slashed a protective arc around her. Just out of reach, the Eian calmly chided her.

"You think hiding among the rotting forn I wouldn't follow?"

The assailant was nearly upon her and Elizabeth lunged at his voice, springing forward on long legs, extending her surprising reach with arm and knife outstretched another meter in front of her. Her wrist buckled as it stopped abruptly against the Eian, but the sharp knife had easily penetrated his abdomen. Still holding the hilt tightly, she lifted the buried knife, slicing upward. Pain erupted from her sprained wrist and she cried out. The stranger had been too surprised to make even a small sound before his insides spilled out over her.

She backed away in shock, dropped to her knees, and began to throw up. The convulsions and shaking continued for sometime, leaving her dizzy and her empty gut aching from dry heaves. Exhausted and unable to find the energy to stand, she lay on her right side, cradling her head in the crook of her good arm, while blood streamed out of her throbbing left arm, and down her hip upon which it rested. After a few minutes rest she forced herself to rise and nearly passed out. She was lightheaded. How much blood had she lost? With sudden panic, she touched her limp arm. It was slick with blood. She struggled to lift it over her head, realizing the need to staunch the flow. Pain shot through her and her knees buckled. Lying on the ground, she managed to rip off her shirt and wrap her arm tightly, using the extra material to form a crude sling. Again she tried to stand, wincing as she put weight on her sprained wrist, then, remembering her knife, she felt around.

Trying to avoid her vomit and the remains of her attacker, she swept the ground from side to side with her good arm. Unexpectedly, she touched the cool metal surface of a small device. Exploring it with her fingers she discovered what felt like a cube with a cylinder protruding from one of the faces. The cube was larger than she could hold in one hand, so she lifted it by the cylindrical part, holding it like an awkward baby's rattle. It must have been a weapon, possibly a club she thought. She put it down next to her and resumed searching for her knife, which she found without any further surprise. Wiping the blade clean, she hid it once again in the sheath along her thigh.

Taking the Eian's device, she stood, struggling not to faint. A steady trickle of blood flowed down her throbbing arm. She knew she needed to tie a better dressing around it, but the chore felt overwhelming...impossible. She was beyond tired and lacked the energy or desire. How long had it been since she slept? Standing alone in the silent darkness, she was filled with profound despair. It penetrated her soul and numbed her mind, but she knew she wouldn't rest until she had found Jasin and Li Sy. Dreadful images flooded her mind and she fought to shake them off. They had to be fine, she convinced herself. Somehow in the pitch black she would find them and they would be all right...she couldn't imagine continuing in the dark alone.

Troubled Dreams

Jasin barely moved his head before feeling a flash of fire sear his brain. Struggling against the pain, he drew a shallow breath. Any slight movement brought a level of agony he hadn't ever experienced. He reached up to run his hand through his blood soaked hair. A five-centimeter gash still oozed, his nose ached, his ears...he couldn't tell what he was hearing, but there it was again. Straining, he tried to concentrate on the sound, distant, muffled, as if his head were wrapped in heavy blankets. It was getting weaker, moving away from him—Elizabeth's pleading voice. His tongue was swollen and bled from where he had bitten down on it making it hard to answer, but without an effort she'd be out of range. She was lost in the dark. He took a deep breath and managed an unintelligible reply.

Elizabeth froze and waited. Where did that come from? From behind her she heard the wail again. Spinning around, she composed herself and headed towards the sound, finally climbing across the rail to join him. "Are you all right?" she asked, settling down in the dirt next to Jasin.

"I bi' ma tongue," he mumbled, "An' I t'ink he boke my nose. Where's Li Sy? The Eian?"

"I haven't found her yet. Can you stand?"

"I can try," he said, rising unsteadily. He reached out for support, grabbing her wounded arm. Elizabeth gasped and pulled away.

"What happened?" cried Jasin, rubbing his sticky blood-coated fingers together.

"He cut me…" she hesitated, suddenly embarrassed. "With my own knife if you can believe it"

"That knife has shed more of your blood than anyone else's."

"Until today," she said softly.

"Come here and let me try and stop the bleeding. Ehh…what smells so bad? You're absolutely retched! Sit back against the rail and I'll fix your dressing. Tell me what happened."

Elizabeth described the attack, while Jasin carefully unwrapped her shirt and felt for the edges of the wound in the dark. Dismayed, his fingers traced a dripping gash as long as his index finger. It would be a substantial scar. Fumbling clumsily in the dark, he cut and tied a bandage from the bloody cloth. He tried feeling for any signs that it continued to bleed, but the cloth was soaked to begin with. "We've got to find Li Sy and our packs. I can't do this without light. Don't move."

Jasin rose, dizzy and disoriented. His nose hurt and his head pounded, but he fought through the pain. Swinging his legs, he walked in ever widening circles. Finally after a few minutes of this peculiar dance, he stumbled upon the packs. Soon, the area was bathed in candlelight.

"Oh…" Jasin gasped, staring at Elizabeth. The front of her thin camisole and pants were caked in dirt, blood, and yellowish-brown gore. A trickle of fresh blood seeped out from beneath the makeshift bandage.

Elizabeth followed his eyes. "Ready for the dance don't you think," she said weakly. "We've got to find Li Sy."

The small towa was unconscious a few meters away on the other side of the rail.

"Is she dead?" asked Elizabeth, as Jasin carried her back and laid her next to Elizabeth.

He ran his hands lightly over the towa looking for any injuries, but once again the alien's physiology made it impossible to tell if she was still alive. He shrugged and brushed a trickle of blood that dripped down his forehead.

"That doesn't look too good. Let me take a look at your head."

"It's stopping. Don't worry about it."

"Always the invincible hero," she teased as she examined the cut to his scalp. "You'll live. But you could use stitches."

"You're the one that needs a seamstress."

"What about her? Do you think she was hit with that?" she asked referring to the Eian object she had found, which now lay next to their packs.

"Well, I don't think that thing is a club. I'm not sure, but I would guess it generates some kind of energy that incapacitates the natives. Humans don't seem to be harmed. Mas and I discovered something that produced a similar effect in the Kull."

Elizabeth leaned over, wincing in pain, and brought the device closer to the light to inspect it more closely. She turned it this way and that using the only hand that was of any use to her. "Then how do we know if the thing is still on? We should get it as far from her as we can" She prepared to toss it back into the darkness.

"Wait! Let me take a look." He took it from her. There appeared to be no moving parts...until he tried pulling on the cylindrical handle—something Elizabeth, in her condition, had not been able to do. It twisted a quarter turn. Li Sy's body suddenly stiffened and she let out a groan. Jasin hastily twisted the handle back to its original position. "I think that's a good sign," he said smiling, putting the device into one of the nearly empty packs. "Might come in handy," he added without much conviction.

"Is there anything we can do for her?" asked Elizabeth.

Jasin shook his head. "I don't know how to help her, but you're still bleeding. We've got to get it stopped."

Elizabeth nodded. It was worse than Jasin suspected and she feared it might become infected before it could be cleaned properly. "How...how's your sewing?" she asked, suddenly feeling faint.

"My what?"

"I think...I'm sorry...just a little dizzy, I think, I think you will need to put a few stitches in it."

"Not me."

"Well, I'm not able to."

Jasin looked down at her bleeding arm. What could he use to stop it? He dumped out the contents of the packs—some clothing, a few hard biscuits, dried fruit, a piece of salted fish. Nothing. What did he expect to find anyway? He examined the pack itself; looking for anything he could use to staunch the flow. Maybe the bindings, they could be used temporarily. She winced as he tied one of the straps tightly around her upper arm. Now what? He knew he couldn't cut the circulation for very long without making matters worse.

He sorted through the clothing. Excitedly he picked up one on his socks. A loose thread dangled from it, but as he attempted to unravel it, he realized the threads were too thin and weak. He examined her spare underwear...again the delicate fabric was too fine. But one of her blouses had been embroidered with a delicate floral pattern. He picked at the edge of the pattern and freed ten centimeters of blue thread. Now all he needed was a needle...and enough nerve to stick her with it.

Glancing over in her direction, he gave her a reassuring smile, but inside panic began to set in. The arm was beginning to look blue. Think, he told himself, small and sharp, small and sharp. He looked over everything in front of him, his eyes coming to rest on the salted fish.

Tearing it apart, he found the largest bone, then using her knife fashioned a crude needle. As carefully as possible, he unwrapped her bandage.

"Don't watch," he suggested.

"Make the stitches as small as possible."

"I'll try," he promised, and then with shaking hands pierced her skin.

She drew a sharp breath through clenched teeth. "Don't stop," she groaned.

Beads of sweat formed on his forehead and ran down into his eyes as he pulled little loops of thread through her skin and muscle, closing the wound knot by knot. He tore new bandages from the bottom of his shirt and bound them tightly before finally releasing the tourniquet.

"Finished?" she asked weakly.

"Rest now, I don't think it would be good to move." Jasin's head throbbed, he felt nauseous and emotionally spent.

Elizabeth's breathing was labored from fighting the pain. "Do...you think...think we can use whatever...the Eian was using...to move on the rail?"

"Perhaps if it's big enough. I'd be happy if we can use it to help us with Li Sy. We'll find it after we rest. Try to sleep." Jasin repacked, and after he was sure everything else was within reach, he blew out the candle. Within minutes his breathing changed; Elizabeth could tell he was asleep.

For Elizabeth, however, the throbbing pain drove sleep away. She turned to lie on her right side, raising her injured arm to reduce the painful pounding she felt at every heartbeat. Her mind sifted through the day's events. She had never even seen the face of the creature she had killed. Did it matter? Somehow it was better that no image accompanied the act.

As it was, Loeton's face still haunted her. During the quiet times before sleep, she often saw his features looming over her, his hands on her, her hands on him, and his chest blown open. No, she wouldn't go back with the lantern to see the Eian. Leave it alone. He was a nameless, faceless creature who had tried to kill them, so she killed him first. Simple survival. Let's keep it that way, she said to herself.

But she couldn't. She had never taken another's life.

In turmoil, she struggled to make sense of her actions, reviewing them, examining her alternatives to see if she could have avoided the Eian's death. Someone's friend, or husband, or father had just died at her hand. Justify that. She was sure that if she could understand why he had to die, the burden she would carry for the rest of her life would be lightened. Death was an easy concept to understand and accept; causing someone's death, she was discovering, wasn't. They had talked about killing and been surrounded by death, but this was their first...her first—a creature so irrelevant, so unimportant that she wouldn't even take the effort to look at his face.

It was better that way, she decided. Not because the life she took was insignificant—she was raised believing all sentient life was practically sacred—but because, at that moment, under that situation, the alien had sacrificed his right to life by his actions. Unfortunately, she had to be the one to extract justice. That was a concept she could accept...it was justified.

But still her dreams were troubled.

Metal Seeds

Julian threw herself from the broken edge of the cliff and swam into the air beyond. With each effortless stroke, she propelled herself forward a few more feet before she coasted to a stop. She used the breaststroke and lifted her head high so she could look around, but there was nothing to see except straight down where the dangerous crystal spires waited for her to fall, waited to impale and slice her apart with their razor sharp edges. Another stroke. She leaned to one side and slowly flipped over. Blackness rotated into view, absorbing her. A million stars assaulted her. Weightless and chilled, she floated in the emptiness of infinite space and she hated it.

Eiton didn't understand sleep or any form of unconsciousness, so when Julian refused to wake after thirty-six hours he grew concerned. He visited her regularly, leaning over to listen to her breathing or gently touching her lips or eyelids to see her reaction, just to be reassured that she was all right, that someone was there inside the still, small body. But she didn't wake. After three days he started to panic and began talking to her, pleading with her to open her eyes. He didn't want her to die. He didn't know why, but she was important to him.

On the fourth day while Eiton moistened her dry lips with water, as he had many times in past days, she opened her eyes. It was peaceful and calm. No one was badgering her for information; no one tore at her hair. Instead, Eiton helped her sit up and drink from a cup he held for her.

He attended to her needs and over time she grew stronger. Unsure about this kindness, Julian often let her anger erupt, hurling plates, food, and insults in his direction, but he was steadfast and never abandoned her. Days passed, she relaxed and eventually they were cordially sharing meals together.

"Eiton, I've been having the most vivid dreams the last few nights."

"Dreams?"

"Thoughts while I'm sleeping."

"That must be wonderful! Nothing to distract you, no one interrupting. When I am working on a difficult problem I must hide from others so that I might concentrate."

Julian smiled. "My dreams are not so productive. I see random images… experience intense feelings."

"It is the *keets*, a concentrated form of the keetah."

"Torture wasn't working so you drug me?" The thought of being controlled by any drug scared her, but keetah frightened her the most.

"The effects are harmless. It is a small amount…to help you, to give you energy. I was afraid."

"What were you afraid of, my dying? I thought you said Eidorf was through with me. I had no worth."

"That is what Eidorf said…not what I believe."

"Why?"

"It seems like a waste. Waste isn't good."

"Spoken like a true engineer." Eiton liked it when she used that word—Engineer—one who makes things work. "Tell me, do you think you might let me go home now. Eidorf doesn't care about me any longer and he was right; I'm not really worth much."

"But…I was hoping you might…I wanted to show you my work. Hadrious is actually quite beautiful, especially above. You might like it here."

Julian stared at him in disbelief. "You kidnapped me, tortured me, nearly killed me, and you think I might like it here! What I want is to leave. The sooner the better."

"But I thought you understood...you've seen too much. You know too much. The transport system, the underground level, isn't it obvious that you will never leave Hadrious unless it is to go to Eian with us? Eidorf would rather see you dead than give you an opportunity to stop the salvage operation." He paused, watching for her reaction. "You can stay here with me. I can show you my work. Maybe I can find something you are capable of doing...something you might enjoy."

"Something I am capable of doing?" she repeated sardonically. "I don't know, maybe I could learn to yank out hair."

"I don't understand."

She stood and walked away from him. "Forget it," she mumbled. "Go now...leave me alone."

Eiton silently left the room, his limp more pronounced than she had yet seen.

Without Eiton's visits the days dragged. She spent most of her time considering her imprisonment, finally determining that escape would be impossible without help from outside. She tried to communicate with those that brought food, but it was apparent that they were either unable to speak Human, or had been warned not to converse with her. Eiton had been the only Eian that dared to be friendly. Finally boredom got the best of her and she asked for the little engineer. A few minutes later he rushed in and stood awkwardly waiting for her to speak.

Julian could not help but be flattered by his willingness to please her. "I was thinking about what you said and I would like to see what it is you do when you're not caring for old women."

"It has been difficult to get all that we need," apologized Eiton, as he led Julian down a narrow corridor weaving between dirt piles and chunks of rock that had fallen from the ceiling. He ran his hand along a smooth blue metal arch that gracefully supported the crumbling roof of the passageway. "We are continually expanding and reinforcing the tunnel system, reworking less important items, reforming whatever metal we can spare into new buttresses, beams, and lintels. The great rail in the Kull could provide all the material we might ever desire, and it lies practically unused in the sand, but it is too visible to the others. It is frustrating, but you know how difficult it is to carry any large amount of material here through the transit system and still keep it out of sight."

Julian smiled, remembering her own experience. "Transit system? It hardly qualifies."

Eiton ignored or didn't understand the sarcasm and limped on silently.

"Eiton, what is wrong with your leg? Are you in pain?"

"It no longer hurts. I injured my mid-joint as a youngster. It was just a silly accident, but it took a long time to heal well enough so that I could walk again. I suppose that's why I am an Engineer." He enjoyed using that word.

"How's that?"

"I couldn't play, so I studied. After it healed, I still couldn't play very well. I read and studied a great deal."

Julian nodded. She had heard that story before in many different guises. Now it came from a different species entirely.

They arrived at a circular disk twenty centimeters thick and nearly two-meters across that stood against a sidewall. It looked massive, but Eiton reached up, grabbed a recessed handle, and easily rolled it to one side, revealing a mammoth, dimly lit cavern, housing the multistory microscope that he had used to study her blood and brain tissue. He led her to the blue metal scaffolding encircled the humming apparatus and they climbed to the viewing platform where he turned off the device.

"I was preparing several new seeds for a series of gears that will be used in the new water generator when you requested to see me," explained Eiton. "I left without shutting down properly."

"Seeds?" asked Julian.

"Metal seeds…patterns."

Julian cocked her head to one side still confused. Eiton stared back, unsure as to what the confusion might be. Finally he tried again, "Microscopic forms for the metal...surely you use a similar technology." Again a puzzled look was all he received. "When you create a metal object such as a wheel or box or let's say a door...you need to shape the material, form it into the proper dimensions."

Julian nodded.

"Well, when you take the unformed metal it has no shape, originally it has no guide or plan to follow, the metal just flows freely. One of my jobs is to determine what is needed and design the proper shape from which the final metal object can grow."

Julian remembered some of her early lessons aboard Tanis. "Before tri-axial plasma forming, humans used hollow molds to flow molten metal into. These molds shaped the metal. But I don't understand what you mean by seeds. What do you mean by growing an object?"

"Come...let me show you."

They climbed down to the lower level where Eiton arranged a small syringe filled with blue liquid and several tiny shallow dishes, each smaller than a contact lens, on a round table whose surface glowed from beneath. From the end of the huge apparatus he carefully removed a triangular slide approximately the size of his small hand. Its surface was covered with hundreds of miniscule dimples. He laid the slide next to the small dishes and syringe, and walked over to a bin where he lifted out a mechanism that he fastened around his head and down along his arm. "This is a simple version of what I do," he explained walking back to the bottom lit table. He engaged clamps, which held his elbow and forehead stationary and using this exoskeleton he manipulated microscopic tools to extract a few of his infinitesimal "metal seeds". He placed them in the small dishes and finished by squirting a small dab of blue into each of them. Only then did he release his head and arm from their restraints.

"Here in the first dish, I placed a single unmodified node." He tipped his head slightly and pointed to the dish on the end. "As you can see it creates a sphere." Julian leaned over and peered into the tiny dish. A perfect little round ball of metal lay in the bottom. He continued, "The second contains a simple equidistant eight point matrix. Again the bonds and faces are left unmodified." Julian looked into the second dish and saw a small cube. The third and fourth were shaped like a donut and a spiral helix. In the last dish, Julian barely made out a complex hollow rectangle with a row of cutouts along the sides.

"What's that one?" asked Julian, amazed at what she had just witnessed.

"They are just random models I chose. Building blocks. I use some as they are, others I modify. The seeds can be manipulated and combined at the molecular level to suit whatever design I need."

She reached across and lifted the syringe. "And this?"

"Simple amorphan, but of course it's non-crystalline and undifferentiated." He took the syringe from her and carefully replaced it on the table. "This sample is pure, laboratory quality from Eian. We have very little that's original. Most amorphan has been recycled hundreds of times. Once you find and remove the seed, it reverts to its fluid state, but the more times it reforms the more viscous it becomes…definition suffers."

Eiton gathered up the demonstration materials and methodically put them away while Julian walked thoughtfully around the end of the enormous microscope. She looked up towards the viewing end of the apparatus nearly twenty meters above.

"Most of the device is for magnification," Eiton remarked, approaching her. "You can't handle what you can't see. Come, I will show you how—"

"Did your people bring this with them from Eiton?" Julian interrupted him.

"No, no," replied the little engineer. "I built this. It took me nearly ten years to collect enough parts. They didn't have time to build any spacecraft large enough or sophisticated enough to bring over something so fragile. We were short on time and tried to save thousands of our people. Instead of building a few large complex vehicles, the Eians of that era built hundreds of simple capsules, not much more than containers filled with people and supplies. It was a one-way trip and the vehicles were all basically grown from the same seed design. The capsules only needed to be used once, but because the hulls were made of self-repairing Amorphan, they arrived in nearly perfect condition. Of course I can't say the same for the people. I understand that a lot of people died coming across. Anyway...the material from the capsules has been used for nearly everything we've built ever since, including the rail in the Kull. Come now, I have much more to show you."

Julian nodded. She had heard him, but leaned back against the rail that encircled the platform lost in thought. The little Eian stood by her side in silence and waited. Finally, she took a deep breath and looked toward the Eian. "You would have liked Tanis. It was the greatest toy an engineer could ever have hoped for."

"Tanis?"

"My home for most of my life." She managed a slight smile. "Another lifetime ago."

"You speak then of your spacecraft. Even in Hadrious, we learned of it. It was a waste to have destroyed it."

"It was very old. Radiation had ravaged the integrity of the hull and the pusher plate was almost completely ablated. Tanis would have probably fallen apart within the next couple generations anyway. We just put it out of its misery."

"But saved the craft in the lake."

Julian shrugged. "I only have your word that it exists. Besides, it has brought me nothing but trouble and pain. It is of little interest to this old woman."

"Eidorf assures me it does exist and it will take us back to Eian where we will build a new ship to rescue our people from this enslavement," Eiton proclaimed heroically.

"You think Eidorf will be able to accomplish that?" Julian couldn't contain the wide grin that grew across her face. "He is a foolish power-hungry creature filled with arrogance and little else. Great deeds are done by the likes of you Eiton, not him. Look at this magnificent instrument you built. You said it took ten years. That's the kind of persistence that overcomes even the most difficult obstacles. If the shuttle exists, fine. Bring it here and use it. Find a way to refuel it. But if I were you, I would build your own ship here. But don't blindly follow Eidorf. Think for yourself. What could possibly be on Eian that you don't have here?"

"Freedom," Eiton replied simply.

"Something you won't grant me." Julian reminded him.

"Something I *can't* grant you."

Supply Depot

Multi-colored light shafts streamed through dozens of fist-sized holes in the tunnel's roof creating a crisscross pattern in the dust filled air. Elizabeth and Jasin shielded their eyes as they pushed the metal sled carrying Li Sy through them. As Jasin had predicted, the Eian's conveyance was barely large enough for the injured towan.

Bright orange rays of sunlight mixed with an equal number of paler greenish-yellow beams from Conboet's reflected shine. It would have been an inspiring sight had they not spent the last two days in oppressive darkness, listening to the nerve racking howl of the wind, fearing the small towa was beyond help. The experience had taken its toll.

They moved hesitantly, sure the Eians were finally going to discover their presence now that they were visible, painted with light from the surface. But as they left the brightly lit section behind and followed the endless rail once again into the darkness in front of them, both realized that they were safe. Elizabeth felt oddly disappointed. Discovery, even if it had meant imprisonment, would have at least provided relief from the near catatonic monotony.

Although not feeling particularly cheerful himself, Jasin tried to lift Elizabeth's spirits with small talk. It was clear from her shallow, rapid breathing and the occasional gasp of pain as she stumbled over unseen rocks and her own feet that she was struggling. Elizabeth was not to be cajoled.

It was easy to believe that the tunnel would never end and they would have to walk on forever, but they knew that the rail was heading straight as an arrow back toward either the Andoree or out to the sea. They just weren't sure where the ancient lava that formed the tunnel had finished its journey. Initially, when they lowered themselves into the tunnel, they hadn't paid close attention to their heading as it hardly seemed relevant, but now as the hours and days dragged on, predicting when or where they would finally run into the Eians monopolized their sparse conversation.

During what they presumed was the third day—for it was nearly impossible to judge time in the dark tunnel—they sensed a rise in humidity followed quickly by the smell of fish and a faint glow in the distance. Jasin carefully lifted Li Sy from the sled and carried her to the tunnel wall where he tenderly laid her on the ground against the tunnel wall.

"If they haven't heard our approach we may be able to check it out without being noticed. Leave everything here," he whispered. "If it's safe we'll come back."

With great relief, being careful not to upset her bound left arm that screamed out at the slightest provocation, Elizabeth slid her heavy pack to the ground. She checked to insure her slender knife still lay snugly against her thigh, frightened at the thought that she might have to use it again.

Cautiously they made their way towards the light. For the last few days they had boldly walked down the center of the tunnel, using the rail to guide them. Now they hugged the outside wall, moving forward slowly, hoping to stay hidden as long as possible. At every unintentional sound, they winced and held their breath. The tunnel brightened. Squinting, they continued until finally they could see where the lava tube had crumbled apart.

It was nothing like what they had expected.

An open-air junkyard, several meters below the actual surface of the Kull, spread out from the rail's terminus. It was surrounded by what appeared to be a natural embankment, but upon closer scrutiny they could tell it was cleverly constructed using rocks and boulders. Jasin estimated it to be at least a hundred meters in diameter.

For several minutes they crouched hidden in the shadows of the tunnel's mouth, surveying the stacks of tattered alien devices littering the enclosure: tubs of blue liquid, containers filled to the brim with pieces of broken technology, and an odd assortment of weathered machinery. The place appeared deserted; the only sign that it was used regularly were several blue-metal sleds, lying at the end of the rail, and a heavily trodden path leading out through the retaining wall's single opening to the river.

After a long minute, Elizabeth stood and took a few steps into the brightly lit clearing. Shielding her eyes she said, "I don't think there's anyone here. It seems deserted."

Jasin, shaking his head, stepped forward to join her. "I wish you wouldn't take chances like that."

"Like what?" Elizabeth smiled weakly, knowing full well that her quick impulsive decisions sometimes bothered him. "I've got to wash. I can't stand myself. Would you mind collecting the packs? There's a change of clothes in mine."

"You shouldn't go alone..." Jasin began, but she had already turned and headed for the water. He rushed back into the tunnel, retrieved Li Sy, and then the packs, leaning them against a large container a few meters from the end of the rail. The towa rested in partial sunlight, and Jasin stooped to examined her.

Except that her shoulder patches were a dull, greenish tint, far from their usual shiny rust color, he could find nothing wrong. He glanced toward the river where Elizabeth was bent over awkwardly scrubbing her face and body with her good hand. He had been sure that they were going to discovery where the Eians were keeping his Mother. By now he should have figured it out, but he was tired and couldn't think straight. There was no time to sleep. He took a deep breath and walked down to the river and splashed water on his grimy face.

"Feel good?" Elizabeth asked, emerging from the cold water. Fresh scarlet rivulets trickled down her arm, but she sounded ecstatic. "I have never been so happy to leave any place in my life." She looked over at Li Sy's still body.

"What do you think we should do? In Panvera she revived in the warm water. Do you think we should soak her in the river?"

"Forget her for a minute. Let me see that arm." He looked over his stitching. Several places had begun to scab over, but it was bleeding where the water had washed several large sections of dried blood away. His sewing left much to be desired; it was going to leave a ragged scar. "I don't know if it was smart to get it wet," he offered.

"The scab was mixed with dirt. It will heal better if it's clean."

Jasin looked doubtful. She leaned down and kissed his forehead. "Trust me, the bleeding will stop, but we've got to keep it clean or infection will set in." She rummaged through her pack mumbling to herself about her lack of clean clothes, then dressed in the blouse Jasin had stolen the string from, and a pair of dirt encrusted pants. "Now, what about Li Sy?"

Except for her discolored shoulder patches the little native showed no outward signs of being attacked.

"Like a baby," Jasin observed.

"I've never seen a baby rest sitting up."

"I meant the coloration." Jasin brushed his own shoulder to clarify. "Newborns have green patches like that."

"When did you ever see a native newborn?"

"Sy Toberry's boy, Sy Jelick. When he was born, Toberry immediately carried him outside near where we were playing. Never saw anything so ugly."

"Well, I haven't a clue what the weapon did to her," Elizabeth said sadly. Do you think it's safe to stay here for a while?"

Jasin didn't hesitate. "No"

"Neither do I," Elizabeth agreed, glancing at the crates scattered about them. "Obviously this is some kind of supply depot. The Eians are probably scavenging bits and pieces of their old technology from the Kull, bringing it here to be reused."

Jasin nodded. "But it still doesn't answer where they are or how they move this stuff from here."

"Let me show you something." Elizabeth led Jasin to where several giant gilia heads had washed up on the bank. The smell of their decay stung their noses. "Notice anything?" she asked.

"Aside from the smell?" Jasin studied the large heads, the tops of which, even in the process of decomposing, stood a full meter tall and reached their waists. Jasin leaned over and stuck his head inside and quickly withdrew it, gagging on the stench.

"No root structure," Elizabeth pointed out.

"Of course not. If the roots were still attached the heads wouldn't have floated ashore."

"But look where the roots would normally attach. Doesn't that look like they've been cut free?"

Jasin studied the edges of the bell shaped plant. Elizabeth was right. Not only had the roots been severed, there were several holes around the bottom edge of the dome that didn't look natural. "What are you thinking? They fill these up with supplies?"

Elizabeth shrugged. "I just think it's strange that these two heads came ashore right here when I haven't seen another anywhere else. They use these somehow."

"Maybe the plants got in their way and they cut them free. My bet is they travel underwater and that's why they've never been seen. Remember Eidorf in Lake Chook. He dove into the water and disappeared."

"There were gilia there as well."

He nodded. "Could be...regardless, it isn't safe here. We could have visitors anytime. We've got to decide what to do with Li Sy and get on our way."

"Get on our way where?"

Jasin pointed at a distant point across the river where smoke rose in a thin wispy tendril. "That's Cernai. We're probably seeing their cooking fires. I figure the trail is about eight kilometers from here. We can either cross here or work our way back along this shore and cross at the islands again. Whatever we do we've got to leave."

They walked in silence back to Li Sy and their packs. Neither wanted to speak about what was apparent to both of them. Li Sy, as tiny as she was, was still too heavy to carry any great distance, and the idea of swimming across the river, somehow holding her above the water, just wasn't possible. Finally Jasin spoke. "I guess we'll have to find a place to hide on this side of the river until Li Sy recovers and hope no one discovers us."

"We have the weapon, and no one knows we're here. We should be all right if we can find food," added Elizabeth. She was glad that Jasin had decided against abandoning Li Sy. She wasn't sure she could have been persuaded to leave without the tiny towa.

As they approached Li Sy they noticed that where her shoulder patches had been exposed to the sun the deep rust color was returning. Jasin positioned her body so that the sun shone fully on both her patches. "I think this is a good sign," said Elizabeth. "Let's give her an hour and see if she can be revived."

"I hope we have an hour," Jasin said somberly, walking over and grabbing the energy weapon. He briefly scanned the area to find the highest vantage point and walked off.

Elizabeth watched him slowly trudge off towards one of the ridges nearest the river. He was clearly exhausted. If only he had joined her in the river. That would have refreshed him. Maybe it would have taken his mind off the disappointment of not finding Julian.

Cernai

Most of the humans had assumed they were being taken to Bistoun as they made their way down the long steppe from the medical facility and were surprised a few days later when they turned to climb past the thundering falls and on towards the Village of Cernai. Except for Initiation, few natives ever ventured into the colder elevations and several of them had stood in awe of the magnificent frigid torrent that fell from the rugged crag three and a half kilometers above. The water fell in a single wondrous translucent sheet eventually splitting into two raging rivers that encircled an immense stone monolith. One couldn't cross the shaky bridges to stand on that solid chunk of rock without imagining the cataclysmic event ages ago when the mass, large enough for a small community to reside upon, broke off and plummeted from the precipice above.

Still nearly two kilometers from the outlaw's village, Mas turned to Nanc, who supported him firmly around his thin waist and pointed out serpentine wisps of gray smoke rising above the enclave. "That's no cooking fire," he remarked, looking among the other captives from the mountain colony to see if anyone else had noticed. Becoming concerned, Nanc immediately called for Wilem to rejoin them.

The young boy, impatient with Mas and his mother's pace often ran ahead to demonstrate his independence. When they first left the Women's Colony, they had been prodded with sharpened lances and forced to march bunched together. But over the last two sleepless days, the weakest had lagged behind and the three of them were now nearer the tail of the long scraggly line of humans that extended over a thousand meters. The towan rear guard was forced to fall back with them.

As the village itself came into view, the origin of the smoke became clear. Several of the larger buildings had been destroyed and several still smoldered. From the shallow craters within the circle of debris it appeared that they were blown apart from the inside. Mas and Nanc were herded into the village center along with the others. A loud argument was in progress between the doctor and one of the natives that spoke very little human.

"If you don't allow us to help them they will all die," argued the doctor, at a volume louder than was necessary, but typical of someone who was not having much success being understood.

"No," replied the towan using the only word of Human he appeared to know. He stood resolute, refusing to allow anyone to approach the few injured humans and nearly dozen burnt towan that lay on the ground. Mas looked at the charred bodies; most appeared beyond help.

"If you allow us to help, I'll treat the towan first," pleaded the doctor.

"How noble of you!" said Beloit McMaster angrily, finally breaking his silence. He hadn't said a word during the destruction of the medical enclave, nor the enforced march to Cernai. The Enforcer had remained aloof, ignoring the human's taunts and poisonous stares. He turned away from the doctor and to the towan guard asked, "Sy Lang?"

The towan pointed down a path that led out of the village center to a small group of huts. Beloit nodded and turned to stare at the doctor and the other tired refugees of the Women's Colony. "If you really want to help, drag the dead to the cliff and get rid of them," he said.

Mas stood aghast, but the doctor moved quickly towards the bodies without a glance at the receding figure. The towan, confused by Beloit's comments, allowed her to examine them one by one. Nanc, Sheelia, and a few others went to help with the triage. They breezed over many that were obviously gone or beyond help. On others they took more time. Those with strong stomachs eventually disposed of the dead at the edge of the cliff. Mas, barely able to support himself without Nanc's help, sat with Wilem contemplating the horrible scene. "Beloit's crazy," he muttered.

"Why is he helping the natives?" asked Wilem.

Mas shook his head. "I'm not sure who is helping who. I don't know…everyone here is probably guilty of disobeying some Prohibition or another. Maybe he thinks he's doing his job."

"And maybe he's gone mad," added Nanc, coming over to sit beside them. She sighed, "None of the burned will make it. Infection will see to that. A few of the towan have pretty deep wounds. More went on here than explosions and fires."

They sat stupefied at the carnage, trying to understand the scene before them, trying to find a reason for their being here, totally unaware of how Sy Lang and the Council, using Beloit McMaster's misguided loyalty to Avram and the Prohibitions, were planning to deal with the human problem.

"The humans of Cernai were prepared," Sy Lang explained to Beloit, who stood feet apart, arms crossed in front of him. "We underestimated their inventiveness. When we entered the buildings, they…" Sy Lang made quick outward motions with his hands and struggled to find the human word. "They broke apart violently and fire flew from the insides. The fire stuck on the towan. The burning did not stop."

"Booby-trapped," said Beloit. "How many of the villagers did you capture?"

"Enforcer…this is very serious. How many humans captured is not the issue. At least twelve towan have died. Your information about this village was not accurate. The humans were ruthless. After the buildings…" again he made an expanding gesture, "booby…"

"Exploded, the buildings were booby-trapped to explode," Beloit explained impatiently.

"Afterward, they attacked with stones and weapons that exploded with fire. Did any towan die that went with you to the mountain?"

"No except earlier, as I explained to you in Bistoun. Sy Toberry died of natural causes."

"It is still difficult to accept his death. Sy Toberry has always been there for us. Two important leaders…gone in such a short time."

McMaster nodded. "Sy Toberry and Avram. He would have been honored to hear you speak of him."

"I speak of Sy Loeton," corrected Lang. "Avram was only human." Sy Lang paused to collect his thoughts. "Your people are dangerous and must be contained. Reports from other council members say many humans are breaking the Prohibitions. Your people are using knives and glow balls. Towan are being mysteriously injured. The colony in the mountain and this village have openly used prohibited technology. The Council has discussed this situation. Thirty years ago one of the options was to isolate our two species. Avram convinced us that the Prohibitions would make that unnecessary. He was wrong. Now it is the Council's desire to find an appropriate location to gather all the humans together so it will be easier to watch your activities. If you continue to help, you will be given special consideration."

Beloit snorted and a broad smile broke across his face. "You're afraid of us. A handful of humans with a few fire bombs scared you."

"We are not frightened—"

"Of course you are, and if the rumors of the shuttle are true you have reason to be."

"There is nothing to fear from you, but young Jasin has disappeared and hasn't been seen in weeks. Without Sy Toberry, there is no one to predict the coming of Rhan-da-lith and the rising of the machine from the lake. Now, are you going to continue helping us gather all the humans together?"

"I am not a traitor!" proclaimed Beloit.

"You think not?" Sy Lang fired back. "That is what your people are calling you. You've exposed Cernai and decimated the medical facility. Did you think your people are going to thank you for those acts?"

"Those particular people broke the Prohibitions. They were all guilty."

"They were, but aren't the makers of glow sticks in Lake Chook guilty. And the knife peddlers in Bistoun, and the herb growers in Panvera, your friend Jasin and the bold whore he travels with—they are all guilty. Most of the humans I have met have at one time or another ignored a Prohibition. Given a chance, I believe all humans will eventually disobey them. Too many towan have died. Humans have disrupted our life. You must all be contained."

"Ridiculous!" shouted Beloit. "You can't be serious."

"What is your decision? Will you help us or do you choose to join those you brought from the mountain?"

"Sy Lang," Beloit replied solemnly, "Avram held you in high regard. He thought you were the most intelligent towan on the Council, but this plan to imprison us is foolhardy. It appears it was difficult to capture even this one small village of a hundred. How do you intend to control a town the size of Lake Chook or Nova Gaia for that matter?"

"Control is simply a matter of instilling fear," answered the Sytonian. "It will be important for you to convince your fellow humans to obey."

"They will resist."

"Then you will tell them about the Village of Cernai," replied Sy Lang ominously.

"Tell them what...that you got your asses kicked?" Beloit asked perturbed, but Sy Lang said no more.

Then, as if on cue, the screaming and crying began. Beloit stared at Sy Lang, who showed no sign of surprise. Beloit ran back to the village center where he had left the doctor and her people. Several armed towans were forcibly herding the small children of the village towards the newcomers. It was difficult for Beloit to see past the natives' broad bodies, but he could tell that the towan held spears to the children's backs and it appeared their hands were tied.

No...as he got nearer he could see that each young boy and girl carried something. He ran around to the front and watched in shocked horror as each village child, prodded by a sharp lance in their back, with silent tears streaming down their cheeks and blood dripping through their fingers, carried the severed head of one of their parents and placed it in a growing pile on the ground.

Cavern

Jasin sat beside the river, alternately pondering the smoke rising from Cernai and gazing out at the slack tide. It was an ideal time to cross, he thought, knowing full well they weren't going to be swimming anytime soon. He was tired and unfocused. Li Sy hadn't so much as moved a muscle, and Elizabeth rested on her back cradling her wounded arm. If only he felt comfortable closing his eyes. He stood and grasped his head between his hands and massaged his scalp, trying to rid himself of the fuzziness. Maybe if he dunked his head. He turned toward the river.

Something was different.

At first he wasn't sure, but then it became obvious. Another giant gilia head had broken free and was floating upright, moving with conviction against the barely perceptible current. It must still be dragging its root, Jasin figured. It veered toward shore, bobbing along the scraggly rock edge. Then suddenly, it disappeared, apparently sucked straight through the solid embankment.

Confused, Jasin worked his way down to where the gilia head had vanished. From his new vantage point, what had appeared as solid rock was actually two overlapping slabs hiding a sliver of an opening. He carefully jumped from rock to rock, avoiding the slippery algae growth, until he was able to lean over and peer through the crack into the space beyond. Artificial light revealed a substantial cavern. The gilia head was being secured to a pier of blue metal at least fifteen meters long by its former occupant. Jasin found himself breathing heavily as the jumbled chaos of past-unexplained sights and disjointed ideas crystallized into a coherent picture. Shocked into action, he ran to Elizabeth.

"We've got company. Gather everything, we've got to find somewhere to hide," Jasin whispered emphatically.

"Where's the weapon?" asked Elizabeth, her eyes sweeping the immediate area.

Jasin spun around. "Damn it!" He started to take a few steps back toward the rocks where he had left the device, then stopped. "There isn't time," he muttered under his breath and turned to lift Li Sy.

"I can't take both packs," complained Elizabeth, slipping one over her good shoulder

"Kick it out of sight. We've got to hurry."

At first Jasin considered leaving the supply depot's enclosure and heading straight toward the river, but there wasn't time. He turned to face the blackness of the tunnel.

Elizabeth could read his mind. "That didn't work so well for us the last time."

Jasin nodded. His eyes swept the supply depot searching for a suitable hiding spot. "There." He motioned with his head toward a corner heaped high with dark purplish rectangular slabs. They quickly took cover behind the largest of them. Jasin leaned Li Sy against a pile of smaller purple modules. Almost instantly, she lurched forward and let out a loud hiss. Jasin dropped to his knees and covered her mouth, checking over his shoulder to see if the visitor, just entering the enclosure, had heard. It was a wet towa...or maybe not. Confused, it took a few seconds to comprehend that they were looking at a female Eian, the identical twin of every towa they had ever seen.

Her tiny eyes swept the supply depot. In one hand she carried her own energy weapon, and in the other, Elizabeth's gore covered clothing. Elizabeth, wide-eyed, turned to Jasin who returned the look. There was nothing they could do. Li Sy squirmed disoriented under his grasp, yet he dared not allow her to move. He forced her against the purple slabs and received a sharp paralyzing jolt along the arm that covered her mouth. For a second, he thought Li Sy had generated the numbing energy, but the towa's eyes bulged in their sockets, obviously also in pain. But he dared not let her free. Holding her tightly, he allowed her to lean forward, away from the alien power cells.

The Eian yelled out a name. Jasin's heart sunk. He hoped Elizabeth wouldn't understand. She needn't know what the Eian searched for. After a brief perusal of the yard, the small female dropped Elizabeth's clothes and walked over to the blue metal sled that stood atop the rail. She slid on with little effort, and with a dozen quick strokes against the rail, moved off and into the lava tube, again calling out her husband's name.

Jasin finally released his hold on Li Sy, who jumped away. "Jasin killing Li Sy? Li Sy must go. Li Sy has told you many times; you must not hold Li Sy. " The towa was infuriated and began to walk away. She took a few steps toward Elizabeth's bloody clothes, picked then up and turned toward Elizabeth and Jasin.

"How do you feel?" asked Elizabeth, ignoring her unspoken question.

"Hungry," she answered, then held up the filthy blouse between her two left thumbs. "What happened here?"

"You're always hungry. Are you sure you're o.k?" asked Jasin, massaging his arm, still numb from the electric shock.

As Elizabeth stepped forward to take the clothing from Li Sy, the native noticed her knife wound and touched it gently. "It is warm. Does it hurt?"

Elizabeth winced at the touch, but smiled weakly. "You are precious," she said sweetly, then turning, she apologized to Jasin, "I'm sorry about the clothes. I just dumped them next to the river. I completely forgot about them."

Jasin nodded. It didn't matter now.

"What was our visitor yelling?" Elizabeth asked.

"I'm not sure," lied Jasin. "Possibly a password or warning."

Elizabeth stared at him. She could sense when he was being evasive.

"She had a weird accent. I've never heard or seen a female Eian before," he added.

"I have," said Elizabeth, looking directly at Li Sy, who stood waiting for someone to explain.

Jasin raised his eyebrows. However different the males of the two races appeared, it was plain that the females were identical. Turning to Li Sy, he quickly summarized the last few days. When he finished it was his turn to apologize to Li Sy. "I didn't realize they were power cells when I sat you against them."

"It may actually have revived you," added Elizabeth.

"Revived?"

"This isn't the time for a language lesson," interrupted Jasin. "Gather our things. I want to show you something."

They moved off toward the river.

"The lava tube tunnel is merely a passageway for the Eians to scavenge supplies from the Kull without being noticed by their big brothers," Jasin began. He tipped one of the rotten heads to see underneath. "They must use these to move up and down river without being noticed. They can drift in and out with the tidal currents. Over there is a huge cavern where they can get in and out of them without being seen. You remember when Eidorf dove into the Lake to escape and never resurfaced?"

Elizabeth understood. There were plenty of gilia heads floating about. He must have simply returned to his and waited for the tide to carry him back to Hadrious. "Hadrious must be somewhere along the river."

"Or Lake Chook," Li Sy added.

Jasin disagreed. "They let us settle around Lake Chook. I think the female Eian came in from the Great Lake. It is one of the prohibited areas. They probably built this place as close to Hadrious as possible. We could try to find it. How far can it be? We still have plenty of light left."

"What we don't have is food and water," Elizabeth argued. "I think we need to head back. We're only a few hours from the islands. We'll rest there and wait for the next slack tide. By nightfall, we'll be across. We can have breakfast in Cernai. We don't have any idea how far away Hadrious is. It could just as easily be out in the sea; we have no way of knowing and it would be foolish to carry on without provisions."

"You're kidding! Julian could be just around the next bend in the river and you think we should turn back. We've come a long way for that. Maybe you should take Li Sy back and I'll—"

"I don't think I can get Li Sy across." Elizabeth said quietly.

Jasin blushed. Even from several paces away he could see how red her injured arm had become. "I'm sorry," he said meekly. "But we're close. I just know it."

"Why don't you take Li Sy? I'll be okay on my own. I'm just afraid I'd be more a hindrance than a help."

Jasin hesitated. He had made this mistake before. Shaking his head, he said, "We can both return when you're healthy."

Slowly, they picked their way through thorny bushes along the river. Elizabeth caught Jasin glancing back toward the supply depot and understood how conflicted he must be. They *were* close. She felt it too. Julian, if she were still alive, was probably just down river, but it would have been reckless to attempt a rescue. It would be far better to report back to the Council, tell them what they had discovered, and then leave it to the Sytonians.

Li Sy had scampered off without a word. Her impulsiveness no longer surprised them, but after several hours they began to worry.

"I think she's run away from you," teased Elizabeth. "Most ladies take a dim view of being nearly shocked to death."

"I don't know…I think I did her a favor. Did you notice how her shoulder patches returned to normal. This weapon actually drains them or something. Maybe it flips something off in their nervous system." He pointed the weapon at one of the plants blocking their way and turned it on. Nothing happened.

"It had no affect on us either." Elizabeth observed. "Whatever it does, it's different than the weapon Eidorf had."

The memory of Sy Loeton's gruesome death flooded back. "Maybe he didn't plan to use it against a native," said Jasin.

Half an hour later, Li Sy returned with a handful of leathery leaves, which she claimed would soothe Elizabeth's arm. They seemed to have no affect, but Elizabeth, afraid of offending Li Sy, kept them bound against her wound as Jasin struggled to make headway through the foliage. Li Sy walked behind them.

"Maybe we should walk in the river. It would be easier than this," said Jasin, more than half serious. He used his arm to wipe the sweat from his forehead.

"Li Sy not walk river," she said emphatically. "We should walk path."

Both Jasin and Elizabeth stopped to stare at the towa.

"Path?" asked Elizabeth. Jasin was too exasperated to speak.

"There." She pointed in the direction she had just returned from. A few moments later they were cruising down a well-trodden path.

"It must lead all the way to Bistoun," Elizabeth remarked cheerfully.

But Jasin was still steaming. "Li Sy...we really have to talk about volunteering useful information without being asked."

"Volunteering?"

Jasin shook his head. Li Sy looked at Elizabeth for guidance, but she just smiled back. "Don't smile at her. It's not funny," complained Jasin.

"Of course it is," laughed Elizabeth.

"You're both strange," Jasin mumbled, quickening his pace until he was alone with his foul mood. Damn, he thought. They had been so close.

Except for the deep claw marks on Jasin's chest where Li Sy had held on for dear life, the river crossing was accomplished without incident. Elizabeth was able to swim on her side and use her one good arm. They rested, on the loose gravel, and warmed up in the late afternoon sun until the forn swarmed in. Li Sy appeared pleased at their arrival. She opened her mouth, expanded her neck folds, and sucked in as many as she could hold. Elizabeth and Jasin swatted the annoying insects, and quickly gathered their belongings. Together they ran toward the cliff trail, Li Sy dawdling reluctantly behind.

Dark shadows fell early along the cliff wall. It had been a long, long day and much to the towa's disappointment, the humans fell asleep, too exhausted to eat. The forn had merely whetted her appetite and she walked off, following a peculiar smell, hoping it would be something that could tide her over until morning. Scrambling between the fallen rocks, she found the source of the odor. Even in the dark she realized it wasn't to be eaten, so she carried it back and placed it between the sleeping humans.

As light filled the narrow canyon, Elizabeth woke. She hadn't slept well and had tossed about looking for a comfortable position that might relieve the throbbing pain of her stitched arm. She turned to look at Jasin. A stranger's severed head stared back.

"JASIN!" she screamed. If Li Sy had hoped for breakfast, she'd have to wait until her companions got over the shock her gift had caused.

"I'm afraid Li Sy is right," reported Jasin, returning from his short walk. "There are over a dozen heads...mostly villagers. I recognized some of them. From the shape they're in, it looks like they've been thrown down from the cliff edge just outside the village. I'm not sure what happened in Cernai, but I have my doubts about making a visit."

Elizabeth's stomach churned, roiled by the mental image and the lack of food. "How else would we get back up?" she asked with mounting fury.

"We'll use the trail, but I think we should avoid contact until we know what has happened."

"Isn't it obvious? You don't think humans did this to each other, do you?" Elizabeth face had become hard with anger. "First they destroyed the Medical Colony and now this..." she searched for a word strong enough, "...this slaughter." She reached for the weapon. Li Sy cowered, unsure of her status.

"You can't be serious,"

"Why not? We aren't protected by law; we have no rights. How else can we protect ourselves? Surely you don't think we should just ignore this."

"We don't really know what has happened here. Besides, we're going to need native help to rescue Julian."

"Forget Julian!"

Jasin jerked like he had been slapped in the face.

"I'm sorry, a lot of people have been risking their necks to help find your mother, but she's just one little old gray-haired lady. Open your eyes damn it! The entire human settlement is in jeopardy."

"Just try to relax."

"Relax! You're joking." Elizabeth raised the weapon. "I think it's time they begin taking us seriously."

"Elizabeth, I want you to listen to me. I understand your anger, but storming into Cernai with that thing isn't going to solve anything. You don't understand the towan."

"And you do?"

"Better than you! The towan don't care if a thousand of them have to die to kill one of us. I saw it in the Kull. Their bones were piled high. Tens of thousands of towan to overcome just a few hundred Eians...and the Eians had all the sophisticated weaponry. Now they are either dead or imprisoned. We can not win a war against the natives."

"Who's talking about a war?" Elizabeth said dejectedly. Her intense anger was giving way to frustration. "I just want a little retribution, a little satisfaction and...and a little sleep."

"And a mattress." Jasin smiled.

"And a warm bath." Elizabeth managed a wry smile and threw the weapon to Jasin. "Here, maybe they'll kill you first."

Reunion

By mid-morning, Jasin, Elizabeth and Li Sy had completed the climb to the edge of Cernai. Leaving the towa with the energy weapon, the humans entered the occupied village and found the towan in charge.

"Son of Elstrada, this is a surprise, I did not expect to see you here in Cernai." Sy Lang looked down at Jasin, then lifted his gaze to Elizabeth, who stared back with unblinking hatred. The towan switched to Human and spoke directly to Elizabeth "You may leave us to have the old woman tend your arm before she dies. Jasin, we will speak privately."

Elizabeth refused to budge.

Jasin said, "Respectfully, Sy Lang, I have kept no secrets from—"

"Perhaps you should," interrupted the towan, who walked over to Elizabeth and sniffed the air around her. "You *will* leave us now," he demanded.

As before, she did not break eye contact, refusing to be intimidated.

Finally, Jasin tried to break the stalemate, "Elizabeth…your arm probably could use the doctor's care and perhaps she knows what happened to Mas and the boy."

"Yes, go now," repeated Sy Lang. "Before you become the forty-first human to die here. You will find your friends and the doctor near the center of this rebel village. For now, the people from the secret colony in the mountain have been allowed to live." Sy Lang turned away from the contest of wills, leaving Elizabeth with only Jasin toward which she could direct her anger.

Elizabeth clenched her jaw. Her arm trembled. How dare he turn his back to her! She fought the temptation to draw her knife and cut off this animal's head, just as he had done to the villagers who had merely defended their homes. Now she was sorry they had left the Eian weapon with Li Sy. Without speaking she stormed out.

"Son of Elstrada, you must take her home. It is not safe for her to be on the trail in her condition."

"The wound will heal. We were heading for Nova Gaia and this village was on our way."

"You should study your Father's maps; there is an easier way to get there."

"But not as direct."

Sy Lang inclined his head in acknowledgement. It was well-studied gesture mimicking a nod and unusual to see in a native. Only Sy Lang's familiarity with humans made it seem almost natural. "So are you prepared to deliver the machine in the lake? We have an agreement."

"Are you prepared to deliver my Mother?"

"We have searched Hadrious. She is not there."

"Perhaps you don't know where to look."

Sy Lang's neck folds expanded slightly. It was clear he understood the insult.

"You needn't worry about the shuttle," continued Jasin. "If Sy Toberry has stopped following me and returned home, I will consult with him in Nova Gaia. I need to know when Rhan-da-lith will occur... unless you know. With that information I will be able to destroy the shuttle when it rises during the next Darkness."

"Sy Toberry is dead. We never had the opportunity to discuss the next darkness. According to your fellow Enforcer, he froze to death on top of Mount Schtolin. Perhaps you will have to move closer to Lake Chook to be ready."

Jasin could hardly believe it. Toberry always had an air of invincibility. Avram believed he was the oldest towan alive and the thought of his death was unsettling. "What was he doing so high up?" Jasin asked, but he already had an inkling.

"He was with McMaster when they discovered the medical colony. I believe they were following you."

The implication was plain. Sy Lang knew they had visited the colony.

"How is it that you, an Enforcer, discovers humans ignoring the Prohibitions and does nothing? Perhaps your father was wrong about you. Perhaps you didn't deserve your father's trust."

"I did not visit or know of..." Jasin paused. The towan's words hurt more than he liked to admit, but he needn't explain himself to this diplomat turned butcher. "What do you intend to do with those you captured on the mountain?"

"Maybe nothing...or maybe we'll send their heads to those who think they can ignore the Prohibitions. Perhaps you should take one of their ugly heads with you to remind yourself how important your job is. But they are not important, the machine in the lake is."

"And Beloit? I will need Mas and Beloit to help me carry out my plan," said Jasin improvising.

"The Enforcer is to be held here until the matter of Sy Toberry's disappearance can be settled."

"If Beloit was guilty, why would he have told you anything? It doesn't make sense. What did he have against Sy Toberry? May I talk to him?"

"Perhaps later, he is presently... *sentlory*, what is the Human word for it?"

"Engaged or busy," Jasin translated.

"The Enforcer is engaged. He will not be released."

"Then at least let me have Mas...and the boy and his mother," he added.

"Perhaps I will allow your friend to go. I understand he did not seek the doctor's help directly, but his companion, the woman who lived in the mountain, she has disobeyed the Prohibitions for years, as have the rest of those that lived in the colony. You should take the boy. If he stays it is likely he will carry his mother's head, and he will need a father."

"I can't take the boy from his mother. We don't do that."

"That's a shame. Then take your friend and your tall female, and leave within the hour. If you think you need more help, I will supply towan."

"That will not be necessary."

Jasin walked past the charred remnants of several buildings and shallow craters, and made his way toward the center of the village. A dozen young children with dirty faces and blood stained clothes ran about recklessly, ignoring Jasin as he tried to speak to them. Along the dense, firegrass perimeter of the village, groups of towan watched for anyone who might want to escape their hospitality. A crowd, mostly women, stood warming themselves around a smoking fire pit that he remembered once had been the location of a large building in the center of town. Jasin assumed they were the refugees from the colony and became concerned when he couldn't immediately find Elizabeth. Her tall, striking figure always made her easy to spot. An older man, his heavily lined face darkened by soot, approached, holding out his hand.

"You have your mother's thick, dark hair. I heard she had a son," the stranger began. "I'm Ada. I'm glad to have a chance to meet you."

Jasin shook the wrinkled man's soft fleshy hand. "Jasin Elstrada...but you must be thinking of someone else. My mother's been gray for over thirty years."

"But as a teenager she had the prettiest raven hair...long and shiny. Beautiful eyes too. Ha, listen to me. I think I must still have a crush on her. But where's my manners? I'm sorry. I hear she is still missing."

It was strange to meet someone who had those kinds of thoughts about your mother. "Hopefully not for much longer. Say, did you see a tall—"

"Then you have news. Have you spoken to Julian? Is she all right?"

"No, but I think we have a good idea where she might be. It's just a matter of getting there. Now I was wondering, have you seen a tall, young woman? She was looking for the doctor."

"Indeed. Nasty knife wound. Over there." He pointed off toward one of the few homes that looked unaffected by the recent events.

Jasin thanked the old man, who offered, if needed, to help find Julian. Silly old man, Jasin thought as he made his way to the hut. The codger would be lucky to ever leave the village alive. Jasin found them behind the hut sitting on large boulders that formed a crude ring.

"Jasin! You fool. Is this anyway to mount a rescue." Mas stood up and the two men embraced.

"I brought her," Jasin said, indicating Elizabeth, who was being tended to by the doctor. "I didn't figure I needed anyone else. Hello, Nanc." Nanc acknowledged him without moving from her boulder. Jasin could still feel the tension between them.

The doctor turned angrily toward Jasin. "Are you the hack that tried suturing this arm? My word, but it looks like you were blind."

"Blind and with a concussion," Jasin replied with mock pride and a smile. "Will she survive?"

"No thanks to you, that I'm sure of," stated the doctor as she finished wrapping Elizabeth's arm with a clean bandage. "It's infected. You've got to tell that towa witchdoctor not to use any more dirty plants. Elizabeth, you have to keep the wound clean. If she wants to use her medicines just make sure they aren't filthy."

"I think it became infected before Li Sy attempted to help. The leaves haven't been changed for over a day and we've been through a lot. Where's Sheelia?" Elizabeth asked.

The doctor shook her head. "Too many needless deaths. Sheelia was killed trying to protect the gene samples. Try to rest now and give it time to heal. It might help if you have an opportunity to expose it to the sunlight. I'm sorry that I don't have any antibiotics. Our towan *friends* destroyed the last of it. Now, the towa's organics are the best we have. Just keep it clean." She rose stiffly from the stone and wished everyone good luck.

"Thank you Doctor. Good luck to you too," replied Jasin

"Yeah," she said taking a deep breath. "Listen…if you are able to find Julian, tell her Misa says hi. Tell her I've missed her, but I'm not sorry about my decision. She'll know what that means."

No one said a word as the feisty old doctor retreated slowly, as if she were walking off to meet her death. Everyone knew it would be a miracle if the towan let her live after thirty years of defiance.

"So, what's the plan? Are they going to let any of us leave?" asked Mas.

Awkwardly, Jasin turned to Nanc. "No one who worked in the colony will be allowed to go. I'm sorry. I got permission for Mas to leave with us, but we've got to get out of here within the hour." Then not able to bear looking at the tears welling up in Nanc's eyes he turned to Elizabeth. "You better find Wilem and see what he remembers."

Elizabeth nodded, but was slow to rise.

Mas shook his head. "You expect me to leave them here alone," he said looking at Nanc who returned his loving look with one of her own.

Jasin was taken by surprise. The thought that Mas could be serious about any woman was as much a shock as Nanc having tender feelings for a man.

Elizabeth, however, was pleased with their obvious affection. She smiled at them then asked softly, "Do you know where Wilem might be?"

Nanc stared at Elizabeth with a vacant look, as if her mind were elsewhere. Suddenly her eyes refocused. "You must take him with you."

"I am staying with you," Mas stated firmly.

Nanc closed her eyes, dropped her chin to her chest and shook her head. With her lips pressed tightly together, she sniffled, and then with a piercing stare directed at Elizabeth, she repeated, "You must take Wilem with you." Then she turned to Mas. "And you must go with him. He will need you."

"We can't do that." Elizabeth replied. "We won't! You can't predict the future. Wilem loves you and it's clear Mas does as well. When we destroy the shuttle, Lang and the

Council will owe us. We will demand your freedom. We will demand everyone's freedom. Wilem has lost too many loved ones. We won't take him from you. We can't. It isn't fair."

"I will most likely die with Misa and the others. If he stays—"

"You don't know that!"

"If you're right and they let us live, then there's little harm done by taking Wilem for a while. He's comfortable with you. He loves you too. But if I'm right...." There was no reason to finish.

"I'm staying with you," repeated Mas.

"Wilem needs you more."

Mas walked to the rock where Nanc sat, knelt down, put his head in her lap and hugged her. "I'm staying," he whispered.

Nanc ran her fingers through his hair and looked off toward the dark edges of the tall grass forest where two towan patrolled. "I think Wilem is playing with the other children in the clearing by the cliff. Bring him here. I will explain."

A few minutes later, Wilem came running and jumped into Elizabeth's arms. She winced as he inadvertently grabbed her bandage. She let him slide down until he stood looking up at her, very small and vulnerable. His clothes were filthy and torn, and his hair carried more than its share of soot and soil.

"Wilem, you need a bath," signed Elizabeth.

The young boy shook his head and turned to his Mother. "Now, we can all go to the lake," he signed accompanied by his flat peculiar speech.

Nanc held out her arms inviting Wilem to join her. The others watched as he reluctantly trudged over. Nanc tussled his hair and everyone laughed as a small cloud of debris flew from his locks. Wilem scowled unhappily.

"Elizabeth and Jasin aren't going that way. They are returning to Nova Gaia, but they've invited you to go with them." She glanced over at Jasin and Elizabeth to insure their acceptance of the little lie. "I think it would be better if you go with them until we can clear up this problem with the natives. Mas and I will join you when we're able. Then we'll go back to the lake if you still want to."

"Elizabeth too?"

"If she'd like, but I think she would prefer to stay with Jasin."

Wilem considered this, and then made his decision. "I think I will stay here with the other kids until we can all leave. We're digging a tunnel into the tall grass. It's Franny's idea."

"It would be best if you go with Elizabeth now," Nanc's signing became more energetic as if she were speaking louder and with more authority.

"I can't leave the other kids. They need my help with the tunnel."

"They will get you into trouble. Go with Elizabeth. I am not asking you. I am telling you."

Wilem looked for a sympathetic face. Not finding one he signed, "No! You can't make me." And with that, he ran off.

"That went well," Mas commented sarcastically. "I'll get him."

"Wait a minute," said Jasin. "There's got to be a better way than forcing him."

"He can't stay here. You've got to take him," Nanc pleaded.

Jasin nodded in agreement. There was an awkward pause as he considered the possibilities. Finally, looking at Elizabeth for support he stated firmly, "We've got to take them all."

Elizabeth stared back at him as if he lost his mind. "Take everyone? With only one weapon? We'll all be dead before nightfall!" Elizabeth declared. Mas nodded in agreement.

"No...just the children. Sy Lang won't care. Many of them don't have parents. We'll take them to Nova Gaia. If they all go, it will be easier for Wilem"

"You're crazy," said Elizabeth. "There's over a dozen kids. We don't have enough food for ourselves. How do you expect—"

"There will be food enough when we get there. Nova Gaia is less than two days away"

"I agree with Elizabeth, you're crazy," Mas added.

Jasin turned to Nanc for support. She smiled back. Then taking Mas's hand, she rose from her boulder. "Come with us Elizabeth," she said, "We'll gather the kids while Jasin talks to Lang." As the two of them passed Jasin, Nanc stopped, looked deeply into his eyes, and kissed his cheek. "I was wrong about you," she whispered.

But as they moved on, Mas looked over his shoulder at his friend and mouthed, "Out of your mind." Elizabeth just stared at Jasin, shaking her head, clearly overwhelmed at the prospect and responsibility the idea carried with it.

Jasin knew it was ridiculous, but he also knew it was the right thing to do. That blank look on the children's faces masked deep pain and confusion. If he could remove the children from harm's way and distance them from where they had watched their parents die, they could begin to heal. Once the idea had entered his mind, he couldn't imagine the kids staying to witness even more murders.

Obtaining Sy Lang's consent was easy. Clearly, he didn't want to deal with the orphaned human children and was pleased to have Jasin rid him of the problem. "Take them all if you want to. It is of no concern. Did you still wish to speak to the Enforcer? He is no longer...occupied."

Sy Lang led Jasin to one of the smaller craters where two towan stood on the rim guarding Beloit. Jasin slid down the side into the depression, kicking up a dust cloud. He stormed over to confront the man he once thought of as a friend and mentor. One of Beloit's eyes had swollen shut and his scalp was bleeding where a large chunk of hair was missing. He could barely raise himself from the ground. The guards were superfluous.

"You're a mess."

"It's nice to see you too." Beloit groaned, trying to shift his weight. "They think I killed Toberry."

"That is the prevailing opinion."

"We were looking for the colony and he got more and more tired. He acted all right when we started out, talking most of the way up, but I guess the cold exhausted him. He froze to death. But you should be glad he's dead. He was a sneaky lying bastard. Everything you did, everywhere you went, he reported it to the Council, but I swear I didn't do anything. I was just doing my job."

"Following me? Imprisoning scores of your own people? A lot of us are probably going to die."

"Avram asked us to help enforce the Prohibitions. The penalty for transgression is death. I didn't make the rules; your father did."

"My father merely agreed to them in order for us to co-exist. But this isn't co-existence; it's the beginning of genocide. I can see removing the technology, but how can you assist them in murder? If we don't value human life, how will they?"

"I did not assist them in any murder."

"Did you try to stop them from killing the villagers?"

Beloit looked puzzled at the mere thought. "I wasn't in the position to do anything. Besides, they would have killed me too. What would that have accomplished?"

"Did you complain? Raise your voice? Anything?"

Beloit stiffened slightly and his eyes glazed over. "You should know they can't be reasoned with. They're perverted savages. There's only one way to deal with them."

"I don't see you doing a damn thing except helping them. Did you tip them off to the villagers here as well?"

"Never! I don't know why they moved against this village, but we both know they weren't innocent," said Beloit dismissively. He looked around the crater with his one good eye. "Though I had no idea the sneaky bastards had developed this kind of capability."

"This whole thing is nuts. You're supposed to be working for us, not them. Why did you follow me to the mountain? How did you connect with Toberry?"

"I ran into him in Bistoun. He had been following you from Fistulee and knew you'd be taking Mas to the Women's colony. I guess he figured I'd like the chance to find a way into there. You know, I've tried before."

Jasin nodded, then shook his head. "I don't know how or even whether to help you now."

"Thanks," Beloit replied sarcastically.

"I'm sorry. Everything we've worked for is falling apart. No one trusts anyone and I can't put a finger on the cause."

"How about the wholesale slaughter of humans? How about the rape and mutilation of Katherine in Bistoun? Jorge in Lake Chook? The kidnapping of Julian? Lot's of reasons why no one trusts anyone now. Have you heard about the shuttle?"

"More than I care to," replied Jasin.

"You don't understand how that one machine could change the balance of power. Hyland fucked us all by not destroying it."

"Well...I'll have to complete what he left unfinished."

"Don't make me laugh. No one is going to get the shuttle. It's like the Holy Grail...forever just out of reach. No Jasin, if the Sytonians don't settle down, we humans will be gone in a year or two. They will find or manufacture a reason."

"You think that's what's going on?"

Beloit shrugged. "I don't know, but in thirty years we've never been at each other's throats like we are today. And I know who will win and who will lose."

"Maybe it's not too late. Like you've said, the shuttle's existence is a major problem. Avram knew that...Hyland didn't."

Beloit nodded.

"Take care of yourself Beloit. Obviously they aren't sure what happened to Toberry either. If they were sure you killed him, you'd be dead already."

Jasin found Elizabeth, Mas, and Nanc watching a small, determined bunch of six children dig their tunnel to freedom. They had managed to scoop out a one-meter deep cavity in the wall of a crater where one of the village's booby-trapped homes had exploded. They only had a half a kilometer to go. The thought should have made Jasin smile, but the children's plan somehow didn't seem so absurd. The children were at least doing something, futile or not. They were oblivious to those that stopped to watch them, including the several towan who stood mystified at the purpose of the children's play.

Jasin took a deep breath. He was fading, completely exhausted. "Well, have you talked to them?"

"These few aren't interested," Mas replied, and then noticing Jasin's somber mood, "I take it your negotiations didn't go well. It's just as well. There's no way you'd be able to manage all the children even if you could get them home."

"You might be right, but Sy Lang thought it was a great idea." Jasin managed a weak smile. "However, he still wants us out of here soon and I would too. I'd like to get through the tall grass and the forest before nightfall. We could camp at the trader's clearing tonight." Jasin paused to look at the children. "Do you know which one is this Franny, Wilem spoke about?"

None of the adults knew, so Jasin made his way carefully down the gravel side of the crater. Upon reaching the cavity he pushed past the kids and examined their tunnel. "Not bad at all," he complimented the filthy workers. "In fact I would say you've done exceptionally good work here. Which one of you is the leader of this group? I would like to shake his hand."

There was an awkward moment while the kids digested this. Finally, the youngest pointed to the far side of the crater where a couple teenage boys sat with a shorter girl and a lanky fair-haired boy. Jasin walked over to them. "I'm told one of you is Franny. I would like to ask for some advice."

"And who might you be?" asked the short, stocky girl who seemed intent on maintaining a hostile demeanor. She threw the heavy rock she had been holding against a large boulder where it shattered with a loud crack.

"My name is Jasin. Are you Franny?" he asked the stone-faced girl.

This amused the others, yet no one offered Jasin any enlightenment. A moment passed while they sized up this new stranger. Finally, the thin, scruffy-faced, blond-haired boy with long legs broke the standoff. "I'm Frank. Little ones call me Franny, cuz my younger sister calls me that. What do you want?"

Jasin indicated the tunnel. "Is that your operation?"

"Why...you interested? Wana buy it? I could have them move it to wherever you might want. Won't cost but a crystal or two." Frank smiled at his own joke.

Jasin smiled too. "No thanks, I've had my fill of tunnels for awhile. But I do have something serious to discuss with whoever might be interested in getting out of here for real."

Frank looked over at the patrolling towan and sneered. "Yeah...and I suppose you think you can just walk right past the towan there."

"I've been given permission to take any children who want to leave. Interested?"

"I ain't a child. Who are you again? And what's the catch. What will it cost us?"

"Don't believe him, Frankie. He's fooling with you," said the girl.

"My name is Jasin. My home is up in Nova Gaia, and you're right...there is a catch." He sat down in the dirt next the young men and explained.

Elizabeth watched Jasin engage the children from across the charred depression that had been someone's home just a few days ago. Initially, there was much shaking of heads and looking off toward the little ones industriously excavating their tunnel, but over time the young men relaxed and the conversation became more animated. They began to respond. Jasin's outlandish idea that they actually help take on the stewardship of the younger children instead of manipulating them for their own entertainment started to take root in their imagination.

"He should have been a teacher," observed Elizabeth from across the crater.

"Or a diplomat like his father, added Nanc.

Mas shook his head. "Never," he declared. "He doesn't lie well enough and I don't think he would have enjoyed living under his father's shadow. Avram's accomplishments and fame have been quite a burden and I'm afraid no matter what he does in life he will never escape that."

Elizabeth gaze drifted back to Jasin. She knew his relationship with Avram had a certain stiffness to it. She had always thought it was a sign of the respect that she knew Jasin had for his father, but her heart told her that Mas was right. So impressed and blinded by the big house and the family name, she hadn't seen the underlying truth and it was shocking. Jasin was afraid he wouldn't measure up, that he would always just be Avram's son. What was it Sy Lang had called him...Son of Elstrada? But things were changing. In the past months, Jasin had begun to discover his own destiny, and with it, increasing happiness. She would have liked to take the entire credit for it, but Avram's shadow had begun to break up like clouds after a storm and light had begun to penetrate. With responsibility and the need for action, Jasin was finding himself, and even in the midst of these trials, she was proud to be his companion. She just wasn't sure his answer concerning the children wasn't lunacy.

Jasin stood and brushed off the dirt from his pants. "We're leaving within the hour. Make sure you tell Wilem you're going." He left the boys alone and rejoined the others.

"How many do you think will come?" asked Elizabeth, afraid of the answer.

"We'll see. I would guess a least four, maybe five." She let out a soft groan and Mas laughed. "You won't even know they're there. It's not as if you were condemned to death. Just think of it as a school field trip. It's just for a day or so. When we get to Nova Gaia we'll find them all homes," Jasin reassured her." He looked back to see if the boys had moved. Lazy teenagers that they were, none seemed the tiniest bit motivated, especially while being stared at. "If we leave them alone, I think they'll move."

Nanc, Mas and Elizabeth rose and the four of them walked back toward the center of the village. Jasin fell in beside his friend and whispered. "Mas...hang back a little... there's something you need to know."

Mas slowed his pace until the women were out of earshot.

"Li Sy is with us. She's hiding just outside the perimeter. I'm going to ask her to stay here in case you need help."

"Just what do you think *she* can do?" asked Mas.

"Kill every towan here." Jasin smiled at Mas's doubtful expression. "We have an Eian weapon. I'll leave it with her. It should drop them like forn in a flame. She'll be watching you. Hopefully, Lang will come to his senses and the bloodshed will stop, but if not…"

"Does Li Sy know how to use it?"

"No…is that important?" The two friends shared a smile and walked on trying to ignore the mounting tension that permeated the village like a thick fog.

Rahfi

Dimness enveloped the gang of youngsters as Jasin and Elizabeth led them to the trader's clearing. Only reflected yellow-green light from Conboet filtered through the trees to illuminate the last few kilometers. With the exception of a few stubbed toes and scraped knees—enough to precipitate tears from the youngest and curses from the oldest—the twelve children emerged in relatively good spirits from the dense foliage to mill around Jasin and wait for instructions. Wilem and Elizabeth were the last to join them.

Frankie and the older boys had agreed to leave the village and Wilem quickly changed his mind, just as Jasin had predicted. Whispered rumors and hushed tales of other towan atrocities throughout the Human settlement had spread among the survivors. No one felt safe. Terrified parents, convinced that Jasin's offer provided the only alternative to having their children witness their deaths, delayed the group's departure. Jasin had refused to leave until everyone made their decision and last minute hugs and emotional goodbye kisses were shared all around.

"Frankie, we'll need a lot of firewood tonight. Can you organize a few teams to search the perimeter of the clearing? It's probably been picked over pretty good," Jasin added, careful to avoid making it sound like an order. So far he'd been successful, but the older boy ignored him. Reacting too quickly was a teenage sign of submission.

"What we need is some food," complained Frankie under his breath.

Elizabeth came up behind and put her hands reassuringly on the young man's shoulders. "Tonight we go hungry, but if we make good time tomorrow, we should eat well in Nova Gaia."

"I hope Rahfi has enough for all of us. I've been dreaming of Suzy's for a week," added Jasin.

"Enough food or enough space?" Elizabeth asked, looking at the crowd of children and remembering the tight quarters of the smoky, open pit inn.

Frankie, uncomfortable with Elizabeth's touch, hunched his shoulders and turned to Wilem. "We need to gather something for a fire tonight, go get some of your friends."

Wilem, unable to make out all the words in the failing light, turned to Elizabeth who made the sign of a fire and reassured him it would be alright to leave her. Wilem wasn't so sure.

"I'll help, "she added. "Come on."

"We don't need your help," Frankie said defensively, grabbing Wilem's shoulder and they walked off to find their own help.

"Frankie is afraid of you," observed Jasin.

"Afraid?"

"Well maybe that's the wrong word…you make him nervous. He doesn't know how to react to someone he's both attracted to and intimidated by."

Elizabeth smiled coyly. "You speak from experience?"

Jasin closed the space between them, smiled, and kissed her. "Absolutely."

"Well maybe I could use a younger model, someone who doesn't act as if the weight of the world were on his shoulders, someone who would make *me* feel like the center of his universe," she teased, realizing too late that she had said more than she meant to.

Jasin stepped back, smarting from her words.

"I didn't mean that…."

Jasin wanted to turn away, but he loved her too much for that.

"It's just that...it's been awhile...and now?" She turned to look at the children.

"It won't always be like this. Things will get back to normal."

"I don't know what normal is anymore," she said, suddenly feeling tears well up. Her emotions had never run so close to the surface before. "I'm sorry; this is a rotten time..." She wiped the moisture from her eyes.

Jasin hugged her tightly, letting her silky hair caress his cheek, feeling guilty that he took pleasure in its softness when he was trying to give her comfort. But she turned and offered him her lips and they kissed deeply, finding a moment of peace and isolation amidst the turmoil.

Later, while watching the shifting reds and oranges of the last dying coals and listening to the rhythmic breathing of the sleeping children, Jasin asked Elizabeth softly, "Did you have a chance to ask Wilem?"

"It was difficult to speak to him while walking, but once, while resting I brought it up. He's blocked out a lot of his father's death. I'm not sure what he remembers. He doesn't want to."

"He's got to. If he doesn't have the entry code—"

"Only the Eians might be able to open the hatch. If that happens, all hell will break loose," Elizabeth finished his thought.

"All what?"

"It's something my dad would say. Hell was a place of chaos where demons and dark souls lived, supposedly underground in the heat and fire of the planet's interior."

"If the Eians use the shuttle's weapons against the Sytonians to regain their freedom, this hell of yours will certainly break loose and we'll get caught in the crossfire. It's one more reason to get rid of the thing. We've got to control it before they do."

Elizabeth closed her eyes and leaned her head on Jasin's shoulder. "Well, I'm not sure Wilem will be any help." They relaxed and let themselves drift off.

Jasin awoke with a jolt. His arm was numb where Elizabeth's head rested, but the rest of him was in a state of heightened alertness. By the position of the stars, Jasin figured they hadn't slept more than four or five hours.

"What's wrong?" mumbled Elizabeth, still sleepy.

"Something's coming through the grasses. See if you can stoke the fire."

Elizabeth grabbed a handful of the firegrass they had used as kindling and broke it across her knee. Then, waited a second until the sap started to ooze, threw it onto what remained of the warm coals. She swore under her breath. The coals had cooled and refused to ignite the volatile sap. Meanwhile, Jasin picked up a rock and crouched low peering into the darkness. A faint shadow emerged...then another. Jasin heaved the rock at the shapes.

"Ow!" screamed the larger of them falling to a knee. "It's just us!"

"Mas?"

"Yeah. Damn it, I think you broke skin."

Jasin and Elizabeth rushed to greet them. They both gave Nanc a big hug, happy to see her still alive. "What happened?" Jasin asked. A few of the youngest children started to fuss and Elizabeth and Nanc walked over to calm them.

"She gets hugs and I get a rock in the face," complained Mas. A small welt was forming near his ear.

"Why'd they let you go?" asked Jasin.

"I made a trade."

Jasin quickly glanced around for Li Sy.

"I gave them the weapon, stupid," said Mas perturbed.

Jasin was speechless. The energy weapon could have protected them from any assault, by either of the other races. Mas could have wiped out all the towan in Cernai, freed everyone and still possessed the weapon.

"I know what you're thinking Jasin, but you're wrong. Unless I was able to kill every one of them, word would have gotten out and thousands would have been hunted us down. You know it and so do I. We saw it in the Kull. Even a dozen weapons wouldn't have been enough to make any difference. This way we're heroes. I told them you found it and that you wanted them to have it. I don't know if they believed me, but Lang understood. It was quite a scene. Once I got the weapon from—"

Suddenly the fire exploded in a burst of flames illuminating the entire area. Everyone turned to see Li Sy calmly sitting beside the fire pit, her big unblinking eyes staring back at them. She held several stalks of firegrass.

"Once I got the weapon from Li Sy, I walked over to Sy Lang, dangling the weapon in his general direction...not really pointing it at him at all...and I explained how you had left this for me to give him as a present, but that you thought it would be nice gesture if he allowed Nanc to go free. All he did was stare at the weapon. I don't think he ever saw one like that before."

"I doubt it."

"But I think he knew what it was...anyway, I just gave it to him. And you know what he did? He thanked me! The butcher thanked me and just let us walk out. Not a question or threat. He could have stopped us, reneged, but he just let us leave."

"Maybe he thinks we have more of them."

"I think he's afraid of you."

"Nonsense! They're not afraid of humans."

"Not humans...you. You're like a wild card. You come and go as you like. You're one of a few that can speak their language. They know you've been in the Kull, and now you show up with this weapon. You are the only human to have been allowed to visit and speak at their council. Now I think the Sytonians believe you know where the Eians are hiding their technology and they're hoping you'll destroy the shuttle before the Eians get their hands on it. I don't think they'll touch you."

"Well, they're right. I think I do know where Hadrious is, and if I'm able, I will still destroy the shuttle. Not just for them...but for all of us living on this frozen hunk of rock. But tonight I think we should rest. Come, enjoy the fire. I'm amazed you were able to make your way through the thick of the forest."

"Actually it was quite easy, we just followed Li Sy. It was as if she could see in the dark."

"Is that right?" Jasin smiled to himself as he led them back to the fire.

Rahfi threw his heavy tongs down on the sizzling grill, shook the sweat off his forehead, and stormed towards them. "You've some nerve showing your face here, Elstrada. Get your butts out. What are you thinking bringing all these filthy little ones here anyway? Hey, don't touch that!" The immense tavern owner swatted Wilem's curious hand away from a charred scrap of meat that remained on the corner of a grill. "It's still hot." If it were possible, Rahfi was even fatter than the last time they saw him…and furious.

"Is that any way to treat your guests? From the looks of this place you could use some paying customers," asked Jasin.

"Paying customers! That's a good one coming from you."

"What's your problem? I've always paid—"

"No one has ever owed me more than your family: fifteen trays of shingals, three serving people for an entire night. Then you all disappear without settling your debt."

"Rahfi…" Elizabeth stepped in, "you know what happened that night."

"I couldn't care less. Someone owes me at least six green. The way I figure it, that means you, Jasin. I didn't push it because of the funeral and all, and I figured you Elstadas were good for it, that you'd eventually settle up. But it's been months. No one knew whether you were coming back."

"Well I'm back now and I have a lot of hungry kids to feed," said Jasin, digging into the depths of his pack. "Six green, huh. Well…" Jasin opened a small pouch of crystals the parents in Cernai had given him. "Listen, I have four green and a couple yellow. They're excellent quality. Not an inclusion in the lot, and I'm home now. I'll bring you the rest tomorrow."

"Let me see," said Rahfi, holding out a greasy hand. Jasin emptied the pouch into it. Whether satisfied with the monetary arrangements or because it was a slow night, Rahfi grudgingly allowed them in.

The voracious travelers split up among the empty tables. Elizabeth thought she recognized the two other patrons from her time with the caravan. The traders were unable to hide their curiosity at the small towa's presence, and they gossiped and lingered over their food all the while providing plenty of nasty looks to the loud ill-mannered juvenile invasion. Elizabeth excused herself and walked over to the their table.

"Sorry if the kids are a little loud. They've had a rough couple of days. I was wondering whether you remember me."

"You aren't an easy one to forget. You rode with Eddie for a while," the man recalled. "Or was that *on* Eddie. He's never stopped talking about you."

"Stop, you'll embarrass her," his woman companion scolded. "Eddie has quite a loose mouth."

"Eddie is also quite a liar, but..." maybe she could turn this to her advantage, "I would like to see him again." She arched her eyebrows suggestively. "Are you traveling together?"

"He and his boy have turned in for the night," said the woman. "That looks like it hurts," she said, referring to Elizabeth's arm.

Elizabeth nodded. "Could you tell Eddie I'm in town, staying at the Elstrada house? The locals can give him instructions. Tell him I'll make it worth his trouble. Tell him I'll pay up my debt and I need something he has." Elizabeth smiled at the innuendo.

"I'm sure he'll be pleased to hear that," snickered the man.

Elizabeth returned to Jasin's side still smiling. Sometimes it was fun to play the loose woman.

"You know them?" Jasin asked.

Nodding, she sat down and whispered in his ear. "By tomorrow you'll have the explosives you've been looking for." She enjoyed his puzzled look, but would tell him no more.

Despite the rude staring, they ate well. Elizabeth could not seem to get enough of the spiced turbak and Jasin, enjoyed several helpings of the grilled sweetmeat washed down with a few large mugs of Rahfi's horrid ale. He leaned back and took stock of the group. Frankie was by far the oldest, eighteen or nineteen Jasin would guess, a natural leader. Frankie sat with the shorter, mean looking girl from the village named Stanya, who for some reason liked to be called Stump. Stump appeared to have done everything possible to hide the fact that she was actually developing into a rather cute, well developed, seventeen year old. Clearly attracted and intensely loyal to Frankie, she easily controlled the other fifteen or sixteen-year-old boys at the table who were mesmerized by the only young woman in their age group, whether or not she was available or interested.

The third table was surrounded by five dirty faces, all about Wilem's age, and watched over by Vanetue and Heather, a pair of plain looking twin girls just flirting with puberty. Jasin had yet to be able to tell which was which although he was sure that if he studied their innumerable freckles he'd find a difference. It was too much work to try, so he referred to them simply as "the Twins". Tonight the Twins had their hands full, for the meat had to be cut and not one of the young ones were able to deal with the rather crude, short culinary knifes allowed under the Prohibitions. Finally sated the adults considered their next steps.

"Sleep," Mas decided. "We're not ten minutes from my place and my mattress is calling my name. It will be cozy with Nanc and Wilem, but manageable."

"I was hoping you might help watch over a few more," said Jasin, beginning to worry that he had over committed.

"Not at my place. What about your cabin?"

Jasin agreed. "We'll sleep in Elizabeth's old room and turn one of the big rooms into a dormitory. Wilem will be happier with the other kids."

As they stood up to leave, Rahfi waddled over and blocked their way. "You won't forget my crystals, Elstrada. I'm not waiting another septet."

"You'll get you crystals," Jasin promised.

"Make sure I do. Stay on the main road. The trader's have been reporting random skirmishes with the natives."

"In Nova Gaia?" Other than Sy Toberry's family, Jasin was unaware of any other Sytonians living in the area.

Rahfi nodded, shaking sweat from his ample forehead. "Since you've been gone, young Initiates have come up. They seem to enjoy setting their untrained cyliths loose. After dark, the streets aren't safe anymore."

No one said a word as Jasin's group began the short walk to the Elstrada compound. They stayed close together, the adults herding the sleepy children ahead through the dimness, moving quickly along the eerily deserted streets, past trader's wagons, heaped with precious goods that hid their suspicious owners and their ever-watchful eyes. The adults traded uneasy glances and tried to ignore the occasional distant cylith howl. Something had changed in Nova Gaia. The illness that infected the entire gorge had made its way to their village.

Sy Jelick

The Initiate had nearly died and it was Sy Jelick's fault. As a mentor, it had been his responsibility to watch for the cylith bitch, but, inexperienced, he had lost sight of the creature until it was too late. Her sharp teeth had already ripped open the younger towan's leg. Using the healing leaves and strips of bark as his father had taught him, Sy Jelick had bandaged what remained of the lacerated leg, then lifted the youngster across his broad shoulders. He had barely managed to carry the Initiate back to Nova Gaia where his mother and Jasin's strange towa could now use their healing knowledge.

As he made his way to the Elstrada compound Sy Jelick looked down at his unbroken horizontal Initiation scar, blood-smeared from the poor boy's wounded leg. There would be no ceremony for either of them now, no cylith pup, and no honor. He had failed where his father had succeeded more times than any other towan in their history.

It had not even been his Initiate. When Sy Toberry failed to join the young towan in Bistoun as promised, the boy had come to Nova Gaia in search of his renowned mentor. Sy Jelick knew his father took the Initiation seriously and it was unlike him to forget his duty without some important reason. And yet, here was this youngster ready for his great moment, ready to brave the cold, ready to capture his cylith companion.

There had to be a first, Sy Jelick had reasoned. A bare unbroken scar also must have stretched across his father's chest when he led his first Initiate up into the cold, those many, many years ago. Now, it was his time. He had been determined not to let his father's absence disgrace his family, but he had never considered that he might bring home such dishonor, or imagined it possible to return with only a mauled Initiate and his own cylith by his side.

Sy Jelick entered the courtyard where he and Jasin had often taken instruction from his father. Several human children glanced apprehensively at him. A few disappeared into the safety of the large house. He sniffed the air and stared back at the few who were bold enough to remain, those refusing to avert their eyes. He did not recognize any of them as being from local families.

Mas entered the courtyard, dragged back by a couple of little ones intent on proving their claim that a scary towan covered in blood had invaded their playground.

"Sy Jelick, you've got to get yourself a mirror!" kidded Mas in Human, knowing full well that Sy Jelick didn't understand a word of their language. "I hope the other guy looks worse than you. Just a minute, I'll get Jasin." Mas picked up a pebble and tossed it at the window in Avram's study. "He's practically lived in there since we got home."

Jasin opened the window and leaned out. Without saying anything he waved for them to come up and join him.

"Sy Jelick, what has happened? Are you hurt?" Jasin asked in the native's language indicating the blood on the young towan's shoulder patch.

"This is nothing. I am unharmed. There has been an accident, but Jelick is fine. Jelick has not had time to wash. Jasin, your towa..." Sy Jelick paused, for that was not correct. He searched for a more accurate description for Li Sy. "Your friend, that is towa, has informed me that you believe Sy Toberry is possibly dead. Jelick came immediately. This knowledge concerning my father can not be correct."

"We are sorry about Sy Toberry," Jasin began, "but he has died on Mount Schtolin. We will all miss him. He was a remarkable towan."

"You have seen his dead body?"

Jasin shook his head. "But I believe what Beloit McMaster has reported."

"Your towa...Li Sy says Sy Toberry ascended Mount Schtolin. Death came to my father in the cold. Is this true?"

"This is what Beloit has said, but Li Sy. Li Sy is not *my* towa. Li Sy is a free towa."

"This can not be true."

"I assure you, Li Sy belongs to no towan."

"Not about Li Sy. This story about my father cannot be true knowledge. Sy Toberry does not like the cold. Sy Toberry would not go up any farther than Nova Gaia and...and there are no free towa," he added as proof that Jasin must be lying to him.

"Jasin is sorry about Sy Toberry, we both are." Jasin repeated, including Mas who stood silently by Jasin's side. "But the story is true."

"But you were not there. You did not see Sy Toberry die? Was my father injured?"

"No, as I said, I did not see him die."

"Then my father may simply be frozen."

Jasin turned to Mas and explained. "He questions whether his father is really dead. He thinks he may only be frozen."

Mas shrugged. "What's the difference? Dead is dead."

"I suppose it might be possible. In Panvera, Li Sy was brought to us completely stiff, I don't know whether she was frozen through, and it was only a single night, but she survived."

Mas shook his head. "From what Beloit was saying, Toberry just got more and more tired until he sat down and died. He didn't get frozen until after he had succumbed."

Jasin translated.

"If this is true, then my father's energy left him before he froze. Sy Toberry is dead. I will tell my mother. Seann Sy thought the black rocks would help."

"Black rocks?" Jasin had never heard of them.

"Seann Sy says she accompanied him when he felt tired to the black rocks beneath the logging camp at the head of the Andoree."

Jasin nodded, recalling a dark stone outcropping on the far shore of Lake Chook. "If Sy Jelick would like, Jasin and Mas would help Sy Jelick retrieve the body from the mountain."

"It is merely cold dead meat. Sy Jelick would not even eat the aspic now. It is for the cylith."

Jasin understood, but doubted there were any cylith hunting for food that high up. Nothing except possibly the field diggers lived in that cold. "Sy Jelick…your father always knew when Rhan-da-lith would occur. Does Sy Jelick know?" he asked hopefully.

Sy Jelick looked about the study thoughtfully. He ran his long center finger over a rusty keetah stain on Avram's desktop and brought it to his nose. "Does Jasin drink the keetah as his father did?"

"No," said Jasin shaking his head. "But lately Jasin has been thinking about it." He smiled, but the young towan was absorbed in his own troubles.

Sy Jelick said, "Recently, it has become clear that there are many things which Sy Toberry was able to do that Sy Jelick can not."

Life in Nova Gaia settled into a comfortable rhythm. Mas and Nanc were enjoying the seclusion of Jasin's cabin, while Wilem spent most nights with the other children in the dormitory that had been Julian's music room. Except for the normal squabbles and fights, the kids had easily accepted the idea of an extended family. After the last few months of continuous travel, adventure, fear, and trauma everyone agreed that rest and rehabilitation were necessary.

Under Li Sy's watchful eye and herbal remedies, Elizabeth's arm healed nicely. She would always carry a jagged scar, but the persistent pain had diminished to a dull ache at night. She found it impossible to sleep on her left side, waking to numb fingers whenever she inadvertently shifted to that side. But that didn't prevent her from getting plenty of rest. Enduring much kidding and teasing, she had begun taking long afternoon naps and loved every unconscious moment.

One day, Elizabeth sought out Nanc. She hadn't planned on announcing her news without informing Jasin first, but Nanc was as close to a best friend and mother she had.

"Are you sure?" asked Nanc.

"I haven't missed since I was twelve." Elizabeth couldn't contain her grin any longer and it burst across her face like a beautiful sunrise.

Delighted, Nanc gave her a big hug and kiss. "I won't say a thing until you tell Jasin. But do it tonight. Secrets like this are to be shared and I don't trust myself not to tell Mas. Make the announcement at dinner, why shouldn't the rest of the family have the fun of witnessing Jasin's expression?"

After hearing the news, Jasin sat glued to his seat, dumbfounded. The teenagers wagged their fingers at him, and Mas lifted the father-to-be out of his seat with a giant bear hug.

"You've been a busy boy now haven't you?" he said, and then whispered in his ear, "Go to her you idiot."

By the time Jasin made it to Elizabeth he was weak-kneed and blind with tears. "I love you so much," he cried, hugging her tightly. He kissed her lips, her cheeks, her neck and kept repeating, "I love you so much. Why didn't you tell me?"

"It seems our little friend was right that morning in the Kull," Elizabeth said looking over at Li Sy. The towa hadn't stopped eating through all the excitement and continued even while returning their gaze.

"A toast!" exclaimed Mas. "Didn't your father leave you any Keetah? If ever there was a fitting occasion…"

"I don't think—" began Jasin.

Mas interrupted. "There is plenty in the study, unless you've been secretly indulging."

The water was heated to boiling and enough Keetah was prepared for all the adults as well as the few older teenagers who dared to burn their mouths. Mas made the appropriate toast and, except for Elizabeth, who out of concern for the new life growing inside her, simply went through the gestures, everyone gulped the boiling liquid and poured what remained in their cups on the floor.

"What a mess," said Elizabeth joyfully, putting her full cup aside before searching out sufficient rags to begin the clean up. Frankie and the other teenagers, for which this had been their first time, laughed and compared the anesthetic effects, bragging to each other over who took the greatest gulp. When Elizabeth returned, everyone joined her on hands and knees to help. Everyone except Wilem, who unnoticed, helped himself to Elizabeth's full cup of the now cooled drink. He wouldn't be left out of the fun. The twins collected all the cups and took them to the kitchen along with all the other tableware.

As they cuddled in bed that night, Jasin confessed to not having the slightest inkling of the pregnancy "I feel guilty not even suspecting anything. Have I really been that unaware of things?"

"I'm only just pregnant. How would you know?"

" Li Sy knew. I should be more sensitive. We've got to make more time for ourselves."

"I've always been right here."

"Yeah, but I haven't. I keep thinking about Hadrious, and that we should be living nearer the lake, preparing for Rhan-da-lith"

"You can't do everything, be everywhere. Right now, I need you to be right here beside me."

"I will always be right beside you" He gathered the warm blanket around her, careful to avoid putting pressure on her arm. He laid his head on her chest and she softly stoked his hair feeling as if, instead of the blanket, she had been wrapped in love and contentment.

In the perfect peace that enveloped them, they listened to the hum of the forn outside until finally Elizabeth, her heart pounding, whispered softly. "Then we should make it official," She feared the thought of becoming a father and husband would be too much for one man to absorb in just a few hours, but Jasin agreed without hesitation.

Wilem

Wilem wrinkled his nose at death's pungent smell, turning his face away from the scorching heat and flames of the pyre that slowly turned his grandfather's body to ash and the smoke that rose to fill the afternoon sky. He lifted his hand to block out the sight of the burning body, but his fingers melted and he screamed. Then, it was his grandfather's voice that he heard. He could see the old man's lips screaming out his name. Leaving his mother's side, he walked across the water to stare at the charred face, now his father's, contorted by agony.

He ran and ran, finally hiding in Elizabeth's trunk at the foot of her bed. It was peaceful here, in the closed chest, nestled in her clothes, the wild flower fragrance she used overwhelming him until he felt like he couldn't breath. He looked down, suddenly embarrassed to be standing barefoot among her underclothes. He threw open the lid and looked up at Franny who pointed and laughed at him. Furious, he flew up and punched the older boy in the nose. Blood spurted out, buckets of blood gushing all over the ground, coming faster and faster, turning the crumbly soil into pools of red mud. Red like the inside of his eyes when he looked at a bright fire with his eyes closed. He could see the tiny spidery veins. They pulsated...like those big veins in his father's neck, straining in agony as the torture machine hummed loudly. The veins bulged and he was afraid they'd burst. He begged for Elizabeth to do something, but she ignored him, sitting calmly in a red puddle laughing. Run away, he thought, but his father held his hands so tightly. He cried out in pain, tugging to free his hands, finally freeing one, but his father held the other and spelled into his palm. And as many times as the dream repeated itself, his father never let go.

When they couldn't wake Wilem, Nanc sent Stump in search of Li Sy. After dashing about, the young girl finally located her at Sy Jelick's home, crushing purplish dried leaves between her right thumbs, and letting the tiny particles fall into the Initiate's wound. Seann Sy looked up at the intrusion.

"Li Sy, you need to come look at Wilem. He won't get up," Stump blurted out.

"Wilem is sleeping. Humans sleep. Li Sy does not know sleep."

"We also wake up and we can't wake him."

But Li Sy could not be rushed. She carefully redressed the Initiates wound and only after a flurry of Native gibberish that Stump couldn't begin to follow, did she follow her back to Wilem's side. Most of the adults had gathered around the young boy, each trying their own remedy to wake the young boy. The children congregated in small bunches throughout the dormitory.

Li Sy leaned over the motionless boy. She looked up and declared, "Wilem is sleeping."

"No he isn't," cried his mother. "This isn't sleep."

Li Sy looked up at Elizabeth who shook her head.

Li Sy leaned over the boy again. Placing one hand on Wilem's forehead, she pulled open his jaw with the other, and stuck her wrinkled nose into the boy's mouth. The kids howled with laughter. Even the adults broke into grins.

"It is keetah," she declared. "Wilem will open his eyes when it is finished."

"He seemed dead," muttered Mas under his breath, now that the thought could be expressed without upsetting anyone further.

"Someone didn't want to be left out," observed Elizabeth. "Let's let him sleep it off. Thank you Li Sy. We were so worried."

"Children should not drink keetah," Li Sy reprimanded. She didn't get any argument from anyone.

Slowly the children drifted out of the dormitory to begin their chores. The adults stood over the still body. Elizabeth put one arm around Nanc and gave her a hug while Jasin and Mas stood at the boy's side.

"He looks so defenseless," Mas said, knelling down to replace the blanket Li Sy had inadvertently knocked to the ground. Mas looked up to give Nanc a reassuring grin, then shifted his gaze to Jasin, who returned a weak smile. "Something wrong?" Mas asked.

Jasin blinked and gave his head a nearly imperceptible shake. "Not really, just thinking. I didn't want to say anything before, but I also could have sworn Wilem was dead."

That evening when all was quiet and everyone else had retired to their rooms and dreams, Jasin climbed the steps to Avram's study and spread the maps open upon the table as he had dozens of times since returning from Cernai with the children. Using several candlesticks and a few cups to prevent the precious documents from rolling up, he examined them. Marvelous workmanship, he thought as he traced the finely inked lines of the Andoree River, looking for any sign of Hadrious or evidence that it had been removed. Here, where the river bulged, could that be it? Or maybe the shoreline has been purposely drawn to hide the fact the river widens. He checked all the maps at his disposal, then stood up, stretched his back, and rubbed his sore eyes. Everything he was studying had been a gift from the Sytonians; he was only seeing what they wanted him to see. What he needed was a survey or map done from orbit, from Tanis, during those years before they were granted the privilege of settlement. His eyes swept the room in vain. He had searched the room, in fact the entire residence, at least three times and knew there was nothing like that. Paper and parchment were rare. Avram had told him about the imaging screens aboard the old ship. Nothing, not even books were ever printed…except of course the disintegrating relic that Hyland had given Avram, the only surviving artifact from Earth according to the old engineer. He sought it out and with care lifted the familiar book from its small niche. He had read from it many times, but still feared harming its fragile pages. Genesis, the origin or beginning…Exodus, Leviticus, he had no idea what that word meant …Numbers…Deuteronomy…so much nonsense. He put the book back and blew out all the candles save one, and walked quietly back toward their room, passing the dormitory on the way. The faint light from his candle revealed Nanc's outline, asleep next to Wilem who hadn't moved a muscle in nearly thirty-five hours.

He hoped Li Sy was right. It wasn't that he doubted her, but he had never seen anything like it before. None of the humans had. If she hadn't enlightened them, he would have been preparing to bury the poor boy. Jasin felt a chill run up his spine. Buried alive, the thought was creepy.

Suddenly a horrible thought took his breath away. What about Avram? Could he have…No, Avram didn't fall into a gradual drugged sleep; his heart blew out and he collapsed. Shaking off the thought he headed off through the kitchen and into the bedroom. Elizabeth was snoring lightly and he was careful not to disturb the covers as he slipped in beside her. He tried to quiet his mind, but something lay just under the surface, a random thought was fighting to rise from his unconscious. He tossed and turned until Elizabeth mumbled, "Can't sleep?"

"I'm sorry. Go back to sleep. I'll settle down"

"What's wrong?"

"Nothing…nothing I can put my finger on." Jasin remained still until Elizabeth's breathing changed. She had fallen back asleep. Damn, he thought. This is crazy. Maybe I'm just….then the ghost of his elusive thought materialized. Beloit had said, "Toberry got more and more tired until he eventually died." Jasin had never seen a towan die of natural causes, but he knew it was proceeded with a general loss of energy to the brain, a sluggishness of thought that according to Sy Jelick, his father prevented with some form of rejuvenation. But Beloit had never indicated that Toberry seemed mentally slowed. Could Toberry have been drugged like Wilem? Could Beloit have poisoned him with keetah without the towan knowing it? For that matter, all they had was Beloit's word that he died that way or died at all. Beloit might have bashed the old towan's head in with a rock. Was Beloit a liar and a murderer? And if so, what did Beloit have to gain by the old towan's death? Perhaps it was just an attempted murder. Jasin tried to shake off the notion that Toberry might be alive. Elizabeth would say it was just wishful thinking since only the old towan knew when the next complete darkness would descend. That was probably true, it was wishful thinking. He simply had no other option. He knew he'd have to find out for sure…and it would have to be soon.

Wilem woke slowly from his long sleep. Disoriented at first, he dragged himself upright. The mattress was wet and he felt ashamed. It had been many, many years since he had had an accident and hoped the big boys wouldn't find out. He could imagine Frankie teasing and he'd have to punch him. Suddenly, memory of the dream he had been having flooded back in and he gasped. He was afraid to venture out of bed in the dark so he lay back on the wet smelly bed, curled himself into a little ball, and started to cry.

Nanc reached for his hand, but when she grasped it, he pulled it violently away. "Wilem…how do you feel?" Nanc could smell the urine and knew he wouldn't want to stay in the bed. She leaned over and kissed his forehead.

He took her hand and told her. "I wet the bed, I had a bad dream."

She stroked his hair. "You're all right now. Come sleep with me tonight." She helped him change into clean clothes and had him lay next to her on the blankets she had spread out next to his mattress.

"I dreamt of Daddy," he signed. "He wouldn't let go of me."

"He loved you very much."

"He held my hand and wouldn't let go. He was trying to tell me something."

"What?"

Wilem tried to duplicate the signs into her palm. "It doesn't make sense to me."

"Do it again," Nanc asked, attempting to understand the seemingly random string of letters.

Again Wilem repeated the signs his father had given him in the dream. "There's a couple of numbers too," he added.

Confused, Nanc asked him to do it once more. It was a jumbled mess. With every repetition the order of the letters were slightly different. Wilem's memory of the actual event, as well as the dream, had faded.

"Let's rest. There are still a few hours before the others get up," Nanc said.

Wilem nestled closer to his mother and closed his eyes, then almost as an after thought he said, "We should tell Elizabeth."

Beloit McMaster

Jasin and Elizabeth jogged slowly down the compacted dirt road that headed toward Nova Gaia, finding a comfortable rhythm that allowed their muscles to stretch and warm up. Their red breathing scarves were frosted except for a round moist circle where their warm breath kept the moisture from freezing. After five minutes, they turned to their right onto the path that took them to the mountain's ragged base. Carefully, they picked their way through the foothills and followed the trail that led up to their favorite promontory. With every stride, the angle of the trail got steeper and they strained against the cold wind blowing down from the distant frigid rim. Snow, having swept through the high passes of Trinity's peaks, stung their rosy cheeks. They drew their breathing scarves higher, as much to block the icy wind as to help soothe their enflamed lungs. Jasin found the flat boulders and sat where they had rested many times before, looking out over the broad vista.

"Maybe we should build our house up here," said Jasin breathlessly.

"You're in terrible shape," teased Elizabeth standing over him and breathing hard herself. "Do you still think it was a stupid idea to run this morning?"

Jasin shook his head. "I didn't say it was a bad idea. I was just worried. What if you stumble and fall? You could hurt the baby."

"You're the only baby that appears to be hurting. Besides, it's just a run. I need the exercise." Elizabeth sat down nest to him.

Jasin glanced off towards the house several hundred meters below. "Wilem looked well this morning. Has Nanc had a chance to talk to you yet? I guess he's remembered something. It didn't make sense to her. Anyway, Wilem wanted to tell you himself. Maybe you'll understand."

"And you think it might be the entrance code to the shuttle."

"I'm hopeful. I don't really relish the idea of using the explosives to gain entry. I wouldn't have the slightest idea of how much to use and your friend Eddie wasn't much help." Jasin shook his head. "What a disgusting character! I'm not sure Samson wasn't better off in Bistoun."

"At least he's with his father."

"Like I said, I'm not sure he wasn't better off alone."

"I don't think it matters."

"Sure it matters. Samson's basically a good kid…"

"No…I meant it didn't matter that Eddie wasn't any help with the explosives. Dad didn't think you could blow your way in."

Jasin shrugged. "Well then, I hope you're right about Jorge giving Wilem the code and he's remembered it."

Elizabeth nodded, then pointed toward town. Two humans were making their way up the well-worn road. "Looks like we might be getting company."

Jasin peered down at the small figures. "Maybe we should just stay here and enjoy the peace and quiet."

"Maybe they're bringing good news. I feel like it's our lucky day," said Elizabeth rising. "Come on, I'll beat you down."

Jasin hurried to catch up, but Elizabeth sprinted through the rocks with abandon, while he trailed behind yelling at her to be more careful.

Avram always took credit for creating the Human Caucus. In private he once confided to Jasin that it was never really supposed to do anything except give the illusion that

Humans still controlled their own destiny, and provide leverage over those naïve enough to believe otherwise. Now that Avram was dead, Jasin wasn't sure who controlled the strings of these deluded marionettes who now stood in front of him with this misguided plan. Jasin recognized the older, thin man as Sandist Lee, one of the original members of the Caucus and a friend of Avram's from the ship. The other couldn't have been more than thirty years old. He had small black eyes and was prematurely balding. Strange that Jasin didn't recognize him. He thought he knew everyone within a few years of himself. Evidently this puppet hadn't attended Advanced Studies.

"I'm sorry. I didn't catch your name." Jasin thought it rude not to be introduced.

"I'm Mordichai, I grew up in Bistoun until McMaster murdered my mother. I've been living in Cernai the last few months."

"You're out of your mind. I was with Beloit when we found the woman."

Sandist explained. "Considering what has happened, we thought it would be good to allow representation from the village."

Jasin was dumbfounded. "How can you believe Beloit had anything to do with that first incident in Bistoun? Who did you say came up with this awful idea?" probed Jasin.

"Well son...we know you're fond of Beloit, but we've thought this through. It's getting worse. There are dozens of reports coming to us from all over."

Obviously Sandist wasn't about to point the finger of responsibility at any single individual.

The elder continued, "In Bistoun, three men and a woman were recently found dead near that tavern along the riverfront," said Lee.

"Sy Fask's place?" asked Jasin.

"No, the one down near the big tree," said Mordichai.

"The greatest number were lost in Cernai," continued his older companion, "but people have also disappeared or been threatened in Lake Chook, and even here in Nova Gaia."

Jasin nodded. He had heard.

"Have there been any reports from Panvera?" asked Elizabeth, walking into the room. "I'm sorry to intrude."

"No reason to apologize. Nothing has been heard from up there, although there have been traders passing through Nova Gaia that were going to head up. Anyway this genocide has got to stop. Over five percent of the entire human population has died or disappeared in just the last few months and if we don't stop this…well, no one believes the natives would care if we all vanished. They are starting to round us up and we have no intention of living in a Human ghetto, but that's just what's going to happen."

"I still don't understand what Beloit has to do with all this. Why make him a scapegoat for human murders he clearly had no part in and the idea that Beloit murdered that woman is ridiculous. I want to know whose idea this was," insisted Jasin.

Sandist Lee shook his head. "The entire Caucus voted on this, and Sy Lang has agreed to allow us to deal with it. Two towan have already brought Beloit back from Cernai. Listen… dealing with our own people is an important step in regaining their respect. Beloit's guilt or innocence in the two murders isn't the question. A public trial and execution should demonstrate that we take responsibility for policing ourselves and that we are serious about the Prohibitions."

"I see that it will be a fair trial," deadpanned Jasin.

"Listen Jasin," Mordichai continued. "As Sandist said, there isn't any question he killed his first wife. And he admits he was the only one with Toberry when the old towan died."

"His wife? I thought you said the woman who died was your mother?" Jasin stared at the young man, waiting. There had to be some mistake, something he didn't understand. Finally, Jasin shook his head. "You're insane. I was with Beloit—"

"You were not with him when he visited Bistoun the first time. You were with your father traveling to Lake Chook for Hyland's funeral."

"But he and I found her dead."

"On his second visit. That's exactly why you're being called to testify tomorrow," said the younger man.

"I still don't understand. You believe the murdered woman in Bistoun was Beloit's first wife? She was mutilated beyond anything I've ever seen." The thought that Beloit was capable of such violence was beyond comprehension. It was absurd. But if the woman was really Beloit's wife why hadn't he said anything? Jasin shook his head. "Where will this trial of yours take place?"

"That's another reason for our visit. This residence is the largest—"

"You want to have the trial here?" Elizabeth exploded. "I suppose you'll want to execute him in the courtyard."

"We will execute him in Bistoun, where the greatest number of both our races will be able to witness it," said Sandist Lee.

"We will all arrive after breakfast, tomorrow." said Mordichai, putting an end to the conversation.

The next morning Sy Hone and Sy Lang escorted a bound Beloit into the large dormitory and presented him to five members of the Human Caucus. His bruises had faded slightly, but his beating was still evident.

The children had stacked their mattresses against the walls and gathered all the chairs and tables from the entire house. It was an odd assortment of mismatched furniture but it would serve for the short few hours everyone assumed the trial would be. Many that had come didn't even bother sitting.

Sandist Lee began. "Beloit McMaster, you are charged with the murders of the noble and highly respected Sytonian, Sy Toberry, and your second wife Katherine McMaster. It is the duty of this Caucus to discover the truth of your involvement and determine punishment if you are found guilty. We thank Sy Lang and the Council of Seventeen for this opportunity to restore faith and trust between our two races. We will begin with your brief response to these charges."

"May I have my hands unbound?" asked Beloit. "It is difficult to plead not guilty when I am being presented like a dangerous man."

"But that is precisely what you appear to be," said Mordichai, running his hand through what was left of his hair.

"May I know who my judges are to be? I have never met you sir."

Sandist Lee nodded. "You are correct on both counts Beloit. See to his bindings; there is no place for him to go." While his hands were being untied Sandist Lee made the introductions. "I believe you know Findley and Yarrow from the ship." Beloit nodded. "Then this is Terrence Winer, from Lake Chook. He took Hyland's place. And this gentleman is the new representative from Cernai, Mordichai McMaster, your first wife's son." A titter ran through the assemblage.

"To my knowledge Katherine had no children and certainly none from me." He turned to Mordichai. "You have no right to use my name—"

"Not really knowing my real father's name, I choose to use my mother's."

"Then use Solend, for that was the name she went by for all but for the briefest of times."

"My name is McMaster. I don't care if it bothers you or not. Now get on with your statement. You are unbound."

Addressing the other Caucus members, Beloit said, "I hardly think it is impartial to have this man, Mordichai, the son of the one of the dead, someone who obviously carries a grudge against me, stand in judgment. I ask that this gentleman be recused."

The Caucus members chatted briefly. Several of them shrugged indifferently, before Sandist agreed. "What can be decided by five can just as easily be decided by four, but Mordichai will be allowed to question you."

"Thank you, Sandist. I am not afraid of his questions."

"Now if you haven't any other complaints, would you be so kind as to begin?"

"Oh I have many other complaints, but to be brief...concerning my innocence in the deaths you mention,

I have but a few simple statements of fact, for I am as baffled today as to the reasons and causes of their deaths as I was when they occurred. First concerning Katherine, we have been estranged for nearly thirty years. I have had little cause to see or speak to her. I have had no direct contact with her all these years. When Jasin Elstrada and I found her dead, well, at first I didn't even recognize her. Her death was gruesome, her face all but unrecognizable. When I finally realized it was she, I was surprised, but not really shocked. She always lived on the edge. Earlier in the week, I had reported the incident to Avram, but at the time I didn't know her identity."

Beloit continued. "As for Sy Toberry's death, for that is what it truly was, not a murder as some have claimed, I was the only one there and I swear he passed away without my involvement in any way. He became tired and died. When I found him he was gone. These are the simple truths."

Sandist Lee thanked Beloit for his briefness and opened the floor to questions from the other members. Terrence Winer started. "I have talked to the young lady who tried to help Katherine. I believe her name is Sherri. She claims to have escorted you back to the victim's house."

"I'm not sure whose house it was."

"You're not?"

"No sir. As I've stated, I was not involved with Katherine."

"She seems to think you knew which of several houses was theirs. You went straight for the correct home without being led. Is this true?"

"It was obvious which was their house. I don't remember why...I think it was the only house that was dark and unoccupied."

"Why did you assume their house would be dark and unoccupied?"

"I'm not sure. It must have been because of what Sherri said or the way she acted. She took no notice of any of the other houses."

"So you aren't sure why you picked the house you did. Is that fair?"

Beloit shrugged.

"When you first met Sherri, she claims you were sure your wife was dead. In fact she says you were shocked to hear she was still alive. Is this true?"

"Katherine was not my wife. I had assumed she was dead. That is what I had heard."

"From whom did you hear this?"

"I'm not sure. I don't remember. Maybe I drew a faulty conclusion, because everyone had said how brutal her attack had been."

"So are you saying no one actually told you that your ex-wife Katherine was dead, yet you assumed it?"

"I'm telling you I don't know why I assumed it."

"Sherri also informs me that you asked her several times whether she had talked to anyone, whether she had said anything. Do you remember asking her?"

"Yes."

"Why were you concerned that she might have talked?"

"I wasn't concerned...I was interested in whether she had possibly mentioned anything that might have been helpful in finding her assailant." The crowd snickered. Many felt the assailant stood in front of them.

"Before allowing others on this panel a chance to question you, let me ask whether the following summary is accurate. You came to Bistoun assuming that your ex-wife Katherine was dead. You were surprised to find out she had lived after the attack and you wanted to know if she had talked. You led Jasin and Sherri directly to her house and there you supposedly discovered that the woman was actually your estranged wife although you didn't mention that fact to anyone until today. Is this accurate?"

"I told you I didn't know whether it was Katherine's house or not. I don't know whose house it was, nor did I lead them there. We followed the young girl."

"Other than that, would you say my last statement was accurate?"

"Misleading, but generally accurate," replied Beloit.

"Thank you, Terrence. I believe Mordichai has a few questions," said Sandist Lee.

Mordichai stood. "If I could ask Jasin Elstrada to clarify a few things…"

"Jasin, would you answer a few questions for us?" asked Lee.

Jasin stood and walked over to face the five Caucus members. As he passed Beloit, he placed a comforting hand on his shoulder. "I am please to help clarify whatever I can. I believe this to be a terrible miscarriage of justice. While I am surprised that Beloit never confided in me concerning the victim's identity, I am nevertheless convinced of his innocence."

"Well, then I'm glad you won't be standing in judgment of him today," replied Mordichai. "Let me ask you whether you were aware of Beloit's general feeling about towan."

"I'm not sure what you're asking."

"Did you ever get an impression he felt one way or the other concerning the male natives?"

"Not particularly."

"Did he ever use any derogatory terms?"

"Well…I guess he had a slight prejudice."

"How's that?"

"Nothing dramatic. I just got the sense that he had run into a few individuals that affected his outlook somewhat."

"Because of what he would say? Let me help you. While in Bistoun, Beloit would frequent a particular tavern near the Big Tree. Do you know the one I'm talking about?"

"Yes."

"Well, it is my experience that Beloit often expressed his opinion of the towan when he thought they weren't around. I have witnessed it several times myself. He would get quite drunk and use the term 'perverted'. Have you ever heard Beloit use that word to describe the towan?"

Jasin hesitated, searching for a way he wouldn't have to answer. "Yes," he finally said. His face flushed.

"What do you suppose he meant by that? What would lead him use that description?"

"I'm not sure," said Jasin.

Then let me ask you another question. Do you have any idea why Katherine and Beloit's relationship didn't last?"

"I…I didn't even…no, I do not."

"What were you going to say?" coaxed Mordichai.

"He never spoke of the relationship. I have no idea why it ended."

"Do you know of Katherine's fondness for…shall we say, unusual attention by several of the natives?"

"I…well, yes. While we were investigating the attack in Bistoun there was mention of the fact that the woman, I now know as Katherine, enjoyed the attention of a few towan."

"Would that qualify as perverted?"

"I…I can't…I won't make that characterization," said Jasin hesitantly.

"Then I will! Beloit McMaster broke off a relationship, a marriage to a woman who enjoyed the attention of another species, and then for no other apparent reason he refers to them as perverted. Do you know who Katherine was entertaining?"

"There was only one that I am sure of."

"Yes?"

"It was no secret that Katherine, as you put it, entertained Sy Loeton."

"And possibly others?"

"I got that impression."

"And Beloit knew this?"

"Knew that the victim entertained Sy Loeton? Yes, but—"

"And now both Sy Loeton and Katherine are dead. Do you think it is a coincidence?"

"Sy Loeton's death had nothing to do with the woman's death. You can ask Sy Hone, or Elizabeth. Beloit had nothing to do with his death."

"What about Katherine's death then, and Sy Toberry's? Did you know Sy Loeton and Toberry knew each other well, that they both came from the same home town; that they got together in Bistoun often? Do you think they may have shared the same desire for Human females? Do you think it's impossible that Beloit knew of Katherine's taste for towan and he killed her for it? That he made sure that the perverts as he called them paid for their attentions?"

"Which question would you like me to answer?"

"Any, which you can."

"We have no answers to Katherine's horrible death, but it didn't look like wounds caused by a human."

"Why do you say that?"

"The wounds to the sexual organs were hideous…as if she were torn or cut apart."

"As if someone wanted to make sure she never made love to anyone again? As if it were some perverted mutilation by a sick individual bent on punishing her?"

Silence

"What's your answer, Jasin?"

"I have no answers. What you are implying is ridiculous," said Jasin softly.

"There is only one answer that ties all these facts together. Beloit is a murderer. He murdered his wife, my mother out of jealousy and Sy Toberry because he and Sy Loeton were enjoying what he could not. There are no other suspects. There are no other scenarios that have been presented that fit the facts. If anyone in this room has a different answer let them speak."

Jasin was speechless and turned to look at Beloit who stared back sadly and just shook his head in denial. Jasin couldn't leave it like this. As convincing as Mordichai's arguments may be, Jasin couldn't bring himself to believe it.

"Are there any other questions or comments that need to be considered before the Caucus rules on these matters?" asked Sandist Lee. He turned to Findley and Yarrow who merely shook their heads. "Then we'll decide by—"

"I just have one other thought," said Jasin slowly, knowing what he was about to say was going to sound desperate. "Are we sure Sy Toberry is really dead?" He looked over towards Sy Lang to judge his reaction. There was a slight turn of the towan's head. "If Beloit is responsible for Sy Toberry's death, why would he be the one to report it? Why say anything? I believe there is a possibility that Sy Toberry is still alive, that he was drugged somehow and merely collapsed on Mount Schtolin and froze. I have seen something similar. If so it might be possible to revive him. Why rush to judgment? Why give up on Sy Toberry? Why kill the only man who knows where to look? I am willing to lead a team to find Sy Toberry's body. If he is alive, as I think he may be, then perhaps the Caucus needs to rethink what it has heard today. Just give me two weeks. Assign whomever you wish to the team. I don't know what happened in Bistoun with the woman. We may never know for sure, but why not at least find out what happened on the mountain? If there has been foul play, then the Caucus can make their decision concerning Beloit. I don't believe that there is enough hard evidence in either case to prove conclusively that Beloit is guilty. I for one believe he's innocent. I know, in my heart, he is innocent."

Sy Lang stepped forward. "The Council has allowed you Humans to deal with this matter, but if there is a chance that Sy Toberry is still alive, we must insist that the possibility be explored. Sy Hone and I will accompany Beloit and young Elstrada to find Sy Toberry's body. We will gather again when we return."

As the Caucus broke up and everyone headed their various directions, Jasin caught up with Sy Lang, Sy Hone, and Beloit who had been rebound and taken back into their custody. "Respectfully sir," asked Jasin in the native's language, "could you include Sy Jelick as well? I believe he would like to help find his father."

Sy Lang spread his arms in agreement.

Beloit leaned forward and whispered to Jasin. "Don't think I'm not grateful, but where did you come up with that crazy idea, because I really believe the old guy is dead."

Jasin shrugged. "Probably. At least I've gotten us some time. Why didn't you tell me she was your wife?"

Beloit looked off into the distance. "Katherine was more of an embarrassment, a lapse of judgment. We lived together less than six months before I realized what a whore she was. The truth is, I really only ever had one wife."

The Code

"Do you believe him?" asked Elizabeth, laying a second clean shirt next to the one Jasin had taken out to pack. "Take this one it's warmer."

"That Beloit didn't kill her?" Jasin carefully folded both shirts into the well-worn pack.

Elizabeth nodded.

"Most of what Winer was accusing him of was nonsense. I was there and I didn't get the impression that Beloit knew where he was going anymore than I did. And Beloit asking Sherri if Katherine had said anything…it was an obvious question. If he hadn't asked I would have. It was Mordichai's questions that were the most damaging. I knew that Beloit didn't like towan, but I never really asked—"

Just then, Wilem walked into the room. Nanc followed close behind. "Are we interrupting?" she asked.

Elizabeth stole a quick glance towards Jasin before answering. "Jasin was just packing." She knelt down and signed to Wilem, "Your mother tells me you remembered something your father tried to tell you." Wilem shrugged and lowered his eyes shyly. Elizabeth lifted his chin. "Wilem, look at me. It could be very important."

"It was just a dream," he signed back. "I don't know what it means." The young boy reached out and took Elizabeth's hand, but before he made any signs into it, he looked at each of the adults for support. They nodded encouragement and he slowly and deliberately spelled out letters. When he was done, he said, "There was something more...a number I think. But I don't remember it."

"Jasin, could you find something to write on?" asked Elizabeth. Jasin returned quickly and she asked Wilem to do it again. Nanc leaned in, watching carefully. Elizabeth spoke the letters as he made their signs in her palm. "X...E...U...D...S".

"Sometimes he uses an 'O' instead of a 'U'," whispered Nanc.

Elizabeth nodded and told the boy to find the kids and go play. But Wilem didn't move. "Are you mad at me?" he asked in his awkward speech.

Elizabeth kissed Wilem's head and gave him a hug. "We all love you...now go play." When he had left the room, she turned to face Nanc; a small tear had formed in the corner of her eye, which she wiped away. "I'm sorry...I don't know why. Sometimes when I think about the time I spent with Wilem at the lake. It's not that it was ever...I mean your husband was a pain..." She laughed a little and sniffled at the same time. "Anyway, you're right. The first time he used an 'O'. Do you have any idea what it means, what Jorge could have been trying to spell out."

"Nanc shook her head. "It's not a word that I've ever heard or seen."

"I have," declared Jasin, looking up from his parchment. "It's both an 'O' and a 'U', and I think the 'E' and 'X' are transposed." Jasin rearranged the letters. "It's a section of the old book Hyland gave Avram. They leaned over to see what Jasin had written—EXODUS.

"What's it mean?" Elizabeth asked. Jasin spread his hands, palms upright in a gesture of ignorance.

"What about the number?" asked Nanc.

Jasin just shook his head. "There are lots of numbers in the book...maybe it's a page number. Maybe Avram wrote something in the book on a certain page. I'll have to check it out."

Jasin hurried to the study and sat down with the ancient book. The edges of the pages flaked off as he opened to the section called Exodus. Taking his time to look for notes or marked passages, he delicately turned each of the fragile pages. Finally, he made it to the end of the section and massaged his stiff neck. Every other page had a numbered subsection and within those, the individual lines were numbered. "Even the numbers have numbers," he mumbled to himself and turned back to the beginning of the section where he began deciphering the text line by line. Many of the words were strange and it was written in a most obscure style. He often had to read sentences out loud in order to understand their meaning. It was a complex story with dozens of names and places. When the light began to fail, he lit several candles to afford him sufficient light to continue reading. After two hours, he began to understand why Hyland had been attracted to this particular story, but he was no nearer to finding the missing number. He was barely a third of the way through the section called Exodus and losing hope when his pulse began to quicken. The slaves were poised on the edge of a sea, their enemies in pursuit and,

"...there was the cloud and the darkness here, yet gave it light by night there; and the one came not near the other all night. And Moses stretched out his hand over the sea; and the Lord caused the sea to go back..."

Jasin read on. Now the words came easily,

"Thus the Lord saved Israel that day out of the hand of the Egyptians; and Israel saw the Egyptians dead upon the sea-shore."

Jasin glanced at the number of the sub-section he had just read—14. He straightened and leaned back in his chair. This had to be what Hyland had in mind when he set the code— Exodus 14, saving one people from the hands of another. It all seemed to fit, the darkness, giving light by night, salvation from the sea, and powerful enemies dead upon the seashore. Just to be sure, Jasin skimmed through the rest of Exodus, but there was not another section as pertinent. Hyland had hidden a powerful weapon in the sea to defeat the enemy and Jasin was the only one who knew the access code. Who else should he tell? A shiver ran down his spine. The few that had known the access code had died. Perhaps it would be better to keep it secret. He closed the book and replaced it carefully where Avram had stored it. If only he knew when the next Rhan-da-lith, the next darkness, would occur. Grabbing the candles from the table he headed back to complete his packing. They would be leaving at sunrise and he didn't want to wake Elizabeth by packing in the morning.

Standing in the doorway his light shone into the room he shared with his wife to be. His pack was finished and lay at the foot of the mattress where she slept with her injured arm exposed above the blanket, her luxurious brown hair framed her perfect face. Jasin was filled with love, but instead of joining her, he turned and quietly retraced his steps to the study where he stood a moment questioning the sanity of his decision. He lifted the ancient bible from its niche and knelt down. Hadn't his father told him that some had thought it a sacred book? That some found solace and used it for prayer? Was this right? He closed his eyes and lifted his head. His fingers lovingly caressed the edges of the thin leather cover, then, when doubt had left him, he opened the bible and ripped out the story of Exodus. He piled the shredded pages on the floor, and set them afire. The dry paper flared up and was quickly consumed. With a strong puff, Jasin blew the ashes away. All that was left of Hyland's secret was a dark smudge on the cold stone floor and what he alone knew.

Toberry's Trough

"You've got to be joking," groaned Beloit, slinging the food pack he was carrying to the frozen ground before collapsing against it. Sy Hone and young Sy Jelick stood quietly at the edge of the precipice with their cyliths nestled against their bare legs. Jasin and Li Sy joined them and surveyed the deep rift that blocked their progress through the mountains. They had made good progress over the last two days, trusting Jasin and the route he had planned using Avram's maps.

Jasin had found three ways to get to Mount Schtolin from Nova Gaia: they could take the normal pass towards Panvera and skirt the mountain range, approaching the base of Mount Schtolin from the high side. They could also follow the Canyon Road to the great valley and approach from the low side as they had done with Mas when he was injured, or they could, as Jasin had convinced them, make their way directly through the mountain range, gradually gaining altitude until they found their way onto the side of Mount Schtolin. Jasin had figured that while more difficult and unexplored, they were all in relatively good shape and this shorter route would save several days while having the added benefit of becoming acclimated in the process. In the back of his mind he also knew he was avoiding the steep incline and strenuous climb that had probably killed Toberry.

"Damn," he muttered under his breath. Turning back was unthinkable, but the heavily foliated gorge that cut across their path insisted otherwise.

"This is a good time to eat," decided Li Sy, coming up beside Beloit to rummage through the food pack. The two towan turned to watch the diminutive female. They didn't understand the Human she spoke, but as soon as her intent became clear, Sy Hone, who carried such a tremendous distaste for the independent towa, turned his back towards her. Jasin smiled at Beloit. They both knew that even if the towan were starving he would have no part in her midday snack. Alone, Sy Jelick may have joined her, but the younger male would never show his disrespect by ignoring Sy Hone's lead.

Before the sojourn had even begun, when Jasin insisted upon taking Li Sy, even Sy Lang had found a convenient excuse to forgo the trip and return to Cernai. To travel in the company of a towa was more than a mere annoyance. For Sy Lang it was unthinkable. He had more important things to do. Besides, he had told Jasin, the pytor could easily guard Beloit and be trusted to return with the truth of Toberry's death. Now, standing before the vast gash that blocked their advance, Jasin was glad Sy Lang wasn't here to see their predicament.

"Think of it this way," he told the natives in their own tongue, "you'll get a chance to explore a part of your world that no one has ever seen. We'll call it, 'Toberry's Trough'." He smiled to himself as the alliteration got lost in their language. "We'll lose maybe eight hours."

Beloit was dubious. "More like eight days. We'll go down easily enough, but going up?"

"Well…a day at most," Jasin relented slightly, "assuming no further surprises. If we get moving we can make the bottom by dimlight."

"It will be a dangerous climb down; this side is already in shadow," complained McMaster.

"I don't want to wait any longer," Jasin insisted.

"What difference do you think it'll make?" asked Beloit. "Toberry's not going anywhere."

Jasin didn't answer. He peered over the edge trying to find the best route into the gorge.

Beloit climbed to his feet. "Snack time is over, Li Sy. Be careful not to slip. It's a long way down."

"Li Sy not fall. Li Sy collect plants," she said looking down into the rich valley below. "But others might fall," she said glancing over at Sy Hone menacingly. Beloit smiled at her audacity. She knew that the towan didn't understand when she spoke Human and was having fun at their expense.

After an hour of picking their way down through rough scrabble and thorny growth that tore at their legs, they rested upon a level stone ledge that projected several meters out from the side of the incline and let their scratched legs dangle over the edge. They could not see a single sign that anyone had ever ventured here. Nature, it appeared, had exclusive stewardship over Toberry's Trough. They peered down from their vantage point, looking for any indication of a trail or runoff, but none presented itself. Instead they found themselves enchanted by the pristine elegance of this rich hidden valley. While it was getting fairly dark on their side of the gorge, on the opposite wall, which Jasin estimated to be over two thousand meters from where they sat, a thin sliver of a water caught the light as it sliced through the thick plant growth and collected in a small lake before spilling over into a rocky creek bed and disappeared into the thirsty gravel. Dozens of purplish shrubs, each of a slightly different shade, grew in clumps on the valley floor still several hours beneath them. Beloit pointed out a circular blue patch, snuggled between two grape-colored clumps, barely visible except for its unique coloration. It had apparently caught Li Sy's attention as well for she stared transfixed.

"You ever see anything like that?" Beloit asked her. By her silence it was obvious that she hadn't.

"Maybe moss or lichen covering a gigantic boulder," suggested Jasin, having convinced himself that it was almost spherical.

A few hours later they discovered it wasn't a rock or anything else natural. Buried beneath hundreds of years of growth, an Eian amorphan capsule lay half buried in the rich soft soil. The small group tried clearing the foliage, but except for a portion along the upper most section of the sphere, the plants had encased the object in a tight interwoven cocoon. Peering between the nearly impenetrable branches, they could make out a small opening in the blue metal. Lying beneath it, nearly invisible in the undergrowth, was a blue hatch that had been released.

"What the hell?" murmured Beloit. "Tanis never carried anything even remotely like this."

"It's obviously Eian technology," said Jasin, looking around.

"Obvious to whom?" Beloit asked.

"It is how...Eian came," Li Sy explained. Losing interest she wandered off to collect seeds and pods from the varied and abundant flora surrounding them.

"Who came?" Beloit asked.

Jasin knelt down and pointed to a pile of bleached bones nearly hidden by vegetation. "I think it is how *they* came," he said trying to clear away some of the surrounding plants. Thick roots had grown beneath the alien bones in the fertile soil enriched by their decomposition. Jasin counted skulls. "At least six must have died on impact. And at least one survived to drag the bodies here. I wonder whether any of them escaped the valley?"

Jasin continued to explain to Beloit what little he knew about the Eians. The two towan were having their own conversation, comparing what each of them had been taught about the Eian immigration.

Beloit McMaster was confused. "Another race? I've been here over thirty years and this is the first I've heard of another race. Even one is too many for this frigid planet...but three?"

"Warren thinks they are the same race," Jasin said, indicating the small bones and then the tall towans standing to their side.

Beloit was skeptical. "Warren knows of them too? Where are these Eians now?"

"Somewhere called Hadrious, but I don't know where—
"

"All of them?" asked Beloit standing and furtively looking over at the natives.

There was something curious in Beloit's tone. "Pretty much...why do you ask?"

"Have you ever seen any of these Eians?"

Jasin nodded.

"Dressed or naked?"

"The few I've seen have been dressed."

"Small like towa, but dressed?"

Again, Jasin nodded. "Up close they look like small males."

"That's interesting." said Beloit thoughtfully. "Before Toberry and I followed you out of Bistoun to the medical colony, we were in the market buying food. Toberry wanted particular things. Awful native stuff, things I would never have eaten. Anyway, I saw what I thought was a towa watching us, wearing a hooded cloak, but I never saw a towa wearing anything before. At the time, I thought it strange, but I just dismissed it."

Jasin shrugged. "Could have been I guess, but they're not supposed to be away from Hadrious."

"No you don't understand. We...we bought all this native food that Toberry eats all the way up into the cold and then he keels over dead."

"He chose the food didn't he?"

"Yeah..."

"So, you don't think he poisoned himself do you?"

Beloit shook his head. "No, but you did say they were an advanced race didn't you."

"It doesn't pay to stand here conjecturing, when Toberry is just a day away. Li Sy should be able to tell us what happened to Toberry."

But the dimness had overtaken them and Li Sy had not returned from collecting her organic pharmaceuticals. Although the towan wanted to push on with or without the towa, Jasin and Beloit decided to rest until brightening. They spread out their sleeping blankets on a soft comfortable spot cushioned by centuries of accumulated humus. Aside from the distant rush of the waterfall the valley fell silent, the dimness thickened, and sleep came quickly.

Eiton

Eiton struggled to lift the last of the thrust diverters from the damaged gilia head and onto the pier inside the hidden cavern. The distended organic float was nearly submerged making the task difficult. Not wanting to make another long trip in the frigid water, Eiton applied himself and with a grunt, muscled it onto the blue metal pier and then left the cavern to find sun to warm himself. His weak leg always ached after physical exertion, reminding him why he had gravitated to his scientific studies and why he so enjoyed when Julian called him "Engineer". It was an affirmation, considering his physical limitations, that he had chosen the correct profession.

He had made many trips up the ice-cold river, delivering the custom metal cradles, reinforced canopy, chains, and of course the compressed air canisters they would need to hijack the shuttle. He was proud of the efficient design, but worried that the unusually large gilia heads they planned to use to transport the supplies might fail like this last one, or because of their size, attract unwanted attention. Now that all the thrust diverters were here, it was just a matter of time before they would move all of it to Lake Chook and retrieve the human's machine. But for the present, he had been instructed to wait at the supply depot until Eidorf returned from Bistoun.

He would have liked to sneak into the town himself; it had been years since he had been allowed the diversion, but with Eidorf also in town he knew that was too dangerous.

One alone always drew curious stares…two cloaked "towa" would be sure to arouse excessive suspicion. He smiled to himself. Too bad he wasn't female; he could have walked down the streets of Bistoun naked and no one would be the wiser.

Eiton stayed in the sun until his shoulder patches were vibrant. He felt refreshed but hungry, so he walked over to the river's edge and sat among the rotting gilia heads where the forn were thick. He inhaled deeply until the insides of his folds were coated with the insects, then he walked back to the cove slowly enjoying his special snack. Hadrious had very few forn. Strong winds prevented their migration, so he relished these opportunities to partake in the delicacy. He settled down again to wait for Eidorf's return.

He never spent much time considering the space trip back to Eian. To him it was a fait accompli, sure that the shuttle would return them in style. Most of his thoughts concerned manufacturing enough fuel to rescue his entire race and return them all safely home. It was strange to consider a place to which he had never been, home, but ever since Eidorf infected him with the idea of returning to Eian, home had become that world in the sky that floated overhead just out of reach. What would Eian be like? No one who was still alive had ever been there. Of course, they all had heard stories, passed down through the generations, of Eian's grand beauty and legends of its vast resources. It was said that unlike this frozen snowball, nearly the entire surface of their moon was habitable and that the temperature was moderate throughout the year. The water was warm and the air, at least until the deep gasses were released, had been rich and soothing, not irritating like Syton's. Eiton was sure that the air would be just fine now regardless of what Julian said. The old human could be so depressing and yet, he was drawn to her logic and enjoyed their frequent talks. He knew he was disobeying Eidorf by not killing her, but he felt he could still learn from her. Occasionally, she surprised him with her depth of knowledge, especially regarding natural science.

"Eiton, you are being careless sitting in full view," admonished Eidorf as he approached hours later. "Must I remind you what is at stake?"

"Of course not. The water was particularly chilly today. I was just warming myself."

"You will need to find another gilia for that deflector or is harvesting beneath the great Eiton?"

"Not at all. As I said, I was cold."

"If you think this is cold, how will you make the long trip to the lake? The water there is even colder. Perhaps we should find someone younger."

Eiton was accustomed to Eidorf's goading. Still, it was annoying. "Perhaps you are right. I'm getting too old for this. Yes…I think you should find someone else for the job." Sometimes it was just easier to agree, and let Eidorf grow tired of the game.

"The deflectors must be ready for transport."

"They *are* ready. Was there some other reason you wished me to wait for you? You could have checked with me back in Hadrious," Eiton probed. "What is the problem?"

"I had to check out something in Bistoun. It seems the towan do have Eican's energy weapon. I fear he is dead. No one has seen or heard from him since he left to return to Hadrious. The sled is here so I assume he was ambushed here at the depot after he emerged."

"Then the towan must know of this place. Our plans are in danger."

"Unfortunately I must agree. And with the weapon…well, I was wondering if there was any defense against its dampening effect. I don't want to be on the receiving side of it and was thinking, as long as we're here…if there were any supplies you might need…" Eidorf turned slightly toward the supply depot.

"I haven't ever given it any thought though I doubt whether anything portable could be constructed. I'll just have to give it some consideration."

"Well, do that. It won't be long now before we might need it."

For the first time, Eiton sensed fear in his superior.

Mount Schtolin

Heavy snow blanketed the upper reaches of Mount Schtolin. Thick gray clouds, impaled and writhing on the mountain's peak, continued to hurl down blizzard upon blizzard, attempting to lighten their loads and free themselves. In the lee of a sizable outcropping, Jasin found refuge. Pulling his cloak tighter, he looked at his sluggish native companions in despair. They had climbed out of the verdant valley healthy and without any serious delay, but then the towan had been comparatively warm. "It's important to drink," Jasin said, trying to catch his breath. His lungs burned and he buried his face in his spent breathing scarf hoping for relief that wasn't there. For the hundredth time today he questioned his sanity for attempting to find and prove that Toberry was alive. He took a few swigs from his drinking gourd before offering it to McMaster.

"Thanks, but I've still got some of my own."

Jasin passed the water to Sy Hone who showed no interest, preferring to keep his hands buried in his cylith's fur. "Here, drink a little," Jasin shoved the gourd into Sy Jelick's chest. With difficulty, the young towan poured what little remained into his mouth

"It's not that much higher," offered Beloit, taking a swig from his own gourd.

"How much is not much?" Jasin wasn't sure he wanted to know.

Beloit stuck his head around the protective stone shield and mumbled something that was obscured by the howling of the fierce wind.

"What?"

McMaster turned back. "I said it's hard to tell...maybe another hour. Everything looks different in the snow." Beloit jammed his hands under his armpits, trying to keep them warm.

Their mittens were nothing more than glorified socks. Jasin wished he had a pair of decent Panvera gloves. He glanced over at Li Sy, huddled in a sleeping blanket; her precious medicine bag lay across her three tiny feet.

The small band had gotten an early start and, while the sun was hidden behind the storm, there was still at least seven hours of decent light left before the mountaintop would be cloaked in darkness. Jasin was resolved to complete their mission during this brightness and be at least a thousand meters lower before resting. He knew they couldn't delay.

"Lead on," Jasin coaxed Beloit. All eyes turned to the Enforcer. At this point he was the only one they could follow.

"I'm not all that sure about where we are now compared to where I left Toberry," Beloit yelled over the wind. "I think the only way to get my bearings is to look down into the colony from the ridgeline. From there I think I can back track."

"After you. It doesn't matter to me where I freeze," said Jasin, managing a weak grin He addressed the natives, "Come on, you're not going to let us inferior humans do this alone are you?" He pulled up his breathing cloth and followed Beloit into the fury of the storm.

The natives with their animals followed, the struggle to move their stiff joints showing on their faces. Li Sy barely left an impression in the snow. Her shallow footprints were filled in almost instantly. However, the heavier towans often sank to their waists and, much to their consternation, needed Jasin and Beloit to help pull them clear. Communication was nearly impossible in the din of the blowing storm so they trudged on lost in their own thoughts and fears.

For Jasin, a single thought accompanied him—a vivid picture of a young wide-eyed girl, the face of his child to be. It was never a boy. She had gotten his brown eyes, but unlike his they were large and beautiful, set off with delicate dark eyebrows, the color of his own hair. Luckily, the child also inherited her mother's sculptured face, Elizabeth's face, which he now saw filled with anger at his refusal to let her come. He had expected her wrath. She couldn't stand to be out of the action, but it was an unnecessary risk especially now that she carried their child. He had no doubt that she would have been physically able to accompany them. She was probably stronger than he...no, if he had to be honest, ignoring his male ego, he knew she was much stronger than he was. But he couldn't help but try to protect her and their baby. It was hard-wired into his being. So he felt he could be forgiven if he occasionally acted as if she needed his protection. The bottom line—there was no need for her to be here. And again, as he had many times in the last few days, he even questioned the wisdom of his own presence.

He took off one glove and rubbed his frozen nose hoping for some sign that blood would once again begin to circulate. He didn't think it was that cold, but the strong wind bit at any uncovered skin. Beloit appeared unbothered by the storm and had pulled quite far ahead. Jasin turned to see how the beefy towan were holding up.

They were gone. Only Li Sy plodded toward him.

Jasin yelled for Beloit to stop, but the Enforcer didn't acknowledge him and trudged on far ahead, alone, unaware that anything was amiss. Or was he? It dawned on Jasin that this was exactly the situation Beloit had described when Sy Toberry had lagged behind on their first passage up Mount Schtolin. Damn this! Jasin had promised Sy Lang he would bring McMaster back regardless of what they found on the mountain. If he turned back to help the towan now, Beloit might just continue towards the ridge. Once there, he could dip down into the shelter of the caldera and make his way to what remained of the colony below, possibly even escaping through the lower passage in the mountain side.

"Li Sy," Jasin shouted, trying to be heard over the wind. "I've got to stay with Beloit. Go back and see what the problem is. I'll come back to find you." But Li Sy didn't seem to hear him either and continued to trudge on mechanically not quite directly towards him. Something was wrong. Jasin took several steps to his side and closed the space between them. Not stopping, Li Sy bumped into him. Jasin crouched over her and stared into her frozen unmoving eyes "Li Sy? Are you all right?"

The towa moved her head awkwardly, seeking out his voice. The towa was blind.

"Come on." He reached down and grabbed her arm. She instinctively recoiled at his controlling grasp, but then relaxed and allowed him to lead her. "We must hurry and catch up to Beloit or all this will be for nothing." Turning, he got a glimpse of Beloit's head just as it sank out of sight. He swore loudly, and with a burst of adrenaline, he plunged ahead through the knee-deep snow, dragging Li Sy roughly behind him. She was like an anchor and Jasin feared he was moments from losing track of Beloit. "Quickly, climb on my back and hold on tightly," he ordered, kneeling down and guiding the near frozen towa. Without waiting for her to settle, he struggled to his feet and leaned into the wind. With the last of his dwindling energy he lunged forward, plowing through the snow, his aching leg muscles screamed for him to stop, his lungs burned, but he lifted his knees high, trying to step over the snow that was intent on holding him still. Finally, he was at the ridgeline. The vast hollow interior of Schtolin fell open in front of him and there, a few steps away hiding from the elements in a protected niche was Beloit.

Jasin knelt down, nearly losing his balance as he helped Li Sy slide off his back. Grasping her hand, he led her over the ragged edge and down a couple dozen steps to join Beloit in the protected cranny. "I was sure you were running away," he said gasping for air, letting Li Sy silently collapse into a tight ball, her frozen face and extremities tucked away to be warmed by her body.

"I am," he admitted with a smirk, looking down towards the wreckage of the medical colony. "Where are the others?"

Jasin shrugged, still trying to catch his breath.

"Probably frozen stiff. You know Jasin...this was monumentally stupid. They don't belong up here. None of us should be this high." He dug a hand inside his heavy coat and withdrew a small water gourd, which he drank from, then offered it to Jasin. The water was laced with Keetah and instantly the burning in his throat was extinguished.

Jasin handed it back. "Avram would approve."

Beloit managed a weak smile. "It should help you breath. Now listen...we've got to talk. See that furrow over there." Beloit pointed to a spot coming off the ridge about three hundred meters away. "That's what I followed down to the colony the first time. There's a cut in the ridgeline just above that. If you go through that and directly down the other side you should find Toberry's body after walking about two minutes.

"I told you I'd help find his body," continued Beloit, reacting to Jasin's questioning glance, "but I'm not hanging around any longer and I don't think you have the energy to stop me. I'm not sure what the body will show, but I didn't kill him. You can see what the cold does to them; their chemistry doesn't do well up here." Beloit stood up stiffly, lifting his pack with a grunt. "Damn, I don't think ours do either. But listen kid.... I don't know what deals you think you have with them, but your first responsibility is to your own people. The natives don't give a damn about you or any human for that matter. Your father forgot that somewhere along the line. He thought you could make deals with them, but trust is a human trait. It's not something that works between species."

"Or between friends?"

"I didn't promise you that I wouldn't take off. I promised them. I promised you that I would show you where Toberry's body was. And I have. " Beloit turned and headed down.

"You're wrong," shouted Jasin. "My father never forgot who he was."

Beloit turned and shook his head sadly. "He made a habit of forgetting who he was. Your father was a great man. I willingly gave up my life for him, for his dream. But he died a washed out addict and I was no better than his pusher. In the end neither of us amounted to anything." He paused and dropped his head, then, lifting it to look squarely into Jasin's eyes he said, "You shouldn't be on this mountain searching for corpses, you should be finding your mother. She's the only one worth saving."

Jasin watched Beloit pick his way down the inside of the mountain. He didn't have the energy or desire to follow. Let him go, he thought. Who really cares? Exhausted and drained, he lacked the moral conviction that had driven him to this frigid outcropping and now, with the cold wind and biting snow, even the need to find Toberry's body no longer possessed him. But they had come so far, and if Beloit had told the truth, Toberry wasn't even half an hour away. He glanced over at Li Sy curled into the small tight ball nearby and smiled.

Suddenly from above, a section of the ridge gave way, raining down a shower of rock and snow. Jasin threw an arm over his head as large chunks threatened to cave in his skull. When he dared open his eyes, there on the ground, mixed with the snow piles and freshly released boulders were the two towan. Bits of ice and snow stuck to their open frozen eyes, and their arms and legs flexed in some strange slow motion dance. Jasin marveled at their perseverance as, with great effort, he dragged them out of the wind and into the relative warmth of the shelter where Li Sy remained curled up.

Removing his gloves, he knelt beside Sy Hone's head and cupped his warm hands over the towan's blind eyes. The great towan's thick arms flailed weakly in a vain attempt to bat Jasin's hands away. He heard growling and looked up at the ridgeline. Sy Hone's cylith slowly approached, but Jasin kept his hands in place until he felt a trickle of water and faint flutter beneath his fingers. The cylith leaned over his master's body and Jasin could smell the foul stench of the animal's breath. He stepped away from the pytor as the cylith lay down next to Sy Hone and snuggled close, sharing his warmth with his master. Jasin warmed Sy Jelick, and his cylith, having observed the other's behavior, also lay down to warm the young towan. Jasin stood up and looked around. Shrugging, he wrapped himself in his sleeping bag and curled up next to Li Sy.

Revulsion

Blood was not evident in the surrounding snow for Toberry's flesh must have been frozen before the small rodents had made their discovery. In the barren heights of Mt. Schtolin, a chunk of Toberry's meaty left thigh and three fingers of the hand that lay exposed had evidently sustained several field diggers quite well. Jasin glanced at Sy Jelick to see how his father's mutilation affected him, but the stoic youngster, perhaps not wanting to appear weak or unduly emotional in Sy Hone's presence, acted unconcerned or at least he covered his reaction well. Jasin, however, was glad his stomach was empty, and looked away from the bare bones jutting out from an otherwise normal hand. Beloit had been right about where they would find the body, and Jasin hoped he was also right about when death had occurred. If not, the towan might have been conscious while the field diggers chewed the flesh from his fingers.

With revulsion, Li Sy approached the body and brushed the snow gently from Toberry's face. She tried to open his mouth, but the body had been frozen too long to allow her access to whatever smells the corpse might provide. It began to dawn on Jasin that the cause of death might never be determined. Turning to Sy Jelick, he expressed his sympathy.

Sy Jelick lifted his emotionless gaze from his father to stare at Jasin. Finally he broke his silence. "My father's cylith…has been dead…a long time, but…he may still honor our animals."

Jasin shook his head. He had had enough. "I don't intend to spend a minute more up here than I have to. It's too cold for any of us, including the cyliths. By dimness we must be a good deal lower. It will be dangerous to spend the night this high."

"It would...would be wrong...not to allow Sy Toberry his...his final gift," argued Sy Hone, having some difficulty getting the words out.

Jasin could see that both towan were having trouble turning their heads and their speech was becoming impaired. "Perhaps, but does it have to be done up here? Let's drag the body back inside the protection of the mountain; it will be warmer there. The longer we spend exposed, the more likely we'll end up lying next to him."

Surprisingly, the towan needed little coaxing. Each found one of Toberry's feet and together they dragged the body back over the ridge and down inside the mountain. Sheltered from the elements, Jasin renewed his appeal to proceed lower. "It's silly to stay up here. Sy Toberry's honor can be served just as well in what remains of the colony below. We still have a couple of hours before full dimness and it's downhill all the way." Finding no disagreement, he turned and led the natives, following the route Beloit had taken toward the colony. Neither of the towan had expressed concerned about Beloit's disappearance. Perhaps they were so impaired it hadn't registered. Perhaps they didn't care or it didn't matter now that Toberry's body had been found. In any case, Jasin was not about to bring it up. He, after all, bore the bulk of the responsibility of returning Beloit to the Human Caucus, not the natives.

The two towan continued hauling the body, feet first, down the steep incline, leaving Toberry's head to bounce and scrape along the rocky makeshift path. Li Sy followed behind.

Even though the temperature at the colony's elevation was at least thirty-five degrees warmer than at the top, Jasin still felt chilled and hurried to start a fire. Much of the debris from the medical complex was flammable and there was even a large undamaged container of lantern oil, which Jasin used to encourage the flame. Taking advantage of the roaring fire, the towan decided to drag the corpse closer so that it might thaw a bit and they could stay warm while bearing witness to Toberry's final act of kindness.

At least the cyliths would benefit from Toberry's death. The loss of Toberry meant the time of the Rhan-da-lith could not be known. It could occur tomorrow or three years from now. Only the old towan had been able to predict its arrival. Jasin would have to move to Lake Chook to be closer and ready for the next total darkness and the rising of the machine. He wondered how Elizabeth would react when told they had to return to the lake. What would they do with the children?

As warmth thawed the body, Jasin considered the irony of sitting in what had once been a center of advanced medical care to watch a barbaric mutilation, and whether he had the stomach to remain and watch. He had always held an abiding fascination with Sytonian customs, but this particular act was revolting. But still, how could he really forgo this unique opportunity to witness their most sacred act? He had slept through Sy Loeton's final gift and never felt guilty.

As the cyliths cautiously circled their evening meal, Jasin couldn't help but wonder if they sensed, as indeed he did, the rare privilege about to befall them. Few humans had ever had the chance to witness what was about to transpire. Still, his stomach turned at the thought of watching the dead towan being torn apart, his insides spilling onto the ground for the cyliths to feast upon. Would leaving now be disrespectful to Toberry's memory? Would he lose the other towan's respect?

Before he could make up his mind, Sy Hone began a deep rhythmic chant, meant to glorify the moment and exalt the memory of Sy Toberry. Jasin felt trapped. After several minutes, Sy Jelick joined the chant and together they repeated it several times, each refrain became quieter and more drawn out. A long hour passed as the towans continued their ceremony.

Then it was time. Jasin averted his eyes as jagged teeth plunged into Toberry's thigh. A horrible cry filled the air. He turned to Sy Jelick, glad that the young towan could finally express his grief, but the young towan stared at his father in silence. Jasin followed his gaze and as the second cylith closed his powerful jaws on Toberry's upper arm, the not-so-dead body flinched and cried out a second time. Sy Hone jumped to his feet and scattered the animals, each carrying a sizable chunk of Toberry's flesh outside the perimeter of firelight.

Now that the body was warm, blood flowed from the open wounds and Li Sy rushed to prepare poultices and bandages to hold them in place over the fresh cylith bites. Soon the strong odor of keets permeated the air to accompany Sy Toberry's moans of agony.

Li Sy pointed to his mangled hand. "It is this damage that Sy Toberry feels. Sy Toberry should not be able to feel the cylith bites covered with keets."

"Then mix some more for his fingers…and his head there where he is bleeding. He's in agony." Jasin pleaded.

Li Sy looked up at Jasin. "Li Sy has used all the keets that we have."

"Then do something else! We can't let him lie there in so much pain."

Li Sy ignored Jasin's last appeal and leaned over the injured towan, putting her nose close to his mouth. "It is aramuth," she said finally, rising and clearing grime from his shoulder patches. "Like keets, except it stops muscles. It is a poison. Beloit McMaster tried to kill Sy Toberry," she proclaimed. "Sy Toberry became paralyzed, the snow eventually covered his shoulder patches, and he froze. There is still a great deal of aramuth in his system."

"Does it take away pain? Does is make you sleep?" asked Sy Jelick.

"No."

"Then he has been aware all these last weeks?"

""No, after his body froze, Sy Toberry was not conscious."

"How can you be sure?" asked Sy Jelick.

Jasin smiled in spite of all that was going on. "You can trust her," he added knowingly. "Do you have anything in your bag to make him sleep?" he asked.

Li Sy thought for a moment before answering. "Yes, I think so, but I don't know how it will mix with aramuth."

"Let's try to knock him out. Now that he is unfrozen, his body will try to heal itself if we give it a chance."

"Why bother?" asked Sy Hone. "Even in this light it is clear his patches are nearly gray. He is dying."

"Then we should let him die without pain," said Jasin firmly.

"He needn't die at all," declared Sy Jelick.

Everyone turned to the towan for an explanation. "We must take him to the black rocks. Seann Sy said he might gain strength from them."

Sy Hone objected. "It is a long trip, several days at least, from here to the black rocks across the lake. I have heard about their supposed healing power from others, but it is a dangerous myth. No one has ever been revived. Either it is a wasted trip or they succumb. Besides, Jasin is right. If we can make Sy Toberry comfortable, if the towa can make him sleep, then we can wait here until his end. No one can live long with gray patches."

"If my father is alive when the light returns, I will carry him to the rocks myself. You needn't help if you don't want to."

Jasin looked at the young towan's proud face illuminated by the fire's flame. So family loyalty, the bond between son and father was truly a universal quality. He looked at the dying towan at his feet. If Jasin could have picked up his own dying father and carried him to be cured, no matter how small the chance, he would have carried him till his legs gave way beneath him, carried him until he died himself. Nothing would've stopped him.

"You will not go alone. I will help you. Tomorrow, at first light we will carry your father to the black rocks. It is something we all must do." Jasin looked at Sy Hone who turned away without saying a word.

Over the next week, Jasin and the small band of natives stopped often to argue and fight over the wisdom of continuing their trek to the black rocks. Without Sy Jelick's unflagging insistence, even Jasin felt he would have abandoned the effort. Between inspiring words and accomplished deeds lay kilometers of doubt. The only reason Sy Hone stayed with them was that each step brought him closer to his home in Fistulee where he insisted he was bound as soon as he could rid himself of the burden, which is what he had begun to call Sy Toberry. To him the aged towan had long since passed on, leaving only a heavy shell he felt somehow forced to help carry. Li Sy spent most of her time checking the color of Toberry's shoulder patches, which never brightened, and making sure he was properly drugged.

On the eighth day, they crossed the shallow water near the black rocks. Li Sy felt strongly that whatever effect the rocks might have on him would be enhanced if he were drug free. So they laid him on the smooth cold pebbles and waited for the towan to regain consciousness.

"Well, I can't just sit here. Who wants to come with me to investigate these so called magic rocks?" Jasin asked.

"You go on ahead, I will stay here with my father. He will need comforting when the drugs wear off."

"He'll need more than that," said Sy Hone, opening his mouth wide to take in a gulp of forn. "Too bad he can't enjoy this swarm. He hasn't eaten in..." The pytor paused trying to calculate when Toberry must have had his last real meal. "Well, it has been a very long time. No wonder his patches never regained their color even in the sunlight. Tonight, we will eat his aspic on this very spot. Jasin, You go ahead. These forn are too fine a treat to pass up."

Indeed, Jasin looked out over the lake where a swarm was gathering. The sky was dark with them yet oddly their reflection in the water seemed to glow beneath them. Why did the forn congregate here, he asked himself? As he studied the dark cloud more closely, he saw what attracted them. Thin glowing tendrils of iridescent plankton rose from the water and were being consumed by the larger bugs.

Mesmerized, he watched the fine threads of glowing organisms grow thicker and more plentiful until their light caused luminous fissures to open in the dark cloud, breaking it apart, overwhelming the forn that had feasted upon them just moments before. And then on the pools of light, darker patches began forming. It was the forn, falling out of the sky onto the surface of the water. Thousands...no hundreds of thousands of the bugs covered the plankton's glow and then these dark patches started to break apart as the microscopic plankton forced their way through, shining like hot molten lava breaking through the crust of dead forn. It was a sight he had never witnessed before.

"Enjoy what you can," Jasin said to Sy Hone, who hadn't stopped eating to watch the battle of the bugs. "It looks like the plankton is winning."

Sy Jelick looked up from his vigil next to his father. "It doesn't really matter. They taste even better than the forn."

Jasin nodded and walked off toward the dark narrow canyon. "I'll be back soon," he shouted over his shoulder. He threaded his way through the black rocks looking for anything that would be a clue as to their next step. After only a hundred meters the passage narrowed until he stood within a small black alcove. Shiny black rocks nearly surrounded him. This had to be the destination they were looking for. Nothing else stood out and there were no other paths in or out. He ran his fingers over the smooth ebony surface of the natural enclosure and tried to see if he could feel anything, but after a few futile moments he had to laugh at himself. Well, it was the journey that mattered. He had helped a son attempt to save his father. It would be the final effort that mattered, that Sy Jelick would remember. He hadn't been so lucky. There were no valiant attempts to save Avram. No memories of bold attempts to save his life, just a dead drug addict lying at his feet. In this, Beloit was right. The Avram that died that night of the party wasn't the Avram that had lived. That hero died long before his body did. Interesting that Toberry's body would also die long after it was supposed to. Was this just the way of things? Jasin hoped that when his time came to make that final journey, he would have the common sense to take his body with him. He turned and walked thoughtfully back to the others.

"Did you find anything?" asked Sy Jelick.

"It's wonderful," he lied. "You could feel the power of the place. We were right to bring him here. What's wrong Li Sy?" The small towa had the contents of her medicine pouch spread out and she was busy sifting through it.

"He is not waking up. Li Sy did not give him very much medicine this morning, but he is not waking."

"Well, he's been drugged for weeks now; lucid for just the briefest moment," Jasin observed. "As Sy Hone pointed out, he must be extremely weak from not eating. If he were human, he would have died many times over." Jasin smiled at their confusion caused by his last statement. "Let's get him to his feet, support him, and see if he can walk."

"Before we try that, Li Sy would like to have him eat this," she said holding up a small vegetable pod." Jasin nodded and helped Sy Jelick force open Toberry's mouth so Li Sy could squeeze the pod's juice down his throat.

"How long—" Jasin was interrupted by Sy Toberry's violent spasm.

"Not long," said Li Sy, flapping her arms.

A groan that seemed to start from deep within Toberry's body roared out and his eyes moved for the first time since the cyliths bit him.

"I've got to get some of that," Jasin muttered under his breath.

While they waited to see the full affect of the stimulant, they peered out over the water and watched the expanding cloud of glowing plankton. It was drifting toward them.

"If we don't move we will be breathing the stuff," Jasin said. A few moments later they were dragging the half conscious towan into the entrance of the narrow canyon, trying to escape from the oncoming swarm.

"We can't let them push us into the canyon. There's no way out," Jasin warned. He had no idea why the microscopic animals were being drawn to the black magnetite behind them.

But Toberry knew. Totally exhausted and overwhelmed with waves of pain, the elder towan knew exactly where he was. He had never been so close to death before, but he could still sense the combined electrostatic charge generated by the billions of infinitesimal organisms. The plankton sought the black rocks to aid in their reproduction. He sought the shiny rocks to survive.

"Take me...take me in." Toberry barely managed to form the words.

Sy Jelick was overjoyed at the sound of his father's voice. "Respectfully sir, they are almost upon us. We should wait until they pass before—"

Toberry moaned. He was in excruciating agony. "Now...take me now."

"I'll show you," Jasin offered the young towan.

Sy Jelick reached under one arm and Sy Hone took the other. Together they carried Toberry down the canyon and into the alcove just as the swarm overtook them. Jasin and Li Sy stepped away from the small enclosure where the three towan were crammed together shoulder to shoulder. There was no room to move. Toberry leaned his head on his son's shoulder and the boy tenderly leaned his head back upon his father's as the electrically charged plankton enveloped them.

At first, the young Sy Jelick wasn't sure what was happening to him. The terrible exhaustion came first, then he felt removed, absent from his own being—somewhere, someone else. His fingers began to burn as if they were aflame and he looked down at them and saw the bare bones of his father's hand. He looked up at his father and seemed to be gazing at himself through his father's eyes. Then his head began to ache...and his thigh. Sy Jelick was dizzy and disoriented, exhausted and invigorated at the same time. Flashes of colored light blinded him and strange images formed from wisps of shadow, flooding his mind, fighting with his own memories as he fainted and woke from a dozen lives, too many lives filled with intense boredom and numbing loneliness. Hundreds of nearly identical faces fought for recognition. He began to feel stronger. Energy flowed into his heavy muscles and his father's memories into his brain. He swung the heavy axe and slaughtered countless tiny Eians, their heads flying in all directions, cutting them down like grass. And he saw himself hiding from enemies and friends alike, mentoring one Initiate after another, mating with dozens of identical towa, always feeling that awful sameness, but driven to mate again, and again, and again, this time with his mother, and then again with the human. He felt revulsion and excitement as he penetrated the screaming woman over and over again. And still the memories came, fighting for space in the corners of his mind until there was simply no room left.

After a long ten minutes, the iridescence faded and the swarm gradually dispersed. Jasin and Li Sy watched the alcove for any sign. Finally, Sy Jelick, disoriented, stumbled out, his patches, like those of his father's were brilliant. Jasin stepped into the narrow opening and helped Sy Toberry out of the enclosure. As they made room in the tiny space, Sy Hone crumbled to the ground. His patches were nearly black. Li Sy rushed into the alcove with her medicine bag, and returned several minutes later with the verdict. Sy Hone was dead as a stone.

Li Sy turned her attention to Sy Toberry, who stood miraculously without assistance. The old towan watched his son stagger away down through the canyon toward the water, the boy's eyes sunk so deep in his gaunt cheeks that Jasin had to look twice to determine whether they were open or closed. Li Sy rummaged through her pouch, but unable to find what she was looking for, turned to Jasin. "He needs nourishment."

Jasin nodded and reached out and touched Toberry's arm. "There's food down near the water. Let me help you."

Toberry broke his gaze and looked down at his mangled hand. "You should have let me die. You have burdened yourself needlessly." He then looked back at Sy Hone's body. "There was no reason for this." Then as if he suddenly became aware of his multiple injuries, he groaned loudly.

Jasin begged, "Come, let's follow Sy Jelick to the river. We will eat and rest there until you are stronger."

"And the pytor's body?" asked Toberry.

Jasin shrugged.

"It must not remain there...perhaps others..."

"Perhaps it will warn others to stay away. Except for yourself, the effects of the black rocks are deadly."

"My son lives," Toberry said simply.

Again Jasin shrugged and then gently shook his head. "At least he isn't dead."

Sy Toberry, supported by Jasin, shuffled toward the open end of the narrow canyon, stopping every couple meters to rest. Each time they paused, Jasin wanted to ask the single question that had possessed him for months— when would the next Rhan-da-lith occur—but he restrained himself. There would be plenty of time while they ate and rested on the shore, just beyond the steep dark walls that now contained them.

Sy Jelick hadn't returned to help. In fact the young towan hadn't even acknowledged his father's recovery as he walked away dazed from the alcove where he had been filled with his father's memories. He strolled along the shore of the lake, lost in alien emotions and images. A shell caught his eye and he lifted it from the gravel. But was it his desire or his father's that he acted upon? Sy Jelick could not tell what thought or action truly belonged to him.

Shouldn't there remain a few secrets between father and son? A few dark corners left unexplored? A barrier of assumed respect should exist. Too much familiarity would destroy that. Some memories, some experiences should not be shared, and his father had lived a dozen lifetimes, had more to be ashamed of, more despicable acts than Sy Jelick, or anyone for that matter, should be made to bare. If his father hadn't discovered the black rocks, he would have died along with his exiled brothers and all the others who overthrew their captors on Syton. His son would never have existed, would never have been forced to learn of his father's chilling deeds or to judge his character. But his father hadn't died.

Where the Eians had failed in their many attempts to control the aging process, Sy Toberry succeeded, and discovered what was missing—the revitalization, the recharging that could occur in the alcove of the black rocks. But his father never experienced it with another that had his gift, his genetic anomaly. Sy Jelick had lived, yet so many other loved ones had died that Sy Toberry had given up trying to share his secret long ago.

Today, the charged plankton, focused by the magnetite, had stimulated one memory pattern after another, and transferred them between father and son. Sy Jelick now knew every horrifying murder, deceitful act, immoral transgression his father had ever committed. And there were hundreds of them, and most awful appeared to be the rape of the human female. She moaned and yelled loudly. Sy Jelick had never heard such sounds. Would he ever be rid of her screams?

"What is wrong? Are you hurt?" asked Jasin, approaching Sy Jelick, who turned to face them. He seemed to be focused far away. "Sy Jelick?"

The dazed young towan held something in his hand, but Jasin could not tell what it was. Sy Jelick approached Jasin and his father. His head reverberated with the woman's groans. Then without hesitation, he slashed open his father's throat with the sharp laskic shell. Sy Toberry's head fell backward, revealing the extent of the fatal stroke. Blood poured out of the wide gash as the most highly honored, most respected towan that had ever lived fell mortally wounded to the ground.

But it didn't help. Sy Jelick dropped the shell and collapsed to his knees. He could still hear the woman's screams...human screams of pleasure.

Jasin took a step back from the gruesome scene as if the additional distance would somehow allow him to gain perspective on the unfathomable act. He looked across the bloody corpse to where Li Sy stood. It was the first time he had seen anything resembling surprise or shock from the little towa and Jasin was sure his expression wasn't much different. He took another step back. If Sy Jelick could kill his father with so little cause....

Sy Jelick finally looked up at Jasin with a queer look, then dropped his gaze to the gravel and retrieved the shell he had dropped. Jasin's heart raced. His chance of escaping the towan was slim, but Sy Jelick's attention refocused on his father's body. Using the bloodied laskic shell, Sy Jelick made a quick incision in Toberry's abdomen, reached in and tore out a dark purplish organ.

"The aspic is always the most tasty," he said, suddenly blasé, chewing off a corner.

"Always? Just how many other organs have you sampled?" asked Jasin weakly, not sure that he would be able to speak at all. It was an easy question, but Sy Jelick appeared confused. The towan stopped eating a moment to consider. Jasin continued, "I can't believe you just did that. We've spent the last two weeks trying to save your father and when we finally do..." Jasin legs suddenly turned rubbery as the full gravity of Toberry's death overwhelmed him. Sitting before he fell, Jasin tried to collect his thoughts, but they slithered away, avoiding examination.

"Are you hungry?" asked Sy Jelick, holding out the remaining piece of aspic as if this were just another mealtime.

Jasin turned his head away. There was no way to make sense of this. He looked across Toberry's mutilated body to the packs he had left leaning against the big boulder beyond. He couldn't muster the energy nor find the desire to cross the few dozen meters. Why hadn't he asked Toberry when he had the chance? Despair filled his heart. Now, he had no way of knowing when the next darkness would come. He would have to leave his home in Nova Gaia and live on the shore of the lake in order to be in place when the machine rose.

Sy Jelick turned to Li Sy, offering her the aspic. She joined him at Toberry's side and made quick work of the small organ. "What is wrong with Jasin?" asked Sy Jelick.

"Your father was important to him. Jasin must be here at the lake when the next Rhan-da-lith occurs. Your father was the only one who always knew when that would be."

Together the natives walked to the shoreline and rinsed their bloody hands. Sy Jelick began to relax. The haunting screams in his head faded. The two natives turned to watch silently as the cyliths begin to devour the body. Toberry had finally honored the cyliths. Sy Jelick turned to Li Sy, "The concerns of the humans seem unimportant tonight."

"The machine in the lake concerns us all," she replied.

Sy Jelick rose from his squat, spread his hands apart, and walked over to Jasin. "You should be prepared. Rhan-da-lith is nearly upon us. In twelve days the darkness will be complete," said Sy Jelick.

"You can not possibly know this," Jasin objected.

With a voice filled with sorrow, the youth answered, "And yet I do."

Rhan-da-lith

Elizabeth cherished any time she was able to spend as a refugee from the mad house. The other adults had accepted the undisciplined free-for-all the Elstrada complex had become, but even now, having run nearly ten kilometers and looking down from Trinity's foothills at the tiny speck that was the residence, she didn't feel she was far enough away. She longed for the time when she first arrived and there was just the four of them. Remembering the quiet talks with Julian and the awkwardness of the budding romance, she smiled, and then wiped the drop of sweat off the tip of her nose with her breathing cloth. Over the last few weeks, with Jasin gone on his foolhardy expedition to find Toberry's body, she had learned that servitude under benevolent management was superior to feigned control over chaos. There was sufficient space within the large structure to bed everyone, but during the brightness, when everyone was up and about, she often sought escape in the foothills where no one else would follow and she could enjoy the solace of isolation. Which made it all the more shocking when the little Eian stepped out, from behind a boulder and limped forward to greet her.

"Don't be frightened," he said in his best Human. "I will not harm you. I just need to talk to you." He wrapped his thin clock about him, but it was clear he remained uncomfortable in the chilly wind sweeping off the snow-covered landscape.

"Who in blazes are you?"

"My name is Eiton. Julian calls me Engineer."

"Oh!" Her joy inadvertently burst forth and she sat, overtaken by the strength of the emotion. "That's wonderful. She's alive then." It was more a statement than question.

"And well, all things considered. I am here to insure that she stays that way. I've grown most fond of her...as I sense you are."

"How have you—"

"I don't have much time. Sorry to interrupt, but I have been gone too long as it is. I am here to warn you and Jasin, or anyone else for that matter, not to attempt to retrieve the shuttle from the lake. Eidorf— I think you have already had dealings with my superior—he will not hesitate to kill anyone who gets in our way."

"We don't understand why you've taken Julian. She never knew anything about the machine in the lake."

Eiton blinked his eyes and settled back upon his middle leg. "We believe this now, but unfortunately she has gained knowledge of a different sort that prevents her release."

"What knowledge, that you have hiding places in Hadrious where the Sytonians can't find you? That you come and go through the supply tunnel in the Kull as you wish? These are not secrets worth holding her for. She is an old woman. If you let her go I will talk to Jasin about not pursuing the shuttle."

"I would, but it is not my decision."

"You apparently can come and go as you wish. Just bring her to us."

"I can not. But I promised her that I would warn her son to stay out of Eidorf's way. We must have the shuttle. We will not let it be destroyed."

"Why do you think Jasin would destroy it?" She was surprised at the depth of Eiton's knowledge.

"It is logical. We know he is in a difficult position and what he must be thinking, but you must tell him that his mother's life, and his, would be at risk if he were to get in our way. Nothing is more important to the Eians than recovering the shuttle. Nothing."

"I will give Jasin your message, but you must let Julian come home."

"I don't see how."

"She calls you Engineer? Then you solve problems. Figure out how to get her home. That is important to us."

"I understand. Now make sure Jasin understands."

Elizabeth nodded her head.

Eiton leaned forward putting his weight back on his side legs. "Such a strange human gesture, this head bobbing," he said and turned to go.

Elizabeth jumped to her feet. "One last question...what are you planning to do with the shuttle? You must realize that the race who controls it, wields extraordinary power."

Eiton craned his neck to look at her and said quite simply, "We plan on going home."

Home...Elizabeth had plenty of time to ponder this as she made her way down to the residence. Upon first reflection, and accepting for the moment that the second moon had recovered sufficiently to support life again, this use of the shuttle actually made a lot of sense. But on second thought, if they possessed the shuttle and the Eian home world weren't safe to return to, all the inhabitants of Syton, including the humans, would once again be in danger of being overtaken and controlled. No, she could see Jasin's reason for eliminating the power of the shuttle. It was too much of a wild card.

But what if the second moon was habitable and the Eians promised non-interference and permanent emigration? Wouldn't that actually be a better solution than keeping the Eians captive on Hadrious? Could they be trusted to keep their word? She knew the present situation would eventually disintegrate. Truly a knotty problem.

And what about this peculiar little engineer? Why did he take the risk to warn them about Eidorf? Was he simply trying to stop the human's efforts as he claimed? Did he come all this way just to protect Jasin or was he attempting to ease his job of capturing the shuttle? Did he really care whether any human got hurt? Perhaps he was being honest. He said he was fond of Julian and that he promised to warn

Jasin for her. Elizabeth decided that this was the simplest and best answer—he was telling the truth. Besides she thought, remembering the time she had spent with the Wynosk family, engineers don't lie very well.

"Whatcha mean, engineers don't lie very well," Henri Membomba chortled after hearing Elizabeth's story. "You think just because some little...whatcha call them little towans?"

"Eians"

"Yeah, Eians...just because some little fella tells you he cares about Julian, you believe him? Foolish, that's what I call it. Just darn gullible. Will you two lay off each other? Blazes! You'd think you hadn't seen each other in years. I don't know what you see in her, Jasin. She's just too darn tall."

"You're just jealous old man. When's the last time you kissed a woman? I mean without paying for it. I bet it's been—"

"None of your business, that's what. Now where's that meal you've been promising Li Sy and me for the last three days."

It was a welcome surprise to find them home, but Elizabeth could have done without the smelly old engineer and his equally pungent animal. When she and Jasin finally had a moment alone she asked, "Don't you think we have enough people around here Jasin? You bump into Membomba and his beast and you have to drag them home with you?" She smiled, "Just when I thought we'd have some private time together."

"In this house? But really, what's one more?" he teased, and then turned serious. "To be honest, I didn't really just bump into him. We actually need him."

"Need that?" She stole a glance in Membomba's direction. "If you expect me to believe that, you've been gone way too long."

Jasin hugged her tight. "I have been gone too long. Have you been feeling all right?"

"For a fat pregnant woman."

Jasin stepped back from her and smiled. Despite the fullness around her middle that only he could feel, she looked more gorgeous than ever. "Yeah, big, fat, *and* ugly," he teased.

"I'm ugly? Look at that mop of hair, and you could have at least bathed. Afraid of the barbers in Bistoun?"

"Only one woman is allowed to cut my hair."

"Or give you a shave." She leaned forward and kissed him. "So?"

"It's happening. We only have a week to prepare and we need the old geezer. He's the only one I know who can fly the damn thing...if he can actually still remember. I swear he's loonier than I remember him being at Hyland's funeral. Anyway, he claims he can and we don't have a choice."

"Where did you find him?"

"I didn't. I mean, I found his blaython in Bistoun. He had sold it to settle a debt and I bought the beast figuring Membomba would be more agreeable if I had something he valued."

"You traded crystals for it?" she asked in disbelief. "Real crystals?"

Jasin nodded sheepishly. "But it worked out. As soon as the animal was free, it trotted down the road to find Henri. All we had to do was follow."

"What were you doing in Bistoun? What about Toberry and Beloit?"

Jasin recounted the last few weeks, sparing her the scene with the cyliths on the lakeshore. She listened intently, interrupting only a few times when Jasin hurried or skipped a detail or two.

"Anyway, I took a chance that Membomba would be there. It was either Bistoun or Lake Chook. There's not many safe places left for us. I was lucky. If he'd been on the trail or up in Panvera, we'd be in trouble."

Elizabeth brushed a lock of Jasin's hair away from his eyes. "Jasin, we *are* in trouble. The Eian's know you are going to try to recover the machine. Eiton said Julian doesn't want any heroics. You aren't supposed to attempt to destroy the shuttle."

"I'm not going to destroy anything…at least not right away. We'll open it up and Membomba will fly it back here. After the Eians bring us Julian, we'll give them what they want."

"But the Sytonians want it destroyed."

"Oh, eventually it *will* be destroyed, publicly, for all to see. You can trust me on that. But not before we use it to trade for Julian. Membomba agreed with your father about doing any damage from the outside, but promises me that the shuttle will be easy to destroy once he has access to the controls on the inside. When we determine where Hadrious is, he can make the shuttle fly there unmanned, rigged to explode. We'll make it appear as if they didn't know what they were doing and caused some sort of accident. No one will ever use the power of the shuttle, except to bring Julian back."

"You don't think in the long term it would be better if the Eians used it to get their people off this world?"

Jasin shook his head. "What if their moon isn't ready to inhabit? The shuttle's power is too great to leave in so few hands."

"Like you being the only one with the entry code?" Elizabeth asked, raising an eyebrow.

"We've talked that to death. I don't want to put anyone else in harm's way, especially you and the baby."

"But if it's as important as you believe, shouldn't we have a backup plan? Give Membomba the code."

"Tell the only person that can operate it how to get in? He's probably the last one who should know."

Elizabeth shrugged. "So what do we do now?"

"Eat! I'm starving."

Elizabeth reached out and pulled Jasin to her. "So am I," she whispered, before sharing a long, passionate kiss.

At dinner Jasin outlined the rest of his plan while stuffing on sweet melon and spice bread. "I haven't missed any of you half as much as this spice bread," he said with a twinkle in his eye. After finishing the last piece, he refilled his cup and pushed back from the table.

"So how many of us do you figure we'll need to make a convincing show?" asked Frankie.

"Well, you can forget about me," Stump said with conviction. If it were possible, she had made herself even less appealing by chopping her hair asymmetrically, leaving the left side not even long enough to cover her ear. "I'll stay here with the young ones."

Jasin disagreed. "The Twins can watch the kids, you and the boys are big enough to help out. Remember, it will be completely dark."

"I'm not stupid. I know what Rhan-da-lith is"

Jasin ignored her. "Mas and Elizabeth will control the diversion at the lake. Nanc...you and the other four, plus anyone else we can convince to accompany you, will take torches and boats out to the center of the lake. Three or four boats ought to keep their attention. The Sytonians will be watching and they must be convinced I'm with you leading some big operation." Jasin looked about to judge the level of acceptance. Elizabeth met his gaze with a scowl. He chose to deal with whatever was bothering her in private and continued.

"You'll want to form a circle; you'll need maybe five boats. Elizabeth, can you borrow that many from your old neighbors near the cabin?" She gave a terse nod. "Bring plenty of lanterns, barrels, rope, and stuff you can throw into the water. A couple of you will need to get wet. Lot's of splashing. You'll have to keep the natives attention for as long as possible. Two, three hours should do it. Then extinguish all your torches and head back to shore in the dark. Leave all the barrels anchored in the middle of the lake for them to see when it brightens."

"Everyone can sleep in the Wynosk cabin that night and head back here when there's enough light." Elizabeth added.

Mas scratched the scar on his forehead. "Who will be left to guard the shuttle if you're successful in flying it back here? It will take us several days to get back from the lake. Someone will hear or see it land," he added.

Jasin turned to Membomba who agreed. "He's right. The exhaust plume should be quite visible. We might be able to avoid Cernai, but folks around here should hear and see it plainly, even in the total darkness."

"Then, we'll land it in the foothills—"

Membomba was shaking his head. "We're not landing that thing in any hills. But you needn't worry. It won't need protection. Unless of course the little folk have something more powerful than we know of." He smiled, showing what was left of his teeth.

"But that's just the problem," complained Nanc. "We don't know what they have and their visit today with Elizabeth shows they can go anywhere without detection."

There was a pause as everyone racked their brains for an answer. Finally Elizabeth spoke. "Take it to Lake Meitalyn. Sink it in the red water and make it rise and fall like Hyland did. They'll never follow you to Panvera and if they did you'll have the protection of the entire town."

Elizabeth's idea held great merit and Jasin agreed that they should all meet in Panvera. "It's a few more days to travel, but it'll be much safer and less likely that we'll be detected. I doubt whether there will be anyone able to follow the shuttle's path if we go that way, especially if we don't head directly there."

Membomba laughed. "You planetborn don't understand the shuttle. We'll take it straight up out of sight, even out of the gorge itself, and then drop straight down into Maylyn. No one except those in Panvera will see anything."

Jasin smiled. "Then it's settled. It looks like Li Sy will get a return visit to the cold."

Li Sy who hadn't said a word since their return looked up from the gourd she'd been gnawing on. "Li Sy will help you, but Li Sy does not want to get cold ever again."

After retiring to their room, Elizabeth exploded. "How dare you send me off as a decoy while you risk your neck without me? How can you even imagine that I would agree to that? Every time you think something will be dangerous, you find a way to send me away. Damn you! You aren't home even a day and we're fighting. And over the same macho crap you've been pulling on me since the beginning.

I'm not some frail thing you need to protect. Maybe your dad felt he had to protect Julian, but I'm not your mother."

"And I'm not my father. Don't be comparing me to him! But is it such a crime to love you? I know you don't *need* my protection…but that doesn't mean I don't *want* to protect you."

"We've had this conversation before. I thought we had resolved this issue."

"No, you resolved the issue and ended up with a knife in you."

"Well, if you don't want a knife in *you*, you'll agree to take me along." She smiled, as usual showing Jasin that any further arguing would be fruitless. "Listen, if you really want to protect me you'll marry me, raise our own kids in this big house, and live happily ever after."

"Like some stupid fairy tale."

"Yeah," she said, taking his hand and leading him to their bed, "Just like a stupid fairy tale."

A few days later, Jasin led his large and raucous gang into town to pick up rope, barrels, and other supplies before heading toward Lake Chook. By the time they left, anyone who didn't know they were preparing for Rhan-da-lith and the rendezvous with the shuttle just hadn't been paying attention. Jasin also made sure to spread the word among the Human Caucus members and casually mention it to Seanne Sy and Sy Jelick as well. Obviously Sy Jelick knew that Jasin planned to recover the shuttle, but Jasin wanted to make sure the Sytonian Council believed he was keeping his word. Moreover, Jasin desperately wanted this misinformation campaign to be believed by the Eians. If they thought that he and their prize would be separated by at least ten kilometers of the Andoree, they might relax their guard at the hidden cavern.

From the onset, Jasin knew he couldn't match the Eian's resources, and had absolutely no faith that his little gang could win a head to head battle against them. In fact, he was counting on the Eian's success, hoping that they would snatch the shuttle out from under everyone's noses even before it rose out of the water completely. He wasn't sure how the Eians were going to accomplish it, but he was confident that they wouldn't tip their hand prematurely and allow the Sytonians, or Humans for that matter, to interfere with their plans. Jasin's brief glimpse into the cavern had convinced him that it was prepared to secretly accommodate something much larger than a few gilia heads; that was where they would find and take the shuttle.

It was the 38th of the sixth septet, two days before Sy Jelick had said Rhan-da-lith would begin. Mas and Nanc, the youngsters, and all their supplies, Jasin, Elizabeth, Membomba and of course, Li Sy, all appeared to be settled in for the night at the trader's clearing. But by the brightening, Jasin, Elizabeth, Membomba and Li Sy were soaking their bruised and bloody extremities five kilometers away in the refreshing water of the Canyon River.

"You youngsters are insane," groaned Henri, examining one particularly nasty scrape along his thigh. "What woulda been the difference if we snuck away and worked our way through the bush during the day? Do ya really think anyone's following us?"

"I wasn't the clumsy one falling half way down the cliff," said Jasin. "Good thing we didn't let you carry the explosives or they'd have been scattered over a thousand square meters like your clothes." Jasin gingerly pulled a two-centimeter thorn out of his sock. The business end was bloody. "I don't think anyone would have followed us down that way, and if they did, we would have heard them. Anyway, we can rest here for a few hours. Just stay out of sight."

"We'll be a day ahead of Mas and the others. If they make it to Fork Camp tonight they will be making good time," Elizabeth added.

Jasin absently nodded, more interested in surveying the surrounding cliffs for any sign of life. He wanted them to get under cover as quickly as possible. "Do you know where Li Sy got off to?" he asked.

Elizabeth pointed ahead. "She's up around the curve there, searching for that stupid milkweed she uses."

"I wish she hadn't wandered off. We've got to get hidden."

"What about the time difference Elizabeth mentioned?" asked Membomba.

Jasin shrugged. "There's nothing we can do about that. Tomorrow should be the eve of Rhan-da-lith. We just have to be ready for whatever happens. We're only going to get one shot at this. If the Eians end up with the shuttle, life here is going to take a turn for the worse."

"Compared to the Sytonians, cutting off our heads?" Elizabeth teased.

"Yeah," Jasin smiled, "worse than that." He had missed her sense of humor on the last trip and was secretly happy to have her by his side. About a half an hour later, Li Sy returned with her medicines, which relieved the pain from all but the deepest abrasions. Jasin had to admit that with what they had been through, she was a special find, a new breed of independent towa. It had become increasing difficult to picture life without her. He wondered whether she would stay with them after the baby was born. It would be nice to have the extra hand, and someone who knew about the herbal remedies, but first things first. She was going to be indispensable over the next couple days.

When he had explained how he wanted her to scout ahead and be their eyes and ears, she had only one reservation—getting across the river. Once Elizabeth offered to swim her across, she was satisfied.

Jasin lay in the shade, making himself comfortable by nestling in a small depression in the ground and within minutes was snoring loudly. Nearby, Elizabeth and Membomba looked at each other amused.

"A true covert operation," Henri declared.

Recovery

Beneath the waves of Lake Chook, under cover of the Rhan-da-lith, Eiton and his crew released air from a few of their many weighted, hollow gilia and descended to the submerged craft. Using glowsticks for illumination they attached a huge fabric canopy to the corners of the shuttle's bow and then inflated the makeshift lifting bag from their compressed air canisters. The ballooning fabric countered the craft's weight while they managed to slide the forward cradle arm underneath. Then slowly so they wouldn't attract attention to the bubbles, they deflated it, and repeated the operation on the stern. Connecting the two cradles together resulted in a stable platform that supported the shuttle. After deflating the canopy once again, and re-anchoring the corners of the dark fabric to the completed cradle, they were able to envelope the entire vehicle within a small pocket of air.

Meanwhile on the surface of the lake, Mas, Nanc, and the children, rowed their small fleet of boats, packed to the gunnels with barrels and rope, out to the middle of the lake. As they began to stage their "public salvage", Eiton and his team, in the frigid water, ten meters below, crawled underneath the opaque, air-filled canopy, and removed their breathing equipment.

The Eians walked along the cradle, holding out fresh glow sticks to reveal the aerodynamic curves and sophisticated design of the human craft. Even covered with thirty years of slime and organic growth, Eiton was impressed. It appeared larger than he remembered from his first surveillance and measurements of the machine. If he had any residual doubt that the craft would be able to take him and his handpicked staff of fellow engineers and fabricators home, it had vanished. Lying before them was the future of his people.

Eiton believed the machine had been programmed to lift-off from the bottom of the lake at precise times and return the craft to the same spot after spending a few minutes on the surface. The bottom thrusters would probably fire just enough to overcome the submerged weight and then turn off gradually, allowing the vehicle to sink smoothly to the bottom.

He counted on the human engineer who had hidden the craft to make it easy to salvage. After all, that was its ultimate purpose wasn't it, to be retrieved and used? Eiton felt that all he'd have to do is move the craft out of position enough that the shuttle's programming would sense that a salvage operation was underway and halt the normal thrusters from firing. At least that was his hope. He had no certainty but it made sense to him. When it was time, he was confident the lifting thrusters on the bottom would fire, but if the positioning thrusters also fired…well that was where the diverters would be important.

The slime build up made attaching the thrust diverters more difficult than Eiton expected. The cone-shaped devices were designed and built to mate tightly to the exhaust ports, but the organic buildup caused a looser fit than he desired. Eiton fussed with them but soon decided the effort and worry wasn't really called for. They probably wouldn't even be needed.

Eiton and Eidorf had debated salvaging the craft days or even weeks ahead of Rhan-da-lith, but they didn't want to tip their hand too early and worried the unusually large flotilla of gilia heads arriving in the brightness would attract suspicion. No, as dangerous as it was, they too needed the cover of darkness.

Eiton fine-tuned the shuttle's buoyancy with a small canister of compressed air until it hovered just a meter above the floor of the lake and within seconds they were enveloped in the gentle grasp of the tide that slowly carried them downstream. Eiton constantly adjusted the volume of air in the canopy to keep them from rising too high or scraping along the floor of the lake.

Then without warning, the bottom engines fired.

With the added buoyancy of the air canopy, they were hurled to the surface. For several uncomfortable moments as the shuttle held itself on the surface, the Eians were trapped under the wet canopy that collapsed over them. Eiton thought he could hear shouting from a distance, but it was difficult to judge from underneath the heavy fabric. Then just as suddenly, the engines turned off and they sunk like a stone. The air that had inflated the canopy had all but escaped, and Eiton and his team were carried into the depths, suddenly drowning. Eiton had just enough time to throw open the air valve and try to reestablish the air pocket before the maneuvering thrusters, stymied by the diverters, fired, turning the water to steam and filling their small refuge with noxious fumes. But now, the canopy, again inflated, lifted the shuttle to the surface a second time. There, the small positioning engines suddenly turned off and the canopy emptied and collapsed again. The craft sunk once more, this time all the way to the bottom. Eiton grabbed hold of the air valve, prepared to shut it down when enough air had filled the canopy, but the air canister had emptied, leaving the canopy only a meager air pocket and the machine resting in the muck of the lake floor.

Eiton was cold and angry. His careful planning had left them stranded. He had failed to understand the shuttle's programming or the speed of their ascents. Now, he didn't know what to do and they sat on the roof of the shuttle in the small air space discussing their plight while the tide reversed itself. The long roots of the gilia swung around them as the floating heads moved with the reverse current.

After several hours, Eiton had an idea and instructed his team to grab hold of one of the roots and together they struggled to pull the head down to them. Once under the canopy they flipped over the head and released the small amount of naturally trapped air. It took about twenty heads, but soon the shuttle gently left the ground. When the tide headed back down stream, they untied the roots that they had used to anchor themselves, and continued to ride the current. Five hours later, the shuttle was safely ensconced in the Eian cavern awaiting the entry code that only Jasin knew.

Across the river, Jasin and Elizabeth's could hear muffled conversation escaping from the cavern. Darkness heightened their sense of hearing and there was no doubt the shuttle had arrived, but Jasin was in no hurry. He wanted the excitement of the Eian success to dissipate, and for Eiton and his crew to leave the area surrounding the shuttle. He needed time to be sure his own group was ready for whatever might arise.

"Elizabeth and Li Sy will go first," he whispered. "Once you're on the opposite shore, Li Sy will sneak into the actual cavern while Elizabeth stays hidden outside, but you must stay within sight of both Li Sy and us." Elizabeth nodded. "When Li Sy thinks it's safe she'll signal Elizabeth by opening the sleeve of the glow stick. Li Sy, remember to direct the slit only toward the opening, like this." Jasin demonstrated. "Elizabeth will relay the "all clear" with her own glow stick and Henri and I will swim across. We will only enter if Li Sy maintains the signal that it's safe. If for any reason Li Sy must hide or leave she will take her glow stick with her and Elizabeth will lower hers. We will wait an hour for a new signal. If it doesn't come, everyone will regroup across the river."

"Li Sy, if it isn't safe for us to come, hide the light and meet back with Elizabeth and she will help you back across. If you get trapped on the other side and you think it safe to try again, flash the glow stick toward this position and we will rejoin you."

"Watch the shuttle carefully. Once we gain entrance, come quickly. We will only keep the shuttle door open for the briefest time. When we are all together inside the shuttle with the door closed, we can relax. Henri will do his stuff. If for any reason we get split up we'll meet either here or if this place is compromised, in Panvera. Everybody understand?"

Elizabeth nodded and gave Jasin a reassuring smile. "Don't worry so much. We'll all be fine."

"You really think they will leave it unguarded?" asked Henri. "It's a big prize and they've gone through a lot of effort to steal it."

"Guard it from whom? They've been using the cavern for years and it hasn't been discovered by anyone except us. It's clear the Sytonians don't have a clue and even if they suspect we might know something. Everyone believes we're two days up river in Lake Chook. Let's get some rest. We'll head off in four hours. It should still be plenty dark."

Elizabeth listened to Jasin with pride. He had become a thoughtful and brave leader, a far cry from Avram's dominated little boy. If that keetah-soaked old man could see his son now…well, at least Julian will have a chance to see this new side of him, and their child will have a father to admire, instead of fear or pity like Avram. She snuggled closer to Jasin and kissed him before lying down.

"Don't take this the wrong way," Jasin whispered, "but I wish you weren't here."

Elizabeth hugged him. There was absolutely no place she'd rather have been.

Jasin waited until Elizabeth signaled before inserting the thinner tube of explosive into the yellow detonator. He looked up into Membomba's wizened and questioning eyes. "Either we are successful or the shuttle must be destroyed. Do you understand?" Jasin placed the vial in his small backpack carefully. "If we manage to take off, the inner tube must quickly be removed from the yellow liquid and if possible, jettisoned. The first thing we do when we get over there is hide the backpack where it will do the most harm, then move it inside if possible. Either we're airborne in thirty minutes, or the shuttle is destroyed. Understand?"

Membomba shook his head. "I thought you'd given up on that. You are one crazy boy if you think that tiny bit of native explosive will really harm the shuttle. More likely we blow ourselves up. You gonna carry that stuff on your back? It's primed. What if you're wrong about the timing?"

"Then it won't matter to me," Jasin managed a weak grin before turning serious. "But just in case, the entrance code is EXODUS14. Don't forget it"

"Just don't expect me to swim next to you."

Jasin ignored him, rose, and kicked off his boots. "Come on, we've got to get going."

In the near perfect blackness they swam toward the faint speck of light that was Elizabeth's glow stick. It was an eerie feeling, sensing but not seeing the water, and Jasin imagined it was like swimming through space itself. Occasionally, they would lower their heads and mistakenly swim toward the reflection of the glow stick in the black water.

Once across, they stumbled over the rocks to join Elizabeth. In the weak artificial illumination within the cavern, they could make out the outline of the shuttle. It was secured against the pier with chains and just behind and off to one side they could see Li Sy's signal.

"Still safe," reported Jasin, more to convince himself than to inform the others who could see the signal for themselves. "You've got to protect our back." Jasin reminded Elizabeth. "Keep twenty or thirty meters behind until we've got the hatch open." She nodded nervously, instinctively feeling for the thin blade strapped to her thigh.

"The interior will illuminate. It will be obvious," added Henri, in a hushed whisper.

Jasin and Membomba snuck quietly along the inside of the cavern using the natural rock features to keep hidden. Elizabeth dutifully held back, continually checking behind them. Finally, they were as close to the shuttle as they were going to be without exposing themselves. Taking a final look around, they darted to the back hatch of the shuttle. Jasin shed the backpack and jammed it into one of the exposed thrusters next to the hatch, where Membomba indicated. Jasin looked at the keypad next to the hatch and his heart skipped a beat.

There was not a single intelligible letter or numeral.

He looked over to Membomba with panic in his eyes. Henri leaned over to take a look, then nonchalantly took the corner of his wet sleeve and rubbed away thirty years of silt away before grinning at Jasin. With a polite flourish, he silently invited Jasin to do the honors. Jasin glanced around and then carefully entered the code.

Nothing happened.

Jasin felt weak in the knees and slumped down defeated, but Membomba reached over, grabbed the handle of the hatch, and gave a mighty tug.

But again nothing.

Henri cleared the keyboard and reentered the code. Then they both grabbed hold of the hatch handle and together they pulled, but to no avail. They inspected the seam where the hatch fit snuggly into the fuselage. It appeared to be sealed with hardened calcium deposits, so Membomba took off his belt and ran the edge of the buckle along the seam, scraping the deposit off while Jasin looked around nervously. They were making too much noise. Taking too long.

They took hold of the handle again and pulled with all they had. Finally, the hatch came free and opened the rest of the way by itself. As Membomba had said, the interior lights came up, and the old engineer slipped inside.

The sight awed Jasin. He had expected to be impressed, but all the sculptured control surfaces and colorful displays were more than he had imagined. He followed Membomba into the shuttle.

"Do you think you can get it to fly?" Jasin asked in a whisper.

For your sake, I hope he can," said a familiar voice behind him.

Jasin turned to see Li Sy framed by the doorway. She held an energy blaster like the one that tore Sy Loeton apart. "Where did you get that thing?" Jasin whispered. "Get inside here." But she leveled the weapon at his chest and didn't move. A male Eian walked up behind her.

"You must be Jasin. We haven't been formally introduced, my name is Eidorf...and I believe you've already met my mate, Li'onna. Now that you have so kindly opened this magnificent machine, I would like you to leave it without touching anything.

Jasin stared at Li Sy, more with astonishment than hatred. "You are Eian?"

"Eian, Sytonian, to us females it is just a matter of allegiance. Now, I suggest you do as Eidorf says and leave the craft before I am forced to blow a hole in you. After all we've been through together, I would rather not."

"I'm not moving. You aren't about to start blasting away inside this precious ship. One miss and it will be disabled." Jasin felt secure as long as he was inside. And there was always Elizabeth.

"Perhaps you are right." Li Sy handed the weapon to Eidorf, and then raised her voice demanding, "Bring her here."

Eiton herded Elizabeth into sight, holding a similar weapon against her back.

Eidorf also turned his weapon on Elizabeth. "If you don't leave the craft—"

The explosion tore through the thruster casing. Metal shrapnel sliced through Li Sy's body, cutting her apart, killing her instantly. The concussion threw everyone else to the ground. Jasin jumped to his feet and started for Elizabeth.

"Get back inside you idiot," yelled Membomba, who stumbled over to the controls and began initiating the lift-off sequence.

"JASIN!" screamed Elizabeth, seeing Eidorf raise his energy weapon. Jasin dove for cover inside the shuttle just as the weapon discharged.

With the two armed Eians between the shuttle and herself, Elizabeth instantly realized she wasn't going to make it and rolled across the narrow pier and disappeared into the black water.

"Damn!" Jasin swore, uncertain what to do, but Henri was already closing the hatch. Mighty engines roared to life and the shuttle lifted off, tearing the pier apart where it had been chained. The craft pivoted and blasted two bursts of high energy weapon fire against the side of the cavern. A flaming hole opened up and Membomba flew toward it.

"Watch out," warned Jasin, but it was too late. The shuttle glanced off the side of the opening before shooting into the clear air beyond.

"What happened to Elizabeth?" Membomba asked.

"We've got to go back for her," Jasin ordered. "She made it into the water. That's all I saw. Bring this thing around." Panic started to creep into his voice.

"The port thruster is damaged," Membomba complained. "You blew the cowling apart."

"I don't give a damn. We've got to land."

"I can't control shit. You probably screwed up the engine pivot too."

"You told me to put it there. Can you fly back? Circle the area. If she escaped the cavern—"

"Jasin…you don't understand. I can't maneuver. I can't make any tight turns. Even if I could, we wouldn't be able to see her. It's still dark. If I try bringing this down anywhere near the cavern or the river we might not—"

"I don't care. We just can't leave her. You've got to try turning around."

"The tightest turn I can make will still bring us back too wide. Look." Membomba activated the navigational plotter and a detailed aerial view appeared on one of the large screens. A record of their crazy course was superimposed in red, their present position was flashing. Membomba showed Jasin a projection of their course.

Jasin cocked his head, staring at the electronic map, trying to orient himself. He could make out the outline of the Andoree and Lake Chook but….

"Our tightest turn would bring us to here, not even close to the cavern. Without both thrusters…on this trajectory we can make…Soto, I think." Membomba pointed to an area just beyond Soto Harbor. "Maybe the pasture lands there,"

Jasin continued to stare at the screen without really focusing. What he had feared most had come to be. He had put Elizabeth in harm's way. He had failed to protect her. He cursed himself. He cursed Li Sy. At least that little bitch got what she deserved. Jasin felt faint and steadied himself.

"Don't be touching the screen. Body oils separate the laminates."

"Fuck the oils!" Jasin glanced down to see if he had really done any harm. "I barely touched it. Jasin pointed at the screen. "What is that?" There was a deformed oval, like a plug dislodged from the mouth of the Andoree.

"What is what?"

"That! What is that? It doesn't belong there. I've studied every map Avram ever collected and that's not supposed to be there."

"I don't know...but it's too far, besides why get marooned on some stupid island. We've got to find tools if we have any chance of fixing this thing."

"We don't have to fix it. We'll just deliver it. Hopefully someone other than the Eians will see us land."

"Land where?"

Jasin pointed at the mysterious landmass. "Hadrious."

"But we just stole it from the Eians. Now you want to give it back?"

"We'll make them a trade. You still think you can get this thing to explode."

"That's easier than ever. You probably blew open a fuel overflow line."

"Then, you've got to get to Hadrious without killing us. Whatever it takes, we've got to land on that island."

Membomba shook his head in despair, but set about making adjustments until Hadrious lay in front of them. Slowly they descended, but then suddenly they began to turn.

"No, no we've got to land," yelled Jasin.

"Oh, we're going to land all right."

Without the port thruster they began to spin, rotating faster and faster. Jasin had just enough time to fall into a seat and grasp the armrests before they corkscrewed into the ground.

Gilia

Elizabeth hid in the scrub on the shore opposite the Eian cavern. She hated indecision, especially in herself, and knew safety demanded she put distance between herself and the Eians. She probably should have left for Panvera immediately as they had planned.

But that wasn't the direction the shuttle had gone. In the darkness and confusion, that was one thing she was sure of—she saw the shuttle's exhaust head toward Soto Harbor, or at least down river, away from Panvera.

She gingerly ran her fingers across her calf, trying to judge the extent of the burn on her leg. The shuttle's raucous departure had served as a diversion, and had allowed her to swim out from her hiding place beneath what was left of the pier, and dive under the pitch-black water. Swimming as hard and far as she could, she had headed for the open river. Although submerged, she heard the side of the cavern burst apart under fire of the shuttle's weapon. Burning chunks of rock fell around her, sizzling as they cooled on their way to the bottom. One hot piece had grazed her leg and even in the frigid water she remembered feeling it burn.

Now, hours later, and still worried about the range of the Eian weapons, she remained hidden behind a thick popper bush and watched the brightness return to the gorge. Rhanda-lith was over.

The changing tide swung the great gilia heads around and they strained against their root tethers, as they were pulled downstream. Two un-tethered heads floated out from the cavern and she knew, just as if she could see through their thick shells that Eidorf and Eiton were inside. Were they following the course of the shuttle or returning to Hadrious? Possibly both.

No longer concerned about being fired upon, she rushed to the water and swam to the largest gilia head on her side of the river. While holding onto the roots with one hand, she used her knife to cut a hole in the bottom of the orb just wide enough to climb through, then she dove underneath, and pulled herself inside. She took a deep breath of the gas inside and immediately felt dizzy and disorientated. Her last coherent thought was to escape before she fell back out through the hole and into the dark green water. The splash of cold brought her around and she managed to claw her way to the surface and gasped for fresh air. Whatever had been inside the gilia, she couldn't breath it.

Holding on to the roots of her gilia, she drifted along almost as fast as the Eians ahead of her. Still, the water was numbing and she knew she couldn't follow like this for long. She struggled to roll the slimy green orb over to see if she could exchange any of the putrid gas inside, but she scooped up unwanted water in the process. With a sigh, she struggled to roll the head over and empty the water when a solution came to her—there was a better way. How silly she had been.

She pushed the gilia in front of her and swam to shallow water along the shore. There, she flipped the gilia head so the hole was on top, and then took her knife and cut off the top third of the sphere, making a little cup or round bottom boat into which she carefully stepped. She pushed off into the current. As long as she sat low and didn't shift her weight, the tipsy gilia head would suit her just fine. They needed concealment. She didn't...unless they were to approach Hadrious. She decided to worry about that later.

Beloit McMaster watched Elizabeth's ingenuity from on top of the cavern's stone roof. She was being foolhardy. These weren't folks you took lightly or pursued unprepared.

In the days he had followed the cloaked towa, or Eian, through the streets of Bistoun, their villainy was revealed. Beloit had seen Eidorf poison a towan and spread the word about how humans were in the area at the time. He had no doubt any longer that he had been victim of just such a tactic. He had seen the Eian trade illegal technology to humans, and then plant clues and evidence of it for the Sytonians to discover. Beloit suspected that the blue knifes, the explosives, and even the glow lights were purposefully supplied to the traders to seed distrust and encourage the humans to break the Prohibitions. It had become clear that the Eians, or this cloaked one at least, had set the two races at each other's throats, manipulating the Sytonians, causing them to murder dozens of humans while remaining in the shadows. What for? Revenge? Were the Eians trying to cause a war, hoping humans would join them against the towans? Or were they creating unrest so humans would be so focused on saving their own necks that they could steal the shuttle without interference. If that were the answer, it had almost worked.

Beloit found himself walking along the shoreline trying to keep pace with Elizabeth's little vessel. The embankment rose and he found that he was climbing steadily. He knew he wasn't allowed on this side of the river nor in the Kull, but he couldn't worry about such trivial issues now that the power of the shuttle and his people's ultimate survival was at stake. Besides, he smiled to himself, who was going to catch him. He realized that he had mentally taken off the Enforcer's cloak, and for the first time in thirty years, felt as if a weight had been lifted. To his complete surprise, he found himself happy.

Hours passed and he grew weary. He hadn't slept since leaving Bistoun to follow the cloaked Eian into the Kull, but now, the tide took pity on him as it slowed and reversed. The Eians tied their gilia roots to stationary heads, keeping themselves from drifting backwards. He watched Elizabeth beach her green boat in the shallows on the far side and crawl out of sight. It was safe to nap for a few hours until the tide turned again.

Crash Site

At first, Jasin's unfocused eyes weren't sure what he was looking at—moving shapes silhouetted against a bright background. Membomba lay close by, crumbled and wedged between the shuttle's controls and his pilot's seat. The confusing scene played out above the old engineer in the large view port, bodies, crowding, peering in.

"Henri!" Jasin stumbled over and carefully inspected Membomba. A purple welt had formed above the engineer's right eye. Other than that, there was no other sign of distress. He must have knocked himself out, Jasin thought. "Henri...wake up."

Grasping Membomba's hands he was able to pull the unconscious engineer away from the seats and the unwanted audience and to an open spot on the floor just in front of a small interior door. For the first time since entering the shuttle he noticed the air inside the cabin had a different smell to it and he took a deep breath. It was quite soothing. Touching a metal plate on the door's frame opened a supply room. Perhaps he could find something to put under Membomba's head. The room was large enough to house half a dozen people. There was a small dining area with rows of numbered bins and lockers. Beyond that were several bunks and he took one of the small pillows for Membomba. Suddenly an irritating alarm began to pulsate from the control room and he hurried back to see what might have set it off. He scanned the monitors and control surfaces in vain.

"What's the damn problem?" groaned Membomba.

"How would I know?"

"Whoa…" said Membomba, laying back again after trying to raise himself. "Come give me a hand. That noise is going to split my head open."

Jasin helped him over to the pilot's seat. Membomba touched a few glowing shapes on the flat surface in front of him and the alarm fell silent. "How long have we had company?" he asked, barely looking up at the faces not two meters away.

Jasin shrugged.

"Well, they are trying to get in using the Exodus code and are setting off the perimeter warning."

"How?"

"Don't worry. I had to dump all the presets and mission programming back in the cavern before taking off. I didn't have time to set up new codes for the door or anything else for that matter."

"But…"

"Listen kid, I'm sure they were observing that panel from every angle back there. You were being played."

"For months I'm afraid. Damn, I'm stupid."

"You won't get any argument from me." Membomba quickly went through a series of diagnostic screens, and then changed the control grid in front of him and brought up the cockpit illumination, darkening the main view port at the same time. "Whatever you're planning young Elstrada, don't count on using this useless piece of crap. It's not moving until the thruster cowling and servos are repaired, which on this snowball means never."

"That's just fine. It doesn't need to go anywhere. Do you still think you can booby trap this thing?"

"As long as it doesn't have to move."

Jasin shook his head. "We will need two codes for the door—one to open and one to detonate…and a silent dead man's switch. If we don't disarm it, I want this thing to destroy itself in four days."

Membomba shook his head sadly as he set about entering the desired programming. "It's a shame you know—giving the shuttle up again now that the natives are showing their true colors. There's a lot here, even if she doesn't fly. These Eians, they're not like the others. They don't care what the natives say. They'll just go on using whatever technology they please. Won't make much difference to an old man like me, but you'll be raising that kid of yours under their control. Write it down, you'll see." When he finished, he showed Jasin how to disarm the failsafe and stop the countdown. "And here are the two codes for the door," he said, pointing to the monitor.

"What, no mythological references?"

"Don't know any mythology."

"Neither do I."

They sat quietly for some time, contemplating what was bound to occur once they left the shuttle and walked into the Eian's hands. If the towan had seen the shuttle's flight and sent a boat to investigate, they could all be headed back home as early as tomorrow. If the Sytonians didn't show up, they'd be at the mercy of the Eians. He just hoped they valued the shuttle more than a couple humans.

"Do you want to take something along for the pain? There's a medicine kit back with the supplies." Membomba asked somberly.

"Sorry?"

"I'm thinking ahead. I'm just not a big fan of pain and I don't suppose they will be too gentle."

Jasin recalled Jorge Wynosk's tortured grimace and knew the Eians wouldn't make the deal for his mother without exhausting all other possibilities. "No, I don't suppose they will."

Beloit woke with a start. He'd been sleeping soundly when his inner alarm catapulted him into alertness. Elizabeth's gilia boat was nearly out of sight down river and he hastened to catch up to it. At a brisk walk he could barely keep up with the current, so he found himself jogging and, when the terrain allowed, running.

After fifteen minutes, he was once again even with the three floating heads and at least a hundred meters above the level of the water. There was no established path along the bluff edge and it broke and fell away often. As he cautiously rounded a curve, Soto Harbor, the forbidden town, came into view.

He had traveled near the harbor only once, while pursuing an errant trader, but he was turned back and chastised by several towan who intercepted him just outside the town. He hadn't thought much about the Prohibition against visiting Soto Harbor. Mentally he had grouped it with the seventh, and since using or owning a boat wasn't ever a desire or concern, he never was particularly curious about a town whose main purpose was maintaining a harbor full of the things. Still, when he could spare a moment from watching his footing and the gilia heads below, he stole glances across the river. The harbor held at least ten single-towan fishing boats like the ones he often saw in Bistoun, and four mammoth vessels that must have been capable of carrying several dozen towan.

Suddenly he was thrown to the ground.

Towering above him, only partially blocking the glare of the evening sun stood a towan, his cylith curled up beside him. The native spoke, but Beloit could not understand a word. He tried explaining his presence, pointing at the floating gilia heads and mimicking the flight of the shuttle. Except for Elizabeth's "boat" the towan showed little interest or understanding. The native reached down, grabbed Beloit's shirt, stood him up, and then pushing Beloit, they proceeded to a small promontory at the very end of the bluff. The vantage point was perfect for keeping watch over the entire mouth of the Andoree, and the boat harbor beyond. Off in the distance Beloit could see the faint outline of an island. It had to be Jasin's mysterious Hadrious. There was no doubt now where the gilia heads were going or where the shuttle had been heading.

The native uncovered a large mirrored surface and flashed a signal across the river. Within minutes a boat left the harbor and headed straight for them.

By the time dimness returned, Beloit was in Soto Harbor, imprisoned and asleep for the night in a small locker with only a few salted fish for company. The next brightening brought an old friend.

"Avram trusted you to enforce the Prohibitions, not to break them," said Sy Lang, in his near perfect Human.

"I'm not sure whether I'm happy to see you or not," said Beloit. "You were going to kill me for murdering Sy Toberry the last time we met."

"I understand that may have been premature. We will just have to find another reason to kill you...such as trespassing in the Kull."

"I thought you were busy removing heads in Cernai."

"And this morning I am here. Do you know who was inside the gilia head you pointed out to the sentinel?"

"I do. But that is unimportant. You must invade Hadrious. Jasin and the shuttle are there."

"You are a liar. Jasin was unsuccessful in salvaging the machine. It is in the lake again. Many saw it rise and sink. But your knowledge of Hadrious is most disturbing."

"Your *ignorance* is most disturbing. There is no time to waste. The Eians have been manipulating both our races and hiding powerful weapons and technology."

"We have heard this claim from Avram's son. We have searched Hadrious. There is no evidence."

"That you can find. This time it will be different. I didn't lie to you about Sy Toberry and you must trust me now."

"Then tell me, who was in the gilia head?"

"It was Elizabeth Tournell, Jasin 's companion."

"The tall one?"

Beloit nodded.

"Why would she go to Hadrious?"

"For the same reason you should. She is following two Eians; she is following Jasin and the shuttle. Why else would she risk her life crossing the water? If we invade Hadrious immediately and with enough force that she feels safe, she'll probably come forward and join us. Hopefully she'll have discovered how the Eians have stayed hidden. Even I can tell you how they travel to and from the island. That's something you have missed for decades. You can not take the chance that the shuttle falls, or perhaps at this point, remains in Eian hands."

"Then, if you know so much, tell me why Jasin has taken the machine to Hadrious?"

"I'm not certain. He thinks his mother is on Hadrious, a prisoner of the Eians. Perhaps he is looking for her."

Rescue

Elizabeth abandoned the cramped quarters of her gilia head by leaning back against an inside wall and rotating the axis of her slimy little boat until the open lip submerged and she slipped into the water. Hiding behind the partially filled head, she waited as Eidorf and Eiton secured their gilia and swam to shore. Elizabeth allowed plenty of time before following from a safe distance.

After months of thinking about Hadrious, imagining what and where it might be and plotting how they might rescue Julian, finally setting foot on the forbidden land was certainly anticlimactic. Elizabeth didn't know what she had expected—weapon fire, throngs of curious Eians, maybe negotiations—slinking up the muddy embankment on her stomach and furtively following a couple Eians was not one of the options she had thought of.

The path from the water's edge was well traveled, but as it was quite a distance from any populated area, and would have appeared to be headed toward the water's edge, any Sytonian inspection party would have overlooked it, as she would certainly have under different circumstances.

The two Eians passed fields of sweet melon and an old deserted stone quarry. Elizabeth stayed far behind and out of sight. After ten minutes, the path began to parallel a smelly pit filled with rotting vegetables and fish remains. It was fed by a fetid canal, an open sewer or garbage drain, which appeared to bring refuge from the town just ahead. Eiton and

Eidorf stopped beside it to converse. Caught off guard, she froze and looked around in desperation for someplace to hide. Even though she was far behind, the only place was inside the pit and she dove for cover.

Her eyes watered and she fought her natural reflex to gag. Forcing herself to stay calm and breathe through her mouth, she watched as Eidorf took a few steps toward the canal and disappeared from her view. Eiton left the path, heading the other way across the open field to their left. Had they seen her? A shiver ran up her spine and she swiveled around to see if someone was behind her. Her imagination was getting the best of her. Relax, she told herself.

Covered in slime, Elizabeth emerged from the garbage pit and cautiously crept forward. Eiton was halfway across the field and hadn't looked back. Eidorf was just gone, either having gone into the pit or into the water. Elizabeth walked along the edge of the pit. There was no conspicuous hatch or opening, no crevice, hole, or entrance into the rotting compost. She circled the pit, and then stood at the edge of the rubbish watching the water flow toward her, delivering more clippings and vegetable shavings. The trash simply merged with the pile, all perfectly normal, except something was amiss. Something she just couldn't put her finger on. The water and refuse flowed into the pit. The garbage stayed, but the water...just disappeared.

How could the canal continue to bring garbage if there was no outlet for the water? There was only one place the water could disappear, the same place the Eidorf must have gone—underground.

She hesitated, feeling anger over her indecision. Which of them should she follow? Following Eidorf made more sense, but what if the water passage was too small for her frame or too far underneath? Why would the Eians make it any larger than it needed to be for them? No, it wouldn't be large enough for a towan to enter and she was nearly the same size. She pictured herself trapped underwater against some spillway or tiny opening trying to fight the current, running out of air. It was suicide. Even if she made it through the water, she'd be entering the underground without knowing anything. For all she knew it was a trap.

Turning away from the canal she followed Eiton. The light was failing, but the path through the scrub was obvious and she hurried to catch up.

Dimness gradually fell across the sparse landscape, but she could still hear Eiton moving ahead of her and she let her ears direct her. The ground rose. The quiet soil gave way to loose gravel. Fearing detection, she hung back, creeping up a long gentle incline. Eiton crested the ridge, becoming silhouetted from a light source just over the hill before descending out of sight.

She crouched as low as she could manage and waited. Conversation and the sounds of activity drifted over the ridge. Curiosity overcame fear and she crept forward on her stomach until she could peer out from the ridge to the plane beyond.

Under blinding artificial lights and surrounded by a dozen of busy technicians, sat the shuttle, embedded in a sculpted swirl of dirt. Eiton huddled over the damaged aft left thruster conferring with several others who were taking measurements with various instruments. Nearby, crates of supplies were being stacked. There was no question they intended to fix the shuttle as quickly as possible and head for Eian just as Eiton had told her during his brief visit on the mountainside in Nova Gaia.

Elizabeth scanned the area for signs of Jasin and Membomba. For the first time since the skirmish in the Eian cavern, she became concerned for them. Once they controlled the shuttle and all its power, she had always assumed they would be fine, never considering that they may have crashed or been forced to give it up, but that was exactly what the scene below conveyed.

Finding a comfortable position from which to watch, exhaustion fought to overcome her. Nearly twenty hours had elapsed since catching that brief nap on the shore and before that…Elizabeth could hardly remember the last full night's sleep, but she worried that Eiton might leave while she slept. He was the key to finding Julian, she was sure of that. In the foothills, when she had first talked to him, he admitted to being fond of Julian. He would return to her. If she stayed awake, he would lead her there.

It was fortunate she had forsaken sleep, for within an hour of arriving, Eiton left with two others, each carried a glowstick. A single technician remained behind to continue working on the thruster. An armed guard hid in the shadows. Elizabeth briefly considered trying to regain the shuttle, but even if she was able to overcome the two small Eians, she had no way of entering or operating the shuttle. No, it was best to follow Eiton and see if she could find Jasin and the others. Together they could return for the shuttle, but from all the activity she had just witnessed, it would have to be soon.

Torture

The halo's glow encircling Jasin's head intensified sending him into yet another spasm. The taste of blood filled his mouth as he involuntarily bit down on his tongue. Eidorf had given up on the hopeless interrogation. Now, he was just enjoying his vengeance.

"Li'onna and I were paired for over twenty years. You could never appreciate the bond we shared. She was kind, and intelligent, fiercely independent. One of a kind," said Eidorf.

Jasin spat out a mouthful of blood. "She looked like every other towa bitch I ever saw."

Eidorf triggered the halo, this time prolonging the effect. "She wasn't a towa. Towa are slaves, hardly more than property," he said loudly above Jasin's loud groan.

An aid rushed in, glanced at Jasin's contorted body, and waited, assuming Eidorf would release the human, but the halo continued to glow. "What is it?" asked Eidorf.

The aid looked over again at Jasin. "Eiton and the others have returned. You asked to be informed."

Eidorf turned off the halo and Jasin collapsed against his restraints, unconscious, a trickle of urine flowed down his leg. "Get help to take this one back. Let the old man see I am not interested in making deals."

Eidorf left the small room and walked down the cramped corridor to Eiton's workshop. The small engineer was strapping himself into his modeling apparatus. Before him, lay the tablets upon which he had recorded his careful measurements.

"Eiton, were the others correct in their assessment?"

"Yes, a new cowling must be formed and attached. The design is complex and the measurements must be exact, but I can do it. We'll be ready by the brightening. Whether we can enter the craft is still unknown."

"And the supplies?"

"Already there."

"Then we will leave when you are done. This is an exciting time, Eiton. We will be home in just a few days."

"Then you have the new entry code?"

"We each have our individual skills. You manage the repairs."

"It will be done." Eiton said. He lowered his gaze and tightened the brace on his forearm as Eidorf left. If Eidorf wasn't successful he doubted he would be able to penetrate the hull without damaging it. There was going to be some serious persuading to do and he was happy not to have to witness it. Hopefully, Eidorf realized they needed the older, wrinkled male alive.

Eidorf left the imaging hall, and proceeded into the central node. He paused a moment, deciding between the seven radiating tunnels, then followed a smaller unpaved one to its end. The small cell where the old woman had been kept was empty. He hurriedly retraced his steps and barged back into Eiton's design station. "I was under the impression that you were keeping the old woman alive."

Eiton carefully extracted the microscopic probe from the seed formation dish. How dare he interrupt him when he was in the middle of such a delicate procedure? Eidorf never understood anything outside his immediate view, outside his own desires. Uncoupling from the eyepiece, Eiton turned to his superior. "Respectfully sir, it was your wish that the woman be disposed of."

"I know you were delaying. Where are you keeping her?"

"Now you have need for her? I thought you wanted her dead." Eiton knew he was close to insubordination, yet he enjoyed whenever his decisions proved Eidorf's irrational ones wrong. He could sense, however, that this wasn't the time to gloat. "I moved her to the older residence section. She is not a danger to us and understands her situation."

"I didn't ask for an explanation."

"No sir. You intend to take her with us? I believe she could still prove to be helpful. She may not have known about the shuttle's existence, but I believe she may know more about the shuttle's operation than she has let on."

"Who comes with us will be my decision. Return to your work. You have delayed me long enough."

Eidorf found Julian focused on a bright cheerful watercolor she was painting from memory. She turned to face him. He glanced about her room. Aside from the painting supplies, he noticed a variety of tablets and personal items. She had evidently been rather persuasive when it came to making herself comfortable.

"You're hair has grown back nicely."

She stared coldly at Eidorf. "Are you here to change that?"

"Your son has delivered your spacecraft to Hadrious."

"My son is here…on Hadrious?"

"He wants to trade it for your release, but there is no reason to trust him."

"His offer is misguided and foolish. May I see him?"

"Why would I allow that? Eidorf walked over to a stack of tablets and looked through them. They were for Eian children. "Are you learning Eian?" he asked, using his own language.

"I like to read," she answered in his tongue. "These are young books."

"These are books for children," he corrected, then switching back to Human, "Eiton says you might know about the machine."

Julian shrugged. "I don't know the entry code, I've told you that many times before. May I see my son?" she asked again.

"I think until this is over I need all you humans in one spot. Come with me."

He led her back to a small dank room. The walls were unfinished stone, as if they had just stopped excavating. Jasin lay unconscious on the gravel floor. Blood trickled from his mouth and down his chin. A cloth cushioned his head. Membomba, shirtless, struggled to his feet to greet her.

"Damn you Eidorf!" Julian said, kneeling next to her son. "Leave us. I will see what I can find out."

Eidorf hesitated, unaccustomed to receiving such direct orders from a female. Regaining command, he warned, "Either we gain access to the spacecraft tomorrow or one of you will die. Your son killed my wife. Don't think I am not serious. It would please me to have him witness the death of his mother. Only having him watch the death of his mate would please me more." At the mention of Jasin's mate, Julian looked up at the Eian, but Eidorf was already leaving.

Membomba looked at Julian. "Ma'am, I'm so very sorry, but—"

Julian put a finger to her mouth silencing him. She rose and hugged the old engineer whispering, "They can see and hear everything." She released him and stood back. "Henri Membomba, you old geezer. You smell like a sewer and look even worse. What have you been doing all these years?"

"Traipsing about this cracked snowball with nothing but my blaython and my charm." He leaned in, covered his mouth, and whispered, "The shuttle was damaged. We've set it to—"

She backed away. "No don't tell me anything you don't want them to find out. I am too frail."

"You look fine to me. I am sorry about Avram. I saw him at Hyland's funeral. He looked healthy enough...I guess you never know."

"We're all getting old, I'm afraid. Now let's see if we can rouse Jasin. There is much I need to know."

Membomba, having just been admonished not to tell her anything, looked puzzled. Julian smiled. "How is it that our captor knows more about the love life of my son than his mother?"

Elizabeth was heartened to see the towans arrive. She had been staying out of sight at the edge of town, spying on the comings and goings of the residents, trying to discover where they were keeping Jasin and the rest of the humans. Seeing the towan approach rekindled a hope that had been burning low. They must have left the mainland before the brightening to have made it here so early in the day, she surmised. The natives of Soto Harbor must have had even a better angle to see where the shuttle had landed. But what really surprised her was seeing Beloit with them. Was he along to arrest and punish Jasin? To help rescue Julian? To help retrieve the shuttle? After Beloit's role in destroying the woman's colony and the massacre in Cernai, considering his trial and eventual escape on Mount Schtolin, the Enforcer's position, his legal status, even his allegiance, were big unknowns.

The towan and McMaster moved into the village as an organized phalanx. She shadowed them, moving through the bushes and scrub, staying out of sight. The Enforcer continually surveyed the horizon looking for something or someone, but Elizabeth stayed well hidden, seeing no advantage in exposing herself. Perhaps the time would come when she needed help. But could she trust him? She knew she couldn't trust the towan leading the group. The last time she saw Sy Lang in Cernai, he had presided over such atrocities she thought murder was the least he deserved. The towan stayed close together in the town center as if fearing an ambush. A few Eians went about their business as if this were commonplace. Others congregated in small groups looking on. Elizabeth hid inside a grain mill waiting for something to happen. The towans also waited. For what, Elizabeth had no idea.

After a few minutes, Beloit conferred with Sy Lang then left the group, and headed back into the countryside. Elizabeth climbed higher inside the mill to watch as he walked off by himself. This was mighty strange, but she decided it would be safer confronting him alone than surrounded by his towan friends. If he got out of line…she reached down and felt the reassuring presence of her thin blade.

"Why are you here?" Elizabeth demanded.

"Elizabeth, you startled me." Beloit feigned surprise.

"I doubt that. Answer the question."

"Looking for you, actually. Have you found where they are hiding?"

"Who?" She looked around cautiously.

"We don't have time to play this game Elizabeth. Jasin could be in trouble."

"Of course he's in trouble. We all are in trouble, as much from that monster you're with, as anyone. What are you doing with Sy Lang?"

"You will have to believe me. He's here to help. If you know how the Eians come and go, or where they are hiding Jasin and the others, you have to tell us."

Elizabeth hated Sy Lang. The thought of trusting Jasin's future...everyone's future to him seemed preposterous, but she needed the towans and was hoping they would arrive. But now seeing Sy Lang, she wasn't sure. "If I tell you, you've got to promise me you won't let Lang hurt any of them."

"Sy Lang isn't the enemy, Eidorf is. Lang is only interested in stopping the Eians and destroying the shuttle, the same as you and I. They need to know where they go when they disappear from the village."

Elizabeth took a deep breath. It was a leap of faith to be sure, but what other choice did she have. "Follow me."

Eidorf

The body of the first towan to squeeze into the stairwell Elizabeth pointed out had to be removed in pieces. Fighting on using the Eian nerve weapon obtained in the trade with Mas, Sy Lang and Beloit soon established a foothold in the subterranean corridor. The zeal and animosity with which the towans infiltrated the Eian underground scared Elizabeth, who pleaded with Sy Lang not to forget that the shuttle's importance, and those that were still being held prisoner.

"If the Eian's succeed in controlling the shuttle, they will dictate the outcome of this conflict whether we win here or not. We need to guard the shuttle," she reminded him. After her third plea, Sy Lang finally relented.

"Do you know exactly where it is?" he asked her.

"Don't you?"

"Your Enforcer suggested we come directly to the city. He felt you would be here and that it would be beneficial to find you first. It seems that it has. But now, if you'd like to take some of the—"

"I won't leave without Jasin and the rest. I didn't come here to protect a piece of metal."

"You are the one who believes we must guard the shuttle at all cost."

"You don't need me to do that."

"They could be headed there now. There must be a back door to this complex."

Elizabeth knew he was right. She had watched Eidorf disappear into the garbage pit. For all they knew, Jasin and the rest may not even be here. Still, it took all of her self-discipline to abandon the immediate search for Jasin, turn around, and along with several towans and captured energy weapons, hurry to the spacecraft.

Amid alarms and confusion, Eiton and Eidorf scrambled to collect their crew and the new thruster cowling.

"Which of the humans should we take?" asked Eiton, knowing the logical answer. But he had never seen Eidorf so upset and couldn't guess what his superior was thinking. They rushed through the tunnels as Eidorf ranted.

"Reports from the surface say the tall woman exposed us. I will kill her myself. I'll tear out her insides and let Jasin watch. Bring them *all* to the surface. We'll use them as shields, and then kill them. When we return with our fleet, we will finish the rest of their horrid race, and then it will be the towans turn. We will finally cleanse this planet of all these parasites."

They burst into the cell holding the humans. The sound of the alarms filtered into the room behind them. Three sets of eyes focused on the Eian leader.

"Come with us now or die here," Eidorf threatened.

"Troubles?" Jasin asked sarcastically. Membomba tried to hide a weak grin.

"We don't need you, Elstrada, or your mother for that matter, so if you want this cell to be the last thing you see, I'd be happy to oblige you. I'd have thought you'd want to see your mate one last time...but no matter." He raised his weapon to Jasin's chest.

"Where are we going?" Julian asked, defusing the situation.

"Out," Eidorf demanded.

Forcing the humans ahead, Eidorf followed with his weapon aimed at their backs. Two technicians joined them in the hallway carrying the blue cowling. Limping along as fast as he could, Eiton brought up the rear. Sound of distant blaster discharges echoed through the tunnels and soon the air was filled with smoke. "They must have found the ventilation shafts," mumbled Eiton.

Rushing on in silence, they finally came to a metal stairway next to a narrow water sluice where the smoky air became putrid.

"Sewer," commented Membomba.

"Up," Eidorf demanded, prodding Jasin in the ribs. "In there."

Jasin, Membomba, and Julian moved into an enclosed section of the sluice with several doors. "Listen carefully," Eidorf said to Eiton and his staff. There isn't enough room in the water lock so we will surface in teams. I will go ahead, then send up the humans, those carrying the cowling go next, Eiton you bring everyone else. We will regroup before proceeding to the shuttle." He turned and threatened the humans. "I warn you not to give me reason to harm you."

Eidorf entered the water lock and sealed the high entry door. He then swung the lower hatch into the flow of the water, which sealed itself against the lower chamber, causing the water lock to fill. It took just a few seconds and then Eidorf opened the main hatch overhead and swam from the chamber. He kicked his way to the surface and waited for the humans to follow.

Eidorf's assistant reset the water lock. "Get in," he demanded.

"There must be another way," complained Membomba. "I don't swim."

"Neither do I," said Julian.

"Just hold your breath and kick for the surface. After coming this far to save you, you don't think I'll let you drown now." said Jasin smiling. His joke broke the tension and they all stepped into the water lock. Jasin pulled the outer entrance door closed. "Don't panic. Everything will be all right," he said, securing the lower hatch. The garbage-strewn water rose around them. "It's a lot warmer than the Andoree," remarked Jasin with a wink. Julian squeezed his hand. "Breath deep!" he warned.

"Do we have to," joked Membomba, his eyes tearing from the fumes of the sewer.

Jasin opened the upper hatch and they pushed off and kicked towards the surface. Jasin helped them to the side of the canal and crawled up to wait for the others with Eidorf. Jasin predicted difficulty with the heavy cowling, but they were able to slowly walk it up the canal wall without any difficulty. He marveled at the Eian's ability to stay submerged for extended periods.

Half an hour later they were on the ridge looking down at the shuttle.

"Damn you Hyland," Julian muttered under her breath. But Jasin was thrilled. His heart swelled when he saw Elizabeth, looking unharmed, standing with six towan. Each of them held a blaster.

"What happens now?" asked Membomba.

"I'll tell you what happens now," said Jasin. He turned to Eidorf. "I'll give you the entry code you'll need to enter. Go to Eian if that's what you truly want. We'll return to the mainland with the towans. I came for my mother. The shuttle means nothing to us. Leave us Humans and the Sytonians to work things out here in the gorge. Build your fleet of ships on Eian if you're able, then come back and take your people home. The alternative is for a lot of us to die here today. You have two blasters. I count seven guarding the shuttle. You do the math."

Eiton looked at Eidorf for direction. "He makes sense, Eidorf. Why take any chances?"

But Eidorf hardly listened to his engineer. His eyes narrowed and you could sense the anger behind them. "Jasin...what did you call Li'onna, a towa bitch? Well, I don't think we're quite even. Your bitch still lives and she's brought ruin on my people. I have another idea. I will give you a chance to save yourself. Go back to the village. Leave us the code; we won't follow you. Take your mother and go. Join the others who are destroying Hadrious. But your mate is mine. It's a good trade. Consider it just retribution, payment for murdering Li'onna."

"You aren't serious," cried Julian.

Jasin walked up to stand before Eidorf. "Listen carefully. Don't make a mistake here. The women leave with the towan…*all* the woman. If you want revenge, I'll stay with you. I killed Li Sy."

"Don't you dare use that towa name. She was Eian. Her name was Li'onna." Eidorf glanced at Julian, then Elizabeth. "I've changed my mind. None of you are going home." He motioned to his one of the Eians who had carried the cowling. Stepping forward, the assistant handed his blaster to another and walked down the hill towards the shuttle. Elizabeth and the towans trained their weapons on the tiny approaching figure.

"According to Li'onna, you and your friend saw how this works in the Kull," said Eidorf. The Eian got within fifty meters of the shuttle before stopping. He knelt down, his hand dropped to the ground and—

The six towan collapsed in agony. A couple of seconds later they were dead. The Eian turned and began to run back to the ridge when suddenly he fell forward. Smoke rose from the hole in his back where Elizabeth's blaster shot had hit him.

Eidorf motioned everyone to proceed to the shuttle. "The math, as you say, has just improved. Let's see how much death your mate can endure?"

Elizabeth watched them approach. Quickly, she gathered up the blasters and hid behind the shuttle. The suddenness of the towan deaths had stunned her. If they could kill them all like that…she looked around in desperation. One of them with a blaster moved off to find a better angle, while a second armed Eian hid behind the humans, using them as shields. If she fired first, she might be lucky again and get the one that had separated, but…they had plenty of replacements.

"Call her over," said Eidorf.

"Never," replied Jasin.

"Do you think she is interested in watching you die?"

"You think that will soften her up?" Jasin managed a nervous laugh.

Eidorf pointed the blaster at Membomba, and then thought better of it, swinging it over towards Julian.

Jasin saw his chance and leapt for Eidorf, knocking the blaster to the ground. As he reached for it, the Eians dropped the heavy cowling they had been holding on his forearm.

Even Elizabeth could hear his bones snap and his involuntary scream of pain. Eidorf took advantage and kicked him in the face. Blood gushed from Jasin's nose. Elizabeth forgot herself and rose to see. A blaster shot clipped the antenna array over her head.

"Enough of this," declared Julian. "Henri, open the shuttle for them. If we keep this up, we'll all be dead, and they'll have it anyway."

"No!" Jasin cried out. "First call off the other blaster. Allow Elizabeth to safely join us here," he begged.

Eidorf agreed.

"I'll get her, and open it myself." Jasin staggered to his feet. Supporting his broken arm, he stumbled toward the shuttle.

Confused, Elizabeth cautiously met Jasin halfway. She tenderly wiped the blood from his face. "What's going on?"

"I love you," he replied, letting his head fall upon her chest. "Go, take care of Julian. I promised them I would open the shuttle." His eyes had trouble focusing on her. He was dizzy and staggered forward.

"Let Membomba do it. I have to set your arm…and your nose or they won't heal right."

Jasin managed a crooked smile and shook his head. "It doesn't matter. It's time to end this and get on."

Elizabeth was about to object, but he was no longer there with her. He stared off in the distance, took a couple of wobbly steps toward the shuttle, and passed out.

The humans rushed to join Elizabeth, who stooped to care for Jasin. Eidorf barked orders and Eiton and his crew set to work attaching the new cowling.

Julian took control. "Henri, open her up. We need to get at the medical supplies." She turned to Eidorf. "As much as I hate to say it, you've won. Membomba and I will get you to Eian and help you build your ships. There is technology aboard this shuttle Eiton will never figure out without us. Membomba is a good engineer and pilot, and I can help as well, but the two young ones stay here. With his broken arm, Jasin will be worthless and she is going to have a child—both damaged goods. You don't need either one. Once we tend to his injuries we can take off. I give you my word."

"Open it up then," said Eidorf.

Membomba walked towards the hatch. "Stop there a moment," said Eidorf. "Eiton, you and your men step away from the shuttle." He stepped back a couple dozen meters as well. "Now you may proceed."

Membomba walked to the keypad and entered the proper code. With all of them in close proximity destroying the shuttle meant too great a sacrifice. The hatch swung open and the Eians returned. Eidorf walked to the shuttle and timidly stuck his head in. The interior lights turned on. He stepped in and looked around. Eiton was right behind him.

"Julian's plan is a good outcome. More than we had hoped for," said Eiton. "The old ones will be more valuable and less trouble."

"How much longer for the repairs?" asked Eidorf.

"Just a few minutes. You were smart to bury the perimeter field." Eiton left to help load the supplies.

Eidorf continued his inspection of the shuttle. Finally, he walked to the open hatch and beckoned for Membomba. "You will teach Eiton everything." Membomba nodded. "Bring Jasin here. You may use the medical supplies."

Membomba left and walked over to join Elizabeth and Julian. "He wants you to treat Jasin inside the shuttle."

"Not a chance," whispered Julian. "Elizabeth, you must take Jasin away immediately. Eidorf has no intention of letting you go."

"What about the medical supplies?"

"Go now, you'll make do without. Henri and I will try to stop them, but—"

It was too late. Two Eians approached. Each grabbed one of Jasin's legs and dragged him to the entrance of the shuttle where Eidorf stepped outside to chastise them. "I said, treat him inside."

Elizabeth rushed over to Jasin, bent down, and gently lifted him up. Without saying a word she turned away from

Eidorf and the shuttle, and began walking away. Suddenly the ground erupted in a shower of dirt and rock as a blaster discharge blew a crater a meter wide just to her right. She hesitated a second, then without looking back, she took another step. A second blast sent chunks of broken stone into the calves of her legs. Bleeding, but still holding Jasin, she stumbled forward and fell to her knees.

"The next one will take your head off," yelled Eidorf. It was a statement of fact, completely devoid of emotion or subterfuge...and she believed him.

The Eians took Jasin and dumped him in a corner of the cockpit. They tied Elizabeth's hands together behind her back, and then secured her to a bulkhead where Eidorf could keep an eye on her. He sent Julian and the rest of the Eians into the supply room. Membomba busied himself with pre-flight and Eiton's orientation.

"Just so you are aware," said Membomba, "this is going to be a one-way flight."

"Explain yourself," demanded Eidorf.

Membomba pointed at a panel. "For thirty years this shuttle has been working off a single fuel load. It has made a dozen trips delivering humans and our supplies to Syton, it has risen countless times from the bottom of the lake, not to mention our little side trip here. I would say that after this fully loaded take-off, and landing on Eian...well, let's hope we don't have to make too many mid-flight course corrections or even a safe landing is questionable."

"That is for you and Eiton to worry about. Get on with it."

Lift-off proceeded without a hitch, the new thruster cowling performed well and within minutes they left the great Syton gorge, cleared the atmosphere and achieved escape velocity. Membomba cut the engines. Silence replaced the deafening roar. "Well that's it. Time to sit back and enjoy the view." said Membomba

Eiton looked at one of the readouts. "I don't understand. Why not continue to accelerate. At this rate..." Eiton did the calculation in his head. "At this rate it will take nearly two days to get there."

Membomba nodded in admiration. "Not bad. You did that in your head? Actually..." He leaned forward changing the display in front of him. "Forty-five point seven hours."

"Answer his question," demanded Eidorf.

"We'll need every joule we have left to set her down safely."

From behind them came the sound of Elizabeth throwing up. The smell of vomit filled the cockpit. Membomba shrugged. "Weightlessness has that affect on humans. It takes some getting used to. I'll clean it up." He unbuckled and floated effortlessly to a supply closet in the back of the cabin. He rummaged about for a moment until he found what he was looking for, then grabbed a portable vacuum and began sucking up the floating mess, moving closer to Elizabeth as he worked. Finally, he took a cloth to wipe her mouth, casually slipping his free hand surreptitiously behind her to brace himself. With this hidden hand, he cut her free from the bulkhead. The orientation of his body covered his actions. It took just seconds and he floated back and replaced the vacuum, slipping the utility knife into his pocket.

"Nothing to it. Happens all the time," he said, dropping into his seat.

The noisy vacuum had awakened Jasin, who groaned and opened his eyes. "You lying bastard," he cursed, when he realized where he was.

Eidorf undid his harness and awkwardly made his way over to him. He pushed his weight down on Jasin's swollen arm. Jasin grunted and shoved the Eian away with his good hand. Flailing and out of control, Eidorf sailed across the cabin and slammed into the bulkhead. Elizabeth couldn't help herself and laughed. She knew it was stupid and clamped her lips together. She diverted her eyes, looking across at Jasin instead. He greeted her with a pained smile.

Eidorf regained control and maneuvered to the center of the cabin. "Eiton, take our friend the pilot into the other cabin with the old woman. Guard them and don't return until I call for you."

Eiton hesitated. "I'm sure I can be more help here. Membomba could—"

"Do as I say. Take a blaster with you and don't turn your back on any of the humans."

"I really should stay," Membomba protested.

Motioning towards Jasin, Eidorf added, "And Eiton, now that he's awake, bind him."

Eiton moved very carefully, found some plastic straps in the utility locker behind the vacuum and bound Jasin's feet together. He looked at Jasin's deformed forearm and hesitated. It was turning purple. Jasin glared at the small Eian. Uncertain, Eiton looked back at Eidorf.

Something felt wrong here. He fixed things. He was an Engineer and he knew Eidorf too well.

"Is the job too difficult for you?" asked Eidorf.

"His arm…"

"That is no concern of yours. Bind him."

Eiton reached across and gently lifted the broken arm. Jasin flinched and drew a sharp breath. Eiton looked into Jasin's eyes, then back at Eidorf, hesitating. Finally he made a decision and loosely wrapped the straps around Jasin's arms, pretending to fasten them tightly.

Grabbing the blaster, Eidorf directed Membomba and Julian into the storage room. He waited until Eiton sealed the door to the supply room behind him.

"All alone. I've waited a long time for this," Eidorf began. "You two have been trouble from the beginning…well, almost the beginning." He moved in closer to Elizabeth. "Remember our first meeting at the lake? I do."

Elizabeth squirmed. She was free of the bulkhead, but her hands were still tied behind her.

"I wonder if…" He reached between her thighs.

Instinctively, she butted his head with hers. He was driven to the floor, but he stood up holding her knife. Jasin tried to stand, but ended up floating at a weird angle. He steadied himself, slowly working his hands free. The pain was excruciating.

Eidorf held the blade at his eye level, admiring it. "Truly one of Eiton's most graceful designs." He placed the tip at the top of her blouse between her breasts and glanced over to Jasin. "Your females and their clothes. Why do you allow it?" He applied pressure and began slowly drawing the razor-sharp blade down. Elizabeth gasped. "I wouldn't move if I were you," Eidorf warned. A thin, red line of blood began to seep into the cut edges of her blouse as he sliced down through the fabric and her skin. Elizabeth gritted her teeth, bravely bearing the pain, afraid that any movement would drive the blade deeper. When Eidorf got to her belly he stopped, lifted her blouse, and turned to Jasin. "Do you want to see if she carries a son? The woman in Bistoun did."

He pushed the knife until a centimeter disappeared into her belly. Blood streamed out, and floated away. Elizabeth was frozen. If she moved he would slice her open with one stroke.

"You sick bastard," cried Jasin.

"You call me sick?" screamed Eidorf. "That mutant Toberry was sick. Loeton was sick. To mate with another species is disgusting. And the female enjoyed it! I did your kind a favor killing her. She was a perverted whore, just like this one. Li'onna told me about her and Loeton. And now she's going to die, and you are going to watch me cut her apart as you did to my Li'onna."

Elizabeth screamed and Jasin pushed off the bulkhead with his feet, freeing his hands as he sailed at Eidorf. The Eian pulled the knife from Elizabeth and turned just as Jasin made contact. The alien blade sliced through Jasin's sternum and heart like paper, and jammed in a rib. His momentum wrenched the knife from Eidorf's grasp. Spinning, Jasin bounced off a bulkhead then smashed into the door of supply cabin before finally coming to rest, floating face down.

The door slid open. Eidorf turned to see Julian standing over her son. Behind her, Eiton and Membomba each held blasters trained on the other Eians. Elizabeth quickly lifted her feet, and slipped her tied hands in front of her.

Julian reached out and tenderly turned Jasin over. She gasped. Blood gushed from his chest forming crimson globules that floated off. Jasin's lifeless eyes stared up in surprise.

The knife had snapped in two. The stub of the blade that projected from his rib began to deform, leaving a blob of blue metal that mixed with the red of his blood. The handle that held the seed floated nearby and, with what little metal it still contained, was reshaping itself into a miniature knife. Julian reached out and with two fingers cautiously picked the tiny blade out of the air. Her eyes narrowed as she stared at Eidorf with hatred.

"Be careful you don't prick your fingers," teased Eidorf.

She turned toward Jasin, hesitating, and then with the utmost care, she placed the tip of the small blade into the blue metal in her son's chest. The knife grew in her hand. She pulled it out and looked back at Eidorf, who glanced frantically about the cabin for a weapon. The blaster lay between the command chairs.

Before Eidorf could move, Elizabeth slipped her arms around his neck. He twisted around, struggling to free himself, but she held his head firmly, pressing his face into her bleeding chest. Julian sailed across the room, coming to rest behind the squirming Eian. While Elizabeth held his head still, Julian slid the thin stiletto into the base of his skull and up into his brain.

Eian

"Lie still," Julian demanded. "You've got to let me tend that cut."

"I can't, Julian, I just can't believe it." Tears welled up in her red eyes again and she brushed them off. Tears, she had discovered, didn't fall in weightlessness. "I'm sorry, but I can't stop. How can you keep it in? I feel like a blubbering idiot."

"I've never been able to cry in public," Julian said softly. "Do you need to see him again?" Elizabeth shook her head, a few strands of auburn hair clung to her moist cheeks. That wasn't Jasin back there, Elizabeth kept telling herself. She was resolved not to revisit the body again. In death it didn't even look like him.

"Then let me close those cuts, you're still bleeding."

While Julian sealed the cuts with a dermal adhesive, Elizabeth leaned her head back and closed her eyes. She felt so alone. At least Julian could have done is acknowledge her grief, lean over and give her a hug or tender touch. What a cold woman. It was her son. What was wrong with her? "Ouch! Isn't there a disinfectant that doesn't sting?" she complained. "With all the wonderful technology contained in this craft, you'd think there would have been something..." she mused. Her eyelids felt heavy. The sedative and painkillers Julian had given her had begun to work.

"Try to sleep now." Julian gathered the few medical items she had taken from the supply room, then floated back to replace them. Membomba was considerate enough to have strapped Eidorf's corpse onto the most remote bunk so neither Julian nor Elizabeth would have to pass it. Jasin's body lay closer to the door and she drifted to her son's side with practiced grace. His chest was a mess. With care, she repaired the wound as best as she was able, working through misty eyes.

"Julian?"

She wiped away her tears before turning to Membomba. "No one needs to see him that way."

He nodded. "We need to make a few decisions."

"The Eians?"

"They're fine. No trouble. That Eiton is a quick study. It's the fuel situation. I don't know if you heard what I told Eidorf?"

She nodded.

"We don't have a lot of options. This baby was almost out of fuel thirty years ago. We've got maybe one powered landing left if we don't have to maneuver too much and Eiton really doesn't have any idea where to put down."

"The atmosphere?"

"Not great...breathable, worse than Syton."

"What about a return?" Julian asked.

"Slingshot?"

Julian nodded. "Maybe, but there's problems with that too."

"Are you human's thinking of breaking your promise?" asked Eiton, joining the conversation. "Isn't this a decision for us all to make?"

"Just what promise is that?" Membomba sneered.

She signaled Membomba to relax. "We're not keeping anything from you Eiton, just discussing possibilities."

"There is only one logical course of action," Eiton began. "If we use fuel to achieve the proper speed and direction to swing around Eian, and then use more fuel to adjust for a landing on Syton, we won't have enough left to maneuver into the canyon, nor for that matter to make a safe landing. We could end up frozen on the surface of Syton. And if by some miracle we bring the shuttle back, our races will kill each other fighting over it. What have we gained?"

Eiton continued. "We only need to slow our speed and drop down to Eian. We can make fine adjustments and get as close to a city as possible, but the entire surface is habitable. A safe landing is assured. If all goes well, in a couple of years we should be able to generate enough fuel for this vehicle and maybe build our own. When we'll retrieve our people, you can return to Syton if you wish."

"You're dreaming," said Membomba. "You'll never accomplish all that with the few of you aboard."

"You could help," suggested Eiton.

Julian made an effort to smile. "Is Eiton correct? Is that a fair assessment of the situation, Henri?"

Membomba had to admit it was. "Then what is the question? I'm exhausted, my head's spinning, and it doesn't really sound like we have a choice, but you two decide. I don't really care on which of these two moons I leave my bones."

Eiton got his way and the two engineers left to work out details of the Eian landing. Julian returned to her son. Through the open doorway they watched her tenderly clean blood from his face. "She doesn't look very well," said Eiton.

"No, she doesn't, but consider the situation." Membomba sighed. "No parent should have to witness the death of their child."

When Eian aligned to obscure the sun's light, the interior of the shuttle was illuminated solely by the glow of the instruments. Membomba fell asleep in the pilot's seat while Eiton studied and experimented with the instrumentation. The other Eians talked among themselves, while Julian kept watch over Elizabeth. Several times already, Elizabeth had emerged from her drugged sleep thrashing at nightmares and tearing open her wounds. Finally, Julian had given her a double dose of the sedative, which had knocked her out cold, but now Julian had to make sure the poor girl continued to breathe. After a vigilant hour, Julian decided it was safe to get some rest herself.

Half a day later, as Eian loomed large, they prepared to alter their trajectory and begin their descent to their new home.

"We'll slow and fall in from the dark side, so don't expect to see anything until we pass the demarcation," Julian explained to Elizabeth.

"Demarcation?"

"The line between day and night. In the Syton gorge we only experienced relative levels of brightness or dimness. Here on Eian it will be different."

"Hopefully, we can get under the thick clouds in the daylight and do a quick survey of the land in our flight path," said Membomba, busily adjusting the sensors he wanted to bring on line. He fired the thrusters that would slow the shuttle, allowing Eian's gravity to begin pulling them down. "Here we go."

The shuttle slipped into the darkness behind the moon. Only the thin atmosphere, backlit from the sun on the opposite side was visible along the periphery.

"How far into space does the atmosphere extend?" asked Eiton.

"Not far, looks like we'll feel its effects in three or four minutes" answered Membomba.

"Then what causes the stars there to flicker off and on?" Eiton pointed towards the edge of the dark moon."

"Where?" Membomba followed Eiton's direction, and then turned to his instruments. He changed the scale of his readouts and muttered.

Julian became concerned. "Henri?"

"Just a minute, I don't know what...."

Suddenly Julian gasped. "That's impossible," she muttered, closing her eyes as if the sight pained her.

"Impossible? What is it?" Elizabeth asked.

Membomba touched a few colored patches on the control surface and a green line of text blinked and almost immediately several dozen additional lines of smaller text appeared beneath it. "We're synced," he said incredulously.

Julian shook her head in disbelief. "I saw it plunge into the sun myself."

Membomba entered data into a console and received a return string of characters. "You saw what Hyland wanted you to see, what he told you, but what you probably saw was Tanis disappear into the blinding light of the sun."

"I watched it until I couldn't any longer."

"Watched what? Could someone please explain what it is?" asked Eiton.

"It's Tanis, the ship we arrived in," Membomba explained.

Julian rubbed her forehead, then nodded to herself, upset that she hadn't thought of it before. "Why hide a shuttle in a lake, if there's no place to take it?" she murmured. "Can we get to it?"

Without any discussion, Membomba fired the aft thrusters and set a course to intersect with the ship.

"What are you doing? You promised to take us to Eian," cried Eiton.

Membomba swiveled in his chair and glared at the small engineer "We're shortening your plans by years. Now sit back and let me show you what a real ship looks like."

Memorial

Elizabeth removed her left boot, shook out the aggravating pebble, and searched the snow-filled rift for familiar signs. Last time, her brother had led through this disheveled territory, while she had inattentively followed, never dreaming that one day she would want to retrace their steps. Through a thick sock, she massaged her cold, stiff toes, then replaced her boot, and willed herself to move on. But without a clear direction she hesitated and took a few swigs from her water gourd, waiting for inspiration.

The weather had been warmer; that Elizabeth did remember. She and her brother had walked along this side of a similar ravine for several hours before turning off and following a creek that cut off their path. If this were the same gully, the creek would be up ahead, still several hours away.

She sighed. This little jaunt had been more difficult than she had anticipated. Perhaps she was just out of shape, or perhaps it was the pregnancy. Absurd excuses. It wasn't difficult to understand why she was having trouble remembering the location of an event she had tried so hard to forget.

She pulled on her mother's thin gloves that Warren had given her and leaned into the wind, feeling its chilling bite, concentrating on her footing, the loose gravel, the purple moss, concentrating on the immediate, staying aware of the present, anything to forget the horrible events and memories of the last week.

Julian had tried to be kind. But as always, true love and tenderness eluded her. "I wish you'd stay," she had said, "at least for a few days." Julian had approached her at Jasin's graveside after the ceremony. Most everyone had departed and in the quiet Elizabeth could finally be alone with her thoughts. No one, except Julian, would have dared interrupt what Elizabeth had hoped would be a private moment. She brushed the dirt from her fingers before looking up. The azure crystal pendant, its presence too strong a reminder of the day their dreams had become a nightmare, now rested safely beneath the soil with him. She had no need for its beauty or the memories it provoked.

"I'm thinking about heading back to Panvera. Membomba said he would fly me. It will be nice to see my dad again," she had replied,

"Membomba will be making other trips."

Elizabeth remembered looking back toward the Elstrada complex, fighting back the tears. "I know, but I think it's best."

There was no place for her there. Honestly, it never had felt like home, never felt like she truly belonged. Oh, there were days with Jasin when she had forgotten whose bed she was sleeping in, but it had become clear they had been living in a fool's paradise, a childish dream. Now, the situation was awkward. She hadn't been Jasin's wife, at least not legally, so she really wasn't his widow. The only formal position she held now was pregnant servant girl. At least in Panvera she was someone's daughter.

Elizabeth remembered the comment that had most disturbed her, that had motivated her return to the wilderness where her brother, Michael, had perished. Julian had remarked, "Beloit's body should have been brought back from the tunnels in Hadrious and buried here with some sort of stone or marker. Avram would have liked that. Beloit should have had more recognition for his years of thankless service."

Julian had been right. It was the idea of recognition, some form of memorial that Elizabeth couldn't get out of her mind. Jasin had received his, Avram too, but what about the others? What about her brother, Michael? He had died and there wasn't so much as a stick or stone to mark his passing. Not even a mound of dirt. It was as if he hadn't existed at all. Of course, she wore his memorial mark, but somehow it felt like a shallow gesture. Why hadn't they done more?

Her father, barely holding himself together, had refused to have a formal ceremony. "Too soon after Sidrah," he had said, referring to her mother's funeral. At the time, she understood. Another memorial service would have taken him over the edge, so Elizabeth had reluctantly agreed. But now she realized she had been wrong.

All of a sudden, the creek appeared in front of her. She had been daydreaming and nearly slid down the embankment onto its frozen surface. Turning left, she followed the white-laced stream as it snaked deeper and higher into the wilderness.

Elizabeth now felt guilty about not doing something for Michael; felt guilty about being so mean to Jorge; guilty about Jasin's death, and Beloit's, wondering whether she'd been right to have shown him the entrance to the Eian underground. It was just one of a dozen questions she was asking herself lately. But as usual, Julian provided the voice of reason.

"Then others might have died," Julian reminded her. "There's no winning the what-if game. You need to look ahead. Think about tomorrow, about the baby you're carrying. It's such a special time for a woman." Then Julian had paused and reflected, "You know what surprised me? The number of kids that showed up today.

It was true—Jasin had inspired a lot of kids. He connected with them, making them believe in a better future. Me? Me he just knocked up, then went and died. What started as a personal joke, struck a nerve and her tears flowed freely, blinding her and causing her to stumble. She wiped her tears away and scanned the frozen land ahead. She was lost. The way forward remained hidden from her.

Cold steep cliffs loomed over her, threatening to release the ice and snow that clung to their ragged edges. She needed to tip her head all the way back to see out of the gorge. Sometimes, if weather permitted and the light was right, you could see wisps of snow from the surface. And that's what she thought she was seeing at first, but realized that only one thing could make a thin straight line like that in the sky. A week ago she wouldn't have recognized the shuttle's trail. She wondered whether it was Membomba or possibly one of the new pilots. She remembered how shocked she had been when Membomba informed her how easily the Eians had learned to fly.

"Eiton and the others are using all the large shuttles," he had informed her. "I never thought I'd be saying this, but I truly have never met a more intelligent or resourceful being than Eiton. His capacity for learning…well, it's been fun to watch him get so fired up. A few of us ship-born are helping with the fueling and relocation. In another week Hadrious will be a ghost town."

Elizabeth remembered the excitement Eiton had shown upon entering the cold, forbidding hulk of the dead ship. How she resented his joy. While Membomba refueled their shuttle aboard Tanis that awful day, the little engineer soared above the dozen other shuttles in the dock. She on the other hand could barely bring herself to leave the shuttle.

Elizabeth reached beneath her coat and scratched the incision on her belly. Julian had done a good job with the dermal adhesive, but the itching was infuriating. She had to move. Dimness was only six hours away. Either she needed to return to Panvera and the safety of her father's home, or choose a direction.

She walked on tentatively, examining each group of rocks, each turn of the frozen creek, hoping that something would be familiar. Finally, she stood in the middle of a clearing. This could be it, she thought, but it had no feeling of familiarity; just another open space. Yet there was something peaceful here. It was almost beautiful, with the partially frozen creek hugging one side and a clear view to the great rim of the gorge. Did Michael's memorial have to be at the exact spot he had died? Did she care? Did it matter? No, at least not to her, and that really was the only opinion that mattered here. She was doing this for herself, to complete what had been left undone, to fill the one void in her soul she had the power to fill.

She searched until she found a large, flat stone about forty centimeters on a side, pulled out her small alien blade, and began to carve Michael's name into the stone's surface. It was easier than she had expected. The soft limestone was no match for the thin, sharp blade. She worked carefully, adding the year he was born and died. He was too young. Jasin was too young. Tears flowed freely and her hand trembled as she finished. She gathered other rocks and stones and placed the tablet on the cairn, then looking at the little memorial, she closed her eyes, trying to bring forth all the good memories she could muster, but her mind remained strangely empty. She knew there were so many wonderful experiences she and Michael had shared, but now....

She fell exhausted to her knees and sobbed. Too many deaths, they all ran together and had taken their toll. She looked at the tiny knife lying on the ground next to her. Anger rose within her; she never wanted to see it again. She took it to the pile of rocks and bridged it across two strong stones, and then using another, she broke the blade in two. One half melted away into small droplets of unformed metal. The other half reformed itself into a minute version of the original. Again, she broke it in half. Then again, and again until there was nothing left. It felt good to be rid of the thing, a catharsis. She turned to go.

And looked into the eyes of a dozen cylith.

Had it been the noise or her smell? Whatever...it didn't matter now. She was probably a lot closer to their initial campsite than she had thought. These were probably the same animals that had attacked Michael. Two different packs of this size wouldn't live in such proximity.

Escape? Run? She looked right, then left. It was futile. She couldn't outrun them or for that matter fight them all. She had just destroyed her only weapon. A strange calm enveloped her. It was over. Knowing her final fate came as a relief, not nearly as scary as she thought it would be. For days, she had already felt dead inside. Oddly, she even relished the coming physical pain—retribution for her mistakes, payment for causing so many deaths on Hadrious.

She would die then. Allow the animals their meager dinner. The natives would be pleased that her last act would be to feed the cylith. She just hoped it would be swift.

The lead animal took a few steps forward, while the others spread out. They had nearly closed a circle about her. Thankfully for her father's sake, there would be nothing left to find. There were enough of them.

Her stomach fluttered. It was a strange feeling. Was she getting sick? Then it happened again—but it wasn't her stomach.

The lead cylith lunged and she instinctively punched upward with all her might. Her fist caught the animal under the jaw and it squealed as it fell. The others hesitated. Elizabeth jumped to her feet and grabbed the flat gravestone as the others leapt forward. She brought the tablet down on the leader, crushing its skull. One animal took hold of her leg and a second struck her back and sent her crashing to the ground. A third came at her face and she turned away leaving the cylith with a mouthful of auburn hair. Disoriented, she couldn't judge where they all were. She struggled to raise herself. Her leg was bleeding badly and as she reached for Michael's stone ragged teeth sunk into her outstretched hand. Blood gushed as the animal's embedded teeth ripped through bone and tendon. Unmanageable pain made her dizzy. The cylith, its muzzle red from her blood, glared at her, waiting for another opening. With her good hand, she grabbed the memorial and swung awkwardly, catching it in the neck. It toppled over dead.

Only ten to go. The absurdity, pain, and helplessness made her cry, then laugh out loud.

And the pack froze.

"Come on you bastards. What are you waiting for?" she screamed.

She brought the heavy stone down across the back of another one. Tears flowed as through the pain and despair, she tried to gain control of herself, but the crying and hysterical laughing erupted again.

A few cylith backed off.

Some of the younger animals veered away, approaching the dead carcasses. It was easier to eat the broken animals, than take a chance with this other wild creature. A single adult took a few steps toward Elizabeth and she lifted the stone over her head and let herself laugh...it worked. The pack shifted its focus to their fallen brethren and began to devour them.

Elizabeth quickly replaced the stone tablet and retreated. Her throat burned and she raised her scarf with her functioning hand and limped off.

Perhaps there *was* something...someone to live for.

Human Caucus

Getting the Human Caucus to agree to a special open meeting was more difficult than Elizabeth had imagined. When she insisted that Eiton be allowed to attend, word came back from the Council of Seventeen, instructing the Caucus to delay until suitable Sytonian supervision could be arranged. That was enough to convince Elizabeth that Sy Jelick had assumed his father's duties as spy on behalf of the Council. It didn't really matter, it was important for the Sytonian Council to hear what she had to say.

As more and more people made their way to the Elstrada estate it soon became evident that even the great hall would not be sufficient to contain all those interested in the rumored topic—the disposal of Tanis. Preparations for the meeting were moved to the courtyard.

Although shuttle sightings had become common over the last week as the Eians were moved off Syton, all eyes, even those of the ship-born Caucus members, were riveted to the descending spacecraft as it gracefully flew in and landed just outside the gates. Wilem, Nanc and Mas stood with the other children. For many of the young, this was as close as they had ever been to an actual piece of their history. Now, all the stories their parents had told them took on a reality they had never expected to have. The door of the shuttle opened. Sy Lang, Elizabeth, and finally Membomba followed Eiton out of the craft and through the gates, slowly, as not to outdistance the limping Eian. For many humans, this was the first time they had ever seen a male Eian.

As Elizabeth approached, Wilem hesitantly stepped forward to meet her. She bent down to embrace the young boy, her dark hair cascading around the two of them. Mas and Nanc joined them. "He's been telling everyone about your scar. I believe you're some kind of hero among six year olds for having a scar that's longer than any towan," whispered Mas.

"Oddity would be more like it," answered Elizabeth, straightening. She gathered her hair back with her good hand before kissing Mas on the cheek.

"Something new?" asked Nanc.

"This?" Elizabeth asked, lifting her wounded hand.

"No…that," Nanc said, indicating the fresh memorial tattoo opposite Michael's.

Elizabeth hugged her. "Where's Julian?" she asked, looking through the crowd. Mas and Nanc looked at each other, each seeming to wait for the other to say something. "She's ok isn't she?" said Elizabeth, suddenly afraid.

"She's fine…physically. Truthfully, she was upset when she heard what you were doing," said Mas.

"She'll be here though?"

"You know her and crowds. This is a little overwhelming."

"She'll be here. This is too important."

The Caucus assembled in a two rows, Sandist Lee, Yarrow, and the other ship-born occupied the first row of seats. Terrence Winer and Mordichai, and several of the younger members sat behind. Chairs, facing the Caucus, were provided for Elizabeth, Eiton, and Sy Lang, but the towan preferred to stand.

Sandist Lee began. "Before we get on with the subject that confronts us today, the Caucus has asked me to address the unfinished business that occupied this body the last time it met. On that occasion we attempted to ascertain the guilt or innocence of our Enforcer, Beloit McMaster. Information obtained over the last few months has cleared his good name of any involvement in the deaths of Sy Toberry or Katherine Solend McMaster. We would like to honor his memory today. He deserves to be remembered in our hearts as a selfless friend who endured our anger and stood guard over our temptations. He insured our adherence to the Prohibitions that allow us to live here in peace." He allowed for a brief moment of silence before continuing.

"Now to the matter at hand. It has become evident that over thirty years ago, Hyland Wynosk ignored direct orders and preserved Tanis. His actions then, including the deception surrounding the destruction of the last shuttle, has pitted our races against each other resulting in the loss of many lives. If he were alive today, he would be dealt with in the most extreme manner. Today, the peace we have enjoyed for so very long is threatened. We are here to correct the situation and restore the trust we once had in each other."

"Tanis is a human problem, so it is up to this Caucus to deal with it. Most of us believe we are faced with exactly the same problem that Avram Elstrada and the original Caucus faced when we first arrived—the need to stabilize our relations with the Sytonians. To do that, we need to destroy Tanis.

"A few weeks ago however, Elizabeth Tournell approached us with an alternative. Because of her role in saving Julian Elstrada, and revealing the Eian plot to put our races in conflict, we have agreed to allow her to address the Caucus."

Elizabeth stood. "It is really quite simple. I agree, with the need to remove Tanis from the equation. It must be destroyed...or it must be removed from this system. Since you would destroy it anyway, we simply ask for permission to take it from this system and never return. Anyone who would like to accompany us is welcome, especially those with experience."

Elizabeth turned to face the murmuring crowd, allowing those present to absorb the idea before continuing. "Most of you believe the situation aboard Tanis is hopeless. You might be saying to yourself, our best engineers couldn't fix the problems that seven hundred years of hard service in space inflicted upon the ship, but I will tell you that you were wrong. Not because I am an engineer, but because our best engineers did not give up on the ship. If Hyland, who was by Avram's own words, the best engineer we ever had, saw value in saving Tanis, who am I to think differently? Who are you? I believe Hyland saved Tanis because he didn't yet have the answers, but he believed in possibilities, he believed in the future, just as I do.

"Avram may not have seen any options, but Hyland knew that didn't mean that sometime in the future the answers wouldn't present themselves. He knew it was impossible...and wrong to abandon technology, to avoid and forget what we have learned. Knowledge, once revealed, cannot be shelved just because it becomes politically inconvenient.

"Neither Avram nor Hyland was aware that the Eians existed, that they had technology of which we were totally ignorant of, that even today we don't fully understand. But we cannot be afraid of new technology. We cannot be afraid of using it to solve our problems or to improve our lives. I have spent long hours in discussion with Henri Membomba, and Eiton, the two brightest engineers we have on Syton today. They believe Tanis can be repaired. We know there are great hurdles to overcome. That we might fail, but they believe we also just might succeed.

"Most of you support the statues quo, believing that change can only bring conflict and unrest. Many of you ship-born are older and might be thinking that Syton is as good a place as any to die. But I have seen too much dying here and not enough living. On Syton, the best we can hope for is a second-class life. We will never be equal, we will never be granted full rights. All I am asking for is the chance to live out my life without someone telling me what I can learn or what to use or make. I am asking to live with the freedom to go where I want, and most importantly, I want to live among those who are full of hope and willing to live life to its fullest, where progress and technology and science is embraced...not prohibited. I am not afraid of dying here on Syton...I am afraid of not living."

Sy Lang stepped forward to be heard. "We have allowed you humans to inhabit our homes and cities. We have permitted your race to share Syton, but you have repeatedly broken your promise to heed the Prohibitions. The very men you chose as Enforcers, violated them on many occasions. Now you meet to consider sharing technology with the Eians. We will not permit this collaboration. We will not permit—"

"Excuse me Sy Lang," Terrence Winer interrupted him. "We are pleased to hear what the Council of Seventeen has to say, but you should understand that we do not need your permission. We will do as we like with Tanis."

"If you would allow me to finish," said Sy Lang. "We will not permit you to collaborate with the Eians while Tanis remains a threat over our heads. At this moment we are still holding over a hundred humans in the village of Cernai. If the rest of you humans leave and we are attacked, either by you or the Eians, they will all die. The rest of you may take Tanis from this system, but those humans will be the price you pay. They will remain here as our guarantee."

"Sandist, may I speak."

All heads turned at the sound of Julian's voice. She slowly made her way forward. Her age showed on her wrinkled face; her sadness and exhaustion felt by all.

"Respectfully sir, you no longer need to imprison those in Cernai. You will have many more than a hundred humans that will choose to remain on Syton even if the Caucus is foolish enough to give Tanis to Elizabeth and her misguided friends. To do so would be suicide and murder, suicide for those that would follow her, and murder if the Caucus allows it. I doubt that any human will allow the Eians to control the power of the ship for revenge or retribution against your race with so many of us, including me, staying behind."

A murmur drifted through the crowd.

Julian continued. "Most of us older humans, who actually know how Tanis operates, realize the ship is a death trap. I plead with all of you not to consider this foolish plan. We, who abandoned it, did so with great reluctance and we will not be returning. It must be destroyed as Avram promised thirty years ago, and as my son recently died trying to do." Julian bowed her head and Mas stepped forward and led her to an empty chair.

"Thank you Julian. As always your input has been most welcome," said Sandist Lee. "Before we vote is there anyone else who wishes to speak?" Elizabeth searched the crowd for support. She had done as much as possible. Repeating any of her reasons would make her look desperate. "Then I think we'll put it to a—"

"Sir...I'm sorry, but I am not familiar with your ways," said Eiton. With difficulty, he climbed up and stood on his chair. "Are you few going to decide the future of perhaps hundreds without examining all the facts? To me it is illogical to waste anything as precious as your starship. I have been told that although important systems have failed, the major problem is metallurgical—your hull and pusher plate are losing their integrity. Material science, especially metallurgical engineering is my specialty. I assure you it can be fixed. It may not be exactly the same ship, and it will probably take several years before Tanis is ready to leave this system, but it can be done."

"If it is going to leave, it must be immediately, before any further Eians can gain access," insisted Sy Lang.

Elizabeth turned to the towan. "Just out of curiosity, and with all due respect sir, how would you ever know?" Silence greeted her question. "You have been so accustomed to controlling us that even when you no longer have that power you try."

Silence followed Elizabeth's final statement and a vote was immediately taken. Elizabeth's plan was soundly defeated and Membomba was ordered to make plans to destroy Tanis in full view of the Sytonians.

"I now know how Hyland must of felt," Membomba grumbled as he, Eiton, and Elizabeth boarded the shuttle. Elizabeth had remained silent and stoic.

"It is a shame no one believed me. I know Tanis can be fixed," said Eiton, fastening his restraint.

"It isn't that they didn't believe you," said Elizabeth, breaking her silence. "They are protecting their positions of power. Allowing humans to leave Syton would diminish their constituency. Why would they vote to lose control of half the population? None of them will ever join us. They know we will have little use for politicians aboard Tanis."

Membomba threw her a glance, which she answered with a smile.

"The Caucus believes it has jurisdiction over Tanis. I say otherwise. We control Tanis, or should I say, you engineers do. If others wish to stay, so be it. I think there will be plenty who will be happy to leave."

Tanis

Julian dropped her head and rubbed her brow before returning her gaze to the old doctor. "Misa, are you out of your mind? You are fortunate to still be alive and you want to join her? I might trust her to run a household, but a starship? As courageous as Elizabeth has been, as much as she's gone through, she doesn't have the training or experience to lead."

"That is why I've come to ask you to join us. We could use your help. She will need you."

Julian shook her head. "How old are you now, eighty?"

"Something like that, who counts? They need us up there Julian. It's filled mostly with planet-born and children, some can't even read."

"We've lost a generation."

"We've lost more than that."

"Don't lecture me about freedom and human spirit. Why would I want to die in space? I'm tired and have had quite enough of it. Besides, Avram and my son are here."

"You mean death is here." Misa poured herself another cup of herbal tea. Julian's hadn't been touched.

"Honestly, yes. I can't have many more years. Why would I want to spend them in the cold of space when I can spend it smelling flowers and going for walks in the sunshine? I've had enough of Tanis and the blackness for two lifetimes. You know, even her father is staying in Panvera."

"For just the same reason. He plans to die here as well. But Eiton and his family have decided to join us. He's arranging to salvage blue metal from the rails in the Kull. You know, I've had a chance to talk to him. He's really remarkable."

Julian nodded absently. She gazed at the distant peaks of Trinity. "I had another visitor a few days ago."

Misa waited for her to continue, but she was off in some daydream. "Jules?"

Julian took a deep breath. "Yeah?"

"A visitor?"

"A young lady from Bistoun...beautiful...long silky black hair. She said she met Jasin once. Her mother had told her where to find me. I didn't recognize the name."

"All the way from Bistoun?"

"I gather she was a barber, or at least that's what she called herself. Said she was going with Elizabeth...that they were going to find a better place. I didn't have the heart to tell her that this was the finest piece of real estate that we humans ever found in seven hundred years of travel."

"The only piece."

Julian nodded and took a sip of tea. "Cold," she made a face and put the cup down.

Misa dumped out the cup and refilled it for her. "It wouldn't have mattered, Jules. She hasn't made her own voyage yet. You've made yours and now you feel as though you can rest. Her life is just beginning, it's her turn and we both must help them."

"Why do you think she came?"

"The young lady? I don't know, maybe for the same reason I have..." Misa turned at the sound of Elizabeth approaching. "Maybe for the same reason she has."

"Don't even try, Elizabeth," Julian warned, as she sat down next to them.

"Aren't you even going to offer me some tea?" Elizabeth said with a tired smile.

"How have you been feeling, dear?" asked Misa. "Are you taking care of yourself?"

"Of course." Elizabeth patted her belly. "Have you told her?"

Julian bristled. "Told me what? It's rude speaking as if I wasn't present."

"We're taking the ship—"

"And who's going to run it?" interrupted Julian. "You think a bunch of engineers and children are enough to command a starship?"

"I have decided to take command of Tanis," said Elizabeth, without a hint of hesitation or doubt.

"You! Are you mad? You have no training, no experience. It takes…forget it. I'm not getting into this. If you think you are able to run the ship, please do. There's no one stopping you."

"Go ahead, Julian, tell me. What does it take to command Tanis? Perhaps I need more skill in hiding or lying, skill in deception perhaps? Maybe that's what I lack. From the beginning you've tested me, challenged me. Don't I measure up to your standards? Just what have I ever done to warrant your disapproval? Wasn't I good enough for your son?"

Julian shook her head sadly. "Look at yourself, Elizabeth—you're smart, beautiful, and tall, men are instantly attracted to you. You command attention whenever you walk into a room. Even the natives notice you."

"How petty of you Julian. How irrational! There is no one that commands the love and respect you do. What happened to you? When did you decide to let Avram take the lead? You gave up everything, just for a chance to live on this damn snowball?

"Hold your tongue, girl!" cried Misa. "How dare you speak to Julian this way? What she did was for our protection. The natives would not have accepted her the way they accepted Avram. It was a courageous and selfless act. I'm sure it—"

"Quiet Misa, I don't need to be defended," said Julian.

"Yes you do!" said Elizabeth. "Your decision affected an entire generation."

"My decisions have always affected entire generations," Julian said in a whisper.

"What are you two talking about?" asked Misa.

Turning to the doctor, Elizabeth asked, "Do you really know why you're here on Syton?"

"Of course, everyone knows."

"Nobody knows." Elizabeth said firmly.

Julian rose suddenly and retreated toward the house. Elizabeth bounded after her, leaving Misa totally confused.

"That was uncalled for," said Julian as Elizabeth caught up to her. "I don't know who you've been talking to, what you think you know, but you know nothing, especially about the demands of running the ship."

"And I've come to ask for help, one last time, from someone that does."

"Never." Julian shook her head sadly, her breathing became labored, and her eyes filled with tears. "I hate that ship…just hate it. It sucked the life out of me. You can't understand. You'll never understand. When we discovered Syton…it was like a gift. Who's to say whether I made a mistake or not? Amongst the death and hardship here, there has also been much happiness." She paused. "How did you find out?"

"Eiton and Membomba have been examining the ship. I think the Eiton was actually disappointed. He had been very excited about the challenge of fixing it."

Julian nodded slowly, her lips pursed. "There's still much to repair. Hyland always had his hands full."

"It's just not as bad as you led everyone to believe. Did anyone else know beside you and Hyland?"

Julian shook her head and said softly, "I had to get off that ship. Only Hyland understood."

"But Hyland loved Tanis."

"Thankfully, he loved someone more."

"And you turned your back on him. Have you ever truly loved anyone like I loved your son, or have all your relationships been matters of convenience like Avram?"

"How dare you. You know nothing of my love."

"That's right," said Elizabeth, her eyes tearing up, "because you've never shown it to me. For that matter, you rarely showed it to Avram or Jasin. You never even came to Hyland's funeral. Whether you realize it or not, I am carrying your only blood relative. The two of us are the only family you've got left and we are going to need your help."

Julian shook here head sadly. "You're wrong."

Months passed, and excitement spread through the human community. Word of the ship's condition had filtered down. Far from being unsafe, it had already provided a bounty to those suffering from health conditions now easily treatable, entertainment beyond all imagination, the collected knowledge of mankind, and for many the simple joy of soothing air they could actually breath. Julian received the news and coaxing from a stream of visitors bound for the ship, including Warren Tournell.

"So you're leaving us Dai Warren?"

"My daughter needs me. I might as well spend my last days being warm and playing with my grandchild...our grandchild."

"Don't try to use that crap on me."

"Why not? You've got more family leaving on that ship than I. You've got more to give them than I. How do you want to be remembered? As some bent, angry, obstinate woman left to walk among the graves of her dead family, or as a sage mentor and loving grandmother?"

"I've never been very good at the loving part."

Julian eventually came up on the very last shuttle with Warren by her side. Elizabeth rushed to give him a giant hug the minute the hatch was opened. She was overjoyed to see them both.

"Blame him," Julian said, smiling at Warren.

Elizabeth was shocked at how frail and thin Julian had become. The deaths of her husband and Jasin, and her imprisonment had finally taken its full toll. She was a mere shadow of herself. The last months of indecision must have also weighed heavily upon her. She walked carefully, slightly bent. They left the hanger and entered the rotating living sections where families hustled about fixing up their quarters. Kids played in the halls.

Occasionally Julian was greeted by ship-born who would nod an acknowledgement or give her a careful hug. She looked as if one strong squeeze could break her ribs. People watched her from their doorways as she made her way into the Medical Bay, where Misa came out to greet her. Together the four of them walked slowly towards the Operation decks where they ran into Mas.

"Well, well, looks like we'll have to open a geriatric department," he joked. "It's good to see you again, Julian."

She smiled weakly. "I'd like to see Jorge's boy. Do you know where he might be?" Julian asked.

Mas led them down a corridor where Wilem and a young dark haired, eight-year-old girl were playing ball. Wilem kicked it and it sailed over the girl's head, coming to rest on a wide stoop in front of a closed double door. Julian approached Wilem, bent over, and asked if he remembered who she was. He looked over at Elizabeth who signed the question. He shook his head.

"He can't hear you," explained the young girl.

Julian nodded. "Elizabeth, will you tell Wilem we need to become better acquainted?" Now, what's your name young lady?"

"Al-hara."

"Well Al-hara, why don't you take Wilem down to the living quarters and play there." Julian stepped carefully up onto the raised step to retrieve the ball. "This really isn't a good area for you to play in."

"You're wrong," the young girl corrected her. "No one ever comes here. It's locked," she said, referring to the doorway Julian stood in front of.

"She's right," said Mas. "Even Membomba can't open it."

"Well, let's see," said Julian. She turned and placed her wrinkled palm on the sintered metal plate on the doorframe.

A few seconds later a disembodied voice announced, "Recognize, Captain Julian Wynosk." And the door slid open.

"Wynosk?" Elizabeth muttered, looking down at Wilem.

Misa grinned. "Your education begins."

As Julian passed through the doorway, the room gradually brightened and dark display panels blinked on. Elizabeth followed her in. The sweet smell of fresh air began to flow into the command center from vents that had been still for thirty years. Julian walked slowly from station to station, idly running her withered fingers along the edges of the dusty consoles, standing straighter and stronger as she made her way around. She paused before a broad view port and the others joined her at the window. Conboet, a sliver of green laced with yellow, was just disappearing behind Eian's silhouette. Elizabeth lifted Wilem for a better look at the thousands of stars that speckled the black space around them.

The End

www.ingramcontent.com/pod-product-compliance
Lightning Source LLC
Chambersburg PA
CBHW051634050726
47502CB00011B/50